Empire of Grass

Empire of Grass

Book Two of The Last King of Osten Ard

TAD WILLIAMS

HODDER &
STOUGHTON

First published in Great Britain in 2019 by Hodder & Stoughton
An Hachette UK company

1

Copyright © Tad Williams 2019

A CIP catalogue record for this title is available from the British Library

Hardback ISBN 978 1 473 60328 8
Trade Paperback ISBN 978 1 473 60329 5
eBook ISBN 978 1 473 60325 7

Printed and bound in Great Britain by Clays Ltd, Elcograf S.p.A.

Hodder & Stoughton policy is to use papers that are natural, renewable
and recyclable products and made from wood grown in sustainable forests.
The logging and manufacturing processes are expected to conform
to the environmental regulations of the country of origin.

Hodder & Stoughton Ltd
Carmelite House
50 Victoria EmbankmentL
ondon EC4Y 0DZ

www.hodder.co.uk

Dedication

If you want to see the full dedication, it's in *The Witchwood Crown*.

If you don't have your copy on hand at the moment, I'll summarize:

This entire story—series—trilogy—whatever you want to call it—is dedicated to my editors (and friends) Betsy Wollheim and Sheila Gilbert, and to my wife (and best friend) Deborah Beale, without all of whom my life would have been different and much less happy.

Acknowledgments

The list of people who have usefully influenced my return to Osten Ard is long, and I apologize in advance if I have forgotten anyone.

Ylva von Löhneysen, Ron Hyde, Angela Welchel, Jeremy Erman, Cindy Squires, and Linda van der Pal all offered indispensable suggestions, corrections, and the occasional smack in the snoot (when I got something really wrong) about the early drafts of the book.

Angela Welchel and Cindy Yan put in a huge amount of creativity and work helping us with other, Osten-Ard-related projects.

Ylva and Ron wrote the synopsis of *The Witchwood Crown*. I edited it a little. Also, Ylva, Ron, and Angela Welchel worked together make the appendix at the end of the book, which is full of chewy informational goodness.

And of course, Ylva and Ron have been godparents to these books since the beginning, because in many ways they (and the other fine humans mentioned above) know Osten Ard better than I do. Hey, I took thirty years off before returning, what do you expect?

In fact, oh, so many people deserve my thanks again this time, because makin' books ain't easy!

Lisa Tveit is the social media warrior making sure that tadwilliams.com remains a bastion of silliness and Tadalia on the internet. And my many friends on the TW Message Board keep my courage up during dark nights of the soul where I wonder if anyone cares about what I'm doing.

Olaf Keith contributes a great deal to the website and also helps me and my work in a number of other ways, and I'm always grateful for his kindness.

Marylou Capes-Platt did her usual excellent job of copyediting on *Empire of Grass*, as well as slipping in the occasional and very welcome note of encouragement.

Michael Whelan painted another fantastic cover. Don't mean to make it sound like it's something I take for granted, no matter how often it has happened. I never do.

Isaac Stewart (with a lot of feedback from ace cryptogeographer Ron Hyde) has again drawn brilliant maps and contributed in many other ways.

Joshua Starr, as always, handled the assembly side of things with his usual skill and good nature.

My agent Matt Bialer takes care of me and my work, and reminds me about things like not biting careless reviewers, no matter how much they might deserve it.

My overseas publishers, especially Stephan Askani of Klett-Cotta in Germany and Oliver Johnson of Hodder and Stoughton in the UK, have been hugely supportive, as always.

And, as mentioned at length in the dedications, none of this would have turned out anywhere near as well without my editor/publishers, Sheila Gilbert and Betsy Wollheim, and my writer/collaborator/partner in crime and life, Deborah Beale.

Thank you, all you heroes.

Synopsis of
The Witchwood Crown

More than thirty years have passed in Osten Ard since the end of the Storm King's deadly, magical war—a war that nearly doomed mankind. *King Simon* and *Queen Miriamele*, scarcely more than children when the Storm King was defeated, now rule over the human nations from the High Throne, but they have lost touch with their onetime allies, the immortal *Sithi* folk. Then *Tanahaya*, the first Sithi envoy since the end of the war, is ambushed on her way to the Hayholt, the ancient castle that is the seat of the High Throne.

While *Tiamak*, scholar and close friend of the king and queen, works with his wife *Thelía* to save Tanahaya's life, Queen Miriamele and King Simon are away from the castle on a royal progress. Currently they are visiting the neighboring country of Hernystir and its *King Hugh* as part of a royal progress to the north, where Simon and Miriamele are troubled by the behavior of Hugh and his new love, the mysterious *Lady Tylleth*. Dowager queen *Inahwen* warns the royal couple's advisor *Count Eolair* that King Hugh and Tylleth have revived worship of the *Morriga*, an ancient, dark, and bloodstained Hernystiri goddess.

Even while accompanying the royal family on their progress, *Prince Morgan*, the seventeen year old grandson of Simon and Miriamele, spends his days drinking and womanizing with his knightly companions *Astrian*, *Olveris* and old *Porto*. Morgan's father, *Prince John Josua*—the only child of Simon and Miriamele—died of a strange illness some years earlier, leaving his wife *Idela* a widow, Morgan and his younger sister *Lillia* fatherless, and the king and queen, John Josua's royal parents, still grieving.

When not nursing the poisoned Sithi envoy, royal counselor Tiamak is collecting books for a library to commemorate the late John Josua, but when his helper *Brother Etan* investigates some of the dead prince's possessions, he discovers a banned and dangerous volume, *A Treatise on the Aetheric Whispers*. Tiamak is filled with foreboding, because the *Treatise* once belonged to the wizard *Pryrates*, now dead, who collaborated with the *Storm King Ineluki* to destroy humanity, though they ultimately failed.

The threats to Simon's and Miriamele's peaceful reign are increasing. In the icy north, in the cavern city of Nakkiga beneath the mountain Stormspike, the ageless ruler of the Norns, *Queen Utuk'ku*, has awakened from a years-long magical slumber. Her chief servant, the magician *Akhenabi*, summons the High Magister of Builders *Viyeki* to an audience with the queen, who declares her intention to attack the mortal lands again. The queen leads a strange ceremony that resurrects *Ommu*, one of the chief servants of the Storm King, though Ommu was thought to have perished forever during the Norns' failed attempt to destroy the Hayholt and the mortal kingdoms.

In Elvritshalla, the capital of Rimmersgard, King Simon and Queen Miriamele are reunited with their old ally *Sludig* and his wife *Alva*, as well as their dear Qanuc friends *Binabik* and his wife *Sisqi*. They also meet the trolls' daughter *Qina* and her betrothed, *Little Snenneq*.

The royal progress reaches Elvritshalla just in time to say farewell to *Duke Isgrimnur*, who dies shortly after their arrival. His last request to Simon and Miriamele is that they renew their search for *Prince Josua* (Miriamele's uncle, Simon's mentor, and John Josua's namesake) and his twin children, *Derra* and *Deornoth*, who mysteriously vanished twenty years earlier. Later Little Snenneq, who is Binabik's apprentice, meets Prince Morgan and predicts that he will become as important to Morgan as Binabik became to Morgan's grandfather, King Simon.

In a castle in southern Rimmersgard where the royal party is guesting on their way home, Simon realizes he has not dreamed in many days. He consults Binabik, who creates a talisman to help him. That very night, Simon dreams of his dead son and the voice of the child *Leleth*, who had once whispered to him in dreams three decades earlier. Leleth tells him "the children are coming back". After Simon frightens the whole household while sleepwalking, Miriamele destroys the talisman, and Simon again loses the ability to dream.

In the still more distant north, the half-blood Sacrifice *Nezeru*, daughter of Norn noble Viyeki and human woman *Tzoja*, is sent as part of a "Talon" of Norn warriors to retrieve the bones of *Hakatri*, brother of Ineluki, the defeated Storm King. Nezeru and her fellows, commanded by their chieftain *Makho*, find the bones being venerated by mortals, but Makho and the Norns take them and escape from the angry islanders. During the escape, Nezeru fails to kill one of their enemies (a child) and is severely punished for it by Makho.

However, before the Talon can return to Nakkiga with Hakatri's remains, they are met by the Norn Queen's arch-magician Akhenabi, who takes the bones and sends the Talon on a new quest to Mount Urmsheim to collect the blood of a living dragon. To aid in this dangerous feat, he sends with them an enslaved giant named *Goh Gam Gar*.

While traveling eastward towards Mount Urmsheim, the Norn Talon encounters a mortal man named *Jarnulf*, a former slave in Nakkiga who has vowed to destroy the Norns and their undying queen, Utuk'ku. Because the Talon has lost its Echo—their trained communicator—Jarnulf, hoping to further his own private aims, convinces the Norns to take him on as a guide. They all travel eastward towards the mountain, last known home of dragons, and on the way Jarnulf overhears the Norns discussing their queen's great plan to defeat the mortals by recovering something called "The Witchwood Crown".

In central Rimmersgard, the Talon encounters the royal party, and Jarnulf is able to get a secret message to Queen Miriamele and King Simon that the Norn Queen is looking for something called the Witchwood Crown. Simon, Miriamele, and their advisors are alarmed, and they have seen enough signs of renewed hostility from the Norns that they take Jarnulf's message seriously, though this is the first they have heard of him.

In the City of Nabban, a Wrannawoman named *Jesa* cares for *Serasina*, the infant daughter of *Duke Saluceris* and *Duchess Canthia*, Simon's and Miriamele's allies. Tensions in Nabban are rising: *Count Dallo Ingadaris* has allied with Saluceris's brother *Earl Drusis* to fan fears of the nomadic Thrithings-men whose lands border on Nabban. Drusis accuses Saluceris of being too cowardly to properly punish the barbarians and drive them back into the grasslands.

Meanwhile, on the plains of the Thrithings, gray-eyed *Unver*, an adopted member of the Crane Clan, and his companion *Fremur*, participate in a raid on a Nabbanai settlement. As they escape, Unver saves Fremur's life, perhaps in part because Unver hopes to marry Fremur's sister, *Kulva*.

Sir Aelin catches up with the royal party, bringing messages for his great-uncle, Count Eolair. *Lord Pasevalles*, Eolair's temporary replacement at the Hayholt, sends his worries about Nabban, and Queen Inahwen of Hernystir sends news that King Hugh and Lady Tylleth are growing ever more open in their worship of terrible old gods. Eolair sends Aelin with this bad news to a trustworthy ally, *Earl Murdo*. But while seeking shelter from a passing storm, Aelin and his men spend the night in a border castle with *Baron Curudan*, leader of King Hugh's private, elite troops. During a storm that night, Aelin sees the dim shapes of a vast Norn army outside the fort, and then watches Curudan meet with humankind's deadliest enemies. But before Aelin and his men can escape with the news of this treachery, they are captured and imprisoned by Curudan's Silver Stags.

In the Norn city of Nakkiga, Viyeki is sent by Lord Akhenabi on a secret mission to the mortal lands with his Builders, but he is accompanied by a small army of Norn soldiers as well. Tzoja discovers that with Viyeki gone, her life is threatened by her lover's wife, *Lady Khimabu*, who hates Tzoja for giving Viyeki a child, Nezeru, when Khimabu could not. Tzoja knows she must escape if she wishes to live.

As Tzoja thinks of her past with the Astaline sisters in Rimmersgard and her childhood in Kwanitupul, it becomes clear Tzoja is actually Derra, one of the lost twins of Prince Josua and his Thrithings wife *Vorzheva*. Tzoja flees to Viyeki's empty lake-house in a cavern deep beneath the city.

Their royal progress finally returned to the Hayholt, Simon and Miriamele ask Tiamak to honor Isgrimnur's dying request with a new search for Prince Josua. Tiamak sends his assistant Brother Etan south to try to discover what happened to Josua when he disappeared twenty years earlier.

Meanwhile, challenged by Little Snenneq, Morgan climbs Hjeldin's Tower, the Hayholt's most infamous spot, and is almost killed. He believes he saw long-dead Pryrates while he was atop the tower, and swears Little Snenneq to secrecy.

With evidence of the Norn resurgence everywhere, Simon and Miriamele realize these ancient and magical foes are too powerful to face alone. They decide to try to contact the Sithi, especially their old allies *Jiriki* and *Aditu*. At Simon's urging, Miriamele reluctantly agrees to send their grandson Prince Morgan with Eolair and a host of soldiers to Aldheorte Forest to find the Sithi and return their poisoned messenger Tanahaya for more healing.

Viyeki travels south from Nakkiga toward mortal lands, accompanied by an army of Norns who plan to attack the mortal fortress of Naglimund. Viyeki is told that he and his Builders are going to excavate the tomb beneath the fortress of the legendary Tinukeda'ya *Ruyan Vé*, called "the Navigator", and salvage his magical armor, though Viyeki does not understand how this can happen without causing a war with the mortals. Tinukeda'ya, also called "Changelings", came to Osten Ard with the Sithi and Norn, though they are not the same as these other immortals. In Osten Ard, the Tinukeda'ya have taken on many shapes and roles.

Prince Morgan and Count Eolair finally contact the Sithi at the edge of Aldheorte Forest. The immortals have abandoned their settlement of Jao é-Tinukai'i and their matriarch Likimeya was attacked by humans and has fallen into a deep, magical sleep. *Khendraja'aro*, of the ruling Sithi Year-Dancing House, has declared himself Protector of their people and refuses to help the mortals in any way, causing friction with Likimeya's children, Jiriki and Aditu. Aditu is pregnant, a rarity among the Sithi. The father is Yeja'aro, nephew and militant supporter of Khendraja'aro.

In the Thrithings, Unver challenges and kills his rival for Fremur's sister Kulva. But Kulva's brother, *Thane Odrig*, does not want to give his sister to an outsider and slits her throat instead. Unver kills Odrig and flees the Crane Clane to return to the Stallion Clan of his mother Vorzheva. Unver, we learn, is actually Deornoth, the other of Josua and Vorzheva's twins. When Unver demands his mother tell him why he was sent away and where his sister has gone, Vorzheva says he was sent away by order of her father, *Thane Fikolmij*, and that Derra ran away shortly after.

Thane Gurdig, husband to Vorzheva's sister *Hyara* and Fikolmij's successor, comes to attack Unver, and in the confusion Vorzheva kills her now old and infirm father, Fikolmij. A giant flock of crows appears out of nowhere to attack Gurdig and his allies, causing many Thrithings-folk to declare that Unver may be the new Shan, the universal monarch of the Thrithings. Unver kills Gurdig, and is then declared the new thane of the Stallion Clan.

Far to the northeast, the Talon and Jarnulf manage to capture a small, young dragon, but then the mother dragon appears. During the struggle Chieftain Makho is badly burned by dragon blood and one of the other Talon members is killed, but the rest manage to escape and begin dragging the captive young dragon down the mountain.

Eolair and Morgan are returning from their embassy to the Sithi to their camp beside Aldheorte Forest, but discover that their party has been attacked and all the soldiers wiped out by Thrithings-men, some of whom are still there, looking for victims and pillage. Eolair and Morgan become separated and the prince ends up lost back in ancient Aldheorte.

Back in the Hayholt, Queen Miriamele and King Simon are invited to attend an important wedding in populous and troubled Nabban. Hoping the presence of the High Throne will help solve the problems between Duke Saluceris and his brother Earl Drusis, Simon and Miriamele accept the invitation. With the increased threat of the Norns and disturbing news from Hernystir they cannot both go to Nabban, so they decide Miriamele will attend the wedding while Simon stays in the Hayholt.

Royal counselor Lord Pasevalles meets his secret lover Princess Idela, John Josua's widow. When she gives him a letter from Nabban he had dropped, Pasevalles sees the seal is broken and fears she has read the letter. He pushes Idela down a flight of stairs and when the fall does not kill her, he breaks her neck with his boot.

In Aldheorte Forest the onetime Sithi envoy Tanahaya at last awakes from her terrible illness and is reunited with Jiriki and Aditu. Despite her recovery, the future seems dark. It is clear that the Norn Queen Utuk'ku intends war on both the Sithi and the human world.

OSTEN ARD

Foreword

As Tanahaya entered the cavern called the Yásira, she was disturbed. Nothing felt right. For a moment, she even doubted herself and her decision.

The bright fliers are here, she thought, looking at the clustered butterflies, *but they are so sad and slow! The stone above and around us hides them from the sun and the wind. They are entombed like the Sa'onsera herself.* She looked at the shrouded body of Likimeya, not dead but not merely sleeping either, and felt a great hollowness. *All the world is out of joint. How can anyone know what is right or wrong at such a time?*

The sacred butterflies clung to the cavern walls and ceiling like a tapestry of living gems, in more colors than even sharp-eyed Tanahaya could count; the gentle rustling of their wings filled the silence like a soft wind caressing the treetops.

Likimeya's daughter Aditu came forward and took Tanahaya's hand for a brief moment. "Jiriki is here, too," Aditu said, and with a feather-light drumming of her fingertips on Tanahaya's palm, told her *Courage, we are with you*, then led her into the depths of the cavern where the rest of the Year-Dancing clan waited.

"Come, Tanahaya of Shisa'eron." Khendraja'aro, the badly scarred, self-elected Protector of the clan, waited at the far end of the chamber just beyond the circle of sunlight admitted by the cave's cloven roof. He sat cross-legged on the naked stone like a war leader, and his closest followers, mostly young male Zida'ya who had never known a life before their exile in the great forest, huddled close on either side of him like bodyguards. "I do not like to leave the battle lines at a time of such threats," Khendraja'aro continued. "Tell me why I am needed here."

The unblinking eyes of his supporters watched Tanahaya with plain distrust, but the faces of most of the rest in the cavern displayed nothing but attention. Only Aditu's brother Jiriki and a few others nodded to welcome Tanahaya.

"It is precisely because of those threats that I wished to speak to you, Elder Khendraja'aro." Tanahaya deliberately did not use his claimed title of "Protector," and she could feel a stirring of interest around her. "At such a time, we cannot afford to drive away allies."

Khendraja'aro's ruined face assumed a more distant expression. "Drive away allies? What allies? We Zida'ya have no allies in this world."

"Nor do we need any!" announced Yeja'aro, Khendraja'aro's young kinsman. Of all gathered in the Yásira, he had the most trouble keeping his feelings appropriately masked. Tanahaya thought Yeja'aro little more than an earnest, angry youth, though she knew there must be more to him, else wise Aditu would not have chosen him to be the father of her child.

"I speak of the mortals." Tanahaya's words caused another stir but so brief and small that only a slight agitation of the butterflies overhead betrayed it. "The mortals who brought me back here so that our healers could save me."

"Yes, of course," Khendraja'aro said. "But surely you and the others did not summon me just to watch some ceremony of gratitude for our healers—or for the feckless mortals."

"No, Elder Khendraja'aro. We summoned you out of courtesy so that I could tell you my decision. I am returning to the mortal lands, to the place they call the Hayholt—our old citadel of Asu'a."

For a long moment Khendraja'aro only stared at her with narrowed eyes, as though he doubted his senses. "No, you are not," he said at last. "By my trust, you are not."

"I fear you have misunderstood, Elder," said Tanahaya. "The trust was *mine*, and it was given to me by Sa'onsera Likimeya's children, Aditu and her brother Jiriki. That task remains uncompleted."

An angry ripple of breath and movement went through the protector's supporters; to Tanahaya it seemed loud as a shout. She willed herself toward greater calm.

"I am the Protector of the House of Year-Dancing," Khendraja'aro said stiffly. "I did not approve your going to the mortals in the first place, and I do not approve it now. My words are law for you."

Now others were stirring, but this new wave of discontent seemed to be centered among the older members of the Sithi, many of whom Tanahaya knew were loyal to Jiriki and especially Aditu as the true scions of Year-Dancing House. "Your words are not law, Khendraja'aro," said Jiriki, but his voice was mild and carefully neutral. "Our father Shima'onari was the last Protector—but he is dead, may the Garden receive him. Our mother Likimeya is the embodied Sa'onsera, and though she is sorely hurt and insensible, she still lives."

"I do not need to hear our history from you, who never saw the Nine Cities of our people's glorious days," Khendraja'aro said, and for a moment seemed to lose the grip on his anger before drawing back into stolidity once more. "In any case, it does not matter. I do not claim every privilege of a Year-Dancing clan leader. But someone must be Protector, and while I serve the clan in that role, it is I who must make the difficult choices—and I choose to let the treacherous mortals go their own way. You will not go to the mortal castle, Tanahaya, and you will have nothing more to do with mortals. None of our house will." He crossed his arms over his breast. "If there are no other matters of import, I declare this foolish and unnecessary council ended."

Courage, she told herself. *What is Khendraja'aro's unhappiness when set against the madness of Queen Utuk'ku and her minions—against the possible destruction of all?* "You misunderstand me, Elder Khendraja'aro," she said. "I am not asking you if I may do this, I am informing you that I will do it. A courtesy, as I said."

Yeja'aro would have leaped to his feet, but Khendraja'aro, though his face showed clear traces of fury and frustration, put out a hand to still his young relative. "No loud words here," he told Yeja'aro. "And no threats. Take your hand away from that sword hilt, young one, or I will banish you. We are the Zida'ya, not brawling mortals—and this is the Yásira." Yeja'aro subsided, folding himself back into a crouch among the others, Khendraja'aro turned back to Tanahaya. "Explain yourself."

She took a deep breath, and suddenly had a strange, dizzying feeling that more was happening beneath this disagreement than anyone present could guess. She looked up to the butterflies above her head and took strength from their presence. *The bright fliers have watched over fiercer conflicts than this,* she told herself. *Yet they still come to us. And we, the Dawn Children, the Zida'ya, still survive.* "It is simple, Elder. You may rule the House of Year-Dancing in most things— but I am not of that house."

He made a gesture of dismissal. "This is art, not fact. You were sent to us by your master, Himano. That puts you under my rule."

"First," she said, "Lord Himano is not my master by law but by my choice— my teacher, not my lord. He is an elder like you, although my respect for him is deep and I owe much to his help." She looked to Jiriki and found some comfort in his grave, thoughtful face. "I was sent by Himano to help Jiriki and Aditu long before Likimeya was wounded and fell into her long sleep. I did their mother Likimeya's bidding in traveling to the mortal's capital, but was prevented from reaching it by an ambush with poisoned arrows. Nothing has changed since then. I serve their interests, not yours."

Khendraja'aro was clearly taken aback. "I cannot understand such talk."

"What *I* cannot understand," Tanahaya said, frightening herself a little with her own bravery, "is why you and your followers, Elder, seem so determined to ignore all that does not coincide with your views. I was sent as envoy to the mortals, whether you approved or not. I was attacked and left for dead, and would have certainly died if several mortals had not worked long and hard to keep me living until I could be brought here. The arrows that struck me, from what I can learn, were black like Hikeda'ya arrows—but they apparently were painted to look that way, not made of true Kuriosora blackwood."

"Your meaning is unclear," Khendraja'aro said, frowning.

Aditu spoke up for the first time. "She means that someone wanted us—or the mortals—to think that the Hikeda'ya were to blame for the attack on our envoy."

"So it was mortals who attacked Tanahaya, not Utuk'ku's folk." Yeja'aro sat up and made a sweeping gesture—*this is just the noise of the wind.* "Which only makes it clearer we should keep them far from us, and ourselves far from them."

"But the poison that was used," said Tanahaya. "That is something to be discussed as well." She turned to a small, silver-haired Sitha woman sitting near Aditu. "Please tell the rest of the Sa'onserei what you told me, Elder Kira'athu."

The healer, who never allowed herself to be hurried, waited several moments before speaking. "The poison that was in Tanahaya's veins was . . . unusual. I have never seen the like. There was no poison left in the wounds, but the signs of it were most strange. Some aspects of *kei-vishaa* were in it, and some of the herb we call Traveler's Hood—the mortals call it wolfsbane. And there was something else as well—"

"This means nothing!" said Yeja'aro, causing a few of the Root and Bough to stir uneasily at his continuous interruptions. "The Hikeda'ya used witchwood dust against mortals in the last war. The mortals know it and what it does."

Kira'athu did not give him the courtesy of a glance. "Yes, the Hikeda'ya have used *kei-vishaa* against men in the past. It is not impossible that the mortals could have discovered its properties, although it is obvious they would have a very difficult time making more of it, with the witchwood trees now all but gone."

A stir of uneasiness seemed to pass among the butterflies on the chamber walls and ceilings, a whisper made by thousands of gently rippling wings.

"But the strangest thing about the ambush is this," the healer said. "Among the signs of the poisoning upon Tanahaya's body I found some that did not come from either *kei-vishaa* or Traveler's Hood. Show them, Tanahaya of Shisae'ron."

Tanahaya turned and pulled up her loose tunic, ignoring the pain from the corruption that had turned her wounds into hollows that were only now beginning to scab.

"Do you see those marks on her skin, like flowers?" Kira'athu asked the assembly. "Several moons after the attack, they are still hot to the touch. No ordinary poison caused them. But they are much like the wounds caused by something else—something that usually only enters the body from the outside. They are like the wounds made by dragon's blood."

Khendraja'aro still looked angry, but his face had also grown a shade more pale. "And what do you claim this means, Healer?"

"I do not claim anything, Protector," Kira'athu said. "I say only what I know."

"Does anyone truly need to ask?" Jiriki said, "It seems plain that someone who can put their hands on both *kei-vishaa* and dragon's blood wants to stop us from sending an envoy to the mortals. That alone would make it worth sending the envoy again."

Khendraja'aro shook his head, slowly but emphatically.

"I do not care for any of this. I do not permit it."

"And as I said, Elder, I do not ask for your permission." Tanahaya spoke as calmly as she could, though her heart was beating fast. "Out of courtesy, I inform you that I will once more take up my embassy to the mortals. Now I must go and prepare."

"Let me help you, heart-sister." Aditu rose to her feet, her belly like a full harvest moon sailing over the horizon. "You are only just regaining your health."

"I fear I will never be truly well again," said Tanahaya. "But I am well enough to do my duty."

They walked out of the cavern side by side, pausing only to pay respects to sleeping Likimeya in her shroud of butterfly silk. The butterflies themselves had grown still again on the ceiling and walls, and for that moment the cave was quiet as the rest of the gathered Zida'ya pondered all that had been said. Still, Tanahaya felt certain the Yásira would not stay silent long after she had gone.

PART ONE

Summer's End

Cruel orb, my foe, the sun,

Glaring upon things
I never want to see again
The proud, lightning-limbed oaks
Of Hekhasor
The shimmering blue waters of Silverhome's lake
And the endless, endless sky
Go away, foul sun! You make me sad.

—SHUN'Y'ASU OF BLUE SPIRIT PEAK

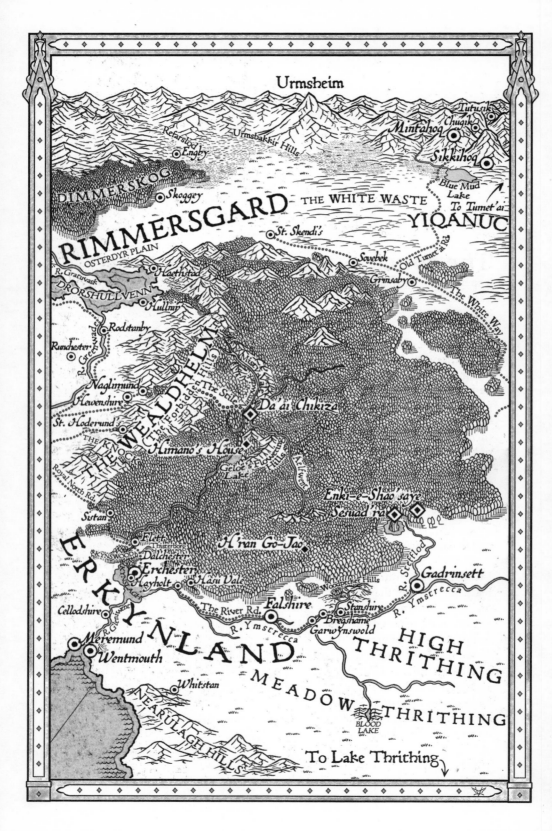

1

Old Heart

The touch of slender fingers frightened Morgan so badly that he leaped off the branch where he had been perched, banged his knee and elbow hard on a lower branch, then half-swung, half-fell to the ground. Even before he rose he was scrabbling forward across the forest floor on hands and knees, his pulse drumming in his ears. Only when he was some dozen paces away from the tree did he dare turn and look.

The moonlight seeping through the ancient trees did not reveal much of the thing that had touched him but cast enough silvery light for Morgan to know he had never seen another creature like it. It was smaller than his young sister, which eased his fears some, but it was no animal he could recognize, neither bear cub nor ape. Its startled black eyes were huge and, before the creature turned and vanished into the upper part of the tree, he even caught a glimpse of hands that seemed to have fingers instead of claws.

Morgan sat on the damp ground as the moon slid out of sight again behind the trees. He shivered, waiting for his heart to slow, wanting to weep but not daring to make a sound. He had no idea which direction he had come from or how long he had run.

I'm lost, he realized. *Alone in Aldheorte Forest. Lost.* It hit him like a blow.

He badly wanted a drink of something strong.

Morgan woke from a harrowing, dark dream of tripping roots and tangling branches, of vines that clutched and dragged him down like vengeful ghosts, to discover that, instead of angry phantoms, a bright blue summer sky peeked at him from between the branches overhead, and the warm morning air was full of the scent of green things.

He had but a single moment to appreciate the relief, the perfect innocence of the day; then as he tried to untangle himself from his cloak he rolled over and fell out of the tree where he had fallen asleep. He was slowed in his tumble by branches beneath; he was lucky to have climbed only a couple of times his own height. Still, branches scratched and gouged him in several places before he struck the ground.

At first he could only lie panting, testing his limbs to see if he had injured himself badly. So much, he thought, for the safety of perching in trees.

Thank our merciful lord Usires I didn't climb any higher!

But his next thought was, *What will happen to me? Is anyone searching? Are any of the others I came with even alive?* He remembered the last time he had seen poor old Count Eolair, and his insides clutched in fear and sorrow for the count and Porto, for Binabik the troll and his family. Morgan did his best to push bleak thoughts away. He was a prince, he reminded himself; he could not let fears or unhappiness unman him. And he had not seen any bodies back at the camp except for Erkynguards, so it was even possible Snenneq and Qina and the rest had survived. But it was hard to believe it.

He desperately wanted a drink. A jug of wine would make the aches go away, and the worries, too. How had he been such a fool as to leave his flask at the camp, when he and Eolair first departed with the Sithi? Porto had probably drunk all of Morgan's brandy. If the old knight had lived long enough.

Morgan was torn between genuine fear for his comrade and the idea that the last of the brandy might have been wasted on someone who wouldn't live to appreciate it.

Now past the first shock of his fall, Morgan climbed unsteadily to his feet and began gathering the things that had tumbled from the branch with him— his sword, water skin, and lastly his dark green cloak, which he had wrapped around himself during a particularly cold stretch in the middle of the night. He sat beneath the beech and laid them all out on the damp ground around him, then untied his purse from his belt and emptied its contents onto the spread cloak.

The pouch that held his flint and steel for making fire were the first thing that struck his eye, and he promptly thanked God. But other than his mail shirt and the clothes he wore under it, he did not have much—his sword and his dagger and the things he had dumped from the purse. He examined the small pile, an unhappily brief inventory.

Flint and steel.

His mother's Book of the Aedon.

A bundle wrapped in leaves that he didn't recognize but prayed was something to eat.

The spiked foot-irons that Snenneq had given him for walking on ice, as useless here in the summer forest as teats on a boar.

But there was still a weight in the purse. He reached in to see what it was. Someone—his squire Melkin or perhaps even Snenneq the troll—had coiled up a few fathoms of slender cord and knotted them into a tight bundle at the bottom of the purse. He was unspeakably grateful to whoever had done it. If nothing else, he could use the rope to help make a shelter.

Or hang myself, he thought, then said a hasty prayer of apology. Why give God ideas?

Prayer over, he swiftly turned his attention to the leaf-wrapped parcel. He and Eolair had last eaten at the camp of the scarred Sitha Khendraja'aro. Morgan had not eaten much, although the food had been very good. It was hard not to curse himself now for having stinted when he could have feasted—but how could he have guessed what would happen next?

For the love of Our Lord, what will I find to eat here in the wood?

To his great relief, the bundle of leaves turned out be food that either old Porto or Morgan's squire Melkin had put there for him—hard cheese, bread, and an apple, all wrapped in grape leaves. But where did the apple come from? Morgan couldn't remember the last time they had been near a tree. Still, the rest of the food would keep a while longer, but the fruit was already softening, so he took a bite and for a moment was almost restored to happiness simply by the taste.

So I'm not such a fool as my grandfather thinks me, he told himself. *Not helpless. Look at what I have with me—a knife, some food, flint and steel for fire.* The moment of satisfaction was interrupted by a memory of his grandfather's friend, Jeremias the Lord Chamberlain, who had strongly criticized Morgan's leather belt-purse.

"It's the kind of thing peasants and pilgrims wear," Jeremias had told him. "And you, Highness, are neither."

Well, Lord Purse-Hater, Morgan thought, *who's right and who's wrong now?* Then he realized he was sitting alone in a huge forest with no idea of how to get home, arguing in his head with someone who wasn't there.

"When you wind up in one of those bad situations," his grandfather had once told him, *"sometimes you just have to get on with things. Just get on with them. Keep going. Keep pushing forward."* Now, years later, the king's words finally began to make sense. Just during the time he had been staring at his few possessions the sun had moved higher in the sky, passing from below one branch to above it, hurrying toward its eventual noon summit, after which it would roll down into darkness again.

The food in his purse would not last long, and Morgan knew nothing of what might be edible in Aldheorte other than a few berries. He had not caught a rabbit since his childhood, while pretending to be wandering heroes with some of the other high-born children of the Hayholt. He hoped he still remembered how to make a snare.

If you remain here you'll starve, he told himself. *You must do something. Think, Morgan, think!*

The most obvious plan was to try to find his way back to the edge of the forest. It had been hard to guess where to go before, but that had been while he was with the Sithi, and doubtless was due to some kind of heathen spell meant to confuse outsiders. There should be no reason now to doubt the sun's path and the directions it would give him.

He bundled everything back into the purse, then looked up in the sky to calculate how the sun had moved before setting out toward what he felt sure was the south, toward the nearby grasslands. Despite his worries—and a fierce thirst for something strong, a thirst that was growing, not easing—he felt brave

enough to whistle as he walked. It was only when he recalled that whoever had
attacked the camp might well be searching for him that he fell silent.

By the middle of the afternoon Morgan could not have mustered the courage
to whistle even if he had wanted to. His stomach was cramping painfully and
his legs ached, but he could not seem to make any progress. After the sun
crossed the peak of the sky he kept the line of its descent to his right, which
should have taken him back to the forest's edge. Instead, as the afternoon wore
on he found himself still deep in the shadows of the tall trees, hornbeam and
lindens and spreading Erkynland oaks, a darkness alleviated only by an occasional sun-scoured clearing or patch of marshy bottomland between hills. He
had walked for far longer now than he could possibly have run the night before,
no matter his terror. But even with the Sithi no longer about, their forest magic
still seemed to afflict him.

   He stopped to take stock, resting against the trunk of a broad beech tree
halfway up a hillside. He'd finished the apple hours before, and squeezed and
sucked the juice out of its core, then crunched up the seeds between his teeth
so as not to waste any of it, feeling almost virtuous as he did so. But now hunger was a constant companion, so he pulled a piece of crust off the bread and
ate it with a few morsels of cheese. That helped a little, but he still pined desperately for some strong drink. The thought of it and the frustration of having
none was a constant misery.

   The problem with where he was going seemed simpler to solve: he knew
that in a general way the grasslands and the Ymstrecca must be south of him
somewhere, but he did not know how deep in the forest he was. He wiped the
sweat from his brow and peered up a nearby slope. If he climbed straight up, it
seemed likely he would see something of his surroundings from the hilltop. He
might even be able to see the edge of the forest and how far he still had to travel.

   The climb took no little while because the slope was steep and covered with
brush and fallen trees. By the time Morgan reached the top the sun had sunk
considerably farther toward the horizon. He made his way across the summit
until he found an open space where the trees fell away at the edge of a stand of
ghostly birches. He looked out at the sea of trees spread below him—a sea with
no shore.

   "It's not fair!" he cried. A jay squawked its disapproval at him. "Not fair!"

   In every direction, the forest stretched away in all directions, nothing but
endless treetops and a few hills here and there like the one on which he was
standing, isolated islands in the green and brown ocean of leaves.

   His eyes misted with tears of frustration and fear chilled him. He desperately
longed to be able to drink himself witless.

   The Sithi called their villages "little boats." How he longed to see such a thing
now. He wouldn't care if it was the camp of that scarred villain Khendraja'aro
himself.

   Morgan's knees felt weak, so he leaned against a birch trunk. The sun was even lower, its light skipping over dark places where the evening mists were already beginning to form. He wiped his eyes, angry with himself for this moment of weakness, but not strong enough to do anything else yet.

I'm going to die here. At that moment there seemed no other possibilty. *Starved, or frozen, or after falling down and breaking my neck. Wolves. Bears. And nobody will ever know what happened to me.*

"Kill the nobleman and take his clothes. He's got nothing else of worth."

Count Eolair, Lord Steward, Hand of the Throne, hero of the Storm King's War, was all but picked up by a sneering Thrithings-man and thrown to the ground.

The rough, bearded men outnumbered Eolair by six to one. His tormentors wore pieces of armor that did not quite match, many of them in dirty surcoats from which the emblems had long ago been torn. The one who had thrown Eolair down stabbed at him with a sword, but it was meant to wound rather than kill—this grasslander wanted sport, first—and the count rolled out of the way so that the man's thrust only pierced his cloak and pinned it to the ground.

One of the other riders dismounted, saying, "Stay your blade, Hurza." The newcomer was young, but Eolair guessed by the easy way he gave the order that he must be the leader. He stared down at Eolair, mouth twisted in a smirk. His cheeks bore ceremonial scars, and numerous small, ornamental bones had been knotted in his fair hair and beard. Like the others, he wore no Thrithings clan-sign, which confirmed for Eolair that they were most likely free-roving bandits. "We can kill him any time we like. I want to know what he's doing here."

"And I will be very willing to tell you," said Eolair, "but I would like to stand up first." He lifted himself into a sitting position. Hurza's blade was still in Eolair's cloak; as the cloth ripped, a piece of it remained tacked to the ground. The grasslander scowled but did not argue with his young chieftain. Hurza withdrew his sword, then slowly wiped the mud from its tip on the count's leg before sheathing it again. "Unless you are all of you afraid of a single Hernystir-man twice your age," Eolair added.

"More than twice mine, I guess," answered the bandit leader, grinning now. "But as I said, there is no hurry in killing you, so tell us—what is a Hernystiri rabbit-eater doing on our land?"

"Is it yours? I see no clan emblem on any of you." Eolair knew he was courting death by such bold replies, but the men of the Thrithings respected courage, and he might as well be killed for a leopard as for a lamb. He also had the feeling that the young one truly did want to hear him out, if only because the chieftain was smarter and more practical than his followers. Also, but not least in importance, Eolair saw three more members of the bandit company still poking around in a disgruntled manner near the fringe of the forest where Morgan had disappeared, and he wanted badly to keep the rest of them distracted. "I am Eolair, Lord Steward of Erkynland. I am here because I was on a mission for the High Throne."

"A mission?" The chief laughed. "To who? The Fox Clan? Or the Sparrows? Or were you on your way to visit the fat villagers of New Gadrinsett?"

"None of those, nor to any other mortals. I was sent to find the Sithi."

Several of the other bandits grew nervous at these words; a few spit on the ground and made signs against evil. "Ha," said the leader. "Now I know you are lying, Hernystirman. Why would anyone want to seek the Forest Folk? And who could find them if the fairies did not wish to be found?"

The men who had been searching the edge of the woods had remounted their horses and were now heading back toward them; Eolair felt a rush of relief. *Great Brynioch, thank you. Keep the boy safe,* he prayed. Perhaps Jiriki was still waiting nearby and would help Morgan to safety. Despite their bad treatment at Khendraja'aro's hands, Eolair thought there were few places outside of the Hayholt where the prince would be safer than with the Sithi.

"We had a horn," he told the bandit leader. "One of the Sithi's. And it worked, because I have only just returned from speaking with the Forest Folk, as you call them, only to find that you have attacked and killed my company."

"I am tired of all this talking," said Hurza, squinting and frowning, but he did not say it loudly, and his leader ignored him.

"This is rare storytelling, sir. Are you sure you are a nobleman, not a bard?"

One of the other bandits, a dark-bearded man older than the chieftain, suddenly spoke up. "By the Thunderer, I think I know this man, Agvalt."

The leader turned. "What do you say?"

"I have seen him before. He knew my father." He looked at Eolair with something like wonder. "I am Hotmer. My father, Hotvig of the Stallion Clan, fought for Prince Josua. Do you remember him?"

"Remember him?" Eolair was astounded, but still cautious. "Of course I do. But Hotvig became a great man in New Gadrinsett—an alderman of the town, I heard. How do you come to be here?"

Hotmer shook his head and his face went grim. "I do not talk of it." He turned to Agvalt. "But this Eolair was an important man even then—the king's right hand, and that was more than twenty summers ago."

"Does any of this matter?" demanded Hurza with narrowed eyes and a sneer. "He has no purse so he has no use. Let us slit his throat and be on our way." A few of the others seemed to agree with him, but the rest of the bandits looked to their young chief.

"It matters if he is worth ransom," Agvalt pointed out. "What do you think, Hernystirman? Does the king care about you enough to ransom you?"

"Of course. If nothing else, he will want news of . . ." Eolair realized that in his exhaustion and fear he had almost said something foolish. "He will want news of my embassy to the Sithi. Yes, King Simon and Queen Miriamele will pay a ransom for me—but only if I am alive and well and can tell them what they want to know."

Agvalt laughed. "Of course. But that is also what any desperate man would say. But though this day has already seen good pickings—" He gestured to a pile of shields and swords and bits of armor on the ground, no doubt looted from dead Erkynguards "—We should not risk missing a bigger prize by hastiness." His scarred face suddenly became canny. "But who was the boy who ran off?" He looked up to the nearing riders and scowled. "The boy my men failed to catch."

Eolair waved his hand. "My squire, a foolish oaf who deserted me when trouble came. I am better off without him." For a moment he wondered if there was some way he could trick the bandits into helping him find Morgan, but could not imagine it without divulging the boy's true rank. This was followed by a longer moment of anguished indecision: which was worse, to leave the prince alone in the wilderness or help him become a prisoner of murderous bandits? Agvalt might well torture and kill them both if the chieftain decided the prospect of ransom was too unlikely or too dangerous.

Agvalt interrupted his thoughts with another question. "And those other boys? The ones we saw in the distance, riding sheep?"

Eolair was astonished but also heartened. That had to be some of Binabik's family, and it seemed they had survived the attack and escaped. "Those were not children but trolls of the high northeastern mountains. A group of them were accompanying us on their way home."

Now Agvalt laughed hard and loud with what sounded like genuine pleasure. "Trolls? Ah, my, what a day this has been! Even if we decide to kill you, Eolair the so-called King's Hand, we will keep you alive at least until you tell us all your stories. Nights on the grasslands can be dreary without a tale or two." Suddenly his face became cold again. "Bind him, Hurza. Not so tightly as to ruin him, but I want no tricks, and he will stay tied until we make camp. He can ride behind Hotmer, who will doubtless enjoy the company of his father's old friend."

Since it seemed he would live at least a while longer, Eolair risked another question. "Where is the rest of your band? You would not have attacked so many armed men with only these."

"The rest of my band?" said Agvalt. "We are not fools." He turned toward the smoldering remains of the Erkynguard camp, where little was left to see but streamers of smoke shredded by the wind. "This butchery was not our work. These were clansmen—and not a few of them, either. A whole clan, on the way to the moot at Spirit Hills, that is my guess. But enough talk. We ride now."

As he was lifted up onto the back of Hotmer's saddle, Eolair took one look back at the spot where Morgan had disappeared, but with evening now fallen across the grassland, he could see nothing of the ancient forest but an endless breakfront of shadow.

All the gods keep you safe, Prince Morgan. I pray you find your way home without me. I don't think I could bear to go back to your grandfather and grandmother with the news of my failure to protect their heir. Better to die here in the wilderness.

At first Morgan kept his sword in his hand, taking an occasional practice swipe at the shafts of sunlight falling through the trees, certain that at any moment he would be surrounded by bandits and forced to fight for his life. But as the day wore on and the forest air became hotter his arm tired and he sheathed the sword again. The bumping of his scabbard against his thigh quickly became another kind of annoyance. Though the sun was halfway down the sky, the day grew hotter until he felt as though he was smothering in his wool cloak. He took it off, rolled it, and draped it over his neck where it protected him from some of the nastier, scratching branches and made only the back of his neck itch instead of all of him.

The itching was the least of his problems. Nothing felt right, everything irritated or disturbed or frightened him. Despite the day's heat and the sweat that dripped off him, he had moments of shivering chills. He could not stop thinking about brandy, wine, even small beer, anything that might ease the pain and numb his miserable thoughts. And on top of everything, he was still hopelessly lost in a strange, dangerous place.

Morgan had never thought much about forests except as places for hunting and the occasional drunken adventure with Astrian and Olveris, like the time they'd gone out to shoot deer in the royal Kynswood and wound up lost, staying out long after dark and only finding their way back with the help of some royal foresters who heard them arguing. But he was beginning to understand that the familiar forest beside the castle was a much different sort of place than this Aldheorte. For one thing, even in the depths of the Kynswood evidence of men was everywhere, hunter's blinds and signs cut into tree bark, stacks of stones meant to mark a path, even the occasional charred remains of an old campfire. Here in the trackless Aldheorte nothing of mankind existed, and he encountered few other living things, just the occasional red flash of a squirrel in the treetops or the swift flutter of fleeing birds, heard more often than seen. He might have been in a new land that had never known a human footstep, yet he could not escape the sense that something—often more than one something— was watching him. He could not even say precisely what made him feel that way, but the sense of being an outsider, of being an object of interest, perhaps even to the great trees themselves, was inescapable.

He had never felt so lonely.

In the Kynswood and the parts of Hernystir's great Circoille forest that he had seen, the woods were never entirely empty of people and human habitations. Forest Folk farmed the trees, coppiced or pollarded them, and chopped some down for fuel, leaving only their stumps jutting from the ground like headstones. The underwood was gathered by charcoal burners, the fallen mast eaten by pigs driven into the woods to feed. Everything was bent to some use. Here he walked completely alone through hot, damp, and silent dark.

By the ending of the afternoon every breath Morgan took seemed to fill his chest without clearing his thoughts, and he fought constantly against a growing sense of helpless despair. Several times, as he crested a rise to see, not a glimpse of the forest's outskirts or a heartening sign of human existence, but only the same apparently endless expanse of trees and tangled brush still stretching before him, it was all he could do not to sink down on his knees and weep.

I can't do that, he told himself, over and over. *I'm a prince. Not allowed.*

He managed to hold the tears at bay, but as the day wore down and it became more and more certain he would not reach anything like the edge of the forest before nightfall, his fear began to rise like floodwater.

> *"That farmer's son took up his sword*
> *And ran to Greenwade's bank*
> *Where stood the Holly King's cruel men*
> *In rank by heathen rank.*
>
> *"The lad he stopped and raised his sword*
> *Close by the foaming flood*
> *And cried 'You'll not take Erkynland*
> *Though the river fills with blood!' "*

Morgan had wanted to sing something martial and cheering, but his voice sounded small and pointless, and—worse—seemed to offend the eternal quiet of the forest, so he gave up before he was halfway through "The Dolshire Farmer's Son." Soon, though, he could not have sung even if he had wanted to. Instead, it was all he could do to keep picking his way through the undergrowth, to ignore the countless bloody scrapes from thorny shrubs overhanging the few animal paths, to keep putting one foot in front of the other.

He spent what must have been an hour in a dense grove of towering, ancient linden trees, some straight and narrow as guards at attention, others so thick with their own new growth that the original trunks crouched in the center like silent grandfathers nodding by the family hearth. When he finally crossed into more open forest he paused to rest. The sun was setting now in the west—it *had* to be the west, or nothing meant anything—and the air was finally starting to cool. He was putting his cloak back on when he noticed a particular ash tree with a wide, angled trunk, as though it had grown in the shadows of some earlier, now vanished giant tree and had stretched toward the sunlight. Morgan could not help thinking, it seemed . . . familiar.

He walked a little closer, then from side to side, and could not dispel the feeling. Something pale on the ground near it caught his eye. It was the stem and topmost bit of an apple. Ants had covered it and the flesh had turned brown, but he knew even before he saw the print of a boot heel pressed into the loamy soil beside it that it was his own, the remnants of his long-ago morning meal.

He had come back to the place where he had started.

Morgan collapsed then, kneeled with his forehead pressed against the ground, and finally wept. The sun was a liar and a traitor, trying to murder him as surely as a knife-wielding assassin. The entire forest hated him, and now he hated it as well. He had walked all day and gone precisely nowhere.

He slept that night—or tried to—in the same tree that had sheltered him the night before. Things moved in the dark forest all around him, and he could hear the murmur of what almost sounded like voices. When he sat upright, heart beating fast, he saw three pairs of large round eyes catch the moonlight, shining on a high branch as they looked down on him, but whatever they were, they kept their distance. After that, Morgan did his best to ignore the rustling and soft murmurs.

The stars he could see through the trees seemed wrong, too—stretched or even unfamiliar shapes in what should have been familiar skies. Where the bright orb of the Lamp should have smoldered in the firmament hung a constellation like a spider or a crab instead, a central bright fire surrounded by radiating lines of lesser fires. It seemed even the sky had turned against him.

Morgan wept again, helpless to stop, but did his best to do it quietly, not wanting to draw the attention of some predator. He no longer feared any human searchers—he would have welcomed something so ordinary. But small noises escaped despite his most powerful efforts, and in the darkness of surrounding trees the invisible watchers murmured softly to each other, as if discussing what strange thing this alien creature might do next.

2

A Wooden Face

"Is that my mother?" Lillia asked, staring wide-eyed at the effigy atop the casket. The image's hands were clasped piously against its breast, the wooden face as rigidly serene as that of any carved saint.

Simon wasn't surprised by his granddaughter's question. He too found his daughter-in-law Idela's wooden likeness more than a little disturbing, with its empty expression and painted eyes that stared up at nothing. "No, little one," he said at last. "It's a carving. Like a doll."

"Why did they make a doll of her?"

"To show what she looked like when she was alive."

"Does she look different now?"

Many days had passed since Princess Idela's death, so the king did not much want to think about it. "It doesn't matter. Your mother's soul is in Heaven. You'll see her again someday, and she will look just as she always did."

"What if I don't go to Heaven?"

"I'm sure you will." He looked around. Other than the honor guard of soldiers stationed along the walls, the royal chapel was empty. A long line of nobles and important commoners had passed through in the previous two days, but it seemed that everyone who wanted to pay their respects had done so. Simon felt a dark astonishment that a woman as full of lively opinions as Idela should lie so long in a covered box, so still, so silent.

"Murderer!" someone groaned—not loudly, but in the nearly empty chapel it was as surprising as a shout and Simon jumped despite himself.

Duke Osric, Idela's father, swayed in the doorway. A few of his men tried to hold him up—he was clearly very drunk—but he pushed them away and walked unsteadily into the chapel. Pasevalles hurried in after him a moment later, begging him to come out again, doing everything he could to restrain the duke without actually laying hands upon him.

"A murderer!" said Osric again. He did not even seem to notice his grand-daughter Lillia or the king, but stumbled past them and sank to his knees in front of the bier. "A murderer walks among us. Walking free! Killed my only d-daughter!"

Pasevalles' face was full of both sympathy and distaste. The duke was sweaty, and the stains on his mourning garments suggested he had not changed them in several days. "I'm sorry, Majesty," he said to Simon, then noticed Lillia and blanched. "By our Lord, I am truly most sorry. His Grace is distraught. He has had too much to drink as well—"

"I can see that," said Simon, but gently. He had not expected Osric, a bluff fellow with little room for sentiment, to be so badly affected by Idela's death. Simon looked down at Lillia, who was watching her grandfather's heaving shoulders with horrified fascination. "But why does he keep saying that word? I do not like to hear such things in front of—" he gestured to Lillia. "Can you help him out again?"

Pasevalles grimaced. "I can only try, Majesty." But his renewed attempts to get the duke's attention were not even acknowledged.

"Come along, Lillia," Simon told her. "Your Grandfather Osric is very sad. Let him be alone."

"But he'll see Mother in Heaven too, won't he?"

"Of course. But he's still sad that he'll have to wait. We all are."

When he got to the doorway of the chapel, Simon left Lillia there for a moment and went back to talk to Pasevalles. Osric was still on his knees before his daughter's casket.

"Can you watch over him? I fear for him in this mood, Pasevalles."

"I will do my best, Majesty. His guards will help me, I'm sure. We will not let him do himself any harm. I think it will pass."

"What does he mean with all this talk of murderers?" Simon spoke softly so Lillia would not hear. "It seems plain that she fell down the stairs. I think it was caused by this terrible custom of wearing such long dresses as the women of this court do. Why they are not all falling down every day, I cannot imagine . . ."

"I do not know where this evil fancy of his comes from, Sire. As you see, my lord Osric is drunk and has not slept well for days. I have sent a coach for his wife, Duchess Nelda, but it is several days travel to Wentmouth and back."

"God our Ransomer, how I wish his good woman had been here in the Hayholt," Simon said. "How I wish Miriamele were here too, now that I speak of absent wives. Still no word from her?"

"You will know the instant any word arrives, Majesty."

"Even if it is the middle of the night."

"Yes, Majesty. Of course."

"Good. I have never had to write such a terrible letter. It brought back . . . it brought back such painful memories." He patted his lord chancellor's arm. "Bless you, Pasevalles. You have been a great help to me at this dreadful time."

"Thank you, my king." Pasevalles bowed deeply. "I only do what any loyal servant would."

Countess Rhona—the Queen's close friend and the throne's trusted counsel— asked him quietly, "How is our wee girl today?"

"Asking questions about death," Simon replied as he watched his grand-daughter walk in slow ovals, following the designs on the tiled hallway floor. "I have told her everything I know, that Idela is in Heaven, that she will see her mother again."

"She needs to think about something else," said Rhona. "I will arrange for her to play with some of the other children—that will take her mind off things."

"I'm not sure," the king said. "I've never met a child so hard to distract as Lillia."

Rhona laughed, but it had a sorrowful edge. "In that way, she is much like her late mother."

"Duke Osric worries me too. Now he is talking as though Idela was murdered."

Rhona waved it away. "I would not let that prey on you too much. Hard, strong men like Osric do not bend well when things go wrong. Sometimes the only way they can survive is to break and then try to heal the broken place."

Simon nodded. "There is something to that, I think." He shook his head vigorously, as if to free himself from a clinging cobweb. "I have a kingdom to see to, dear, good Rhona. Keep a close eye on the child, will you? I cannot help fearing how clear-eyed and sensible she is being, at a time when her mother has just died."

"Not to speak ill of the dead—" Rhona looked around to make sure none could overhear—"but her mother was never so close to Lillia in the first place."

Simon made the sign of the Tree. "Please. Just watch over my granddaughter, Countess, and please do not say anything like that to her."

Rhona smiled sadly. "I would never say such a thing to a child, Majesty."

When she had taken Lillia away, already fending off the girl's questions about the decomposition of the dead, Simon made his way back to the retiring room that served as a place of work when he did not wish to brave the usual din of the Throne Hall with its crush of courtiers and petitioners. He was weary and considering a private nap, so he was a little annoyed to find Tiamak, his Wrannaman friend and counselor, waiting there for him.

"How is your granddaughter, Simon? Is she bearing up?"

"Better than I am." He groaned as he sagged onto a chair. "This has quite unmanned me. And that it should happen the very moment Miriamele is too far away to do anything. And we sent Morgan away as well! My poor grandson does not even know his mother is dead!"

"You sent the prince away to meet with the Sithi, an important task, and the queen agreed—although I admit that it was not with much grace. Do not be too hard on yourself."

Simon sighed. "And now Duke Osric is staggering around the Hayholt, stinking of wine and raving that Idela was murdered. What next? Will Eahlstan's dragon come back to life and burn us all? Will Pryrates reappear too, and the lights of his tower glow red again at night?"

Tiamak did his best to suppress a shudder. "Please, Majesty—Simon—do not say such things. I do not believe you can summon bad fortune simply by speaking of it, but I doubt that your god or any of mine like to be challenged."

The king slumped back against his high wooden chair. Tiamak took up a seat on the far side of the writing table. "In any case," Simon said, "I do not want Osric crying 'Murder!' up and down the hallways of my castle. Nothing good will come of it, and it makes people fearful. That is the last thing we need when we already fear an attack by the Norns."

"We are preparing for the possibility of an attack," said Tiamak carefully. "We do not know anything about their plans for certain yet."

"Now you sound like Pasevalles." Simon scowled. "Caution, caution, make no assumptions. Am I the only person who remembers what those creatures are like?"

"I do not think so, Simon. Many faced that terror with you. They all remember, I do not doubt."

The king looked at his counselor with irritation. "Do you mean to shame me, Tiamak?"

Tiamak shook his head, and Simon saw streaks of gray in his friend's dark hair, something he had not noticed before. "No, truly, I do not mean anything like that. I too am frustrated and worried, I have problems of my own. But I won't burden you. Instead, let us talk about important matters of the kingdom."

"Such as?"

"For one thing, Simon, you have requests from both the Northern Alliance and the Perdruinese syndicate to rule on shipping rights in the waters between Erkynland and Nabban. Countess Yissola of Perdruin has even demanded an audience."

He groaned again. "Is she coming here? I do not need such aggravation."

"So do not invite her."

"I won't. Merciful Elysia, people say she's a hard, obstinate creature, and I need none of that. What else?"

Tiamak pointed to a large stack of parchments on the corner of the table. "All of this, my old friend. Did you miss it? I put it there for you to look at this morning."

"I woke up to my granddaughter poking me in the chest. What sort of guards I have, I don't understand—it was plainly an assault of the sort they're supposed to protect me from. She wanted to go to the chapel and pray that Idela would remember her daughter's saint's day even now she's in Heaven, because she'd promised Lillia a new dress as a gift."

Tiamak nodded, smiling. "Your granddaughter is a strong-willed child."

"Isgrimnur had a friend named Einskaldir who loved to kill enemies like most of us love eating supper. *He* had a weaker will than Lillia."

Tiamak's smile slipped a little. "Ah, you have reminded me. I put it off until we had discussed the most pressing matters, but now I need to speak of it. Of Idela's death, I mean."

This time Simon's groan was deep and heartfelt. "By the good God, what now? I confess I did not love her as much as I could have, but I was a good father-in-law to her, I think, and I have done everything I could to treat her with proper respect and mourning. What have I failed to do?"

"It's not you, Majesty—Simon. It's only that I have a few questions of my own about her actual death."

"You too, Tiamak?"

"Do not look at me that way. It is my responsibility as your counselor, or secretary or whatever I might be, to ask questions on your behalf, and to accept no answer that does not have the ring of truth. But let us make that the first question—is it not my given task?"

"Yes, yes, of course it is. Merciful Rhiap, you are as bad as Morgenes. Always setting me puzzles and questions, trying to get me to answer the way he wanted, leading me by the nose like a dull beast."

"You were never a beast, Simon—but in fact Morgenes was doing his best for you. That method of teaching is old and time-tested."

"I know, I know. I'm not a kitchen boy any more, Tiamak."

"Most of the time, no, you are not, Majesty."

Simon scowled. "Feel free to tease me as much as you wish, just because I'm not the sort of king who cuts people's heads off when they anger him."

"I do, Simon. I do, and I and many others thank the stars, the fates, or even the gods that you and Miriamele are not those sort of rulers."

"If you keep speaking of "gods" instead of "God," it won't be me you need to worry about but Mother Church."

"She may be an admirable parent, but she is not *my* mother, Majesty. And the strong never need to silence the weak, or they prove that they are the truly weak ones. Now, do you have the fortitude to listen to me, or do you need to complain a bit longer about how poorly everyone treats you?"

Simon laughed despite himself. "Good God, man, you do have a sharp tongue. Even Morgenes wasn't so mean to me."

"Because when he was your councilor, you were still only a kitchen boy. I am councilor to a king. The stakes are much higher."

Simon waved his hand. "Very well. You win. I will sit humble and silent while you describe my faults."

"That is not my purpose. As I said once already, I have questions about Idela's death. For one thing, I still do not understand exactly why she was on the stairs leading up to the uppermost floor of the residence."

"Why shouldn't she be? She was the mother of the heir. She was allowed to go where she pleased."

"You miss my meaning. Why was she *there*? There is nothing on the upper floor that should have attracted her interest. The rooms there are empty bedchambers, seldom used except when a large party of visitors arrive—something that has not happened in a while, I might add."

Simon groaned. "Are you going to fault me for not having more guests come to the Hayholt? I thought that was only Miri's favorite song. It's expensive, you know, all those visitors, and they always want to hunt and feast and have musicians every night—"

Tiamak cleared his throat. "I'm not faulting you for anything, merely wondering what Idela was doing on the stairs between the third and fourth floor."

"Who can guess? Perhaps she was meeting a lover up there. I have certainly heard it rumored."

The Wrannaman gave him a keen look. "Rumored that she had lovers, or that she met them in the upper part of the residence?"

"Had lovers. Not that I begrudged it to her, not after the first year or so. I would actually have been happier if she hadn't remained my son's eternal widow." He looked up. "You're staring at me again. What did I do wrong?"

"Nothing. But we do keep wandering away from the point, and I am always aware that I have your undivided attention only for a short time, and then the rest of the duties of kingship will wash in like a rising river and my business with you will be obliterated."

"Then talk faster—less scolding, more getting to the point."

Tiamak nodded. "Fairly spoken. I had the maids go through the rooms up there. All were clean, as if unused. But one—the large one in the center where the old chimney makes one wall—was cleaner than the rest."

Simon cocked an eyebrow. "Cleaner than the rest . . . ?"

"No dust. As if it had been tidied more recently than the others."

The king shook his head. "It seems a small thing."

"Perhaps. But none of the maids or other household servants can remember having cleaned those rooms since early in the spring, while you, the queen, and the rest of us were still traveling in the north."

"Very well, but if Idela was meeting a lover there, perhaps she was also keeping the room clean herself. She was always fastidious." He paused for a moment, a thought suddenly occurring to him. "Pasevalles found her. Are you saying he might have been her lover? That he was going there to meet her?"

Tiamak shook his head. "I would need to learn a great deal more before I would even dream of dragging anyone's name into such flimsy suspicions as I have. In fact, as far as I know, Pasevalles has never taken a lover from among the ladies of the court—but I do not pretend to know all the gossip."

"I've wondered about him myself, I'll admit," Simon said. "Whether he might be one of those, you know . . ." The king colored. "The other sort."

Tiamak smiled again. "I understand, sire. But I ask your leave to inquire around the castle—discreetly, I promise you—about Princess Idela and any lovers she might have had, especially in recent days."

"But why? You don't believe the drunken nonsense that her father is spouting, do you? That she was murdered?"

"In truth, no, because I can see no purpose to it—no gain for anyone. But there is still something about her death that troubles me, and she was part of the royal family, after all. Any crime against your family—any *possible* crime, I should say—is a threat to you and the queen as well. And preventing or uncovering such things is certainly a part of the trust you have placed in me."

"I suppose that's so." Simon let his head fall against the high back of the wooden chair. "I imagined all sorts of things could go wrong while Miriamele is in the south, but never this. And I also never imagined how tired I would be, just trying to do it all without her. I miss her, Tiamak. I miss her badly."

"We all do, Majesty," he said. "But I'm certain you feel her absence more deeply than any of us."

Pasevalles knocked at the door of Duke Osric's chambers. He told the servant who opened the door, "Get the duchess."

"But she is sleeping, my lord!"

"It makes no difference. Get her now."

The servant went off shaking his head, which made Pasevalles want to shove a dagger into the lazy, disrespectful fool's back and leave him bleeding and weeping on the floor.

Patience, he told himself. *Cultivate patience at all times.*

He went back down the hallway where the duke was sitting on the landing of the stairs, head in hands.

"Your Grace," he said, gently touching the duke's shoulder. Osric might be drunk, but he was still a large, strong man and there was nothing to be gained by startling him into anger. "Your Grace, please get up. Your wife is coming."

"Nelda?" Osric stirred, looked around, then lowered his head to his hands again, as if the weight was too much for his neck. "What is she doing here?"

"She arrived this morning, Your Grace. You greeted her yourself."

"No. Don't want to see her . . . don't want her to see me. Like this."

Pasevalles suppressed a noise of frustration. "She's coming, my lord. You might as well straighten up."

Duchess Nelda appeared in the corridor. She wore a nightcap and voluminous nightgown despite the late hour of the afternoon. Her long journey from Wentmouth had exhausted her, and seeing her daughter's body lying in state had been enough to send her weeping to her bed. But she was still the more alert and composed of the two. "Osric? Osric, what are you doing? Get up now. Come to bed."

The duke groaned. "Oh, my dear, what are you doing here?"

"What are you talking about? I've been here since early this morning, as you'd know perfectly well if you hadn't drunk so much. Come now. Aedon save us, it is hard enough . . ." She looked torn between anger and a flood of tears. "Come now. Come lie down. I will stroke your head."

At last Osric allowed himself to be coaxed to his feet, and with the help of the servant and Pasevalles, was led to his bedchamber. To his hidden disgust, Pasevalles even had to help the duchess pull off Osric's boots. The duke's feet were cold and gritty and stank of dried sweat.

"Thank you, Lord Pasevalles." Duchess Nelda's doughy face looked as though it might collapse into grief again at any moment, but she did her best to smile. "You are very kind."

"This has been a terrible blow to all of us, Your Grace." He left her trying with the servant's help to get her husband's legs under the bedcovers, but the duke was already snoring loudly, limp and heavy as a dead codfish.

Pasevalles retreated to his chamber and washed his hands three times to remove the smell of the duke's flesh.

Twenty years earlier, Pasevalles had also washed his hands more than once, but not in such luxurious surroundings. On that day he had knelt beside a stream in the Kynswood, washing a dead man's blood from his hands and clothes. Afterward, he left the woods and made his way into Erchester, then up Main Row and through the castle gates with the tradesmen and workers who were entering the Hayholt for the day.

Once inside the walls he had stopped to look over the great common yard where his father Brindalles had died during the last battle in Erkynland of the Storm King's War. Even at that early hour of the day the yard between the castle's outer and inner baileys had been full of people, servants and soldiers, tradesmen and farmers, none of them paying any attention whatsoever to the fair-haired youth in ragged clothes standing just inside the shadow of the massive gate tower.

Pasevalles hadn't known how he would feel about this place where his father had been hacked to death by Norns, but after the years of imagining it, he surprised himself by feeling almost nothing, just the same dull resentment he had long held over the way that life or God had favored some—but not him.

Still, he had come to the Hayholt for a purpose, and he knew that purpose would not be served by standing on the common, brooding. He needed to find a crack he could use to enter in the system—someone to whom he could attach himself and make himself useful. And it should be someone with powerful friends.

Within a short time he had found the ideal candidate—Father Strangyeard, the gentle, one-eyed priest who was a close associate of the High King and High Queen and now acted as their chief almoner, disbursing the throne's money to various worthy causes. Because Pasevalles with his noble upbringing could read and write and speak well, he had quickly secured a position as a cleric working with the account books of the castle's busy Chancelry, and made himself as useful there as he could. Father Strangyeard soon took a liking to the young Nabban-man, in part because Pasevalles was often still bent over his accounts long after the other clerics had left, candle burned down almost to nothing. The old priest would sometimes bring him a cup of wine and share stories of the fierce, frightening days of the war, when Norns had moved through the Hayholt by night and the mad King Elias, with the aid of the dreaded red priest, Pryrates, had almost brought the undead demon Storm King back to life.

Pasevalles had always listened to Strangyeard's tales with apparent fascination, and in turn shared some carefully altered stories of his own life, about his sorrow at his father's early death and the cruel way he had been thrust from his patrimony by an evil relative. Pasevalles had practiced making faces in a looking glass most of his life so he would be able to appear as other people did, and as he relayed these stories he wore a mask of deep sadness combined with a bit of a yearning expression that suggested a young man trying to lift himself above his sorrow and do something useful with his life.

Strangyeard always enjoyed "our talks," as he called them, and the courteous, hard-working new cleric had quickly become one of the priest's favorites. After several months had passed, Pasevalles shyly—or at least that was the face he had chosen—admitted that he was the nephew of Baron Seriddan of Metessa and son of the man who had heroically masqueraded as Prince Josua in the last great fight and lost his life doing so.

Strangyeard was stunned. "The nephew of Metessa? But that means you're— don't tell me, I know his name, I swear I do—Brindalles! You are the son of Brindalles! But why didn't you tell me, young man? Why didn't you tell me?"

"I did not want to presume on old acquaintances," Pasevalles told the old priest. "I wanted to show what I could do on my own, like honorable Sir Fluiren in the stories. Besides, I am no knight, and my father was only the baron's younger brother."

"But you have more than proved your worth!" Strangyeard assured him. "And it is not more warriors we need in these thankfully peaceful days. We need men of learning willing to take on hard work, like you, young man—just like you!"

This additional mark of family heroism had only done Pasevalles good in the old priest's eyes, and as the years passed he had risen swiftly through the ranks of the Almonry. When the old Lord Chancellor died, Father Strangyeard became the new Chancellor—complete with a noble title that the old priest never used and hardly even seemed to remember. Of course, he took Pasevalles with him. And when the Red Ruin felled Strangyeard himself, it seemed only natural to King Simon and Queen Miriamele that Pasevalles, Strangyeard's chief assistant, whose history was now known to all, should succeed him as Lord Chancellor. He was gifted with a title of his own and the income from a barony in Hewenshire, and for the first time since his father and uncle had died, he had money of his own.

For a little while he had simply enjoyed the greater freedom, the better food and drink and clothes, the admiring way that people looked at him, but after awhile even those pleasures were not enough. Weary of hard work in the Almonry and Chancelry, he briefly contemplated a life as a peer of the realm, but the idea of living in a small castle in windy, rainy Hewenshire was not worth considering. And in any case, he had developed other interests, some of which were best indulged in a large city like Erchester. More diversions were to be found in the old scrolls and papers and books that filled the castle, many of which had not been examined for generations. From those records, and from documents he obtained by other methods, he learned more of the castle's history, and—more importantly—of the history of what lay below it. Then the desire to see for himself became stronger than his caution, and he began to explore. And what he found there had changed everything.

"Baron Pasevalles! My Lord!"

Startled out of his memories, he took a moment to compose his features before turning. Duchess Nelda, now wearing a more suitable embroidered robe and slippers, was hurrying after him down the hall, swaying like an overloaded oxcart.

"Yes, Your Grace? Is everything well?"

She stopped beside him, already a little out of breath. "The duke is sleeping. I wanted to thank you for your help. You are very kind."

He smiled, wondering what else was on her mind—he could not imagine the stout duchess hurrying herself just to thank him. "No need, my lady. The duke is a good friend."

She hesitated. "You won't tell the king, will you? I mean, how you found Osric? It is just that my husband is so distraught over our poor Idela . . . !" Tears welled in her eyes, and to stave off that unpleasant display, Pasevalles laid his hand on her arm.

"It will remain between us." He did not bother to tell her that Simon already knew about the drunken duke's behavior. It was always useful to have a favor in hand.

"Oh. Oh, thank you." The duchess was still trying to catch her breath. "Bless you, my lord. The king has so much on his mind already, with the queen away in Nabban and all."

It was interesting, he thought, how women seemed to cope with troubles better than men. Only Pasevalles himself saw everything, but in general, women saw more than men did, and were better at keeping it to themselves. He wondered how he could make Nelda's gratitude useful. "The secret is safe with me."

She thanked him again and turned back to her bedchamber and the slumbering duke.

Pasevalles watched her go. His face showed nothing, but he was thinking about secrets, thinking about favors, and, as always, thinking about what he would do next.

Already the city of Meremund was falling away behind them, the harbor small and pretty as a jewel box, the great spire of St. Tankred's just a slim dagger's point poking above the housetops. Miriamele stood at the quarterdeck rail and watched the froth of the *Hylissa's* wake and the seabirds hovering above it, gliding and flipping like leaves tugged from their branches by the wind. Being on the open ocean at last gave her an unexpected sense of freedom, a feeling that she could at any moment simply change direction and keep going, sail away from every responsibility and care. The sea went on forever as far as anyone knew, and there were moments when that seemed like exactly the right amount of distance to put between herself and the cares of the High Throne.

But I could not go without my Simon. And I would not leave him behind to deal with my responsibilities. He never wanted anything but me, poor fellow. I wanted both him and the throne.

"Come away, Majesty, please." Lady Shulamit and two other of the queen's female companions had come out on deck. It was a fairly warm morning, but Shulamit was dressed as though for a bitter storm, wound in a thick cloak that had been reinforced with at least two woolen scarves, one around her neck and the other covering her ears and the underside of her chin, so that she looked like a lumpy nun. "It isn't safe. There are kilpa about. See, there!" Shulamit pointed out into the sun's glare with a shaky hand.

Miriamele frowned. "First of all, those can't be kilpa, not this far north and not so many. Secondly, even if those were kilpa, they do not climb onto large ships, so we would not be in danger." But a black trace of memory suddenly came to her, a nightmarish vision of hooting, gape-mouthed phantoms.

That was more than thirty years ago, she told herself. And the Storm King's return had made the dreadful sea-creatures restless and dangerous in those days. Still, she stared at what Shulamit was pointing at, low bumps dragging white ripples. They might be sea otters, which often moved in large family groups. Kilpa did not. *So those couldn't be kilpa. Simple.* But she did not feel as comfortable in that certainty as she would have liked.

"Come, Majesty," said Shulamit. "Denah must have put out something to break our fast by now. You must be hungry."

Her two other ladies-in-waiting agreed that, yes, Miriamele must be hungry.

"But I'm not. Not yet. I think I will walk on the deck a little longer. It's a bright, clear day and I'm enjoying the view, but the rest of you look cold. You go ahead and I'll join you soon. And don't worry." She smiled at Shulamit, although it was a little forced—Miri hated to be mothered. "I promise I won't lean over the railing, in case the kilpa have learned to leap like dolphins."

When she had at last persuaded her ladies to leave her, Miriamele walked back to the starboard rail and stared out across the coastal breakers to the darker green of the ocean. Within an hour or two they would be out in the open sea, and then the deck would be colder and the motion of the ship a great deal rougher. She was not going to be hurried away from a calm morning.

As she stood watching the blue of the sky deepen, she felt rather than saw or heard someone standing beside her. One of the ship's boys was waiting for her attention, a youth of perhaps ten years, his eyes wide and his mouth clenched tightly shut as if to protect himself from accidentally saying something treasonous or heretical in front of the queen. The thought amused her.

"Y'r Majesty," he said when he saw her looking, and then made a strange half-bow, as though he wasn't quite sure whether he should try it at all. "Begging pardon. A message, that is. I mean, that's what I have. For you."

"A message?"

"Yes'm."

She looked at him. He stared back, hair wild from the wind's handling, eyes still wide as wide could be. "And the message is . . . ?" she asked at last.

"He wants you to come see him. Said to tell you . . . *secret*-like." Only now did he think to look around, although *Hylissa's* sailors were far too busy making ready for the open sea to pay attention even to their monarch.

"And who is 'he'? The captain?" She had a thought. "Escritor Auxis, perhaps?"

The boy looked alarmed, as though he might have been tasked with messages from those worthies as well and had somehow completely forgotten them. "No'm. Don't think so, no. From the Niskie-fella. He's in the hole. Wants to talk to you, if Y'r Majesty finds it confident." He frowned, then brightened. "*Convenient*. I mean."

"The hole? Ah, do you mean the Niskie Hole? Tell me where it is, and I'll go directly." But she was not as blithe as she made out. Memories of the hooting kilpa clambering onto her ship, of flames in the sails, and above all, of a keening, desperate song, were now besieging her in earnest. "I did not know we even had a Niskie on the ship."

"Came on at Meremund, he did. We take 'em on much farther north nowadays." He was proud of having a seaman's knowledge beyond his years, but there was something else beneath his words, something fearful. "I'll show you where. Thank you, ma'am. Your Majesty, ma'am."

"Very well. And what's your name, young sir?"

Again the eyes widened. He clearly did not know why she was asking, and for a moment she thought he was considering giving her a false name, but at last fear or training won out. "Ham, Majesty. Like the back of y'r leg." He colored, suddenly and brightly. "Not *your* leg, 'course. Not Y'r Majesty's. But someone's." He started to turn around to point at the back of his leg, then thought better of it, and stood looking completely dumbfounded. It was all Miri could do not to smile.

"Very well, Sir Ham. You have delivered your message most bravely. Now lead me to the Niskie Hole and I will give you a fithing-piece for your services."

Ham escorted her to a small door at the end of a narrow passageway under the forecastle. After the boy had been generously rewarded and had hurried off, she knocked on the door and was invited inside.

The cabin was small even for shipboard, and unadorned but for a thin pallet and a sack laid out upon it. A slender person in a gray hooded cloak, who had been bending over the sack, straightened at her entrance. He was smaller than she was, with long, thin fingers showing at the end of his wide sleeves, a deeply tanned face, and huge, dark eyes. Even if his size and shape had not suggested it already, those gold-flecked eyes would have told her this was a Niskie.

"You do me an honor, Queen Miriamele," he said, but did not bow or take her hand, almost as though they were equals. "Forgive me not coming to you, but it is never good to court unnecessary talk on a ship. I am Gan Doha."

She started. "You have the same name as another of your kind I used to know."

He nodded. "Gan Itai. My great-great grandmother."

Something too large to express suddenly welled inside Miri's breast. "She saved my life."

"I know," said Gan Doha. "It is one of our clan's proudest tales."

The powerful tide of memories did not prevent a sudden bite of suspicion. "Gan Itai died with the *Eadne Cloud* in the middle of the Bay of Firannos. How could even her family know of it?"

"She did not—not exactly. But sit, please. Even a sea watcher cannot keep a queen standing." He smiled, but it was an odd, half-hearted thing. He pushed a low stool toward her, a gesture that reminded her so strongly of his ancestor and herself in a tiny cabin much like this, that she struggled against tears. But she still wondered how this Gan Doha could know anything about what had happened on that ill-fated ship all those years ago—a lifetime ago.

Before she could ask her first question, the Niskie held up a long forefinger. "First let me tell you what I know and why I know it, instead of playing at riddles. When you were young you ran away from your father, pretending to be a commoner. You were taken up by Earl Aspitis, whose ship *Eadne Cloud* was my great-grandmother's responsibility—her *instrument*, as we Tinukeda'ya say. Latterly you found out that Aspitis was an ally of your father and planned to force you to marry him. My foreparent Gan Itai decided—and for more than one single reason—that she could not stand by and see it happen. So instead of singing the monstrous kilpa *down*, as is our usual task, she called them *up* instead. She summoned them, and they came to *Eadne Cloud* in terrible numbers. Does this all have the sound of truth to you, Queen Miriamele?"

"Yes, yes it does. But how do you know this?"

"I am reaching that. When the burning and crippled ship at last began to sink, my great-grandmother was determined to sink with it—she had betrayed her trust, after all, and helped to destroy her instrument, however important her reasons. But a wave swept her over the side, and she could not reach the ship again, so gave herself to the sea. But she did not die—not then. Later, in the early hours of light, another ship found her still afloat but dying. Before she breathed her last breath, she told everything to the sea watcher of that vessel, and he brought the tale back to our people in Nabban. When you and your husband the king at last were victorious, we thought of our foreparent's part in it all and were proud. And you have not disappointed us—although that is not true for all those who have ruled in your name here in the south."

Miriamele did not at first know what to say. She had thought for so long that Gan Itai's death had at least been swift that she was overcome by learning the truth, and now tears did come to her eyes. "She saved me. She truly saved me!" was all she could say.

Gan Doha did not try to soothe her or silence her, just waited patiently until she had dabbed her eyes dry. "I did not tell you this to make you sad," he said at last.

"I do not mind. I owe Gan Itai more than I can say—more than I could have repaid even if she lived. Is there something I can do for her family? I should have thought of that before—should have tried to find her relatives." A spate of fresh tears came. She blotted them with the sleeve of her gown. "I have done badly by your family, Gan Doha, and I apologize. The truth of being a monarch is that you are always disappointing someone, cheating someone else, though you never wish to do it." *I sound like my husband*, she thought, and a fresh pang of missing him added to her sudden unhappiness.

"We want and need nothing from you," the Niskie said, "—at least, nothing in the way of reward or thanks. But our elders wish an audience with you when you reach Nabban. They say it is important to both your people and mine. That is why they sent me to Meremund to sing for *Hylissa*, so that I might have this chance to speak with you. I did not think I would be lucky enough to manage it so soon. Will you come to them in Nabban without making much of it? The elders said to tell you that they think secrecy is better than openness, at least until you have heard what they have to say."

"Of course," she told him. "As I said, I owe you and your people far more than that. But how will I know where to come, and when?"

"That will be made clear when the time is closer," Gan Doha said. His wide eyes hinted at some amusement she did not understand. "Do not be surprised. We have ways to communicate even within the great Sancellan Mahistrevis itself."

When she left the Niskie and made her way back up to the forecastle, Miriamele was so full of confused new thoughts and old memories that she did not at first hear that someone was calling her. It was Denah, her pretty young maid, and the girl had been searching for Miriamele long and hard enough that her round face was flushed and her curly hair had come loose and spilled from beneath her headdress.

"Your Majesty, there you are! I've been looking everywhere! The captain wants you."

Miriamele rolled her eyes. Barely an hour out of port and already she was being batted from place to place like a shuttlecock. "And does the captain expect me to hurry to him, like a tavern maid?"

"No, Majesty! He's right there! See, he's coming!"

Captain Felisso was indeed bounding up the ladder from the main deck, waving something white in his hand. "Majesty, Majesty, a thousand pardons— no, a hundred thousand, because we could not find you!" Felisso was Perdruinese by birth, and when excited or angry his old accent strengthened, so for a moment she couldn't understand what he'd said.

"But I'm here, Captain. I did not fall off the ship and no matter what my ladies might have said, I was in no danger of being snatched by a kilpa."

He gave her a surprised look at that, but quickly recovered his aplomb. "Just so, just so. But I am still so very dreadful sorry I could not find you, in case there was a message back. But wait, of course, the messenger is still on board. He came in a little boat of his own. Foolish me. Yes, of course you can send a message back. He said it was very important."

"Who said? I confess I don't know what you're trying to tell me, Captain."

"A messenger set out from the port only moments after we were casted off. We saw him and did our best to wait until we could meet him with our own boat. He had a message for you—from the king, he said. From your husband in Erkynland, the king himself!"

"Yes, my husband is the king, that much is certainly true." Already she was looking at the folded white sheet of parchment with trepidation. "May I have it, Captain, if it is truly for me?"

Felisso jumped as if someone had swung an ax at him. "Oh, by the saints, Majesty, of course. Forgive me." With a sweeping bow, he handed her the letter.

The seal was Simon's. The hand was his too, both the legibility and the spelling as usual leaving something to be desired. She read the first line, then the second, then read them both again. A hole seemed to have opened in the middle of her body. She thought she could feel cold air blowing right through her.

"Majesty?" said Denah, frightened by Miri's face. "Are you ill?"

"Please, Majesty, can I give you my arm?" said the captain. "I pray it is not bad news."

"Oh, but it is," she said, then realized she had spoken so quietly that they might not even have heard her. "I fear it is," she said more loudly. The day seemed to have turned into something unreal, a dream, a mistake, something that should be discarded and started over. "My husband writes to say that Princess Idela, the wife of our son—and the mother of the heir to the High Throne—is dead."

She left the captain standing, sputtering out sympathy and protestations of grief. When Denah wanted to walk with her, she waved the girl away. She did not want to speak to anyone.

Everything. Nothing. She felt everything and nothing. The world she had greeted that morning was not the world she had thought it was, and she was lost and alone on a world of water, agonizingly far from home.

3

The Hidden

"Do you know how your father lost his hand, Derra?" her mother had once asked, with the tone of someone about to reveal an important secret. She often said things like that, suddenly and out of nowhere, as though she were answering angry voices only she could hear.

"In a war," Derra—as she had then been called—answered. "He said it happened a long time ago, before he met you."

"He lost it for a woman," Vorzheva continued, as if her daughter had not spoken. "A woman he still loves, a woman he keeps in his heart like a treasure."

"What a ridiculous thing to tell a child," her father said, laughing, but his face looked a little angry. "I was fighting to protect my brother's wife. Our caravan was attacked and she was killed, so it is a sad thing to talk about. Killed by Thrithings-men, as a matter of fact—your mother's people."

Her mother turned on him. "Not my clan! My clan fought on your father's side!"

Derra had stopped paying attention, because she had heard it before. She had already begged her father for the story until he'd told her. She couldn't remember how old she'd been when she first noticed that other men were not like her father, that most of them had two hands, but from that moment on she had burned to know the story. Her brother Deornoth, strangely, had not, and had walked away when her father began to explain.

But Deornoth had always been that way. He did not like bloodshed, not even in stories. Once when they were smaller he had hit Sagra, a boy who lived near their parents' inn, and bloodied the child's nose. Deornoth had run home and hidden under his blanket, refusing to come out even when Sagra himself came by later in the evening to ask him out to play.

But Derra had always loved stories. She didn't care that her father had only one hand, or that he had once been a prince but had decided not to be—a story her mother told often, sometimes as evidence of his love for her, sometimes as evidence of the reverse, especially when she was feeling oppressed by what she called "this wretched-smelling, watery place!"—Kwanitupul, their home on the edge of the swampy Wran.

*   *   *

It seemed strange to think about those days now, especially when she could not have been further away from them—not in plain distance or years. The lengthy, winding road that had led her to this hiding place in the deep blackness beneath the great mountain Nakkiga was only bits of separated memory now, like beads on a necklace.

When their father had not returned from his journey, her mother Vorzheva had despaired. After months of rage and recriminations against her vanished husband, she at last decided to take Derra and Deornoth north—although with what plan she never told them. She had sold the inn called Pelippa's Bowl and its unexalted reputation for very little—even Derra, despite being only ten years, had known they were being cheated by the fat merchant—then set out with all their remaining goods piled on a single cart. But they were captured on the road by Thrithings-men, who had been mostly interested in Vorzheva's purse, then heard her muttering under her breath in her original tongue, which was also theirs. Only a few days later the entire family—minus any valuable belongings and the proceeds from selling the inn, of course—had been delivered to Vorzheva's horrible father, Thane Fikolmij, ruler over much of the High Thrithings. From that point everything in Derra's life had gone from merely bad to dreadful. Her twin brother Deornoth was sent away to live with another clan—he did not even get to say goodbye. And Derra and her mother became no better than slaves to Fikolmij, laboring from dawn to dusk and beyond with the other women in her grandfather's camp.

Derra might have been able to put up with even such a dire change in fortune, but with each day after Deornoth had been taken away, her mother seemed to lose life. Vorzheva's eyes became dark-circled and her face gaunt—she could barely force herself to eat. She even lost interest in Derra and began to avoid her. Derra's kindly Aunt Hyara, the only good thing that had happened to her since her father vanished, tried to tell her that Vorzheva was not angry at her, but that each time she looked at her daughter, she saw the absent twin as well, her son, and it broke her heart.

"She will come back to you," Hyara had said. "Give her time."

But time had been the one thing Derra had not been able to give. Every day felt like being buried alive. She was not even allowed to mix with the other children—her grandfather deemed her too old for play when there was work to be done.

And worse, her grandfather had begun to notice her in other ways, ways Derra could not talk about with her mother, who hardly spoke to her at all, or even with Aunt Hyara. And when the old man's furtive squeezing and pinching and poking began to keep her from sleeping at night because she was terrified he would come to her bed, she decided she would run away from the camp, from the wagons, from her monstrous grandfather and her silent, brooding mother, who acted as though she had lost both children and not just one . . .

She stopped, startled by a noise from the underground lake. She had been walking nearly aimlessly, adrift in memories, but the sound reminded her that she was down in the underground depths beneath the city of Nakkiga, and discovery would likely mean death. Or worse.

She folded the glowing sphere called a *ni'yo* deeper into her hand, until it showed as only a faint red glow in the web of her finger and thumb. Then she stood in silence, listening. She heard a splash. Perhaps only a fish, but it meant she had wandered too close to the shore of the underground lake. As far as she knew, there were no other people in any of the other lakefront dwellings, most of which belonged to rich nobles who only made the long journey out from the heart of the city during festivals. But back in the Enduya clan house, Khimabu, wife of her lover and master Viyeki, must have realized by now that Tzoja had fled. So she could not afford to be noticed even by some gardener or servant preparing for the arrival of a rich master—not by anyone who might mention to masters that he had seen a mortal woman near the lake.

And what if the splash were something else entirely? Things moved down here in the dark tunnels that even Viyeki avoided talking about, and he was magister of the order that had excavated these deep places.

She crouched unmoving. With her light-sphere hidden, the only glow came from the strange, shining worms that dangled above the lake on strands of luminous silk. Tzoja had been thinking of the old days, her old life when she had still been called Derra, and for a moment she could imagine the glowing creatures as something else, as stars in the broad sky over lands she had not seen in many years.

The Thrithings, she thought, *and Erkynland, and last in Rimmersgard, with Roskva and the Astalines. Sky as far as I could see in all directions, the mountains so distant they were only shadows . . .*

The splash came again, making her heart speed, but now she was almost certain a sound so small must come from a fish or a frog; she felt her fear ease. Tzoja knew she might have to start thinking about catching fish soon; the food she had brought from the clan-house pantry would not last too much longer. She had eked out her supplies as carefully as she could, though it was difficult to know how much time was passing in a dark house in a cavern far beneath the ground, a place where she dared not even light a fire for fear of someone seeing it.

Living day after day alone in a pitch-black house in a pitch-black cavern, with only the ghost light of the worms for illumination, Tzoja had begun to feel as though she was trapped in some terrible dream from which she could not awake. So she had begun her daily walks around the lake to a rich manor house some distance away. By its outer decorations and the spiral on the door, the house seemed to belong to somebody well-placed in the Order of Song. She would never have dared to cross the threshold of such a place, but whoever owned the house had placed a very fine water clock in a grotto on the outer grounds of the property. The clock was a mysterious arrangement of gears and troughs and several stone jars of water, but she could mark by the movement of the decorated dial in the center of one of the largest gears how the face of the moon was changing in the sky above the mountain, on the far side of an incomprehensible weight of stone.

Still, the noises had unnerved her, and she decided to give up this day's visit to the water clock and turn back.

It's the darkness, she told herself as she retreated, shielding the sphere in her hand so that only the tiniest needles of light illuminated her track. She thought she had learned all its tricks and cruelties while living in Nakkiga, but as bad as things had been in the gloomy Hikeda'ya city, this was much worse.

But I can survive. I must. She had to stay alive until Viyeki returned. If she was caught, Khimabu would see that she was killed. But even that meant nothing to Tzoja compared to the true horror: Khimabu would not be satisfied with destroying Tzoja alone, but would want herself rid of Nezeru as well, her husband's half-mortal bastard.

Nezeru, her daughter Nezeru, so strange and so beautiful, a fierce little animal from the very first moment she had emerged into the world. Tzoja had never pretended to understand her child, but that had never prevented her helpless love.

I will not let that witch harm my daughter, she thought as she made her way quietly up from the main path and through the modest grounds of Viyeki's house. For a moment a rush of anger dissolved all her fears. *I will die with my fingernails in Khimabu's eyes and my teeth in her throat if I have to.*

She was so caught up in imagining it that she did not stop to listen at the door she always used, which opened on the back gardens. Instead she was halfway down the hall before she heard noises coming from the kitchen.

Whispers.

Tzoja stopped so quickly she almost fell down. A thousand ideas rushed into her head at once—it was the Hamakha Guard, looking for her, or robbers who would kill her before despoiling Viyeki's house, or even ghastly shades out of the depths. But was it really whispering she heard, or was it something else? She paused again, listening with fast-beating heart to the wordless sounds—squeaking, chittering, and the rattle of small things being pushed across the kitchen's stony floors.

Rats! Oh, Usires and all the other gods, what if they've found my food?

Tzoja felt around just inside the door until she discovered one of Viyeki's walking sticks, then edged down the corridor, sliding her feet across the polished floors to move as silently as possible. The closer she got to the kitchen, the more clearly she could hear the strange sounds; for a moment she almost thought she heard a cadence to them, like speech.

She lifted the stick high, then pushed open the kitchen door and lifted the *ni'yo*. A slight pressure of her fingers made it flare into brightness and paint the entire scene in an instant.

Eyes. Eyes and grotesque shapes, staring at her—a waking nightmare.

Tzoja gasped and almost dropped the sphere. The figures in front of her suddenly burst into life, squealing and hissing as they scattered in all directions to escape the sudden glare. She saw eyes, hands, limbs, but all in a mere moment before their owners scuttled into the dark corners of the kitchen or past her into the hallway, so that she could not immediately make sense of what she had seen.

They were not rats, that was dreadfully clear: she had seen faces. Mortals like herself? No. Hikeda'ya? No. In that panicky instant she could not even think of a prayer, though she sorely wished to make one.

She had fallen backward at the first shock; with her fingers loosened, the light of the sphere began to die. All around her she could hear clatter and scratching as its glow faded, then she was surrounded by darkness again and in another moment, by silence as well.

Monsters, was her first real thought, remembering the mad things the flare of light had revealed. Small monsters, perhaps, but what else could you call them? There was one like a naked child with one limb bizarrely long, others with no real limbs at all, as well as fat, toadlike creatures with human skin and bulging but still human eyes. Already the details were sliding from her memory—it had all been too swift, too violently strange, too unexpected.

What could they be? Why did those horrors come here? I have lost my sanctuary. Her thoughts were like an avalanche of stones. Monsters, and they were still all around! She straightened up, half-certain she would feel hands grabbing at her ankles at any moment, then she squeezed and rubbed the sphere until its full radiance burst forth again, but in its yellowy light the kitchen was empty and silent.

No, not silent, she realized after a moment. Beside her own hitching, terrified breath, she could hear another noise, a soft, wordless moan from deeper in the large kitchen. What were those things? She was grateful that they seemed as startled and frightened as she was, but she did not trust it would last.

I should leave this place this very moment, she told herself. *Whatever they are, the house is no longer safe. It certainly isn't secret.* But she had spent days learning the house's plan by darkness, had found hiding places for all her belongings so that nobody arriving suddenly would know she was here unless they actually caught her. Where would she go if she left? To another house beside the lake, probably just as full of hairless cavern rats or whatever those ghastly things had been? Another festival house that, unlike Viyeki's, might become occupied at any time?

She heard a noise coming from the brick oven, a strange, thin sound like an animal gasping for breath or a baby beginning to cry. It did not sound as if it came from anything large, so she felt around for the walking stick she had dropped, then slowly and quietly got to her feet. The kitchen was long—when the house had been occupied, people owning the place often brought large contingents of servants to stay as well as guests, and the kitchen had to provide for them all.

Tzoja made her way across the polished flagstones in darkness, marveling at how long it took her to cross it. As she drew closer to the oven, her foot crunched down on something and the muffled whimpering abruptly stopped. After the initial shock and a stifled scream, she reached down hesitantly and discovered what she had trod on—a heel of bread. She squeezed hard on the light-sphere to increase the glow.

Whatever was making the hitching sound went silent again. The heel of bread was the largest piece of food on the floor; the rest were little more than crumbs and a few gnawed ends. With a sudden upswelling of horror and despair, she ran back across the kitchen, heedless now of the light that would be visible to anyone outside the house nearby, and threw open the chest in which she had hidden her supply of bread, several large loaves, enough to last her for weeks.

Gone. All gone. A few fragments of dried fruit and sausage scattered among the crumbs and gnawed crusts confirmed what she already feared, but she doggedly dragged out the covered basket where the food had been kept and discovered that all but a single waxwing sausage and a few tiny morsels of cheese were gone.

It was all Tzoja could do not to let out a howl of rage and misery. All her stores, so carefully obtained and hidden, food that should have lasted her until Sky-Singer's Moon, or even Tortoise, now gone.

She would have to go back into Nakkiga or risk starvation.

Her fury rose again. She swung the *ni'iyo* around the wide kitchen until its light fell on the round bread oven. Whatever hid inside began making soft, terrified noises again. Angry, frightened, gripped by feelings she couldn't even name, she reached down and shoved the ball of light close to the oven door as she leaned forward, careful not to get too close in case whatever was hiding there had claws. Then she pulled the door open.

An infant stared back at her from the oven's depths, not human, not Hikeda'ya, but not impossibly far from either. A naked, big-eyed infant with a swollen belly, no mouth between its nose and receding chin, and a slit throat— a horrible slash of red across the center of its neck.

Tzoja recoiled in horror and almost fell again. The thing in the oven gave a soft, startled shriek, but did not try to escape. She leaned toward the opening again. Huge eyes stared back at her, dark as lumps of coal.

It wasn't a wound across its neck at all, she saw now with a mixture of disgust and astonishment, but a mouth, which for some unfathomable reason opened in its neck instead of its face. For a moment, everything she had ever heard about demons and monsters came back to her, from her mother's tales of unnatural grassland fiends to Valada Roskva, her friend and teacher, warning about restless things that watched the living from beyond the veil of death. But then the unnatural mouth of the thing in the oven pressed together in a wrinkled pucker before opening again to emit a wail of terror, and despite her fear, she became a mother again.

"Here now," she said, suddenly realizing that the noise might be a bigger

danger to her than even the strange little creature itself. *"Hush. Stop that."* Without noticing, she had slipped back into the tongue of her own childhood, her mother's words straight from the grasslands. *"Hush. The Night Eater will hear."*

And then, as if to prove her words, Tzoja heard a strange, uneven noise in the great hallway beyond the kitchen—*thump-drag, thump-drag, thump-drag.* Whatever was making the footsteps was no tiny monstrosity like the oven-beast, but sounded larger than any mortal or Hikeda'ya.

Gripped again by terror, Tzoja only remembered the other door to the kitchen when it swung open. She lifted her light even as she stumbled backward. A huge, two-headed shape that could only have leaped out of nightmare or madness swayed in the doorway. It threw its misshapen hands up before it and let out a rumbling noise of rage as it lurched toward her.

The sphere dropped from her nerveless fingers. For a moment the falling light seemed to make everything leap into the air, then the *ni'yo* struck the ground and went out.

Tzoja clambered after it, groping with both hands, and when she found it she lifted it and held it before her like a weapon as she squeezed it into shining life. A huge shape loomed above her, but fell back, groaning as though the light was painful as fire. The thing wiped frantically at its eyes with the back of a massive forearm as she pushed herself back out of reach. The creature's vast face turned toward her, eyes tightly shut. It was as bizarre and misshapen as a grass-land shaman's demon mask, the mouth slack, the face hurt and angry but as incomprehending as the lowest animal.

"Do not fear," the monster said in oddly-accented Hikeda'yasao, but as if to prove that terrible face truly was a mask, the slack lips did not move in time with the words, or at all. "We do not harm you."

Now she finally saw the second head that she had glimpsed in the doorway, as large as the first but canted at a strange angle and thus slightly hidden from her at first. This head, despite being nearly as grotesque as the first, hairless and with round, slightly crooked eyes, seemed actually to be watching her with interest, and when the voice came again and the lips moved in time with it, she saw that this head was the speaker, not the first one. "Please do not make the light bright again," it said. "It hurts the eyes, mine and Dasa's both."

She had just been about to make the sphere glare as brightly as she could, but the speaker's tone was reasonable, almost apologetic, and she hesitated. She pushed herself back a little farther, and only then did she see that what had come through the kitchen doorway was not one creature with two heads, but two creatures, one carried by the other. The head that spoke lolled atop a shrunken, almost infantile body whose legs ended in stumps just where the knees should have been. This nodding oddity was curled in the crook of a powerful arm that belonged to a carry-man, one of the nearly mindless Tinukeda'ya bred for servitude, but this carry-man had a badly withered leg, and she now understood the step-and-drag sound that had announced its arrival.

But there was no such thing anywhere in Nakkiga as a crippled carry-man, let alone one of infant-sized with no legs—the Hikeda'ya would never allow such malformed creatures to live. Even Viyeki, the kindest she had met, would have had them dispatched in an instant.

"Who are you? *What* are you?" she demanded, voice trembling.

"Naya Nos am I," said the malformed infant. "This is my brother-in-claim, Dasa. He does not speak." The swollen baby face looked grave. "What we are is Hidden Ones—but that is not something to concern you. Our young ones stole from you. We are sorry, but they have gone long without food, and it has been a poor season for both gathering and gifting. We will do our best to make good what they took from you."

The day's events had been so shocking that Tzoja could only watch in stunned silence as the infant-sized creature called to the remaining Hidden, who scuttled out of the oven and other hiding places, eyes wide with fear, then crawled past her as swiftly as they could, as though Tzoja were a sleeping predator instead of the victim of their raid. The small horrors followed their rescuers out of the festival house and in moments had vanished into the darkness. She pushed the door closed behind them, then stumbled back to the kitchen to pick up the few crumbs that remained, weeping silently as she pressed the salvaged remnants into a single lump that would be that night's supper—perhaps her last meal for a long time.

Nonao, the secretary who had replaced poor Yemon after his execution, was unobtrusive even by the exacting standards of the Hikeda'ya, but Viyeki still noticed him as he stood just outside the simple, slanted wall of fabric that was the magister's tent. Viyeki did not look up or acknowledge him in any way, but continued to read his much-handled copy of *The Five Fingers of the Queen's Hand* with what must have looked like great concentration. At last even Nonao's patience began to stretch beyond the fraying point: the secretary made a small movement, a silent shift of weight from one foot to the other.

Viyeki looked at him just long enough to make certain Nonao saw him, then dropped his eyes to the book again. "What do you want?"

"This worthless servant begs your pardon, High Magister, but the queen's relative Prince-Templar Pratiki has arrived."

"Ah." Viyeki kept his eyes on the words, though he was not truly very much interested in them. Like all in his caste, he had committed the famous tract to memory long before he reached adulthhood.

"Do you not wish to greet him, High Magister?"

"Of course! That is why I have returned to the words of venerated Xohabi."

To remind myself of what is expected, what is right." He held the book up as though Nonao might not have seen it before. "You have read *The Five Fingers*?"

"Of course, Master!"

"So full of wisdom. So full of help for every situation." Viyeki began to read. *"The Five Fingers are the tools the Queen, the Mother of the People, uses to feed and shelter and protect her people. Without a knowledge of these tools and how they are used, without an energetic determination to act for the good of all the People, a noble can only hinder, not help, the Queen in her great work.'* You agree of course, Nonao?"

"Of course, Master. They are the words I live by, and which are always uppermost in my thoughts as I strive to serve you and the Mother of All."

"Good, good." He ignored Nonao's increasing anxiousness. "How wise was great Xohabi! Give your ear to this, Nonao-tza—the elegant simplicity of his words entrances still, all these Great Years later! *'Loyalty to the People is the first finger. Without dedication to your own kind, you are no better than a solitary witiko'ya in the wilderness, hunting without a pack, dying alone of starvation.'* So true! Who would reject his own people? And what else should be the lot of such a fool or traitor but death?"

"Yes, Master."

"And how much joy I get from revisiting these words, no matter how often I have read them before. Loyalty to the race! Loyalty to the city! Loyalty to the order and, of course, loyalty to our queen and the Garden that birthed us . . . !" He shook his head in mock-wonder. "I have heard it said that in this one slender volume is written every word needed for a good life. I shall never tire of it."

Nonao was wringing his hands together, too anxious now even to hide it. "No one reveres Xohabi—or *you*—more greatly than I do, Master, and please forgive my unpardonable interruption . . ."

Viyeki decided he had tormented his servant long enough. He did not dislike Nonao personally, but he knew beyond doubt that the new secretary was passing information to the relatives of Viyeki's wife Khimabu and doubtless to others as well. It would have been virtually impossible to find someone utterly honorable and incorruptible to fill the position—there were very few such creatures to be found in all of Nakkiga, and none of them had the talent or intelligence to do a good job with anything more challenging than spreading oil on a slice of *puju*—so he was content with a secretary he knew from the start not to trust.

But my old master Yaarike would have warned me not to treat him too badly. Better a casual enemy than a determined one. And if I make too much obvious sport of the Five Fingers, he'll report that to the listening ears as well. The book was an object of near-religious veneration among the noble classes, although Viyeki had no doubt that many of its most noisy proponents were no more inspired by Xohabi's legendary fawning than he was.

So we make liars of ourselves, and by doing so, prove Xohabi a liar also.

It was a new thought, and one that brought him a pang of what felt like sudden fright. Was he losing his mind, that such heretical thoughts came to him so easily these days?

The Sacrifices stood lined up at one end of the camp in their martial rigor, along with Viyeki's Builders and the rest of the company, as the prince-templar's party made its way up to the hilltop beneath the deep blue of a clear night. All expression absent from his face but serene satisfaction—the only proper look for a high noble in the presence of the very highest noble family, the queen's—Viyeki observed that the prince-templar was dressed in the full panoply of his sacred station, robed and hooded in white with yellow ornamentation. His Serene Highness Pratiki wore his white hair long and unadorned. His skin was so pale it almost seemed to glow from within, like the wax of a burning candle, but the prince-templar's eyes, though calm and almost sorrowful in appearance, watched everything carefully. He was of the queen's Hamakha clan, but of much more recent generation than most of the queen's most trusted servitors, in fact just a little older than Viyeki himself. Viyeki had only met the prince-templar a few times—before he had become a high magister their circles of acquaintanceship had barely intersected, and even afterward they seldom frequented the same gatherings—but he had heard nothing to make him think badly of Pratiki. Still, the princeling seemed to be here to lend some kind of official support for what Viyeki thought a rash invasion of the mortal lands, so he knew he would have to treat the royal clansman with gracious caution.

Surprisingly, for one of the ruling caste, Pratiki had not brought much in the way of an entourage, just a hand of Hamakha Dragon Guards and a few clerics. Nor did he unduly drag out the welcoming ceremony. Viyeki went first, greeting Pratiki with all due respect but avoiding flowery speech, which he had heard the prince-templar did not like. That bit of gossip seemed to be true, as Pratiki then watched with little enthusiasm while General Kikiti, lean and tall as a stork, made lengthy protestations of loyalty to the queen and Clan Hamakha, then was followed by Sogeyu and her Order of Song minions welcoming him with all their own ancient and ornate formulas. When they had finished, Pratiki said, "I am certain there is more important work to be done than seeing to the comfort of a mere religious official, but I thank you on behalf of the Mother of us all. You may all go now. My servants will see that I am housed. Oh, and High Magister Viyeki, will you grant me the courtesy of a short audience?"

This was intriguing, if a tiny bit worrying. Viyeki waited as the prince-templar's tent was erected—it had more sides than Viyeki's own simple lean-to, but was otherwise quite spare and unassuming—then Pratiki sent his clerics away.

"How goes the queen's task?" he asked Viyeki when they were alone in the tent.

"I have little progress to report, Prince-Templar." Viyeki framed his words carefully. "The time for my Builders to do their part has not yet come. Although of course I do my best every hour and every day to serve the Mother of All." General Kikiti had told Viyeki that they would be excavating the tomb of legendary Ruyan Vé the Navigator himself, hero of the Tinukeda'ya race, whose grave had lain hidden for years beneath the fortress that mortals called Naglimund. Naglimund stood only a short distance away across the valley, but at the moment, several thousand mortals still occupied the fortress, many of them well-armed soldiers. Viyeki did not know exactly what such a task would entail, and also could not imagine any way, short of open warfare, that the tomb could be reached. But those were not the kinds of questions he was going to ask a lord of the high Hamakha.

"Of course," said Pratiki with what almost seemed the hint of a smile. "I did not mean to suggest you should have finished it already, High Magister. I know you are a loyal supporter of the queen. You are Clan Enduya, as I remember. An old and worthy family with a long record of service to the throne."

Viyeki could not help wondering whether another meaning swam beneath the prince-templar's words, but said only, "You are kind, Serenity."

"We will be thrown together frequently, you and I," said the prince-templar. "I know you will serve the queen with wisdom and courage. I wished only to say to you that I am aware sometimes it is difficult to reconcile the needs and wants of different Orders, and that this may be one such time. Please do not hesitate to come to me if you need assistance or advice."

"I will think of you as though you were the queen herself, gifting me with time and attention I could never deserve."

Pratiki nodded, but did not seem entirely satisfied by the answer. For his own part, Viyeki could only wonder why a member of the queen's own family was here in the middle of nowhere, on the eve of a new war against the mortals. And what could the Mother of All want with the remains of a long-dead Tinukeda'ya, even such a famous one as Ruyan the Navigator?

He bowed to an appropriate depth before the prince-templar. "All praise to the queen, all praise to her Hamakha Clan," he said.

4

In the Storm

In his dream she stood over him. He could not see her, but could feel her presence, straight and cold as a sword's blade. He could feel her perilous anger, too, but it did not seem to be aimed at him—or at least he prayed that was so.

The winds are too strong, she said. *They blow my words back at me, or carry them into darkness to be swallowed and forgotten.*

Morgan knew he was dreaming and desperately wanted to wake, but it felt as though something pressed him, held him down in sleep, helpless as a swaddled child.

You must tell them. You must tell them for me. The winds are too strong.

He had felt this angry presence before, but in his dream he could not put a face to it, perceived only swirling shadows and splashes of light, like a shattered church window, the mournful saints in fragments, mournful eyes, weeping, moaning mouths.

Who are you? He did not say it, but the presence seemed to catch his thought.

You know me, mortal child. You know me. First Grandmother knew your grandsire. I feel the touch of her on you—and something else . . . the taste of the Dreaming Sea . . .

And then he woke, bereft and alone once more—lost, lost, lost in the endless Aldheorte. He did not weep this time because he no longer had the strength, but he wished he could. Anything to wash such bleak strangeness out of his head. He could not bear to think about it. He knew the forest was trying to drive him mad.

Hot, wearying days and chilly nights crawled by, each as hopeless as the last. Morgan found himself daydreaming of wine, of brandy, even of weak beer, anything wet that would draw a curtain over his miserable thoughts. He brooded over the memories of every pitcher or tankard that had been spilled in his presence. He wanted something other than water to drink so fiercely that he would gladly have licked the filthy floor of the Quarely Maid just to get what had dripped or splashed on it. His hunger had gone away, but only because it was replaced by a miserable flux that gripped his hollow guts and emptied them again and again, long past the time when there was anything to empty. His head seemed to smolder like a hot coal.

Hell is no wine, he thought. *Hell is a dry mouth and a burning head.*

After the sun had risen and set a few times, the unholy craving began to diminish, but he still felt ill, and ached as if he had been beaten. Still, Morgan forced himself to keep walking, trying to hold to a straight line southward, but although he did not find himself back at his beginning as he had the first time, each exhausting day ended the same way, with Morgan still in deep forest.

He thought often about discarding everything he carried that had no use or purpose but which pulled on him—his sword, his mother's Book of the Aedon, the ridiculous irons that Snenneq had presented to him. And the heavy armor? What use was armor against despair? What use against starvation and the stealing of his wits? But although he took off his weighty shirt of chain mail, he could not bring himself to discard it, so he wore it draped over his shoulders and pretended to himself he might want it again. A last, a still sensible part of him knew that if he began to discard all that seemed useless he would not stop; eventually he would be naked but for a few rags, eating leaves and grass and drinking dew, like a broken-minded hermit. He would leave nothing behind when he died but his skeleton, and even those who found him would never know who he had been.

The naked prince. Prince of Bones. Morgan the Pointless, last of his line.

Something kept him from surrendering, and after another day or two the wild, unreasoning craving for strong drink at last faded to a dull ache, a small but constant regret. Hunger and despair were now his greatest enemies. As he stumbled along the forest tracks that animals had made, or cleared undergrowth with his sword, he had to force himself to keep going. *If I'm still moving, I'm not dying,* he told himself, though he was not completely certain that was true. And over and over as he staggered on through the long days, he thought of what his grandfather had often said—*"You don't know you're in a story until someone tells it to you afterward."*

Was he in such a story? And was it only a story of his death? Perhaps something unforeseen might still change things. Perhaps some of the Erkynguard had survived and would come looking for him. Perhaps his grandparents would send searchers.

Yes, perhaps, a sour voice whispered. *And perhaps the trees will dance and the mountains will sing.*

He was still sleeping on the wide boughs of large trees, oaks or ash, for fear of what might walk the forest floor at night, and he had learned to wake up long enough to adjust his position while remembering that he was high above the ground. The wide-eyed watchers, the treetop whisperers who had surrounded him the first night were still often present, but in smaller numbers now, so that he seldom heard them, and only very infrequently saw the moony gleam of their eyes. It felt as though they too, whatever they might be, were beginning to give up on him.

Is it the fifth or the sixth day? Morgan wondered as he followed the course of a nearly empty streambed. *The seventh?* That fact that he didn't know frightened him, and he did his best to go back over everything that had happened, but the bitter sameness of the days defeated him.

He had eaten every scrap and crumb that had been in his purse, and although the flux was gone, the pain in his stomach was even more overwhelming. He had found elder berries and hawthorn berries, which eased the pangs a little, and in one small, sunny forest clearing he had stumbled across a sun-bright fizz of dandelions and devoured them all, flowers and leaves. He was chewing the last one now, and though it did not taste much like the sort of food he had begun to think of in every waking moment after the flux finally deserted him—red, juicy beef, hot loaves of bread, puddings, pies, and fragrant cheeses— it quieted his ravenous hunger a little. But Aldheorte's forest cover was too thick to rely on finding many sun-loving dandelions, and eventually the berry season would end too. He had found nothing like a walnut or chestnut tree, although he had been looking. His knowledge of how to feed himself was as exhausted as the rest of him.

What did my grandfather eat when he was lost in the woods—these same woods? Not for the first time Morgan wished he had listened more closely. But who could ever have dreamed the same thing might happen to him?

You don't know you're in a story until someone tells it to you afterward.

He sang a little song to himself, *"Morgan died with an empty gut, his mouth wide open and his eyes tight shut."*

He was far too hungry to laugh. *Is that Your idea, my Lord God? Do you mean to humble me, bit by bit, until I renounce my stubbornness and say my grandparents were right? Well, then, I was wrong. I was a fool. Lead me to the forest's edge, or a crofter's hut. Send me a dying deer, or better yet, a bow and some arrows so that I can kill my own food.*

But God, the Almighty Father of the World, did not seem to be listening, or if He heard, He was not yet ready to forgive His errant child Morgan. He swallowed his curses. If he ever needed God's forgiveness, it was now. Just thinking about what real hunger would feel like terrified him. He could find water on the dewy grass, but soon the autumn would come, then the winter . . .

Winter! He had astonished himself. Already he was thinking about the chance of not getting out of the Aldheorte before winter. *But I will never live so long.*

Something finally changed in the late afternoon of what might have been the seventh or even the eighth day, but it was not the sort of change Morgan would have wished. The sky began to darken beyond the high forest canopy. The trees started to sway, especially the topmost branches. A summer storm seemed to be coming in.

He had little beyond his cloak to keep him dry, and knew that being wet and cold in the wild would likely be a death sentence, so he began to search for a place where he could sit out a bad storm. He did not want to be near a tree, because any fool knew that trees attracted lightning—especially oak trees, which carried the shape of the thunderbolts in their very limbs. As the darkness grew and the winds strengthened, he almost forgot his hunger in his growing fear of being caught in the tempest. Though the sun hung high in the sky behind the clouds, the forest had already gone as dark as evening and the trees were writhing and thrashing above him. Drops of rain fell like stones, and although even after days wandering lost he was sure the month could be no later than Tiyagar-month, it felt cold as winter.

Morgan headed upslope, searching for a drier spot to wait out the storm. Already the rains were beginning to soak his wool cloak, making it even heavier than the mail shirt. As the loamy forest soil turned to mud, his boots kept sticking, slowing him down, as though evil children ran behind him, snatching at his feet. Once he pulled his foot entirely out of one boot, and then had to sit down in the muck with rain beating on his head and use both hands to drag it out. All the time the sky grew darker and the voice of the wind grew more shrill.

At last he reached a group of ash trees on a rocky slope, ancient sentries guarding a limestone outcrop as big as a church. This miniature mountain jutted at an angle from the forested hillside, and Morgan found a crevice in the base of it not much bigger than himself. At last he could escape the rain, though the space was too small to light a fire and the deadfall wood that lay along the slope was already soaking wet. He dropped his armor shirt to one side, then took off his cloak and sat on it. His knees close under his chin, he watched the muddy earth leap in wet gouts as the rain beat down. He stayed that way, shivering, his thoughts numbed with misery, until the true dark came and he could no longer see anything farther away than the dim shape of his own feet.

In the night the storm strengthened, the ash trees creaking, branches snapping. The rain blew almost sideways, so that he had to force himself deeper into the small crevice to stay dry. He wondered what had happened to the tree-murmurers he had heard and seen. Did such creatures have a nest or burrow they could go to? What did squirrels or birds do in storms like this? Did they simply cling to branches, or did they have dry, safe places to hide? It was something he had never thought much about, but it seemed important now.

If I can't light a fire by tomorrow, I think I will go mad.

Porto and an Erkynguard sergeant named Levias were watching over a small troop of Erkynguards as they brought back levies of food from the nearby shire seat at Leaworth to the camp where the soldiers waited for Count Eolair and the prince to return from their mission to the Sithi. The levy had taken longer than expected, because the local baron had protested every requisition, and had even angrily stated that he would inform the High Throne of the outrage being practiced upon him until the Erkynguard quartermaster produced the order signed by Duke Osric and countersigned by the king.

"If that baron ever has to feed a real army instead of just this little traveling company," Levias suggested to Porto, "he'll likely have a fit and fall down dead." Porto had laughed in agreement.

Sergeant Levias was a friendly sort, a round-faced, stocky man about a decade past the end of youth. Porto liked the man's company and was also enjoying the day and the sunshine. After passing nearly a month in the saddle since they'd left the Hayholt, Porto was comfortable riding again, despite the occasional ache in his old bones. He was concerned about Morgan, of course, after the prince and Eolair had been gone so many days in the forest, but that was in God's hands, not his own. He could only wait with the rest of the Erkynguard and hope for the best.

As they followed the course of the river on their way back from Leaworth, going slow because the carts were laden with grain and beer and other useful things, they saw the first smoke drifting on the southern horizon, a dark plume above the grassy hillocks that stood between them and the camp. At first Porto thought nothing of it—what was a military camp without fires?—but after a moment Levias saw it too.

"That's wrong, that is," the sergeant said, but he didn't look very worried. "Too much smoke, too dark. One of the wagons must have caught fire."

"God help us," said one of the foot soldiers from under his milkmaid's yoke, "let's hope it's not the cook wagons. I need my supper. This is hard work."

"Do not throw the Lord's name about," Levias told him. "Your complaining stomach is nothing to Him."

"So the priest told me too, back home." The guardsman, a young fellow named Ordwine, had proved to be fond of his own voice. "But when I let out a great fart, it seems God changed his mind, because the priest threw me out of His church!"

Porto laughed in spite of himself, but Levias only gave the young soldier a disgusted look. "You will learn to fear the Lord one day. I only hope that it does not come too late."

Instead of continuing what was obviously raillery of long standing with his superior, young Ordwine stared into the distance, his eyes suddenly wide. "Look, now, Sergeant. The smoke is getting thicker."

Porto turned even as Levias did. The black cloud was like a thunderhead. The rest of the guardsman had stopped to look, and even the drovers brought their wagons to a halt, faces gone suddenly pale as suet.

A part of the dark cloud broke loose from its base and came hurrying toward them across the uneven meadow. For a moment Porto was frozen with fear, cast back in an instant to the Norn lands and the terrible magic of the White Foxes that had brought cookfires to life, collapsed great stones, and even moved mountains. But what was speeding toward them was no rogue cloud of smoke, he saw a moment later, but horses—Erkynguard horses running in terror, eyes rolling, hooves flashing in the late afternoon glare, many still wearing their blankets emblazoned with the Twin Dragons of the royal house.

"By the Aedon, what happens here?" said Levias, forgetting his own rule against using holy names in vain. "Has the whole camp caught fire? Ordwine, you and the rest get after those horses before they escape. See if you can calm them and get them harnessed—once they escape into the grasslands we'll never catch them." He turned to Porto. "Keep with me, Sir Porto. Something is amiss!"

Afterward, Porto could remember little of the scene they saw as they galloped toward the smoke, except that for a brief instant he could have almost believed that the green, peaceful grassland had opened up and vomited forth demons from Hell. The Erkynguard camp was beset by men in armor, perhaps a hundred ragged but well-armed Thrithings-men on swift horses. The Erkynguardsmen were fighting back from behind wagons but they were much outnumbered, and many of the wagons had already been set ablaze by the attackers' fiery arrows. The fast-moving nomads seemed to range on all sides, so that many soldiers who thought they were hidden from danger by a wagon or tent died with arrows in their backs.

Levias spurred his horse toward the melée, but to Porto it was already clear that the battle was over. Perhaps half of the guardsmen in the camp were already dead and the rest surrounded, but very few of the attackers had been killed or even wounded.

He lay his head close against his horse's neck and spurred after Sergeant Levias. "Turn back!" Porto shouted. "Turn back!"

"We have to help them!" Levias cried, his words barely audible above the shouts and screams.

"And who will help the prince?" Porto shouted, reining up. They were still far from the camp. Half the wagons were now blazing high and hot, and several others were beginning to burn. "Who will help the heir to the throne when we are dead?"

Levias slowed, then a moment later half a dozen of the whooping clansmen saw them and broke off from the main group. Levias pulled back hard on his reins, then turned his horse and sped back toward Porto, the Thrithings-men closing rapidly behind, their braided beards bouncing, their red mouths open in cries of battle-joy.

It is Hell indeed, Porto thought, turning his horse to flight.

Arrows were humming past them like hornets, and Porto knew that the Thrithings-horses were all but tireless and would catch them soon. He shouted to Levias to head toward the forest, their only chance for escape, but realized a moment later that they were far downstream from the ford and would have to cross the Ymstrecca in full flow.

An arrow flew past him close enough to bite at the skin of his neck. They crested a low, grassy hill and as they flew down the slope on the far side, suddenly more riders were on top of them, springing up as if from nowhere. For a moment Porto's heart skipped and seemed to stop. But before he could even draw his blade, these new riders rushed past with loud cries, heading up the slope toward the trailing Thrithings-men, who had just arrived at the top of the rise, and Porto realized these new riders were the Erkynguards— Ordwine and the others that Levias had sent to catch some of the fleeing horses—and he breathlessly praised God. It was clear from the way they rode that these soldiers were not horsemen—most of them had been farm boys before joining the guard—but he had seldom been so glad to see anyone. Screaming with rage, almost with madness, Ordwine and the rest crashed into the trailing Thrithings-men. Porto could not leave them to fight alone, so he turned his mount in an abrupt, shuddering half-circle, then followed them up, determined to sell his death for a good price.

Men tumbled through the air as the two troops met and their horses reared or stumbled. Horses fell, crushing men beneath them. Axes and swords rang on shields or clashed blade on blade, or blade on flesh. Men screamed. Blood sprayed. In that little trough between two rolling greens swells an entire battle began and ended before the sun had set. Luckily for Porto, the battle went better for his side than the fight at the camp.

When it was over, the only survivors were Porto and Levias, both wounded but not too badly, and two of the Erkynguards—young Ordwine and a smaller, beardless soldier named Firman. None of the Thrithings-men who had chased them would see their clans again, but that could scarcely be called a victory.

When they made their way back toward the camp, the rest of the nomad army was gone and most of the fires had burned out, leaving only a few flames wavering here and there, like drunks staggering home from the tavern. The ground was littered with corpses, but the dead were almost all Erkynguardsmen and Thrithings-men: Porto saw no sign of the trolls among them.

Nobody spoke but Sergeant Levias, and his only words were a string of sickened, angry curses.

When the newcomers first came toward them out of the woods, distance made size confusing: Porto drew the sword he had only just sheathed and called out to Levias and the others to be ready. A moment later he saw that the leader was riding, not a shaggy Thrithings-horse but something smaller and stranger—a white wolf, in fact—and he lowered his blade. He hailed Binabik and his troll family with relief, but the guardsmen with him seemed less joyful. Many of the soldiers had regarded the Qanuc with superstitious fear from the moment the company had left Erchester, and if ever there had been a day of disastrous luck, this had been that day.

"I did not think to see you alive again," Porto said as the trolls rode up.

Binabik swung down from his mount, then looked over the smoking remains of the camp. "We were being in and out of the forest all the day, looking by the chance that Prince and Eolair had been coming out somewhere different." As he spoke, his wife, daughter, and the large troll named Little Snenneq looked around in grim silence.

Porto nodded sadly. It had been almost a sennight since the Sithi had taken the prince and Eolair away and the whole camp had been unsettled by the lengthy absence. Only military discipline had kept them relatively calm.

"It will be just us waiting for them now," Porto said. "We must pray those grasslanders do not return."

"There are Thrithings-men and other grasslanders on the move in great numbers all around," Binabik told him. "But mostly distant from this place, on the far downs." He gestured toward the low hills along the southern horizon.

"Grasslanders are coming this way, you say?" Porto was terrified at the idea of having to fight again. The strength of desperation that had fueled him had ebbed back out of his body, and every weary muscle and every old bone he possessed seemed to be aching.

"Not this way." Binabik crouched, running his fingers through the bent grass, eyes narrowed. "All heading toward the west they are, but also away from this spot. The Thrithings people are making a great clan gathering at the end of summer each year. Perhaps this attack was by some clans on their journeying to that gathering. Ah!" Binabik held up what at first looked like nothing so much as a gobbet of mud. He cleaned it with a handful of dewy grass. "Look," he said. "A tatter of cloak, and it is of fine weave."

Porto shook his head. "What good is that to us?"

"To wear, no goodness at all," said Binabik with a crooked half-smile. "To see and think about, perhaps it is being more use. Look with closeness."

"I can't see close things so well," Porto admitted.

"Then I will be telling you. This is a cloth of very clever stitching and make. No broadweave, as we Qanuc say of the garments we make during the summer, but fine work. I mean no impoliteness when I say these are not the garments of one of your soldiers, let alone the cook or his helpers. This is the cloak of a nobleman. Sisqi! Qina! Help me."

Together the three trolls moved slowly outward from the spot where Binabik had found the piece of cloth, staying low to the ground, examining the muddy, torn turf. Porto and the guardsmen looked on in puzzled silence. Little Snenneq, still mounted on his huge, slow-cropping ram, wore an expression like a hungry child forced to sit through a long prayer before eating.

Sisqi stopped and called to Binabik.

He leaned close and then nodded. "And see—it was Count Eolair. He was here during the battling or just after. See how the mud has been trampled back over the bloody ground."

"But then what of the prince?" asked Porto in sudden fear. "Sweet God and merciful Elysia, was Prince Morgan here too? Oh, God, is he dead?"

Binabik's face was somber. "I pray to all my ancestors he is not. But you and your men go to there, Porto." He pointed to the far end of the muddied battle-ground, where some of the men had fallen back from the original camp in their futile resistance. "We will do the searching here. Be looking at all the dead. I am praying none are Morgan or Eolair, but we must be knowing with certainty."

Porto stood over the last of the dead Thrithings-men. This one was a thin fellow with long mustaches and the bloodless look of a drowned rodent. His guts were out, and they stank. After staring a moment, Porto turned away to collect himself. The sun had all but vanished in the west. He could see a thin haze of mist rising from the distant meadows.

"I am bringing perhaps hopeful news!" Binabik called, walking toward him. "But first, what have you found?"

Porto listed off the number of each side's fallen. "All the Erkynguard are dead, Levias says, but those who went with us to Leaworth. They also killed the camp servants, mostly young boys." A wash of pure hatred went through him. He had almost forgotten what it felt like, the helpless, burning heat. "But, praise God, none of the dead are Eolair or Prince Morgan."

Binabik let out a deep breath. "I mourn the others, but the absence of the prince and Eolair is making the meaning of my own discovery more certain. Come see."

He led Porto and the guardsmen back across the twilight battlefield. They had been among the dead long enough that Porto had begun to feel as though they walked in the afterlife—as though they were the ones who had died, and were waiting for their fellows to rise and join them in eternity.

Binabik took a brand from the fire Little Snenneq had built and began to walk along the edges of a torn but less brutalized section of meadow on the forest side of the camp. Porto, who was long-legged even beyond most men, towered over the troll and had to take small, almost mincing steps to avoid tripping over him.

"There, and again there, and again there." Binabik was now leading him out from the camp toward the ford, gesturing at things Porto could only barely see, even with the torch held close. "Footprints that came from there." He pointed toward the shadowy tree-wall of Aldheorte across the river. "Prints of two walkers, both in boots well-crafted. But before they reach this camp, there is being confusion—and here." He pointed again. Porto could at least see that the ground was much disturbed. "One set turns back to the forest. The sky rained the night before last, do you remember? These are prints being made since that night, as with the others around us—or just *after* yesterday's battling."

Porto tried to consider all these ideas. "After the battle? What does that mean? And what do the two sets of tracks mean?"

Levias, who had been listening silently, said, "It means one of them turned back to the forest."

Binabik nodded. "Good seeing, Sergeant. I too think it so."

"It was Prince Morgan who went to the forest," Snenneq said.

Binabik again nodded. "That too I am hoping now. If the prince and Eolair

were coming from the forest and saw the battle, Eolair I am thinking would
have made the prince run to safety, the only safety that was there for his seeking, in the great forest. But the piece of cloak and no blood there, and no body
of the count, tells me—what, Snenneq?"

"That someone took the Count of Eolair prisoner," Snenneq said immediately.

"Yes," Binabik said, nodding. "So we will all pray to our ancestors and gods
they are both being still alive—Prince Morgan in the forest, Eolair with his
captors." He stood and put his hands to his mouth, then called, *"Vaqana, hinik
aia!"*

It seemed no time at all before the wolf appeared, tongue dangling and eyes
intent, clearly enjoying the smell of blood and burned flesh more than the humans did. The troll bent and put his mouth near the beast's ear; it looked to
Porto as if they were conversing quietly. The idea, though strange, did not seem
impossible—the leader of the trolls had shown several times that the wolf
understood him even better than a horse did its rider.

Now Binabik climbed onto Vaqana's back and seized the ruff of fur at its
neck, then called something to his wife Sisqi. The wolf leaped off so quickly
that grass flew into the air behind him, carrying Binabik back toward the scene
of the original attack.

"Where does he go?" asked Sergeant Levias. "Does he desert us?"

"The trolls are not that sort," said Porto.

"My husband says of something he heard," Sisqi explained. "He hurries to
see, and tells us to follow with carefulness."

Levias exchanged a look with the other two Erkynguards, and they stayed
close together as they rode eastward along the Ymstrecca's bank. Bodies lay
scattered across the meadow like the tumbled statuary of a lost race. He heard
a cry and looked up, squinting in the evening darkness until he could make
out the distant conjoined shape of Binabik and his wolf hurrying back toward
them.

"Come to me!" Binabik cried as drew nearer. "With swiftness!"

As the others approached, he turned the wolf away from the river and led
them back across the grass, just beyond the last sad tangle of dead Erkynlandish
soldiers. "Here, you see?" he said. "A large force of Thrithings horses were
passing here—look, here is a shoe-marking from one." He pointed at a muddy
half-circle. "They lead away west and south, toward the place that is being
called Spirit Hills, where the grassland people have their gathering."

"I don't understand," Porto said.

"Are you suggesting we should try to attack them, with our paltry numbers?"
Levias asked.

"I am suggesting only that you cannot understand until I am left to finish,"
said Binabik with an edge of severity. "There is more to see."

They followed him again, this time east along the periphery of the bloodied battleground, until they found another, smaller confusion of hoofprints, this one leading away in much the same direction, but in a slightly wider angle.

"What do you say, daughter?" he asked the smallest of the trolls.

She got down on one knee to touch the grass. "Men who took Eolair Count," she said.

"Just so," said Binabik. When he saw the look on Porto and the Erkyn-guardsmen, he grimaced. "The more small troop—the men who took Eolair—have passed this way. It is my guessing that they did not wish to come with much closeness to the ones who attacked our camping place, but they follow toward the same direction. Spirit Hills."

"You think the ones who took Eolair might be another clan or something like?" asked Levias. He seemed to be viewing the trolls a little more respectfully now.

"It is being possible. Not all grasslanders are being the same—not all are even being part of the horse-clans."

"Then we must follow them," said Levias. "Perhaps we can wait until they sleep and steal back Count Eolair."

"But what about the prince?" Porto said in dismay. "What about Prince Morgan? Didn't you say he'd gone back into the forest? We can't just leave him to the bears and wolves!"

"And that is being exactly the puzzle we must solve." In the light from Ord-wine's torch, Binabik looked tired and miserable. "We should not be surrender-ing either of them, Morgan *or* Eolair." He made a gesture with his fists against his chest. "But no matter how I fear for Count Eolair, I cannot be leaving Mor-gan the prince. He is my true friend's grandson and I am sworn to protect him."

"So am I!" Porto declared. "I'll go with you."

"But so were we, his guards," said Levias. "The troll is right—we cannot desert the heir to the throne."

"We cannot leave Eolair to the Thrithings-men either," said Porto. "Ser-geant Levias, you take your men and follow the tracks of the ones who took him. I'll go with the trolls."

Binabik shook his head. "I am sorry, Sir Porto, but if Morgan is not to be found just within the forest border, your horse will not be able to follow us to all the places we will go searching for him. I give salute to your brave heart, but you should be riding with the guardsmen after Count Eolair. You tall men and your horses will have better traveling on the open plains than in the deep woods and undergrowth. Also, I am having some knowledge of the woods where the Sithi live, but you are not. Distances and directions there can have a most deceptive appearance."

"But the prince—!" Porto began.

"Will have best service from those of us who can be following him in tan-gled woods," said Binabik. "And experienced trackers some of us are, too. Also, Vaqana's courageous nose will be of great usefulness as well."

Porto was not happy. "Lord Chancellor Pasevalles himself said that I must protect the prince at all times! I can't leave him and go after someone else. I can't. It would betray my trust." And despite his genuine fear for the prince, he could not help thinking of the gold he had been promised, too, gold that would have saved his failing years from wretchedness. Who would support a soldier who was too old to fight and who had failed his only mission?

Binabik turned from a quiet conversation with his family to look him in the eye. It was strange to feel intimidated by one so small. "Good Sir Porto, we are all understanding your unhappiness," the troll told him. "This is not a choice any of us wished to have. But you will only be making us move with more slowness if you come with us. If you do not wish for following Eolair with the sergeant and his men, then at least you must ride back to the Hayholt with all the speed that is possible."

"Back to the Hayholt?"

"Prince Morgan lost in the forest and the lord steward stolen by Thrithings-men, who also killed many of the royal Erkynguard—this must be told to the king and queen!"

"I cannot do it." Porto shook his head, so empty inside he thought a strong wind might blow him over. "I cannot leave the prince *and* the Hand of the Throne both. Send one of the guardsmen back to Erchester instead."

Binabik frowned, thinking, then began to search in the bag he wore over his shoulder. He came up with a piece of dried and polished sheepskin. "That twig, Snenneq—give it to me." Stick in hand, Binabik held it in the flame of Ord-wine's torch—the guardsman had to bend so he could reach it—and then began to write with the charred end on the scrap of pounded skin. It took a long time, and Porto had to force himself to be patient.

"There," the troll said at last, and handed the strip of hide to Porto. "Send this with whom you are choosing. It is for taking to the king and queen. It tells them of what has happened. Now we must go to our different ways."

"But . . ." Porto began, but he had no good argument against the troll's piti-less reasoning. "Very well," he said at last, though it felt as though his heart was splintering, "if it must be so, it must be."

"You are a good man in truthfulness, Porto," Binabik said. "But now we can waste no more breath and no more moments." The troll waved to his family, who urged their rams into movement once more as he followed on his wolf. "Ride well—and hunter's luck," he called back to the knight and the three Erkynguards. "May happy fortune be watching over you all and bring you home with safety again."

Porto, suddenly not just melancholy but fearful that he was watching some terrible thing happening, something he did not entirely understand, only raised his hand, but words of farewell caught in his throat.

What have we done? he wondered. *We were a large, fine company—a company of soldiers guarding the prince and one of the highest nobles of all Osten Ard. Now we are a tatter, a few threads, and they're all being pulled in different directions.*

The trolls rode off north toward the great forest, a spectacle that at other times would have been almost comical—several small, stocky people mounted on sheep and wolves, like a proverb illustrated in the margin of a religious book. Levias and the other two soldiers began to discuss what they should do next, but their quiet, halting words sounded to Porto like children's fearful voices in the darkness.

In Morgan's dream the outcropping had become a thousand times larger, a true mountain. At the top, beyond his sight but not beyond his hearing, she was speaking to him again:

The others cannot hear me now, not even the blood of my blood. Why can you?

I don't know. I don't even know who you are! Part of him wanted to climb the great stone, to come face to face with this creature haunting his dreams, but he could feel her power and her age and it frightened him.

You know me, child. I spoke to you in the place of my helpless rest and you heard me. But here, where I stand in the doorway, there are no names. I cannot give you what I do not possess.

He woke suddenly, startled by the noise of wolves howling outside of his stony refuge, but after a heart-pounding moment he realized no animal could make a sound so loud. It was the wind, risen to a fierce pitch, moaning and shrieking, and even the forest seemed terrified. The trees he could see bent and waved their limbs. He could hear cracking, and the sound of branches falling.

The first light of dawn was coloring the violet sky, just ahead of the sun itself. The rain had weakened a little, but still blew sideways like the arrows of an attacking army. He had only a moment to feel grateful for his small portion of shelter, and another moment to worry about what would happen to him if the storm did not abate, then he heard another sound that pierced even the shrill anger of the wind.

"Reeeee! Reeeee!"

It was nothing he had heard before, not loud but clear even through the storm, so he knew it must be close by. It sounded like a hawk calling, or perhaps like some small animal screeching its terror as a predator snatched it up. He pushed himself as far back in the shallow crevice as he could manage. Whatever might be hunting out there in such unholy weather, he did not want to meet it.

He was only just starting to slide back into uneasy sleep when he was startled again, this time by a loud crack and what sounded like several branches falling, or perhaps even an entire tree brought down by the wind. He squinted out into the dim dawn light and saw a tangle of ash limbs that had just crashed to the ground near his rock, and in the midst of all the limbs and flapping leaves something small, round, and solid. It began to scream again—*Reeee! Reeee! Reeeee!*—but it did not crawl out of the fallen branches.

Morgan watched the pile of branches for what seemed a very long time. The shrill cries of distress grew fainter but did not stop. Dismay clutched at his stomach—not fear for himself, but at the clear sound of distress, of a small, terrified thing in pain. Still, he did not move, though every cry hurt him.

When the wind at last began to die and the diminished rain was falling at a more ordinary angle once more, Morgan crawled out of his crevice. The entire slope in front of the limestone outcrop was covered with fallen limbs and great piles of leaves that had been ripped living from their twigs, but the clutter of ash branches and the thing which had fallen with them had finally gone still. Morgan approached with caution, sword in hand. As he drew nearer, he saw that what had fallen was a single large and crooked limb that had brought down several others with it. He leaned over the tangle of broken branches at its outer end and saw something small and brown prisoned inside them, something that was still alive, because it turned its round, dark eyes toward him, semicircles of white showing along their edges. Then it began to thrash, but with the helpless weakness of something that had already tried and failed to escape more times than he could imagine.

It was no larger than a human baby, but he could see little else of the creature except its reddish-brown fur and a hint here and there of pink skin, because most of it was covered in mud and leaves. He reached out with the tip of his sword and lifted one of the covering branches, then broke it off near its base. The thing watching him did not stir, but the wide, terrified eyes never left him.

Within a few moments he had cut or broken enough branches to free the small creature. He stepped back to allow it to make its escape, but it did not move. He wondered if it was frightened of him or badly injured. He looked around, but the rest of the slope seemed empty of anything but the wreckage left by the storm.

"*Reeeee*," the little thing whined, and this time it seemed like the bleat of something dying.

Caught up by something he could not have explained even to himself, Morgan slowly and carefully lifted the rest of the twigs off it until he could see the creature whole. He was no master of woodcraft, but the animal was utterly unfamiliar, and when he saw the tiny, long pink fingers on its forepaws, he had a sudden start. This, or something like it, must have been what touched him during his first escape into the forest. He guessed it must be one of the treetop watchers that had followed him through the woods.

Despite its almost human hands, the creature was no ape. It had the harelip and long, flat front teeth of a rat or squirrel, but its large eyes were set too far forward for either of those, and its small, round ears were low on its head, giving it a curious, manlike appearance almost as unsettling as the pink fingers. Its small chest was pumping in and out, in terror or its last extremities, but he feared it would bite him if he tried to help it any more, so he sat back on his haunches and watched. Still the little animal did not move.

He was about to give up and let it live or die on its own, but when he stood, the creature suddenly bared its teeth and screeched "*CHIK!*" loudly, then

"Reee! Reee! Ree!" again, startling him so that he took a step back. He heard movement in the trees and looked up. He thought he saw a glimpse of red but couldn't be sure.

"Chik!" the little thing barked once more, but then its head lolled back as though it had exhausted its final strength.

He bent toward it, this time wrapping his cloak several times around his hands. When he lifted it loose from the last branches it hissed and *chik*ed again, struggling weakly in his grasp, but did not try to bite him, although he suspected that if it had been stronger it might have. Now that it was in his hands Morgan could feel it trembling through the wool of his cloak, and without thinking he wrapped it up and lifted it into the crook of his arm. He heard more movement in the trees overhead, but no voices answered the little thing's quiet *ree-reeing*. He carried it back to the crevice, wrapping the cloak so that the little beast's head protruded but its limbs were held against its sides, like a swaddled infant. When he reached his sanctuary he sat down with it in his lap. The struggling gradually ceased and the thing's large eyes closed, but its chest was still rising and falling beneath his hands.

"Reeeeeeee . . ." it breathed, then fell silent again but for the thin whisper of its breath. He held it against his chest to warm it, and remembered the days when his sister Lillia had been a baby, when the only thing that had brought him even a moment's relief from the horror of his father's death was to hold her and watch her innocent face.

For a little while, he even forgot his hunger.

5

The Pool

Dragging, pulling, and shoving a live, bound dragon down a mountain, even with huge Goh Gam Gar doing most of the work, seemed a nearly impossible task. Despite the giant's laboring from hours before the sun rose and into the darkness after it had set, at the end of the first day's efforts the huge, trussed worm had been moved only a demoralizingly short distance down the mountain. Dragging its monstrous bulk over obstacles and across patches of rocky ground between the snows had left Goh Gam Gar exhausted, and the dragon's groans and gurgles of pain through its bound jaws almost made Nezeru feel sorry for the great worm. Its eyes, each as big as a serving platter, rolled desperately in its sockets, froth dripped from its vast mouth. The Singer Saomeji was careful to keep it insensible as much as possible with compounds of *kei-vishaa* that he forced between the dragon's massive jaws. Even in stupefied slumber the great beast writhed and groaned like a sleeper beset by nightmares. As Nezeru listened to the ropes that bound the monster creaking with its every shudder and twist, she wondered what would happen to them if Saomeji's store of *kei-vishaa* ran out.

If the captured dragon was suffering, Nezeru and Jarnulf were not much better off. They had spent the day carrying the burned and crippled body of Hand Chieftain Makho in a sling made from Jarnulf's cloak. Despite what must have been hideously painful injuries from dragon's blood, Makho had remained senseless all day, giving no more sign of life than the occasional moan or small movement. Nezeru did her best to ignore the growing misery of her cramped fingers. *Jarnulf was not Sacrifice-trained as I was*, she thought. *The pain must be worse for him.*

Only Saomeji had not carried anything down the mountain, keeping his hands free at all times to threaten the giant with the pain he could summon from the stone rod. As a Sacrifice, Nezeru had been taught always to bow before authority; as a survivor of a crippled expedition, she was less enthralled that one of their number—a half-blood like herself, too!—should go free of burdens. But as long as Saomeji controlled the giant, he was the leader, and Nezeru's unhappiness remained unspoken.

★   ★   ★

When they finally stopped for the day, Saomeji ordered Jarnulf off to hunt for food. "Make sure you bring back enough for the giant *and* the worm, Huntsman. The rest of us can get by on very little, but we need both animals alive."

Jarnulf scowled. "I am nearly falling over after carrying Makho all day. You could do it yourself, Singer." He pointed at the giant. "Look. He's too weary even to stand. He is no danger to us."

Saomeji looked back at him with a flat, unconcerned stare. "You would never have survived the first day in the Order of Song, mortal. The other acolytes would have fed on you like the dumb brute you are. Nobody watches over the giant but me, and now that the hand chieftain has been struck down, I am also the one who gives the orders." He turned to Nezeru. "You, Sacrifice—tend to Makho. Give him water. I do not think he will want food for a while, but he must have water. Clean his wounds with snow, but be careful. I will look him over later, when I have rested. And you, mortal—why are you still here? I said go and find something to eat."

Jarnulf hesitated, anger clear on his face.

"If you speak another word," Saomeji said, "I will make the giant swipe off your head. He is not too weary for *that*."

Jarnulf turned away and walked into the woods.

Hours later, when the Lantern was high up in the midnight sky and the Wolf was chasing its tail toward the horizon, Nezeru sat on the cold ground and watched as Jarnulf finished pounding the last of the snow rabbits and grouse into an ugly paste of meat, bones, fur and feathers so that he could push it into the dragon's bound jaws. Nezeru's own charge, Chieftain Makho, slept on. His burns were still bright crimson, but the livid patches of skin between them were beginning to take on the dull look of death.

Saomeji bent over the wounded chieftain to shake droplets of something from a small jar into Makho's gaping mouth. Nezeru could not understand the point of this: surely, even if the chieftain survived such dreadful burns, he would never be able to serve the queen again. One of his eyes was gone, nothing left but a hole surrounded by angry red flesh, and ragged holes pierced his cheek and chin where the blood had burned through the skin all the way to his teeth, like a candle flame through old parchment.

On his way back from feeding the dragon, Jarnulf paused to stare down. "Are we truly supposed to carry him all the way down the mountain? He's as good as dead."

Saomeji gave the mortal a look that was almost amused, if one ignored his eyes. "Convincing, yes. I know how much you love Makho."

"I don't care about him enough to hate him, if that's what you mean, Singer. But I want to get down off this mountain before the summer ends and the *real* cold and winds come. In other words, I would like to live. Makho is a burden we can't afford. Nezeru and I could do much—"

Saomeji's hand snapped up. "No. You will be silent now. I am weary and I

have other, more important things to attend to than your babble." He turned
to Nezeru. "Sacrifice, tomorrow the giant, the mortal, and I will go cut down
trees so that we can make a sledge to haul the dragon more easily. You will stay
here and tend the chieftain and the dragon."

"I am no Healer, to be left with such duties," she said, struggling to contain
her fury. "I am not of that order."

"You are of whatever order I say," Saomeji returned calmly. "My master
Akhenabi, as well as Her Majesty Queen Utuk'ku—may she reign forever—
have charged me with bringing back a living dragon so that they may have its
blood. Do not doubt that if you resist me or interfere in any way, I will happily
kill all of you but the giant and get my last use of you by feeding your carcasses
to the worm."

This time Nezeru did not look at Jarnulf or anywhere near him, afraid to
give Saomeji even a hint of her rebellious thoughts. Instead, she made her face
into something without expression.

"I hear the queen in your voice," she said—the old, safe words.

With the first filtered rays of dawn in the gray sky, Saomeji led Jarnulf and the
giant away from the camp in search of wood to build a sledge, leaving Nezeru
alone with the dragon and the burned chieftain.

As she cleaned Makho's wounds with snow and dressed them once more, she
could not help wondering that she had seen more of daylight in the last moons
than in her entire life before that—so much that sunlight was beginning to feel
almost ordinary. During the first days the brightness had sometimes blurred
everything she saw into a dazzling, shimmering whole, parts of which could
not be separated, leaving her blinking and motionless.

She had grown used to it, but she still felt as though she had wandered into
a completely foreign world, and it was more than just the constant light. All her
certainties were fractured. She no longer trusted those above her, all the rungs
of the ladder between her and their great queen, high above. What had seemed
solid and eternal now seemed terrifyingly shaky.

Saomeji had claimed the right to give orders, but she felt no confidence in
this mad, dangerous journey down the mountain. Did he not realize that even
if they managed to reach the bottom without killing themselves or the dragon,
even if they reached their horses and added their strength to the giant's, the
sheer size of the creature would make it impossible to cross the great, snowy
plain east of the Gray Southwood before winter returned with blizzard strength?
That even if she and the others survived the weather, they would never be able
to keep a bound dragon alive across the empty plain, let alone all the way back
to distant Nakkiga? And on top of everything else, Saomeji had increased the
risk of failing the queen by making them carry Makho's useless weight home.

She took a deep, slow breath to calm herself. A handful of snow had melted
in her clenched fist, dripping through her fingers onto the sleeping chieftain.
Was she angrier about this unwanted task because she despised Makho, she

wondered, or because she was outraged by the risk to the queen's mission he represented? What had happened to the proud Sacrifice she had been, that she should even feel such doubt?

She discarded the slush, scooped up another handful of snow, and was patting it onto Makho's wounds when his eye suddenly opened.

"You carry no child," he said in a rasp that she could barely hear. His remaining eye fixed on her, dark as mountain glass. "No child. *They* told me."

Her heart caught in her throat before she remembered they were alone. In any case, she reminded herself, her pretense of bearing a new life was no longer necessary: a halfblood like Saomeji had no rights to her body, and she could easily claim that the fight with the dragons had killed what had been growing inside her. She took a breath and continued to tend Makho's wounds. He gave an agonized grunt but did not speak again, and his eye rolled up until only the dark purple rim of his iris could still be seen beneath the lid. She ignored the terrible stink of his wounds, trying to work swiftly.

Suddenly she felt his jaw tremble beneath her fingers, then his whole body began to shake until she thought he must be dying, perhaps simply from the pain of what she was doing. She would have given him some *kei-vishaa*, but Saomeji had declared the small amount of the powder left could be used only to keep the trussed dragon quiet, and had it on his person at all times.

Makho's shivering suddenly eased. Nezeru tried to finish tending his raw-meat-red and waxy yellow wounds, but a voice abruptly sighed from his open mouth.

"*Darkness has a true name.*" This new, whispering voice did not sound like Makho or his way of speaking. "*It is wound all through the whisperless whispers, in places where the stars look down with cold cruelty on everything that moves and lives.*"

Her heartbeat stuttered. She felt like a small animal frozen beneath an owl's shadow.

"*It is Unbeing,*" said the breathless, murmuring voice. "*It is the enemy of life. They told me. It is the unbinding force.*"

She looked around, for once actually hoping to see Saomeji approach, but she was still alone on the mountainside with Makho and the motionless dragon.

"*All waits for the aspects of the Crow Mother to become one.*" His words floated out like the cold vapor of his breath, like a poisonous smoke. "*She is three—She Who Waits Outside, She Who Stands In The Door, She Who Never Enters. She is three and must become one. Only when the three are one will Unbeing and Being contest. The voices tell me. The voices weep like lost children. The voices . . .*"

Makho fell silent.

What have I become part of? Her heart was still rabbiting so quickly that her chest hurt and her ears hummed; in that instant, she wanted nothing more than to be ignorant again. She was no longer a glorious part of the holy Sacrifice army but a single, lost thing. She floated in untethered darkness, without kin or place or understanding.

By the Sacred Garden, what is happening? And what have I become?

As Goh Gam Gar hacked down trees with his massive ax and shaved away the branches under Saomeji's constantly threatening supervision, it fell to Jarnulf to tie the trimmed logs together into a platform strong enough to support the dragon's immense weight. It was clear that he was quickly running out of rope, but building the sledge seemed at this moment to be the least of Jarnulf's problems.

As he wound the last of the slippery Hikeda'ya cord around the trunks, securing each with strong knots, he began to wonder whether his goals might not be best served simply by killing Saomeji now, finishing off Makho, and perhaps giving a swift and painless death to the female Sacrifice Nezeru as well. Only a few moons earlier he would have rejoiced at sending five Talons to their deaths, and fate had already dispatched two of them without Jarnulf raising a hand. But now fate was beginning to look a bit greedy, and Jarnulf did not want to join these mad Hikeda'ya in death.

My God, my sweet Ransomer, I do not care for my own life at all, but somehow I must survive so I can do Your work.

Now that he knew Queen Utuk'ku herself still lived, his earlier determination to single-handedly rid the world of as many Norns as possible seemed a simpleton's plan. The Hikeda'ya were preparing for war—a great war, from what he could tell. Uncountable mortals would die, and Jarnulf's enslaved folk would die too, forced to fight for Nakkiga and their Hikeda'ya masters. The oaths he had taken to avenge Father, the priest who had adopted him, and to avenge Jarnulf's own family as well, seemed meaningless now. The only thing he could do that might avert the Norns' coming war on mankind was to kill their monstrous queen. And returning to Nakkiga in the triumphant company of the Talons who had achieved the queen's greatest tasks was the only way he could imagine getting close enough to the ageless witch to destroy her. Jarnulf had no doubt he would die himself in the doing of it, but if he succeeded the angels would sing up and down the roads of Heaven when he arrived. Father would be proud of him. His poor, dead brother Jarngrimnur would be proud. And God Himself and His holy Son Usires would be proud.

"Why do you malinger, mortal?" Saomeji shouted across the slope. The sun had gone down, and only a glowing lavender veil lit the western skies. Behind the sorcerer a tall pine was swaying violently with every one of the giant's heavy ax-blows. "We must still drag the sledge all the way back up to where the dragon lies, and we cannot do that until you finish it."

"*We?*" bellowed the giant, pausing between swings. "You are a lying turd, Singer. You mean that poor old Goh Gam Gar will carry it."

Jarnulf waved his hands in exaggerated frustration. "I have used all the rope you gave me, Singer, but the sledge is not finished. If you can tell me how to make more rope out of air, or perhaps send demons speeding back to Blue Cavern to fetch some, please do."

Saomeji gave him a blankly annoyed look. "There is more. I have kept some back." He turned to the giant. "On with your work, beast, or you will taste something you won't like." When the giant had bent to his task again, Saomeji made his way across snow and rubble toward the unfinished sledge.

"You should have told me earlier, mortal," he said. "I will bring you what I can spare, but after that you will have to make double-headed pegs when we return to the camp."

"With what, my fingers? My battle-blade? You are generous with the work for everyone else, Singer. Anything more you wish from me? Shall I carry you back up the hill on my shoulders as well?"

If Saomeji was stung he hid it behind his stony expression. "In fact there *is* another task for you, mortal. While I am fetching more rope, you may take the time to hunt—and don't let a little weariness talk you into half-measures. Just as I cannot let the dragon perish, I cannot let the giant die from hunger—not yet, when I still need his strength. But you are nothing so useful, pink-skin, and you are certainly not under the protection of our Exile's Way like Chieftain Makho and Sacrifice Nezeru. If I am forced to destroy you, we can still complete our task without you. And do not think you can escape me by fleeing, because the giant could catch you and kill you before the moon sets. Now go."

Jarnulf briefly considered what it would be like to push his sword blade through the Singer's snow-white robe and into his black Hikeda'ya heart, but it was a fantasy he could not afford to indulge. Instead he merely nodded, then went to collect his bow and quiver and don the jacket he had taken off in the heat of work.

O, my Ransomer, he thought, and it was not quite a prayer so much as a complaint, *my loving Lord, I know You cannot expect me to feel even an instant's pity for these inhuman creatures, who would deny You and murder Your children, but could You ease my hatred just a little so I do not lose patience and betray Your greater works?*

By the middle of the following day the massive sledge was finished. Grunting and sputtering, the giant managed to drag the great body of the dragon onto it, then they secured the beast with a great length of Saomeji's remaining rope. All Nezeru wished now was to survive this broken expedition and return to her home and her people. Unless the Singer actually put the queen's mission into fatal danger, she felt bound to obey his orders.

Several more days passed as they made their laborious way down the lower slopes of the mountain. The weather sharpened, blinding them with flurries of snow and turning the nights cold enough that even Nezeru began to feel truly uncomfortable despite her heritage and training. They also spent hours every day struggling with the dragon's weight on treacherous slopes, difficult problems of engineering that would have given her own father pause, even with all his Builders to help him.

Even Saomeji seemed to recognize that time and the deepening chill of approaching winter was against them. "We need more than you diminished lot to do the queen's will," he said one night as they all huddled on an unprotected slope around a small fire, Saomeji's only concession to the bitter weather. "If I but had Kemme and Makho to lend their strength, we would be on our way across the plain already."

"But you do not," said Jarnulf. "Kemme is a broken, frozen lump in the snow somewhere high above us, and Makho is scarce better off. What you really need is the Echo you lost the day I met you, to call for someone to help us."

"Ibi-Khai," said Nezeru promptly, surprising herself. She had scarcely known him, but he had been part of their Hand and had a name. She wondered if fearing her own likely disappearance in these trackless wastes had made her speak. *Does it matter whether our names are remembered?* she wondered. *We will still be just as dead. We will still have failed the Mother of All.*

"Just so," Jarnulf said. "If we had his mirror, or whatever trinket it is that Echoes carry, we could communicate to your masters in Nakkiga how badly their mission goes."

"Like all mortals, you talk needlessly and foolishly about things you do not understand." Saomeji's voice was full of scorn. "But your words have helped me to make up my mind. It is true we must find help soon, before winter storms make it impossible to reach Nakkiga. And I think I know a way."

"What will you do?" asked Nezeru.

"You have no need to know that—you will see it when the time comes." The Singer glanced over at the place where Makho lay bundled in his cloak on a rock that had been cleared of snow. "How is your dragon-burned charge today? Does he show any signs of recovery?"

Nezeru was astonished by the question. "Recovery? He lies on the threshold of death. His wounds are terrible, and I doubt he will live more than a few more days. When he is awake, all he does is whisper and sing. His mind is gone."

"Sing?" For the first time Saomeji seemed to be paying attention. "That is interesting. I will look him over myself later."

Two long days later they finally reached the mountain's broad skirts. The slopes here were a little easier to negotiate, though the task still exhausted them all and tested even the giant's great strength to its uttermost. When the day's travel was finished Goh Gam Gar could do little but eat and then sleep. Makho rode on the dragon's sledge, submerged in almost continuous slumber, and despite the days' passing, his wounds did not heal or even scar. Nezeru felt certain the chieftain was on the edge of death, and wished it would happen sooner rather than later.

As they descended the broader slopes Saomeji began collecting round stones like those that he had filled full of fiery heat and used as weapons against the mortal bandits on the Hand's journey to the mountain. Every stone he collected—and there were dozens—was added to the growing pile on the sledge, much to the giant's irritation. Saomeji paid no attention to complaints. Occasionally the Singer picked up a different kind of stone, jagged shards with clear and obvious veins of brighter, more translucent stone running through them, and these he piled on the sledge with the others.

It was mid-morning when Saomeji stopped them, the sun shrouded in iron-gray clouds and flurrying snow. "Here," he said. "We will go no farther today. The time to seek help has come, and I have difficult labors to perform."

Nezeru had not expected them to make camp until long after dark, and she was even more puzzled when the Singer ordered the giant to dig a pit in a level space at the center of a stand of leafless birch trees.

"What?" growled Goh Gam Gar. "You wish me to break my hands as well as break my back?"

"There is soil under the snow," said Saomeji. "It is frozen hard, but you will manage. Do you complain of your burden? Do you wish help to carry the dragon to the queen? Then dig, monster, dig."

The shrouded sun was high in the sky when Goh Gam Gar had finished digging the pit in the frozen ground, and his great, hairy hands were filthy and bleeding. The Singer sent him away from the hole, then began to remove the stones he had collected on their journey from the sledge. As Nezeru watched, Saomeji walked in a wide circle around the spot where Goh Gam Gar now sat. As the giant stared at the Singer with bleary distrust, Saomeji set the stones in a wide ring around the giant so that none was more than a pace from the next, singing softly as he did so. When Saomeji had finished the first circuit he went around again, and this time picked up each stone, moved it to the nearest stone in the circle until they clicked together, then did the same with the stone that had already been there, until he had touched, clicked, and moved each stone one space around the circle, still singing the same soft, strange song.

"I have an important task to do now," Saomeji said to the giant when he had finished surrounding him with the ring of stones. "A task that will take much of my strength. But even should I have a moment of inattention, monster, do not think it will do you any service. Should anything cross the line of my stone circle I will know it instantly. And I will not wait to see what it is, but will burn you from the inside out."

Goh Gam Gar stared at him from beneath the great shelf of his brow. "What if I do not move, but something else crosses it? What if a bird flies through your Song-circle?"

"Then as soon as I see that is true, I will stop your punishment. I do not wish to kill you if I do not have to—not while I need your labor."

The giant's eyes flashed green like marsh-fire, then his massive arm shot out as he reached for the nearest stone, with the likely intention of dashing out Saomeji's brains. The Singer's hands were hidden in his sleeves and Nezeru saw no sign of movement at all, yet a heartbeat later Goh Gam Gar toppled over as though he had been poleaxed and lay twitching and panting, gasping in pain.

"You will stay inside the circle until I let you out again," was all Saomeji said before turning his back on the writhing giant.

While Nezeru watched, wondering, Saomeji took more of the round stones he had gathered and filled the bottom of the pit that Goh Gam Gar had dug, then he bade Jarnulf and Nezeru bring armfuls of snow and dump it on top of the stones. Last, Saomeji arranged the more jagged rocks that he had gathered into several odd configurations at the center of the pit, then piled snow on top of them as well.

"I will have silence now," Saomeji said. "Do not speak to me or approach me, if you value your lives." He rucked up his robes and sat down beside the snow-filled hole. As Nezeru and Jarnulf watched, he lowered his chin to his chest and began to sing.

At some moments what he sang seemed almost understandable to Nezeru— she thought she could hear distorted versions of the Hikeda'yasao words for "pool," "dragon-scale," and "fire"—but at other times she could make out only guttural noises in bizarre cadences, repeated over and over. Once she looked up and caught Jarnulf staring at her intently, his expression quite indecipherable. Caught by surprise and annoyed by her own startled, almost guilty reaction, she looked away.

The song went on, and steam began to rise from the heaped snow. The white heaps filling the pit began to move a little, settling. Saomeji was heating the rocks to melt the snow, that seemed clear, although little else was. The Singer's eyes were fixed above the pit, focused on nothing Nezeru could see. His hands were held out flat, palms down in the rising streams of vapor.

When the snow in the pit had melted into a steaming pool, she saw gleams of subtle light moving through the water—not-quite-possible colors, greenish reds and purplish yellows that circulated in the bubbling depths like clusters of fireflies. She also felt something changing around her, a sudden tightening of the air like a held breath, and a weird echo seemed to play around the edges of all sound. Saomeji had begun to perspire heavily, something even halfbloods almost never did; sweat ran from his long chin and dripped into the pool, but the Singer was oblivious, lost in his trancelike state.

He's making a Witness, Nezeru abruptly realized, and was astonished. Stones and scales, pools and pyres—she had heard Ibi Khai recite the litany several times, and now she understood what Saomeji was trying to do. *But how is that possible? Surely no Singer except perhaps Akhenabi himself could be that powerful! Not even a trained Echo could make such a powerful tool out of nothing!*

The tightening air abruptly seemed to harden, becoming almost as solid as ice or glass. For a moment Nezeru could barely breathe, and it pushed other thoughts from her mind. Tiny, almost invisible hairs on her arms and neck rose, and shivers ran along her limbs.

And then *he* was there, sudden as a stooping hawk. Nezeru could feel the cold presence and knew in a heartbeat that Saomeji was reaching out to the Lord of Song, Akhenabi himself. She actually shrank back, as though in fear of being touched by the ancient masked magician, but it made no difference: he was everywhere at once, all around her, an invisible presence.

Akhenabi spoke then, and though she could not hear the words in her head she could feel each one of them, as though she were wrapped in a rotting burial shroud and spiders walked across her face.

She could not make out what he actually said, nor Saomeji's replies, but she could sense them conversing and could feel fragments of meaning—the dragon, the mountain, the silver-masked queen—and a feeling of something else as well, a waiting something, dark and old, but growing ever stronger. If Akhenabi was a cold breath on her neck, this was an icy blast from the endless white wastes beyond Nakkiga. If Akhenabi was a deadly enemy, this was Death itself, implacable and final.

The Whisperer . . .

It came to her as not quite a word, or even a name, but a sensation, and it brought tears of horror to her eyes. It was a hole in everything, draining away light and life.

Then the contact ended, and both the Lord of Song and the greater, colder presence that had hovered behind him were gone.

Saomeji staggered to his feet and swayed like a drunkard beside the steaming pit. "My master will aid us to complete our task," he said, each word an obvious effort. "He will send horses and warriors to us at the foot of the mountain. Now I must rest. I have done a mighty thing today. Our people will speak of it with awe in time to come."

Nezeru's tears had turned to ice on her cheeks. She felt hollow, as though something had reached into her and torn away all that gave her life and hope. As Saomeji stumbled off to sleep, she scraped the tears from her face with the back of her hand, but could not otherwise move or speak for a long time.

6

Meeting the Bride

Escritor Auxis came to Miriamele's cabin on the *Hylissa* to offer his condolences. Her ladies—all but Shulamit, who had been seasick for two days and was moaning in her narrow bed—scuttled to the back of the small room and stood behind the queen's chair like a choir of painted angels around Holy Elysia's throne.

Miri did not much feel like the mother of God or in fact the mother of anything. She had a hole inside her that seemed far greater than all her feelings for her dead daughter-in-law.

"Your Majesty." Auxis went down to a knee, then bowed his handsome head to kiss her extended hand. "I come to give you the condolence of Mother Church, and to share my own sadness at your bereavement as well."

This would make a pretty painting too, she thought, but felt too numb even to amuse herself. "Thank you, Escritor. Please, sit with me."

"You are kind, Majesty, but I will not intrude on you so long."

She did her best to smile. Auxis was a tall man, and had to bend beneath the low ceiling that was just high enough for Miri and her ladies to stand without striking their heads against the timbers. "Even so. But are you allowed to take off your hat? I fear you will injure it, or it will be smeared with pitch."

This caught Auxis by surprise, and he struggled for a moment to decide whether he was being mocked. "I take your point," he said. "Perhaps I will sit, if only for a short while. Your Majesty is very kind." He lowered himself onto a stool, which vanished beneath his magnificent golden robes. "The Sacred Father, I'm sure, would want me to extend his gratitude that you will continue your journey to Nabban. He would understand, I'm sure, what a sacrifice it is on your part."

"Not such a sacrifice," she said, her strange mood driving her toward honesty, even with this man she did not much like. "We will reach the Port of Nabban tomorrow. Even were I to turn back immediately, I would not be in time for Princess Idela's funeral."

"Of course, Majesty. But still, it must be a terrible time for you."

"It is more terrible for my husband. He has our granddaughter to care for, who must be comforted over the loss of her mother, as well as the people of Erkynland."

Auxis nodded. "And your grandson, Prince Morgan?"

Miri wondered at this. Was it only because she had not mentioned him, or was there something else to the escritor's interest? "He is on a mission for the High Throne. It breaks my heart to think he has likely not even heard yet about his mother's death."

Auxis shook his head in sorrow. If it was an imposture, the escritor was an even better mummer than Miri suspected. "We can never be prepared for death, except that we stand in the light of Usires, our Ransomer."

She decided to take him at face value, at least for now. She needed the lector and Mother Church to help her make peace between Nabban's feuding factions. "Oh, have no fear on that score, Eminence—Princess Idela was a devout Aedonite. She read little but religious tracts, and of course the Book of the Aedon was her constant companion, may she already stand in God's grace and light." Miri made the sign of the Tree, and Auxis joined her before she had finished the first stroke. "If anyone was prepared for the fate that comes to us all, she was."

"It makes my heart glad to hear that, Majesty. It is balm to the soul of those left behind, to know that our loved ones are with our Heavenly Father."

Despite her better instincts, Miriamele was tiring of this round of platitudes. "You have been most kind to visit, and to bring me the Church's condolence. Please keep Princess Idela in your prayers."

The escritor, as much courtier as churchman, knew when he was being excused. He stood, holding his tall hat in place, and backed toward the door. "It is always a privilege to speak with you, Majesty. I hope we shall continue our acquaintanceship, the demands on your time notwithstanding, when you have reached Nabban."

"I am sure I can depend on the reliability of your counsel." *The reliability that it will be entirely selfish,* she thought, but that felt a little unfair. The man had done nothing but what was necessary and right. Still, she was in a mood to trust no one, least of all one of the leading powers of Mother Church. Although what Simon had said of Idela's death had made it sound no more than a terrible accident, it also felt like a blow against safety and security—a blow she felt strongly on this journey to a divided and dangerous country. Dangerous even for the High Queen? That was something she would know better when she could feel and hear the mood of Nabban for herself.

What was it my grandfather used to say? Patience is the greatest tool of a king. Patience and a long memory.

On those occasions when Duchess Canthia was being dressed in the full panoply of her title and position, when her retiring room was full of happily talking women, Jesa could feel for a moment at least that she was back home in the Wran. On the day of a wedding the women there would gather in the hut of the bride's parents and help the bride through the rituals.

Today's gathering felt something like that, and even Jesa joined in the merriment. Because she was Canthia's friend and childhood companion, instead of looking at her like something that should be sent out of doors, the ladies-in-waiting treated her as though she belonged among them. But even though the room was full of excitement and glee, Jesa did not feel like laughing very often. She could see that her mistress was fretful, though trying not to show it. Even the broadest smile that came to Canthia's face looked like something carefully created. Jesa wondered if she alone noticed, or if others knew the duchess well enough to be worried.

Not that anyone was truly calm today. Queen Miriamele's ship had arrived and the queen was coming to the Sancellan Mahistrevis this morning. Ever since the news of her visit had been brought to Nabban a sennight ago, on a fast merchant ship, the entire Sancellan had seemed to Jesa like a tree full of birds suddenly aware a snake was making its way up the trunk. Worried, she had asked Canthia if the queen was someone to be feared, but Canthia had promised her that Queen Miriamele was very kind and that the queen and Canthia were on good terms. The duchess assured her the excitement in the ducal palace came only from the concern to make a good impression.

Which was a relief, but Jesa's real worry was about the duchess herself, who had seemed troubled for many days, beginning long before the news had come. Not that Canthia did not have reasons for worry. Riots were still taking place in the city, and quite a few people had been killed. The enmity between the two main parties, the duke's Kingfishers and the Stormbirds of Dallo Ingadaris, even divided the Dominiate, where the noble families met to make law. Jesa heard these recitations directly from the duke every night—though he spoke them to his wife, not her—when she brought little Serasina to her parents so they could bid the baby goodnight.

But Jesa thought her mistress seemed to have even more dire things on her mind than the warring families and unrest in the streets. Duchess Canthia was normally quite courageous, trained by a terrifying mother to maintain her composure in all circumstances, as she had often said with dark amusement. Jesa thought whatever was bothering her now seemed almost like one of the spirits who troubled the people of Red Pig Lagoon, the hungry ones who drank up people's lives at night, little by little, like a dog lapping water.

If I were home, I'd go to one of the healers and have her make up a charm against hungry ghosts to put beneath my lady's pillow. Of course, many of Jesa's people lived in the city of Nabban, especially near the docks—perhaps she could find such a one. But how? She certainly would not be leaving the Sancellan Mahistrevis while the queen was visiting—not unless the duchess herself set her some task that took her out into the city.

She had run many such errands of late for the duchess, mostly carrying letters. To her silent but genuine pleasure, several of them had been to Viscount Matreu, the handsome brown man (as she always thought of him, only realizing when she did how long she had been surrounded by paler faces) who had saved Jesa, baby Serasina, and the duchess from disaster when they were caught in a riot.

In other circumstances Jesa might have suspected herself the go-between in an illicit romance, but she could not believe that of her mistress. Canthia showed none of the feverish excitement of love, only the deep, hidden sadness that Jesa found so disturbing, and Canthia seemed to treat the letters to Matreu no differently than those from her other correspondents. For that matter, the duchess wrote more to ugly old Bellin Hermis, the earl of Vissa, than she did to the handsome viscount.

Jesa was also disgusted because even though she did not believe her mistress cared anything about Matreu beyond friendship and gratitude, she still felt a little jealous about their communications.

The viscount asked you to come work for him, foolish girl, that's all, she scolded herself. *Maybe he would have taken you to his bed, too. But nothing beyond that. Would you leave your friend and her daughter, sweet Serasina you love so much, to be a rich man's plaything?*

When Duchess Canthia was dressed and powdered, she sent her ladies out. "I must have a moment to catch my breath," she said, propping herself on a tall stool. "These skirts are so stiff! Here, Jesa, bring me my little darling."

But one of Canthia's attendants had stayed behind, clearly seeking a word with her, so Jesa waited. The duchess, understanding they were not alone yet, made a weary face before turning. "Yes, Mindia?"

The young woman hesitated. "It is just, Your Grace, that I heard my uncle, the baron, talking to some of the other men."

"I'm not a priest, dear one. I cannot absolve you of eavesdropping."

Lady Mindia colored. "It is not that. I just . . . it is what he said. He told them that he fears Count Dallo and his faction will make trouble at the duke's brother's wedding. They are planning something, he said, because Queen Miriamele will be there."

Canthia looked at her with flat disbelief. "At Drusis's wedding? A wedding that Dallo himself is paying for, and which benefits him more than anyone? Who would disrupt a wedding for such petty ends? I cannot believe it."

"Nevertheless, my uncle told his men to lay by arms in case there is trouble."

Now the duchess was angry. "These are the kind of tales that can make things happen, Mindia. You should know better."

"I'm sorry, Your Grace. I only wanted you to know—"

"And I do know. I will speak to my husband about it. But I do not want you carrying that tale anywhere else. Promise me you will speak no more of it to anyone."

The lady looked troubled, but said, "Of course, Duchess."

Jesa thought that sounded like a very unconvincing promise. She held infant

Serasina a little closer. Surely the duchess was right, though—no matter how bad the Ingadarines were, it made no sense that they would risk anything dangerous at their own festivities.

When Mindia had gone out, Canthia again asked for her daughter. As she held the child, one of the nurses brought in her son, young Blasis, also dressed for the state occasion in his finest clothes, but fidgeting as if he wore not silk and velvet but itchy grass. He was a handsome little boy with clear, dark eyes and a high forehead, but few children his age cared anything for meeting important people, and the duke's son was no exception.

"And there's my other darling," the duchess said when she saw him. "What a fine young man you look!"

"Thank you, Your Grace," said the nurse. "He fought every bit of it, though I beg pardon at having to tell you."

Blasis scowled. "I want to shoot my bow and arrows."

"And you will, my brave little son, but first you must meet the queen. She is a very wonderful woman, a good friend to Nabban. Did you know she is half Nabbanai herself?"

Blasis only looked down at his new slippers.

"Ah, well. Take him out and keep him clean, please, at least until the queen sees him looking tidy."

When her son had been conducted out again, doing his best to scuff those slippers with each dragging step, the duchess looked back down at Serasina. "And here is the smallest angel," she said, pressing her face close against the baby's pink skin. "She smells so lovely! Is there any fragrance to match it?"

Jesa, who had a greater familiarity than the duchess with the tiny girl's less pleasant smells, only smiled and shook her head. "No, Your Grace."

Canthia gave her a sharp look. "Is something troubling you as well, Jesa? Do not tell me otherwise—I know you too well." She set a few delicate, nibbling kisses on her baby's ear. "Out with it."

"It is what Lady Mindia said."

"Ah." She sighed. "Did you hear what I told her? There is no reason to fear. Yes, some of Dallo's Stormbirds might make trouble in the streets. They will use the excuse of public celebration to pick fights and perhaps even riot in the poorer quarters. Drink makes the peasants loud and full of themselves. But nothing worse will happen, I promise."

Jesa fought against a moment of resentment at the word "peasants." What was she herself but a different sort of peasant, a child of the savage Wran and thus little more than a trained animal in the eyes of most at the court? But she knew Canthia's heart was good, and that the duchess would never understand how her words could sometimes hurt her friend. "Then why is Lady Mindia's uncle so worried? Why should his men have weapons put aside?"

Canthia made a noise of exasperation. "Because her uncle, Baron Sessian, has ambitions of his own. He would love to turn some disagreement into an attack that he alone was prepared to defend. He wants to become my husband's indispensable man. I think he sees himself taking Envalles's place as the duke's principal counselor."

"But Envalles is the duke's uncle!"

"Exactly. So Sessian looks for anything that will make him seem more important, and prepares to fight against phantoms of his own ambition, like little Blasis shooting his bow and saying, 'Take that, dragon!'" Canthia laughed. "You know so little of these men, Jesa. They are full of wind and fire, but only when they can be so without risk."

Jesa felt a bit better. "You are certain, my lady?"

"Mark me—the wedding, though ridiculous in itself, will go smoothly. The Ingadarines are so happy to bind Drusis to them that they would ignore the Sancellan Mahistrevis itself catching fire and burning to the ground as long as the vows were completed."

The news about Princess Idela's death had swept through Duke Saluceris's palace ahead of Miriamele's arrival. As she made her way along the apparently endless lines of nobles waiting to meet her on the courtyard steps and in the Sancellan's great outer hall she was given almost as many words of condolence as of greeting.

She had spent much of the last day overwhelmed with sorrow for her grandchildren and anger with herself about having thought (and said, at least to Simon) so many unkind things about the dead woman. She was also troubled by the idea that her husband would have to bear the burden of Idela's death alone. Miri knew such things were painful for him, that Simon could not put on and off the mask of his position as easily as she could, who had been raised to it in a royal childhood.

Oh, my dear man, what I would not give for us to be together now. She was more than a bit shamed that she had pushed so hard for him to stay home while she came to Nabban. Yes, there were important things here to be done, but it seemed as if God wished to remind her that few obligations were more sacred than family and marriage.

In a moment when nobody stood directly before her, she discreetly made the sign of the Tree and offered a silent a prayer to the Mother of God.

Elysia, raised above all other mortals, Queen of the Sky and Sea, intercede for your supplicant so that mercy may fall upon this sinner.

The great bell in the Sancellan Aedonitis, the nearby palace of the lector, had tolled the hour two times before Miriamele finished making her way through the crush of well-wishers, attention-curriers, and the merely curious, and could finally retreat with her company of supporters to an inner hall of the Sancellan Mahistrevis to take refreshment. She had been pleased to see Duchess Canthia again, who had kissed her heartily on both cheeks. Duke Saluceris, though more reserved in his greeting, had said all the right things with admirable sincerity, and Miri, gratified, had made a dignified fuss over both the children. The duke's handsome, arrogant brother Drusis had kissed her hand and welcomed her too, although she could sense by the stiffness of his smile that he was not entirely pleased by her presence.

Feeling more secure, surrounded now by both her own soldiers and the duke's Kingfisher Guard, Miri realized how tired she was. Her dress seemed made of wood and her feet were aching, but there was no opportunity or place in the chamber to sit down. As her ladies talked excitedly among themselves, pointing out this or that well-known Nabbanai earl or baron or the best-known ladies of the court, measuring their flaws and favors, Miri moved a little apart to study the large paintings that dominated the high back wall of the chamber.

Three huge pictures were arranged in a triangle with the center image higher than the others. The outer paintings were of Nabban's two greatest leaders, Tiyagaris, who had founded the Imperium, and Anitulles, who had converted to the Church of Aedon and forced his subjects to do the same. Tiyagaris was shown in full martial regalia, helmet beneath his arm and a dim scene of armies on the move behind him. Anitulles wore clothes that looked more scholarly than warlike, though he had been willing enough to chastise unbelievers with imprisonment and death. He held in his hand the Edict of Gemmia, the declaration that all under Nabbanai sway would now observe the True Faith.

At the center, lifted above the others, either because he stood figuratively on their shoulders, or—more likely, she thought—because he was the progenitor of the current ruling house, hung a picture of Benidrivis the Great, who had captured the throne and begun the Third Imperium. The artist had given the bearded patriarch both a scroll and a sword. She wondered which one was supposed to be used first.

As she studied the huge portrait she sensed a presence behind her. Assuming it was one of her ladies, she said, "Just give me a moment more."

"Of course, Your Majesty."

A little startled by the male voice, she turned and found herself face to face with Count Dallo Ingadaris. She had not seen him in many years, but she could not help thinking that time had been unkind to him. The master of House Ingadaris had grown plump, but though he wore a narrow beard on his chin like a young buck, his exquisite green doublet and ceremonial sash could not hide his protruding stomach. He looked, she could not help thinking, like a dandified toad.

"Your Majesty!" he said, then made a deep bow, not without a small grunt of effort that Miri scented rather than heard in the noisy chamber. He had been chewing mint, which was some relief. "What a pleasure it is to see you again, Cousin—if I may be so bold as to call you so."

At once, all her dislike of him came flooding back. "Of course you may, Count Dallo. I have many cousins here in Nabban, but few as distinguished as you."

His eyes were small and shrewd in his wide face. "You flatter me, Majesty. I am most grateful you should come so far to honor a humble family wedding—especially at a time of such tragedy."

She sensed something else in his smile, a glint of a private jest. Did he know something about Idela's death? Could he in some way have been involved?

That makes no sense, she chided herself. *None at all. Do not let fear and the whispers of anxious courtiers drive you to hasty conclusions.* "My daughter-in-law died when I was on the way—I only heard after we had left Meremund. I would not have been able to return in time for her funeral in any case."

"Still, I know that family is important to you—as it is to all of us." He bowed again. "And I can guess how much you must wish you could be there. We shall do our best to make certain your visit is pleasurable. I know that your mere presence will do much to calm our agitated subjects."

She gave him a look, uncertain whether this was mere flattery or had some other purpose. "And why is it that your subjects—the duke's subjects, to be more precise—are agitated?"

Dallo put on a look of regret. "I'm certain you have heard many tales, and it is true that some foolish, hot-headed folk have clashed with the duke's men. But I assure you, they do not act in my name."

Only with the Ingadarine albatross crest for their banner, she thought. For a moment all her other thoughts were pushed aside by an unexpected wash of pure relief. If she had been raised a Nabbanai instead of half-Erkynlander and a queen in her own right, as the head of her mother's family this puffed-up fellow a decade or more younger than herself would have decided all matters of her life. It almost made her shudder, but she covered the moment with a sip from her cup of wine. *But things did not come to pass that way. And this man is only a greedy troublemaker, while I am queen and the mistress of the High Ward that rules Nabban and the other nations.*

"I am glad to hear you object to such behavior, my lord," she said. "I hope that while I am here we can work together to make the streets safe and the duke's subjects happy again."

"I will certainly drink to that," said Dallo, lifting and draining his own cup with almost indecent haste. Something was odd about his speech and posture, but she could not put her finger on it. "I know you have much else to do, Majesty, and many other people wish to give you their greetings and good wishes," he said, wiping his lips with the back of his hand, "but may I beg one last favor of you?"

Was it really so obvious I was about to make an excuse? she wondered. *Miriamele, your statecraft has become rusted in Erkynland's more placid court.* "And what might that be, Count Dallo?"

"Please, let me just bring someone I wish you to meet. It will take scarcely a moment, Majesty. May I have your grace to do so?"

"Of course."

She fortified herself with another sip from the wine, over-watered but still of fine vintage. She would send one of her women later to find her a jug of the stuff, so she might at least have a few more cups and sleep tonight without troubling dreams or nagging regrets. Perhaps she had better send Shulamit, she decided. It would do her good to move about after she spent most of the voyage in bed, complaining of her stomach.

Dallo Ingadaris returned through the crowding courtiers, who quickly moved to let him pass. With him was a pretty, very young, dark-haired girl. For a moment Miriamele could only stare, wondering whether Dallo had taken a new wife, but by the time they reached her she had realized who this must be.

"Your Majesty, may I please introduce to you my niece, Lady Turia Ingadaris. She is to marry Drusis, the duke's brother—the reason for your kind visit."

The girl, who had eyes as wide and dark as a fawn's, made a low courtesy and remained there until Miri gently told her to rise. Turia took the queen's proffered hand and placed a careful, dry kiss on it, then stood up and regarded her with open interest. She did not seem much awed to be in the High Queen's presence, Miri could not help noting.

That thought tugged at another, but she did not wish to be distracted and pushed it away. "Much joy to you, Lady Turia," she said. "I wish you and Drusis many happy years and a large, healthy family."

"Thank you, Majesty." The girl was quite lovely, especially when standing beside her toadlike uncle, but Miri knew her to be just twelve years of age and thought she seemed far too delicate for marriage or much of anything more serious than playing at dolls in the garden. Still, for all her frail, elfin appearance, the bride-to-be carried herself with the calm possession of a much older woman. Miri wondered if that might have something to do with having been raised as part of Dallo's ambitious and often cruel family.

"You may go now, Turia," Dallo said, "—if the queen permits it, I mean. Of course."

"It was a pleasure to meet you," Miri told her. "We will talk again, I hope, when I am not so pressed with other duties."

"I would like that," the girl replied, but despite her charming smile, Miri could not help sensing something else, a sort of masked indifference.

Well, only God and our Ransomer know what nonsense Dallo and Drusis have filled her head with, Miri told herself. *I will sound her thoughts if I get the chance, and perhaps teach her that there are other ways than Dallo's. So young as she is, she may wield some power here in Nabban through our Morgan's reign and even beyond. It would be good to have an ally among the Ingadarines.*

When Dallo and Turia had retreated again, she finally understood what had troubled her about the count's manner. Dallo was a powerful man, yes, but only a noble. He had made a noteworthy alliance with Drusis, the duke's brother and rival. And as the leader of House Ingadaris, Dallo certainly knew that Miri was here in large part because of the troubles in Nabban.

But it was Miri herself, along with Simon, who had put the crown on Duke

Saluceris. Although she would never have done so, as the queen Miri could make an excuse any time and have Dallo locked away. He had long ago made himself an enemy to the High Throne and everyone knew it.

Why, then, had he shown not the slightest fear of her? Instead, he had been confidence itself, as though he had the power and not she. And his grand-daughter had been no different—a mere child, she had looked over the queen of the High Ward as though sizing up a rival.

This thought disturbed Miri the rest of the day, but in the press of courtiers and official duties she was given little time to think too deeply. When she escaped to the great suite prepared for her at last, it was with immense relief and a strong thirst.

7

Dust

Tiamak locked the door to the chambers he shared with his wife before sitting down at his table. Thelía was down in the garden and would probably be happily at work among her plants for some time, but he did not want to be surprised by her or one of the castle servants.

He carefully took the box from the hidden drawer and set it on the table, but did not immediately open it. Instead, he examined its outside more carefully than he had the first time. The pearwood coffer was a little longer than a man's foot and almost as wide and carved with scenes from old stories—musicians, dancers, and lovers disporting in sylvan settings. It was the kind of thing a highborn woman might keep her jewelry in, but the fact that it was locked and had been hidden behind a wall panel in Prince John Josua's library suggested it probably held something other than necklaces and brooches. Why would a prince hide jewelry in his own chambers in his family's castle?

It did not look as though it had been touched in the seven years since John Josua's death. Tiamak took a settling breath, then picked up a hammer and chisel and, with several increasingly heavy blows, managed to break the lock. He then slipped on a pair of leather gloves he used to handle the hot crucible when he was making medicines, before opening the lid. Tiamek held his breath, beset with a sudden vision of an evil cloud rising from it, as in his people's story of Dika's Jar, but no cloud of angry spirits appeared, only a drift of dust.

A workman had found the box in the days after Idela's death as they were clearing the apartments that had once belonged to her and John Josua, and Tiamak was grateful it had been brought to him instead of to the king. The apothecary Brother Etan's discovery of Fortis's horrid, forbidden book among the prince's other effects had been preying on Tiamak's thoughts since the spring. He already felt like a traitor for not having told Simon and Miriamele about their son John Josua's possession of *Treatise on the Aetheric Whispers*, but every instinct told him he should examine what was in this locked casket himself before letting anyone else know.

On a day more than a score of years gone now, the people of the castle had sealed up Pryrates's tower and burned every article of his that had been found, including several of the priest's infamous, costly red robes. Not a person in the castle was free of the superstitious fear of anything belonging to Pryrates—not even Tiamak himself—but for some reason the young Prince John Josua had found and kept the book. Tiamak could only pray that the prince had not found any other of the red priest's possessions.

As he examined the box's contents, turning things over delicately with a gloved finger, Tiamak's first sensation was one of relief. Although the box was full of small articles, none of them were books, and none of them had obviously belonged to Pryrates. Instead, he found a collection of odds and ends that seemed almost like a child's treasures—broken bits of jewelry, odd-colored stones, and other objects he did not immediately recognize but which seemed harmless. But then he found a circle of carved wood at the bottom. After he had lifted it out and stared at it in puzzlement for little while, he finally recognized it, or thought he did. A chill scuttled up Tiamak's back, and for a moment he found it difficult to breathe.

The work of the day was only just begun and already Simon was weary of statecraft, especially statecraft of this niggling variety. The mayor and aldermen of Erchester had much to say and seemed determined to say all of it at the same time. The king's head was ringing.

"Can you put your objections into a few words," he said at last, "and perhaps choose just one of you to speak them?"

Thomas Oystercatcher cleared his throat. He was a round, self-important man who had made a frightening amount of money in the beer trade. He was mayor of Erchester by election of his peers, "Lord Mayor" only because he styled himself that way and had applied to purchase the vacated title of Ealmer the Large, Baron of Grafton, who had died without heirs after strangling on a chicken bone.

"Your Majesty must know that the city fathers find this new tax outrageous," said Oystercatcher.

"It's not a new tax," Simon told him. "Pasevalles assures me this is the law, that it has been the law since old King John's day but has not been enforced. Well, now it will be. You wish the protection of the High Throne so that Erchester and its port remain free? Then someone must pay for the privilege."

"You steal from us to give to the peasantry!" cried one of the aldermen, but Thomas Oystercatcher gave him a hard look before turning back to the king.

"Forgive my colleague, but it *is* hard, Majesty, that you lower the taxes on the peasantry then expect our merchants to make up the shortfall, all to keep a standing army against years of tradition. Do you not see that this appears to us like the actions of the tyrant Elias all over again?"

Tyrant. Even hearing the word made Simon want to growl like a bear, but to be compared to Elias . . . ! These wretched, grasping men! "We have lowered the taxes on the peasants because many of them are all but starving after several dry winters, and the harvests this year will be even smaller." Simon was doing his best to stay patient. He had discussed it all with Pasevalles and felt certain of his position. "While in the last years, you Erchester guildsmen with your tariffs and tolls have taken larger and larger shares of their market produce. That is to say, in truth, *you* lot raised the taxes, and so now you must yourselves pay more for the common good."

This reasoning, of course, quieted them not at all. Simon wished he could rub their faces in the real threats they all faced, especially the renewed threat of the Norns, but that was largely still a secret.

"Enough!" he said at last, silencing them for a moment. "Do you not remember I buried my daughter-in-law scarcely a sennight ago?" He gestured at his mourning clothes. "Do you think I wear black because I like the fashion? Go away now and come back to me with something other than loud complaints. I have my own figures, you know, so don't try to fool me—you are not the only ones with a counting house and clerks to make sense of all these numbers."

When Oystercatcher and the aldermen had been shown out, murmuring among themselves, Simon leaned back and wagged his hand for the page. "Wine, and less water in it this time," he said, then turned to Tiamak, who had been watching silently throughout the discussion. "There are times I can almost understand Elias—before he went mad, I mean. A little harsh discipline would not go amiss with men like that."

Tiamak made a discontented face. "I wish you would not say things like that, Majesty."

"I'm not talking about hanging them, man, I'm talking about a broomstick across the backside like Rachel the Dragon used to give me."

"I understand what you mean, Majesty—Simon—but the Hayholt is as leaky as a cane basket. Everything you say will eventually be whispered around Market Square and other, farther places, and they will not believe you were talking about a mere spanking."

"Well, damn everything to Hell, who could put up with this?" Simon glowered. "There's a reason I used to let Miri do most of this sort of thing. She's better at it than I am."

"Let us say that she is less surprised by how difficult people can be," Tiamak suggested.

Simon gave him a long look. "Something is bothering you. And it's not just how I barked at Oystercatcher."

Tiamak looked a bit guilty. "What makes you say that?"

"Knowing you for more years than I can tell. What troubles you?"

"Nothing I would trouble you with in turn. That is my task, sire, to take care of small matters so you may act on the large ones." Tiamak waved his hand, trying for a gesture of airy dismissal, but looking instead a bit unsettled.

Simon wanted to pursue it, but he was tired and hungry and the day's work had just begun. "Well, then, let us have something to eat and some cheerful talk before we must begin this nonsense again." Tiamak looked relieved, and Simon couldn't help wondering at that. "By the way, your lady wife, is she well?"

Tiamak nodded. "Very busy with inquiries and work of her own, but otherwise happy and fit."

"And your own health? Robust, I hope?"

"Yes, Majesty, and thank you for asking."

The king glared at him, only half-serious. " 'Majesty,' again? With no one else around?"

He bowed his head. "My apologies. Yes, Simon, my wife and I are both well, and thank you for asking."

Thelía was writing a letter to her old mentor and friend the Abbess of Latria, but when she noticed the look on Tiamak's face she put her quill down. "What is it? You look as though you have seen something dreadful, my husband."

He groaned and slumped into a chair. The stairs up to the fourth floor had made his leg ache. "I have. Or at least, something that makes me feel that way."

She brought him a cup of burdock wine. "Here, drink up and share your thoughts with me."

He had not planned to share his discovery with anyone, but Brother Etan, who had found the terrible book, was gone and the burden of so many secrets was beginning to exhaust him. Tiamak made a swift decision and prayed to He Who Always Steps On Sand that he would not regret it later. "Stay a moment," he said. "Let me get something that I wish to show you."

Thelía looked over the contents of the box, which Tiamak had taken out and arranged across a piece of cloth on the table.

"I had not wanted to make you a part of keeping a secret from the king and queen, but I begin to distrust my own judgement."

"What are those?" she asked, reaching a hand toward a trio of latticework silver balls. He had discovered as he set them out that they rattled.

"Do not touch anything!" he said, louder than he had intended.

She looked at him in surprise. "Why such a tone?"

"Because we still do not know what killed Prince John Josua, and we do not know where these things have come from—and these were his. That is why I put on gloves."

"You think they are evil?" She moved a little farther back from the table.

"I cannot say—I am not even certain what that would mean. But there could be something on them that made the prince ill." He took a breath, then slid the box a little closer to his own seat. "As to what those silver balls are, I cannot say. Bells from a horse's bridle? Beads from a necklace? But I have a question for you." He gestured toward the collection. "Have you ever seen anything like these things? Could they be from the time of the Nabbanai Imperium? Or even ancient Khand?"

Thelía gave him a strange look. "How would I know?"

"Because to me, they all have the look of Sithi work."

"This castle was built atop a Sithi city. You may well be right about that—but what is your concern?"

He took up the gray wooden circlet in his gloved hand, held it to the light so she could see it better. "The carving is old, but every cut is still sharp. And see the color! I think this is witchwood."

She squinted. "It is beautiful, in a way. But I ask you again, why the concern?"

"Because as I told you, the box was hidden in John Josua's study. Hidden like that dreadful book by Bishop Fortis."

"You should have told the king and queen about that," she said. "As I already said."

He sighed. "There are many things I might have done, and it may be true that I *should* have done them. But the reasons I chose not to speak up are still real. I do not want to go to Simon and Miriamele with troubling news about their dead son until I am sure of my facts."

"John Josua had a forbidden book," Thelía said with a shrug. "He hid a box of gewgaws that *might* be Sithi-made. Neither of those things seem unusual or unlikely for a scholar-prince living above the ruins of an old Sithi city."

"That book belonged to the wicked priest Pryrates, enemy of mankind, who plotted with the Norns . . . and with worse things. These objects—well, if they *are* Sithi, where did John Josua find them? The tunnels underneath the castle, at least those that lead to old Asu'a, were sealed off at the same time as Hjeldin's Tower was filled with stones and locked, twenty years ago and more. We scoured the castle for anything belonging to Pryrates and destroyed all we found. How did John Josua get any of these things?"

"I still do not understand why this box troubles you so."

"It is not the box, my good wife. In fact, it is particularly this." He again held up the carved circle of silver-gray wood. "Can you guess what it might be?"

She stared for a moment. "A frame for a small picture, perhaps? Or for a hand mirror?"

"Yes—a mirror. Exactly." He set it down again. "Do you see this thin crack—as if it broke just enough for whatever was in it to be removed?"

"You are making me fearful, husband. Your face is quite frightening."

"That is because I am frightened. The Sithi used mirrors like these to speak to each other—and, as we guessed from what we know of Pryrates, such mirrors, called Witnesses, could also be used to speak to . . . things. Things we do not understand. The sort of dark, nameless spirits that are spoken of in Pyrates's book—which John Josua also had hidden away."

For a long moment Thelía did not speak. "You think he may have found a Sithi mirror," she said at last. "One of these things you call 'Witnesses' . . . ?"

"I fear it, yes. Worse, I fear such exploration may have had a part in his death."

"Then you *must* speak to the king about all this." Her face now mirrored the strain he felt, the helplessness. "You must! If this is true, he and Queen Miriamele deserve to know."

"I know," Tiamak said. "And that is what most frightens me." He took another long swallow of his burdock wine. "Some truths, I cannot help thinking, are best left unlearned, and some secrets undiscovered. But I *am* the League of the Scroll now, for all purposes, since I will not hear from Binabik for many months, so it falls to me to worry and to decide."

"Not just you, husband," she said, and got up from her seat to come and put her arms around his shoulders. He pushed the box away where she would not brush against it by mischance. "You are not alone in this world," she said, her cheek against his. She smelled of rosemary and lavender and other growing things. It almost made him weep. "You have me to share your burdens."

"And that frightens me most of all," he said. "Oh, Thelía, I wanted you nowhere near any of this. But I fear I have grasped too much and now it is all spilling from my hands."

8

ReeRee

Morgan floated up out of what seemed like a dreamless sleep. The hillside around his hiding place was covered with broken branches and damp leaves blown into mounds like ruined castles, but the storm had passed and the sky was a brilliant blue between the trees.

His first waking movements started the small, warm bundle against his chest squirming. Long fingers reached up and pulled gently at his whiskers, which he had not shaved since the day before leaving with the Sithi, and the events of the stormy night came flooding back.

He unrolled his cloak a little to look at the thing he was holding. As the light fell on it, the little animal made soft noises of pain or discontent—*ree, ree, ree*. It seemed to be favoring one of its forelegs.

A pang of hunger dug at him, and for a moment he was looking at himself as if from outside, a lost young man making a pet out of a wild creature while he himself was starving. *It's the size of a plump hen*, he thought. *Or a rabbit that could feed me for days.* But even as one cold, sensible part of him considered this, another part of him was horrified by the idea. The creature looked up at him, hare's mouth gaping in concern, as if it understood his thought. Its eyes were far too much like a real child's, with a frightened ring of white around the edges. A wave of revulsion rolled over him.

This was madness. This must be the kind of thing his grandfather had told him about, when someone had been alone too long. Soon he would be talking to himself, perhaps even to imaginary people.

"I won't," he said out loud. "I won't let it happen."

Morgan leaned out and set the little animal down on the ground just in front of the crevice. It looked at him with wide eyes but made no effort to run or even crawl away.

"Go on," he said. "Off to your tree. Go!" He made a shooing motion, but the creature only stared back in wide-eyed alarm. Full of anger fueled by the stupid nastiness of hunger, he picked the little thing up roughly—it squeaked in pain—and carried it down the slope, then set it down in a dry spot and walked back to the crevice, resolutely not looking back.

When he got back to the limestone outcrop he could still hear it crying.

It was not the whine of a deserted puppy or the piping of a kitten, but a series of high-pitched moans, with hitching breaths between each forlorn "reeeee!" that sounded so much like a human child it made the hairs on his neck stand up.

I have to find food, he told himself. *I have to get out of this cursed, endless forest. I can't afford to care about some animal.*

But in Morgan's mind there now seemed a mysterious connection between the creature that had fallen from the tree and his young sister; it almost felt as though he had left a weeping Lillia behind in the forest.

When he returned to the wreckage of the tree, he discovered the little animal curled silently on the ground, trying to hide its face against its own belly with indifferent success. For a moment Morgan thought it had died and his heart stuttered, though the sensible part of him still wondered why he even cared. But when he picked it up it opened its eyes and looked at him gravely.

"*Chik,*" it said in a scolding tone, then more softly: "*Reeeee. Ree.*"

"Maybe you're a nighttime creature," he said. "Maybe I need to let you go when it's dark. But what are you?" He turned the animal on its back; it barked angry little *chik*s at him and kicked and squirmed. It had the twin rows of teats down the belly and nothing in the way of an obvious pizzle. "So you're a she-Ree, not a he-Ree." He laughed, then wondered if that might be a sign of encroaching madness. "But what kind of beast are you?" Morgan had never seen anything like her, apelike in some respects including the fingered hands, but with limbs and snout more like a rabbit or squirrel, and the stub of a tail at the bottom of her backbone. "What do you eat? And, for the love of our merciful Lord, what can *I* eat?" He hadn't seen any berry bushes, nor anything else he recognized, and hunger was making him want to give up, lie down beneath a sheltering tree, and sleep. But he recognized the danger.

That's how it begins, he told himself. *Someone told me that—you're hungry, then you're not so hungry, then you're just sleepy. Then you die.*

Probably something his grandfather had said. Which reminded him—beetles? Had his grandfather once said he'd lived off beetles in the woods? His shrunken stomach fluttered at the idea, but whether from revulsion or hunger he could not say.

Morgan's new companion was reaching out over his shoulder, as if trying to snatch at something, her clawed hands stretched wide. He turned and saw a sort of gall or nut he hadn't noticed growing on a bush near him, an object about the size of a chestnut and covered in thorny, tight-fitting scales. She waved her paw at it again and he reached out and twisted it loose from the branch. He gave it to her, but she could only use one of her forelegs—the other was still tucked protectively against her chest—and the nut or seed or whatever it was fell to the ground.

Annoyed, Morgan bent and picked it up, then held it prickling against his thumb in place of her injured leg while she held the other side. She began gouging at it with her long teeth, and soon had peeled off a good portion of the skin.

The inside was a pale cream color, like nut meat, but the smell was something more fruity.

When she had eaten about half of it she let it go as though it no longer existed. Morgan picked it up, wiped away the dirt, then peeled off a bit more of the armored rind with his thumbnail. It didn't smell sweet like a berry, but it still had a wholesome scent he liked. He nibbled a little bit and thought it tasted like nothing much, but at least it was not bitter. He waited to see if he had poisoned himself, but when a little time had passed and he felt nothing except the renewed awareness of how little was in his stomach right now, he peeled and ate the rest, then plucked the last few that the birds and insects had not attacked and ate another one. He offered a piece of it to his passenger, but she was apparently sated, at least with this particular delicacy.

"I suppose I'll have to give you a name. Who are you? Chik-ree? ReeRee?"

He decided that she should be called ReeRee, which sounded like a name, but she was *a* chikri, since he had seen others of her kind, perhaps even her family. He wondered for a moment if they missed her, but that made him think of Lillia and the rest of his own kin, and he did not want to linger on such thoughts. He cradled the beast in the crook of his arm as he went searching for more things to eat.

Thus, a partnership was formed. Morgan let the little animal choose things she seemed to like, and in most cases it turned out he could eat them too. A few did not work out, like a cluster of red berries that ReeRee downed with glee but which Morgan vomited up a hundred steps later. But he found most of her diet edible, if not exactly what he would have chosen.

Together they stripped the leaves off a flowering plant—they were peppery and made Morgan's mouth water—and later found a tree whose fruit looked like small brown apples, but tasted like book paste and crunched like a honeycomb when you ate them. Acorns were too bitter for Morgan to eat more than a bite, but on the shaded ground where the acorns lay he found little grassy stems that ReeRee ate happily and Morgan managed almost to enjoy because they were moist.

By the time they had reached the top of the hill behind the rocky crevice the sun had nearly topped the trees on the western horizon, and a wind had sprung up. He could already see that the top of this hill would not reveal anything beyond him but more forest—the crest was only halfway up a wide valley, with higher ground blocking his view of the distance. He decided that even though the storm had passed, he would sleep again in his rocky crevice.

When they arrived back at the base of the outcrop he made a sort of bed for the little animal in his cloak, then, after long search to find dry wood, built a fire on the slope in front of his refuge. He had no meal except for a couple of the scaly fruits, and no meat to roast or wine to soothe his worries, but for the first time in at least a few days his stomach was not aching. As he sat and warmed his hands in front of the flames, he felt something inside him he could only think of as peace.

He took out the Book of the Aedon his mother had given him, and by the light of the fire read one of the Hymns of the Precentor out loud. The creature curled sleeping on his cloak did not seem much moved by the Book, but the familiar words reminded Morgan of sitting in the chapel between his mother and his father, listening to Father Nulles, and that was a memory worth falling asleep to.

Qina thought Little Snenneq was the finest young man she had ever met, far better than anyone else on Mintahoq or any of the other mountains of Yiqanuc. He knew so much more than any of the other Qanuc men her age, but could—with coaxing—admit he did not know everything. Most endearing of all, he admired her parents as much as she did. She had never imagined she would find someone who fit her needs so perfectly.

But with all that said, sometimes she still felt a powerful urge to hit her *nukapik* with a large, heavy stick. "But surely I should be the one to cast the bones," he was saying for perhaps the third time. "It would be excellent practice for me."

"You will make my father angry," she warned him.

As usual, once Snenneq had a grip on something, he was not inclined to let go easily. "But I have a special duty to Prince Morgan . . ."

"You have a special duty to listen and learn." It was a relief to her to speak her own tongue. Qina had grown tired of being the one who could barely express herself to the lowlanders. "And as far as I have seen, this 'special duty' is all on your side. Morgan the prince did not agree. And now you have a duty to do what my father, the Singing Man, says . . ."

"Nobody honors your father more highly than me—" he began again.

"Qina, Snenneq," Binabik called from the far side of their forest campsite. "I have thrown the bones. Come and join me for talk."

Her mother Sisqi was off bathing herself in the creek, but Qina and Snenneq settled themselves beside the circle Binabik had drawn in the dirt. Her father stared down at the jumbled knucklebones with a look Qina knew well, frustration in the furrow of his brow and the squint of his eyes. He held up his hand for quiet—a gesture clearly meant for Snenneq, who was almost quivering with the need to talk. The wolf Vaqana padded over and, after making a few small circles, lay down next to her master and put her huge white head on his lap. Binabik stroked her, but kept staring at the tangle of his third and final casting.

"The first declaration the bones made was *Unnatural Birth,*" Binabik said. "Yes, Snenneq, I remember that is what you also threw for the prince. Give me another few moments to think, please." He tilted from side to side, studying the yellowed shapes from different angles. "Since we seek Morgan, that gives a certain sense. Whatever cloud you sensed in his sky, Snenneq, still remains on his horizon. But I do not sense that is the whole story."

"It could be, though," said Snenneq, unable to hold himself back any longer. "It could be that the prince is coming close to the time when something will change and he will lose what was expected."

Binabik's smile was measured. "Yes. That could be." He turned back to the bones. "But the second pattern was *Unexpected Visitor.* That is strange to me because that same uncommon result came up when I threw the bones for Morgan's grandfather, King Simon, in the days we first knew each other. That was long ago, at the beginning of the Storm King's War."

"What does it mean, Father?" asked Qina, as much to keep Snenneq from talking again as anything else. Her betrothed badly needed to learn that just because her father seemed equitable on the outside did not mean he was in a good mood.

"I don't know," Binabik admitted. "But it is such an odd result that after the king's declaration, I went back to the scrolls of Ookekuq, that I carry with me, to see if I had forgotten anything important. It only said what I remembered, that it is related to the casting *No Shadow*, and suggests there is or will be involvement from an unforeseen quarter. Still, it is important because, as the second declaration, it suggests how perhaps we can better our chances." He smiled. "The fate the bones see is not unstoppable, my daughter, but like a great stone rolling downhill, it has much force. To alter its course takes luck and good timing."

"I agree, Master," said Snenneq, Qina's betrothed.

Binabik's smile shrank a little. "I am pleased to hear that, Snenneq."

Qina did not enjoy it much when her father and betrothed were at cross-purposes with each other. She got up and began to examine the edges of the clearing, avoiding the places where she knew Vaqana had been sniffing and trampling and urinating. "I am listening," she assured them. "Continue, please."

"Here is that thing which puzzles me the most," said Binabik. "Look—the final declaration of the bones is *Unwrapped Dart*, and I can make no sense of that at all. Tell me what you know of it, Snenneq."

She could hear her beloved take a deep breath, finally given a chance to expound on things he had learned, and was grateful Binabik had taken pity on him. In fact, she could learn something from her father's patience, she thought: The chances were good that she would be spending a significant portion of her life annoyed at her husband. Snenneq was kind and clever, but he was also a bit full of himself. Her father sometimes even called her betrothed a "braided ram," but not when he thought she was listening.

"'Unwrapped Dart' can mean many things—" Snenneq began.

"Yes," said Binabik. "You are right. Tell me just those you think might have meaning for us here and now."

"It can mean that your enemy is closer to hand than you believe, which might be meaningful here, especially if someone beside ourselves is searching for the prince."

"Good. Go on."

"It can also mean that preparations need to be made, that those seeking to protect themselves have been slack in constructing their defense."

Binabik frowned, but it was a frown of contemplation. "That is a useful meaning, Snenneq, and you are right, but I do not believe that is the case here. It is too mild to represent what we should fear, in a time of so much danger from so many directions."

If Snenneq felt hurt to be contradicted, he did not sound it; instead, his reply was thoughtful. "You show me something I had not thought of, Master."

As she bent to examine some broken branches in the undergrowth, Qina sent her betrothed a silent thought of love and pride. *Well done, Snenne-sa. You are learning, you truly are.*

"But I do not have any greater insight myself to bring at this time," Binabik said. "It is a strange cast for a final declaration. The prince seems to have as many possibilities hanging above him as a man walking bareheaded into the Icicle Gallery back on Mintahoq." He gathered up the bones and returned them to their pouch. "We will continue to think. Snenneq. If an idea comes to you, do not hesitate to share it." His tone was light again. "Unless I am sleeping, of course."

Now that they had finished, Qina called, "Come here, please, all of you. I think you should look at this."

She had wandered a few steps beyond the edge of the clearing. At her urging, Binabik kept Vaqana back. The wolf complied, but with a look clearly meant to shame everyone involved.

"What have you seen, daughter?"

"This." She pointed down, and her father squatted at the edge of the faint animal track. "Now, look up here where the branches are broken. Something large has passed—not a deer, and certainly nothing smaller."

"It could be a bear," said Snenneq quickly. "This part of the Aldheorte is home to many bears, and they are large enough to break branches so."

"Interesting," she said. "Come a few steps farther and tell me, my betrothed, do the bears in this part of Aldheorte also wear boots?" She pointed at an undeniable crescent dent in the mud. "Before you tell me it is the slot of a deer or even a cow, please notice the marks left by the stitching of the sole just beside it."

"I see them, Qina," said Snenneq in a grumpy voice.

"Do not be cross, daughter." Binabik smiled. "You have made a wonderful find. Somebody wearing boots has indeed passed this way. You have found our next track to follow."

"You always had the sharpest eye," Snenneq told her, with only the barest hint of envy.

"Thank you."

After Qina's mother returned, her dark hair still wet and her eyes bright with pleasure at her bath, they followed Prince Morgan's spoor, losing it at intervals, especially when he traveled over hard or open ground, but with the help of Vaqana's nose and Qina's eyes, they found their way forward each time.

It was late, late afternoon, the sun hovering above the horizon and the forest filling with shadows, when Vaqana stopped, growling softly, hackles uplifted. Binabik calmed the wolf, signaled for Qina and the others to wait with Vaqana and keep her quiet, and then dropped to hands and knees to crawl up the slope. He moved slowly to keep the breeze in his face and to avoid anything that might make noise. Within moments he had disappeared from sight, but before Qina had time to worry more than a little, he clambered back down into view, signaled them all to follow silently. When Vaqana reached him, Binabik took the scruff of the wolf's neck-fur in his hand to keep her close.

Just below the top of the rise he gestured for them to stop. The light was all but gone now, the sky beginning to darken. On the far side of the hilltop a bear and two cubs were ambling along, working their way down the edge of a large berry bramble. The wind shifted, and a few moments later the larger bear rose on her hind legs to look around. She sank down and turned until she was facing the spot where the Qanuc were hiding. Qina felt a stab of fear: the she-creature was big, almost as large as some of the ice bears back home. She also had cubs to protect, which made her very dangerous.

Beside her, Snenneq was pulling one of his many pouches from his bag.

"I have just the thing," he whispered. "A dart, tipped with the Strong Sleep."

Binabik's words were swift and harsh. "Put it away."

Snenneq stared in surprise, still fumbling at the wool that would be pinched around the butt of the bone dart to make it fit the blowpipe, as if his hands had not yet heard from his ears. "But I will be careful. I will stay upwind . . ."

"No." Binabik scowled and waved his hand urgently. "Put it away. We will speak of this afterward."

Snenneq was doing his best not to look hurt again. "Wait until he unfolds his thoughts," Qina whispered to him. "He does not say such things carelessly."

They watched as the bear, evidently sensing no immediate danger, tipped forward onto to her forelegs once more and continued on her rambling way, stopping between mouthfuls of berries to gently cuff one of her cubs out of the thicket and back into her line of sight. They were a long time finishing, but when they finally wandered off down the hillside in a direction perpendicular to the track the trolls had been following, Binabik let out a sigh of relief.

"Now, I can talk," he said. "Please, tell me your thought, Snenneq. You were going to use a dart."

"To protect us—to protect Qina too!"

" 'The Strong Sleep,' you said."

"Surely. Anything weaker might only have made the bear angry."

"But now the bear is gone. And not angry."

"Do not set puzzles for him, husband," said Qina's mother. "It is unkind."

Snenneq pursed his lips in frustration. "Things could have happened differently!"

"And if they had, we would perhaps not be having this discussion."

Her father brandished his own walking stick, which Qina saw he had disassembled so that he could use it as a blowpipe. "I had a dart of my own, Little Snenneq, but I did not want to use it. Can you tell me why?"

Snenneq shook his head wearily. "No, Master. Not without guessing, and you do not like guessing."

Binabik smiled and most of the irritation slipped from his features. "I do not mind guessing, but it must be based on knowledge. Here is knowledge. If you had darted the bear, she would have slept, yes? Well past the setting of sun and into the dark hours."

"Yes, I suppose so."

He nodded. "And her cubs? What would they have done? Stayed beside her in the cold, unprotected. They could not find their den without her."

"But she would have woken up after a while."

"And what if a male bear came while she slept, Snenneq? Some of them eat cubs that are not their own." Binabik's smile now had a mischievous edge. "It is of course impossible to understand wanting to do such a thing, but there it is—it happens. That is one reason the mother watches them with so much care, and that they are so far away from the best feeding grounds."

"They are only bears," said Snenneq, unable to keep a little sullenness from his voice.

Binabik appeared to take pity on him. "You are a very clever young man, and I have no doubt you will someday be a fine, fine Singing Man, Snenneq, but there is still much you do not know. You are not just in any place here, and you are certainly not at home on familiar Mintahoq."

"Again, good husband," said Sisqi, "I ask you not to set puzzles for Snenneq. Help him see what you mean."

"I am trying to do just that, my beloved," he told her. "This is the Aldheorte, Snenneq—and you too should understand this, Qina—and nobody can lightly take a life here. This part of the forest is wound through with the songs of the Sithi, songs to confuse outsiders and to hide them from those who would seek them. That is hard enough to guard against, even with all the teaching I received from Ookekuq and even the Sithi themselves.

"*But*—" he raised a finger, "—there are older powers in Aldheorte, older . . . presences."

"Like what?" said Snenneq, and his hurt was lost in his newfound interest.

"I do not know. And I do not talk of them when I am among them, in any case. This is not our home. This is not our place. We are guests."

Qina's betrothed no longer looked upset, just uncertain. "Are you saying that if we hurt the bears, something bad would happen to us? What if we take a rabbit for dinner, or a quail?"

"I'm saying that taking a life to eat is one thing. Harming an animal from impatience or laziness . . . well, I suspect that would be viewed differently."

"You keep saying things like that, Master, but I fear I don't understand. Viewed by whom?"

"If I knew, it would be different. As it is I only have feelings and old tales to go on. And those tales—and my feelings—suggest that except for small animals and birds for eating, we should harm nothing that does not threaten us." He considered. "Perhaps it would even be safest if we harmed nothing at all, not even to fill our stomachs. We have some small store of food with us."

"But that is only bread and dried fish!" Snenneq, who liked nothing better than a stewed rabbit, could not suppress a look of horror.

"Bread should be fine. And I do not think the forest watchers care about the fate of a fish that has been dead since last summer," said Binabik cheerfully. "I think you may also have as much of that as you want."

Morgan had a strange dream in which he was a dragon in a garden where all the plants and trees hung with jewels that glittered in the sun, gems red as blood, green as grass, oranges and yellows as bright as gold coins. In the dream he knew the garden was his and his alone, but as he lay coiled in the center of his treasures he heard leaves rustling and the sounds of small things moving. Someone had come to steal from him, and he woke with his heart beating fast and a fierce desire to protect his property.

In the first groggy moments after waking, his eyes still blurry with sleep, he heard small noises just as in his dream. His first thought was that little ReeRee had wandered away, but she was curled up against his belly as she had been when he fell asleep, the fingers of one small paw curled tightly around the edge of his jacket. He leaned forward to look out of the crevice and see what might have made the noises; she murmured a sleepy *chik* in protest. At that, whatever was making the other sounds retreated in a sudden patter of movement, followed by silence.

He leaned farther out of the crack in the outcrop, holding ReeRee close to keep her quiet, but saw no sign of anything unusual. He set her down on his cloak and crawled out into the weak dawn sunlight to discover a small pile of nuts and fruit that had been carefully assembled on the slope a few paces away.

Morgan kneeled beside the pile for a moment, staring without understanding. The pile was no bigger than what he could hold in both hands, but the clusters of berries and rough-shelled nuts had been set on leaves, as though tiny servants had prepared a breakfast and put it out for him as he slept. Only after a moment did he think to look up, and caught a brief glimpse of dark eyes watching him from the trees, the same sort of creatures as ReeRee, then the watchers disappeared into the higher branches.

He gathered up the offering, for it seemed as if it could be nothing else, and climbed back into the crevice. His assumption seemed to prove true when ReeRee took everything he offered her, not merely without suspicion but with positive excitement. Despite all the foraging they had done together Morgan was hungry again, painfully so, and although he let her have her choice, he took the lion's share for himself. For a while they ate together, silent except for ReeRee's contented noises and the crunch of nutshells, as the world warmed around them and the day-sounds of the forest swelled; first birds, then the hum and click of insects.

The chikri creatures had made him a gift. For the duration of the meal that thought made him feel almost warm and safe. It was only when they had finished, and ReeRee was contentedly grooming the fur of her belly and arms, that he realized it was more likely that the food was a sort of ransom, like the tribute paid by villages to encourage troops of bandits or landless knights to pass them by without harming them.

They're afraid of me, he realized, and then he had an even stranger thought: *That's how we lived in the castle. We had the swords and the horses and the armor, and so everyone gave us food and gold. We always thought they loved us—but what if they didn't? What if they don't?*

His dream of being a dragon floated up to his thoughts again. He could still remember the feeling of lying torpid and suspicious as small creatures scuttled in the shadows.

Is that how they think of us back home—the people we rule? Not as their rightful lords, not as their saviors, but as monsters they must convince not to kill and eat them?

It was an uncomfortable thought, and one that did not quickly go away.

9

Appetite

Afternoon was waning on the mountainside. The melted snow in the Witness pool had finally stopped bubbling and was beginning to ice over. After the labor of making the Witness and using it to speak with his master Akhenabi, Saomeji had stretched out at the base of a tree to rest with eyes closed, his strength exhausted. Goh Gam Gar, who had pulled the bound dragon all day and then dug the deep pit for the Witness out of the frozen ground, lay curled on his side within Saomeji's fence of magical stones. The giant might have been a stone himself, a massive boulder covered in dirty white hair, the rumble of his slumbering breath echoing along the hillside. The bound dragon and the crippled chieftain had also gone quiet.

Nezeru took a long, deep breath and let it out, still shaken from the Singer's Witness ceremony but grateful for a rare moment free from the demands of others.

Jarnulf gathered up his bow and quiver. "Now I must go hunt."

"I'll go with you."

He did not hide his surprise. "Truly? What of your ward, Makho?"

"I have done all I can for him today and with little result. I do not see how he can live much longer." She began pulling on her gloves.

"But what of Saomeji and the giant?"

"If one of them wakes up and kills the other," she said, "then that is one less for us to worry about."

Jarnulf's look seemed almost admiring. "You have changed, Sacrifice Nezeru. You sound as though you have embraced Genathi's Gift."

She was impressed by his choice of phrase. It was a reference to the blind Celebrant Genathi, one of the first born in the new land after the flight from the Garden, who had famously said, *"Living in darkness is a gift, since the darkness will take all some day and we who cannot see will be least troubled by it."* It was the kind of sour jest her father's father might make. "You may think what you will, Huntsman," she replied. "A Sacrifice is practical, and I have an appetite."

They found a small lake nestled in a saddle of the hills, an hour's walk from the camp. A flock of geese lay on the moonlit water like a rumpled blanket, and before long they had each taken a fat bird. Neżeru's better eyes let her take a resting one with a clean shot; Jarnulf had to bring his down from the air with an arrow through its wing, then break its neck. The rest of the flock went flapping and honking to the far end of the water, so Nezeru and Jarnulf started back toward the camp. On the way they shot a brace of rabbits as well, but snow was beginning to swirl around them as they tracked the second rabbit's bloody attempt to escape.

"We had better hurry," Jarnulf said as they found the dying creature and added it to their bag. "Even you won't be able to see your way through this soon."

"I cannot see well now," said Nezeru. "And there were places as we came out that I would not want to cross again without being able to see what was before me. I think we should take shelter until the worst has passed. The sky was clear a short while ago. This kind of mountain storm lasts only a little while."

He looked dubious. "Saomeji will think we ran away."

"But we haven't," she said. "Either he will send the giant to look for us or he will wait to see if we come back. You are not wearing a painful collar, Master Huntsman. You need not fear the Singer's anger."

He shook his head. "You do seem changed, Sacrifice Nezeru. I am not entirely certain I like it."

"And I am not certain I care. Keep your eyes open. I remember there were some caverns, or at least openings in the rocks, somewhere just ahead."

They found a deep hole in the cliff face, and once inside they huddled together, watching the snow fall.

"I wish to ask you a question," Jarnulf said at last.

"Why do you need to announce your asking instead of simply asking?"

She felt him shake a little—a laugh. "I suppose I'll find out. You are not carrying a child, are you? But you told Makho you were."

Nezeru was startled. "How do you know anything of that?"

"We travel in a small group, day after day. I speak your tongue. It is not such a mystery. I saw how Makho and the other Sacrifice Kemme treated you— carefully, but without kindness. It suggested to me that they might be restraining themselves because you were useful in some important way, but they showed little evidence of that either. You were merely given duties that would not tax your strength, but neither coddled or protected you. I grew up among your people. I know how cautiously Hikeda'ya women are treated when with child. It seemed the most likely thing."

He had surprised her again and Nezeru did not like it. For a moment it soured her independent mood. "So tell me, clever mortal, how you knew that there was no child in fact?"

"Oh, I heard Makho talking about it when you were away from his side— you know how he raves sometimes. I didn't understand much of what he said, but I did hear him say, 'The halfblood lied. There is no child—not yet. The prophecy is not fulfilled.'"

"The prophecy?" She was honestly astonished. "What nonsense is that? And what makes you think his babbling has anything to do with me? There are other halfbloods in the world."

He gave her a shrewd look. "Come, Sacrifice, since the dragon's blood burned him, Makho only speaks of two things—the end of the world and you."

If Makho's words somehow *did* refer to her, Nezeru could not imagine what they meant.

Jarnulf broke the silence at last. "Why did you tell them you were carrying a child?"

"So Makho would leave me alone." She found herself suddenly enjoying this chance to speak freely. "Now you tell me something. Why are you with us?"

"You already know."

"Simply to serve the queen? Liar. That makes no sense. Makho knew it from the first, and I suspect Saomeji does too. Let me tell you what I think. You wish to re-enter Nakkiga, for some reason. You have offended someone powerful, or broken a rule, but you are tired of exile."

He nodded slowly, his face a pale, moon-silvered shadow. "Yes, I am tired of exile." He spoke carefully. "You have most of it right. But that is all I will say. Still, I admit you are more clever than my first guesses."

"As you are cleverer than mine." She felt something bubbling a bit inside her, and realized she wanted to laugh. It was an absurd impulse that she did not understand, but she could not deny its strength. "So, here we are, two enemies who underestimated each other. What is next?"

"Two enemies? I thought we fought for the same side."

"We are being honest here, in this cave in the snow, mortal. Jarnulf. You know our two kinds can never be anything but enemies, whatever temporary accommodations we might make. We Hikeda'ya must enslave or kill your people if we wish to survive. You must wipe us from the face of the world if you wish to do the same."

He was silent then as they both watched the snow dancing in the moonlight. At last she moved closer, until she was pressed against him from hip to shoulder. She reached out a finger and traced his profile. "Like, yet unlike," she said. "Do you think we were created by the same hand, that we should look so similar?"

His voice was gruff, almost angry, though he did not lean away. "I do not think so, Sacrifice."

"You seem very certain. How can that be?" Her fingers now trailed down his neck to the collar of his jacket. His skin was so warm! How could mortals be so warm-blooded and yet take cold so quickly?

"What are you doing?" he asked at last.

"Touching your skin. It is different than mine. Differences are interesting, are they not?"

"What happened to honesty? I do not think you are speaking the truth."

"Not the whole truth, perhaps." She paused to consider. She had been watching Jarnulf for days with a sort of growing admiration, not for what was human in him, but what was like the Hikeda'ya—his near-tirelessness, his willingness to do what needed to be done, his patience while dealing with the giant and Saomeji. Whatever his true goal, a lesser mortal would not have put up with the suffering Jarnulf had endured on this trip, nor would a lesser mortal have saved her and the others as many times as he had done.

He should have been a Sacrifice, she thought. *He has the making. He has the mind and the purpose, but the wrong blood—mortal blood. Like my own, but without the Hikeda'ya portion to offset the weakness.*

"You . . . interest me," she said at last. "And after so many days now without Makho and Kemme looking over my shoulder, always waiting for me to make mistakes, I find that interest has increased to something more. 'Appetite,' I said earlier. 'Appetite' is as good a word as any. I am as surprised as you are to find I crave comradeship—a particular kind."

"That is not . . ." He stopped when her fingers closed gently in his hair. "Not a good plan, Sacrifice," he said quietly. "Not for either of us."

"We will not know for certain unless we try. Do you mortals never couple unless making a child? Is it as joyless for your kind, then, as it has been for me, a half-blood who owes the use of her body to her people?"

He gave her an odd look, as if it surprised him that she might display any resentment at all about her lot. And this mood of hers *was* unusual, Nezeru realized. She had been in a distracted, angry state ever since Saomeji had spoken to Akhenabi, and she had felt their conversation in her own thoughts and blood. Everything reminded her how little she mattered to them—that she was not truly the queen's Talon or even Finger as far as the Order of Song was concerned, but more like a single ant in a nest, something to be used, sacrificed, discarded.

Sacrifice. The meaning of the name had never seemed so clear. And this was what she had spent her entire life trying to achieve—the right to be sacrificed. It had been one thing when she had believed utterly in those above her, from Queen Utuk'ku herself all the way down to Makho, her hand chieftain. But it all felt different now.

She realized they had both been silent for some time. "It is not your questions that have changed things. Do not flatter yourself, mortal. It is my own answers to your questions that trouble me."

"You are in depths I do not understand, Sacrifice Nezeru."

"Nor do I understand them myself. It is both frightening and . . . exhilarating." She leaned back against the rock wall behind them. She could feel the length of his leg and torso against her. "What do mortals do when they are lovemaking?"

She could feel him start in surprise. "What do you mean?"

"You heard me. My mother calls it lovemaking. There is little of that in any coupling I have done with Makho or other Sacrifices since I reached womanhood. I cannot quite imagine it." She laughed, a harsh, clipped sound. "So tell me, what do mortals do?"

He was silent for long moments. "I am not the one to ask."

"Is that a joke? Or are you truly so innocent?"

"I did not say I was innocent. Only that I was not the one you should ask." He stared at the swirls of white spinning in front of the cave mouth like downy feathers from a torn cushion.

"I do not care much," she said at last, "whether you lovemake well or badly. I told you, I have an appetite—a hunger of the body, and something more. A hunger of the spirit, I suppose. I am tired of being alone in the world, with only those who despise me. Whatever else we are to each other, enemies, doomed allies, I do not think you despise me."

"No. No, I do not despise you, Nezeru." His voice was tight with discomfort, more than she would have expected. "But there is no true connection possible between us."

"I said nothing of 'true connection.' I said 'appetite.' I wish to be soothed. I wish to be distracted. Now, show me what mortals do. Do you touch mouths?" She leaned closer, enjoying the smell of him, strong and lively yet not unpleasant, like a horse after exercise. "Do you do something else? Makho would only mount me and enter, like a conqueror taking possession of a town he had no interest in governing."

For a moment Jarnulf sat motionless as she breathed warmly on his cheek, then he slowly turned his head until his mouth brushed her skin. He pressed his lips against hers—tentatively at first, the skin dry and cold, but as several heartbeats passed their mouths warmed.

In such a narrow space the mortal could not easily move the arm that was pinned against her side, but his free hand slid up her leg—slowly, as if he did not truly control it—then over her hip and onto the curve of her ribcage below her arm. For a while they only sat like that. Nezeru found it awkward but fascinating. Her childhood had been spent in the Order-house of Sacrifice, where little affection passed between the young troops, and any coupling had been swift and secret, a matter of stolen moments. The Hikeda'ya of her parents' caste did not show physical affection in front of others—even an embrace was considered crass and showy when others were present—so this was utterly new to her. Still, she could not help feeling that something was wrong. Jarnulf, despite his rapid heartbeat and uneven breathing, despite every other sign of emotion, seemed content merely to sit like this, his mouth pressed against hers, his arm around her in an embrace that did not seem much more than brotherly.

She took his hand from her ribs and lifted it to her breast, pressed it firmly, even squeezed his fingers as if showing a new Sacrifice how to properly grasp a sword hilt. As she did, his mouth opened a little, and they pressed themselves closer together. His hand on her breast was beginning to make her feel warm, to stimulate the longing she had been feeling into something more serious, something that made her squirm a bit. She opened her lips wider and let her tongue touch his. As their mouths mingled she felt almost vulnerable.

Strange, so strange, she thought. Was this what mortals valued—not the sensations themselves, but the surrender to risk?

But the sensations were nothing to scoff at; the pressure of his fingers as he gently squeezed her breast was making her feel increasingly heavy between her legs—sensitive, like a bruise just beginning to heal. She wanted to push herself against him, wanted to rub on him like a bear scratching itself against a tree, and the ridiculousness of that idea almost made her laugh. First she undid the front of her jacket so that he could touch her skin, then she tried to lie down and pull him with her, but the cave was too small for them to stretch out. Still, she wanted more of this unusual feeling, so she reached up and folded her fingers around his hand again—he lifted it away suddenly, as though caught in the commission of a crime—then slid it down across her belly and into the fork of her legs so he could feel the heat at the center of her, the heat that was now making her squirm and rub against him everywhere they touched.

But the moment she closed her thighs on his hand to press his fingers tighter, he yanked his hand away and pulled his face from hers. He even began to clamber out of the cavern, which she only prevented by wrapping her arms around his waist and holding on.

"Stop!" she said. "What are you doing?"

"No." He was talking as if to himself, not her. "No, no. It cannot be."

"What cannot be? Coupling? Don't you like it? Isn't that what you've wanted from me all along?"

He shook his head violently. "No. I wanted nothing of the sort. You don't know."

"Don't get up."

"I'll do what I want to—what I need to—!"

But she felt him relax a little, so she let go of his waist. "Do not be so foolish, mortal man. If you don't want to couple with me, nobody will force you. I think even among your own folk a woman does not have to beg for someone to mate with her."

He disentangled himself and pulled away as far as he could, not in revulsion exactly, but more as if he needed the space between their bodies to think clearly. She wondered if there was something else about mortals she did not understand. Were there formalities before coupling? Religious rituals? It was strange how little she knew about the creatures who were her own people's greatest enemies.

It was stranger still that she had just been trying to couple with one of them.

"The weather is not so bad now," he said without meeting her eye. "We need to go back. Saomeji will be angry if we stay away too long. He will be suspicious."

It was plain that nothing further was going to happen between them—not here, at least, not now. "Very well." She tied her jacket closed again as he looked out into the fluttering snow. "Lead the way, then."

I have made some mistake, she thought as she followed him. Although Jarnulf was only a few steps ahead of her, she could barely see him through the flurries. *There is something here I do not understand—perhaps he never thought of me as anything but a Sacrifice, as a Hikeda'ya, the people who enslaved him. But more than anything else, I feel frustrated again. And alone.*

At first the scratching sound seemed only part of Tzoja's dream. When she opened her eyes, the blackness around her was so complete that for long moments she did not know where she was, but the furtive noises continued even as she lay in quiet panic.

Finally memory returned, but the scraping went on. She turned over, her heart beating at a fierce, frantic pace, then crawled out of the parlor and down the twisting hallway toward the door.

The scratching had stopped by the time she reached it, so she put her face to the keyhole and, to avoid making the slightest sound, held her breath while she peered through. By the ghost-light of the glowing worm threads above the lake she could make out a bulky silhouette with what looked like an extra head, and knew it was Naya Nos and his silent steed, Dasa. She opened the latch as quietly as she could, then stood out of the way so the huge carry-man Dasa could shuffle in.

"What do you want?" she demanded in a loud whisper when the door was closed again. "Why have you come back? All my food is gone."

"To make repayment," said Naya Nos.

"Repayment?" she asked.

"Some of the other Hidden have come back from the water—the 'lake' you call it—with a good catch of . . ." He frowned, his childish face puzzled. "Swimmers. Swimmers, I think you call them." He made a sinuous side-to-side motion with his hand.

"Fish?"

"Yes. Fish. Swimmers? But you are invited. Come to eat." He smiled broadly, but his companion Dasa's face remained empty as a spilled bucket. "You will meet her."

Tzoja's alarm returned. *"Her?* Who is that?"

"The Lady of the Hidden. She knows of you already. We told her."

"I don't understand."

"You need not. Because she is good and kind. She is our Lady! And she wants to meet you." He grinned again and drummed his little legs against Dasa's broad chest. "Say yes. We wish to make good the wrong we did you."

The idea made her fretful—every instinct she had told her to stay hidden, to stay away from these strange creatures—but if she could not find more to eat here beside Lake Suno'ku then she would have to return to the city to steal more food. The idea of fresh fish was also appealing—in fact, her stomach was already growling with anticipation at the thought.

"Very well," she said at last. "I'll come with you. But only for a little while."

She let them lead her down to the edge of the lake, then followed in the carry-man's footprints as he made his way around the water's muddy verge through banks of ghostly white reeds. Dasa's massive, shadowy shape suddenly turned to the side and vanished into a crevice in the cavern wall; Tzoja stopped in confusion. It was not merely a crevice, she saw as she stepped closer, but an actual gap that passed deeper into the mountain's stony skeleton accompanied by a wide finger of the lake, and she allowed herself to enter. The glowing worms had also hung their glassy strands above the water here, so that she was accompanied into the depths by a dangling forest of small, cold lights.

After a short, cautious walk behind the carry-man and Naya Nos, Tzoja found herself in a large cavern with the channel of lake water in the middle of it, the stony floor as uneven as butter swirled in a churn. But as she stared she could make out movement here and there.

"Fear not, brothers and sisters," called Naya Nos. "Come out! This is not an enemy but a friend."

Tzoja, still bitter about the loss of her supplies, was not quite willing to go as far as that, but she was distracted by the sheer number of creatures who now began to creep out from behind stones and out of crevices in the floor and nooks in the walls. Having discovered at least a half-dozen pillaging the kitchen in the festival house, she had assumed there might be twice that many Hidden all together, but in just this chamber she could see scores of them, all smaller than Dasa but in many different sizes and shapes.

By Usires the Aedon and Dror the Thunderer, she thought, astonished. *How do they all feed themselves? Especially when there is no one like me to steal from?*

"Are these all your people?" she asked.

"Not all, but many," he said. "Most! Some are out looking for more food. But they know we will feast today, so they will come back soon." Naya Nos waved his spindly arms, clearly overjoyed by the idea of the bounty that awaited them. "And the rest are in the Lady's Chamber, which is just there." He waggled his hand at the place where the stream and the dangling glow-worms vanished into a dark oval at the far end of the large cavern. "She blesses the food!"

"I hope she cooks it, too," said Tzoja, but too quietly for Naya Nos to hear. She had caught and eaten a small fish out of Lake Suno'ku the day before, too impatient to carry such a small thing all the way back to Viyeki's festival house and then build a fire. Anything was better than starving, but sucking the tiny bit of clammy flesh off the bones had been a less than delightful experience.

The Hidden all shrank away from her as she followed her guides deeper into the chamber, but their eyes followed her every step. The creatures seemed as weirdly individual as those that had robbed her stores, ranging in size from nearly as large as Tzoja herself to some even smaller than Naya Nos, and in skin color from dark to pale. Many of them had features that resembled either Hikeda'ya or Tinukeda'ya—in a few cases, both—and most of those who had eyes shared the same color, an almost luminous yellow. Otherwise Tzoja could see no obvious commonality between them, except that all would have been culled without pity from the slave pens of Nakkiga.

At Naya Nos's suggestion she seated herself on a flat rock by the side of the water. Dasa slowly sank to his knees beside her. His rider clambered down, wiry little arms doing most of the work, then pointed to the far end of the cavern and clapped his hands in glee. "Look! See, they come! The feast begins!" He leaned toward Tzoja. "Do not fear—a special portion has been put aside for you, because of the wrong our young ones did to you."

She watched a couple of the larger Hidden approach with a dripping bundle between them that looked like a fishing net. As she watched the puddles that formed beneath their burden every time they stopped, Tzoja's heart sank. So much for the meal being cooked.

"Ah, so tasty," said Naya Nos. "Swimmers are my favorite."

"Do all your people speak Hikeda'yasao like you do?" she asked, trying not to think too much about cold, raw fish. "I haven't heard anyone else say anything."

"Some do. Most do not, or will not." His animated face became grim. "Many were punished severely for making any noise at all."

"Punished? Who by? Where did you come from?"

"The Lady will tell you all you need," he said. "Do not fear—she knows everything that can be known about the People and the Hidden and everything that happens in the Sea Definite and Internal. But here, now, here!" he called to the approaching Hidden with their dripping net. "Let us serve our guest! Just here, then you can give out to the rest."

The two wide-eyed servers seemed torn between staring at her in fearful wonder and avoiding her return gaze. Both were naked except for rags around their loins, and both were achingly thin, with ribs and hip bones so prominent that one of the slender, graceful Hikeda'ya would have seemed overfed beside them. They set the net down and let it fall open. A pile of wet, wriggling shapes slid outward in all directions. Even in the cavern's dim light, she could tell by the lumpy bodies and short, fat tails that they were not fish.

"Pollwags," she said. Her stomach knotted. "Frogspawn."

Naya Nos smiled, misunderstanding the tone of her voice. "We are lucky—so lucky! They breed near the place where the hot water comes up from below."

She looked down at the wriggling, mostly legless globs. She would have to eat some. It would be foolish not to. She couldn't guess when she would next find food.

"Bless us and bless this bounty," she said, repeating the prayer the Astalines had taught her to say at every meal, but unable to make herself sound either enthusiastic or truly grateful as she scooped up a wet, squirming handful.

The last mouthful was no better than the first, but Tzoja had been hungry many times before in her life, so she shoveled it in like the rest and tried not to feel the swimmers that were still wriggling on their way down.

"We are lucky today!" said Naya Nos. "You brought us this luck, maybe. But look, she is coming out now!"

A stir went through the cavern as a little procession emerged from the chamber beyond, a scurrying parade of freakish shapes. Several of them were leading a larger figure by the hand, and as this newcomer appeared in the pale light of the glowing worms, Tzoja found herself staring. This was no crippled thing like the others: instead, this woman had the look of Hikeda'ya nobility in her height and graceful presence. Only her dark hair and large yellow eyes suggested a more complicated heritage.

"*Uvasika!*" cried Naya Nos, and others around Tzoja echoed him from mouths of many different shapes, reverentially and over and over, until she realized they were not calling out some word of welcome but the name of the one who seated herself on a rounded rock beside the narrow span of water. Instantly, just by the dignity of her presence, that rock became a throne.

"Come," said Naya Nos. "Uvasika will want to meet you." He scrambled up onto Dasa, who had been kneeling as patiently as any horse cropping grass, then together they led Tzoja across the cavern.

"You may bow to her," said Naya Nos quietly, then raised his piping voice as they neared the rock. "Uvasika, Lady of the Hidden, we have brought you an outsider—one of the People."

Tzoja made a clumsy courtesy. She had never learned any kind of court etiquette during her years among the Astalines in Rimmersgard or her childhood in Kwanitupul and the Thrithings, and her Hikeda'ya captors expected nothing from slaves except obedient silence, so she could only hope she was being properly respectful. She looked up to see Uvasika's reaction, but found herself gazing into eyes that, despite their bright golden color, seemed as shallow as water on a flat stone. *Is she blind? Why does she stare that way, as though she doesn't even see me?* "I am pleased to meet you, Lady Uvasika," she said, but the dark-haired woman did not reply.

Naya Nos chortled from Dasa's arms. "She will not speak to you, oh, no. She does not speak. Not for ears to hear."

Uvasika's placid stare turned to Naya Nos.

"Yes, my lady, thank you," he said a moment later, exactly as if she had uttered some pleasantry aloud. "She is, yes. This is the one. The children stole her food." He nodded vigorously. "Yes, she was given first fruits of today's fine catch!"

Confused, Tzoja looked around at the other Hidden, who were watching their mistress with obvious admiration. Could they hear her, too? Was it only Tzoja herself who was deaf to the Lady's words?

"The Silent Princess speaks only to me and a few others," explained Naya Nos proudly. "Do not be ashamed. She welcomes you and wishes to make amends for the mistakes of her children."

"*Her* children?" Tzoja could not help asking, looking around the wide cavern at the dozens of odd, malformed creatures.

"We are all her children," said Naya Nos proudly. "Not of her body, but of her heart. She protects us—and the Dreaming Lord protects us, too." He turned his attention back to Uvasika. "Of course," he said, smiling his wide, toothless smile. "It would be an honor, Mistress."

And indeed, as if they had all heard her clearly, the other Hidden began crowding closer, until Tzoja was so tightly surrounded she began to feel a bit panicked.

"The Lady asks me to make this a Story Day," Naya Nos announced, and his audience murmured like excited children. "For the honor of our visitor, our mistress will tell the story of our kind, and I will speak her words aloud."

"Once the People lived in a garden," he began. "They lived happily, and all the trees and plants were there for them, and they ate what they wanted and made what they wanted. The People became many, and so at last they built themselves a great home that they called the Star, and they lived there a long time in happiness and peace.

"But although they did not know it, they were surrounded by enemies they could not see, and these enemies hated them because before the People came, the garden had been only theirs, unshared. So the enemies sent great beasts to attack the People—beasts of the water, air, and land—but the People were brave. They fought those beasts and triumphed. Then the enemies grew even more angry, and brought forth even more of those fearsome creatures that were the first dragons, and set these terrible worms upon the People to destroy them. But the People would not be overcome, and at last the dragons were defeated. Those worms that survived fled to the far reaches of the garden because they feared the People.

"The enemies of the People had no more fearsome creatures to send against them, so they came forth themselves, but in humble form, and pretended to make peace. At first the People trusted them, and together they built the Star into greater and greater beauty and size, and the People became even more numerous. But their enemies, who called themselves *Vao*, never meant true friendship. Instead they plotted in secret to drive the People from the garden or destroy them. As the years went by the Vao pretended to be the People's allies, but all the time they were making a great and terrible magic, the greatest and most terrible ever done, called the Un Being. But when the Vao summoned the Un Being out of the void, they found that even they could not contain it or control it. Un Being began to devour the garden, and even the People with all their wisdom and craft could not make it stop.

"At last it became certain that the Un Being would swallow everything, the garden and every tree, plant, and creature in it, that it would destroy the great dwelling-place Star and at last pull each mote of the garden away from every other until nothing remained. So the People built great ships, hoping to escape the end of everything, and set sail for the Unknown West. They took with them all they could of the old garden—even their enemies, the Vao.

"Eight great ships brought the People here to this land, where the days were short as moments and the years flickered past like the wavering light of a fire. The People began to build again, and for a time the Vao worked with them, and it seemed that together they might make a world almost as perfect as the lost garden. But then the leader of the Vao was revealed to have plotted against the People once more, stealing from them what was theirs, and so he was cast into chains for his crime. His subjects fought against the People and were driven away, so the Vao went wandering, never again to have a home of their own, and all because of their own treachery.

"But the People survived. The People will always survive. And as long as we are loyal, we Hidden will survive, too. The silver-faced Queen protects us. The Dreaming Lord perfects us."

"All praise to them. All praise!"

The Hidden replied obediently to Naya Nos's invocation, but even with so many of them in the cavern, their voices remained faint, little more than a whisper. "All praise!"

The triumph they spoke of, and the Silent Lady's protection, must seem very fragile, Tzoja thought, if they dared not make much sound even here in the depths of the earth. *In truth, these Hidden seem no better off than I am,* she decided, but the thought gave her no satisfaction. Knowing that others suffered did not make one's own suffering any easier.

She was confused and a little disturbed by Naya Nos's story, and the meal in her stomach was not resting easily, either. She staggered to her feet and said, "I have to go."

Naya Nos was clearly distressed. "But we have taken much food from you. You must let us repay you."

"We will see each other again, I promise. And I thank you for your hospitality." She made a small bow to silent Uvasika, who regarded her with the blank face of a wooden doll. "Thank you, Lady. I wish you and your people health and good fortune."

"We will guide you out," said Naya Nos, but she waved him off.

"I can find my own way. Enjoy the rest of your feast."

It was only when she had made her way back out to the shore of Lake Suno'ku again, tracing her steps back along its stony shore and trying to ignore the noise of frogs because it reminded her of her meal, that Tzoja suddenly understood one of the things that had been bothering her about the story.

The Hidden were clearly telling themselves some version of the Hikeda'ya's own story—the Lost Garden, the city called Tzo, or "Star," and the Great Silver

Queen, who could only be Utuk'ku herself. But they were not themselves
Hikeda'ya. She also wondered who the Dreaming Lord was, and why the name
tugged at her memory?

It only came to her as she reached the festival house and made her way inside. *The Dreaming Lord . . . could they mean the queen's mad relative, Lord Jijibo?
He's called "the Dreamer."* Viyeki had told her that the Dreamer had as many
secrets as Akhenabi and his entire Order of Song. But why would someone as
powerful as the queen's odd kinsman be concerned with the broken and malformed Hidden?

She could find no answer, and when the time came to try to sleep, she was
haunted by the memory of empty eyes.

10

A Familiar Face

Sir Aelin, grand-nephew to Count Eolair, was grateful to the gods of Hernystir for keeping him alive, but he was not entirely pleased with the situation in which they had left him—a prisoner of King Hugh's Silver Stags.

Dunath Tower had nothing so sophisticated as a dungeon, but it did have a great, windowless storeroom with a heavy door and strong iron locks, and that was where Aelin and his men were being kept after being captured by Baron Curudan and his Silver Stags. Curudan had left for Hernysadharc with most of his troop, having decided not to do anything irreversible with the prisoners before consulting King Hugh. He had left a dozen men behind under the command of his lieutenant, Samreas, to watch over Aelin and the rest of his imprisoned company.

Samreas had made it very clear he was in favor of simply lopping off their heads and burying the bodies somewhere in the surrounding woods, so Curudan's caution was keeping Aelin and the rest alive. Aelin had hated surrendering, but the baron's force was three times as large, and if Aelin and his men were killed in this far-off spot the message they were carrying from Aelin's uncle, Count Eolair, would never get to Earl Murdo and nobody would ever know what Aelin and the others had seen—the bizarre meeting between the Silver Stags and the White Foxes, mankind's direst enemies.

So I thank you and praise you, lords of the world, he prayed. *But I would not be shamed to take any additional assistance you might care to offer.*

One of the guards banged on the doorway and bellowed for the prisoners to stand back while the food was brought in. Aelin signaled his men to make no trouble, ignoring the anger he saw on many of their faces. His squire Jarreth and several of the others had been Aelin's companions since childhood, so although the days of confinement and pain of the shackles made them short-tempered almost to the point of rebellion, they still heeded their liege-lord's commands and backed away from the door. Three guards came in. Two carried a steaming pot, though the smells that rose from it were less than appetizing. The other carried a bucket of water and bowls, which he handed out to the prisoners. Each received a bowl of water to drink, then when they had finished, they were allowed to fill the same bowls from the pot of thin stew.

Aelin sipped at his, wondering at a broth so thin he could not tell if it the original source had been rabbit, squirrel, or rat.

"I think I actually taste some meat in this," said Jarreth. "Somebody count the men and see if someone's missing."

The guards only smirked and backed out. The door swung closed and the bar and lock loudly slammed back in place.

While the prisoners finished their meal, young Evan dragged his shackle and chain over and sat down beside Aelin. He was the youngest of the company, but had already proved himself no fool. As the youth lowered himself to sit against the wall and lifted his bowl to his lips, Aelin asked him, "Do you Aedonites not say a prayer before every meal?" He had only discovered that Evan was a follower of that religion the day they had all been captured.

"Yes, but we need not say it aloud." The young man wiped his mouth with his fingers, then licked them clean. He fixed Aelin with a strange look. "Do you hate me?"

"What? Why?"

"Because I am a heretic. An Aedonite."

Aelin shook his head. "You are also a Hernystirman. Our country has been surrounded by Aedonite believers since long before Tethtain's day—although not so many live within our own lands. I do not pretend to understand the things you believe, but you have never given me anything but good service, Evan. And whether many gods command us or just one, men are still men. Some do good. Some do evil. What they call themselves and what they believe seldom seem to matter much."

The youth smiled a little. "You are a very wide-minded man, Lord Aelin."

Aelin smiled back, glad to entertain a pleasant memory. "Blame my uncle, Count Eolair—my great-uncle, to tell the truth of it—whose errand we were on before Curudan's Stags waylaid us. Those are his words, more or less, though he puts a finer polish on them than a soldier like me can do. But I saw the truth of what he said early on and have never lost it."

Evan looked carefully from side to side. The other prisoners were eating and arguing among themselves with the weary disinterest of confined men. Evan moved a little closer. "What then would you say if I told you that one of the Silver Stags is also an Aedonite?"

Aelin swallowed the last of the weak broth. "Are we talking about faith, or about something else?"

"It is Fintan, the youngest of the Stags. He is unhappy with what Curudan and the others are doing. He thinks that making a bargain with the White Foxes is no different than making a bargain with the Great Adversary."

"The Great Adversary?"

"The Prince of the Deeps, the enemy of God."

Aelin nodded, though he had never really understood what Aedonites be-lieved. "So this Fintan is unhappy."

"More than that, he thinks it is wrong that fellow Hernystiri who have committed no crime should be held prisoner—and that there is talk about simply killing us because we are inconvenient."

"I am not happy with such talk either." Aelin considered. "How do you know this?"

"He talks to me through the door when he is on duty." Evan inclined his head toward the grill of iron bars. "But only when the other guard is far away. There are always two guards on duty outside."

"And he simply began speaking to you? Telling you his treasonous thoughts, as his comrades would see it?"

Evan shook his head. "He saw me make the Sign of the Tree one day when we were fed and recognized me as another of the faith. We have a saying: 'Any stranger who believes is my brother'."

Beyond orders, beyond blood, Aelin thought. It felt dangerous to him as a noble, this idea of a secret fellowship between strangers that could overthrow the rule of order, but just now he could not afford to let such feelings rule him. He looked around the cell at his men, who after only a few days in prison already had the pale, distracted look of longtime captives. "Do you think there is a chance he would help us?"

Evan hesitated. "Yes. Yes, I think so. He is devout. I think you should speak to him."

"Me? But I am not of your faith."

"No, but he knows you by reputation—he has heard you are a good and truthful man, Sir Aelin, and I confirmed it. And you can promise him protection if he helps us. I am merely one of your soldiers. You are our liege lord."

"Not much of a lord. Not much of a leader either, I fear, or we would not be in such straits." But he knew what his great-uncle Eolair would do, so he knew what he must do as well. "Of course I will speak to him. Tell me when he is on duty and we will discover whether there is some way out of this mire."

It took six days for Eolair and his bandit captors to cross the High Thrithings into the Meadow Thrithings, site of the Thanemoot. Eolair did not have a comfortable journey, since he spent much of it with his hands trussed, riding the back of Hotmer's saddle, but other than the occasional sneer, shove, or harsh jest, his captors heeded their chief Agvalt's orders and did not harm him. The bandits fed him as well as they fed themselves, if not so promptly, and while Hotmer was not a particularly witty companion, as long as Eolair did not press him on the subject of why he had left his family and New Gadrinsett to return to the wildlands, the Thrithings-man was willing enough to talk.

"I have heard of the Thanemoot, of course," Eolair said as they crossed a grassy hilltop, marveling again at the broad sky and the unpeopled width of the plains spread before him, "but I thought only men of the clans would go. Half the men here in Agvalt's company are not even from the Thrithings."

Hotmer spat, courteous enough to aim it away so the wind would not blow it into the count's face. "People come to Blood Lake from all over the grasslands—many kinds of folk. It is the greatest gathering of the year." He shrugged. "They come to buy and sell, to find brides, to get news. There are riding and wrestling and other contests, and people make great names for themselves at those. Also, traders come from Kwanitupul and even Nabban."

"But, and I mean no slight, you all—you men of Agvalt's company—you are not traders or even clansmen, but outlaws."

"We are a free company." Hotmer sounded offended. Eolair could not help but wonder at a man who would carry a bound prisoner who had done him no ill, with no purpose more noble than ransom, yet balk at the name "outlaw."

"As I said, I meant no slight."

"The grasslands are not a place of roads and rules." Hotmer took a piece of dried chewing skin from his pocket and offered it to Eolair, who politely demurred. "Not like New Gadrinsett," he said, jaws working at the stiff hide. "The clans move, the people move, sometimes men leave one clan for another. And sometimes they join no new clan, but a company like ours instead. We all must live somehow."

"So you never have problems from the clansmen at these gatherings?"

Hotmer huffed a laugh that Eolair could feel through the man's back. "Problems? Do you mean fights?" He laughed again and held up an arm, displaying the long, curving scar that ran from just below his index finger and under his bracelets to his elbow. "A Roebuck-man gave me that because he said I was trying to steal his woman. I gave him back worse before they pulled us apart."

"And were you? Trying to steal his woman?"

Hotmer shrugged. "I said she could do better with a man like me. He didn't like the truth."

Eolair shook his head. "So there are fights."

Hotmer smirked. "Of course, Hernystirman. Do the men in your cities who drink and argue never fight? Never kill each other over foolish disagreements?"

Eolair had no ready reply to that.

The grassy Meadow Thrithing, which had for the first part of their ride seemed as empty as the drifting sands of Nascadu, was now becoming more crowded. Eolair saw wagons and people on foot coming together from all directions. It seemed a formless scatter at first, but narrowed until most of them were following a few sets of well-worn tracks toward the place of the great gathering. Some of the larger clans seemed like whole cities on the move, wagons bumping along one behind the next like a string of colorful beads, in lines stretching as far as the eye could see. Many were piled high with the belongings of their owners, tied in improbable, swaying bundles taller than the wagons were long. The carts themselves were often painted in bright colors, or covered with carvings, banners, and ribbons. It was hard to watch the more ornate examples, awash in bright colors, piled high with possessions, often with at least one or two small children sitting on the top like successful mountaineers, and not feel the urge to smile at the sheer, colorful improbability of it.

It is like someone took all the wooden carvings hanging in the Taig and put them on wheels, Eolair thought.

But if the conveyances were often charming to behold, many of the riders who guarded them were less so. Eolair saw clansmen more frightening than any of Agvalt's freebooters; big, scarred men with curved swords like mowing hooks, tattooed so thoroughly that faces and arms were almost black. More than a few had tasseled their saddles with what looked like human scalps, and some displayed even grislier trophies: one glowering giant wore a necklace made of shriveled human hands. Eolair did not stare for long before looking away. He was never surprised by what men did to each other, but that did not make him like it.

With little else to do on the back of Hotmer's horse, except keep his balance, Eolair watched the parade of passing nomads, salted with the smaller, less ornate carts of the Kwanitupuli peddlers and the wagons of the Hyrka horse traders, which sometimes outdid in decoration even those the most powerful Thrithings thanes. But the count had spent most of his life as an agent of royalty and power, so even as he took in the spectacle he was making note of everything around him.

It was hard to estimate numbers, especially on the outskirts of the gathering. The main wagon tracks, now growing stickily deep in mud, were surrounded by a delta of individual wheel ruts as incoming grasslanders tried to avoid the mire. There were clearly hundreds upon hundreds of wagons, and a very rough headcount showed at least a woman and a few children inside or on top of most of them. Counting the wagons, and taking a high guess at as many as two mounted men for each, Eolair estimated nearly a thousand grasslanders just from the travelers he could see near him, without counting the encampments stretched more than halfway around the lake.

Five thousand riders, perhaps, at the Thanemoot, was his first guess—armed, hardy men, ready to fight. The clansmen's love of fighting among themselves was the only thing that kept Nabban safe, he thought. And Erkynland, too, for that matter.

May Murhagh One-Arm continue to fill them with anger at each other, he prayed. *May they cheat each other and steal each other's women left and right. But keep them strong, too, else the Nabbanai will overrun us all someday.*

"Where exactly are we going?" he asked.

They had almost reached the top of a hill, and Hotmer didn't bother to answer him until they reached the crest, where he stretched out his hand. "Here," he said with his usual economy of words. "Blood Lake."

The ground fell away before them in a slope thronged with pines and other trees, forming a bowl of grass surrounding a glassy lake that was, if not the color of blood, at least red-tinged by what Eolair guessed was iron in the ground beneath it. The long, reddish lake looked like a lady's hand mirror dropped and forgotten, and the scene reminded him of the Cuihmne Valley east of his home, which brought a sudden twinge of homesickness.

Will I ever see those places again?

The lake's grassy banks, shaded in many places by stands of willow, birch, and other trees, were full of people and wagons, little more than spots of color and movement from this distance. As Eolair looked over the throngs camped on the shore and those farther back under the eaves of the woods that almost touched the lake in several places, he revised his estimate upwards.

As many as ten thousand men of fighting age, perhaps? That is more I think than all Erkynland could muster.

Like most men of the cities, Eolair was used to thinking of the Thrithings-men only when they committed some new outrage along the borders, usually the result of a small group of clansmen out for plunder or simply excitement. Only twice in recent memory had they provided any greater threat, during the first and second Thrithings Wars, and both times there had been enough other clans willing to side with the city-men to keep the fighting mostly confined to the grasslands. King John had bargained with Fikolmij, a powerful thane in the High Thrithings, which was how Prince Josua had met his wife—Vorzheva, the thane's daughter. Years later another angry clan chief had started a rebellion on the western edge of the Meadow Thrithing and King Simon and Duke Osric and others had been forced to take an entire army against the rebels to keep the horsemen from burning and pillaging their way into southeastern Erkynland. As always, the grasslanders had been their own worst enemies, seeming almost to compete to see which clan could betray the others first. That time a thane named Rudur of the Black Bear Clan had been the winner. With Rudur's help, a rebellion that could have been far more dangerous had been put down with an acceptable loss of life among the Erkynlanders. Acceptable to all but Simon and Miriamele, of course, who had bitterly regretted their dead; Simon in particular had become angrily determined to find better ways to deal with the Thrithings-men afterward.

For if they ever turn against us all together, the king had said, *we may not be able to push them back.* Eolair was inclined to agree with him.

But now, he thought, *foolish Nabbanai nobles led by Drusis are rattling their swords in their scabbards, talking daily of "chastising the barbarians" while pushing their new farms and settlements deeper into Thrithings territory. Thank all the gods that Duke Saluceris has more sense than the rest of them. Especially if the Norns are rising again in the north.* He thought for a moment—and only a moment—of what it would mean to be caught in a pincer between barbarian grasslanders and White Foxes, and shivered under the bright sun as though a fever had entered him.

By tradition, outlanders were allowed a place only at the thickly forested eastern end of the lake, where the shadows hung all morning below the hills and the land was marshy and damp. All the traders, as well as those visitors of less obvious purpose, like Agvalt's bandits, collected under the trees at that end, ignoring each other by general agreement. The bandits and other clanless fighting men—many of whom lived by hiring themselves out to one clan or another during feuds, and the rest of the time preyed on travelers and those who lived on the fringe of the grasslands—made a festival of it, drinking and boasting late into the night, and bringing back such unclaimed women as they could find. The traders from the west and south were more discreet, pursuing their business as quietly as they could, intent only on earning what could be made during the Thanemoot and then escaping safely back to Kwanitupul, the Wran, or lower Erkynland with their lives and profits intact.

Because the land around the lake itself was so full of camps and the main road (little more than a wide trail) was so crowded with wagons and riders, it took a long time for Agvalt's bandit troop to make its way to the shadowed eastern end. Because they were only a small company and not clansmen, Agvalt frequently had to lead his men off the road into the trees to allow larger bands coming from the opposite direction to pass. By the time they had traveled halfway around Blood Lake, the sky was beginning to darken.

Another large group approached, so Agvalt's company stepped off into the woods. Fires burned in many of the camps and wood smoke filled the air, making it even harder to see. The smell of meat cooking made Eolair's mouth water. He hoped he might get more to eat tonight than the thin bean porridge the bandits had been feeding him; his mind was on the rabbits several of the bandits had shot. He prayed he might get at least a bite or two—he was desperate for something substantial. The memory of the Sithi banquet, strange as it had been, seemed a summit of happiness he might never see again.

Eolair idly noted the emblems on some of the wagons and the fetishes and pennants carried by many of the riders. He saw Bison, Fox, and Grouse clans, all from the High Thrithings as he remembered, but saw signs of Crane and Polecat too, clans he thought were from the Lake Thrithings, closer to Nabban.

A large and well-decorated pair of wagons caught his attention, the back one tied to the front, the whole drawn by a double team of horses. The sides of the wagons were decorated with a painted golden horse, a totem he recognized from the Hayholt's throne hall: Clan Mehrdon—the Stallion Clan, Prester John's old allies from the first grassland war. As he watched, one of the women riding on top of the double wagon leaned forward to shout something to the driver. Her gray hair was cut so short it almost looked as if it had been a punishment, but there was something about her handsome, spare features that seized him and would not loose its grip. Eolair leaned out from behind Hotmer to get a better look, but already the great wagon was trundling away and trees were blocking his view. He had seen that face before, or something much like it, he felt sure.

"Bagba bite me!" he said, suddenly and loudly enough to startle not just Hotmer but even the bandit's horse, which whinnied and did a little quickstep. "That is Vorzheva herself—Josua's wife—or I am a blind man! Hotmer, follow that wagon!"

"Are you mad, Hernystirman?"

"No, I know that woman!"

Hotmer did not even look. "We follow Agvalt, not some trollop who tickles your fancy."

How could he explain? What could he say that would make them even care? Still, even after twenty years and more, he was as certain as he could be that he had just seen Vorzheva alive and well, less than an arrow's shot away. "Agvalt!" he called. "Agvalt, please! Tell Hotmer to take me after that woman who just passed! It is important to all of us."

At the head of the company, the bandit chief looked up in annoyance. "Why, Hernystirman? Do you think that we must feed you *and* help you to dip your *skeem* in the local waters?"

"I tell the truth! It is a matter of great importance—the king of Erkynland will reward you beyond your dreams!" He was shouting now, conscious that with every moment the big wagons were carrying her farther away, deeper into the horde of grasslanders. Perhaps they were even leaving the Thanemoot entirely! "I order you to help me in the name of the High Throne!"

Agvalt nudged his horse in the ribs and it trotted forward until they had caught up with Hotmer and Eolair. Agvalt leaned in, his young face strangely calm and considering, then slapped the count across the side of the head so hard that Eolair fell from the saddle and onto the ground. With his hands tied, he could not soften his fall, and struck hard on the trampled ground, squeezing all breath from his chest.

Agvalt climbed out of his saddle and crouched beside him as Eolair gasped. The chieftain's face still seemed unconcerned, but Eolair saw that his eyes were flat and lifeless. He had not seen Agvalt like this, and was suddenly reminded of how precarious his position was.

"Do not ever seek to tell me what to do." Agvalt's voice was not much more than a whisper. "I am sure your king will still pay to have you back even without your hands and feet. And you are a clever fellow, too, I'm sure, able to write and read, so you could give him your news even without a tongue. If you speak that way to me again, even once, you will go back to your king a whimpering remnant of a man. Do you understand me?"

Eolair still had not caught his breath, but nodded. A moment later Agvalt's knife was out and the tip was on Eolair's cheek just below his eye. "I did not hear you, Herynstirman. Do you understand me."

"Yes." He did not have the wind for anything longer.

"Good." Agvalt swung himself back into his saddle with the nimbleness of a cat and turned to the rest of his men, who had been watching Eolair's chastisement with interest and even pleasure. "The road is ours again. Ride on."

In the end, the plan of escape went more smoothly than Aelin could have guessed, and with the help of Skyfather Brynioch and all the gods, without any bloodshed.

The Aedonite soldier Fintan agreed to Aelin's proposal, and when he was next on guard duty, while the rest of the Silver Stags took their midday meal, he gave young Evan the signal. Aelin and the rest quietly loosened their muscles against the weary lassitude of confinement and waited. When the other guard slipped off down the corridor to the privy, Fintan quickly unlocked the door to the great storeroom and passed them the key to their shackles. Once freed from the chains, Aelin hid behind the door with his squire Jarreth, just out of sight of the iron grille, while the rest of his men moved to their assigned positions.

When the other guard returned at last, complaining loudly about a second night on duty during mealtime, Fintan brought him over to the door on the pretense of one of the prisoners looking ill. As the guard squinted into the darkness—the storeroom was lit by only a single, guttering torch—Aelin suddenly shoved the door open and, with Fintan pushing and Jarreth pulling, they dragged the struggling guard inside. While Aelin stood over him, he was swarmed by the others, then held on his back on the floor with several hands clapped over his mouth—and at least a couple of fingers poking his eyes, which was only to be expected after the harsh treatment the prisoners had suffered.

"Bind him tight. And gag him tightly too, at least until we have the others. He will have time for breathing later on."

"Do not hurt him," said Fintan, who was already beginning to show signs of second thoughts.

"Nobody will be hurt who does not try to harm us," said Aelin. "Not even Samreas, though I would gladly put my sword through the traitorous bastard. Go on, shove that one into the corner and tie him to something—I do not want him working that cloth out of his mouth and raising the alarm. Then follow me. Quiet as the Fair Ones, all of you. Not a sound."

The guard secured, Aelin and his men moved out into the narrow passage, then down to the armory with Fintan's keys to recover their weapons.

In the main hall, they paused outside the door. Aelin knew there would be no more than half a dozen men there, and two more on the battlements keeping each other company through the windy evening, but the odds were still too close for his liking, so he signaled his men to hang back along the wall and wait. Before too long one of the other Stags came lurching out into the passage. He wore no helmet and his armor was half undone. He was still jibing drunkenly at the men in the hall as the door fell shut behind him, and he realized too late that the shadows were full of armed men. Aelin did not bother to try to capture this one carefully, but instead, even as the man opened his mouth to cry out, lifted his sword and dealt him a hard blow in the middle of his forehead with the pommel.

The Stag made no noise, but Aelin's sword scraped against the stone wall. He and his men stood and listened, but nobody else seemed to be coming.

When they had tied the senseless soldier's hands behind his back, Aelin listened until he heard their captors' voices rise again, laughing and shouting.

I hope you've enjoyed your meal, he thought. *Because it is the last one you will like much for some time.* He lifted his hand and gave the signal.

They were through the door and into the hall in a heartbeat. Curudan's men sat at the long table, the bones of rabbits and small birds piled high before them, the fire muttering and flickering in the large fireplace. Their hard-faced leader Samreas was quicker than the rest and had risen to his feet, sword already out of its sheath, when an arrow splintered the back of his chair, quivering between his arm and his belly. From the corner of his eye Aelin saw Evan nock another arrow.

"Put your blade down!" he told the Stags. "Put up your weapons and you will all live. Show us steel and you will die. A simple choice."

Samreas glared at him, his eyes quickly taking in the odds. Half his soldiers were still sitting, dumbfounded, and Aelin's men hurried forward to surround them with long billhooks, each of which ended in a spearlike point of sharpened steel. Samreas scowled. "This is treason against the king of Hernystir."

"Is it?" Aelin moved closer, sword lifted toward the man's throat. "I have nobody's word for that but yours. In truth, I think many in the court would be interested to hear what you were doing."

Samreas remained imperturbable. "We do the king's bidding."

"You do Curudan's bidding. I saw no royal seal saying the baron could take us prisoner while I was on a lawful errand for the High Throne."

"The High Throne is a lie!" cried one of the other Silver Stags. "Foreign dogs have no right to rule us!"

Aelin shook his head. "So that is the tune of your treason? It makes little difference. Will you put up your weapon, Samreas?" Beside him, Evan moved a couple of steps closer, arrow on bowstring.

Samreas saw the young Stag Fintan and his lip curled. "So the tales were true, you bastard Aedonite—you are a traitor to the king and to the old faith, both."

"Don't speak to him," Aelin said. "Sheathe your sword or die, Samreas."

After a moment more, the hawk-faced man let his blade fall to the floor. "You will all be hanged for this."

"Or you will all be burned for giving aid to the White Foxes," said Aelin, then turned to his men. "Tie them all in turn, two of you for each prisoner." He returned his attention to their enemies. "Since you were kind enough to give us accommodation, we shall return the favor."

When the Silver Stags had all been restrained, Aelin and his company leveled their billhooks and prodded the new captives down the stairs and into the storeroom, where the guard they had captured still lay, struggling with his bonds. Only Samreas was left out in the passageway as Evan and Jarreth shut the storeroom door and locked it with the heavy key.

"You might do your brother Stag a favor," Aelin called the prisoners, nodding toward the first guard, "and take the gag from his mouth. He can then explain to you how he wound up in this sad condition. Meanwhile, we will be on our way."

"What, you will leave us to starve?" cried one of the Stags. "Kinder just to kill us now!"

"Oh, you will not be left here long enough to starve—not if Samreas truly cares about you." He poked Samreas with the tip of his sword. "Off we go, Lieutenant, or however you style yourself. You will accompany us, at least for a while."

The shouts of the prisoners echoed in the passage as they went out again.

"So, the nephew of high-minded Eolair is a murderer but does not want to admit it," Samreas sneered.

"Do not judge me by what you would do." Aelin smiled. "You will have time enough yet to comprehend my vengeance."

If Samreas was outraged at being captured and bound like a common pick-purse, he was almost apoplectic when he was lifted up and unceremoniously dumped, belly-down and arse-up, across the back of Aelin's saddle. "Fintan," Aelin said, "it seems you are with us now. Take your fellow Aedonite, Evan, and fetch the rest of the Silver Stags' horses and harness them together. Even if the Stags escape somehow, they won't catch up with this troop on foot."

"And shut your mouth," he told the upside-down Samreas, who was still making bitter threats. "Unless you like swallowing dust."

They made their way out into the valley, headed toward the main road. Aelin wanted to put distance between his company and Dunath Tower, so he urged them to ride swiftly. When they reached a main road he led them north toward Earl Murdo's castle at Carn Inbarh.

"Still running your uncle's errands?" Samreas jibed, breathless as he bounced up and down on the saddle. "Little good his schemes will do him. King Hugh has not trusted him in a long time."

"Then King Hugh is getting bad counsel. I suspect Baron Curudan is to blame for that."

Samreas did his best to laugh, though it was undercut by the inelegance of his position. "You know nothing. You have *no idea* what is going on—what is to come."

"Nor do you," said Aelin. "I may still decide to cut off your treasonous head, so I suggest you make yourself right with the gods while you can."

His captive fell into a sullen silence.

When they had been riding for a good two hours and the sun was beginning to settle into the western sky, Aelin called the company to a halt. He helped Samreas off the saddle, none too gently; the hawk-faced man fell to the ground like a sack of wet laundry and lay cursing. Aelin gestured to his squire Jarreth to remove the prisoner's bonds, and after a doubtful look at his lord, Jarreth complied. Samreas got up, rubbing his wrists, eyes roaming to the trees on either side of the road as he prepared to run for his life.

"Here," said Aelin, and tossed Samreas the heavy ring of keys. "You may walk back to Dunath Tower, and—if you have any fellow-feeling—release your men before they starve. We have your horses, so unless you all prefer to march back to Hernysadharc, I suggest you wait for Curudan to return. I'm sure he will be pleased to see you all." He waved to his men to ride on, then pulled at his reins to turn his horse.

Something flew past Aelin's head, missing him by inches, then caromed off a tree branch and rattled into a broad spread of blackthorn. He reined up and turned back to Samreas, who stood glaring.

"And now you have thrown the keys into the thorns." Aelin shook his head in mock-sadness. "I cannot imagine you will enjoy fishing them out again, but so be it. Farewell, Samreas. I cannot say 'Give my best to Curudan', because I will reserve my intentions for him until we meet face to face."

"I will kill you myself, long before you see the baron again," Samreas called.

Aelin waved to his men to continue, then fell in behind them.

11

Bucket of Eels

The duke and duchess had given Miriamele the largest set of chambers in the newer wing of the Sancellan Mahistrevis. As a makeshift throne room, where she could receive visitors, she chose the pretty solar with its high, wide window and its carved and gilded furniture made of southern walnut.

"It is lovely," said Count Froye, admiring the blue and gold wall hangings. "I hope you are comfortable here, Majesty."

"I am, my lord, thank you." She liked Froye. Those who did not know him well thought him fretful and distracted, but she knew him for a shrewd observer of the complexity of the courts at both Sancellans, the duke's Mahistrevis and the lector's Aedonitis—"two squirming eel buckets of intrigue," as Froye had once memorably named them. The High Throne's envoy was a philosopher at heart, and observed both palaces as a studious alchemist might study a new and unusual mixture, more interested in learning new things than in being right. But he was clearly worried about the current state of affairs in Nabban, and that worried the queen in turn.

"I think I have imposed on you long enough, Majesty," the count said. "I imagine nothing I have said is completely new to you. It is only that I would rather err on the side of too much rather than too little, at a time like this."

"Do you really think things are at such a dangerous pass?"

"I'm afraid I do, my Queen. Which reminds me—ah! I have been negligent! I have left a friend in the antechamber who wished a few words with you. He is Viscount Matreu, a good friend to the High Throne, and since he could not be here when you arrived, I think you have not met him."

Miriamele nodded. She remembered that Pasevalles had mentioned the viscount as a useful person to know if ever she felt herself endangered. "Of course. I have heard good things from the Lord Chancellor about him."

"I can only echo his praise. Matreu has been a good friend to the High Throne."

A servant was sent and a few moments later the viscount came in. "Your Majesty is very kind to see me," he said with a sweeping bow. He paused at the finish, appearing to accidentally strike a statuesque pose, then kneeled and kissed her hand.

You like the way you look, don't you? Miri thought. Still, she couldn't say he was wrong to do so. Matreu was quite a handsome man, tall and well-built, with strong, even features and skin the warm color of chestnut wood. He had made some effort at tidying himself, but there was no hiding the fact that he still wore his traveling clothes: the hem of his cloak was spattered with mud. She wondered if his casual carelessness was for show.

"Rise, please, Viscount," she said. "No need to be overly formal. We have heard good things about you back in Erkynland."

"Thank you, Majesty," he said. "I am a devoted servant of the High Throne." He stood. "In fact, it is that which led to me asking for this audience."

"Then speak, Viscount, by all means."

He nodded. "You are of course aware that I am an ally of Duke Saluceris— a very committed ally."

"As am I," Miri said, smiling. "I see nothing controversial in that."

"I am certain that Count Froye—and others—have already told you at length about the tensions that divide us here in Nabban. And I believe the duke has done everything he can to keep the peace, especially when it is his own brother Drusis who most threatens it."

Ah, Drusis. Miri sighed inwardly. *Holy Elysia, give me strength! As if I had not heard that name enough today.* "And do you, too, have something to say about him, lord?"

He smiled, shaking his head. She imagined a lot of young women had felt flattered to be offered that smile. "Not about Drusis, Majesty, or at least not him by himself." His face turned serious. "My worry is that I do not think Drusis and Dallo Ingadaris are alone in this."

"In this *what*?"

Matreu made a vague gesture with his hands. "I do not have the wisdom to say, Majesty. Whatever ploy they have concocted to increase their power in the Dominiate and under the High Ward."

"And why do you say that, Viscount?"

"Things have happened too quickly of late. People know things more swiftly than they should. It is hard to explain." He wrinkled his smooth brow in frustration. "Forgive me for telling you about the land of your own mother's birth, but those of us who live here are used to the struggle for power between *Honsae*—the noble houses—which is constant. And we all have spies in each other's strongholds, of course, but generally they are only servants and such. Most of the more skilled players know better than to speak loosely in front of anyone outside their trusted circle."

"None of this comes as a surprise, Viscount Matreu," she said. "The perilous nature of keeping a secret in Nabban is well known."

"Yes, but times are worse here now—as bad as they have been since before the Storm King's War, I think—worse than any time before you and your husband ascended the High Throne."

"To the point, please, Viscount," said Froye. "Much as we value your counsel, the queen has several more people to see after you, and the day is wearing away."

"My apologies, Majesty." Matreu bowed again. "Here is my concern, wrapped in a tidy bundle. I fear that someone among the duke's closest allies is not simply untrustworthy, but is carrying tales of everything that goes on in the Sancellan Mahistrevis straight to Honsa Ingadaris. If it was only a servant spying, I would not worry—no servant can make himself privy to every important detail. But someone who is a member of the inner circle—*Matra sa Duos!* That is a real danger."

Miriamele could not help a quick look around the chamber, as though someone might be lurking behind one of the arrases, but only the three of them were present and her own Erkynguards were stationed outside the door. "Do you have a particular suspicion, my lord, or is this only a general fear?"

"I would not denounce a fellow noble to the High Throne on such thin wisps of suspicion as I have at this moment. But I beg you to remember my warning and be cautious of who is listening to you if you speak any secrets."

"In other words, trust no one?"

"Excepting your countryman Count Froye, yes," he said, and bowed to the envoy. "And of course the duke himself."

"I take the point." Miri felt a prickling of uneasiness. Already she was wishing she had not come back to Nabban. Bucket of eels? Bucket of venomous serpents, more like. She pulled together a smile. "Thank you for your warning, my lord."

"I am ever your servant, Majesty." Matreu bowed, then gave her a bold look. "And of course your husband's as well. We are all sorry King Simon could not come with you."

"Not half so sorry as I am," she said, and in that instant it was so true that it almost made her dizzy.

After Froye and the viscount had gone she sat for a time reading the *Promissi* in her Book of the Aedon, troubled for reasons she could not completely understand. A few of her ladies came in and strongly suggested she should eat something, but she sent them away again. Her stomach roiled and she did not feel she could eat or listen to their talk just now.

Shortly afterward, one of the heralds came in from the antechamber and announced the duke's uncle, Marquis Envalles. Miriamele had known Envalles since before Saluceris had inherited the throne, and though she was not much in the mood for another audience, he was usually full of amusing gossip. He was also a man whose wisdom she respected; she had thought on more than one occasion that he would have made a better duke than either Saluceris or the duke's late father, Varellan. But capability always bowed to blood, especially male blood, and Envalles had not been in the direct line.

"Send him in," she said.

One of the marquis's little tricks was always to dress like a harmless old man, affecting slippers and a warm shawl even on a day as hot as this one. He shuffled in, made a slow, creaky bow, and then came forward to kiss Miriamele's extended hand. "Your Majesty," he said, "you have not aged at all."

"What, since you saw me across the great hall two days ago?" She laughed. "Until they finally start hanging people for excessive flattery, you will remain the wickedest man in the south, my lord. Please, seat yourself and talk to me."

Envalles laughed. "Sadly, Majesty, I cannot now, although I pray we will find a good long time to converse before too much longer. I miss your company—and your husband's, too. He always makes me laugh."

She could feel her smile was a little crooked. "We all miss Simon—the king, I mean. But why can't you stay?"

He shrugged. "Busy times, my queen, and many responsibilities—though none as onerous as yours, God give you grace. And this audience, instead of being for my own pleasure, is so I may dispatch my duty as an envoy."

"An envoy? For whom?"

"All will become clear very soon, Majesty." He slid something out of his jacket. It was a Book of the Aedon, and not a particularly new one by the look of it, its pages foxed and the leather cover scratched.

Miriamele could not prevent a surprised laugh. "That is very kind, Envalles. Do you worry for my soul? As you see, I have my own copy right here in my lap."

"Ah, but this is a special copy, Majesty—my own. And you will see why it is special when you read it. But please make certain you're alone when you do so, or at least as alone as a queen is allowed to be." He gave her a look that she could not quite fathom. "Now, I beg you to excuse me. I will apply in the usual way for an audience, and then you and I will have a proper talk and make fun of all those around us who so dearly, dearly deserve it."

When Envalles had gone Miriamele sat for a moment wondering at the strangeness of his visit. She lifted the book and opened it, but could see nothing that made his copy exceptional. Then, as she riffled through the pages, she encountered a folded piece of parchment, stiff and new.

The message was not signed, and it was not long. It read, *"You are invited to the Sea Watchers' Guild Hall."* The date of the invitation was for noon on the next day. *"Bring as many guards and courtiers as you wish for your comfort and safety. Arrangements will be made."*

For a moment she only stared at it without understanding. Then she remembered that the Sea Watchers' Guild was another name for the Niskies.

Jesa had just finished putting little Serasina down in the corner for her nap. The great bedchamber was full of women, all surrounding one small boy, son of the duke and duchess, who was outraged at being dressed in velvet on such a warm day.

"I don't like it," Blasis said, trying to shrug his way out of his doublet even as one of the ladies-in-waiting tried to button it. "Take it off."

"Just be still, my little frog," said his mother, laughing. "You look so handsome!"

"Want to play with my soldiers," Blasis replied, frowning dreadfully. "Don't want to see the queen. I *saw* the queen! She said I was a fine young man." He pronounced the words as though they had been a cruel epithet.

"And you are," the duchess told him. "Even if you do squirm and wiggle."

"And how will you wear armor someday if you can't even wear a nice jacket without fidgeting?" asked Lady Mindia. "Armor is *much* heavier."

"Yes," Blasis explained patiently, as to an idiot. "But then I'll have a *real sword.*"

Jesa had edged near to Duchess Canthia. "My lady? May I go out to the market?"

"Whatever for? There's so much to do and dinner is in only a few hours. What about Serasina?"

Jesa gestured to the cradle. "She sleeps, my lady. I will come back before she is awake."

Canthia did not look pleased, but at last she nodded. "If you must. But do not linger. And be careful! There are all kinds of ruffians out these days. Serasina would be heartbroken if she lost you!"

What about you, my lady? Jesa wondered. *Would you miss me too?* But it was a mean, selfish thought and she secretly pinched herself. All she had in the world was because of the duchess—her clothes, her meals, this astounding, rich palace in which to live. Not to mention Serasina, the beautiful little baby girl who sometimes felt like Jesa's own child. It was wrong to be ungrateful.

She took her purse from its hiding-place before making her way down into the great entrance hall, which was full of scurrying activity, servants and courtiers all looking busy and worried, as though the Sancellan Mahistrevis were threatened by invisible flames. Jesa patted her purse and felt the reassuring chink of her money. When she ran errands for the duchess she was sometimes given a small coin by the recipients of Canthia's letters, and she saved them all carefully for just such moments of freedom.

Outside it was a lovely day, the heat of the late Tiyagar sun soothed by the wind off the ocean. The road at the base of the hill was a great river of humanity, surging with folk of many colors. The two things Jesa could never get used to were the sheer amount of people that lived in Nabban and the stink they made around themselves. Between the animal and human waste dumped directly into the street, the complicated smells of the markets and shops, and the strong perfumes most of the nobles drenched themselves with to ward off the other stinks, Jesa sometimes wished her nose was as blind as the eyes of Old Gorahok from back home.

She could not stay out long—there was too much noise in the duchess's chambers today for Serasina to sleep more than an hour—so she made her way swiftly across the Mahistrevis Market directly to the stalls on the less popular, unshaded southwestern end where the Wran folk set up their blankets. Back home it was almost time for the Wind Festival, and although the celebrations among the Wrannafolk in Nabban were much smaller, those of her people who could afford it would buy new clothes for the festival days, so the blankets would be piled high with rainbow-colored garments.

Jesa was not going to a Wind Festival feast. She doubted Canthia would let her even if she were invited to one, but she enjoyed thinking about going back to Red Pig Lagoon some day to show her family and neighbors what had happened to the little girl they had sent away. How could she do that without a fine dress to show them how she had prospered in the household of the duke of all Nabban?

She walked slowly past a dozen places selling brightly dyed cloth, most of them overseen by a single Wrannawoman or Wrannaman. Some had surrendered to the powerful summer sun and slept sitting up, legs crossed, a leaf or a piece of cloth draped over their heads to keep off the sun and the flies. At the last such stand at the end of a row, a roll of brilliant fabric caught her eye, reddish-yellow as a flame, with vigorous designs in dark red and brown along its edge. The color was so magnificent that Jesa almost laughed out loud. Could she imagine herself wearing something so beautiful, so fierce? What would the people of her village think? That she looked like a queen, or like the mistress of a rich drylander? No, it would never do. But it was lovely to think about. What if the duchess lent her one of her beautiful necklaces to wear with it—the one with the crimson stones that glowed like coals from a fire? Jesa would be the finest thing the Red Pig Lagoon had ever seen! Let the old ladies cluck. Let the men talk behind their hands. They would never forget her, *that* was certain.

The owner of the stall was an old woman as thin and brown as rawhide cord, who watched Jesa with a sharp eye, as if she expected the young woman to snatch up the cloth and run away.

Doesn't she see my clothes—palace clothes? This is a dress that the duchess herself once wore!

But she smiled and said, *"Good day, Mother,"* in Wran speech.

The old woman's expression did not become more welcoming, but she nodded her head, then replied in Nabbanai, "And to you, daughter."

"You have some very beautiful things here."

The woman nodded again, as though it were only the obvious truth. "My son owns a fine shop in Kwanitupul. He sends these to me. The drylander women love them."

Jesa wondered if those drylander women actually bought anything. She could not imagine one of Duchess Canthia's ladies wearing anything so vivid. "I'm sure." She bent down and gently touched the flame-colored cloth. "I have never seen anything like this since I've been in Nabban."

The woman did not reply, and when Jesa stood she saw that the stall owner was staring at her even more openly than before, her mouth a little open. "I know you," the woman said.

Jesa was surprised. "I beg your pardon, Mother?"

"I know you, girl. You live in the Great Lodge." That was how the Sancellan Mahistrevis was called by the Wran folk. They called the other palace, the Sancellan Aedonitis, "the God Lodge."

"I do." She could not keep the pride from her voice. "I am nurse to Duchess Canthia's daughter."

But the old woman shook her head. "Bad. That is bad."

Jesa gaped. "What do you say?"

"It is a bad place. A bad time. You listen to old Laliba, girl. Ask anyone here, they know me." She spread her scrawny arms to either side. "They know Laliba only tells the truth."

"What truth? What do you mean?"

Laliba glanced around again before leaning forward. She looked like a snake preparing to strike, and Jesa backed away. The woman was still staring fixedly at her, but now her reddened eyes terrified Jesa.

"If you do not listen, it will take you too!" she declared. "The Great Lodge will burn from the inside. I can see it! Many will die."

All thoughts of cloth and jewels gone, Jesa turned and began to run back toward the Sancellan Mahistrevis. She realized that the people she passed, many of them her own folk, were staring at her in curiosity, so she forced herself to slow down and walk, but she badly wanted the safety of the palace's walls around her once more.

Duke Saluceris did not like the idea of the Niskies' invitation at all. "The Sea Watchers? That guild hall is in the worst part of the Porta Antiga."

"I have guards, Your Grace—quite a few," Miriamele pointed out. "And we have a harbor in Erchester as well, not to mention in Meremund, where I spent my childhood. I am not naive about the sort of folk one is likely to find there."

He frowned. "That is not what I mean, Majesty. It is not just the danger of being attacked but of disease. The place is filthy, and the Niskies—well, the plague has started there several times in the past."

Plague had appeared in many harborside communities over the centuries, both in the south where Niskies lived and in the north where they did not, so she thought it unlikely sea watchers were the cause. "I owe them my respect, Your Grace. One of them saved my life when I was younger."

The duke swallowed another argument. "I cannot gainsay you, Majesty, of course. But if you must go, take a carriage—take mine if you wish. I would not want you and your men on foot in that low place. It is treacherous and full of danger—a nest of eels."

Miri was greatly amused to hear him use almost the same phrase about Porta

Antiga that Froye had used to describe the two Sancellans. "Thank you, sir, but I will use my own, just to make sure my coachmen are not enjoying themselves too much and entirely forgetting their work. I will be careful. And I will keep my eyes wide open—that I promise."

Despite the duke's worries, Miri found the old harbor district quite lively, at least on its outskirts. People of all types thronged the streets, merchants, traders, sailors, prostitutes, as well as all those who worked for them or dealt with them. The crowds had a rough-and-tumble look that reminded Miri of brawling Meremund, a place she still dreamed of, though she had not lived there for any long stretch since her childhood. But as the coach rolled down the hilly streets toward the docks the streets became emptier and quieter. Most of the largest ships, the great merchant caravels and cargo barges, now docked at the Porta Nova, a league away on the other side of the city.

The old harbor at Porta Antiga dated back to the time of the imperators, and perhaps even earlier. During the days of the Second Imperium the nobles of Nabban, always frustrated by the Niskies and their unwillingness to bargain— which meant unwillingness to be bullied into accepting what the nobles offered, Miri felt sure—had convinced the imperator to build a new harbor. Now the only ships that regularly called at Porta Antiga were those of fishermen and the poorer merchants.

The Niskies, however, had refused to move out of their immemorial home to be closer to the new harbor. And when the nobles and traders found they still desperately needed the Sea Watchers' Guild to keep the predatory kilpa off their ships, they had been forced to begin a ferry service between Porta Nova and the old harbor just so that the Niskies could reach the ships they protected in a timely manner.

There was a lesson there, Miri thought, but she was not quite sure what it was. Stubbornness and consistency was part of it—even wealth and the rights of high birth had to bow to necessity in the end.

The clacking of hooves on cobblestones lost its steady rhythm as the coach slowed to a halt. The guildhall was not particularly impressive, a ramshackle, two-story edifice, made mostly of wood, stretching along the main roadway between two piers, though the roofline was covered in carved sea beasts and fanciful fish. Miri thought it felt different here than in the outer part of the neighborhood. Many Niskies were in the street, though almost every one of them seemed to be on the way to somewhere else. She found it hard to tell which were male and which female, since they all wore the same heavy, hooded sea-cloaks, even in this warm weather.

"It looks as though it might fall down in the next storm," said Sir Jurgen darkly. The young knight clearly did not approve of the Niskies' hall. "Can they not come out to you, Your Majesty?"

"What better way to promote understanding than to force them out of their hall and make them bend a knee in front of the queen on the street?"

"What understanding are we trying to promote?" wondered Froye, but since he asked it as though he truly wanted to know, she took his question at face value.

"Whatever understanding that has prompted this invitation," she said. "Do not forget that I owe the sea watchers a great debt."

Froye nodded, but Jurgen did not know the story. "Truly, Majesty?"

"Truly, Jurgen, and I will tell you about it some day. But now I must go in, because that is the noon bell ringing."

A group of what she took for Niskie dignitaries were waiting inside the hall, dressed in the same heavy cloaks as the others she had seen, but with richer fabrics and less muted colors. She was pleased and surprised when the youngest of them stepped forward and pulled back his hood.

"Greetings, Your Majesty," he said. "You honor us with your presence."

"Gan Doha. It's good to see you again." She looked around the high-ceilinged chamber, its walls decorated not with paintings or tapestries, as would be the case in other such places, but carved wooden shapes that reminded her of those hanging in the Taig in Hernystir, except that she could not tell what these carvings were meant to represent. She began to glimpse a pattern to their arrangement, but before she could give it much thought Gan Doha bowed and then extended his hand.

"Let me lead you," he said. "The elders wait for you in the Talking Hall downstairs. I fear the invitation is for you alone, Majesty, not your soldiers." He shook his head sadly. "My people are very particular about such things. Our secrets have been kept for centuries, and though we will gladly share them with you, honored queen, there are limits. I apologize."

"Preposterous!" said Froye. "The queen does not go anywhere without the Erkynguard!"

"Then we must regretfully say that we have asked the queen here for no purpose," said Gan Doha. "Would the Church of Usires allow soldiers into the lector's private chapel? Do not fear—no harm will come to Queen Miriamele while she is here. That I can promise you."

"You can't do it, Majesty." If Sir Jurgen meant to whisper to her, the young knight reckoned without his anger. He was was loud enough to make some of the Niskies take a step back. "I can't let you go off on your own with these . . . people. For one thing, your husband would never forgive me if something happened to you. And I would never forgive myself."

Miriamele looked at him for a moment, then at Count Froye. At last she turned back to Gan Doha. "Could I bring one guard with me? Sir Jurgen was ordered by my husband to be my special protector."

Gan Doha thought about it for a moment, wide, heavy-lidded eyes downcast. At last he looked up. "I think it can be done. But your guard will have to stay silent. And if he harms anyone in his zeal to protect you, the elders will be very angry. Angry with me, I hasten to say—not you, Majesty."

"Very well. Do you hear, Sir Jurgen?" She did her best not to smile at the knight's fiercely serious face. "You may come along, but you must be silent and try not to kill anyone without asking me first."

The knight looked from her to Froye, then surveyed the hall as though making certain that assassins were not already lurking and waiting. "Your wishes are all that matter to me, my queen."

"Good," she said. "Froye, I beg your pardon, but I must leave you here for a little while with the rest of the guards."

"How long, Majesty?" The count was clearly not happy.

Miri looked at Gan Doha, whose sun-browned face showed little expression. "Perhaps an hour of the clock," he said. "The elders can be slow to come to the point sometimes, but they know that Your Majesty's time is precious."

"Very well," she said. "We are agreed. Lead on."

Gan Doha took a torch from a sconce on the wall, then led Miriamele and Jurgen through a nondescript wooden door that opened onto a narrow stairwell with unfinished wooden walls gone gray from years of salt air. They descended several flights, until Miri saw that the wooden walls had become rough-cut stone and realized that they must have left the guild hall. They were climbing down into the bedrock of the Porta Antiga itself.

Jurgen stopped on the next landing. "Is this a trick?" he demanded. "Does this stairway never end?"

"I told you that the elders were waiting downstairs." Gan Doha sounded amused.

Even Miri feeling a bit reluctant, they followed him farther down, and at last reached the bottom. Gan Doha led them through another door and into a chamber that quite beggared Miriamele's expectations.

The vast space had been cut into the very stone of the promontory on which the Porta Antiga was built. In places along the base of the wall and floor Gan Doha's torch revealed chisel marks, but the upper surfaces had been carefully smoothed and covered in painted pictures. Miri thought she could make out big-eyed creatures and strange, misshapen ships ranging all the way up the wall from eye level to the shadows of the high stone ceiling. Strangest of all, though, was the single immense decoration that hung from that ceiling, a slender, curving object almost as long as the chamber itself—so long that at first Miri took it for the backbone of some impossibly huge fish or a whale. It shone in the torchlight, as smooth as if every inch had been lovingly polished by thousands of hands. Jurgen stared at it with his mouth open.

"What is that?" she asked.

"It is called the Spar," Gan Doha told her. "It is the only remaining piece of the great ship that brought our ancestors to Jhiná-T'senei, before it was swallowed by the sea. You know of the Eight Ships, do you not, Majesty?"

"The ones that carried the Sithi and . . ." for a moment she could not think of the proper name the Niskies used for themselves, ". . . and the Tinukeda'ya here from their old land."

"From the Lost Garden, yes." Gan Doha nodded, and for a moment they all stared up at the gleaming timber. "It is a beautiful thing, is it not?"

"It's so big!"

"So were the Eight Ships, the stories tell," said Gan Doha. "Big as cities. Now let us go to the elders."

And even as he spoke, a light bloomed at the far end of the great stone chamber, and for the first time Miri saw a table there, with a number of shapes seated around it.

Did they only now light a lamp, she wondered? *Have they been sitting here in the near-dark, waiting for us?* She felt a little superstitious shiver.

Almost two dozen Niskies were ranged around the long, rough table. Gan Doha introduced them, but the names slid past her in a flurry of unfamiliar sounds and only the last one captured her attention.

". . . And this is Gan Lagi, the eldest of my clan," Gan Doha finished, indicating a squat, extremely weathered woman. The elder's eyes were large and hooded like a sea turtle's, and she scarcely moved except to incline her head toward the queen.

"Thank you for coming to us, Queen Miriamele," said the old Niskie woman in hoarse Westerling. "We welcome you beneath the Spar."

"I am honored," Miri said. "And I will be forever grateful to your clan. I will never forget Gan Itai, and I would like to do something to honor her memory."

"You honor her well simply by taking us seriously," Gan Lagi told her. "And we know that you have little time before your absence makes those who came with you fretful." The old Niskie stole a sly glance at Sir Jurgen, who seemed caught in a strange and disturbing dream, glancing from the assembled Niskies and then up to the mighty Spar, then back to the sea watchers again. "Now we must speak of the things my people need you to know."

"Do you rule over all the Niskies?" Miri asked her.

"Me? Rule over all the folk?" Gan Lagi shook her head. "I do not even rule over my own clan. They ask me for advice and I give it. Sometimes they even show wisdom and follow it."

Miri heard Gan Doha make a snorting noise beside her—a quiet laugh, she realized. "Very well. And is it advice you wish to give me?"

"Not advice, Majesty. A warning, perhaps."

Miri felt Jurgen stiffen beside her and inch closer. "Go on," she said.

"You know a bit of our history, I think. My kinswoman Gan Itai told you some of it when you were together on the *Eadne Cloud.*"

"Yes. She told me about you, the Tinukeda'ya, but I do not remember much. I learned more later on from the Sithi."

"The Zida'ya do not always tell the truth about us," said Gan Lagi sourly, "but that is not to our point today." Her eyes were sharp in their nets of wrinkled flesh. "It is important for you to know that we Tinukeda'ya have some gift for seeing and for understanding. Sometimes we know things before other mortals know them. Sometimes we have even glimpsed the days to come in ways that our Keida'ya masters could not."

"Keida'ya?"

"An old name for the tribe from which both the Zida'ya and Hikeda'ya spring—those you call Sithi and Norns. But even when we see what is coming, we Ocean Children are not always believed." Some of the other elders made quiet moaning noises.

"I fear I do not take your point," Miri said.

"It is coming," Gan Lagi promised. "In long-ago days, before Nabban rose, many of us lived in the island city of Jhiná-T'seneí. We foresaw a great disaster would come to that city, and we warned our masters who did not believe us; so countless Keida'ya perished when the earth shook. Jhiná-T'seneí was swallowed by the sea, and in the north mighty Kementari was thrown down as well, all its columns and walls broken into dust. By the time your grandfather grew up there—Warinsten as the mortals now call it—only rubble and old stories remained of the immortals' great city of Kementari. But many Tinuka'ya escaped those two disasters and settled here on the coast."

"I have learned a little about those ancient days, but not much."

"The history is not so important. I tell you about it only so you will understand that we Tinukeda'ya sense things others often do not. That is important to know, because of late our people have been greatly afflicted with visions and voices."

"Visions?"

"And voices, yes. They come to us mostly in our dreams and call on the Tinukeda'ya by our ancient names, and always they summon us north. And it is not only the scryers and horizon-watchers among us who have these dreams. They come to many, including some folk of Nabban who have only a little Niskie blood in them."

Miriamele was puzzled. "Voices that summon you north? What do these voices say, exactly?"

Gan Lagi shook her head emphatically; her hood slipped backward a bit, revealing her sparse white hair and the rough, almost scaly skin of her neck and cheeks. "The voices do not often use *words*, Queen Miriamele, so it is difficult to explain. They put ideas in our heads, ideas of being safe from earthly woes, or about a great cause—the dreams are different for nearly everyone. But the meaning is always clear: *Come north! You are summoned!* And the dreams are very strong, very . . . convincing. Of course, most of us do not trust them—I certainly do not, not after all the evil that has come to us out of the north. But we felt you and your husband should know of these dreams that summon us." She made a simple gesture, spreading her hands toward the other Niskies, two dozen pairs of wide eyes listening in silence. "You are the only ones we trust."

"But why would you be summoned? Do you think the Norn Queen wants you to fight for her?"

Gan Lagi shrugged. "We cannot say. When the dreams first started we sent some of our clansfolk north to investigate, but none have returned. All is mystery, but we thought you should be told what we know. That is all I have to say." Gan Lagi bobbed her head—almost a bow, but not quite. "The other elders and I thank you for honoring us with your presence."

Niskies did not seem to make courtly small talk. The conversation finished, Gan Doha led her and Jurgen back across the great chamber and up the stairs once more. Miri was puzzled and troubled by the strange warning, and it was only when they reached the last flight that she realized Jurgen had been silent the whole time. "Are you well, sir?" she asked him.

He did not reply for several more steps. "I am your sworn bondsman, Majesty. I know all the good you and King Simon have done, and I have heard all the stories of the strange things you two have seen. But I am not sure until today that I truly believed them."

She was amused, despite her concern over the Niskies' strange message. "And do you now?"

"I must thank you, Majesty." Then, to her surprise, he tried to drop to a knee in the narrow stairwell.

"Get up, Jurgen, please."

He rose. She could see his cheeks were flushed as Gan Doha opened the door and let in the light of the guildhall. "I beg your pardon, Majesty," the knight said. "But I want to thank you. I had wondered if I would ever see something as astounding as what you and the king have seen. Now I have. I . . . I do not know what else to say."

"I am glad it brought you pleasure," she said, "but I hope you never have to see some of the less enjoyable things Simon and I encountered." Froye and the guards were hurrying toward her, the count's face showing his fulsome relief that she was safe. "There are many I wish every day that I could forget."

12

Blood and Parchment

Seventeenth Day *of Tiyagar, Founding Year 1201*

My dear Lord Tiamak,

My greetings to you. I hope that God gives good health to you, your lady, and our king and queen.

I write to you from Kwanitupul, which I reached two days ago after a voyage that seemed to stop at every port on every island and every inch of coastline. More specifically, I write from the common room of the inn that was once Pelippa's Bowl, but which is now called The Welcome Harbor, a grossly deceitful name—

Brother Etan looked up at the noise of the inn's front door creaking open. "Where are you going, Madi?"

His erstwhile guide, who must have crossed the common room with unusual stealth to get so far before being noticed, turned in the doorway with a look of profound disappointment on his face. "What do you mean, Father Etan, my darling? I am just stepping out into the dooryard for some air. It is a power of hot today, you see. God love us, but I am sweating like a dray horse."

"I suspect you are more dry than hot, especially in the mouth and throat. God hates a drunkard, Madi." Etan gave him a hard look. "But I will be writing for a while here and have nothing for you to do at present. If you wish to go out, you may. But take your children with you." He waved at Plekto and Parlippa, who were stretched on the floor, slowed by heat, lazily tormenting the inn's old three-legged dog. The beast showed the two young bandits its teeth but seemed to have no more interest in getting up than they did.

"Ah, but Father Etan," said Madi, "it would do them a world more good to watch you at your work—a Godly man doing Godly things. I try so hard to give them proper instruction, especially about the Lord Usires and the Execution Tree and such, but they do not listen to me." He dutifully made the Sign of the Tree on the breast of his none-too-clean jerkin.

Whether Madi actually gave his children religious instruction was open to question. The closest Etan had heard was him telling the children that if they did not do what their father said, God would kill them—but he could not dispute that the two creatures were sorely in need of correction. During a day's stopover in Repra Vessina he had actually stumbled across them at work in the town square. They had tied up Parlippa's leg so only one limb showed below her ragged shift, and Plek was begging passersby to help his crippled sister with a coin or two.

"Perhaps we will read together from the Book of the Aedon later on," Etan said. "I think we might all take a useful lesson from the tale of Mamarte and the Deceivers. But for now, take your children with you so that I may work in peace."

Madi shook his head. "Ah, that is hard, Father Etan. Terrible hard, my dear one."

"And for the last time, I am not 'Father,' I am a 'brother'—*Brother* Etan. I belong to the Sutrinian Order."

"And a fine order it is, too," said Madi hopefully. "Charity, kindness, alms for the poor—all those sort of thing, bless you and keep you."

Etan gave him a stern look. "I know you spent less than half of the coins I gave you yesterday on this room, so don't bother to ask for more."

Madi went out the door, still shaking his head, his progeny now in train. "Travel is supposed to broaden a man, bring to him wisdom and great-heartedness," he called over his shoulder. "What happened to the generous soul I met on the dock in Erchester? I fear for the change in you, Brother."

You were right, my lord, to say that I would see things on this journey that would change me, and that I would remember forever. My first sight of Nabban as we rounded the headland astonished me, and I could not help thinking of St. Velthir in our Book of Prophets, who first saw that great expanse of white towers from the mountains and said, 'Here is a city as great as a nation, as big as the sea. The men who live here must be mighty indeed and more in need of the word of God than any other place on the teeming earth.'

The neighborhood of Josua's old inn, where we are presently lodging, is no different from most along the waterfront of Kwanitupul. In truth, because of its many canals, houseboats, and rows of stilt-houses extending out into the swamps, almost everywhere is waterfront in this city on the edge of the marshes.

The inn that Josua formerly owned has had at least four owners as well as two other names since then, as far as I can discover, and there may have been more of both. All of yesterday I spent searching out the oldest residents of the street even to be sure this truly was the place that had once been Pelippa's Bowl, since that name is all but forgotten. It is owned now by a man so thin and sour-faced that I marvel anyone without an errand like mine would ever stop here. But neither that old miser nor anyone else seems to have any useful memories of the prince, his wife, or their children, let alone where any of them might have gone, although one old woman told me she remembers a man who had 'the same name as the old king's son', and said he was 'a handsome, tall fellow'. You might think that she would have realized he had not only the same name but the same missing hand. But perhaps I expect too much from ordinary folk, who have their own worries.

I fear that though my search has begun here in Kwanitupul, the trail is too cold to follow to any good effect. To be honest, my dear friend and mentor, I am not even certain I will be able to send this letter to you until we are back in more civilized lands where I might find a post that can reach the High Throne in Erchester.

Kwanitupul is the strangest place I have ever seen, although I am sure I can tell you nothing of it you do not already know. The people are the most perfect mix of so many different races, Wran-men and Nabbanai and islanders from farther south, and they dress in every sort of clothing that can be imagined, many in hats meant to keep off the fierce sun. These hats are wide, strange things like grain baskets, woven from reeds and decorated with feathers and even serpent skins. All these people live together in what seems to be a harmonious agreement to leave each other alone and instead bleed every possible coin from travelers. Between Madi's thieving children and the Kwanitupulians—or is it Kwanitupulis?—I have already gone through far more of my money than I should have. I dread to think what will happen when Madi is set loose in the fleshpots of Nabban and Perdruin. I concede that his command of local dialects and his knowledge of the places we have traveled have both been very useful to my mission, but he and his family have worried me almost into despair.

A last thought before I go out and try to find a ship bound for Erkynland to carry this message to you, my lord. I have carefully read the letters that you gave me from Prince Josua, and in the last one he said that he was sending to Lady Faiera in Perdruin to learn what she could tell him of "certain aetherial whispers." Do you think he was speaking of the thing we both know but that I will not name here? Is that possible, or is the cursed thing preying on my thoughts? I ask you with hope you will tell me if my speculations are too fevered. That thing and our discussions of it are much on my mind. Am I seeing enemies and specters in every shadow?

Tiamak folded Etan's letter carefully and slid it under the belt of his robe. He was distracted at the moment and would have to read it again later, but it certainly seemed as though Those Who Watch And Shape, the shadowy powers that ruled his people's lives, were trying to tell him that he could not keep Fortis' dreadful book secret from the king any longer. The box he had found hidden in John Josua's library only made that more clear.

It was, however, something he most decidedly did not want to do.

"Please, Majesty, try not to be too angry—"

"Angry? I am far more than just angry, I am *furious!*" Simon was red-faced and wide-eyed, disturbed in a way Tiamak had not seen. Not even Thomas

Oystercatcher had ever angered him so. "You discovered that my son had one of the most feared books in Aedondom—a book that belonged to Pryrates himself! How could you dare to keep this from us?"

A host of explanations rose to Tiamak's lips, but he kept his mouth closed and instead, carefully lowered himself to his knees on the retiring room's hard stone floor.

"What are you doing?" The king's anger was muddied now by another kind of discomfort. "Get up, for the love of Usires, or at least kneel on the carpet. I'm not a tyrant! But I am angry—and I have every right to be!"

"Yes, you do, sire." But Tiamak stubbornly remained kneeling. "And I beg pardon from the bottom of my heart. I made a decision that I thought was in the High Throne's best interest—in your best interest, Simon. I regret it now."

"What are you talking about, my best interest?" The king's temper was fiery, but seldom lasted long, although nothing seemed sure when the subject was his dead son, John Josua. He and Miriamele were both still in terrible pain, even all these years later. "How could you even think not telling me about this book was in my interests?" His scowl was profound. "God's Bloody Tree, man, get up off the floor and talk to me, will you?"

Tiamak did, although slowly and with a calculated show of discomfort. He hated to remind Simon of his infirmities—he didn't like being pitied any more than the king did—but some situations called for every resource. Once Tiamak was perched on a stool they sat in silence for a moment.

"Look at yourself, please, Simon," he said at last. "You are trembling—almost weeping with rage. That is why I did not tell you about the book before. I did not know what it signified, and I did not wish to cause you and the queen heartache until I could learn more. Not because I was trying to deceive you, or make my own work easier, but because you are my *friends*."

Simon stared for a long moment, brows pulled low as though he suspected a trick. At last he sat back and slapped his hand hard on the chair's arm. "I always want to know, Tiamak." His voice was still full of fury, but it was layered with other sadness now. "God save me, John Josua was all we had."

"I know. And keeping anything about him from you and the queen made me sick inside. But it was precisely because I did not want to plunge you into grief again that I kept my discovery of the *Aetheric Whispers* from you. That is the burden of any king's counselor, Simon—deciding what to tell and what not to tell, what burdens to add to those you already carry and which to keep to myself." He held out the box. "But now there is more, and I dared not keep it secret any longer."

Simon took it gingerly, as if it held some venomous beast. "Is this something that also belonged to Pryrates?"

"Don't you recognize it?"

Simon stared at the carved and inlaid cover, rubbing his finger over the cloaking dust and grit. "Yes, God love me, I think I do. Miri gave it to our son when he was getting his first beard. It held a razor, a whetstone, scented unguents, a piece of sponge-rock from the south for rubbing away whiskers, things of that sort. He must have liked it—he was clean shaven until the last years . . ." He trailed off, eyes suddenly overspilling.

He Who Always Steps On Sand, Tiamak thought, *keep my own feet on a safe track, because far more than this good man's feelings are at stake.* "Open it, please. But do not touch anything, I beg you."

Simon tipped up the lid, then stared at the contents. "What is this? Broken rubbish, it looks like."

"I believe they are Sithi things your son found in the depths beneath the castle."

"Under the castle?" The king looked stunned. "When would he have been there?"

"I don't know. But remember how much of this place you explored when you were young, and you did not have a prince's privileges of movement. And where else would he have found all these things?" He pointed out the strange, big-eyed faces on some of the bits of carved stone in the box. "These look like the Dwarrows or Dvernings who supposedly built the castle Asu'a for their immortal masters," he said. "And the silver bells or beads and the other objects also have the look of Sithi-make. But it is this little, harmless-looking thing that worries me most." He reached in, using the fold of his sleeve to pick up the broken frame and hold it where the king could see. "I think this might have been a Sithi mirror, though the glass is no longer in it. And not just any mirror but a *Witness*, as they call it. You carried one for a time, Simon, so you know what they can do—"

"Good God. Good God!" Simon made the sign of the Tree. "Do you think John Josua tried to use such a thing? Could that have . . . ?" He bunched his hands into fists and pressed them against his temples. "I cannot tell Miri this about our son. She will be horrified—heartbroken!"

"It is far too early to even guess at anything of the sort, Simon, but this is why I felt I had to tell you now. It is exactly the sort of thing of which the *Aetheric Whispers* speaks."

"That foul book! Pryrates' book!" The king had reddened again and was tugging at his beard as though he meant to pull it out by the roots. "Curse that wretched sorcerer! And curse King Elias for bringing him here! The book must have come from the priest's bloody tower somehow. We should have pulled the whole cursed thing down after the war ended, stone by stone, and seeded the ground with salt!" He sat up straight. "Well, I will do it now! I will have the damnable thing destroyed!"

"But the dilemma has not changed, Simon," Tiamak reminded him. "If we pull down Hjeldin's Tower and expose the tunnels beneath it—tunnels that run beneath all of the Hayholt—who knows what kind of things the red priest captured and imprisoned there might be set free? Who knows what poisons he made or found? What kind of terrible spells?" He shook his head. "This castle may be our home and the seat of the High Throne, but it stands on the ruins of the Sithi's greatest palace. It is a strange, haunted place beneath the cellars, and nothing so dangerous as pulling down the tower can be done without much care and thought."

Simon's knuckles had gone white where he clutched the chair arms. "I don't want to hear about 'care and thought.' Care and thought may have killed my son!"

Before Tiamak could reply, the door to the retiring room opened, and a herald and a guard stepped in. And before she could be announced Lady Thelía pushed past them and hurried toward the king and Tiamak. She did not even make a courtesy, but said, "I beg pardon, Majesty, but a messenger has come for my husband saying that there is a dead man in the gatehouse and that he carried a message saying the prince's company was attacked."

"The prince's company?" said Simon in confusion. "My grandson?"

As soon as he had seen the look on his wife's face, Tiamak got to his feet. "Is he safe?" he asked. "Is Prince Morgan safe?"

"I could make little sense of any of it," she admitted. "But the messenger also said that Duke Osric has lost his wits."

His leg still in pain from kneeling, Tiamak took his wife's arm and hobbled after Simon, who had already reached the door.

Osric stood just outside the doorway of the gatehouse, howling like a wolf. "They've killed him! The savages have killed him!"

"For God's sake, take him in hand," Simon told Sir Kenrick. He felt as if his own sanity was being held together by something thinner than cobwebs. "Even if the worst has happened . . ." For a moment he could not speak, but he swallowed and tried again. "No matter what has happened, we cannot have the Lord Constable shouting like a madman in view of everyone. It will terrify the people."

"It looks as though people already know, Majesty." Kenrick gestured toward the crowd on the Erchester side of the gate, dozens of pale, worried faces turned toward the gatehouse. Rather than reassuring them, the arrival of the king seemed to have made them even more frightened; some began shouting to Simon, asking what had happened. He forced his way into the gatehouse, elbowing past guards who stood in the doorway like uneasy cattle. Tiamak and his wife followed, letting tall Simon clear the way.

Half a dozen more guardsmen and a barber-surgeon had gathered around a man lying on one of the tables where the guardsmen shared their meals. Thelía and Tiamak stood beside Simon to look at the dead man. Thelía let out a sigh of pity.

The young soldier wore the tattered, stained surcoat of an Erkynguard, although the white dragon on one side of the Holy Tree was so drenched in blood that the two beasts on the insignia had become scarlet twins.

"I fear it's too late, Your Majesty," the barber-surgeon said as Tiamak stepped forward to feel the man's wrists and throat for a heartbeat. "You can see he's shed too much blood. He must have ridden miles with that wound."

"Yes, the poor fellow is dead." Tiamak looked around at the gaping soldiers. "Who here found him?" he demanded. "Did he speak?" For a moment no one answered.

"God blast you all to the depths!" Simon shouted. In his fright, it was all he could do not to strike out at the useless, fearful faces around him. "You heard Lord Tiamak—answer! Who found this man?"

"He . . . he rode into Erchester," said a soldier, one of a trio who wore the blue and white of the City Guard. He spoke hesitantly, as though he might be accused of the murder himself. "People saw that he was hurt and called to him but he would not stop. He made it all the way down Main Row to the square before he collapsed. We brought him here. We are sorry, Majesty. We tried to help him."

"Did he speak at all?" Tiamak asked again. "What did he say?"

"He could hardly talk," said the soldier. "As we carried him, he told us his company had been attacked by Thrithings clansmen—by grasslanders. That they were taken by surprise, and the Erkynguards were slaughtered almost to a man."

"Are you sure that's what he said?" Simon's heart beat so fast and his head felt so hollow, he thought he might topple over like a felled tree. "Curse you, Osric, stop your shouting, I cannot hear the man!" He turned to the soldier who had spoken, and must have looked fearsome indeed because the man shrank away from his king like a terrified child. "Tell us, damn it!"

Simon was about to shout at Captain Kenrick to drag the duke out of the guardhouse if necessary, but realized Kenrick was beside him now, staring at the pale face of the dead man.

"I know him, Majesty," the guard captain said heavily. "That is Ordwine of Westworth. He went out as part of the company with Prince Morgan and the lord steward, Count Eolair."

"God save us all," Simon said quietly. He felt fevered, his head scalding hot while a frozen lump inside his chest grew more and more heavy by the moment. All he could think, over and over, was that Miriamele would blame him, and she would be right to do it. "What have I done? Sir Kenrick, please remove everyone but those who brought the man here."

Tiamak turned to the barber-surgeon. "Help me get his mail shirt off." Simon's long-serving advisor, at least, was not giving in to the helpless terror that seemed to have gripped almost everyone else.

Simon was desperate to do something, to make something happen, but not even a king could bring a man back once the life was out of him. He could only wait and pray that a mistake had been made. So pray he did, but it felt no more useful than a child's wall of sand raised in front of an incoming tide.

With the help of the surgeon and another soldier, Tiamak wrestled the shirt and mail off the dead man. When the corselet came off, Ordwine's head fell back and hit the table with a terrible, harsh crack. A few of the remaining soldiers cursed at this indignity, but Ordwine was beyond suffering. Tiamak peeled away the bloody arming-shirt beneath to reveal a huge, ragged hole in the man's chest close to his right arm.

"What use is all this?" Osric had slipped into the chamber while Kenrick was clearing out the other unwanted watchers. The duke sounded bewildered now, and for a moment Simon's anger at him cooled a little. "The Thrithings barbarians have killed my grandson," he said, but then his voice rose again to a shout of despair. "We should have burned them out years ago. Oh, God, merciful God!"

"Kenrick, take some soldiers and get the lord constable out of this place. If he argues, tell him it is my royal order. Get some strong drink into him until he quiets, then take him back to his chambers and keep him there until I say otherwise. By the saints, tie him to the bed if you have to. And do not let Duchess Nelda talk you out of doing what you must." He wished he too could leave, but he needed to be strong now—strong for Miri, strong for everyone else who needed him to be the king, no matter the horror and grief that threatened almost to stop his heart. He had never felt more alone than he did at that moment.

Tiamak was testing the wound with his fingers, but stopped to roll back his sleeves, though the cuffs were already soaked in blood. Lady Thelía stood beside him, gathering bits of tattered shirt as Tiamak plucked them from the wound, and though she was clearly troubled, her face was nearly as composed as her husband's.

"Made by an arrow, that is my guess," Tiamak said, probing again. "The wound is too small for a spear or even a sword. But the hole has been torn outward. Ordwine pulled it out himself, if I am any judge, so that he could keep riding." He nodded slowly. "Poor, brave man." He turned to the Erchester town guards. "We are still waiting for an answer. Think very carefully. What did he say to you?"

"That they had been surprised by clansmen, my lord," said the soldier who had spoken earlier. "That the Erkynguard had been slaughtered almost to a man—that was his word, 'slaughtered'—that only a few had survived—"

"So some of them lived?" Simon felt a surge of hope, though he knew it was foolish.

"I think another guard accompanied him, bringing the message," volunteered one of the other city guardsmen. "When we first picked him up from where he fell, he said, 'They caught up with us.' And he said someone else was dead. Firman! I remember. 'They caught up with us,' he said. 'They killed Firman.'"

"Firman—he was with the prince's company too," said the first guardsman. "Firman Ostler's Son, that's what everyone called him."

Tiamak finished examining the wound and began to search for other injuries. "You said he rode through the town. Someone find the horse and bring it here."

The captain of the Nearulagh gatehouse had arrived only a short while before, a grizzled older soldier with a well-trimmed beard who was clearly abashed to have missed so much. "You heard Lord Tiamak," he told two of his men. "Get that horse before someone steals it."

Tiamak was holding Ordwine's right hand, which was clenched in a bloody fist. He was trying to open the dead man's fingers but not succeeding. "I need help," he said, but when one of the soldiers would have moved in, he shook his head. "Thelía, I would rather you do it. Gently. He will not be stiff yet, but he was holding tight and still is."

Ignoring the blood, Lady Thelía helped her husband work the dead man's hand open, revealing a crumpled object almost entirely soaked in red. Tiamak lifted it out and set it carefully on the table. "A parchment," he said. "No, something cruder." He carefully began to tease open the wadded mass. "There is writing on it," he said. "But see, a great hole is torn in the middle."

Simon pushed in closer. "Why would he do that?"

"I do not think he did, Majesty. I think he carried this message in his breast, beneath his armor, and the arrow went through it. It was so important to him that he pulled the arrow free from his own body to save it."

"Brave man!" Simon said, fighting back tears for fear he would not be able to stop. "He will have a hero's funeral. But what is it? Tell me, man, what does it say?"

"A moment, Majesty," Tiamak said. "It is very torn and stained, and I do not want to harm it any more—see, already much of the writing is destroyed. Save all those small pieces," he told his wife. "We may find a word here and there."

"Tell me what it says!"

Almost everybody flinched at the anger in Simon's voice, but Tiamak would not be hurried. "First I need a clean white cloth," he said. "And a knife. I seem to have left mine in my chambers."

It was all Simon could do to stay silent while soldiers hurried to find a suitable piece of cloth—it was not the sort of thing ordinarily found in the Nearulagh gatehouse. At last one came back with a white arming shirt. "It is new—my wife just sewed it for me," he said dejectedly as Tiamak took it.

"Give it over, man," Simon growled. "We will get you another."

Tiamak laid the shirt out on one of the few unbloodied parts of the table, then spread the rumpled message upon it. He then folded the shirt over it and pressed down as the soldier who had donated the garment looked on sadly.

Now that some of the blood had been soaked away, Simon could see the letters more plainly. It was no polished parchment meant for courtly missives, but a piece of stretched skin with crudely irregular edges. Simon had seen such things before, and he also recognized the small, bold runes, although he had never seen them so hurried and slapdash. "I know that hand," he said. "It is Binabik's, praise God, so perhaps he still lives. But what does he write?"

Tiamak squinted. "'Set on by Thrithings men on forest's edge,' is the first part, but then we reach the bits that were torn by the arrow. Thelía, can you make out the next?"

His wife leaned close. "'The prince,' I think it says just before the hole. And after that is 'Eolair,' I believe. Is this from the troll? His writing is very odd—I have seen nothing like it before." She pursed her lips, studying it. "On the other side it says, 'taken by clansmen, perhaps for . . .'" She shook her head. "I cannot make it out."

Simon now felt his heart thawing, if only a little. "*Ransom,*" he said. "I know Binabik's hand. That is 'ransom.' Does he mean Eolair and the prince have been captured, not killed? All praise to Almighty God if that is true!"

"Yes," Lady Thelía said, "I believe you are right, Your Majesty. 'Ransom.' Below the hole, I can read, 'and my family follow him. We will not . . .' That is all I can read."

"Are you certain it is Binabik's writing?" Tiamak asked, then laughed, a short bark with no mirth. "I am a fool. Of course it is—who else in that company would be traveling with his family?"

"So Binabik and his kin are alive—and perhaps Morgan is alive too." Simon could not remember having feelings so mixed in all his memory, full of dread and yet suddenly hopeful when he had been certain only moments before that no hope remained. "And Count Eolair, too—God and his sacred son keep them all safe! They are in the hands of grasslander barbarians. Still, that is better news than I first feared. I will tell Duke Osric that we need not give up yet." He had a sudden, intensely painful thought that brought despair rushing back in. "But, oh!—merciful Aedon, now I will have to write to the queen and tell her this terrible news."

13

Life in the Treetops

Between the occasional offerings from
the secretive creatures in the trees—ReeRee's family, as Morgan supposed—
and what he was able to find with the little animal's help, he managed to keep
starvation at arm's length. Still, an hour did not pass when he didn't think of
real food, of great slabs of beef or venison, red and dripping, or a cheese tart,
the crust as breakable as the ice of an early frost.

You miss things so much when you can't have them . . .

He thought about wine, too, and brandy. In the first days in the woods his
thirst for such things had been so strong that sometimes he feared it would drive
him mad. But after hacking angrily at tree trunks with his sword, then having
to sharpen the blade again, he had done his best to stop thinking about such
impossible things, but it did not keep them from haunting him.

In dreams now he often found himself a child again, his father alive, his
mother still with nothing but time for her young son. He ran again through the
endless halls of the Hayholt, where everything was giant-high. He crawled on
the floors across carpet or cold stone, which had always been closer to his child's
life than the walls or ceiling, the provinces of looming adults. Sometimes he
found himself to be something other than his own younger self, a kind of animal perhaps, scuttling along the forest earth, clambering over huge roots or
mountainous fallen trees. And when he dreamed he was an animal, he was
always hunted. Something out there was searching for him, and despite all his
hurrying and scurrying he could never outrun it.

Morgan was in the middle of such a dream when he woke bolt upright in
the near-complete darkness of his tree-canopied crevice to discover that little
ReeRee was gone.

For a confused moment he felt himself to be both the dream-Morgan, a
creature pursued, and the child Morgan, lost and missing his parents. Then
both phantoms receded and he remembered where he was and what had happened. As he scrambled out of the crevice a sound made him stop.

Whimpering. It came from upslope and to his right, where the trees leaned
close to the granite outcropping that had more or less become his home.

As he made his way cautiously around the base of the great stone, as uneven ground and tangles of underbrush made a puzzle of shadows by the tree-shuttered starlight, he heard the noise again. He made his way to the base of the tall beech tree that grew beside the stone and saw what he felt reasonably sure was ReeRee's small, huddled form on a branch and close against the trunk, three or four times his own height off the ground.

The small creature turned to look down at him and her eyes were two pale yellow disks glowing in the starlight. He opened his mouth to scold her for getting into a place where she could not get down, then it occurred to him that maybe she had tried to join the rest of her kind, but weakness or her slow-healing injury had prevented it.

She wants her people, he thought, *like I want mine*—although he knew it was ridiculous to think of animals as "people." He was about to call her when he heard a rattling in the trees behind him. For a sliver of an instant he thought it might be ReeRee's fellow creatures come to take her back, but the noise was too loud: something large was shoving its way through thick shrubbery and slender tree limbs, and it was coming closer.

Morgan looked up at ReeRee's perch in sudden panic but saw that even if he jumped his highest, the lowest limbs were beyond his reach. Even as he cast around for another route of escape he heard himself uttering panicky curses, as though it was someone else speaking. He'd left his sword back in his sleeping place.

The large thing in the trees moved again. A single thin sapling snapped and fell forward into a puddle of starlight—it was now a dozen paces away at most. Was it a wolf? A bear? Or something worse, something he had not ever heard of except in the servants' ghost stories . . . ?

"Climb something, idiot!" he told himself out loud.

Whatever was skulking in the trees heard him. For a moment it was completely silent, then the sound of crackling branches became loud and steady.

He could not reach the branches where ReeRee crouched or find a climbable tree before whatever it was caught him. Given little choice, he turned and began to scale the stone outcropping itself.

It was a terrible choice: he knew even as he grabbed for his first handhold; the mass of stone jutted from the hillside at such an angle that it was like climbing the prow of a large ship. Even though he managed to haul himself up off the ground, and found a place to lodge his bare feet, each successive movement up the rock tilted him farther and farther backward, until it became harder to hold on each time.

The rattle in the trees ended in a crash of brush as a large shape burst out of the vegetation into the clearing in front of the stone. The unwanted visitor was a bear, dark gray in the dim light and at least twice Morgan's size. When it saw him clambering up the rock it stopped and reared onto its hind legs, throwing its front legs wide. He saw wisps of gray at the end of both forefeet—claws as long as paring knives.

As the bear lumbered toward him, Morgan turned back to the outcrop, heart thundering and hands slippery with sweat. A piece of stone broke loose under his hand and in a desperate scramble he almost fell down and into the creature's open jaws. He was able, however, to cling with one hand until his feet found purchase. Still, he was hanging upside down like a spider on a ceiling.

The bear waddled to the base of the stone and reared again, snapping at him, its massive head so near that he could smell the strange, sweet stink of its breath. He could not find anything above him to grasp, and knew he did not have the strength to hang for long where he was. He saw only one chance and took it, crouching with his weight against the footholds while continuing to hold on with one hand. His knees and legs were trembling so badly that for a moment, nightmarishly, he could already feel himself failing, his leap falling short even before he began it. He put all he had into a single uncoiling of his legs, leaping away from the stone with his arms outstretched and his back toward the ground.

He caught the lowest branch of the beech tree and slipped a little, then held on. Beneath him the bear snarled and swung huge but impotent paws. Gasping, Morgan dragged himself onto the branch and clung with both arms and both legs, quivering all over, then slid along it until he reached the trunk and could make his way up, branch by branch. ReeRee was waiting for him, making soft fear-noises. Below, the bear paced back and forth, grumbling and growling. It even climbed a little way up the trunk—Morgan's heart again thundered—but failed and slid down again. Even after that, the beast would not leave and continued to waddle back and forth around the base of the stone. ReeRee fell silent and for a long while Morgan could hear no sound except for the bear's snuffling breath.

He finally dropped into a sort of half-sleep on the branch next to ReeRee. He did not tumble out, though dreams of doing just that kept waking him, his fingers gripping the branch beneath him so hard that they ached. He did not truly sleep, nor did he want to. At last, after weary hours, the cold, damp dawn arrived, and he started awake out of another doze to discover that the bear had gone.

It was clear he had to move on. Before it gave up, the bear had pulled most of Morgan's belongings from the crevice in the rock and scattered them across the slope. And though there was nothing for the monster to eat and no damage done except for scratches and bite marks on his leather purse and boots, he felt sure it would come back. He decided he would be safer sleeping in the trees from now on, no matter how uncomfortable that was.

Morgan made a bed from his folded cloak for ReeRee, and set it in the depths of the crevice as he gathered up his belongings, but he found himself lingering over his sword and shirt of chain mail. Neither had been much use to him thus far, although he had used his blade on more than one occasion to chop through underbrush. But as he held it in his hands and remembered his foolish childhood dreams of using it in battle instead of as a makeshift scythe, he could not bear to leave it behind. The blade had been his father's, given to John Josua when he had been made a knight and passed to Morgan at his father's death. His father had never drawn it in anger—unlike King Simon, John Josua had never shown any inclination for the warrior life—but it was still a treasured possession.

What son leaves his father's sword in the forest? And what prince, especially, would ever do such a thing? What if, next time he had to fight a bear, not hide from it? His knife, useful as it had been elsewhere, would be worth nothing in such a moment.

So although the sword had so far been more of a hindrance than a help, he sheathed it and strapped it around his waist. The armor, though, was a less compelling burden. It did not keep him warm at night, and in the summer days' heat it weighed on him. It might save him from a bear's claws or a wolf's jaws, but only for a moment. He hung the armor from the branch of a tree—a flag that declared, "Prince Morgan was here," to anyone who might be looking for him, although he was becoming more and more certain that if anyone had been, they had given up by now.

As he picked up the various other scattered articles and stuffed them back in his purse—his muddied Book of Aedon, his coil of rope—he found the spike-covered climbing irons that Little Snenneq had given him. They were certainly heavy, and there seemed very little chance he would be walking or climbing anything icy, unless he was lost in the forest until winter—an ugly possibility he still did not want to consider—and he was about to toss them away, but an idea suddenly came. It seemed so mad that he actually laughed out loud, but the more he examined the irons the more interesting the idea became.

He put them on, though it took him several tries before he could remember the correct way Qina and Snenneq had shown him. When he had laced them firmly over his boots, he walked in an awkward fashion back to the tree where he and ReeRee had spent the night.

He could now dig the spikes that protruded from the toe of his boot into the bark, but found the trunk was still too slippery; he only managed to climb a few feet before his own weight pulled him back. He pulled the toe-spikes out and slid clumsily back down, disappointed. But then a memory of the steeple-jacks at the Hayholt and their elaborate harnesses came to him.

Morgan went for his coil of rope and found a suitable stone that he could knot at one end. Returning to the tree, he swung the rope and let the stone end spin around the trunk. Then he pulled the ends even and grasped them tight. He could now dig his toes into the bark and pull back on the rope around the trunk, supporting his upper half at the same time.

After a few failed attempts, including a painful landing on his fundament that he was glad no one he knew had witnessed, he was able to climb even the smooth trunk of the beech to a point where he could grab the bottommost branch. He let himself down—going backward was even harder than going up, but faster—and then did it again. The third time he managed to scramble up to the nearest branch so quickly that when he reached it, he let out a whoop of joy that echoed through the trees. ReeRee came wide-eyed out of the crevice, still favoring her injured foreleg, perhaps wondering why he was bellowing and capering on a branch that she could reach with so little effort.

"I live in the trees!" Morgan shouted and for the moment didn't care that he was proclaiming it to no one but himself.

The days that followed were some of the strangest and yet happiest Morgan had spent in a long time. ReeRee grew stronger and more interested in climbing on her own, and would leave him for long stretches to search for delicacies only she could locate. But now he could climb up after her, and often they spent hours together in the branches. Morgan found he could also use the cord to tie himself to the trunk at night and sleep without fear of falling. He was still hungry, still lost, still miserably without human company, but if he could climb high enough into the slenderer branches by sundown he no longer had to worry about whatever was out hunting on the ground.

ReeRee seemed to enjoy the new arrangement too, chittering at him to come see something she had found, or curling up on him when she was tired. He could not go everywhere she could, and sometimes, when she leaped from one tree to the next where the branches were too slight to hold his weight, Morgan had to descend one tree and climb the next. They moved slowly. He had largely given up on finding his way out of the forest, so he did not care. The order of the moment was simply to find food and stay alive.

It quickly became clear that ReeRee's troop had stayed close to her and her odd, clumsy companion. The Chikri seemed less shy of him now that he was often in the trees as well, and though they still kept their distance, he could observe them closely. ReeRee's first excited reunion with the troop was a particularly joyful thing to see. They all frisked and rubbed against each other, even rubbing noses, and one of them was so reluctant to let ReeRee go again that Morgan felt certain it was her mother. His own mother had been that way once, anxious whenever he was out of her sight, especially in the first months after his father's death. He could not help feeling sorry for the fear he must have caused in the small animals when they saw their offspring carried away by giant Morgan, presumably to be eaten.

As the forest days crept by the Chikri lost almost all their fear of him, and came closer and closer until whatever tree he was in was usually crowded with the furry creatures. There seemed to be a couple of dozen in the troop, and the more he watched them, the more convinced he was that ReeRee was still young. Most of the others were at least half again as large as she was, and their coats had lost the oblong spots that covered hers. And while ReeRee and one or two of the other small Chikri were endlessly full of curiosity and mischief, the larger ones seemed interested only in gathering food and resting.

The troop, with ReeRee now a part of it once more (though she also stayed close to Morgan) began to move steadily though slowly in one direction through the woods, resting each day a half a mile or so from where they'd begun. When he tried to lead ReeRee another way the other Chikri scolded him, and when he let her choose the direction she followed her family or tribe. He no longer trusted the position of the sun after many frustrating days of circular travel, certain that the Sithi had bespelled this entire part of the forest, but the Chikri seemed to be heading in what he would have guessed was a northwesterly direction. His father had told him once that many animals had paths they traveled every season, just like human roads but invisible to the eye, so he guessed that the creatures were following an ancient food-gathering trail. For now he was content to move with them, though he often had to scramble to keep up. The Chikri did not come down from the treetops if they could avoid it, and then only to feed on some particularly succulent bit of forage like newly-discovered berry brambles or a hazel shedding ripe nuts before scurrying back into the branches again.

Once the troop came across a solitary apple tree, which stood in the middle of a stand of ashes like a lone cuckoo in a nest of blackbirds. The apples were small and sour but the taste made Morgan ache for home. He put several down his shirt for later, and even cried a little when he ate one that night, with ReeRee chuntering quietly in her sleep as she lay curled against his belly.

The strangest thing of all, though, was how *alive* the treetops were. Morgan had never thought much about trees before, only climbed them as children do, usually with an objective in mind, such as pilfering fruit or hiding from a tutor who never thought to look up while searching for escaped pupils. When Morgan had thought about the treetops he had more or less assumed that, other than birds and a few squirrels, the heights were empty, nothing but leaves waving in the wind. Instead, as he was now learning, an entire world existed there, and it felt as if he alone had discovered it.

The first things he learned was that the trees themselves came in dozens of kinds beyond the common ones like ash, oak, beech, and elm. Each one was different, especially for climbing and sheltering. Some, like silver-barked hornbeams, seemed to present their boughs to the climber like stairs, regular and sturdy. Beeches had hard, slippery bark. But some lured him toward the heights and then left him stranded far below the crown, with all the tree's best sights, fruits, or nuts still out of reach. Once an old pear tree tempted him with fruit in its high crown, but the branches proved thorny and, even worse, as fragile as kindling. He got scratches all over his legs and on his belly from that lesson, as well as a limp for most of a day, when his rope caught him during the fall and swung him hard against the trunk. Worst of all, the single pear he had plucked before he fell was so sourly unripe that he could barely swallow it and felt ill for hours afterward.

Morgan had never imagined how many animals, birds, and bugs made their homes or at least spent a large part of their day in the trees. He saw snakes entwining through the upper boughs, green and shiny as damp grass, and sala-manders squatting contentedly in the rainwater puddles that collected where broken branches had left a hollow. The treetops were an entire little world, and now that world contained at least one lost prince as well.

Qina was on her hands and knees, examining the welter of different prints that covered the clearing in front of the granite outcrop. She lifted a fallen leaf with the edge of her knife.

"Here is a good sign," she said. "We are lucky there was a storm while he was here, so the ground was wet and the prints are deep. Prince Morgan's foot-print lies on top of the bear's track and looks newer, but it is hard to tell for certain with so many other prints, especially all of these *kunikuni*. Daughter of the Mountains! All of those creatures I have ever seen are small, but some of these prints look much bigger than of those that live in the trees at Blue Mud Lake."

Binabik was examining Morgan's armor where it hung on a tree branch. "The strange part is not the *kunikuni*, daughter, but where the prince has gone. There are many of his tracks to say he stayed here some time, but he is not here now and beyond this clearing the footprints simply end."

"At least we know he was not carried off by the bear," said Qina's mother Sisqi, who had coaxed a small fire into being. "There would be some sign."

"I think your thought is a right one," said Binabik, "for which I give thanks. I see no evidence of a fight. And I think it has been several days since he was last here. But how did he go away without leaving footprints? It is as if he learned to fly."

"It is certainly a puzzle," said Qina, her face so close to the ground that her nose almost touched the earth. She looked up at the sound of Snenneq's quiet chortle. "What are you doing there? What is funny?"

"I am remembering when you spoke Westerling to the prince. '*Oh, Morgan Prince, that is a terrible puddle,*' you said." He poked the fire happily. Because he thought they would be at least a day examining the rock and Morgan's camp, Binabik had given Snenneq permission to hunt and cook food, and Qina's be-trothed now had a pile of several birds wrapped in wild grape leaves beside him. " '*Puddle,*' Snenneq said again and laughed.

"Not all of us spent so many hours learning the flatlander tongue," she said, scowling. "Some of us had more important lessons to master, like learning to read tracks."

"A Singing Man must be able to speak to those beyond his own tribe," was his lofty reply. "And my skill with their tongue helped us in many ways on this journey, and made us friends among all the flatlanders—even the Croo-hok!"

"Oh, yes, the Croohok loved you," Qina said. "Especially those who tried to beat your head in." She waved her knife significantly. "Remember, even a sheep's bladder puffed full of air can be emptied with one swift poke."

Snenneq took a mock-stumble back from the small fire and toppled slowly onto his back where he waved his arms and legs in the air. Vaqana, Binabik's wolf, gave a bark of annoyance. "Ah! Ah!" Snenneq cried. "My betrothed has stabbed me and let out my air! Ah! Save me, Binabik—your daughter has sharp claws!"

Qina rolled her eyes. "Are all men such fools?" she asked her mother. "And does it grow worse or better once they marry?"

"I think your father chose Little Snenneq to be the next Singing Man because they were so much alike," Sisqi told her. "They both love to tell jokes that no one else finds funny but themselves."

Binabik shook his head, frowning. "May I remind you, wife, of the words of my own master, Ookekuq? He told me once, 'There is only one creature in all the world more ridiculous than a human woman.'"

"And that creature is?"

"Oh, a human man, of course." Binabik turned from his examination of Prince Morgan's mail shirt and began once more to pace the clearing in front of the outcrop. "I must climb this rock, I fear. Perhaps that is the way Morgan left, and thus no tracks were left for us to find, although it seems too steep."

Snenneq stood and brushed himself off. "My birds will not go in to cook until the fire has burned down to coals. I am a good climber. Let me do it."

Binabik waved his hand. "If you wish. But do not be so busy talking about your climbing skills that you muddle any tracks or signs there might be."

"But why must we climb the rock at all?" Snenneq said, walking around the side of the outcrop until he was out of Qina's sight. "Here is a tree right beside it," he called. "It would be possible to throw a rope over one of those branches, I think, and reach the top of the rock that way. Perhaps that is what Prince Morgan did." He inspected the trunk. "Look, Qina, here is something strange. Have you ever seen woodpeckers make this sort of hole?"

She came to his side. "It does not look like a woodpecker hole to me, O Singing-Man-To-Be. Woodpecker holes are rounded, the result of many strikes of the beak. This is only a single very narrow strike, like a knife blade." She stared at the twin punctures in the bark. When she turned to Snenneq he was chortling again. "What has seized you? Has my mention of a knife reminded you how nearly you escaped being punctured, my beloved bladder?"

"No, no. I am thinking instead that I know what Morgan has done, and why we cannot find his tracks beyond this place. Wait here." He trotted quickly to where his great ram Falku was tethered, nibbling on damp grass, then began to root around in his saddlebag. Hurrying back, he showed her: "Look," he said, "and then tell me your *nukapik* is not wise beyond other men." He lifted the climbing-iron, its rawhide straps trailing, and set it against the trunk. Two of the front spikes fit the holes in the trunk as though they had been made for them.

"Kikkasut's Wings, I think you are right!" she said. "Father, Mother, come look!"

Binabik and Sisqi examined the holes and the spikes of the climbing iron. "That was indeed a clever idea, Little Snenneq," Binabik said. "I see now why we see no tracks on the ground." He shook his head as he looked up into the high branches. "But how do we follow him now?"

"Vaqana's nose might follow him, even without tracks," Qina suggested. "It has been days since he passed, but the wolf might still catch his traces if we move now, without waiting."

"But my birds!" said Snenneq, clearly heartsick. "The coals are almost ready!"

"Wrap them well and perhaps when we stop tonight we may still enjoy them," said Binabik. "Morgan must rest at sunset—he may have learned to travel through the trees like the *kunikuni*, but I am guessing he does not leap from limb to limb in darkness. So Qina is right—now we must go."

Snenneq mournfully wrapped each of the wood pigeons in an extra layer of leaves and placed them carefully in his saddlebag, as though he were holding a funeral for tiny but beloved friends.

Morgan awoke in the darkness of deep night, although at first he didn't know what had wakened him. The Chikri surrounded him in the branches, silent in sleep, with ReeRee curled on the branch where he had tied himself to the trunk. But something was strange, and it was only when he realized that he could hear a voice speaking quietly—no, not speaking, he realized, so much as singing or chanting—that he noticed that the stars speckling the sky above him were completely and utterly unfamiliar.

He stared at the alien shapes of the constellations—no Staff, no Horned Owl or Lamp, not even the sky-shapes of winter, which would at least have suggested earthly skies—and was certain that he dreamed. The singsong voice murmured on, not from beneath him as he had first thought, or even from the treetop above, but inside his own head. Morgan became even more certain that he was still asleep, although he could not ever remember a dream quite as real as this one.

After a while he began to take meaning from the quiet, musical collection of sounds, as though they had paraded before him wrapped in cloaks, then threw off their disguises to reveal their true selves. As he came to understand the words, he also realized it was a voice he had heard before, but this time it did not speak just to him but, it seemed, to the sky itself.

O, stars of our home! it said, and that single phrase seemed to strike his thoughts with such a feeling of loss that he almost wept. Loneliness swept through him like wind through branches.

O, stars of the vanished land that even my grandmother never saw! Here in this no-where place I can only see your shapes as she gave them to me, in word and thought and song! I ask you to grant me the strength of the true light, whether the sky-lamps of the fallen land or these, the phantoms of our lost Garden!

I see the Pool, and the Swallower, and the Bend of the River. So they must have glimmered above Tzo, the city named for their light, when it first fell upon our eyes so many ages ago! The Blade, the Well, the Dancer, the Reaching Hand—all lost! Do those stars still shine somewhere, or did they go dark when Unbeing took the Garden?

Morgan could not move, could only listen and stare up at the unfamiliar lights. If this was a dream he could not awaken from it, no matter how he tried, but could only listen as the words that echoed in his head grew even more sharp, more sad. Slowly he came to realize that he was not truly hearing words but ideas: somehow the voice was speaking some tongue he did not know and could not speak, a thing of strange melodies, but still he understood almost all.

But why mourn this way? said the voice in his head. *No one can hear me. My beloved mate is gone, my people are lost to me. My children and my children's children are beyond my reach, and I am caught between one world and another, between life and what comes after. Why mourn? This is our lot, the way of the People, to see too late what they should know in their hearts from birth. Grandmother, I was wrong not to heed you. The voices lie until lies become truth.*

And in that instant, Morgan finally knew who was speaking. When she had spoken to him before it had been in dreams and had frightened him so that he did not think about it when it ceased, fearful of going mad. But now he remembered the words from what seemed another life, in the cave where he had gone with Eolair and the two Sithi, Aditu and her brother.

All the voices lie except the one that whispers, she had said then, and Morgan had heard her though her lips had not moved and her breath had not carried the words. *And that one will steal away the world.* This could only be the mother of Aditu and Jiriki, who he had seen lying near death, covered in a shroud of butterflies.

The voice continued, growing ever quieter. *So it must be permitted, it seems, neither to go back nor to go on, with no one to hear me, and a world in pain.*

Thus will end Likimeya Y'Briseyu no'e-Sa'onserei, guttering like a candle . . .

"Likimeya!" Morgan said out loud, and found himself sitting upright on the branch where he had fallen asleep, straining against the rope that held him as though he might burst loose and fly over the trees toward those unfamiliar stars. Beside him, ReeRee had wakened too, and stared at him with a worried look. The stars above the treetops, though still stretched and strange, were once more the night-fires he knew. The Lantern again hung high in the sky, tilted as if it were falling away into an unimaginable abyss, but still the same recognizable star that had heralded summer's arrival all his life. And the voice that had awakened him was gone, as if the candle to which she had compared herself had truly been extinguished.

Morgan shook his head and pulled ReeRee close, his heart beating fast, his cheeks wet with tears he could not entirely understand. Despite the warmth of the little animal's body and the dark shapes of her fellows perched on branches all around him in the forest night, Morgan felt like the last and loneliest person in the world.

14

A Sip of Cloudberry Wine

"To the Mother of All." Prince-Templar Pratiki dipped his finger into the wine, then lifted it to his lips and gently blew upon it.

Viyeki did the same. "To the Mother of All."

"And to the White Prince, whom we celebrate today."

"And to the White Prince," Viyeki echoed.

It was a great honor to be invited to drink cloudberry wine with the queen's noble clansman for the celebration of Drukhi's Day, but Viyeki was not altogether happy. For one thing, a mission given to him by the queen herself, with the clear imputation that he would be the leading figure, had turned out to be something stranger and less satisfying. General Kikiti and his soldiers were preparing to launch an attack on the castle mortals called Naglimund, but Viyeki and his builders were only there to dig. And now, for no reason Viyeki could understand, Prince-Templar Pratiki was here too. Viyeki had no particular dislike of Pratiki, but it had not escaped his attention that he had been superseded in yet one more way. Still, he knew better than to complain.

"You are kind to share this day with me, Serenity."

Pratiki waved his finger, flicking the idea away. His posture was astonishingly good, and as part of honoring the day, the prince-templar wore his long white hair like an ancient warrior-priest, the braids tied with bird-leather straps, so that he looked more like a statue than a living Hikeda'ya. Still, what Viyeki had heard over the years inclined him to like Pratiki, though that counted for little in the deadly world of Nakkiga politics.

"So how has time behaved to you here in the wilderness, High Magister?" Pratiki asked. "You must find it hanging heavily while you wait for the Sacrifices to discharge their part in the queen's mission."

"Time has been tolerable. I think about the problems we may face when it is time for my Builders. And I read *The Five Fingers*, of course, because it never grows old in its wisdom."

"Of course," said Pratiki, but a shadow seemed to flit across his face. It was always difficult, even for another noble like Viyeki, to guess at the thoughts of a Hamakha clansman—the queen's relatives made a particular fetish of inscrutability—but for an instant he thought Pratiki had looked disappointed.

Is he trying to trick me into saying something foolish? Is someone in the court whisper-ing against me?

Perhaps sensing Viyeki's discomfort, the prince-templar gracefully changed the subject. They talked of small things, of favorite spots in Nakkiga, of mutual acquaintances—the small number of those testifying to the different circles they inhabited—and of court life. The cloudberry wine was clearly of some magnificent ancient vintage; it eclipsed even the bottle that his old master Yaarike bequeathed him as a reminder of a significant drink they had once shared. This wine was even more bitterly tart than Yaarike's, but also had more flavors than Viyeki could count, tangs of smoke, flint, even slate, all swimming in and out of the berries' sweetness like a school of swift silver fish, and it over-whelmed his senses.

He knew he should decline a second glass, because the headiness of the first was urging him to let down his guard and relax in the presence of a convivial and apparently like-minded companion. Viyeki knew the penalties of such inattention too well—he had seen friends of his father's executed for humorous remarks that had later been judged treason. He accepted a second glass—the urge to caution had to be measured against not offending someone who had a great deal of power—and only touched it to his lips from time to time.

"Myself," Pratiki said, "I often marvel at the naked ambition you see in some of the folks at court, saying or doing whatever they think will allow them to reach into more pockets and kiss more noble feet." He shook his head and showed a thin smile, then began a long and outwardly humorous story about the greed and duplicity of several different nobles. Viyeki smiled or shook his head in disgust at the correct moments, but his own worries were making it hard for him to pay attention. He wondered whether he could make some ex-cuse and depart before too much longer; he had many reasons not to offend Pratiki, but he was surprised by how much the prince-templar was willing to talk. Viyeki began to long for silence.

"But you know how these things are, High Magister Viyeki!" said Pratiki. "What puffed-up fools some of our fellows are. What was it the poet said? 'My brains are in my purse / You can hear them clink / Silver is what I am / Silver is what I think.'"

Something about the words tickled at Viyeki's memory, but the conversation was interrupted by the silent entrance of one of the prince-templar's Hamakha guards. Once through the tent flap, the snake-helmeted soldier fell into mo-tionless attention, as though suddenly frozen by a gust of icy wind.

Pratiki gave a small nod. Formally invited to exist, the guard now made a gesture of apology. "Sacrifice General Kikiti wishes to enter your presence, Serenity."

"Send him in, of course," said Pratiki, but he shot Viyeki a quick look that almost seemed to say, "And here's one of the fools I was talking about."

If General Kikiti was a fool, Viyeki had to admit that he did not look the part; he was unusually tall and harshly handsome in the bony, beak-nosed way of some of the oldest families.

"You are welcome, General," said Pratiki as Kikiti kneeled before him. "Rise! I wish you good tidings on this Drukhi's Day. I hope you are free to take some wine with me later—we have much to discuss."

"I hear the queen in your voice," Kikiti replied, glancing briefly at Viyeki. The general did not look overjoyed to discover the magister and prince-templar talking together. "I would be honored, Serene Highness, and we do indeed have much to discuss. The remainder of our forces have now arrived and taken their positions. We are ready to begin our conquest of the mortal fortress."

Once again, Viyeki saw clearly what small importance Kikiti and the Singer Sogeyu and the rest gave him. Kikiti had not greeted him, and now he was announcing an attack on the mortals—essentially starting a new war—without even the pretense that Viyeki had anything to say about it or wielded any power whatsoever. The queen's orders to Viyeki were meaningless.

Meaningless. It was an arresting thought. *Did the queen lie? Is that even possible? Is it only that others bend or flout her words, or does she sometimes say things that are not true even while knowing they are not true?*

It was so shocking to consider that Viyeki felt almost light-headed. Despite his earlier promise to himself he took a long sip from his rock crystal goblet of cloudberry wine, and was relieved to feel his heartbeat slow as the drink worked its way through him like cold fire. "Your pardon, General Kikiti," he said suddenly, emboldened a little by the complicated taste of the wine and the reputed drops of *kei-mi* said to be put in each cask by the vintners of the Order of Gatherers. "You say the remainder of our forces have arrived. This is the first I've heard of this. May I ask where they come from and who commands them?"

"Of course you may ask, High Magister," said Kikiti in a tone that belied his words. "They were sent from the forts of the Northeastern Host, under the command of General Ensume."

"The Northeastern Host?" Viyeki had never heard of it. "And why did they not accompany us from the first?" He turned to the prince-templar. "I beg your pardon for this unseemly interruption, Serenity. Perhaps the general and I should have our conversation elsewhere. We shame ourselves by sullying your hospitality on this sacred day."

Pratiki looked amused again, and lifted his cup for a long, savoring sip. "No, by all means, continue, High Magister."

Kikiti now assumed an appearance of calm courtesy. "My officers and I have been watching the mortal fortress for some days. We decided we needed a greater force to ensure quick and complete success of the queen's mission."

Which meant no prisoners, Viyeki guessed—no mortals escaping the conquest to spread tales of the attack. Perhaps this Northeastern Host was a group of specially trained killers. "Ah," he said. "As expected, the Order of Sacrifice is full of foresight and wisdom." He rose and bowed to Pratiki. "Many thanks for the generosity of your time and counsel, Highness." Just to make Kikiti think, he added, "I will consider carefully what you said about the motives of some who claim to be trustworthy. Your words were instructive." He then turned and made a much smaller bow to Kikiti, emphasizing the difference in their nominal rank, even if it seemed to mean nothing here in the wilderness. "And good tidings to you on Drukhi's Day, Host General. Please give your officers my wishes for the queen's favor."

It was only when he had escaped the silken confines of Pratiki's tent and stood once more on the windy hillside, knee deep in waving grasses, that he realized why the prince-templar's earlier words had troubled him.

He quoted that bit of doggerel—"My brains are in my purse"—but it was written by Shun'y'asu, whose work is forbidden by the queen. Viyeki was not completely astounded. He knew that those in the highest families sometimes bent the queen's rules here and there as a symbol of their power and pride. But it seemed a strange thing for the prince templar to say to someone he did not know, someone he definitely had no need to impress by being daring. *I may be the high magister of an order, but compared to Pratiki I have no importance at all. My magistracy could be given to another this very day, and I doubt anyone in the Hamakha Clan would even notice. So why would Pratiki quote Shun'y'asu to me? Does he wish to make me think he is somehow an ally, or a potential ally? Is he trying to trick me into a traitorous remark? And if not, what other purpose could he have?*

It was even possible that the prince templar might have no purpose at all, might just be the sort of powerful noble who enjoyed flouting rules he considered petty, secure in the protection of his bloodline.

Viyeki stood, motionless and silent, and watched clouds silvered by the moon sail across the purple sky. Now that nightfall had made the Hikeda'ya army's movements all but invisible from the fortress across the valley, the hillside encampment was full of brisk but silent activity. Kikiti's Sacrifices were pulling down their shelters and removing all traces of their stay, a trait of Viyeki's race since the earliest years here in the new lands, when Viyeki's people had been few and dragons had been everywhere.

But then we only fought to protect ourselves. Then we fought only when we had to, so that we could keep our race alive. Now we seem to fight for something different. Is it only revenge we seek now? Does anyone in the queen's palace actually believe we can defeat the mortals?

But those questions had no answers. Viyeki returned to his own shelter and bade his secretary and servants gather up his things in preparation for whatever would happen next. He felt certain that if he waited for Kikiti and the rest to warn him they were departing, he would most likely rise from his next sleep to find himself alone on an empty hillside.

In the days that followed, Tzoja shared several more meals with the Hidden. The pollwag feast was not the least appetizing thing they served, but some foods she liked, especially the clump of white fungus strands called Cave Icicle. She preferred such things cooked, but because they did not make fires, everything Naya Nos' folk ate was cold and raw. Tzoja had dreams nearly every night about the joy of eating even dry, charred puju bread, but she had to admit the Hidden were doing their honorable best to make up for the destruction of her supplies by their hungry, roving young.

Over the course of several meals she also heard more of Naya Nos's stories, which all seemed to be about the history of the Hikeda'ya themselves, stories full of racial pride and a worship of purity that seemed to have nothing to do with the distorted creatures who listened so raptly to them. She also could not help wondering why the Hidden were here at all, living like wild animals so deep beneath the city.

"You tell so many fine stories of the People," she finally said to Naya Nos. "But there are many things I don't understand."

The childlike creature was enthroned in Dasa's broad lap so that he looked like a little king, and there was even a touch of condescension in his voice as he answered. "The stories are all true."

"I'm sure. But . . . are *you* the People?" She spread her hands to indicate all the strange creatures around them, gathered to share the story. "Are these stories about you?"

Though they never spoke to her, at least a few of the others could apparently understand Tzoja's Hikeda'ya speech, because they groaned. She was afraid she had said something insulting, but Naya Nos had a strange expression on his face—not anger, but a deep sadness.

"Alas," he said. "We are the Incomplete. We are the Ruined and the Misshapen—the mistakes. But with help from the Lord of Dreaming, someday we will be true men and women of the People, and on that day we will come out of hiding."

Tzoja had known since the first time that the Hidden were telling themselves a version of the Hikeda'ya's story, but they were too bizarrely misshapen to be Cloud Children, or even Tinukeda'ya. The changeling Ocean Children took many shapes, but as far as she knew, only the shapes into which they were bred. She had never seen any as grotesque as the Hidden. How had they been allowed to live?

They also talked of the Lord of Dreaming who would save them. That might be the queen's strange kinsman, Lord Jijibo, but what why would someone like him be revered by the broken and malformed Hidden? Why would he collect his people's deformed, despised children? Charity did not seem a likely answer.

Even with the Hidden's fairly regular contributions, Tzoja still had to find new ways to feed herself. She did not enjoy the taste of the mosses, lichens, or other plants that the Hidden gathered along the lake's edge, but by watching carefully and eating only what Naya Nos and his people ate she was seldom made sick. She even constructed a net out of an old rag she found in one of the festival cottage's bedchambers and managed to catch a few small fish with it. The first time, she was so hungry she gobbled them whole, but as days went on her fishing improved and she began taking them back to Viyeki's house. She carefully cleaned them outside, buried the entrails in the garden, then ate them raw with a little of the parchment-twist of salt that remained to her. At such moments she felt almost content.

Days and then weeks went by, the passage of time in this timeless place measured only by her daily visits to the distant water clock. She took some of her meals with the Hidden, but they were too strange to provide much companionship. Most of her days were spent in the secure darkness of the festival cottage instead, often in a half sleep full of dreams of other days, often about the place in Kwanitupul where she had spent her earliest years, or of her grandfather's wagon, more a prison than a home. She also dreamed of her time living with the Astalines, of the years of growing happiness there, and the single night of horror that had ended it.

At thirteen years of age and still with no name but Derra, she had run away from the Stallion Clan, from her dreadful old grandfather Fikolmij, his casual cruelties and his unwanted touch. It had meant leaving her mother as well, but the distance grown between them and Vorzheva's constant, angry misery had helped with the decision.

It had not been easy to get away from her grandfather's camp, and she had planned it from the First Green Moon to the Third—an entire spring. She picked out the gentlest horse in the paddock, a yearling named Sefstred, and began secretly feeding her bits of leftover food.

Stealing the horse was no small crime: her grandfather and the other clansmen regarded theft of their valuable stock as an attack on themselves, and if she was caught the very least she would receive was a brutal whipping. It was even possible she might be put to death, so when the night came for her to sneak out of the wagon and make her way to the paddock, Derra went as slowly and silently as honey dripping from a comb.

She had picked a night when she knew one of the laziest of the Stallion clansmen would be guarding the paddock, and as she had hoped, she found him sleeping. She did not know what terrible punishment his inattention earned him after her escape, and had never much cared. Nearly all the men of the Stallion Clan had treated her like a slave, and only the fact that she was the thane's granddaughter had protected her from being raped, but it had never stopped their leering and fondling.

She had made her way north on her stolen horse, fording the broad Umstrejha that ran along the forest fringe before turning west toward Erkynland; where she knew her father had been born, where his "ungrateful friends" (as her mother always termed them) lived in the great castle called the Hayholt.

She reached the capital city of Erchester at last, overwhelmed by its size, stink, and the constant, seemingly pointless bustling of its citizens, but the Hayholt castle guards turned her away from the gate each time she tried to enter.

The money she had made from selling Sefstred was running out, so she begged for a position at the inn where she was staying. She became the taverner's girl-of-all-work, and could have become his mistress too if she wanted, or filled that same position for any number of the inn's visitors. She was a handsome girl, and everybody who knew her seemed to agree—everybody except Derra herself, who did not like the strong, hawklike nose she had inherited from her mother. It seemed odd to her that in later years it was one of the things Viyeki always cited when he talked of her beauty—the most Hikeda'ya thing about her, he often said.

After a few months she was lured away from her tavern work and into the service of a wealthy fur merchant named Herwald, who hired her to act as a sort of ladies' maid and child nurse for his wife, a loud, vain, proudly ignorant, but often kind woman named Leola. Derra spent many months in their employ, and they even took her on one of their trips to Rimmersgard to buy furs at a market town named Hudstad. Traveling in the north was an overwhelming experience: she had never seen heavy snow or mountains, except from a very great distance, and could not imagine how anyone could live in such a cold, forbidding place—though she would find out soon enough.

The merchant Herwald suffered a terrible loss when he bought a load of what he thought were illicit young fox skins, then discovered after they had traveled miles from the market that he had bought only a few actual fox skins, the layer on top, and that the rest were the dyed pelts of rats and other vermin. Herwald might not have discovered the swindle until he was back in Erkynland, but a rainstorm washed off the dye, and the wagon shed a continuous stream of red into the roadway until a rider who had come upon them from behind warned them that something in their wagon was dripping a great deal of blood.

Herwald was alternately furious and weepy about how he had been tricked, but it was too late to do anything: the traders he had bought from were not bonded guildsmen and would be long gone with their takings. At the next inn he sold Derra, without even telling her, to a trio of fur traders arriving late for the same market and in a hurry to get rid of their wares in the few remaining days.

The fur traders, thick-bearded, uncommonly silent men from Vindirthorp in the east of Rimmersgard, worked her hard and fed her little, but at least did not molest her. That was probably because they were all related to each other somehow, and Derra was a joint purchase—an investment. One of them had brought his wife and young child along on the journey, and the wife was ill and too weak to care for the child. There was more to the story than Derra ever learned but the wife told her some of it during the moments when she felt well enough to converse: the traders were grim men from the stoniest outer lands, places where dragons and vicious trolls still roamed, and they did not waste their masculine conversation on women and servants.

But after Derra had been with them little more than a sennight, the wife let slip that the trading brothers were preparing to return to distant Vindirthorp and that Derra would go back with them.

The idea of becoming a kitchen slave again for men not very different from her grandfather and his fellow clansmen terrified her, so on the night before they were planning to depart she ran away.

The people of Hudstad were no more or less charitable than other Aedonites, but most of them were poor and there was no work to be had now that the market had ended. Derra received a few crusts of bread and spent two nights out of the snow in the chilly, wooden church, but it was a suggestion from the church's sexton that truly saved her. He told her of what he called "a nunnery" just outside the town; he called it Saint Asta's.

It took Derra most of a blustering winter day to make her way there, and by the time she arrived at the old sprawling farmhouse she was half-dead from cold and shivering too much to talk. Several women, some young, some old, but all dressed in simple shifts, brought her to the large kitchen where a fire leaped and crackled. After she had been given a cup of hot broth, which tasted like liquid white magic to the cold and hungry young woman, she was given a simple linen shift of her own, a wool blanket, and a place to sleep for the night.

The last thing they told her after showing her to an empty bed in a chamber where several other women were also sleeping was that the helpful sexton had been wrong: they were not nuns. "It's true we Astalines are an order," one of the older women explained. "But we have no religious practice, and we are not part of Mother Church."

Just to be on the safe side Derra murmured as many prayers as she could remember, Aedonite and Thrithings and even a charm against She Who Waits To Take All Back, learned from a neighbor in Kwanitupul, before sleep dragged her down into healing darkness.

In the morning, after a simple breakfast shared with several dozen other women, all talking quietly but merrily, she was taken to meet the founder of the order. Valada Roskva was a windburned woman of some seventy years, round and sharp-eyed, her short hair mostly hidden by a simple linen coif. She looked the newcomer up and down and asked her name.

"Derra, Mistress."

"Derra." Roskva nodded and smiled. "Star. I knew you were coming, but I didn't know who you were! Now I know."

Derra didn't know how to reply to this.

"Well, child, are you on a journey? Have you been hurt or attacked? Or have you simply lost your way?"

Derra had to think about that for a moment. She had set out to find her father, or so she had told herself. But she had also fled from the Stallion Clan and her mother, then let life sweep her on and on, away from any chance of finding him.

"Lost my way, I think," she said at last.

"Well, you have found something, at any rate." Roskva made a sound that from a younger, less important woman might have been a giggle. "You are definitely somewhere now. Would you like to stay?"

"Yes. Oh, yes!" She did not have to think about it. She had seen very little kindness since her father had left them and had not realized until now how much she had been aching for it. "Yes, Valada Roskva. I will work very hard if I can stay. I am a very good worker."

The old woman smiled again. "Call me Roskva. 'Valada' is a title, and I don't necessarily agree with it, either." This time she laughed, although again Derra did not understand why. "You and I will talk again. Now go and tell Agnida—the woman who brought you to me—that you are staying with us for a while, and she will take you under her wing."

She knew almost nothing about the order she was joining, and the more she saw the more questions she had, but she never doubted her choice and never had reason to.

Derra lived with the Astalines for several years, learned much about the arts of healing and weaving, and eventually had most of her questions answered. Two hundred years earlier a Nabbanai noblewoman named Asta of Turonis had renounced her vows and left the convent where she had lived much of her life. But instead of marrying, or otherwise doing what would make her family happy, Asta had devoted her life to making sanctuaries for women. The first Astaline house was outside a remote village in Nabban, but by the time of the founder's death, a dozen such houses had sprung up all over the country—even one in the heart of the city at the base of the Redenturine Hill.

The order had grown in the years since, spreading across Erkynland and Warinsten and even parts of Rimmersgard and Hernystir. Roskva's house had been one of the first in the far north, and the women there had come from all over Rimmsergard. They grew most of their own food, but the bulk of their income came from weaving: when Derra first saw the great barn full of looms she was astounded by how many there were—at least two dozen, she guessed—all clacking away as the Astalines worked.

She had never imagined that such a thing could be—women living together without having to ask anything of men. It set her thinking in a way that had never ended, making her consider things she had never considered before. In the end, although the Astalines helped keep her alive and even to heal her heart—which she had not known was broken—the most significant thing her time with them gave her was the understanding that things could be different than expected, that even what seemed as unalterable as a mountain could change.

★　　★　　★

It all ended, of course, on the worst night of her life.

The Astalines had lived near Hudstad for long enough that the people of the market village thought no more about them than they would have a true religious order. The villagers came to the Astalines sometimes when they were ill, or when they needed advice on medicaments for their livestock or children, and of course the farmers brought the wool of their sheep to be made into cloth. A few villagers talked darkly from time to time of "those women" and even whispered about witchcraft—people in this part of Rimmersgard were very religious—but they had eyed the balance and had seen the good that the Astalines did. And there was also the money their weaving brought.

Thus, when Derra and the others were awakened late one Novander night by screams that the house was on fire and armed men were inside the retreat, the Astalines were caught by surprise. But the shouting, ax-wielding men were not townsfolk but Skalijar—bandits.

Derra never found out if the raid had been prompted by something—the Skalijar were pagans and had attacked Aedonite convents and monasteries before—or was simply an assault on a weak target. It hardly mattered. By the time Derra made her way out of the house many younger Astalines were being dragged off by their hair and thrown across the saddles of the invaders. Some of the older women tried to save them, but were all killed.

Derra fled toward the nearest trees, moving from shadow to shadow as cautiously as she could. The last thing she saw of the place where she had lived so long and so contentedly was the roof blazing high above the house where Valada Roskva's chambers lay, then falling inward in leaping flames and a whirlwind of sparks.

Her caution ultimately did her no good. She was caught within an hour by bandits following the prints of her bare feet in the snow, then snatched up and dumped across a saddle like her Astaline sisters.

She could remember little of the month she spent in the Skalijar camp in the largely deserted western reaches of Rimmersgard, but that was intentional: when she did recall things, every memory was colored in gray and black and blood red. She was raped by several of the bandits and treated as the lowliest of slaves. She was given picked bones to gnaw on and little else, and beaten without reason.

Derra was so desperate during that time, so overwhelmed by hopeless horror, that she planned making one last escape, this time by hanging herself from a rope fashioned from her ragged dress, but was prevented when a Hikeda'ya outland patrol discovered the bandits' camp. The battle was terrible, mostly silent except for the screams of mortally wounded Skalijar, but so much blood flowed that by moonlight the snow of the campsite looked more black than white.

The Norns were the strangest people Derra had ever seen, immortal creatures she knew only from her father's stories. The dead-faced soldiers carried her and the other captive women back to Nakkiga, all of them bound for the slave pens. As she was marched through the mountain's vast, bronze-hinged gates and into the dark city beyond, a prisoner of far more terrible captors than even the murderous Skalijar, a single leaden thought went through her mind, over and over:

Nothing good can happen in a place like this. Nothing—not ever. My life is ended.
But, astonishingly, that did not turn out to be true.

15

Among the Grasslanders

Sergeant Levias cut the last Erkynguard badge from his surcoat, leaving a strange array of darker patches on the cloth. Before pulling his outer clothes on he wiped dirt and mud across to make himself look more like the kind of masterless soldier who would be wandering the fringes of the great Thrithings gathering.

Porto made a few holes in his own garments, then removed the Tree and Dragons emblem. "I hate to do this," he said sadly. "It was a proud day when I first took the High Throne's service."

Levias didn't need to add much dirt. His face and whiskers well demonstrated the effects of a many days traveling and sleeping rough across the meadows of the High Thrithings. "You are still in service, never fear," he said, flicking a bit of mud from his beard. "We are still the High Throne's men. But now we are spies and must go unmarked."

Porto eyed his comrade's waist, which he thought just a little too portly to belong to a supposedly impoverished mercenary, but said nothing. He had grown fond of the Erkynlander in their time together. It occurred to him that in recent years he had kept company with almost no one but the knights Astrian and Olveris—and Prince Morgan, of course—and had forgotten how to do much beside drink and listen to their jests. Jests of which Porto himself was usually the butt, although he did not mind too badly: after years of loneliness following the death of his wife and child, he had been happy to find any companions at all, and he did not believe that even Astrian's cruellest jibes were anything worse than rough barracks humor.

By God, were I to shun everyone who has ever mocked my height, my figure, or my drinking, I would have to go a-hermit in some deep forest.

Thinking of deep forests reminded him of the lost prince, and Porto felt a stab of fear. *I pray you Lord Usires, our Ransomer, help the trolls find Morgan safe and bring him back to the king and queen.*

He and the sergeant had halted to improve their disguises atop one of the hills that hemmed Blood Lake on the east. From where they stood they could see a great throng of humanity reduced to the size of fleas as they milled on the valley floor, a city with no walls or permanent buildings.

"They are so many clansmen!" Porto said. "Who would ever have guessed?"

"Anyone who fought in the war against them," Levias answered, now rubbing his dirty hands on his sleeves. "I did not, but I heard my father's stories."

"Your father was a soldier?"

"Like me, yes. An Erkynguard, too, and proud to be one. He and his fellows held the line before the Ymstrecca when the grasslanders thought they had won—hundreds of horsemen sweeping down, screeching like demons, but the brave Tree and Dragons held firm. The Thrithings-men almost captured King Simon during that battle, you know. But did you not fight? You are, if you will pardon me saying so, more than of an age."

Porto shook his head. "I fought grasslanders, yes, but I was in the south then, warring for Varellan, Saluceris's father. We were sent against the southern Thrithings-men along our border and had many a battle, I can promise you. They told us we would catch the pony-riders from behind and pinch them between us and the Erkynlanders. Later I began to think we were only helping Varellan to drive back the clansmen along the Nabbanai border, and the rebellion in the north never even knew of our fight."

"Such things are beyond me," said Levias cheerfully. "I go where I am told and do what they bid me, and of course trust in God. The plans of kings and ministers are beyond me."

But those plans of kings and ministers are why men like us live or die, Porto thought. He was still bitter toward Varellan, though the Nabbanai duke was years dead. A thousand soldiers from Perdruin had marched out under Varellan's banner, but less than half had returned home afterward, sacrificed to protect the lands of Nabbanai noblemen. It had been one of the things that drove him north to King Simon and Queen Miriamele, who at least seemed interested in protecting all their people and not only the rich ones.

Levias wiped his knife on his breeks, then examined himself in the reflection on the blade. "Well, we look like proper outlaws now. Shall we go down and join them in their merrymaking?"

"Is that all this gathering is? A festival?"

Levias slipped his knife back into its sheath. "I told you, I know little beyond what I have heard. Every year the clans join together here at this lake, next to these hills they hold sacred. They trade with outsiders, barter between themselves for brides and horses, settle disputes, and sacrifice to their savage gods. It is the only time they come together, except when one of their great chiefs dies—a 'Shan,' as they are called. But grasslanders have not had such a leader for many years, not even in the last war. That is why we need not worry about their numbers. The only thing the Thrithings thanes hate worse than us city folk is other thanes. They do mischief to each other constantly, and each thane has more blood feuds than a hound has ticks. Now, come, Sir Porto." He shouldered his bag and began to lead his horse down the narrow, winding trail. "It is not the grasslander thanes we need to think about now, but Count Eolair."

Porto followed, doing his best to ignore the ache in his knees each time he took a step downhill. Thinking about Eolair was all well and good, but that would not make it any easier to find him here in the midst of thousands of city-hating grasslanders.

"My God," whispered Levias, startled once again into taking a holy name in vain, "did you see that one? Half her bubs are on show! I thought the horse-riders kept their women hidden in their wagons."

Porto had also turned to watch the broad-hipped Thrithings-woman who had just passed them, fascinated as much by her confident stride as by her ample cleavage. "Perhaps she is trying to find a husband."

"I hear they sometimes take more than one wife, these grassland men." Levias leaned close, since they were surrounded on all sides by the objects of their discussion. The sides of the muddy track were lined with wagons, some modest, some as opulent as wheeled palaces, and many of the large ones had makeshift paddocks full of horses, cattle, and other animals. "It seems to flout the Lord's will," Levias said. "I wonder what my wife, God rest her, would have thought of sharing me with another woman."

"There is enough of you to go around, I think."

Levias stared at him. "A jest!" he said, and grinned. "Porto the Dour has made a jest. Not a good one, but still . . ." His attention was distracted by a large wagon rumbling down the center of the track, driven by a grimacing, full-bearded man who clearly did not care whether he ran them over or not. Levias and Porto scrambled to get out of the way but could not avoid being splashed by mud from the wheels.

"We could simply have waited and let these cursed wagons make our disguises," Levias said, wiping the worst of it from his knees and shins.

"Where do you think the bandits might be?" asked Porto.

"That is what we must discover. I have not the least idea."

It was not going to be easy, that at least seemed clear. They were in a teeming and temporary city neither of them had ever visited. Campsites extended as far as Porto could see, from the base of the hills to the far end of the lake and all around its shore, with haphazard tracks wandering between them, some merely the ruts left by a few wheels, others broad, deep swathes of mud as wide as Main Row back in Erchester. Smoke from countless cooking fires hung low, making Porto's eyes water. In places it was so thick on this mostly windless day that camps more than a dozen paces away were all but invisible.

Another stinging insect landed on Porto's hand. He smashed it, rubbing it onto his shirt where it left a little smear of blood—not his own, he hoped. The winged vermin were everywhere here beside the lake, massive horseflies, mosquitoes, and other nasty things he did not think he had ever seen before. As he stared in disgust at the insect's remains, he was startled by the sound of shouting close by, but it was only two clansmen wrestling in the mud and punching at each other while spectators hurried toward them, shouting and jeering louder than the angry combatants.

"Wherever Count Eolair may be, we must find him quickly," he said. "I do not like this place." A family with a small, open cart trudged past them in the opposite direction. The children on the cart stared at the two outlanders as though they had never seen anything like them, their expressions not so much curious as openly mistrustful. "We are in the middle of ten thousand enemies."

Levias said, "The Book of the Aedon tells us, 'Even when I am in the midst of my foes, I will keep Your name in my heart, O my lord, Keeper of the Heavenly Garden, and I will be well.'"

Porto said nothing. He knew from long experience that when men with swords and axes came for you, God's name in your heart was not enough to keep you safe. The deaths of far too many godly men had proved that to him.

As they followed the wide, muddy track that served as the road around the northern side of the lake, the wagons jostled so close to each other and the paths were so full of different kinds of people that it seemed to Porto even more like a city. He saw dark-skinned Wrannamen, some with wagons as ostentatious as the clansmen's, while others carried everything they owned, including their trade goods, on their backs. Many had families trailing behind, and even the smallest children carried burdens as big as they were. Each time Porto saw someone who looked to be neither a native grasslander nor one of the Wrannaman traders; he watched carefully to see where they came from and where they were going. He knew that it was not only grassland bandits who came to the Thanemoot, but also fighters and troublemakers from all over Osten Ard, many fleeing from the law. These sold their swords to various Thrithings clans, both those who had plans to overrun their neighbors and those who feared it being done to them. The work never lasted long, since the feuding season was limited, but for the dregs and mercenaries of the surrounding nations, it was a way to make money, to stay alive.

Something we all need, Porto admitted to himself. *What have I done that was different, except stay with the lords who paid me to go a-soldiering? A few more nights being caught drunk, or away from my post—God forgive me, there were many times I could have become a lordless knight, especially during my dark years—and I would be here too, begging for work as a sell-sword. A very weary old sell-sword.*

But he was not. Instead, he was the one watching. Traders from Nabban seemed to stay almost entirely in the areas that were clearly meant as markets, The seamier outlanders, many with the scarred look of fighters, were concentrated at the eastern end of the lake, beneath the very hills Porto and his companion had just descended.

"Had we known that when we started, we would not be walking all the way around this cursed lake," Levias said, wiping sweat from his eyes. Porto ignored him, looking toward the lake's western end—the clansmen's end—and nearby hills the sergeant had told him of that morning, crowned with an old stone the grasslanders called the Silent One, and it was their holiest place.

On the lake shore beneath the western hills stood the biggest compound of all, full of wagons, people, and more animals than Porto could count. A pair of Nabbanai traders walking nearby were discussing it, and Porto heard enough to learn that this was the camp of Rudur Redbeard, thane of the Black Bear Clan and much of the Middle Thrithings, the closest thing the Thrithings had to a ruler.

Perhaps Eolair is in there, Porto thought, *just a short distance from where we stand. Binabik said he was likely taken by bandits coming to the Thanemoot separately from the clansmen, but who could know that from a few tracks? And even if the troll was right, might his captors not take the count to this Rudur to buy favor with him?*

But another look at the two dozen large men guarding the camp, all armed, suggested that if Eolair was held there they had little chance of freeing him.

And that is if he is still alive. Porto felt overwhelmed by their mission. It hadn't occurred to him how many grasslanders would be at the gathering, how dangerous a place it was for two soldiers of Erkynland.

As they passed the front of the Black Bear Clan's sprawling camp, Porto saw that people were gathering along its lakeside fences like spectators waiting for a parade. "Look at all these folk," he told Levias. "Do you think they might be gathered to see Count Eolair brought to this Thane Redbeard? Not that we could do anything if that's the case."

"Perhaps," said Levias. "Let's find a safer place and see what happens. At least we'll know where he is."

To Porto's eye the swelling crowd did not have the look of people expecting violence so much as excitement of some less deadly kind, although it was hard to tell for certain with Thrithings clansmen, who were even more fond of rough sport and rough punishment than were city folk. Neither Porto nor Levias spoke the grassland tongue, although Porto retained a few words from his days fighting along the borders of the Lake Thrithings. However, there were enough outlanders in the crowd who spoke Nabbanai and Westerling: soon Porto understood that a meeting or parley was happening—that Rudur had summoned one of the other clan chieftains, perhaps to reward him, perhaps to chastise him.

The sun disappeared in a red blaze behind the hills, and a shudder of excitement ran through the crowd.

"You are tall, but not so big!" someone shouted in Nabbanai. Jeers began, but Porto could not make out their target at first. Then he saw, approaching the Black Bear compound, the dark-haired head bobbing along the track above the watching crowd. The man was pale for a grasslander, but he dressed like a headman in furs and bone necklaces, and his posture suggested that he cared not at all what the crowd might be shouting. A dozen other riders followed behind him, most wearing the insignia of the Stallion Clan, the High Thrithings' most powerful, with a few others from clans Porto did not recognize. All of them had weapons, but kept them in sheath or belt as they approached the gate.

A young man riding beside the leader stood up in his stirrups and called something to the guards on the other side of the heavy wooden gate. After a moment the gate opened, then the Black Bear clansmen on the far side parted to let in the tall, dark-haired man and his company. The newcomers made their way across the grass toward where the largest wagon and the colorful tents that surrounded it stood at the back of the compound.

"He'll be put in his place, you wait and see," someone said in Nabbanai. "Rudur lets no one get too high-flown but himself."

Porto turned to look at the men behind him, a threesome dressed in dirty robes that had probably been spotless before the marketing trip began.

"Who was that who passed?" he asked the bearded man who had spoken. "The Stallion Clan leader."

The merchant gave him a quiet, suspicious look, but said, "He is named Unver—a thane of the northern clans who has ambition to be more than that. Apparently he has made a name for himself, and Rudur wants to meet him face to face." The man squinted in the near-darkness. "And who are you, friend? I don't recognize you."

"Sell-swords," Porto told him. "Looking for work."

"We might have need of such ourselves." The merchant looked them over. "Though I must say you are not the most impressive mercenaries I've encountered. You, sir, are very old, and your companion is a bit fat. You cannot expect full wage, either of you."

Levias stirred. "What are they saying?"

"They want to hire us," Porto reported, half-amused.

"Tell them we don't need their stinking work." Levias apparently spoke enough Nabbanai to recognize the word 'fat.'

"My companion thanks you for the offer, but we have already been hired," Porto said. "But one more question, please. Why would so many people gather to see one thane come to meet Rudur? It must happen often at such a gathering as this."

"Not really," said the merchant, and he looked around in a way that was almost furtive. "This one, this Unver—there are people who say he is the Shan returned."

Porto had heard the title before—it meant a great king, a thane over all thanes. "And is he?"

"Aedon preserve us." The bearded merchant made the Sign of the Tree on his breast, very broadly and emphatically, and his round face looked genuinely troubled. "We had better pray he isn't or all our cities will burn."

Frustrated and in increasingly sour temper, Eolair pulled his cloak tighter around his shoulders and leaned toward the fire. He was grateful it was summer, but he was no longer used to sleeping on the ground and his craven old flesh and brittle bones were letting him know it. Also, the stinging creatures that lived around the lake seemed to carry a personal grudge against him. Worst of all, with his wrists tied it was difficult to scratch the bites. A little conversation seemed the only thing that might distract him from all these woes, but deep-bearded Hotmer was not much of a talker.

"So why is it so interesting that Rudur Redbeard is meeting someone?" Eolair asked again, since he hadn't received a reply the first time.

A large number of Agvalt's bandit company were away from the camp that evening, pursuing whatever pleasures the Thanemoot and their purses could provide. Several had gone off toward Rudur's Bear Clan camp at the base of the sacred hills because of rumors about Redbeard and the new thane of the Stallion Clan.

Hotmer took a long drink from his skin bag before offering it to Eolair, who managed to suck down a draught despite the clumsiness of his bound wrists. "Not interesting," the outlaw said, then considered for a long, silent time before adding, "I hate those people."

It took Eolair a moment to understand. "The Thrithings-folk? But are you not one of them?"

Hotmer made an angry sound. "Not of the clans, me. Not of the Gadrinsett city-folk either."

Eolair put that aside for a moment. "But who is this Enver and why is everyone talking about him?"

His companion spat into the fire and watched it sizzle. "Unver, not Enver. Because some say he is the Shan."

Eolair had heard that word, but not for a long time, not since his youth. "Some kind of war leader?"

"God-chosen. Meant to bring all the tribes together. They say the signs follow him like birds behind a farmer sowing corn." He took a breath, then tilted the skin back and had another swig. "But it's all shit."

It was more than what he could usually wring out of Hotmer. "It sometimes seems to me that the gods cannot be as busy in our lives as we would like to think them," Eolair offered. "Do they really listen to every prayer? Do they grant one man's requests but deny another's? My people say the gods argue and even fight among themselves sometimes, just as men do. Do you think that is so?"

"Don't know. Don't care." Hotmer fell silent, brooding on thoughts of his own, and would not speak any more. Eolair was just about to drag himself to his sleeping spot in the center of the camp when the chieftain Agvalt wandered up, clearly just returned from somewhere in which liquor was in ample supply. The fair-haired young bandit stopped, grinning, and looked down on the two men.

"Did you keep the fire warm for me, Mother?" he asked Hotmer. "Did you cook me some cakes on the hot stones?"

Hotmer said nothing. The chieftain turned to Eolair. "Here. Give me your hands."

The count didn't trust the man's drunken mood, and was anyway slow to rise these days, which angered Agvalt. "By the burnt fingers of Tasdar, be swift about it, man! You make me regret doing you a kindness."

When he at last presented his hands, Agvalt worked the knot loose and let the rope fall from Eolair's wrists. "There. We don't want your hands to turn black and fall off, do we? Not if we want to get the most gold for you we can. Go on, rub the blood back into them. This freedom won't last long."

"Nevertheless, I thank you." His hands felt as if they were being poked by invisible needles.

"If you want to show gratitude, do nothing to make me regret it. I would prefer to ransom you whole, but that's not the only way it could happen. Do we understand each other?"

"We do."

But Agvalt remained, swaying a little. "I have just seen the so-called Shan," he announced. "He marched into Rudur's camp with a dozen Stallions, arrogant as you please. He is a fool. Rudur will eat him like a spring lamb and throw away the bones."

"You don't believe he's the Shan?"

Agvalt turned his slightly unfocused attention back to Eolair. "When has anyone calling themselves the Shan ever been one?"

"I have heard tales of a man who once united the clans."

"You mean Edizel. Yes, he was called Shan." Agvalt belched, then wiped his mouth with his fist. "He died back in my great-great-great grandfather's day—killed by his own son and guards after another lost war against the stone-dwellers. What kind of Shan is that?" Agvalt belched again. "Now give me your hands, Count of Nad Wherever, and I will tie you again so you won't get up to any mischief." He turned his slightly bleary gaze toward Hotmer. "He is your responsibility, Stallion-man."

Hotmer made a noise of distaste. "They are not my clan."

"Then, man, you are lucky to have found such fine companions as us. It is dangerous on the grasslands without someone to guard your back." Agvalt slapped Hotmer on the shoulder, hard enough to make him grunt again, grinned unpleasantly at Eolair, then made his unsteady way across the camp.

16

The Two Sancellans

His Sacredness Vidian II, Lector of the Aedonite
Church, was a small man a decade older than Miriamele. He had a cheerful
smile, but he seemed to use it as a porpentine used its quills, to keep others at
a safe distance. Vidian might have been mistaken for a moderately successful
shopkeeper if not for his expensive robes, intricately embroidered in silver and
gold. Here in his own apartments deep in the Sancellan Aedonitis, the lector
also wore a black skullcap instead of one of his tall hats, to add to the pretence,
Miri supposed, that this was merely a meeting of old friends who just happened
to be two of the most powerful people in Osten Ard.

"I'm so pleased we are having this chance to talk, Your Majesty," Vidian
said, petting the creature on his lap, which was largely hidden in the folds of
his heavy robes. "It is good to see you again in happier circumstances."

Miriamele tried to smile but could not quite manage it. Seven years ago,
Lector Vidian had come to Erkynland for John Josua's funeral, and although
she had been grateful for his presence then, it was not a good memory. "It
pleases me too, Sacred Father," she managed at last. "I only wish we had a longer time to spend together today."

"Ah, yes, of course, the wedding." Vidian rearranged the lump of fur and fat
on his lap, now revealed to be some sort of very small bulldog with protuberant
eyes and a jutting lower jaw. "We wish we could be there, don't we, Fraxi?" He
looked up and saw Miri staring at the dog. "His formal name is Ferax because
he is so fierce." He smiled and scratched the dog's underslung chin. "In any
case, I am very sad I cannot attend today's festivities, but my infirmity prevents
it." He gestured to his swollen left foot, propped on a cushion. "*Podegris*, the
learned men call it, but everyone else knows it as 'gout.' Please do not think it
is from excessive drink, Majesty. You may ask Escritor Auxis if you doubt
me—I am abstemious, like a flower that drinks only water."

Miri knew that his infirmity was not Vidian's true reason for avoiding
the wedding of Earl Drusis and Turia Ingadaris. The lector's connections to
the bride's uncle Dallo were well known, so the lector wanted to keep at
least a nominal distance between himself and a ceremony that benefited the

Ingadarines far more than the Benidrivines. She said, "I do not doubt you are disappointed, Sacredness."

"But surely, Your Majesty, you do not have to leave yet? You have a coach, do you not? Dallo's estate is but a short ride. Let me have Father Fino bring up more wine—at least for you. It pleases me to see someone else, at least, enjoy the things that I am denied."

Like burying a child? Miri wondered, shocking herself with her own sudden anger. Where had that blaze of fury come from? Vidian was no saint, but he was no monster either, and he had seemed genuinely sad at John Josua's death. She covered her discomposure by patting her lips with a napkin. "I would like to, Your Sacredness, but I am afraid I cannot stay. The hour tolled some time ago, and I must leave soon."

"Of course, as you wish." He seemed disappointed. He lifted his own cup, sipped, and made a rueful face. "Sage water is not really a man's beverage, I have to say. But I suspect God means to keep me humble, using my illness to remind me nothing stands firm on His Earth without Him holding it up." As if to make up for his own deprivation, the lector offered a crust of bread to Fraxi. The bulldog's eyes bulged so grotesquely as he swallowed that Miri actually feared they might pop loose.

"I truly must leave soon," she said again. Vidian nodded and smiled, but began a story about how Fraxi had wickedly barked at the lector's secretary, startling the man so badly that he knocked over an inkwell.

Miriamele had grown up the daughter of a prince, and now she was queen. She did not often worry about making others wait for her, but the wedding of Drusis and Turia Ingadaris was not only important, it was fraught with dangerous ill-feelings as well. Miriamele was beginning to wonder if Vidian might be making her late on purpose.

Another strange idea, she told herself. *Only back in Nabban a short while, and I am seeing plots everywhere.*

Somewhere high above them, the bell in St. Tunato's tower tolled the half hour, but Lector Vidian chattered on like a jay on a branch.

Jesa had not felt so excited and terrified at the same time since she held Blasis after Canthia had given birth to him. She was full of anticipation for the wedding, thrilled to be part of it and pleased to know that after the main feast she and the other servants would be given a fine meal of their own. But she was frightened to be in Count Dallo's great house, a walled stronghold full of soldiers clad in the Ingadaris Stormbird livery. Still, though she might be surrounded by the duke's enemies, Jesa told herself that nothing bad would be allowed to happen to the duchess or any of her company while they were guests in the count's own home.

The retiring room was crowded with the flower of the Benidrivine nobility, all but Duke Saluceris himself, who had gone north to visit the family estates in Ardivalis. It seemed strange to Jesa that the duke would not attend his own brother's wedding, no matter what differences they might have, but she knew Saluceris to be a wise, fair-minded man, so she assumed it must be for the best. Certainly the duke was not frightened of anything that might happen here, or he would not have allowed his own wife and their two children to attend.

Silly girl, she told herself. *Remember, Queen Miriamele will be here too—the queen of all the lands! Nothing bad will happen.* But the queen had not yet arrived after her visit to the lector at the Sancellan Aedonitis, and Duchess Canthia was becoming fretful.

"I promised I would wait for her," the duchess said. "Where can she be? Why would His Sacredness even invite her on a day when so much else is happening?" She waved away one of her ladies who was trying to reattach the veil of her hat, which had fallen across the right side of Canthia's face in a very odd and distracting way. "Not now, Mindia!" she said. "Blasis, you stay here with your sister and Jesa. I do not want to see your clothes spoiled before the wedding even begins."

The boy gave her a look of supreme disgust, but edged closer to Jesa and Serasina. Jesa did not get to see much of the duke's son—his care had been given over almost entirely to male tutors—but she was fond of him, although she had to admit he was terribly spoiled. She knew that back in Red Pig Lagoon Blasis would have been dropped off the rooftop into the water a few times by now for making such faces.

"By our good Lady, there she is!" said Canthia, on her tiptoes as she looked out the window and across the front of the great house. She turned and hurried to take a seat, then composed herself until she seemed as calm as if she had not moved for the last hour, which Jesa knew was quite the opposite of the truth.

The queen swept in, surrounded by several ladies in waiting and trailed by a pair of soldiers in Erkynguard livery.

"I swear that in all the years since I was crowned and married I did not ride in as many carriages as I have here in Nabban." She had already thrown off her cloak. "Forgive me, Duchess. I fear you'll have to wait longer still—the street cobbles have knocked my hair and cap askew. I am in a wretched condition."

As Canthia's ladies joined in to help the queen repair herself, little Serasina awoke and began fussing quietly. She was hungry, but the duchess had sent her wetnurse off on some other mission, so Jesa moistened her finger and slipped it into the baby's mouth in place of a nipple. She hoped the nurse came back soon, because nobody would want to hear a baby crying during a wedding. In the Wran it was quite ordinary during any celebration, but the Nabbanai seemed almost to think of it as bad luck.

Jesa looked down at Serasina and gave the child a kiss on her small, round forehead. How could such a precious thing ever bring anything but good luck?

"I beg pardon for keeping you waiting, Duchess," Miriamele said as the ladies buzzed about her like bees around a patch of clover. "I kept saying, 'Sacred Father, there is the matter of the wedding . . .' and he kept saying, 'Of course, of course. Do you know, I officiated at Count Dallo's marriage? It's a shame I couldn't do the same for his niece, but my foot, you know . . .' and on and on. I thought he would never let me go." But Jesa thought the queen's expression suggested a deeper discontent than merely being bored by the lector.

"His Sacredness does like to talk." Canthia tried to keep her voice light, but it was clear she was anxious to get downstairs. "Is all well now, Majesty? Shall we go?"

Queen Miriamele surveyed Canthia in her pale blue wedding finery, then glanced down at her own deep green dress and frowned. "I look like a pine tree," she said. "But I feel fairly certain there is no law saying that a pine tree cannot be queen, so off we go."

Queen Miriamele went first, preceded only by two guards and their captain, the stiff-backed, serious-looking young northerner Jesa had heard called Sir Jurgen. Behind them came Duchess Canthia and her closest friends and kin, followed by several more of the queen's guards and the rest of both women's ladies in waiting. Sir Jurgen, who had clearly worked hard since his arrival a few hours earlier to learn the estate's every twist and turn, led the sizable company through the large manor house. From one of the wide windows on the lower floor, propped all the way open to let in the warmth and light of a splendid summer afternoon, they could see the rest of the guests already assembled in Count Dallo's fine gardens. Jesa could even make out young Turia Ingadaris, waiting under an arbor with Escritor Auxis in his golden robes. She thought the bride seemed little more than a child, slender and small.

"All the saints be praised," she heard the duchess say quietly behind her, "they have not started without us."

"They would not dare," said the queen. "After I bumped over cobblestones all the way to get here, I would have their heads off if they did!" Despite the monstrousness of the remark, Jesa was still not entirely certain the queen was jesting. She did not sound as if she was.

The company made their way down a narrow, winding staircase and into an open arcade between one part of Dallo's sprawling house and another. Stairs descended from either side of the arcade, one set leading to a path on the right that Jesa thought must connect to the front of the house, the other leading down into the lush greenery of the count's garden. The baby was beginning to complain again in Jesa's arms, and when Queen Miriamele suddenly stopped just at the top of the garden stairs and raised one hand, Jesa was certain that she was about to be scolded. But Sir Jurgen turned—he had already gone several steps downward—and mounted back up in an instant to stand beside the queen, one hand on his sword hilt.

"Majesty?" he said. "What—?"

"Soft," she said. "Someone is coming."

Jurgen tilted his head as the duchess, the rest of the guards, and the ladies-in-waiting bumped to a clumsy halt behind them.

"Your Majesty," asked one of the her ladies, "why do we stop?"

"Be quiet." Queen Miriamele still held her hand upright, like a priest blessing a crowd, but her face looked suddenly drawn, even weary. "I heard the sounds of swords rattling."

Everyone could hear the noise of feet now, and it was all Jesa could do to stay silent and clutch little Serasina to her breast, but her heart was beating so fast that she feared the baby must feel it.

A group of men came around the corner from the front side of the house, at least a dozen or more headed for the stairs and the arcade where the queen and others had stopped. They were an unruly-looking crew, clearly dressed for a fight—several carried swords, and the rest had clubs and short, nasty-looking spears. Jesa's heart seemed to scramble up her throat until it blocked her breathing.

"Behind me, Majesty," said Jurgen.

The queen ignored him. *"Stop!"* she called out in a voice so loud that it startled little Serasina into a moment of breath-holding silence, then a shocked wail.

The interlopers, who had just seen that the arcade was full of people, had slowed anyway, but at the queen's single word they halted.

"Out of the way!" cried one of them, a dark-bearded man with eyes bright under bony brows.

"Majesty," said Sir Jurgen under his breath, but the queen did not even look at him.

"Gentlemen, I do not see your invitations to this celebration," she said loudly. "Perhaps you would show them to my guards so we can all go together and wish the bride and groom well."

"If you don't move your arse out of our path, we'll just go through you, milady," said the bearded man, curling his lip. "And your guards too."

"Sir Jurgen," said Miriamele, "give me your sword."

For a moment the knight couldn't even respond. "Majesty?"

She extended her open hand, still staring down at the bearded man. Even Jesa could see that, for Jurgen, it was like cutting off his own hand to surrender it, but at last he drew the blade from its sheath and held it out to the queen, hilt first. The two groups, courtiers and guards on one hand, armed bravos on the other, could only stare at her as she took it. "I am Miriamele," she said, speaking slowly but very clearly, "daughter of High King Elias, granddaughter of High King Prester John. I myself am Mistress of the High Ward. If any of you have the courage to attack your lawful queen, come and do so. I promise you that whatever happens, you will not escape unbloodied."

"Your Majesty, no!" cried Canthia, but she received no more response from the queen than had Jurgen.

"And I see that at least one of you wears the Kingfisher crest," the queen continued, staring at one of the bravos in the back, whose tunic had gaped open to show the duke's emblem. Some of the swordsmen were staring up at her as though they had suddenly discovered their path blocked by a mythical monster, and even the bearded leader looked dismayed by what was happening. "Guards, keep that one alive, whatever else happens. The royal torturers will find out if he wears that insignia honestly or not." She turned to her soldiers. "Do you hear me? Alive. We cannot make him scream if he is already dead."

For a moment it seemed everything stood on a swaying balance, like a market scale. Jesa was quietly edging back the way they had come, preparing to take the baby and run. At the duchess' side, little Blasis asked in his piping voice, "Who are those men, Mama?"

Then the balance tipped. The man with the Benidrivine crest under his jacket suddenly turned and sprinted away back up the path, headed for the front of the estate, and within a few heartbeats most of his comrades had joined him. The bearded man had only time to throw a curse at them all, then followed after them at a dead run.

"What do you wait for, Sir?" the queen said to Jurgen, handing him back his sword. "I will get the ladies to safety. Go and catch those fellows. We may not actually have a royal torturer, but I still want that man wearing the duke's crest left alive to be questioned."

Jurgen looked completely discomfited, but at least had the presence of mind to take his men and hurry after the escaping bravos, shouting for aid as he went. Within a moment they had vanished down the path, and now Jesa could hear other worried voices calling from the garden below.

Jesa realized she was shivering like a willow tree in a strong wind and sat down on the first step, cradling little Serasina. She held the baby close, crooning wordlessly into her ear, still not quite able to believe what had just happened. It had all taken place so quickly!

Someone was leaning over her. Jesa looked up to see the queen. Her face was quite pale. "Do not fear. She will do better than the rest of us. They understand little at this age, and remember less." Queen Miriamele let out a long, ragged sigh. "Oh, my knees are weak and shaking. Threatening armed bandits with a sword when I have not used one in years and years! What was I thinking? Here, move over, child. I must sit next to you or fall down. Damn this stiff dress!"

After the ceremony, Count Dallo Ingadaris approached Miriamele. The master of the household looked genuinely distressed, but few men rose to the summits of power in Nabban without being able to tell a convincing lie. "Your Majesty," he said, "I have heard of your brave act, and I thank you from the bottom of my heart. Benevolent God alone knows what those men planned."

"You need not thank me," she said. "I only did what I thought best. Sometimes men who would happily cut a throat will be awed by power and titles."

"Such bravery." He shook his head wonderingly. "Your husband—our king—would be very proud."

"My husband would call me an idiot," she said and laughed a little despite herself. Miri wanted only to hurry back to the Sancellan Mahistrevis and crawl into her borrowed bed—her moment of bravado was costing her dearly—but she was determined to make it through the meal before leaving with Duchess Canthia in the duke's coach. "And he would be right."

"I am unhappy to report that most of those cut-throats escaped," Dallo told her, "although a few were killed. We will get to the bottom of this, Your Majesty, I promise you."

"Please keep me informed, my lord." On the other side of the garden the new bride Turia was greeting a line of well-wishers. Her husband Drusis was nowhere to be seen. The young woman looked so delicate that Miri felt unexpected pity for her. *She will have to learn to put up with so much more of this. So much more.*

Dallo thanked her again, then returned to his guests. As she watched the count's portly but lightfooted progress across the garden, Miri wondered whether she was right to see him as entirely a villain, or whether it was only the demons of her childhood fleering at her.

In truth, she told herself, *nobody in this city should be trusted.* She found herself missing her friend Rhona, who would have helped her to laugh at the obvious insincerity of the Nabbanai courtiers.

Sir Jurgen sidled over to the large ceremonial chair where Miri sat and bowed, but before he could begin she called Count Froye to join them. Froye was holding a cup of wine in each hand, and offered one to the queen, who refused it. He handed it to Jurgen instead, who seemed only too happy to accept and downed it in one go, as though he had been waiting a long time for something like it.

"I heard what Dallo said," Jurgen began quietly. "Yes, a few of the intruders were killed, but the leader got away, and none of those who fell were wearing Benidrivine livery under their clothes."

"But you saw it too, didn't you?"

"Yes, Majesty. The Kingfisher, plain as day."

"So either they were sent by someone in Saluceris's employ, or they are members of his party that acted on their own . . . *or* we were supposed to believe they were one of those."

"You think it was a false banner, Majesty?" Froye had also lowered his voice, so that in the midst of the garden, as music played and children ran back and forth trailing stolen ribbons and bunting, Miri felt like a conspirator.

Ah, Nabban, she thought sourly. *How quickly you draw us into your webs.* "I certainly think it possible," she said. "Never take anything here for its appearance. Which does not mean things are never what they seem, but it is definitely the more uncommon outcome."

Jurgen looked shocked, and his whisper was almost too loud. "But why would Count Dallo have someone attack his own house?"

"To blame on his enemy—his ally's brother, of course," said Froye promptly. "But we do not know that is true—do we, Majesty?"

"No. But as they say, never wager against treachery when you are climbing the Five Hills. My aunt Nessalanta taught me that and I have never forgotten it." Miri offered a grim smile. "She knew it well, the good Lord knows—the most treacherous old bitch I've ever met." She turned to Sir Jurgen. "How did they get in, Captain? Has anyone found out?"

"One of the gates was open, and the count's guards there had been struck senseless."

"The premise being that one or two of them climbed over, silenced the guards, then opened the gate for the rest." Miriamele considered. "Odd that men bent on bloody, perhaps even fatal mischief would not have slit the guards' throats to make certain they did not wake and give the alarm. How was it that so many of them escaped with you after them, Jurgen? And you were helped by the count's guards, too, I assume, because you made enough noise going after that Dallo's men must have come to see what happened."

The knight looked shamefaced. "Bad luck. Just at the moment the sell-swords or whatever they were ran for the gate, another noble arrived with his entourage and we became tangled up together, all mingled. People were shouting and cursing. By the time we could get clear all but a couple of the intruders were onto their horses and away."

"Horses?"

"They had them hidden farther down the hill, behind a wall."

"So this was no group of drunken troublemakers come to spoil the wedding," said Froye. "This was well planned."

"Perhaps even more than we can see now," Miriamele said. "Who was the late-arriving noble?"

"The islander fellow. You've seen him." Jurgen was clearly embarrassed not to be able to summon the name.

"Viscount Matreu?" That seemed strange. "Does it not feel convenient that he should arrive at such a moment?"

"Majesty," said Froye, almost shocked. "I assure you that Matreu is as trustworthy as I am! He has been a staunch ally of the High Throne for all the years I have known him. In fact, he saved Duchess Canthia not long ago from a street riot."

"In any case, Your Majesty," said Sir Jurgen, "how could anyone have known those men would meet you only to flee just then?" He colored. "I beg your pardon, but I confess I thought you had lost your wits, my queen, when you asked for my sword. I thought you were going to leap down the stairs at those ruffians like something out of an old story."

Miri laughed, but now that her blood had cooled, the thought of it frightened her. "Bluff, Captain, bluff. That is what I learned from my mother's people. Never admit weakness, never show fear, and stick to your lie even when it seems everyone must see through it." She sighed. "You may be right about Matreu, Froye. I fear since coming here I see conspiracies everywhere." She looked up and let her gaze slip from face to face. "Even now, I suspect that everyone in this garden is looking at us, wondering what we're saying, guessing and arguing about it."

"Sadly, Majesty, you are probably correct about that," Froye said.

"Then let us put this aside until we are back in the Sancellan Mahistrevis. I will have a better idea of things, I think, if I can be there when Duke Saluceris gets the news."

"He will likely have heard before he returns from Ardivalis, Majesty," said Jurgen. "But surely you don't think the duke could have had anything to do with this?"

"My good captain," she said, a little sharply, "Have you not been listening? If you are to be of use to me, you must learn to suspect everyone and everything here, lest one day you find a knife in your back and I must begin searching for a new protector. This is the most treacherous country in Osten Ard, and has been since long before Imperator Crexis hung Our Lord upside down on the Execution Tree."

Sir Jurgen and Count Froye both made the holy sign against their breasts.

And may He help me to get back to the Hayholt and my grandchildren alive, she thought. *I wish I had never come.*

17

A Scent of Witchwood

The afternoon sun vanished behind dark, threatening clouds as Jarnulf and the rest finally returned to the cave near the mountain's foot where they had left their horses. To Jarnulf, that day seemed so long ago that it might have happened in another life.

Goh Gam Gar had been forced to pull the sledge and the dragon's immense weight back uphill at several points so they could make their way around obstacles during their descent, and even the giant's great strength was utterly exhausted. When they reached the shelf of stone beside the cave, the monster immediately let go his burden, groaned so deeply Jarnulf felt it in his teeth, then curled himself into a shaggy ball to sleep.

Saomeji was only a few dozen paces away with the rod that kept Goh Gam Gar tame, but Jarnulf still made a wide circle around the giant. The huge creature had been weary and out of temper for days. He might fear punishment, but that would not stop him from lashing out in sudden anger, and even a glancing blow from the giant's hand could mean broken ribs or worse.

Jarnulf stepped over an expanse of mud that had pooled at the entrance to the cavern and made his way inside, where he saw to his relief that all the horses were still alive. Kemme would never ride his again, and dying Makho seemed no more likely than Kemme to return to the saddle, but finding the cave again made Jarnulf almost hopeful. His white horse Salt looked bony, almost spectral, and the cave stank of dung and urine, but he and his mount had both survived his long, deadly trip up and down the mountain. Jarnulf could almost believe his life might resume its ordinary course again. *But that ordinary course is toward death*, he reminded himself grimly—*one way or another. Defend me, O God, until I can do Thy will.*

Nezeru entered the cave behind him. Their eyes met, but Jarnulf looked away. She went to her own steed and felt its ribs and belly, then leaned close to whisper quiet Hikeda'yasao words into its ear.

Why am I the one who turns aside? Jarnulf wondered. *If anyone is wicked here, it is the Hikeda'ya, who stole my blood family from me one by one, and who murdered Father's family as well. And I did no wrong to this shameless female—it was she who offered herself to me, like any mortal whore.*

But though he could feel the righteousness in his head, he could not make himself feel it in his gut as well. Every time he looked at the halfblood woman Jarnulf felt shame, as though he were the one who had done something wrong.

He led Salt out of the cavern and past the trussed bulk of the dragon, which seemed, like Makho, to live entirely in half-sleep now. It was astonishing to see any living thing so large, to see its breast, big as a fishing boat, rising and falling as breath rasped in and out of its bound jaws. *What a world this is, where such a monstrous creature can become commonplace to me!*

Nezeru emerged and saw him staring at the dragon's huge, half-lidded eye. "Do you think they dream, Queen's Huntsman?"

He still could not look at her. "They dream of eating us, Sacrifice Nezeru. Of devouring everything that walks on two legs or four." He could not keep bitterness from his voice. "But at least the creature will save you for last, because you are the most tender of us."

He led his horse to a spot on the slope where a few shoots of green grass still grew among the brown and left it to feed while he sat down to rest. Saomeji, who had taken Makho from his hammock on the sledge, laid him down with little care and looked up.

"What are you doing, Huntsman? Do you not see the skies? You must find food before the storm is on us."

Much as he despised him, Jarnulf knew the Singer was right—there was not much time before an early night fell—but he had something important to do. When Saomeji had walked away Jarnulf sat himself straight and closed his eyes, turning inward until he no longer noticed the noises around him or even the cold bite of the wind.

My Lord God, my Redeemer Usires Aedon, hear my prayer.

I am full of confusion, but I wish to do only your will. Must the woman Nezeru die too? She is one of them, a slave of the Witch Queen, but I believe I have opened her eyes. She is different than when I first met her—she asks questions, even seems to think for herself. No longer is her every word one of praise for her superiors and her queen.

It was strange, this sort of prayer. He almost felt that he was bargaining with the Lord God, which was surely the error of pride grown to its largest size.

Her father is a powerful man. Should she not be spared to take her questions back to him and to her people some day? Who knows when and how such a seed might sprout? Or must she die? Lord, I am weak. I am foolish. I almost lost sight of my oath. But at the last moment I opened my eyes to the light. Help me now. Send me a sign. Should she live, or must she die? Forgive me, O Lord, because I am weak and wish to spare her, but fear that if she remains alive she will be a threat to Your work.

His prayer finished, he sat in silence with the cold wind on his cheeks, hoping for God's guidance.

"Look, you shirking mortal, look!" Saomeji's words pierced the quiet. "The shadows have covered the mountain. You must go now to find food for the worm. If you wait too long you will not find your way back, and I shall have to send the giant to find you and tear one of your arms loose."

Jarnulf opened his eyes to see spinning flakes of white dance past his face like ashes from a fire—but no one had lit a fire. Snowflakes were swirling down from the bulging black clouds overhead.

"Very well," he said calmly. "I will go. Sacrifice Nezeru, will you join me? It will make the hunting go more quickly to have two sets of eyes."

She looked at him, her face unnaturally still, her eyes intent, as though trying to see what was in Jarnulf's thought.

"If you will clean Chieftain Makho's wounds, Saomeji," she finally said.

"Yes, yes," said the Singer. "Go. But hurry back!"

Was this strangeness she felt but could not understand only in Jarnulf, Nezeru wondered, or was it something common to all his mortal kind? Except for her mother, she had little experience with the Sunset Children, but this long journey had put her much in the huntsman's company.

At first, their being thrown together so often had seemed deliberate on his part; later it became deliberate on hers. Partially it was because he was the closest thing to a trustworthy companion—which was perhaps the strangest twist of all. But he had not wanted to couple with her, and that she did not understand. She was not misshapen or ugly: if she was, one of her Sacrifice rivals back in the Order-house would have shamed her for it. And mortals could not be strangers to the act, or why were so many of them spread out across the lands like hungry insects, devouring all before them? His rejection made no sense.

But whatever the obstacle might have been, the mortal seemed in no hurry to talk about it, and they had been hunting for over an hour in silence. They had taken several rabbits and a sitting mountain goat, but the snow began to fall heavily. Jarnulf looked back over his shoulder, down the hillside they had just climbed.

"Sacrifice Nezeru," he said, "the People's eyes are better than mine. Can you see our horses' hoofprints behind us?"

It was a strange question. She glanced back. "A few. Most are already covered. Do you fear you won't be able to find your way back to the others? You need not concern yourself with me along."

"Ah, of course," he said. "You were trained in tracking back in the order-house. Where they taught you also to kill the queen's enemies."

"Of course," she said. "What else should they teach me? Why are you so strange . . . *Jarnulf*?" The name felt ungainly in her mouth. She could not remember if she had ever spoken it aloud before. "Is it because I invited you to couple with me? Let it leave your thoughts. Already for me it is as though it never happened."

He turned to stare at her, then patted his horse on the neck. The snow was swirling. "Do you truly wish to hear the truth?" he said after a while. "I seem to remember that you do not enjoy it."

"Those were *your* truths, not mine. I fear no word you might utter. Why should I care what a mortal thinks?"

"Not all your kind hate mortals," he said. "Your father loved one enough to make a child with her."

Nezeru was startled. Her father had confessed to her once, when she had been angry with her mother's hopeless sentimentality, that though it was difficult to admit, he cared for Tzoja as more than a servant, more than simply a bedmate plucked from the slave pens. How could Jarnulf know that, or was it just a chance strike?

"So," she said at last. "Tell me this 'truth' of yours, Jarnulf. Soon we will be among my kind again, and I will not have the freedom to flout the laws of my people in this way. So speak."

"Then listen well," he said. "Much of what I have told you was true. I was raised in the slave barracks of White Snail Castle on the flanks of the mountain. My brother died of cold, my mother and then my sister were taken away by your people, our masters. I learned swordplay from the great master Xoka, who trained me in the same spirit as a noblewoman might train an ermine to nuzzle her cheek and eat from her hand." Nezeru thought the mortal's face was so hard, so expressionless, that he might have been a death-sung Sacrifice like her. "When I was old enough I escaped, and after coming close to death in the wilderness beyond Nakkiga, I fell in at last with the Skalijar, those Rimmersgard bandits we fought against on our way to the mountain. Their leader Dyrmundur—the one you saw recognize me—made me his servant." He saw her expression and smirked. "Do not think I murdered an old friend just to keep my secret, Sacrifice Nezeru. Dyrmundur was a cruel, drunken beast, and when I was young he used me badly in every way. Not everything was pain, though. He taught me skills that even Xoka could not, the ways of treachery and ambush, of living off the wilderness and off my fellow men, because that is how the Skalijar live—by robbery and pillage.

"So one day I ran from them too, and made my way east into the outer plains of Rimmersgard, stealing from mortal farmers, hiding out in the forests and fields. But after so many shivering nights of my life I had come to hate the cold, so as I went from place to place I moved ever southward, looking for a land where the sun shone."

The wind had grown harder as he spoke, so that the snow was flying almost sideways. Jarnulf urged his horse into the lee of a rock outcrop and Nezeru guided her own mount to join him there.

"Let us wait until the wind dies down," he said as he swung himself down from his saddle. "You may not feel its bite, but I do. The sun is gone now and our tracks are covered by snow, so it will make no difference if we wait a little longer."

She could sense neither his mood nor his intent, but could not see any harm in it, so she dismounted and seated herself beside him, her back against the stone so that it felt as if the world itself was her chair. She could tell he was not done speaking, so she waited in silence as the horses nuzzled at the snow-powdered ground, looking for grass to crop.

"I made my way at last into Erkynland at the south of the Frostmarch, where my life changed. I came to rest in a good-sized town with a market and several churches, so I was able to add to my thefts with food given me by a kind watchman at one of the churches, and there my destiny found me. Because that is where I met Father."

Nezeru was surprised. "You met your father in Erkynland?"

He shook his head, the phantom of a smile on his lean, sun-browned face. "No, that is only what I called him. He had been an Aedonite priest, and from him I learned much of the catechism. Other than the church watchman and a precious few villagers, he was the first person who was kind to me. I became his companion, and we wandered from town to town, begging bread for Father, reciting from the Book of Aedon. Sometimes even giving a bit of a sermon, though he was not always up to it. He had suffered some terrible shock before I met him, and at times he wept in the night. When I finally had the courage to ask him, he told me that all his family had been murdered, and that it had been the soldiers of the silver-masked queen who had done it." He did not look at her. "Your people."

"Why do you tell me this?"

"Because it is the truth, Sacrifice Nezeru. Because I said I would speak the truth to you, and I will—this of all days." He had one hand in his jacket, protecting it from the cold, but he raised his other hand as though swearing an oath. "Now listen, Sacrifice, because what I say next concerns you closely.

"Years later, when I lost Father, I swore an oath that I would devote my life to repaying everything he had done for me, especially for what turned out to be greatest gift of all. You see, through Father I found my lord Usires Aedon, who ransomed all mortal men from God's wrath by dying on the Execution Tree."

"You are an Aedonite?" Nezeru was confused and disturbed not just by his words, but by his heedless urge to vomit all this out, as though he did not expect to live much longer. "That cannot be. You are a Queen's Huntsman."

"I was never a Queen's Huntsman." He withdrew his hand from his jacket and clapped it across her face, throwing his weight onto her and bearing her to the ground. Nezeru tried to scream her rage at this treachery, but the powerful smell of something sweet and yet slightly foul filled her nose and mouth, the odor of something that had died long ago in a locked room and had then become dust. The powder-sweet scent of sacred witchwood flooded her nostrils, and she could not breathe the choking fumes out again no matter how she tried. Nezeru struggled to pull Jarnulf's hand away from her face, but he was sitting on her now, kicking out with his legs to keep his balance even as she struggled to get free.

She tried to reach up and scratch his eyes but could not, because she could barely feel her limbs now. Both her movements and her thoughts grew slower, and the struggle began to seem unimportant, something happening far away, like the sound of Jarnulf's voice.

"You see, I swore an oath to the Lord God that I would revenge the theft of Father's family and my own by destroying every Hikeda'ya I met. But then I discovered from a corpse-giant that the queen of death herself still lived . . ."

Nezeru did not hear the rest of his words. The world dropped away beneath her and she tumbled down into nothing.

At first she could only sense that she was something separate from the blackness, and for a while that was enough. Then, as memory returned, she began to struggle to escape.

Her oath came back to her before her name, but at last the name came back as well. Slowly, as if donning a set of familiar, well-worn clothes, Nezeru slipped back into herself, though her thoughts were still as halting as if her head was filled with thick caterpillar honey.

Kei-vishaa. She could still taste its sickly-sweet taste in her mouth and nose. *Where did he get it? And why would he use it on me?*

She was on her stomach, she realized, and something was holding her so tightly she could not move anything between her knees and neck. Her face was pressed against something rough—the shoulders of a horse, she suddenly realized. Jarnulf's horse, by its scent. She twisted her head as far as she could and discovered she was tied to the saddle and bent forward against the horse's neck, held by tight coils of silvery Hikeda'ya cord.

"I do not know whether Saomeji might track one of the Nakkiga horses—your horse—with his Singer's skills," Jarnulf said from just beside her. His voice seemed to echo in her ears, as if from down a deep hole. "So you are being given my greatest gift—Salt, my faithful friend and companion. He has carried me all over the north."

She fought to make words, but her tongue was as thick and useless in her mouth as a leather scabbard. When she finally spoke, even she found it hard to understand. "Why . . . are you—"

"Call it Aedonite mercy." He gave a last pull on the rope, which she felt across the small of her back, then tied the ends in a knot. She could see only his hands and the edge of his face.

"You said . . . you not a Queen's—"

"Huntsman," he finished. "And I am not. But that is the last truth I will share with you, Sacrifice Nezeru. I think you are clever enough to work yourself loose after a time, but we will be long gone by then. I wish you luck—at least of a sort."

She struggled to free herself, but the ropes were looped many times around her and tied tight. "But why? *Why?*"

"Take a deep breath, Sacrifice." Jarnulf was out of her sight now. "You will thank me for it later. Goodbye to you, old friend." She felt a moment of outrage that he should dare call her 'old friend,' but then he shouted "*Laup*, Salt!" and must have slapped the horse on the quarters because it sprang forward as if jumping from a cliff. It was too late for Nezeru to take that deep breath; the horse was already running, crushing her against its back and the saddle with every surging step, driving the air from her lungs.

She fought to keep her head up, to see something of where she was and where they were going, but she was so dizzy she could barely even think, and now the point of her chin was striking the horse's back like a hammer against a warm, hairy anvil. She let her head sag forward and tried merely to breathe as the horse pounded downhill.

So many knots . . . so many webs. She didn't even know what the thought meant. The *kei-vishaa* was still in her. The horse's hooves sounded loud as thunder, thunder that shook her and shook her until she could hear nothing but endless roaring. After a little while her thoughts began to fall apart, and she slid into the blackness once more.

Jarnulf's return out of darkness was hastened by the pain of his cheek. It wasn't a single pain, the ache of a rotted tooth or a healing wound, but the same sharp pain, over and over, growing in discomfort as he made his way back toward the light.

"Tell me, you mortal fool! Where is she?"

The *kei-vishaa* Jarnulf had breathed made Saomeji's pale face, looming above him, appear as broad as the moon, and he could not help staring. Something about the face was so strange—the golden eyes, like little suns, but how could there be suns on the moon?—that he almost laughed. The shadows in his head were beginning to drift away like smoke.

Another hard blow to his cheek. *"Speak!"*

"Stop!" Jarnulf felt weak as a child. "What happened?"

"Do not pretend innocence. What did Nezeru do? Where is she?"

Jarnulf groaned and rolled onto his side to protect himself from any more blows. "I don't know. I don't know!" He tried to get onto all fours to lift himself up, but the world swayed beneath him and after a fumbling attempt to crawl, he slumped back onto the ground. The stars overhead told him it was evening, which meant he had been insensible for some two or three hours.

The Singer clutched a *ni'yo*, dimmed to a mere glow that showed Saomeji's bones black beneath the rosy skin of his hand.

Saomeji abruptly made a noise of fury and snatched something from the ground where Jarnulf had been lying, lifted the torn piece of cloth, examined it by the glow of the lightstone, then lifted it to his nose and cautiously sniffed. "*Kei-vishaa*—curse her! I knew some of my supply had gone missing, but I thought I had merely spilled it in my trance. May she spend centuries in the Cold, Slow Halls, the treacherous bitch."

Jarnulf licked his lips without thinking, and tasted the foreign sweetness.

around his mouth. It tingled against his tongue. He raised himself enough to spit it onto the ground. "I was kneeling, taking a stone out of her horse's hoof," he said, his words as slurred as if he had been drinking wine all evening. "Then . . . then I don't know."

Saomeji's fine-boned face was dead white with rage, which made his dark-circled, golden eyes seem even more alien. "She must have planned it since I made the Witness," he said. "But why?" He looked at Jarnulf for a long moment. "Did you have a pact? Did she betray you?"

Jarnulf's thoughts were still so fuzzy that it was easier just to shake his head. "I was taking a stone out—"

"Yes, yes, I heard. Only a mortal would let someone get so close without being alert to danger."

Jarnulf sat up. He needed to behave as he always did if he wanted to convince Saomeji of his innocence. "That is a fine jest coming from a Queen's Talon who I saved after they camped atop a *Furi'a* nest." He groaned and held his head. The *kei-vishaa* was still making him feel grossly ill and almost stupefied. He was even more impressed now with how quickly Nezeru had recovered her wits. "Where is the giant?"

"You—silence." Saomeji stood and shouted Goh Gam Gar's name; an answering bellow came from lower on the hillside.

The snow had almost stopped falling, but it was thick on the ground and thick on Jarnulf's garments as well. He shook it off as he got unsteadily to his feet. He realized he had been lucky. What little he remembered of the lore of *kei-vishaa*, the potent poison made from witchwood pollen, had been taught to him by Xoka many, many years ago. If Saomeji's mixture had been a little stronger, or Jarnulf had breathed in only a little more after sending Nezeru on her unwilling ride, he might easily have frozen to death before waking up.

The giant appeared, shoving young trees out of his way as he climbed. "The snow covers all," he rumbled. "It dulls her scent and the scent of the horse. There is not enough smell even to make old Gam hungry, and I love to eat horse more than anything beside manflesh."

Saomeji looked at him in distaste. "Pick this fool up and lift him into the saddle. I do not want to leave Makho alone for long, even in the cave. As for Nezeru, she may escape us for the present, but she will find a traitor's death at the end of her road. Soon the mortals will be gone and the all world will be Nakkiga. She will have nowhere to hide." He turned to Jarnulf. "Some of your kind might be spared destruction—there is always a need for slaves—but it will not be the stupid or the unfit. If I did not need you, you would not leave this spot alive."

"And I give you a good day as well," Jarnulf said heavily. Still swaying a little, he looked around as if in surprise. "Where is my horse?"

He almost did not hear the giant behind him until the huge hand had closed around his waist. He found himself suddenly lifted in the air, then was set down on the back of Nezeru's gray horse.

"She stole it," said Saomeji. "You said you were taking a stone from her horse's hoof. Perhaps she did not want to risk it going lame, or perhaps she thought a mortal's horse would be harder for me to find." He shook his head, his face resuming its usual stony lack of expression. "As if I would waste time hunting for a mere deserter. She will be stricken from the Order of Sacrifice and her name will be a curse to all. I almost feel sorry for her father—poor Magister Viyeki will be humiliated."

They began to tramp back across the snowy hills.

I took a great risk to send the woman away, Jarnulf told himself. *To spare her from the vengeance I plan on the others. Was it worth it?*

The horse jounced across the rocky hillside. His stomach wanted to empty itself, and his head throbbed. *I will likely never know,* he told himself. *Not until the hour of my death, when I stand before my Creator at last, and all questions are answered.*

18

A Burning Field

"Before we go into the throne hall," Simon told Tiamak, "I would have some words with you. There are so many matters filling my head, but I feel as if there's a hole in my skull and my wits are running out."

He nodded. "Of course, Simon."

Before either of them could say more, a herald announced Pasevalles. Simon waved the Lord Chancellor into the retiring room, ignoring a look of concern from Tiamak. "Come in and sit down, Lord Pasevalles—we will go in to the others presently. Have some wine—I suspect it will be thirsty work today." He gestured to one of the servants.

Tiamak was trying to give him a significant look, but Simon ignored it. *Does he think he is my only councilor?* Simon was still unhappy that the Wrannaman had kept important news from him. *The Norns are making trouble again and my poor grandson is held prisoner by grasslanders. The times are too dangerous for my advisers to fight with each other like children for my attention.* "I want to know about several things, Lord Tiamak," he said, "but I fear the day ahead will be entirely taken up with Morgan and the Thrithings. Did you and your friend, that factor fellow, ever learn anything about the kitchen worker who tried to kill Count Eolair?"

Tiamak shook his head, but he looked troubled. "You mean Lord Aengas. He is himself from Hernystir, and he says the man only babbles things from old tales about demons and the Morriga—"

"At the moment, that seems a madness common among the Hernystiri," Simon said, interrupting him. "Well, the fellow will do no harm now that he is locked up. I hate to punish a madman, but a would-be murderer cannot run free." He turned to Pasevalles. "Did you have something urgent, my lord, or may I finish my business with Lord Tiamak first?"

Pasevalles shook his head. "I await your pleasure, sire." He lifted his cup to his lips.

"Good. And one other thing, Tiamak. I have been thinking about our earlier talk." The Wrannaman's pleading looks were beginning to annoy him. "About John Josua, as I'm sure you remember. We must see if there are other ways down into the tunnels under the castle, and not just because of what happened to my son."

He was silenced by a loud clank and clatter. Pasevalles had dropped his cup. Wine splashed across the floor. "I beg your pardon, Majesty!" He hurriedly got down on his knees to pick it up, as if he feared he would be upbraided for interrupting.

"Worry not, my lord," Simon said, waving his hand. "Easily repaired—and, thank God, we have more wine." He waved to the servant. "Clean that up, please, and bring Lord Pasevalles a fresh cup." He turned back to Tiamak. "I think we need to go through the castle and find out if there are entrances to the old Sithi ruins that we have missed. If so, they must all be sealed. Perhaps Pasevalles can help with the project. We can use the Erkynguard—those we don't send to the grasslands."

"I would like to speak of this later, Majesty." Tiamak seemed as upset by Simon's words as Pasevalles had been at spilling his wine.

"Very well," he said, "but it cannot wait long. What if the Norns should march south? I wager the White Foxes know the depths underneath the Hayholt better than we do." He drained his own cup, then stood. "Now, gentlemen, let us take ourselves to the throne hall. I fear we can avoid our allies no longer."

I miss Miri more than ever. If ever a problem called out for careful thought, for a knowledge of power and how best to use it, Morgan's capture was such a problem. Simon knew his own limitations all too well.

She'd see the most important bits right off. He glanced down the length of the Pellarine Table at the members of the Inner Council. Countess Rhona had the combination of experience and caution closest to his wife's, but she was only a single sensible voice. A new face, Father Boez, sat beside her, a quiet, slender young priest who seemed old beyond his years. Boez had taken the place of Archbishop Gervis as Chief Almoner now that Gervis was to be made an escritor. He had been cautious about speaking in front of the rest of the council.

The same was not true for Earl Rowson, of course, who had no problem speaking up but was unlikely to offer anything useful. And Rowson's ally Baron Evoric and the other landed nobles of the Inner Council usually believed as Rowson did—that they should be left in peace to work their peasants into early graves and to defend their hunting preserves against poachers.

God forbid a poor man might take a deer out of Evoric's private forest to feed his family, even though the baron himself never goes out to the country at all. But I suppose Miri would say I am always siding with the common folk no matter the crime, and ignoring the rights of the nobles.

But it was Duke Osric who truly worried Simon. After days spent stalking the castle corridors, full of dire words like an Aedonite prophet stumbling out of the wilderness to proclaim God's growing anger, the duke had finally bathed and shaved. He seemed more or less sober as well, but Simon still thought he saw something distant in the duke's stare, something fierce that seemed beyond mourning or ordinary anger. Pasevalles, however, said the duke had regained his wits, and even Tiamak had argued strongly that Osric must be present at any meeting of the Inner Council.

It wasn't Osric's loudly stated desire to punish the grassland barbarians for laying hands on his grandson Morgan that worried Simon—he would have liked to do something bold and sudden for his grandson too. Simon was not used to being the one to counsel patience—that was generally Miriamele's role, Simon was not practiced at it. But he was terrified by the thought of doing something that might endanger Morgan's life.

And I fear for Eolair, as well. The problems seemed all but overwhelming, and he was moved to sudden prayer. *Help me, O Lord. Help me, Usires our Ransomer. Give me the wisdom to choose the right course. Give me the strength to be cautious, if caution is what is needed . . .*

"Who else but Duke Osric can be sent—*should* be sent?" Baron Evoric asked loudly, dragging Simon's attention back to the conversation. The baron was a fleshy, bearded man with a port-wine birthmark across his nose and cheeks that gave him the unfortunate appearance of perpetual drunkenness. "It is his grandson who has been captured. And he is the lord constable, after all."

"The lord constable's calling is to protect the Hayholt and the throne," observed Countess Rhona.

"But those barbarians have taken the heir!" Evoric cried. "Is that not an attack on the throne itself?"

On another day Simon would actually have agreed with the baron—a nearly unheard-of event—but it was not Osric's sworn duty that concerned him today but Osric's state of mind. He bowed to the inevitable. "The duke has been waiting to speak," he said. "Please make your thoughts known to us, Duke Osric."

Osric ran a hand through his beard, which was still damp and curly from his recent bath. "Before I say anything else, Majesty, I owe you and the High Throne an apology."

Simon raised an eyebrow. "Why is that, my lord?"

"You know the reason, Majesty. I have not been myself. My grief over my daughter's death, and now Morgan—now this—!" He balled his fingers into a fist, then slowly unclenched them. "I have shamed myself. And I have drunk to excess, as my wife has informed me." He smiled in a shamefaced way. "Informed me many times and very loudly." When the polite laughter ended, he shook his head. "There is no escaping it, Majesty—I have failed the throne and my family. And I crave your pardon before anything else."

Simon did not like having such a conversation in front of the entire Inner Council. "You have my pardon, of course, Your Grace. We're all grieving, but there's no doubt you and your wife have had the worst of things."

Tiamak gave the king an approving nod. Pasevalles was still carefully watching Osric.

"Then if I am forgiven, Your Majesty," the duke said, "I would ask that you let me take a large company to the grasslands to rescue our grandson. I promise I will not fail you. I will not fail Erkynland."

Simon sat back in his chair, uncertain of what to say. Around the long table many of the council members darted glances at each other. "Do not be silent, sirs and ladies," Simon said at last. "You are the Inner Council. You heard the Lord Constable's words. Let me know your thoughts."

In the hour that followed, most of the members of the council felt compelled to speak in support of Osric—not surprising with Osric sitting beside them. When Simon called a temporary halt to allow the councillors to relieve themselves and the servants to clear the table and bring in a fresh round of fruits and sweetmeats, Tiamak spoke quietly into Simon's ear. "You can see as well as I that Osric may have washed and trimmed his beard, but he is still badly frayed—with dangling threads at all his edges."

Simon was annoyed. If anyone should be arguing forgiveness it should be Tiamak, who had recent sins of his own. "Morgan is Osric's grandson too," he said. "I would go myself if I could."

"Questioning his fitness is not the same as questioning his right," Tiamak said.

"Do not lecture me, please. I am trying to do what is best."

After everyone was in their seats again, Pasevalles asked Simon's permission to speak. "Before we decide who will be sent to parley with the Thrithingsmen," he asked, "should we not speak more of what the soldiers who go with him will do once they get there?"

"They will defend His Grace, the duke," said Tiamak. "And make it clear this is a serious matter to us. What else should happen at a parley?"

"But why should we pay ransom to barbarians and thieves?" complained Earl Rowson. "We should put as many of them as possible to the sword. They will be quick enough to bargain then. If Osric is not well enough to go, I would be honored to lead the Erkynguard myself, Majesty. Rest assured, I will chastise the barbarians well and properly."

For a moment Simon feared he wouldn't be able to swallow his anger, that he would lean across the table, wrap his hands around the earl's throat, and yank Rowson out of his chair. "And what if the barbarians decide to pay us back by murdering the prince, my lord?" he demanded. "What if they should kill my grandson, the heir to the High Throne? Who then will have been most chastised?"

Rowson's mouth worked for a moment as he realized that he had waded in deeper than he had planned. "Oh, we must secure the prince first, Majesty, of course. That goes without saying. I am only talking of afterward."

Which the earl had plainly *not* been doing, but Simon felt that if he said any more he would begin shouting and perhaps not be able to stop. "Whatever happens, there will be *no* attack against any of the grasslanders until the prince is free and safe. Count Eolair, too. If that is not clear to anyone, speak up now." He glared up and down the table. "Good." He looked to Pasevalles. "Were you finished, my lord?"

"In fact, Majesty, I had a suggestion. No matter who is sent—and I agree with most here that Osric should be the one, yes. But we must have more than one strategy in place. What if the grasslanders will not bargain? Or what if there is no thane who can speak for those holding Prince Morgan and Count Eolair? What if your grandson has already been taken somewhere else?"

"What if, what if—!" Simon forced himself to take a breath. "Do you have a suggestion, my lord, or do you merely seek to make us feel hopeless?"

Pasevalles nodded, sober and careful. "I might have a plan, sire. You see, two of the Erkynguard have been keeping a watch on Morgan for some time, at my bidding. But they did not go with him on the mission to the Sithi, so they are available for our use now."

"Use? What use? And who are you talking about?" Simon demanded.

"I speak of Sir Astrian of Poines and his friend, Sir Olveris, our two Nabbanai knights," said Pasevalles. "They fought in the south along the edge of the Thrithings for many years in the skirmishes that followed the Second Thrithings War. Astrian speaks the grasslander tongue passably well."

"What do you mean, they have been watching Morgan?" Simon asked. "It seems to me that they have been the ones leading him astray!"

"Appearances can be deceiving, Majesty," said Pasevalles. "I will be happy to explain all after the council meeting has ended."

"But what are you suggesting?" asked Tiamak. "Not that these two should be in charge of the mission, I hope."

"No, no." Pasevalles shook his head emphatically. "But when our forces go into the field, our army—and it must be an army of sufficient size to show we mean to ruin them if they play us false in any way—should not be the only tool. If we send the two Nabbanai knights with them, they can make their own way into the grasslands, passing for sell-swords. They may then have a chance of finding out where the prince is being held and perhaps even of rescuing him with no cost to the throne."

"I don't care a fig about cost," said Simon. "But your idea isn't a bad one."

The discussion that followed stretched through the best part of another hour, but the king grew less and less interested in what even his closest advisors had to say. He could see now what common sense decreed, and delaying it any farther would serve no purpose.

"Enough," he finally said, then waited for the table to fall silent. "Here is what we will do. We will send a force of Erkynguards and other mustered soldiers to the River Laestfinger on the eastern border. Duke Osric and Captain Zakiel will recommend the size of the force to me. Osric will lead them." He paused a moment while Osric made the Sign of the Tree and blessed Simon in a loud whisper. "The duke and our forces will camp on the Erkynlandish side of the river and demand a parley with that Redbeard fellow or whoever it is who speaks for the Thrithings-folk these days. And as Pasevalles suggests, Astrian and his friend will cross the river in secret and make their way into the grasslands, with the idea of finding out as much as they can about the prince's whereabouts." He paused and fixed first Pasevalles and then Osric with his hardest, most steadfast gaze. "While Prince Morgan is a prisoner, *nothing* will be done about beginning any sort of fight with the Thrithings-men without my approval—even if you must write to me first and wait for my reply. Is that clear, Your Grace?"

Duke Osric nodded vigorously. "Of course, Your Majesty, and I thank you for your confidence in me. I will do nothing more than you order. I would not risk our grandson's life, never fear."

"I will say that precisely to Astrian and Olveris, my king," Pasevalles agreed. "Your words alone will guide them."

"Good." For the first time in days Simon was not exhausted, did not simply want his responsibilities to end. Horrible as it was, Morgan's capture at least presented him with important decisions to make and a course of action. "Come back to me by this time tomorrow with your recommendation on how many men we can send, Osric—and you too, Captain Zakiel. His Grace will need your help with the muster rolls." He paused at a new thought. "And somehow we must find the gold for this as well. Pasevalles, you must help Osric and Zakiel to assemble the money to do what must be done. It may mean more taxes." He looked around. "Are you all willing to shoulder that burden?"

There was a moment of silence as the nobles contemplated paying higher taxes.

"You have only to ask us, King Simon," said Countess Rhona suddenly, "and we stand ready. We want only to bring the prince back safely, and to protect the High Ward."

"The Hernystirwoman says what we all believe," said Earl Rowson, trying as he usually did to drag himself back into the center of proceedings.

"I am glad to hear that," Simon said, doing his best to let go of the anger he now seemed to feel toward almost everyone. Surely it was Miri's absence that made the world feel so out of joint.

But our Lord of Angels, he prayed, *please let me have Morgan here alive and well to greet her when she returns! Please, Elysia Mother of God, show mercy on a poor sinner like me and bring our grandson back safely! I'll build you another cathedral, or feed the hungry . . . or both! Just show me a sign.*

Simon stood to show that the council was ended. Several of those gathered around the Pellarine Table looked worried, Tiamak more than any of them, but Simon could not afford to doubt the choices he had made. Something had to be done, and it was almost impossible to imagine denying Osric a leading role. But if the duke could be managed carefully and kept on a short leash, he would do well. Simon knew he had made the sensible choice—the kingly choice.

But he avoided Tiamak's company as he left the Throne Hall.

"You're supposed to come back now," said Aedonita. "Nurse Loes said so."

"I don't have to," Lillia told her. Aedonita was her favorite friend, but some-times she acted as though she was the real princess.

"You do! She said you were supposed to come right away. She said you didn't eat any of your porridge."

"I happen to be thinking about my *mother*," said Lillia. "She died, you know. Right up there."

Aedonita looked up the stairwell in dawning horror, then vigorously made the Sign of the Tree. "You shouldn't be here, Lillia! Lady Rhona said you weren't supposed to come near the stairs."

Lillia rolled her eyes. "I have to go on these stairs *every single day,* silly. Don't be stupid. And Lady Rhona isn't even around today. She's been with my grand-father all morning."

"But I'll get into trouble!" Aedonita was unable to keep the whine of fear out of her voice. "The nurse told me to bring you back."

"I'll come when I'm ready," said Lillia. "Tell her I'm praying for my mother's soul. Go on. You won't get in trouble if you tell her I'm praying."

Aedonita clearly wasn't as confident about that as Lillia was, but she turned and trudged back down the stairs toward the residence's main hall where the children were imprisoned.

All but me, thought Lillia. *I'm not going to go running just because Nurse calls.*

She had not been lying to her friend—not entirely. She really was here on the stairway because it was the place her mother had died, or so everyone told her. The spot fascinated her, in part because of the strong feelings she had whenever she came near it or thought about what had happened to her mother. It made her sad and scared, but she *wanted* to think about it, too—like an itch inside her head that she had to scratch. Sometimes she had been so mad at her mother that she'd wished Idela would go away somewhere, but then she did. Had it happened because Lillia had wished it?

But I also wished for her to be nice to me, and to give me a ruby necklace. Those things didn't happen.

It was all very confusing and frustrating.

Lillia went back into her own bedchamber on the third floor to look for her lady doll. It looked a little like her mother, although the hair was the wrong color; she wanted to make it slip on the stairs and fall like her mother had, even though she knew stupid old Loes and even Auntie Rhoner would say it was a wicked thing to do. But as she was leaving the room Lillia heard footsteps on the stairs, so she stopped and peered out between the door and the frame, wor-ried that the nurse might have come to fetch her. It was only Lord Pasevalles though. He was coming up quietly, like he didn't want anyone to hear him, so she stayed behind the door and watched as he climbed past the floor with the royal chambers and up the steps toward the top floor where all the empty rooms were.

Lillia knew Nurse Loes wouldn't dare scold her if she was with Lord Pasevalles, so she left the doll behind and wandered out into the third floor hall to meet him when he came back down. Maybe if she asked him he would tell her more about what happened to her mother, because none of the women who took care of her ever would. It soon became clear, though, that Pasevalles was not coming right back down, so she decided to go to the top floor and find him.

Lillia went up the steps lightly, not because she was trying to be quiet but because she was thinking about her mother slipping and wondering where exactly it had happened. She was still frowning and thinking about what it might feel like to fall down such steep stairs when her head rose above the fourth floor landing, and she saw something that made her stop where she was. Lord Pasevalles was kneeling in front of an open door at the far end of the passage, holding a candle very close to the ground as he stared at the floor of the room.

Lillia thought he must have dropped something, but seeing him there made her uneasy, though she could not have said why. It just seemed . . . *private*. She backed down a couple of steps and leaned against the wall, suddenly breathless.

Then she heard a grunt from the corridor above; she thought it must be Pasevalles getting to his feet again. She didn't want him to think she was spying on him—although perhaps she had been, just a little—so she turned and hurried back down the stairs as quietly as she could, then down the next set as well before moving to the edge of the second floor landing. She could see several of the children gathered in the hall below her. Aedonita was trying to organize a game there, without success; Lillia thought that she could do it better. She almost forgot about the stairs and Pasevalles when a hand came down on her shoulder, making her jump a little and squeak.

"You scared me!"

Lord Pasevalles smiled. "I beg your pardon, Princess Lillia. I was just upstairs looking for the Mistress of Chambermaids. Was that you I heard on the steps?"

"No." She wasn't certain why she told the lie. She was the princess of the whole castle—why shouldn't she be on the stairs if she wanted to be?

"Ah." Pasevalles nodded. "I thought perhaps you were pretending that I was an evil ogre or a robber king—that you were spying on me to find out the truth of my terrible deeds." He said it in a light, teasing voice, but something still seemed wrong to her.

"Don't be silly," she said. "I'm just watching the other children down in the hall. I don't want to play the game they're playing."

"Have you been up here long?"

He definitely seemed suspicious of her, and now Lillia began to wonder what he had been doing on the top floor of the residence, if it might be something to do with her mother's death. Maybe Lord Pasevalles was trying to find out how her mother had fallen down the stairs, but he didn't want her to know that. "No, I just came up here," she told him.

Pasevalles was still playing the spying game, or pretending to. "Well, if I really were a bandit king like Flann, or a huge, frightening ogre," he said slowly, "do you know what I'd do to any spy I caught?"

"What?"

"Oh, something very, very bad." He leaned down so his face was close to hers. "But you don't need to know what that might be, do you? Because you're a good girl and not a spy. Isn't that right, Princess?"

He smiled again and bowed. Then, without waiting for an answer, he turned and climbed down the stairs to the main hall.

He has a secret, she thought, and felt a flutter of excitement, along with a pinch of worry that she always got when she knew others wouldn't approve of what she was thinking. *And I want to know what it is. Because nobody should be allowed to keep secrets from the only princess of the whole castle.*

19

Footsteps

After so much time lost in Aldheorte, Morgan was beginning to understand why the Sithi called their forest settlements "little boats" and the city they had abandoned, "The Boat on the Ocean of Trees." The great forest really was a sort of ocean.

He stood in the upper branches of a great ash, its crown looming over the other treetops like a church steeple above a village, its great trunk creaking in the wind. Morgan felt as if he were on the edge of some great understanding. Most of the forest seemed to lie beneath him, but only its surface, an endless seascape in a hundred different greens, with here and there the early gold of late summer leaves starting to turn.

From the ground the upper reaches of the forest were as unknowable as what lay beneath the waters of any ocean. And from above, where he now stood, the earth and all its byways were just as hidden, just as secret.

Passing winds ruffled the treetops below him like a hand stroking a cat's fur.

All my life I've looked at the outsides of things and thought I saw them whole. All my life I've seen forests and never wondered about the things that happen in them every moment—every creature with its own life, no matter how small, every tree and plant trying to find the sun.

So many new ideas filled his head but he had no one to tell them to. How would anyone who lived alone ever know if they were mad? Again Morgan thought he might be losing his wits—how else could he hear the words of a dying Sitha in his dreams? Other times he wondered whether this was how his grandfather and grandmother had felt during the Storm King's War, as if important things were happening but people themselves were too small to understand those things.

He had hoped that climbing this tall, gray-barked ash would at least give him some idea of where the edge of the woods might be, but even from up here, nothing met his eye but the endless canopy of treetops, reaching out so far it seemed they must extend to the end of the world.

Morgan knew the ancient wood could not stretch on forever, but at the moment that was very hard to believe otherwise. For him, the forest had become everything.

Days went by, each the same but for the small particularities of life with Ree-
Ree's troop. The Chikri might not be people, might not cure the ache of
loneliness that had become Morgan's constant companion, but they were lively
and individual in their way.

ReeRee's front leg had entirely healed now. She scampered up and down
trunks and from limb to limb beside the other young Chikri with an energy
that exhausted Morgan just to watch. He was beginning to recognize some of
her most frequent playmates, and he was certain now that the adult he had
named Stripe must be ReeRee's mother. Stripe was the busiest Chikri, as far as
he could tell, stuffing her cheeks with tidbits of food until they bulged, then
sharing with ReeRee and some of the other young ones. Stripe had at first
regarded Morgan with extreme distrust, and would *chik* warnings at ReeRee
every time she approached him, but the little Chikri would not be dissuaded,
and at last Stripe grudgingly accepted him, going so far as to drop nuts or other
treats in front of him from time to time, as though he were just another young
one who could not be trusted to feed himself properly.

The males of the troop ranged far above and beyond the rest, taking picket
duty, alerting the others with loud, rasping chirps and squeals when danger
appeared on the horizon. Lynxes seemed to be the greatest threats to ReeRee's
kin, although the tuft-eared cats were slow climbers compared to the Chikri.
But on the ground they were just as fast and much larger than their prey. Morgan and the rest of the troop had watched in dismay once as a lynx cornered
and then killed one of the young members of the troop. The other Chikri had
screeched and thrown down nut husks and sticks, but the cat had only ducked
its head between its shoulders until it was close enough to spring. It landed with
one paw on its prey's back, crushed the little Chikri's neck between its jaws in
an instant, then carried the limp body off into the underbrush, as unconcerned
as a tax collector he had seen one time, from the window of his grandfather's
carriage, carrying off a poor family's goods.

It was only afterward that Morgan realized that he was not a Chikri, that he
was many times larger than the cat and was carrying a sword as well. He had
probably been too far away to help in any case, but the knowledge that he had
watched and done nothing filled him with shame long afterward.

Morgan had moved his scabbard onto his back so it would not interfere with
climbing. The belt, now a makeshift harness, chafed uncomfortably, but he was
still unwilling to give up his father's sword. It felt like one of the few things that
tethered him to his old life, as if without it he might become a tree-creature in
fact as well as by current circumstance.

Bored, frustrated, and hungry for something beside nuts and leaves, Morgan
went out of his way from time to time to climb down out of the trees and catch
a rabbit, then, like a human being, make a fire to cook and eat it while the
Chikri watched him from the branches. The death and consumption of a creature not hugely different from themselves did not seem to alarm them as much

as he would have guessed: the troop watched with wide, curious eyes and sniffed the rising smoke, as though this were only another strange thing the giant Chikri did, like standing up on a branch to piss or tying himself to a tree trunk before he slept. But it was important to Morgan. He was still a man. He might be lost, friendless except for a few forest creatures, hardly a prince at all—but he was not an animal yet.

He was sitting on one of the lower branches, a little more than twice his own height from the ground which, after many long days in the trees and more time on the branches than on the ground, felt like almost no height at all. Nearby, Stripe was grooming a recalcitrant young Chikri, giving it so much "elbow," as his grandfather liked to say, that Morgan almost feared she'd scrub the poor little thing's whiskers off. ReeRee crouched on the ground below him eating a mushroom she had found growing on a log, her small, nimble hands turning the white wheel of the cap from one side to the other as she bit pieces from it. Morgan was hungry, as usual, but he had learned the hard way that he could not eat everything the Chikri could. The last bits of mushroom he had tried, an offering from Stripe, had made him so sick he had spent the rest of the evening vomiting down into the bushes below, even though he had only nibbled at a very small piece.

One of the male Chikri stood on a branch high above, leaning out into the wind like a sailor atop a mast. The sun had all but disappeared behind the trees off in what Morgan would have called the west in the old world of certainties; the little creature's reddish fur caught the light, glinting like a living flame. The troop had fed well that day while covering a great deal of ground on their mysterious, seemingly northward pilgrimage across the forest, and soon it would be time to sleep. Morgan felt a strange contentment, but a moment later he realized that he did not want that feeling, that even a moment's simple happiness filled him with unease.

I'm turning into one of them.

He looked down at ReeRee, reminding himself that if he was ever going to be a person again he would have to leave her and her troop behind. As he did, a movement along the ground caught his eye. He stared, unable at first to make out what had caught his attention. He was about to look away when he saw it again, an odd linear flickering along the edge of the log where ReeRee sat.

It was a snake, a crossed adder, bigger than any he had ever encountered in the Kynswood or the fields around Erchester. Its gray, black-laddered body was as thick as his forearm and it was almost as long he was tall. The snake was headed toward ReeRee with surprising speed, gliding through the leaf mulch as smoothly as a loose thread being pulled out of a garment. Morgan shouted a warning but ReeRee only looked up at him for a startled instant, then returned to her meal. The serpent stopped and drew its head back, bending its body like a curving mountain road. Its tongue snicked in and out. ReeRee finally noticed it and froze, the remains of her mushroom still held in front of her mouth.

Morgan jumped down from the branch. He landed badly and rolled hard against the log, but was up almost immediately, reaching over his shoulder to find the hilt of his sword. He managed to pull it free while the snake drew itself back in a threatening arc, its raw, pink mouth open to bite. He had not grasped the sword hilt properly, but he swung it at the attacker as hard as he could, catching the adder mostly with the flat of his blade. ReeRee gave out a little *squeep!* of terror and bolted up into the nearest tree, but Morgan did not take his eyes from the snake. It had a bloody gash on its side where he had hit it, but was otherwise uninjured, and it darted its head at him again and again.

Now he had his hilt properly in his hand, he lashed out backhand to keep the snake from striking. Its head bobbed as it tried to find an angle to lunge, so he kept swiping. Finally, on his fourth or fifth swing he caught it with a full cut. It flew to one side from the strength of the blow, landing in two pieces, both of which continued to writhe on the ground.

Disgusted and frightened, he hacked at it until he had made it into several smaller pieces, and they had all finally stopped moving. For a fleeting instant he wondered if he could eat it but decided that it must be full of venom. He lifted the truncated pieces on the tip of his sword and, one by one, flung them away into the underbrush, then plucked a handful of poplar leaves and wiped the blood off his blade. His father had been far too modest and practical to name a sword he used only for one ceremony, but Morgan thought it deserved a name now.

"Snakesplitter it is then." He was surprised at how strange his own voice sounded to him, how loud and unfamiliar. He sheathed the sword and scrambled back into the tree, although he discovered he was so shaky that even the short climb was difficult. ReeRee, Stripe, and the rest stared at him and chattered in quiet awe as he reached them, as though they were humble townfolk who had been menaced by a dragon and Morgan was the great Sir Camaris. And in that heady moment, he almost felt as though it were true.

More days passed by in stripes of shadow and sun. Morgan had long since lost track of what month it might be in the world outside. Anitul? Septander? Even those names had nearly lost their meaning. His time was measured instead in movement and sleep, in the soft murmurs of the Chikri as they settled in at night and the excited squeals of the youngest who woke him from his tethered sleep every morning by climbing onto his chest to share the apparently astonishing news of the sun's return.

The troop kept moving steadily northward. One happy result of their pilgrimage was that they finally seemed to move out of the disturbing dreamworld of the Sithi. Morgan could trust the shadows now, and read directions from them, but he no longer had any idea where in the great wood—a forest as big as an entire country—he might be, so he continued following the Chikri, while they in turn followed whims Morgan could not understand. A few times he tried to change the troop's direction, or simply set off on his own, but within a few hours ReeRee would find him and chatter at him in heartfelt distress until he followed her back to the rest of the troop and what she obviously considered the safety of their shared journey.

The forest lands they crossed were changing too, from the gentle hilly slopes at the edge of the Thrithings to steeper hills, heights crowned with pine trees and firs, most with branches too close together for Morgan to climb. He began to wonder where this long march would end. If he stayed with the little beasts long enough, would he finally reach the end of the forest, or—as he had long feared—were they only on some long, roundabout trek that would eventually return to the forest's southern edge again when the seasons had turned? He no longer feared starvation, but it was neither a diet that satisfied him very much, nor a life he wanted to live forever.

I'm a man, he told himself again and again, as though he did not completely believe it. *I'm not a squirrel or a bird. I can't live in the trees forever. People are missing me.*

Foremost in that imaginary group was his sister Lillia, of course, who had never known their father and who, like Morgan himself, had a mother who did not overflow with doting kindness toward her children. He owed it to his small sister to try to get back home. But how? Such thoughts came and went every day, but increasingly seemed to be matters of philosophy, like what the stars were made of, rather than real problems like feeding himself and keeping up with the Chikri.

He could not follow the troop across every stand of trees and often had to walk a good part of a morning or afternoon before being able to join them again in the heights. But his comfort in the trees was growing. His body was becoming strong in places he had not realized he was weak. His back, shoulders, thighs, and even hands grew knotted with muscle from the constant climbing. His hands, once barely callused, the rigors of youthful arms practice undone by hours spent in taverns or in soft beds, were now almost as tough as tree bark. He could hang by one arm far above the ground for long enough to find just the right place for his other hand before pulling himself up onto a limb, when only a few short weeks ago he had struggled for each upward span. Now, though he still could not match the Chikri, he would fling his loop of rope upward each time, so quickly that he barely paused on his way up the trunk in a vertical hopping motion not that different from a climbing squirrel. The Chikri, who had once watched his efforts with a worried interest that looked much like pity, had stopped paying attention, and this was perhaps the thing that made Morgan most proud.

Still, he asked himself, what use was it to be a prince who could climb trees better than any other? Especially when he was the only prince—in fact, as far as he could tell, the only person—trapped in the heart of the great forest.

They'll find my bones in a tree one day, he sometimes told himself. *I'll be a puzzle for the philosophers, that's all. That will be my legacy.*

It was a disheartening thought, which was why, some days, it was best not to think too much at all.

★   ★   ★

Morgan did not hear Likimeya's voice in his dreams any more, although he often wondered about her. He could not understand how the sleeping Sitha—if it was indeed her, and not just a phantom contrived by his own madness—could speak to him, and why she had chosen him of all people. Was it because he'd touched her? But surely others had done that too. Because he was a prince? But the Sithi had made it all too clear that they thought little of his grandparents, mortal rulers of all Osten Ard, so how much less did his own title mean?

One night he fell asleep early after a long, exhausting day and woke in darkness, still safely trussed to the linden's trunk and supported by a basket of branches. The moon had risen while he slept, and sat full and fat atop the trees like an enormous yellow egg, though the branches around him, which had been loaded with Chikri grooming and eating when he fell asleep, were now empty. He was alone.

Morgan sat up and was unknotting his rope when he heard a deep, rumbling drone drift down from above, as if a bumblebee the size of a wild boar hovered not far away. The moonlight was strong enough for him to see that the branches near the top of the tree were bowed with the weight of almost every Chikri in the troop, a bountiful harvest's worth of rounded, furry fruit. Those he could see were motionless and silent, though the low drone persisted, and he wondered if they had been driven farther into the heights after spotting some predator. Curiosity and concern overcame weariness, and he climbed up the trunk toward them, not even bothering with the rope because the branches made such useful steps.

When he had gone as high as he could without overtaxing the increasingly slender limbs, he saw that the troop members were all crouched along a pair of branches, and that above them, like a priest saying the *mansa*, sat a single Chikri, one that Morgan called Grey since most of his fur had gone that color. Grey moved with greater deliberation than most of the others, and the youngest ones liked to tease him sometimes until he drove them off with angry *chiks*. But they weren't teasing him now. Like their older relatives, the young Chikri watched with what looked like reverent attention as Grey continued to make the deep sound Morgan had heard. It had something of the feeling of a loud cat's purr, though it rose and dipped in a way no cat's purr ever did. In fact, it had a cadence almost like song or prayer, which made him think again of a priest blessing his congregation.

Then Grey paused and, after a long moment of silence, the rest of the Chikri began to purr back to him, almost in chorus, nearly startling Morgan into losing his grip. It felt as if he had stumbled onto a well-hidden secret, as though the Chikri had only been pretending to be simple forest creatures but now were unmasked as something much more subtle.

Grey began to buzz and murmur again. The others responded. After watching and listening for no little time, Morgan decided that he would never know what it was or what it meant. A few Chikri looked at him again as he made his way back down to the tree, but only briefly. All their attention was on Grey and his song of moonlight and forest.

The troop's murmur drifting gently from above, Morgan secured himself and fell asleep again. He dreamed of a place on the moon where only Chikri lived, feeding on moon moss and moon berries in a land of plenty, where they were never hunted, and where Morgan himself was happily one of them.

As if to remind him that even such a strange summer as this could not last forever, the mists began to creep across the forest. Each morning he woke to a world of murky gray beneath the treetops, and some days it did not disperse until well after the sun had reached its peak. Deer and other animals appeared as if summoned by magicians, then vanished again just as quickly and completely. Some days, descending to the misty ground when he could not follow the Chikri from tree to tree, was like diving into a colorless sea.

Is it getting colder because autumn is almost here? he wondered. *Or because we are moving north?*

The longer they traveled, the more hurried the Chikri seemed to be: the troop stopped less often these days and scarcely ever slept more than once in the same place before moving on. Some nights Morgan could hear the young ones complaining softly because there had been little time during the day's progress to look for food. Nothing seemed to be pursuing them, and as they traveled increasingly in high hills the food became more and more scarce as evergreens replaced the other trees, but still something drove the Chikri onward.

Or leads them, he told himself. He, on the other hand, was beginning to wonder whether it might be time to go his own way. He had learned much from the little animals, but if they were bound for the white wastelands of Rimmersgard, Morgan knew he would not survive. Unlike the Chikri, he had no furry coat, only his now tattered and threadbare cloak and the clothes he had been wearing since everything had gone wrong. His boots were beginning to rub through where he tied on his climbing irons, and the idea of still being lost in the woods when the cold rains came, let alone in winter's snows, filled him with dread.

The Chikri had begun a long climb through a part of the forest dominated by steep, rocky hills, and each day brought new hazards for Morgan. There were no roads, of course, and in most places not even animal tracks to follow, so when he had to leave the trees he was forced to make his way as best he could. Many times when he caught up to the troop he had the distinct feeling that Grey and the other Chikri were growing tired of waiting for him. Only ReeRee still seemed to think his presence was important, and when he staggered down from whatever rocky obstacles had slowed him and climbed wearily into the tree where they had stopped for the night, she would come to him and groom his hair and eyebrows, muttering softly the while, as if scolding a beloved but daft old relative.

★　　★　　★

They finally came to a place where Morgan knew he could not follow them, a narrow valley that stretched south to north, with high slate walls. Morgan did not much like the look of it: it was so full of mist it might have been a gateway to the netherworld, and the western side of the valley was mostly sheer stone cliffs. He hoped the troop would find a different route, but Grey and the others headed right for it. Worse, instead of simply traveling through the valley itself, or going past it to find an easier way north, the Chikri seemed determined to make their way up onto the towering eastern edge of the valley where, unlike the far side, trees grew along the steep, rocky walls. As Morgan watched in dismay, the little animals clambered through the evergreens that grew in tiers along the valley's nearly vertical walls, leaping from one tree to the next. Morgan knew that climbing through the close-knit branches of the pines would be almost impossible for him, and that the journey would only grow more perilous as they made their way through the trees along the valley's wall of crumbling slates. Even if he managed to go directly from tree to tree, Morgan could see that he would be high enough above the ground that a slip would drop him a killing distance down to the mist-cloaked valley floor, and he had no idea how long the valley was. They might be climbing along side it for days.

As the rest of the Chikri scrambled up the vegetation of the steep wall, Morgan turned away. He would have to make his way through the valley itself, which he felt sure could not be as deadly as the climb, even if the valley was inhabited entirely by hungry bears.

To his surprise, the Chikri troop took notice of him retreating to the forest floor and began to chatter and *chik* at him in alarm, but he ignored them, scrambling down the last yards of the slope. Just as he found his footing back on level ground, something ran up his back and became tangled for a moment in his cloak, making him trip and fight for balance before tumbling to the damp ground.

It was ReeRee, and when he unwound her she had a look on her strange little face he had never seen before, lips pulled back, eyes wide.

"*Chik, chik chik!*" She hopped around him as he picked himself up, her every movement a clear expression of fear and unhappiness.

"Leave me alone," he told her sternly as he climbed back onto his feet. "I can't climb that cliff. You go. I'll meet you and the rest on the other side." He pointed, but she only redoubled her scolding, and he realized he was arguing with a creature that could not understand him. He bent down to reassure her, but she leaped into his arms and clung, little claws scratching him through his thin clothing.

"Stop, ReeRee!" But she would not let go, only gripping him more tightly. He pulled her loose and dropped her to the ground, a bit more roughly than intended, but he was tired and worried about going into a place that the Chikri were so obviously avoiding, and he wasn't going to take the little one with him.

"You go back," he told her. The little animal crouched, eyes wide, looking at him in a way that filled him with shame, as though he had just knocked over a small child in the street. "I promise I'll see you on the other side, ReeRee. Go with the others." He turned his back on her and walked into the swirling mist. The last he heard was a single, distressed squeal—*"Reeeeee!"*—a final warning, he assumed, or perhaps a cry of misery.

It was only late afternoon, but within a few hundred paces into the valley he had left the sun behind along with the Chikri; darkness fell sudden as a blow and the air lost its late-summer warmth. The mist, thicker now with his every step, formed strange, ghostly shapes that billowed around him as he headed into the gorge. Nor was that the only thing that set his heart speeding and made him decide to draw his sword from the sheath on his back. The valley was also pre-ternaturally silent—no bird's cries, no hum of insects, not even the noise of wind rustling the branches. Even the broad river in the center of the valley floor flowed as smoothly as molten glass, without a burble or splash. Except for the occasional dull glint in the moving water and the dancing mists, the whole vale seemed still and empty as a plundered tomb.

Once he thought he heard a soft noise behind him and looked back, half-hoping and half-fearing ReeRee was following him, but though he stopped and stood motionless he saw nothing and heard nothing but his own heartbeat, a muffled drumbeat of blood throbbing in his veins.

The jagged valley walls looming over him were made of near-vertical bands of slate, like a stack of parchments set on end. The clifftops were jagged and broken slates piled everywhere: the valley was so narrow that it almost seemed as though giant hands had reached down and pulled the earth apart like curtains. Even the trees on the river's banks seemed unnatural, trunks growing at bizarre, tortured angles, roots spreading in interlaced webs over the damp, dark ground, and the branches of neighboring trees tangled, as though they fought each other in some impossibly slow, impossibly ancient battle. Most of the vegetation was strange to Morgan's eyes, black grasses topped with nodding gray catkin puffs, pale yellow moss that hung from the trees in clumps like the fleeces of sickly sheep. Some trees had blotchy, silvery bark and fruit as dark and shiny as lumps of tar. Morgan could not imagine ever being hungry enough to try one of those gleaming things, even though an unsatisfying meal of nuts early in the day no longer sustained him.

A glimpse of movement on the riverbank just ahead of him made him slow and stop. When he saw what had caused it, he was momentarily relieved by its small size, but sickened again a moment later by its shape. It was a salamander or something like it, but it had no eyes and as many legs as a centipede. It wound slowly across the open ground, each leg seeming to grope forward individually, toes flexing, before it disappeared into the black grass.

As he stood staring after it, the ground shook beneath his feet, a tremble so slight he might have believed he had imagined it but for the swaying of the black fruit on the branches. He began to walk again, watching the cliff walls above him for rockfalls.

The mists grew thicker still. Morgan's way grew darker, and what little sky he could occasionally see over the valley had begun to turn from blue to twilight purple. He cursed himself for his foolishness at entering the valley with no idea of how far he would have to walk. He still had his flint and steel and could start a fire, but he doubted he could find any dry wood for a torch along a damp riverbank in this unending sea of mist. The idea of being here when full night descended made him hurry his steps. He suddenly wanted to be out of the gloomy, narrow valley more than he had wanted anything in a very long time.

Then the ground lurched beneath him again, stronger this time. He stumbled and almost lost his footing, and had to steady himself against a rock slimy with moss. Something in the moss stung his fingers, and he was so busy wiping his hand, trying to get the rest of the slimy stuff off his skin that he was caught flat-footed and unbalanced when the earth trembled for a third time, spilled him off his feet, and left him sitting in the mud. A snake as long as his leg— which in full sunlight might have been colorful, but was now banded only in shades of gray and purple-black—slithered out of the grass near him and writhed past so suddenly that he did not even have time to pick up his sword before it was gone.

He scrambled to his feet and looked up for the chunks of valley wall he felt sure must have broken loose, but saw only a scatter of small, flat stones cascading down the cliffs, making ripples in the mist where they fell.

Thoom! The fourth tremor was the strongest yet, and came with a sound like thunder. As he began to climb back onto his feet Morgan had a sudden realization: each rumbling shake had been the same as the one before, but louder. Like footsteps. Like footsteps coming toward him.

Slimy with mud and nearly blinded by the thick mists, he felt something leap past his ear with a noise like a hornet's buzz. An instant later he saw an arrow juddering in the bark of a willow tree that overhung the river—it had only missed him by a hand's breadth. As he stared in stunned surprise, two more shafts flew past him, hissing like a drover's whip, and snapped into the tree just above the first one, the three in an almost perfect vertical line up the smooth gray trunk.

Morgan ran deeper into the mist, away from whoever was shooting at him, his sword still useless in his hand. His thoughts sped and fluttered madly—all he could think of was the next arrow, the one that would strike him in the back and end everything for him forever, here in this dismal, swampy valley.

A fifth great tremor struck then, and if it was a footfall the foot must have been as large as a house. The ground bucked under Morgan's feet, and he tumbled forward into water that had sloshed out of the river and drowned the black grass along the bank. As he struggled forward on hands and knees, desperately trying to gain purchase in the muddy grass, dirty water streaming into his eyes, he looked up and saw an impossible thing.

Something unbelievably huge was coming slowly down the valley toward him. In the dense mist it almost seemed a vast section of the stony cliffs had broken loose and come to life. He could hear trunks breaking as the monstrous shape approached, great bursts of sound as trees the size of the Festival Oak back home shattered into flinders. He could make out little through the murk except that the shape had two legs, and above the legs a shadowy body as wide as the prow of a great ship.

Morgan turned and ran back the way he had come, no longer concerned about arrows. The terror of the monstrous shadow was on him and he could think of nothing else, only escape, only staying ahead of the world-devouring, giant *thing*.

On he ran until he saw the entrance to the valley before him, a delta of light against the pearly mist, but the monstrous footsteps seemed even closer behind him now and he could not keep his balance on the shuddering ground. A few more arm-flailing steps and he fell. He tried to get up, to stagger forward—the end of the valley was so close now!—but he could not make his mud-coated limbs work properly. He could barely even think at all and began crawling onward on his hands and knees like some crippled animal, certain it was useless, that it would be only moments until he was crushed by that impossible thing like an ant beneath a human boot heel.

Then something caught him from above. His belly was squeezed as though gripped by a terrible serpent, and it forced the air out of his lungs as he was jerked up into the swirling mists.

PART TWO

Autumn's Chill

What is this land?
The seasons here change as swiftly
As a scholar turns a book's pages
Spring becomes summer, summer fall
Then winter again kindles spring
A year in this land is a fire that burns, dies, and burns again,
Forever consuming itself

—BENHAYA OF KEMENTARI

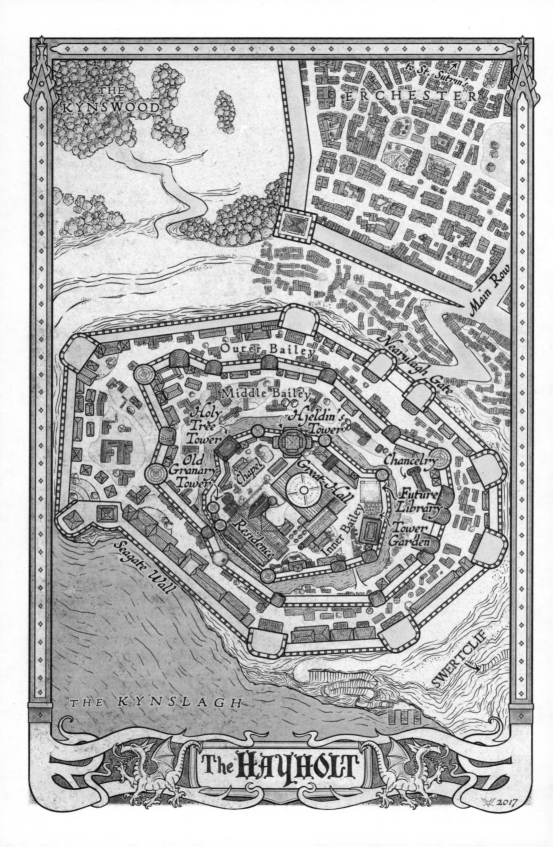

THE KYNSWOOD

ERCHESTER

to St. Sutrin's

Main Row

Outer Bailey

Nearulagh Gate

Middle Bailey

Holy Tree Tower

Hjeldin's Tower

Old Granary Tower

Chancelry

Chapel

Great Hall

Future Library

Residence

Inner Bailey

Tower Garden

Seagate Wall

SWERTCLIF

THE KYNSLAGH

The HAYHOLT

2017

20

The Summer Rose

Fremur shrugged. "It does not matter what you or I think. Unver does what he wishes, and he listens to no one. He has never been different."

A lifetime among the men of her clan should have prepared Hyara for his words, but she still felt a hot rush of anger. "But you are his friend! Don't you care? If Rudur Redbeard gets Unver in his power he will kill him."

Fremur wore a look of careful disinterest. Hyara had hoped the young thane sitting next to her would be different than the other men, but it seemed she had misread the few words they had passed together. "Friend?" he said. "Unver has never had one. Just because I am the closest thing to it does not make me his friend." And at last, to her immense relief, he betrayed something of what he was feeling, a flash of anger, a glimmer of fear. "The difference between Unver and Redbeard is, Unver Shan has honor, which he holds above everything—even friendship." He looked at her now in a way that seemed almost beseeching. "Surely you know that," Fremur said. "He is your sister's son, after all."

"Sister's son, yes, but I have not known him since he was a child. And I scarcely know my sister Vorzheva any better. She is many years my elder, and went away to live in the city with her Prince Josua while I grew. When she left our father's camp, I thought she had triumphed—met a man who cared for her, who wanted more for her than a wagon full of bawling children. Then years later she came back, face dark as a thundercloud, bringing her twins with her. My father sent young Deornoth away—that was Unver's name then—and told us he would beat us bloody if we ever spoke of him again." Hyara could still feel how that day had all but silenced Vorzheva, like a spell turning her to stone. "Our father," she said, tasting the bitterness. "I am glad he is dead."

"There," said Fremur, with a hard laugh. "That is something Unver has done for you at least—killed that old monster Fikolmij."

"You do not know as much as you think." She looked around, but nobody in the Stallion Clan's camp was paying any attention to them, all busy with plans of their own during the short but all-important festival beneath the Spirit Hills. Thanemoot held too many distractions for anyone to care much about the quiet conversation of others—boasts to make, horses to trade, *yerut* to be drunk with old friends or old enemies, until everyone involved had forgotten which they were, friend or enemy, and could only stagger out from beneath the merchant canopies and try to find their way back to their camps. Still, Hyara lowered her voice. "Unver killed my husband Gurdig, yes." She paused, remembering, and a little of that unspeakably strange day came back to her. "The spirits aided him, that is sure. I saw that with my own eyes."

"I know of Unver and the spirits," Fremur agreed, with no little feeling.

His words hung in the air. "Then you understand me," she said at last. "But Unver did not kill my father—my sister Vorzheva did. I saw that with my own eyes too."

Fremur looked surprised, even shocked, and in that moment she could see that he was still young, that however much he might want to be just another clansman, hard and cold as a blade, there was still a part of him that felt things. "Truly?"

"She had sworn she would one day."

"Then why do people say Unver did it?"

"Because he lets them. Now that Fikolmij is dead nobody will speak out against him, so he takes her crime on himself. Besides, everybody hated my father and most were glad to hear he was finally gone. The only thing they would hate more is the idea that a woman dared to raise her hand against her own father. If the others in the Stallion Clan knew, my sister would be staked out for the wolves."

Fremur laughed, and it was Hyara's turn to be surprised. "Ha! Well, they will not hear it from me. How did she do it?"

"With a cooking fork in the throat and a knife in the chest. He did not die well, but I did not raise a finger to help him." She could not bear to tell this near-stranger about the terrible things her father had done, so she hid a shiver of rage, drawing her shawl close around her shoulders though the evening was warm. "But all this is off the path, Thane Fremur."

He laughed again, but it felt different this time. "Thane. I cannot grow used to it. In fact, after the moot has ended I doubt anyone will still be calling me that. My clansmen do not care much for me *or* for Unver."

"But for now they follow you. And friend or not, you must keep Unver from going to Rudur's camp. Everyone at the moot is talking of Unver and what he has done! Rudur Redbeard cannot let a rival like that leave the Spirit Hills alive. And then the rest of us, all who came with Unver, will be murdered or made slaves."

Fremur reached out and took her hand. Hyara was both startled and strangely gratified by the younger man's touch. Her husband had not treated her as anything but a brood mare for long years before he died, and even then not as his favorite. "I cannot stop him, Hyara," Fremur said slowly. "The spirits are in him and no man alive can talk him out of anything, especially where his honor is concerned." He shook his head. "Rudur has invited him, and every man in every clan at this moot knows that. If Unver does not go, no matter how wise a course it may be, they will whisper that he was afraid of Rudur."

"Who cares what the others think?" She almost shouted it, then struggled to bring her voice back under her control. "Is it better to be dead and honored than to be alive?"

"For some, yes." Fremur took her hand again and squeezed it, then rose from the logs where they sat. "Even though I will almost certainly not be a thane by the time the last Yellow Moon wanes, I am a thane now, and I must see that my people will be safe tomorrow."

"And you?" Hyara asked, and hated herself for how much she cared about the answer. She scarcely knew this young man, who must look on her as an aging widow. To need was to be weak, and just as among the animals of the grassland, the weak attracted predators. That was a lesson she had learned from her terrible father, and she took it seriously. "Will you be safe, too? Or will you follow Unver in his foolish, deadly need to keep his honor?"

"He saved my life," Fremur said. "Honor is not only a way for men to find their deaths, you know. Your sister acted with her own honor when she killed Fikolmij, it seems to me—I have heard tales about him. We all do what we must to live inside our own skins."

She could not bear to look at him, so she lowered her eyes and nodded. "Then may the Grass Thunderer look over you." Hyara remembered he was not of her clan. "And the Crane," she began, but could not remember the spirit's proper name.

"The Sky Piercer," he said, and this time he smiled. "Yes, I hope that all the spirits will watch over us tomorrow. Do not give up all hope, lady. I saw the wolves surround Unver, saw the leader of the wolfpack pay him homage. He is not like other men."

And neither are you, Fremur Hurvalt's son, she thought as she watched him walk away. *So your death at Redbeard's hands will be mourned by few but me, I fear.*

Members of many clans lined the path that a thousand hooves had beaten into pockmarked dust to watch Unver and his followers ride past, heading toward the Black Bear camp at the end of the lake. Fremur saw that women and children stood among the men, as though this were a feast day, and most of the watching faces were full of excitement. Whether it came from seeing the now-infamous Unver Long Legs in the flesh or at the prospect of Rudur Redbeard's killing a rival was difficult to say. Many shouted as they passed, mostly in mockery—here and there someone called "Tell Redbeard we want our pasture lands back!" or "Rudur is a thief!" as though they hoped Unver and his band of a dozen clansmen would take up their grievances.

Fremur spurred his horse forward until he reached Unver, who rode with negligent grace and a hard, impassive look that might have been carved from wood.

"We are fools to ride into Redbeard's camp," Fremur quietly told Unver. "If you have a plan, at least let me know. I was the only one who took your side from the start."

"I have no side."

Fremur cursed silently. The events of the last moon had only made Unver less talkative, if such a thing was possible. "Rudur Redbeard will not think so. He will kill me and the rest of my men just as dead as he will kill you."

"He will not kill me. We are his guests." But the way Unver said it did not sound so much like belief as indifference, which was little help to Fremur's stomach. He had felt all morning like a serpent was wrapped around his innards, slowly squeezing.

A man pushed closer to where they rode, shoving others out of his way. He was large and very drunk but also young, his mustache still downy.

"Hoy, Long Legs!" he shouted. "Hoy, Unver! That is your name, isn't it? 'Nobody'! And that's what you are!"

Unver turned his horse so abruptly that the young man had to jump back to avoid it. Unver leaned down from the saddle like a hawk watching something small and full of blood scuttling through the grass. The young grasslander had not expected this reaction and stared up at him, still as stone, eyes wide, dazzled.

"No one calls me 'Nobody' unless they are *somebody*," Unver said. "Are you?"

The young man could not answer. Unver nodded, as if in agreement and turned his horse back toward Rudur's camp.

When they reached the gate the Black Bear Clan had erected for the Thanemoot, Fremur looked back at the men following them. "Where is Gezdahn Baldhead?" he asked. "He said he would be here."

His Crane Clan men shrugged.

Unver dismounted and tied his horse to the fence, then walked across the grass toward Rudur's huge tent as his other companions secured their mounts and followed. Fremur had to take swift steps to stay abreast of Unver, but he was determined that if it came to a fight he would not be thought a coward by any, even if that meant today would be his last day alive. Unver had come back for him when he could easily have left him to die. Fremur could not pay for a life with anything less than a life risked in return.

Grand as it was, Rudur's tent was only a small part of the Bear Clan camp. A wide awning stood beside it at the center of the encampment, twenty paces long on each side and open at the front; on the other two sides of the awning, Rudur's wagons served as makeshift walls. A large banner of the clan's totem, the Forest Growler, hung from the wagons at the rear, so that the man on the high stool seemed to wait for them in the bear's red, toothy mouth. Half a dozen more men sat at his feet; rough, bearded warriors, thanes of their own clans but also Rudur's bondsmen. Fremur knew them all at least by reputation, and could not imagine raising a sword against them as anything other than a form of self-slaughter.

The man on the stool, Rudur Redbeard, seemed both like and unlike his followers, although his thick gold armbands and the golden torque around his neck marked him out as more than just an ordinary clansman. Rudur was not overly tall or overly bulky, but the muscles in his tattooed arms were taut as whipcords. He had a thin nose and eyes narrow as knife-cuts, but did not glare or glower like the thanes who surrounded him. Instead he watched Unver's approach with a half-smile on his face and the keen attention of a hunter. Rudur was neither old nor young, perhaps a decade beyond Unver at most, and his famous red beard showed grey only in streaks on either side of his chin.

Fremur could see men and even some women at work around the camp, but saw no other armed Bear clansmen in sight, and none of Rudur's folk stood staring like the grasslanders who had watched their approach. Was Unver Long Legs coming to Rudur's camp really so uninteresting to them? Or did they fear violence? And was that why Fremur's clansman Gezdahn had not accompanied them after saying he would?

"Ah, here he is," said Rudur loudly at they approached. He had a shaman's voice, as though each word took on greater meaning than if spoken by another. "Unver of the Stallion Clan, come to pay his respects. Or is it Sanver? I hear you had that name once. I hear you even have a stone-dweller name as well, though I cannot remember it. And are you Stallion or Crane Clan? Many are talking about you here—asking questions about you—but perhaps you will tell me—what are you, exactly?"

"I am what you see," said Unver. "And I did not come to pay respects, although I bring no disrespect either, Redbeard. I came because you asked me to."

"I did, I did!" Rudur seemed pleased with the answer, grinning, though the rest of his expression remained cold. "I thought, 'How could the Thanemoot pass without meeting this one I have heard so much about?' And here you are."

"Yes," Unver agreed. "Here I am."

A quiet moment passed while the two men regarded each other. "Take a cup of wine with me," said Rudur at last. He clapped his hands and a trio of women appeared from his huge tent, each carrying a silver tray that, by its intricate design and fine workmanship, suggested it had been looted from the home of some Nabbanai noble. Instead of allowing himself to be served by the women, Rudur leaned out and picked up a cup and one of the ewers before pouring for himself and swigging it down. He then poured for Unver and each of the thanes sitting at his feet, who drained their cups without the slightest show of welcome or celebration.

"Fear not," Rudur said, "there is no poison here, only good red wine from the southern hills."

Unver took his and stared at it for a brief instant, then swallowed some and swirled it around in his mouth. "Wine?" he asked. "Have you given up drinking *yerut* like your father and grandfather did?"

Rudur laughed. "Do you call me soft because I like to drink what the Nab-banai drink? And am I less of a clansman because I make Nabbanai noble-women into my bed-slaves?"

"If you fell in love with one and turned away from your people, then yes—you would not be much of a clansman."

"Hah!" Rudur drained his silver cup and waved it for more. One of the women hurried forward and poured for him. "That is a rich jest, friend Unver, coming from one who is only half a clansman at all!"

Unver shrugged. "I am not responsible for my blood—or my father's deci-sion to go back to the stone-dwellers when I was young. I have lived my life as a clansmen, riding, raiding . . . and drinking *yerut*." He handed his cup to the nearest serving woman, who looked to Redbeard for permission before taking it from him. "This drink of yours is too mild for my stomach. I will wait for something more to my taste."

Rudur nodded as if at a well-shot arrow. "Then we will waste no more time on courtesies and speak of other things. I am told you call yourself the new Shan, like Edizel come again."

Fremur felt his men suddenly grew tense as drawn bowstrings, and one or two dropped their hands to their sword hilts.

"I call myself nothing but a man," said Unver. "I am no more to blame for what others say about me than I am for the stone-dweller blood that runs in my veins."

"You are not the reborn Shan, then? You do not claim that title?"

"I claim nothing."

"Then you must answer your accusers like any other clansman." Rudur clapped his hands; the serving women took their trays and scurried back to the tent, then Rudur clapped again and called, *"Volfrag!"*

The man who came out of the tent wore a shaman's robes. His black and gray beard was longer than Rudur's and hung all the way to his waist. A star had been tattooed on each of his cheeks just below his temples, and a staring eye on his forehead.

"Yes, Thane of Thanes?" the shaman asked in a deep, rumbling voice that might have come from an unsettled bull.

"Bring our other visitor."

Volfrag nodded and returned to the tent, then reemerged a moment later leading a man who wore a tattooed insignia of the Crane Clan on his arm. The newcomer looked at Unver, Fremur, and the rest, but would not meet their eyes for more than a moment.

Fremur leaped to his feet. "Gezdahn Baldhead! What are you doing? Have you betrayed us?"

At Fremur's movement the half dozen thanes sitting around Rudur all rose to their feet. The men behind Unver did the same, curved swords rasping out of scabbards. For an instant or two it seemed that bloodshed was unavoidable, but Rudur stood and glared at all of them.

"What has happened to you? Have you forgotten our way of justice? Gezdahn of the Crane Clan will speak and you will listen. No swords will drink here beneath my roof." He pursed his lips then and whistled, a single shrill blast like the call of a thrush, and suddenly a couple of score of Black Bear clansmen came spilling onto the shaded field from behind the wagons and around the side of Rudur's tent. Clearly they had been hiding and waiting for the signal. Fremur damned himself for a fool, and Unver too. These clansmen had bows and took only a few steps toward Unver and the rest before setting arrows on strings and taking aim.

"Now," said Rudur, "we shall have peace to hear what this Gezdahn fellow has to say."

"Peace? Curse you, Redbeard!" cried Fremur, for the moment more angry than he was fearful. "We are guests beneath your roof!"

"And if you offer no harm, no harm will come to you," Rudur replied. "Any man has the right to defend himself in his own camp. If any of you move from that spot, my men will kill you."

Gezdahn Baldhead had clearly not expected to complete his treachery in full view of those he was betraying and stammered so under Rudur's questioning that one of Redbeard's pet thanes stood up and held a knife against his ribs to encourage him to speak more loudly and plainly.

"I will ask again," Rudur asked, and pointed to Unver. "Do you know this man?"

Gezdahn nodded. "He is Unver Long Legs. He killed our thane, Odrig, and the groom at the wedding where all were celebrating, then named himself Thane of the Crane Clan."

"Liar!" cried Fremur. "Unver fought only to defend himself, and both fights were fair!"

"The crows helped Unver to win!" offered one of Fremur's men. "The spirits were for him, just like Edizel Shan. We all saw it!!"

"Silence," said Rudur. "I am the thane giving justice here. And I declare that this Unver is an outlaw and no true clansman. He can be no guest, since he came to me under a false name and on false grounds. Bind him."

While the rest of the Black Bear clansmen kept arrows trained on Fremur and his band, several stepped up and pulled Unver's wrists behind his back, then tied them with rawhide. "Now bow to Rudur," said the one who knotted the cord. "Bow to the Thane of Thanes."

Unver spat on the ground. "I would rather bow to the king of the demons."

"And so you may soon enough." Rudur nodded. Unver's captor lifted his sword, and in despair Fremur lurched forward, not even thinking of the certain

storm of deadly arrows. But instead of taking Unver's head off, the man re-
versed his blade and struck him on the skull with the heavy pommel, toppling
Unver senseless to the grass.

"You call this treachery *justice*?" Fremur shouted. "Attacking those you have
invited to guest under your roof? The spirits of the grasslands will judge you
and condemn you!"

Rudur examined Unver's supine form with a ghost of a smile before answering. "It is nothing *but* justice. And as to the spirits—well, Fremur-also-called-
Rabbit, we will see what the Forest Growler and the rest think in truth. I will
not do anything so crude as behead this pretender, much as he might deserve it
for his murdering ways. No, the spirits themselves will judge him."

"What nonsense are you talking?" Fremur demanded, but a sudden memory
had come to him and the icy knot in his stomach pulled even tighter.

"You believe he is the Shan," Rudur said loudly enough for all to hear. "And
he did not discourage those who named him so, however little he had done to
deserve it. Edizel Shan and many others before him who claimed Heaven's
favor were all put to the test of the Summer Rose and the Long Night. Only
Edizel survived. So we will give Long Legs the same tests, and the spirits of
Heaven themselves will decide his fate." He turned to the shaman. "Volfrag, is
the hour for the ordeal come now?"

"It will be here soon, Thane of Thanes," the bearded man rumbled.

"Good." Rudur stretched his limbs like a man who had been kept from his
real business too long, then looked down again at the man lying stretched before him. "Throw some water on him and get him to his feet. He will be taken
out to where all those who bark his name can see his fate with their own eyes.
They think Unver Long Legs is the Shan returned, do they? Let us see how he
likes the kiss of the Summer Rose."

Two open wagons, flanked by Rudur's warriors on horseback, rolled along
the main road of the camp, circling the lake so Redbeard could show off his
prisoners. Fremur and the rest of Unver's followers had been shoved into the
second wagon and sat on the damp boards, bound and tumbling against each
other with every bump of its wheels. Unver was in the first, still senseless, with
Rudur standing over him. Because the Thane of Thanes was with him, the
crowd hurled only insults at Unver, but Fremur and the rest, not so lucky, were
pelted with mud and offal.

Where are the rest of my Cranes? Fremur wondered. *Are they all traitors, not just
Gezdahn Baldhead? And what of Unver's own Stallions? Does Redbeard not fear to
provoke a fight?* But when he wiped the mud from his eyes and looked back, he
saw what looked like every man from Rudur's Black Bear Clan and hundreds
more from the clans that supported him walking half a dozen abreast behind
the wagons, and knew why Rudur Redbeard did not fear to display what he
had done.

The circuit of the lake took hours in the hot afternoon sun, and by the time they returned to Rudur's camp it seemed like the whole of the Thanemoot was following them. Fremur and the rest of his men were lying down in the wagon now, weary of being splashed with filth and deafened by shouted curses. The wagons rolled past the Black Bear camp and headed toward the base of the largest and most sacred hill, called the Silent One after the nameless spirit who had created humankind from atop its crest in the days before time began.

The horses snorted and dirt flew from beneath their hooves as the two wagons climbed the winding track. The crowd scrambled after them like ants over a fallen log, picking their way up the slope however they could, almost frenzied at being allowed on the sacred hill. The caravan stopped near the summit on a great natural shelf of grassy earth. At the center loomed a massive standing stone, said to be the place where the spirits first met to learn their places in the world made by the Silent One. Some of Rudur's men had ridden ahead to drive a wooden post into the ground in front of the holy stone; Fremur's blood went cold when he saw it. This was the place where enemies of the clans had been sacrificed for years beyond counting. No execution post had been mounted on the hill since the end of the last war with the stone-dwellers, but Rudur seemed bent on showing the whole of the grasslands that he was the only Thane of Thanes.

Several more of Rudur's clansmen climbed into the wagon and lifted Unver then carried him toward the post. He was awake now and fought them, but they were too many. They tore off his shirt, then pushed his face against the post. With several men grasping each arm, Rudur's warriors cut the bonds on Unver's wrists and ankles and pulled his hands to the far side of the post before retying them, so that he could only stand helplessly with his belly against the naked wood and his back exposed.

Rudur inspected his prisoner, then walked to the front of the plateau where the crowd, following, met a line of grim Black Bear clansmen and stopped. The onlookers continued to struggle among themselves for a better view, shoving and shouting.

"In the old days," Rudur called out, "there was a cure for those who tried to take what was not theirs, whether another man's horses or the title of Shan. It is called the Summer Rose." He turned and waved his arm. "Bring it to me, Volfrag."

The bearded shaman stepped forward with an armload of slender branches of so dark a green that they looked almost black even in the bright, late afternoon sunshine. Rudur took one end of the rope-bound bundle, thick as a man's wrist, and lifted it in the air. The flail of long branches dangled almost to his knees. "Wild roses blessed by the Silent One, grown on His hill," said Rudur. "A fit punishment for one who would put his name in the mouths of the spirits."

The wild rose branches had been soaked in brine, Fremur knew, until they were as supple and strong as braided whipcord. But the treatment did not soften the thorns at all, his father had told him, leaving them instead as hard and fierce as fish hooks.

"This is what the spirits think of those who would tell lies in their names, Unver No-Clan," Rudur declared, loud enough to be heard far back in the throng. "This is what their anger feels like!" And he swung back the branches and then snapped them forward, raking Unver's back in a broad swath. Unver did not cry out, but his muscles clenched beneath the blow like a fist, and for a moment his legs did not hold him, though the knots around his wrists did. Blood began to dribble from his back in some places, but in others the thorns had bitten more deeply, so that red streamed out in rivulets and began to drip down his legs.

"One hundred strokes of the Summer Rose!" crowed Rudur, and the crowd gave back a noise like animals waiting to be fed. Here and there Fremur thought he heard a few of them cursing Redbeard, but they were isolated sounds in a sea of approval. "That will test his claim. Edizel Shan survived it—surely you, with your high ambitions, can do no less!"

"That is only an old story!" cried Fremur, finally staggering to his feet to stand at the back of the wagon. His clansmen tried to pull him down but he would not be silenced.

"You call the history of our people only a story, Fremur-the-Rabbit?" Rudur shook his head, still swinging the rose-branches slowly back and forth. "Do you envy this traitor so much you wish to join him? We can always put up another stake."

"If you like stories, Redbeard," shouted Fremur, "then remember what happened to the thanes who were false to Edizel!" If his men hadn't been tied they would have clapped their hands over his mouth to silence him, but as it was they could only jostle him and try to kick his feet out from under him as he kept shouting. "Remember what the spirits did to *those traitors!*"

Rudur nodded to someone Fremur couldn't see, and a moment later a large hand seized his neck and slammed his head forward against the rail of the wagon. His wits swirled in a dark whirlpool, and he tumbled backward, feeling as if the entire hill had fallen on him.

As he lay helplessly on the wagon bed he heard Rudur say, "Next time I hear your voice, Crane-man, you will join this weak-blooded fool."

Unver's whipping went on and on. Fremur heard Rudur bring others of his chosen thanes in to take turns, but he did not see it, since he could not get his legs to support him. It was only as the last of the strokes was falling that he managed to climb to his feet again. Unver, who had not cried out once, was now far beyond making any noise at all. He hung limply by his tied wrists, his back a hideous, red-smeared mass of deep furrows and tattered skin. Even the crowd had fallen silent.

"Take him down," said Rudur. "Volfrag, does he live?"

The shaman bent over Unver and held a small, shiny object before his face. "He still breathes, Thane of Thanes."

Rudur laughed. "Then the spirits decree he has not suffered enough yet. They want to take a hand! Tie him with his back to the post."

Unver did not resist as his tattered, bloody back was pushed against the stake, and his hands were tied once more. Now Fremur could hear a voice screaming curses at Rudur from somewhere in the crowd.

"One of Unver's women does not like the entertainment," said Rudur to the other thanes. "Or perhaps she is already searching for a new man."

"I'll kill you myself, you coward!" the woman cried, and now Fremur could hear others trying to make her stop. "You are no bear, Redbeard—you are an ox! You gave up your balls to the city-men years ago!"

Rudur was clearly annoyed by the woman, but the disruption was far enough back in the crowd that he could not easily silence her. "I made peace, you bitch—peace for all the clans! I saved our lands!"

"The stone-dwellers take more of them every day!" someone shouted from another part of the crowd. "The Nabban-folk push us out of the places our fathers rode!"

"Silence!" Rudur bellowed. "You mewling children know nothing. Any more braying from any of you and we will water this sacred ground with *your* blood as well." He barked an order to his thanes and several gathered their men and waded out into the crowd, pushing and even hitting those who would not get out of their way fast enough, but the onlookers were crushed too close together and Rudur's men had to stop after penetrating only a little way.

Rudur Redbeard seemed to recognize that the spectacle had gone on too long. He strode to the front of the level place and stared down at the throng until those nearest him fell into uneasy silence. The sun had dropped behind the rounded top of the Silent One; for most of the observers he could not have been much more than a dark shape, like one of the spirits' first attempts to make people.

"Unver No-Clan will hang here through the night," announced Rudur, then strode to where the prisoner slumped at the base of the post. Rudur lifted Unver's head and seemed to like what he saw in the man's face, for he laughed then.

"I think the blood is already drying," said the Thane of Thanes. "That will never do. We want the wild creatures of the Spirit Hills to know that a gift has been left for them—an offering." He bent and pulled a long knife from his belt, slashed at Unver's cheeks and forehead, then made three horizontal cuts across his chest. Even after all the blood that had coursed from Unver's back during the whipping, more flowed from these wounds.

Rudur straightened. "Spirit Hill will be surrounded by armed men tonight," he said, voice booming out over the now quiet, uneasy crowd. "Any one who tries to bring this traitor water or anything else will be killed. Only the spirits themselves will decide if he lives or dies. Now go! Back to your camps! You will see the results tomorrow at dawn."

After a few moments the wagon holding Fremur and his men lurched forward and then turned in a slow circle to head out of the hills. The last Fremur saw of Unver was a darkened shape crumpled against the post at the base of the great stone, motionless but for a slow trickle of blood down his chest. He seemed lifeless as the husk of a dead beetle.

21

Among the War-Shrikes

Nezeru came back to herself at last, bound, betrayed, and groggy. She was tied into the saddle, her face against the neck of Jarnulf's horse, and the pounding of its hooves shook her until she could barely think. And each moment that passed carried her farther into unknown reaches.

Nezeru struggled against her bonds, but could find no quick way loose. Jarnulf might be a traitor to the queen and Nakkiga, she thought in disgust, but he knew how to make a knot. As the horse thundered on she grunted and stretched her arms against the ropes, ignoring the pain as she began the long process of freeing herself.

The white horse had finally slowed to a canter by the time she worked one hand free. Her face still pressed against the horse's sweating back, Nezeru began working the rest of her arm back and forth, gripping a loop of her bonds for leverage. As she did so she felt a lump beneath the coils of cord and began to dig under the rope, trying to work her hand between the tight coils, and was at last able to touch something hard with her fingertips. It took no small time to wriggle it loose, but by the time she could wrap her fingers all the way around it, she could tell it was her own knife, still in its sheath. Jarnulf had gone out of his way to tie it just within her reach—he must have known she would find it eventually. Which meant he had given her a way to escape.

He is truly mad. Mortal thought, at least his, seemed far beyond Nezeru's understanding.

She cut the bonds holding her tight to the horse's back, and could at last sit up straight. Ignoring the terrible ache of her muscles, she grabbed at the pale mane and pulled back until the horse stopped and reared, whinnying. A moment later she slid off in a mess of uncoiling cord.

Nezeru hit the ground hard and rolled. For a dozen swift heartbeats or more she could only lie on her back staring up at the trees and the darkening sky as she struggled to get air into her chest. She heard the horse stamping anxiously nearby, then it turned and went crashing through the forest, still performing the task its master had set even after its burden was gone. Nezeru tried to rise but her legs were wobbly as willow branches, and she could only

take a few steps before she stumbled and fell to her knees. She let her forehead
sag to the ground until the blackness cleared. When she next looked up, she
could no longer hear the horse's hoofbeats on the forest floor.

She remembered that she still had *kei-vishaa* on her face from Jarnulf's attack,
so she took up a handful of earth and leaves and scrubbed at her mouth and
chin. As her head began to clear she crawled back to the spot where she had
fallen with the idea of gathering up the rope, but quickly saw that something
else lay half-covered in the splay of coils—a sheathed sword.

She recognized the scabbard immediately; the incised runes on the witchwood blade only confirmed what she already knew. *Cold Root, Makho's fabled
sword,* she marveled. *The blade of General Suno'ku herself! By the Blood of the Garden, the mortal has given me that as well!*

Nezeru crouched, stunned. She did not know where she was and could not
understand why she had been chosen by Jarnulf for this incomprehensible treatment, but had a sudden, icy premonition that after this, nothing in her life
would ever be the same.

Three nights and three days alone in the woods did nothing to further Nezeru's
understanding of why the mortal Jarnulf had kidnapped her. Not that it mattered; she was bent only on finding her way back to the rest of her companions
to denounce him and see him get the punishment he deserved. She even hoped
she would be allowed to do it herself—separating Jarnulf's treacherous head
from his neck would be the only truly satisfying thing that had happened to her
since she had left Nakkiga. But she did not know how far his horse had carried
her, or what path it had taken—the hills were covered in slabs of white granite
that showed no tracks, even to the trained eyes of a Talon. She could only hope
she was still in the foothills of Urmsheim, close to Saomeji and the giant, but
the position of the sun and nightime stars suggested that she was instead far
south of any place she remembered—and now she was on foot as well. She
knew it would take an overwhelming effort to catch up to her companions
before they met up with the company that Akhenabi had promised to send from
Nakkiga, so she forced her bruised body into a rigorous march. She scrambled
over fallen trees and leaped from one flat place to another like one of the mountain sheep that inhabited Urmsheim's most inaccessible slopes. She was hungry
and remembered a small supply of *puju* in her jacket. The unwanted ride on
Jarnulf's horse, however, had crushed it to a powder that she had to swallow in
dry, dusty bites. It barely kept her going, but she dared not take the time to
hunt, not if she held any hope of catching up with the rest of the Talons and
settling accounts with the mortal huntsman.

Nezeru hurried down the sloping foothills trying to remember everything
that had led up to Jarnulf's act of treachery. Each riddle she examined seemed
to have another set of questions nested inside it, layer after infuriating layer. The
mortal had often tried to confuse her with questions that had no sane answers.
She swore now that she would get her answers from Jarnulf himself—if that was

even his name—in the true, time-honored Sacrifice manner, with a blade at his throat, before she ended him.

The purple of dawn was the first thing Nezeru saw when she opened her eyes, but it seemed a bitter hue. More time lost. The *kei-vishaa* seemed to be lingering in her blood: when she had stopped to rest she had fallen into a sleep deeper than any she had known. Now it was clear that hours had been wasted.

But even as she struggled to order her groggy thoughts, to rise and begin again, a hand coiled in her war-braid and something sharp pressed against her throat. "Do not move, deserter," said a voice in quiet Hikeda'yasao, "or your sentence will be rendered here and now."

Nezeru stayed motionless, but her heart skipped a beat in relief. She had been found by her own people—perhaps even the soldiers sent to meet Saomeji and the rest with their prisoned dragon! "I will give no resistance," she said promptly. "I am no deserter, either. I am a Queen's Talon, on the queen's business. Let me sit up, and I will keep my hands lifted so you can see that I hold no weapon."

"You may not hold a weapon at this moment," the voice said close to her ear. "But you have a sword you are not grand enough to carry, I think, and I see another blade at your belt. Wait until my fellow scouts join me before you move or I will let out your blood." The sharp point against her throat pushed harder, a sting like a horsefly's bite. "Sit and be silent."

Within moments two more shapes glided all but soundlessly out of the trees. They wore pale garments smeared with mud and pine needles, so that they almost seemed part of the forest. Nezeru was grateful to have been found, but ashamed to have slept so deeply that ordinary Sacrifices could surround her without waking her. Still, after the shambles her own Queen's Hand had become, it was almost soothing to find a troop of her order performing their duties with grace and skill.

The first scout gave her a nod to say she could sit up, but did not let go of her hair or take the knife from her throat.

"I am Queen's Talon Nezeru, a Sacrifice of Chieftain's Makho's Hand," she said. "Why do you treat me like an enemy?"

"Speak only to answer," he told her. "What are you doing here, prowling near Fortress Dark Lantern?"

She did not recognize the name. She turned slowly toward him. His skin was pale as birch bark and a stripe of black had been daubed from temple to temple, surrounding his eyes like a mask, but she guessed by the shape of his face that he was probably a halfblood like Nezeru herself. "Who are you, Sacrifice?"

He met her stare with defiance. "I am Scout Rinde of the Legion *Sey-Jok'kochi*—the War-Shrikes."

"Were you sent to meet our Hand?"

He shook his head. "No more questions from you, Sacrifice. Our commander will decide your fate." He stood up and slid his slender bronze knife into a sheath on the arm of his muddied jacket. "Now stand and walk before us. My companions both have bows. If you move too swiftly they will put half a dozen arrows in you before you can escape."

"I have no interest in escaping." She let them prod her onto her feet, then walked with them, the one called Rinde at her elbow and the other two pacing silently behind her down the slope.

Tzoja's days in hiding by the underground lake were long and she had little to occupy her thoughts but memories. She thought often of her daughter Nezeru, but after a year of not knowing where in the world she might be, that was more like mourning. She also thought about Viyeki, who at first had been only her master but now seemed much more to her—a husband, almost, though his peers would have been disgusted by the idea. But Viyeki was not like the rest of the Hikeda'ya, for which she was very, very grateful.

When he had first chosen her from several slaves sent by the barrack master for his perusal, he had drawn the process out over hours, asking the mortal women strange questions such as whether they dreamed, or had they ever been south of Rimmersgard. He must have liked Tzoja's answers best—*yes, vividly,* she had told him; and *yes, as far as Kwanitupul.* The dream part was not really true, since after her capture by the Skalijar and then the Hikeda'ya, Tzoja generally fell asleep like someone stumbling off a precipice and came back up like a drowning woman reaching for the light. Her slumber was haunted by shadows, angry voices, long bleak vistas through which she walked and walked, but even these faded quickly when she woke. Still, she would have said or done anything to escape the squalor of the slave barn, and inventing dreams for an eccentric fairy nobleman seemed a small price to pay.

Her answers had seemed to please this Lord Viyeki, and after deliberating silently for a long time he at last chose Tzoja and sent the others back to the frigid barns. The rejected slave-women did not even look up as they were led out.

"So," Viyeki had said, "Do you know why you are here? You are young, but not that young, I think. Tell me your name again."

"Derra."

"An awkward sound. We will consider that. Please take off your clothes. Put them by the door—they will be disposed of. There is a bath in the next chamber. Do you know what that is?"

She had barely been able to confine herself to a demure nod. She had not been clean for longer than she could remember, and the idea of hot water had been as welcome as the thought of seeing sunlight again.

Of course, the water was not hot, nor even warm. She learned the first of many lessons about the Hikeda'ya nobility: they preferred to bathe in the icy water that sluiced down from the mountain's cap in numerous rivulets, although they also had it hot from deep springs, steaming, frothing water that coursed through Nakkiga like veins of blood. But though they scorned hot water for bathing, the Hikeda'ya did use soap, or at least a strange, flaky stone that did the same job, and though she could not force herself to squat for very long in the shiveringly cold water, she at least managed to scrub the grime from her skin.

With nothing to dress herself in, she had gone naked out into the main chamber and found Viyeki waiting for her. To her eye he could have been a young man of thirty summers or even less, but she had learned enough about the immortals to know he might be hundreds of years old. That had been too strange to think about—it still was—and she had pushed it away, determined to do whatever was needed to stay in this warm place for as long as possible.

Their first lovemaking, or "coupling" as Viyeki called it, was nowhere near as painful or humiliating as she had feared. Since being captured, she had been taken to the beds of several other Hikeda'ya, and most of them had been perfunctory at best in their attentions, treating her more like a necessary but uninteresting tool than a partner. Viyeki was different. That first time and afterward he seemed interested in her as more than just a receptacle, pausing to look at her face, smell her skin, even rub his cheek gently against her neck—the closest thing to a kiss she had experienced as a bed slave—

Tzoja was startled out of these memories by a scratching sound at the door, just loud enough for her to hear. She darkened the light of her crystal sphere, then crawled by feel into the hallway. Had it been a less familiar sound she would have hidden, but she had already recognized the noise: it came from Naya Nos's little fingers, and it meant that the Hidden were at the door.

Still, she rose to peer through a slot in the door, no bigger than a finger. The wormglow of the cavern revealed the tall, two-headed silhouette she expected, the small one held in huge Dasa's arms. She opened the door as quietly as she could and beckoned them inside, but they did not move.

"I am sorry, friend," said Naya Nos in a strange, unhappy voice, then the two-headed shape moved to one side and someone else stepped forward and jabbed a long shadow at her face. Tzoja barely had time to take a startled step backward before something snapped shut around her neck and then, with sudden, almost casual brutality, she was yanked forward off her feet and onto her hands and knees.

"There are no words to say my sorrow," Naya Nos murmured. "He would kill all my people—all the Hidden. We had to give you up to him. Even the Lady Uvasika agreed."

The collar was chokingly tight, and at first she could not even swallow. The thing that held her was a slave pole, a long rod with a neck-catch at one end. As she tried to move her head and loosen the grip on her throat, a bright flash blinded her—a *ni'iyo* in the newcomer's hand. When Tzoja could see again she discovered that her captor was a tall figure dressed all in black, as bony and grim-faced as any Hikeda'ya, despite his ruddy skin—another mortal like herself.

He held the lighted sphere close to her face and studied her. "You are the one known as Tzoja, the property of Clan Enduya." It was not a question.

"No," she managed at last. "I ran away from the slave barns." At least the penalty for a slave trying to escape was a quick death.

The hard-faced man did not bother to refute her hasty lie, but pulled up on his tether-staff until she had to rise or choke, then he led her toward the door. Outside she saw shapes in the darkness. Naya Nos and the rest of the Hidden, she presumed, here to see her life exchanged for theirs.

"Cowards!" she cried, but her captor silenced her with a twist of the pole, squeezing her neck even more cruelly. She had not worn a slave collar since Viyeki had taken hers off during the first days she spent in his clan house. She had forgotten how horrid it felt, not just the discomfort, but the knowledge that you were owned, that your very life was now someone else's property, to be disposed of as they wished.

She wondered if she would be able to divert this grim man's attention enough to jerk the pole out of his hand as they climbed one of the steep staircases on the way back to the upper levels of Nakkiga. Killing herself by jumping from the stairs was likely the best alternative left to her—at least it would be by her own choice.

"Please forgive me for speaking," she said in as servile a tone as she could manage, "but I am curious. If I have nothing else left, I might as well satisfy that. Who are you?"

"I am a Queen's Huntsman." He dragged her stumbling away from the festival-house and across the cavern, then up one of the winding corridors. To her dismay, she realized he had chosen a covered passage meant for litters and wagons, with closed sides and only shallow slopes.

"Queen's Huntsman—but you are a mortal!" she said.

He walked for a while in silence, keeping the collar tight against the back of her neck by tension on the pole. "You are ignorant," he finally said. "Most of the queen's huntsmen are mortals. Why would the People stoop to chasing runaway slaves? Slaves are good enough to catch other slaves."

"Then you are a slave like me?"

"I am on the other end of the catchpole, so obviously I am not." But she heard something alive in his voice for the first time, some glimmer of human feeling, even if it was only contempt. "So do not seek to play on my fellow-feeling, woman. I would not be the queen's chief huntsman of the lower depths if I had any. Now be silent and stop trying to distract me. We are following the cart-route instead of the stairs, so there will be nowhere you can escape or destroy yourself." He felt her stumble, and when he spoke again she heard a poisonous note of satisfaction. "All you fools are the same."

Tzoja had been so long in nearly complete darkness that when they reached the dim, lantern-lit streets of Nakkiga it seemed almost as bright to her as a mortal city. The Hikeda'ya nobles and soldiers in the street did not bother to look at her as she was led past, but the slaves did, some only sneaking fearful glances, others staring openly—and doubtless thanking their gods, Tzoja thought miserably, that they were not the ones at the end of the huntsman's tether.

As her grim-faced captor marched her through the outskirts of the Harvest District, past the long, narrow warren-houses of fungus pickers and grub gatherers, Tzoja became more fearful with every step. When they turned at last onto the Avenue of the Fallen and approached the guardhouse at the deepward gate of Clan Enduya's compound, it was all her trembling legs could do to keep her upright.

The huntsman was taking her back to Viyeki's clan house—but Viyeki was no longer there. The only one waiting for her would be her master's wife, Khimabu, the beautiful monster who would happily torture her for daring to bear her husband a child when his Hikeda'ya wife could not. Tzoja tried to pull away, but a surprisingly small twist of the pole yanked her off balance so that her head cracked hard against the compound's stony outer wall. She sagged, then was throttled into rising again, coughing and breathless, by another twist of the collar.

She should have been beyond shame, but seeing the faces of Clan Enduya guards she recognized while they looked back blandly, as though they had never seen her before, hollowed her out completely. As the huntsman rapped out a few words to them she could only stand shivering, caught in a waking nightmare.

One of the guards disappeared into the clan house; a scant few moments later the lady of the house swept in like something from a nursery tale, her diaphanous pale green dress billowing around her like forest mist, her face as icily perfect as an artist's masterpiece. When she saw Tzoja, Khimabu's matchless lips parted just a little, turning up at both ends in a small but immensely satisfied smile.

"My lady," said the Queen's Huntsman, "is this the escaped slave Tzoja, servant of Lord Viyeki's household?"

"Oh, yes. Oh, yes, it most certainly is." Khimabu stared at Tzoja like a delicious meal. "A very wicked slave she is, too, but do not fear—I have thought of many suitable punishments for her. *Many*." She reached out a long-fingered hand, her movements graceful and measured, but the gleam in her bright eyes gave her away. "Give her to me now, huntsman—I cannot wait. Do you need payment? I will have my cleric take you to my lord's counting room . . ."

"No, my lady, you may not have her," said the huntsman, surprising both women. "That is all I need of you—you have confirmed this is the slave Tzoja. She will not stay here any longer. She is not your prisoner."

Khimabu's expression turned icy and her lip curled as if she would bite out his throat. "What nonsense is this from another mortal slave? My husband the High Magister is away on a mission for Queen Utuk'ku herself. In his absence, my word rules this clan house."

The huntsman bowed again. "I am a slave, yes, my lady, but this creature is now the queen's prisoner—the Mother of All personally ordered her capture. Do you take precedence over the queen? I think not."

He left Khimabu stuttering in confusion as he led Tzoja away.

At first Tzoja had a moment of hope, unlikely as it seemed, that the huntsman might have lied, that he might wish to keep her for himself. She was relieved to think that rape followed by death might be the worst thing she would suffer—a horror, but far better than what Khimabu meant for her. As they made their way up the great staircase to the upper level, approached the labyrinth that was the royal Omeiyo Palace, then marched through its great carved gates, Tzoja realized the huntsman had been telling the truth about taking her to Queen Utuk'ku and she abandoned hope entirely.

Even on horseback—Nezeru rode behind Rinde with her wrists bound—it still took them almost two full days to reach the War-Shrike Legion camp, and that was only the first surprise.

With no warning, Scout Rinde stopped and dismounted in a small forest clearing on the side of a wooded hill. He made a trilling sound with pursed lips and a slab of rock that had looked to be half-buried in the earth rose upward, revealing another Sacrifice lifting it from beneath. Nezeru was forced onto her hands and knees and made to crawl into the hidden tunnel. It seemed like an elaborate arrangement for a mere Sacrifice camp and she wondered if the secrecy meant they were close to mortal lands. Certainly they seemed to have traveled eastward far enough. But she had never heard of Hikeda'ya encampments so far from Nakkiga.

The passage beyond the opening was much larger than Nezeru would have expected, large enough for her to stand up and for two or maybe even three Sacrifices to walk abreast. Rinde and the other scouts prodded her forward. Here and there, holes in the passage ceiling let in light. When she looked up she saw a complicated arrangement of sticks and leaves that disguised the holes and would prevent anyone above from seeing down. As they walked through the tunnel Nezeru could see it was crossed by other passages just as high and almost as spacious, the work of much digging and bracing. Many Sacrifice soldiers passed them, and although a few cast curious looks in her direction none spoke. When another two almost ran into each other in a crossing just in front of her, they stepped apart without a word and went their separate ways.

They're under silence discipline, she realized.

This was no mere camp she had arrived at, but a fortification meant for long-term survival in enemy territory. She knew Jarnulf's horse had carried her a long distance, but could it have carried her almost all the way into mortal lands? Even so, she had never heard of such an elaborate underground fort so far from Nakkiga, nor knew of any reason for such a thing to exist.

She was led to a door—something clearly crafted in Nakkiga and brought here. Rinde left her in the tunnel with the other two scouts while he went inside, then a short time later he emerged and gestured for her to enter.

A surprisingly large room had been dug out of the earth and walled in wooden boards. A single Sacrifice officer stood over a wide table (another piece of woodwork too fine to have been crafted in the field) looking down at a collection of abstract shapes made from wood and set in clumps on a rolled-out tapestry. She did not look up. Rinde, who had accompanied Nezeru into the lamplit chamber, stood at silent attention just inside the door.

Nezeru could see that this was no common officer but a league commander, a Sacrifice rank just below general. The room was lit by several small lamps, and stools were set around the table, suggesting a war council had just ended.

The commander seemed in no hurry to acknowledge Nezeru but moved slowly around the table examining the arrangements of wooden shapes from different angles. She was lean and fit, her age apparent only in the thinness of her skin. But she held her left arm against her chest at an odd angle, as though it were injured.

At last the commander paused and straightened, then turned hard, coal-dark eyes on Nezeru.

"You claim to be a Queen's Talon," she said without preamble.

"It is no mere claim. I am Sacrifice Nezeru, one of the Queen's Talon commanded by Chieftain Makho. I have been kidnapped from my camp . . ." She hesitated then, reluctant to admit she had been bested by a mortal. "If you give me assistance to return to my Hand, you will be doing the queen's will."

"I do nothing *but* the queen's will," said the officer. "Do not tell me my duty, Sacrifice. Rinde?"

"Yes, Commander Juni'ata?"

"Find this Sacrifice a place to take rest if she needs it, but she is not to leave the fort under any circumstances unless I command it. Is that clear?"

"But I have a mission! The queen's mission that she gave to us!" Nezeru could not believe even the most confident officer would risk the queen's ire without more information. "You have not even asked me what our task is!"

Juni'ata turned, the movement displacing her shoulder cloak to reveal a stretch of strange weathered yellow between her left glove and sleeve. Juni'ata noticed her staring and shrugged the cape aside, then pulled back the sleeve. At first Nezeru could not make sense of what she saw, but then she realized the commander's forearm was not flesh but a single piece of what looked like walrus ivory.

"A giant took my arm," Juni'ata said, but she was not looking at Nezeru anymore: the shapes on the tabletop had recaptured her attention. "Bit off everything below the shoulder. But after I killed him, one of his leg bones was carved to provide me with a new arm." The officer shook her head with something like dissatisfaction, as if wishing she could do it all again but even more artfully. "Scout Rinde, take the prisoner away now. I am working."

"Yes, Commander."

"Prisoner?" Nezeru was having trouble keeping her voice respectfully calm. "I am on a mission for the queen herself! How can you interfere?"

Commander Juni'ata gave her a look as empty as a broken jug. "Anyone could claim that. We will discover what is real. If you speak the truth, Sacrifice, you will be allowed to return to your Hand. If you are lying, you will receive the full penalty for your broken oath." She made a small hand-sign and Rinde took Nezeru by the arm, then guided her out again.

"She is hard but fair, our commander," the scout said quietly. "But may the Garden protect you if you ever lie to her."

She had no answer. Nezeru knew by experience that the cold discipline of the Order of Sacrifice would prevail, no matter what she said or did.

22

Misty Vale

Something squeezed the breath from Morgan's chest
as it yanked him upward into the air—squeezing him so tightly that though he
tried to scream in sudden terror, he could only summon enough breath to
squeak.

He jerked to a halt but still swung helplessly. The mists surrounded him,
hiding both the ground and the treetops above so that he seemed to float in a
swirling white netherworld. As the first moment of astonishment passed he
realized he was not being held by gigantic fingers but by a rope around his
chest, and that as he thrashed and fought to free himself the rope was working
its way higher up his body—and that rope was the only thing keeping him from
falling what he felt sure was a fatal distance.

Morgan stopped struggling. His arms were pinioned, the rope pulled painfully tight around his arms just above his elbows, but he had a swift nightmare
vision of the loop suddenly sliding all the way up to his neck. For a long moment
all he could think of was the thief he had once seen on the public gallows in
Breakstaff Square in Erchester. Inexpertly hanged, the man had wriggled like a
fish for an achingly long time as he died. Morgan's tutor (who along with several
guards had been letting the young prince explore the marketplace) had tried to
pull him away, but the last sight of the legs kicking in mid-air had never left him.

He looked up into the tree, but the leaves hid whoever or whatever had
snared him.

Just then the branches rattled and the whole tree shuddered, as if a hammer
as big as the moon had struck the ground. As Morgan swung violently back and
forth he remembered that the rope on which he dangled like a plumb bob was
the least of his problems.

That thing . . . the giant . . . !

It was still coming toward him, a monstrously huge shape made unrecognizable by mist and angled light. It was far too big to be real—but it *was* real, it
was, and moving closer. Then it stopped. In that moment of stillness he could
make out something of the thing's squat shagginess—or at least its shaggy lower
quarters, since the rest of the massive thing was still hidden by the swirling
white haze. Its legs made shadows as big as grain silos.

Morgan held his breath and let himself go limp, though his heart was thumping. He prayed to God and Usires and his Mother Elysia that the giant could not see him hanging there like a fat quail curing above a crofter's door. For an achingly extended moment nothing moved except Morgan himself, gently swaying. Then the massive shadow turned and trudged back into the depths of the canyon, each thunderous step accompanied by the snap and crack of small trees being crushed.

The rope around his chest tightened as Morgan began to rise again, rattling upward through the branches until he could see the other end of the rope was stretched over a sturdy branch, and held by a cloaked and hooded figure. His captor pulled him higher, then pushed him gently to one side as he rose until he felt something solid rub against him—a wide branch—then he was lowered again until he was sitting on it. The hooded figure reached out once more and, with a single flick of the hand so swift he couldn't follow it, loosened the rope that held him. As it fell into coils his captor quickly reeled it in. No longer held in place, Morgan felt a momentary loss of balance and flung out his aching arms to grab at the branch.

The shape jumped down beside him, landing so lightly the branch did not move. The agility made him think this might be one of the Sithi, but that only slightly reassuring thought was followed almost immediately by another: *Or it might be one of those White Foxes.*

Before Morgan could get his bloodless, tingling fingers to close on the hilt of his knife, the cloaked figure put a cool hand across his mouth; the grip was much stronger than the slenderness of the fingers suggested. He tried to struggle free, but the stranger kept one hand over his mouth, then reached out with the other hand—which meant he or she was crouching unsupported on the branch—and gave Morgan's ear a painful but silent twist, like a furious tutor with an unresponsive pupil. Then it pointed down into the mist below.

One last time he opened his mouth, but when the hand pinched his lips closed Morgan finally understood. He stopped fighting and tried to make his breathing as shallow and quiet as possible. Something else was coming, that was clear. Something was looking for him, or for the one who had pulled him up into the tree, or for both of them.

Such a long time passed that he began to wonder if his hooded and still unknown rescuer had been mistaken, but just when he was about to risk a whispered question he saw shapes in the mist below, only a few dozen yards from the tree in which he and his rescuer crouched. The shapes moved as silently as shadows, as ghosts, but they were no phantoms. Morgan held his breath until it burned in his chest.

He had never seen a live Norn before, but he knew the three figures on the ground could be nothing else: their hair, faces, and hands were so pale as to be almost luminous in the day's failing light. They wore armor made of what looked like lacquered wood, held long black bows in their hands, and seemed perfectly at home in this wild place, their steps soundless, their movements graceful but precise. As Morgan stared, one of them paused, his head tipped to one side as if listening, and Morgan felt his breath turn into scalding steam in his lungs. A dozen swift heartbeats sounded in his chest—two dozen! He needed to breathe so badly, but did not dare. The other two Norns waited like statures. Then, at last, the one who had stopped began moving again. Within a few moments the Norns had all slipped away into the mist, bypassing the mouth of the valley without a look.

Morgan was shaking so badly now that he was afraid he would slide off the branch. He let out his long-held breath and drank in a glorious new one. His rescuer threw back the cloak's hood and said softly, "Gone. We were fortunate. *You* were fortunate."

Morgan stared. He had been right—it *was* a Sitha, golden-eyed and golden-skinned, with long, white hair pulled back in a simple braid. At first he couldn't tell whether his rescuer was male or female, but a delicacy in the features at last convinced him this was a Sitha woman crouched beside him. "Who are you?" he asked.

She looked at him curiously. "You do not recognize me? You and your fellows carried me a long journey back to my home."

"You're the one who was sick? Poisoned, I mean?"

"Yes. My mother named me Tanahaya. And you are Morgan, grandson of the *Hikka Staja*, so I am pleased we finally meet."

He had only ever seen her pale and insensible, so ill that it had been hard to look at her because it reminded him of his father's last days. In fact, this creature had looked so close to death the last time he saw her—carried into the Sithi camp—that it seemed nearly impossible to believe this could be her. Even more confounding, she had hauled the whole of his weight up into the tree by herself.

"Tanahaya," he said, experimenting with the sound. It sounded flatter and heavier when he said it. Morgan suddenly had a sense of what a mad picture this would make to someone else, him sitting on a tree branch exchanging pleasantries with a fairy after an impossibly huge monster, and then several demons, had just tried to kill him. "What was that huge thing?" he asked suddenly. "A giant?"

"Not the kind you know—not what mortals call '*Hunën*.' The thing that lives in Misty Vale is something different, and jealous of its privacy. Murderously jealous. Only a mortal would try to enter that valley—all my kind know it is forbidden."

"Forbidden by whom?"

She shook her head. "How can it matter to you? The place has been forbidden since Amerasu Ship-Born's time, or even before. But it is not merely the word of our elders that keeps us out—the smashed and broken bodies of those who wandered into that valley by mistake are warning enough."

Morgan knew that he was certainly never going to go near the place again. In fact, he was ready to get farther away as quickly as possible, and said so.

"Not yet," said Tanahaya. "The Hikeda'ya scouts are still close by. We will stay here until after nightfall."

"*Hikeda'ya.* That word means 'Norns,' doesn't it? Those were Norns."

"Yes, your people call them Norns, just as they call us 'Sithi.' But I do not know what they were doing here, so far from their own lands. They have been tracking you for a day or two, I think."

That made Morgan's blood turn icy cold. "Tracking *me?* Why?"

"How can I say? I do not know why they are here in the first place. But I came upon them first and followed them until I found you, so I feel certain it was you they hunted." She finally unfolded from her crouch and lowered herself onto the branch beside him. "You are luckier than you know that they did not catch you before I did. I think it is only your smell that confused them. You do not smell like a mortal anymore, but more like those Tinukeda'ya you were journeying with."

It took a moment—so many new words. "Hikeda . . . Hikeya, Tinkedaya. All these 'Daya's!' I don't know what any of it means. What are Tinka—the last thing you said?" A sudden idea came to him. "Are you talking about the Chi-kri? The little animals I was with?"

She shook her head emphatically. "They are not animals, they are Tinu-keda'ya."

"You keep saying that word." He vaguely remembered hearing it before, perhaps as part of one of his grandfather's stories. "You're talking about the creatures in the trees? They looked like some kind of squirrels to me."

"I have never seen Tinukeda'ya in forms so crude and animal-like, but they were still Changelings, I promise you." She put a hand on his leg. "You are damp from these fogs. I think it has been long enough now that we can go down. I have a place that will be safe for tonight."

He was conscious of her hand in a way he had not been of anything in a while. "Damp?"

"You mortals die if you become too wet, don't you? You take fever and die."

"Not if we're just a little wet."

"Still." She was perched atop the branch again in moments, balanced and sure-footed as a bird. He caught his breath to see how nimble she was—it made his own hard-won climbing skills seem small indeed. "Your people saved my life. I could not allow you to die without trying to help."

She climbed down first, jumping the last ten cubits to land almost perfectly balanced. Despite his weeks in the trees, Morgan could not hope to match her, but he did his best not to seem like an ordinary clumsy mortal.

"What do you have on your feet?" she asked after he reached the ground.

He showed her. "The troll Snenneq made them. They're for walking on ice, but I used them to climb the trees." He said it with more than a little pride.

"Strange," was all she said, then "Follow."

It was all he could do to keep up.

★   ★   ★

The Sitha led him to a cave nestled in the rocks at the far side of the entrance to the Misty Vale. "We cannot make a fire," she said as she ushered him in. "The Hikeda'ya would smell it if they are still anywhere close."

Morgan looked around the cavern. It was little more than an empty space in the midst of a jumble of boulders, but the entrance was hidden by a spread of gorse. He thought of ReeRee and her troop and felt a momentary ache of loss.

"Changelings," he said out loud, remembering what Tanahaya had called the Chikri. "What does that mean?"

"Do you know the Niskies of the south? The sea-watchers?"

"Yes. I've seen them."

"And the dwarrows who live in deep mountain places?"

That sounded familiar, but only barely. "Perhaps."

"Then you know the Tinukeda'ya. They are called Changelings because they grow to fit the places they are, the way they must live."

"But the things I was in the trees with—they were animals!"

"It is true I have never seen any Tinukeda'ya so far different from the shapes I know, but I swear by my calling as a scholar that I could not mistake those eyes, those voices."

Morgan remembered the night he had found all the Chikri listening to the oldest of their troop and the strange shiver it had given him to hear them and to see their rapt attention. Animals? Fairy creatures? It was all too much for him, and he realized he was so exhausted that he could not think without effort. He slid off his sword belt and used the scabbard for a pillow, then pulled his cloak tight around him.

"I just need to close my eyes," he said. "Only for a moment."

"Then sleep, mortal." He thought he heard something almost like fondness in her voice—something he had not heard from any other Sitha except the beautiful Aditu. "I will watch over you."

In his dream, the tree in which he perched was full of singing angels, wispy shapes he could not see. Their soft, wordless voices filled the treetops, and he wanted nothing more than just to listen, but something large was moving in the great darkness below, searching for the singers, and only he seemed to realize it. He tried to call out and warn them but his throat had clamped shut and no matter how he tried he could not make a sound.

"Silence," said a voice in his ear, and he realized that someone was holding a hand over his mouth. He stopped fighting, then opened his eyes to see the shadowy interior of the cave, the tumbled rocks a myriad of colors in the soft morning light filtering through the bushes covering the entrance. He remembered where he was.

Tanahaya took her hand from his mouth. "You were crying out in your sleep. That is not a good thing to do when Hikeda'ya could still be somewhere near."

"I'm sorry." He felt the last of the dream dissolving like the mist of the strange valley. "It was . . . that giant thing."

"The ogre of Misty Vale." She nodded. "I am not surprised. We are among the few who have seen it and lived, I think."

"What did you see? What was it?"

She made a movement like a snake shedding skin. He took it for a shrug. "Nothing but shadow," she said. "The mist was too thick."

"But what *was* it?"

"Better to turn your mind instead to what we will do next. There are other dangers here in the great woods beside the ogre."

He felt chastised and it made him angry. Hadn't he survived for a long time in the forest on his own? Again he remembered the way Jiriki had talked down to him, as if he were a foolish child, and also the contempt of the scarred chieftain Khendraja'aro for all mortals, even the grandchildren of kings and queens.

Yes, she saved me, he thought. *But that doesn't mean I have to love the Sithi.*

But as the dream faded, so did much of Morgan's irritation. For the first time in a long while he thought how nice it would be to have a cup of wine. No, not just a cup, he thought, but an entire cask to himself, and the leisure in which to drink it all. Instead, Sitha or no Sitha, he was still lost in the middle of the forest and his stomach was aching.

"Is there anything to eat?"

Tanahaya seemed amused. "None of the things your people eat, I think, but there is bread and a little honey wrapped in that leaf beside you."

There was, and Morgan fell on it like a beast, devouring it so quickly that he barely tasted the glorious sweetness of the honey as he hurried it down his throat. As soon as he had finished he wished he could start all over again. "We mortals eat honey and bread too." He licked the last honey from his lips, then searched his beard for crumbs. "That was good. Is there any more?"

"I gave you what I would have eaten myself," Tanahaya said, but without rancor. "I did not expect to have a guest."

"I didn't expect to be anyone's guest either." So much talking made his head ache a little, but it was exciting to be with someone who could actually answer him. "Why did you save me?"

"Why? What a strange question. Your people saved *me*, did they not?"

"I suppose."

"When I set out from H'ran Go-jao I came across your trail at the forest's edge, but it led in the opposite direction from where I was told Jiriki had taken you. I did not know the reasons you had turned around—and still do not, although I saw fires out on the meadowlands, so I can guess—but I could not leave you alone to die in the forest. That would be a poor return of the favor your people showed me."

"I wasn't dying. I found things to eat. I lived with the Chikri."

"If you mean those Tinukeda'ya, I have seen the evidence so I must believe you. Perhaps Jiriki and Aditu were right about this too—there is more to your kind than we Zida'ya sometimes wish to believe."

A memory of Likimeya's voice in his head came to Morgan suddenly, but he did not share it. Tanahaya might just have saved him, but he didn't truly know or trust the Sithi, however much his grandparents might favor them.

And it makes no sense in any case, he thought. *Why me? Why would a Sithi monarch speak to me, a mortal? And would she speak to me in dreams?*

I will keep this to myself, he thought. *At least for now. I am a prince, after all. I can keep my own counsel.*

"Are you still hungry?" Tanahaya asked. "This is the season for dove eggs. I could find some for you."

"Do your people eat eggs?"

She smiled gently, as if remembering something. "Sometimes. Only when they have not quickened." She saw his expression. "Only when they will not become a young bird."

"But how do you know without cracking them open?"

"By smell, of course." She gave him an odd look. "But perhaps you cannot smell anything because of your own scent, Morgan. It is very . . . pungent."

He sat back, still thinking of honey and bread, but eggs had now made their way into his imagination too and were causing quite a commotion there. "You said my smell was why the Norns couldn't find me, so that's good, right?"

"Perhaps. But now that we travel together I cannot smell anything *but* you. I will have to consider which is the greater asset, your invisibility from our enemies or my ability to know those enemies are near."

"Then we're traveling together?"

"Unless you know how to find your own way home—yes, Morgan of Erkynland, I believe we are. For it is back to your grandparents' dwelling I am bound, to fulfill the duty my friends laid upon me so many moons ago. You would be wise to travel with me."

Suddenly the light sifting down into the tumble of stones seemed warmer, splashing the colors of an inspiring day all over the uneven, rocky burrow. "I do want to go home, by all God's angels. Yes, I'll go with you." He suddenly remembered. "And thank you. Thank you, Tanahaya, for helping me."

She nodded.

"What month is it?" He knew he was talking a lot, but he was thrilled to have a partner for conversation and was reluctant to be quiet again, although he sensed she would have preferred it. "What day?"

Her clear golden brow furrowed ever so slightly. "I do not remember the name for the ninth month in your tongue—is it 'Septander'? By my reckoning, it is the eleventh day of the Sky-Singer's Moon."

"*Septander?*" He and Eolair had left the Erkynguards to go with the Sithi in early Tiyagar-month. "Elysia's Mercy, have I truly been in the forest that long? Two months?"

"It is a noble feat that you have lived so long without help. Be proud. Your people will certainly be proud of you."

"Yes, perhaps." But he was not entirely certain of that. He could imagine how his grandparents would feel when he returned with the news that only he had escaped, that the troop of Erkynguards and Count Eolair were all dead and the mission had been a failure. "Perhaps."

"There is no sense spending the daylight hours talking here," she said. "You would rather travel in daylight, I suspect, and it is definitely better for avoiding Hikeda'ya scouts. Let us start walking."

As the morning warmed they made their way up into the rocky heights that formed the northern side of Misty Vale by dint of sheer hard work, much of it requiring the use of hands as well as feet, and reached the top not long before noon. They stopped so Morgan could remove his climbing irons; Tanahaya, who had been climbing in bare feet, took her soft boots from her belt and put them back on. Even in full sunlight, Misty Vale was a trough of billowing white below them, and Morgan was relieved he couldn't see anything. As he got back to his feet, he wondered where the Chikri might be in that grim, dangerous expanse, and felt another pang of worry for little ReeRee.

Now that the worst of the climbing was over and he didn't have to worry about falling, the events of the previous day kept spinning through his mind, over and over as they made their way through the woods. Despite Tanahaya's clear preference for silent travel, he could not stop himself from asking more questions.

"Why are there Norns here? My grandparents and their company were also attacked by some coming back from Elvritshalla. What are the White Foxes doing so far from their mountain or wherever it is they live? Will they make war on us?"

"Their presence is a bad sign," she agreed. "When I heard from Jiriki and Aditu what happened to your grandparents' caravan, it made my decision to return to the Hayholt clear. Something strange is happening—something frightening, I think—and it seems plain to me that Dawn Children and Sunset Children must work together to protect ourselves."

"Dawn Children. That means . . . ?"

"My people, the Sithi—the *Zida'ya*. And yours are called *Sudhoda'ya*—Sunset Children."

"Why 'sunset'?"

He could not see her face, but she sounded as though she was growing tired of answering questions. "Because this world is better shaped for your kind than ours," was all she said.

An hour later they came down another long slope cluttered with deadfall. Morgan could hear the sound of rushing water. "What's that?"

"We have caught up to the course of the *Dekusao* again, the river that runs from Misty Vale. You would call it 'Narrowdark.' That will be a good place for you to wash the stink from you."

"But I thought you said my smell was useful."

"I said I must think, and I have thought—and you must wash." She sounded like Countess Rhona now, or one of the other no-nonsense women from back home. Morgan could not help recoiling a bit—that tone never brought anything good for him. "Yes," she said sternly, "it shields you somewhat from the noses of Hikeda'ya scouts, but it keeps me from scenting anything myself, and on top of it, I have just realized that since you smell so strongly of—what did you call the climbing Tinukeda'ya?"

"Chikri."

"Yes, the 'Chikri'—I have realized that the creatures who eat the tree-dwellers, wolves and bears, must also smell you everywhere you go. And I do not wish to fight a bear."

"I did! I fought a bear!" He was about to tell her a version that emphasized his bravery and resourcefulness, but felt compelled for some reason he could not explain to tell the truth instead. "It almost killed me. That's why I was up in the trees in the first place. That and ReeRee."

"ReeRee?" As she tried the name they emerged from a copse of aspen trees and he could finally see the river, wider than the name "Narrowdark" suggested, glinting jade green in places, but black as tar where it ran deep. "What is a ReeRee?"

He explained how the small creature had first come to him and how he had lived with her troop. "Strange," she said as she led him down the slope to the river's broad, sandy banks. "All of it. But you did well."

"And I can show you all kinds of things that are safe to eat!"

"We will eat later. Now, I think this is a good spot for you—a quiet backwater. You may bathe the stink from your skin."

"Are you sure . . . ?"

"Yes," she said firmly.

He sat down and took off his belt and sword, then doffed his cloak and pulled off his shirt before he saw that Tanahaya was still standing and watching. Morgan was not unduly modest—countless guards, servants, and more than a few tavern girls had seen him naked—but something about the Sitha abashed him.

"Are you going to watch? I can clean myself."

Tanahaya stared at him for a moment as though she did not understand, then nodded in a distracted way and moved farther down the riverbank until he could not see her anymore.

The river was wide and strong, but Tanahaya had picked a bend where the current was slowed by rocks and spread into a shallow, relatively placid pond on the near side. He stripped off the rest of his clothes and waded out. The water was so cold that the first thing he did was curse and retreat back into the shallowest edges, but he braced himself for the chill and manfully waded back in until it was above his waist. Every part of him below that point felt like it had been packed in snow.

Still, once the worst of the shock was over he found himself almost hungry for the feeling of water on his skin as weeks' worth of grime washed away. In fact, for a brief moment the lost familiarity of getting clean seemed so satisfying that he began to sing one of his grandfather's Jack Mundwode songs. But before he had sung more than a few hooting words he remembered the patient, death-pale Norns that had walked right beneath them like stalking cats, and he abruptly fell silent.

There was no sign of Tanahaya, so he climbed up the bank and gathered his clothes, then brought them back to the river to wash. He did his best, but it was clear that none of them would ever truly be clean again. Still, it was pleasant to know he had at least removed most of the fleas and spiders and clinging leaves. When he finished he looked for a place to dry them, but the sun had slid behind the trees and the bank was in deep shade. He waded to the edge of the back-water and then scrambled from one rock to the next until he reached the bend, where the shining sun beamed across the river bank without impediment. He was laying out his breeks on a pair of wide, flat stones at the river's edge when he heard the sound of someone singing.

It was a trill of melody he did not recognize, and although he could sense the shape of words in the flow of sound, he could not understand them. It must be Tanahaya, he realized after a moment. He sloshed a little way through the shallows until he reached a pair of tall stones standing straight in the water as if they had been set there. He could see her in the river just ahead. She was wash-ing herself too, a slender expanse of golden skin in thigh-high water.

A part of him wanted to warn her that he had stumbled onto her bathing place, but he was captured by the unexpectedness. It was strange, too, to see the whole shape of her at once, the hidden nakedness of someone he had scarcely thought of before that moment as female. He felt a stirring in his chest. She did not have the womanly shape he most fancied, curvaceous and wide-hipped; despite her long, wet, white hair, he thought Tanahaya looked more like a boy, her supple back tight with smooth muscle, her legs long beneath her small backside. But she was graceful in her every movement—oh, so graceful—and the river water sliding down her skin seemed to catch every ray of the sun and send it bouncing outward again, cloaking her in a shiny dazzle that sparkled with rainbow colors.

Morgan did not think he had made a noise, but somehow the Sitha heard him behind her and turned. She did not cover herself or look surprised—she did not even look embarrassed—but only gazed at him with the kind of offhand interest another solitary bather might have felt to discover herself observed by a deer or a squirrel. After a moment she turned away again, not to hide, but to continue what she was doing. Morgan sloshed back against the slow current, looking for a less problematic spot—for him if not for the Sitha—to dry his clothes.

*   *   *

"How long will it take to reach the Hayholt?" he asked that night as they ate a meager and not particularly satisfying meal of boiled acorns and dandelion leaves.

"I do not know the answer to that, Morgan. In fact, I think I will take you someplace else first."

He didn't like that sound of that at all. "What do you mean? Where?"

Finished with her food, she fixed him with a sharp, steady gaze. She had not mentioned his appearance at her bathing spot, and he had not wanted to bring it up, but it now seemed to hang between them somehow, or at least so it felt to Morgan. "Just my finding you has changed things already. I suppose that your grandparents and the others must still think you lost."

"I still *am* lost until we get out of this forest," he reminded her, a trifle cross.

"I gave you most of the dandelions," she replied. "Did you mutter at your Chikri friends too for not supplying you with a sufficiency of hazelnuts?"

"No. I'm sorry." But he wasn't really, not too much. How long could he be expected to eat the sort of things sensible farmers plowed under before he went mad from hunger?

"In any case," she continued, "I need to tell my friends that I am with you. Jiriki and Aditu might be able to send word to your family somehow, but even if they cannot, they still will be relieved to know you are safe. It is also important they know I have seen Sacrifice scouts as close to them. As near as Misty Vale."

Morgan was pleased to hear that not *all* the Sithi wanted him dead. Still, the idea of anything other than heading straight home undercut the relief he had been feeling since Tanahaya had told him her plan that morning. "God save us, you're not going to take me all the way back to those Sithi villages are you? They must be leagues and leagues away, and in the wrong direction!"

She showed something that again seemed nearly a smile. "From following your trail, I suspect you are not the best person to decide which direction is which. The Veil of the Sa'onsera snared you and would not let you free."

If she meant the mad untrustworthiness of the sun and stars, he didn't want to talk about it. "I didn't ask to be lost."

"True. No, I do not intend to lead you back to H'ran Go-jao. With only a slight alteration to our path we can reach the Flowering Hills on our way to your home. My teacher Himano has his house there, and I have not seen him for so very, very long."

"So we'd go out of our way to visit some old friend of yours?"

She gave him a look this time that could only be irritation. Apparently, Morgan decided with a small thrill of triumph, the Sithi were not as emotionless as they wanted everyone to believe. "Have you not listened to what I said?" She spoke carefully, as though to a bad-tempered child. "I wish to tell those who need to know that I have found you, and that there are Hikeda'ya Sacrifice warriors roaming much farther into the great woods than before. My teacher Himano will have a Witness. Do you know what that is?"

He was about to say that, yes, he certainly did know, because his grandfather
had told him all about them, but then he realized that he could scarcely recall
a single detail of what King Simon had said. Humbled, he said, "A bit. Some
kind of magic mirror?"

Tanahaya made a hand-sign he hadn't seen before, a quick touching of all
her fingertips, almost as though she were folding her hands in prayer. "I have
never understood what your folk mean by 'magic,' because they use it to describe not only impossibilities seen only in your children's tales, but also things
we Zida'ya do every day, even those who are untutored. Yes, Witnesses, especially the smallest ones often appear to be mirrors, but they can be many things
of many sizes—'Stones, Scales, Pools, and Pyres' as the saying goes."

"I've never heard that saying."

"Because you are . . . young." She hesitated before choosing the last word.
"The Witnesses are a way to speak through the between places over great distance, so that our voices do not have to travel through the naked air. But all that
matters is, with Himano's Witness I can speak to Jiriki and Aditu and tell them
what I have discovered."

She gave him another stern look, her golden eyes intent as a hawk's, and for
a moment Morgan almost felt afraid.

"Do you understand? Or will we argue more?"

"Yes, yes, very well." He tried to surrender with good grace—she had saved
him after all. "I suppose it makes sense."

"It does, so that is where we will be headed tomorrow, although I doubt we
will reach it in daylight." She paused. "And if you are not going to finish eating
those leaves, I will have them."

23

In the Root Cellar

By the time Miriamele reached the deep part of the Sancellan Mahistrevis—which most of its inhabitants called the root cellar, though it had been more than a century since it was used for something so ordinary—she and her guards had collected a crowd of dismayed functionaries, all trying to tell the queen where she should not go go, which happened to be exactly where she was going. A pair of sentries in kingfisher livery stood on either side of the heavy, barred door. At the sight of her they blocked the door and lowered their pikes.

Sir Jurgen stepped in front of her. "Put those up, you fools! Would you have it said you threatened the High Queen?"

"But the duke said nobody may pass," declared the braver of the two.

"Am I nobody?" Miriamele asked, struggling to keep her temper in check. "Or am I somebody? Think carefully before you answer, because it will be judged by these Erkynguardsmen, loyal servants of the High Throne."

The sentries looked at each other, then at Miri's guards, who looked quite capable of dispatching a pair of such trivial obstacles. At last one of the sentries reached up a gloved fist and knocked loudly on the door, then stepped back and lifted the bolt. Jurgen stepped between the duke's men and pushed it open; Miri swept in after him.

It was much as she had imagined: a man chained to a post at the center of the low-ceilinged chamber, sagging, chin on his chest, with a hooded jailer on either side of him. Coals in a brazier lit one side of his body in hellscape red, but the embers were clearly meant for more than light: a trio of metal instruments rested on the brazier's edge, heating for eventual use.

Duke Saluceris, who had been sitting on a stool at the far side of the root cellar, now stood, unfeigned surprise on his face. "Majesty! What are you doing here?"

She looked around at stone walls hung with chains and various devices crafted to cause pain and damage to human bodies. "Rather I should ask that of you, Your Grace." She looked at the prisoner's cut and bruised head, his face largely masked by drying blood. "Especially since everything you do, you do in my name and my husband's. I see you have not yet removed anything from this man that will not heal, and for that I give God thanks. Now unchain him."

Saluceris shook his head, half-angry, half-worried, uncertain how to respond. "Your Majesty, I understand that you are upset, but this is not your concern."

She glared at him. "You dare say that to me, Saluceris?" She fought to remain calm. "Who put you on the throne? Who has kept the Benidrivines in the Sancellan Mahistrevis all these years? My grandfather John could have exiled your entire family or worse after he defeated Adrivis, but instead he handed them back the reins of power. No, I think this is utterly my concern." She stepped forward. Several more of the duke's soldiers stood in the shadows, as many as the guards Miri had brought, who now crowded into the chamber behind her, but even in her current fury she could not imagine the Nabbanai soldiers offering resistance.

She leaned over the prisoner. "Who are you, man?"

"He is a criminal, Majesty," said the duke. "That is why he is here, because he will not give us the names of his associates."

Miri gave him a look, then turned back to the bloody man. "Speak. Tell me only the truth. Your name?"

"Yuvis, my lady," he wheezed, a little red bubbling at the corner of his mouth. "Called the tailor's son."

"This man knows the bandits that were hired to attack the wedding party and cast blame for it on the Benidrivine House," Saluceris said angrily. "He protects them because some are his relatives. Please, Majesty, do not interfere."

"I interfered at the wedding, and that is likely why your wife and children are still alive, Duke." She was doing her best to remain calm. "If you think you know the names of some who were actually responsible for the planned attack—an attack that did not happen, remember—arrest them. Get your information from their mouths, not his. Dozens of people have sworn to me that this man is guilty of nothing more than having a criminal cousin. His wife and five children are on the steps of the Sancellan Aedonitis now, crying out to Heaven to save their father from the monstrous duke."

"But, Majesty . . ." Saluceris was desperately trying to stay between her and the prisoner, as if hiding what had been done to the man would make it go away. "I know that sometimes what must be done in the search for justice is ugly—that women and the gentle-hearted cannot bear . . ."

Miriamele jerked up her hand to stop him, clenching her teeth so hard to avoid shouting that she bit her own cheek. "Let us step outside and talk, just the two of us, my lord," she said when she had regained her composure. Without waiting for his assent she strode to the door and pushed it open, hitting one of the sentries who had been listening at the doorway. She knocked his soup plate helmet off.

"Step inside with the others," Miri told the other sentry as the eavesdropper crawled across the floor trying to retrieve his clattering helmet.

"Yes," said Saluceris, perhaps hoping to regain a little control. "You men, inside."

When the door had closed and they were alone in the corridor, Miriamele held up her hand again. The duke's nostrils flared but he remained silent. "Did you learn anything about this man you have tortured other than what was told to you by an informant?"

"What do you mean?" Saluceris barely remembered to add the words, "Your Majesty."

"I mean that if you had bothered to speak to the local people before snatching this fellow out of his shop and dragging him here, you would know that this Yuvis is an important man in his neighborhood. Respected by all. But as Count Froye discovered by asking only a few questions, Yuvis the tailor's son is also a loyal supporter of your dukedom and of the High Throne. His cousin, the one you are torturing him to learn about, is the shame of the family. There are dozens you could have arrested and questioned about this, but you have somehow chosen the only one who would have defended you to the rest of his kin and fellows."

"But the informant—"

"—may have been lying, may have been mistaken, or may simply have told you the first thing he thought of because he feared getting the same treatment from your torturers."

"I have no choice, Majesty. We cannot let the Ingadarines get away with such a thing, sending bravos and killers to a wedding, putting my own family in danger—"

"This is not practicality, Saluceris, this is pride." She said it quietly, but she made sure that he heard each word. "If you cannot stand to think people might tell lies about you, you should hand over the ducal crown today. It is part and parcel of being a ruler."

"But Dallo Ingadaris wants—"

"Please stop making me interrupt you, my lord. It is nothing so simple and stupid as a woman shuddering at the sight of blood. What makes me shudder is how you are doing exactly what the Ingadarines want. If you respond to every provocation with this kind of gross, heedless violence, the streets of Nabban will be ablaze before St. Granis' Day. Do you understand? Count Dallo *wants* you to do this, until innocent people are afraid and murder is answered with murder, until the people no longer trust you to keep them safe. And all the time, without having to say a word, he offers them your brother instead. Can you not see that? Even if you trace this back to Dallo, you will never prove that Drusis was in any way involved. A bitter fight between you and Honsa Ingadaris will still leave your brother the last one standing."

She was almost out of breath by the time she had finished. *Look at me*, she thought. *Oh, Simon, we are old now, but they still have learned nothing. How do we keep them from taking what small good we leave behind and turning it into ruin?*

Saluceris swallowed, no more interested in a shouting match that others might hear than Miri was. At last he said, "What do you wish me to do, Your Majesty?"

"I want you to speak to me before you take any more steps like this."

"But you will not be here in Nabban much longer now the wedding is over." He didn't sound like the prospect saddened him much.

"Long enough perhaps to help you. And that is what I'm trying to do, Duke Saluceris, whether you know it or not." She paused. "You must let this man go. You must apologize to him."

"Apologize?" His eyes widened as if she had just suggested he ask the fellow to dance.

"Yes. And you will have your most discreet servants pass the word around that he was denounced by one of Dallo's hirelings—that the entire thing was Count Dallo's revenge on the tailor's son for not supporting the Ingadarines."

Saluceris paused, for the first time thinking of something beyond his own frustration. "Do you think it will be believed?"

"At least it will be another story—and one that will make more sense to those who know this man as one of your supporters. Let them do your work for you. Clean him up, let him rest for a day, then send him home with a bag of gold. You have not harmed him in some way I did not see, have you?"

The duke shook his head like a sullen child. "No. He was barely touched, just cuffed and bruised."

"Lucky man—and lucky us. But do not forget the apology, I beg you." She considered. "When he can think clearly again, tell him you did not know you had such a loyal supporter in the Cloth District, and that you are heartbroken by the mistake. The arrest was all a terrible trick played on him by the his enemies among the Stormbirds."

"I suppose it is best, if what you say about him is true."

"I do not act until I know as much as I need to." She tried not to show the bitterness she felt. "You might find it a more practical method in dealing with Count Dallo and your brother than what you've been doing."

Ever since she had seen the queen frighten a dozen armed men into running away, Jesa had been in awe of her. In this foreign land of women who hid behind veils and pretended, at least in public, not to understand anything to do with either violence or lovemaking, it was the first thing that had reminded her of her own upbringing in the Wran. Jesa had once seen her mother, small and plump and with no weapon but a wooden spoon, chase a large, drunken fisherman with a grudge against her father off the family jetty.

"Be glad my husband was not home!" she had shouted after him as the other women stood in the doorway laughing. "He would have given you more than a poke in the eye!"

Not that what Queen Miriamele had done was the same—it had been much braver, much more dangerous. But Jesa had not seen that spirit for some time, and it reminded her of how much strangeness she had come to take for granted.

But it also made her shy, and when the queen and her envoy, Count Froye, visited with Duchess Canthia, Jesa took the baby to the next room but left the door open. She was doing her best to calm Serasina, who had a tooth coming in and would not sleep. Jesa could hear most of what was being said, but Miriamele's firm voice brought her to the doorway with the infant in her arms.

"Canthia, I think it is time for you to leave for Domos Benidriyan," the queen said. "Take the children and stay there."

"I do not understand, Majesty." The duchess was quiet but stubborn. Canthia was trying to hold young Blasis on her lap but the boy was squirming and struggling to get down. "This is our city. The people are our subjects and we have been nothing but good to them. Why should I fear them?"

"First of all, never make the mistake of thinking that because nobody says anything bad to your face, nobody is saying anything bad about you at all."

Jesa could see that Count Froye was silently trying to get the queen's attention but the queen ignored him. "At this very moment," Miriamele went on, "Dallo Ingadaris and your husband's brother are saying many bad things about you, and not just in the Dominiate where all can hear. Their servants are poisoning the marketplaces and guildhalls all over Nabban with talk of how the duke doesn't care if his subjects are robbed and killed by Thrithings-men."

"But none of that is true!" protested the Duchess.

"What is *true* doesn't matter, Canthia. That is what I am trying to tell you. And your husband is already making mistakes—I'm sorry, Froye, but don't wave your hands at me like that," she told her envoy sternly. "It has to be said. Canthia, your husband is already letting Dallo's tricks and treacheries anger him. Imagine what will happen if some band of so-called outlaws were to attack you and your children. The Duke would lose his wits and strike back without thinking, and then the city will burn. The Sancellan Mahistrevis itself will not be safe."

Jesa gaped at the queen's words and a sudden chill made her skin prickle. She held little Serasina close, frightened for her—frightened for all of them. It was just as the old woman Laliba had told her in the market! *"The Great Lodge will burn from the inside . . ."*

Canthia started to rise from her chair, as though even now armed ravishers might be at the door of the retiring room. "You are frightening me, Your Majesty."

"Good. That is the first step toward wisdom."

Blasis, still held prisoner, had begun to cry, his round face red. In his struggles he kicked his mother's knee. "Stop!" Canthia smacked him on the forearm. "You hurt me! Blasis, what is wrong with you?"

"Even when children do not understand everything that's being said," the queen suggested, "they understand when people are frightened or angry." She went to Canthia. "May I hold him?"

The duchess seemed surprised, but lifted the boy so the queen could take him.

"Do you know, Blasis," said Queen Miriamele as she sat down, wrapping her arms gently around him, "that I once had a little boy just like you?" He looked at her with distrust. "I used to sing to him sometimes. Do you know what a wishing fish is?"

He turned away from her and shook his head, scowling.

"You don't?" The queen's voice, so grim moments earlier, had become light and sweet. "Truly? Because it's a very magical kind of fish."

"Fish swim," said Blasis, as if someone had insisted otherwise.

"They certainly do. And people catch them. But if you catch a wishing fish and let it go, then it will grant you a wish. Do you know what a wish is?"

Blasis was reluctantly listening now, and had stopped thrashing. "No."

"It means you can ask for something, like a favor, and then someone gives it to you."

"Honey cake?"

"Yes, you could wish for honey cake if you wanted. Or a bow and arrows."

"Have a bow. Arrows, too."

"Aren't you a lucky young man? Well, when my son was small, I used to sing a song to him that I learned from my nurse. It's about a magical wishing fish. Would you like to hear it?" Queen Miriamele did not wait for his reply, but leaned toward him and sang in a low, tuneful voice.

> *"O, little fish, little magical fish*
> *What will you give me, your life for a wish?"*

She changed her voice for the fish, making it shrill and comical, so that even Blasis smiled a little.

> *"Please, and you throw me back into the stream*
> *I'll give to you all things that your heart can dream*
>
> *"O, little fish that I took from the water*
> *What if I wish for a son and a daughter?*
> *I'll give unto you girl- and boy-child, so fair*
> *That all will come running to see such a pair."*

Blasis had stopped wriggling, and though he still frowned and tugged at Miriamele's sleeve, he also seemed to be listening. The queen pulled him a little closer as she sang.

"O, little fish that I took from the river
What if I wish for a handful of silver?
I'll give you such riches that all will crowd 'round
To beg for your alms when you ride into town

"O, little fish that I caught in my boat
What if I wished for a castle and moat?
I'll give you a castle so big and so strong
That you will be safe there for all your lifelong

"O, little fish that I brought to the shore
What if I wish for a thousand things more?
All that you wish shall be yours to command
If you will return me to water again . . ."

There were a good many verses as the wishing fish worked its way out of the stewing pot and was eventually released back into the river by the fisherman, who asked only for a blessing. By the time the queen had finished the song Blasis was calm and had begun to look sleepy. Miriamele handed him back to the duchess. The child curled himself tight against his mother, clasped a tress of Canthia's unbound hair in one fist, and closed his eyes.

The queen looked at him fondly, but Jesa thought she saw the bright trace of tears in Miriamele's eyes and wondered at it. "You must take your dear children and go, Canthia," the queen said in a quiet voice. "Go to a safe place. Listen to one who knows too well that they are more important than anything else."

"Your Majesty." Count Froye had waited patiently through the queen's song, trying hard—but failing—to hide a fretful expression, "I wonder if I might have a word with you in private?"

"Count, you are a good man." Though the queen still spoke softly there was a hint of iron in her words. "I value your wisdom and your discretion more than you know. But this is between the women here. We are talking about the safety of Duchess Canthia's children. For once I do not want to hear what a man has to say. I will meet with you later. You may go."

The count bowed low, first to Duchess Canthia then to the queen. When he had left there was a long silence.

"Do you truly think we are in such great danger?" the duchess finally asked.

"I hope not, but hope makes a flimsy armor," the queen said. "That's what my grandfather used to say—and he was right. Every outrage, every rumor, every disturbance or street fight is to Dallo's advantage, because it bespeaks turmoil, and for most people the only cure for turmoil is a new ruler. A *strong* ruler. Your husband is a fair-minded man, but he is not seen as strong, not like his brother Drusis."

"But I cannot believe we are in danger here—not in the Sancellan, our home."

To Jesa's astonishment, Miriamele dropped to her knees beside the duchess and took her hand. "By the love of our Redeemer, I do not seek to frighten you, my lady, but to warn you. I have seen things like this before, especially during my father's reign—may God forgive him his crimes. A city can be turned into a bubbling pot, and as the fire is poked and poked by those who desire chaos, at last it *will* boil over. It is too late then to lament the scalding."

Jesa bent her head close over Serasina's tiny round face, whispering mean-ingless sounds, suddenly frightened for the child in a way she had never been before. What if the old Wran-woman had been right? Would it change any-thing if Jesa begged the duchess to listen to what the queen said? Would Can-thia heed her, or would she send her away for daring to speak up like a friend instead of a servant? Who would protect Serasina then?

I love this little girl, she thought, suddenly aware in a way she had never been of the complicated ways she was tied to the duchess and her family. *I must take care of her. And if bad things happen, she will need me. I cannot risk speaking up.*

Miriamele was standing now; her stiff dress of gold and gray, Jesa thought, made her look like a sturdy doll made of woven reeds.

He Who Always Steps on Sand, she prayed, *please let the duchess trust her as I do!*

"It is your children I fear for most, Canthia," said the queen. "You have a beautiful, strong son and daughter. They are the future of Nabban and of the duke's house. Your husband will stay and keep order—or try—no matter what happens, but I wish you would consider going to your house on the Antigine Hill or even out of the city entirely."

After the queen had gone out again and the rattle of the guards following her down the hallway had faded, Jesa was startled to hear the duchess quietly weeping.

Miriamele was uncomfortable meeting Count Dallo in Vellia's Garden but she had little choice. She did not fear for her safety, not here in the heart of the Sancellan Mahistrevis with a dozen of her own men posted among the trees and paths that meandered between overgrown hedges, as well as a hundred more of the duke's guards within shouting distance. What she disliked about such surroundings was the near impossibility of knowing for certain whether anyone was listening. Built for Vellia Hermis, the wife of Imperator Argenian, the garden covered an extensive section of the grounds where the old impera-torial palace itself had once stood, but the trees were planted so thickly along the paths it was hard to see more than a few paces in any direction.

At another moment Miri might have felt glad for the chance to spend some quiet time in the garden, a masterpiece of its kind, with dozens of quiet nooks and long walkways shaded by quince and other fruit trees—even a burbling stream of sweet water meandering through it, pumped up from below by some mechanism to make the gardens seem even more a part of nature. But just now Miri had her husband's most recent letter folded in the bosom of her dress, pressing against her chest like a knife, and she felt very weak and very worried.

Simon had been careful with his words, more so than was his wont, but the simple facts were clear: the Erkynguard company escorting Eolair and their grandson Morgan had been attacked by Thrithings raiders, leaving only a few survivors, and the best hope was that Morgan had been taken for ransom. Miri could only pray that whatever bearded headman among the grasslanders had received this prize understood how important Morgan was. She knew Simon would pay any ransom to get their grandson back safely, but she felt quite ill to be so far from the Hayholt now.

She slid her golden marriage ring up and down her finger, wishing it were the kind of ring she had heard of in childhood tales, a magical token that would take her in an instant to her beloved's side. But she knew that whatever magic might actually be found in the circlet of entwined golden dragons—the subtler magic of love and marriage—would not carry her an inch beyond the bench on which she sat. She could only wait for more frightening letters, more dreadful news to come to her like birds of ill omen alighting one after another on a branch.

First Idela, now Morgan, she thought, and a shadowy fear abruptly became clearer. *Is it our family? Are these truly just horrible accidents or is someone striking at our family? But who?*

She let herself down onto a bench, desperate for a little shade on this hot day. The disturbing new idea would not be ignored, especially when she knew that one of the men who would gladly see her family thrown down was coming to meet her.

I should leave for Erkynland today. It was the first thing that made her feel a little less helpless in the long hours since Froye had brought her Simon's letter. *I should call for my carriage and leave now for the port. With a fair wind I would be home in less than a fortnight.*

But she couldn't—not at this moment. She still had important things to do here, and Simon had already made the decisions on his own. No, she had to be a queen—she had to be *the* queen—and push forward with what her people needed, however much her heart was aching, however much she feared the days to come.

"Your Majesty! You do me great honor. I know you have many more important things to do." Count Dallo had appeared from around a turn in the path. It had happened too suddenly to be an accident—he must have been waiting.

She let him come to her and kiss her hand. He was dressed in exquisite fashion, as always, but it did not suit his amphibian appearance. Miriamele did her best to smile. "I always have time for my loyal subjects, Count—especially when they are also members of my family."

"Ah, now you do me even greater honor! There is not an Ingadarine in all of Nabban who does not swell with pride to know that one of our own sits the High Throne." He smiled, enjoying the exaggerated flattery.

Miriamele almost shared his amusement—they both knew it was rubbish— but her heart was not in this kind of courtly two-step today. "Is there something I can do for you, cousin, or is this purely a social pleasure?"

"Oh, no!" He affected horror at the thought. "No, Your Majesty, I would not take up your time just for the pleasure of conversing with you again, not with all the demands upon you. But I spoke of honor earlier, and honor demanded that I ask for this audience."

"Honor?" Was he going to pretend she had insulted him somehow, or that Saluceris had? Surely things were too far gone between them for that sort of shallow bickering.

"Of course! Just days ago my niece was married to the duke's brother. Yet within my own walls an outrage almost occurred to spoil the day. Without your astonishing bravery, Majesty, only God knows what terrible crimes might have been committed against my guests. My honor demanded that I thank you in person, my queen. You have saved my dignity, and perhaps many lives as well."

Miriamele was slightly taken aback. "I did what any queen would do when her subjects were threatened."

"Ah, I think you underestimate what you have done. Certainly people all over Nabban are talking of it—they cannot stop! A warrior queen like Xaxina from the old stories! All Nabban is agog."

Now the flattery was beginning to annoy her. "Xaxina was an imperator's wife, as I remember—or to be more precise, an imperator's widow. But otherwise I take your meaning and I thank you." She was tired, she realized, and wanted nothing more except to carry her husband's letter back to the privacy of her chambers and read it again, hoping to find, amidst Simon's labored scrawlings, a few bits of hope that she might have missed.

Dallo executed a quick bow, as though someone had momentarily let his puppet strings go slack. "You have other things to occupy your thoughts, I see. Forgive me for one last trespass against your kindness, Majesty, but my niece is waiting. She wished to thank you herself."

Miriamele momentarily considered saying no, but at that instant a dove fluttered down from a nearby tree and walked bobbing across the path.

Sacred Elysia's bird, she thought. *The bird of forgiveness . . . of peace.*

"Of course," she said.

He waved his hand in the air and a servant whom Miriamele had not even seen stepped from behind one of the hedges. "Tell my niece she may come now," Dallo said. As the servant slipped away down the path, Miri wondered how the count *and* his servant had come into the garden without any of her own guards seeming to notice.

She saw a flash of bright color on the path as two large soldiers stepped into the sunlight, one on either side of little Turia, who wore a brown velvet dress ribbed with jewels.

Dallo guards that girl like a precious gem, Miri thought. One of her own Erkynguard stepped onto the path behind them and looked at the queen inquiringly, as if he had only just noticed Dallo's soldiers. She nodded to let him know that all was well and he stepped back again.

Turia waited silently for Miriamele to turn to her, then dropped into a deep courtesy. "Thank you, Majesty," she said, "for keeping my wedding day safe. Thank you for what you did." She spoke without deep conviction, like a child being trotted out for older relatives—which was, in a way, exactly what she was. Miriamele almost felt sorry for her, but there was something flat in the way the new bride looked at her that seemed more disturbing than pathetic. She could only imagine the upbringing the girl must have had in Honsa Ingadaris under Dallo's unpleasant patriarchy.

"You are welcome, my lady," Miri replied, "although I think my role was smaller than it is being made."

Now that she had begun, Miri had to carry out the rest of the ritual. She invited Turia to share her seat on the bench. As Dallo and the guards stood by, she dragged the child bride through a clumsy exchange of small talk.

"I am glad things went well, Lady Turia," Miri said at last, signaling an end to something neither of them seemed to be enjoying much. "And of course I wish you much happiness in your marriage."

"I beg your pardon, Your Majesty," the girl said. "But I am Countess Turia now."

Miriamele was caught by surprise. "Of course," she said at last. "I did not mean to offend. I wish you and the earl your husband much happiness."

Turia folded her hands over her stomach, almost protectively, and for a moment Miri wondered if she was pregnant already.

"How much longer will you be with us, Your Majesty?" Turia asked. Miri could not help thinking she had been supplied the question by her uncle.

"Yes," chimed in Dallo. "We are delighted to have you, but we know there are many matters back home which call for your presence."

He knows, Miri thought. *The news of what happened to Morgan must be all over Nabban by now, even though I myself have only just learned of it. Too many sailors coming down from the north to keep secrets for long.*

She put on her most serene face. "Fear not, my lord, I will be with you long enough for the signing of the lector's covenant." It was what kept her in the city despite all the terrible things happening at home, the promise she and Simon had wrung from Lector Vidian in return for her attendance at the wedding. She knew that no document would end the power struggle no matter who signed it, but it was an important public gesture that would at least help to make clear what the High Throne expected of the warring Kingfishers and Dallo's Stormbirds.

"Ah. That, of course, is a relief to all of us," said Dallo. "The unrest in this city has been greatly calmed by your presence."

And you are a liar, sir, she thought.

"May I ask you one more question, Your Majesty?" Turia asked, her little heart-shaped face turned up to Miri's like a child prettily asking for a sweet.

"Of course, Countess."

"When those men came, and you stood before them . . . were you frightened?"

It was the first time that any of Turia's words had seemed charged with actual interest, and her heavy-lidded stare seemed bright and curious. "Was I frightened?" Miri weighed several possible answers, but the moment seemed somehow significant and she decided on the truth. "Of course, yes. It is a long time since I have swung a sword in anger, and although my guards are well trained and brave, there were far more bandits than there were of us. So, yes, I was frightened. But as you will discover, courage is not so much being unafraid as it is doing what you must, no matter how you tremble inside."

"The queen is very wise," said Dallo. "Very wise indeed."

"Thank you, Majesty," said Turia, making another courtesy. "I truly wanted to know."

At last Dallo, his niece, and his servants—several more had been loitering about the gardens, it seemed—departed with their guards.

Miriamele twisted her wedding ring on her finger, aching again for her husband, her brave kitchen boy, her closest friend. Nabban, the source of a major tributary of her family's blood, a place where everything seemed louder, brighter, and usually more dangerous, now had begun to seem like a prison.

24

The Tebi Pit

The more days and nights Nezeru spent in Fortress Dark Lantern, the more puzzled she became. The underground warren of tunnels was so extensive that it took a long time simply to walk from the place where she slept in one of the dormitory wings to the low-ceilinged central hall to receive her daily ration of puju bread and dried fish. The more she looked, the more the Builder magister's daughter became convinced that cave-borers—many-legged digging beasts from deep in the earth—must have been brought all the way from Nakkiga to do the work.

But that did not answer her larger questions—why was it so big, and why had it been built here? As far as she knew, the fort was in a region between two great forests on the outer fringes of mortal territory, perhaps as much as a hundred leagues away from the Hikeda'ya's own lands. As for the soldiers under Juni'ata's command, they seemed just as much of a mystery. Nezeru had been taught Sacrifice Order history, but she had never heard of the War-Shrike Legion, yet here she was in their midst.

She could remember rumors about carefully chosen recruits who trained on their own and did not take their oaths with Nezeru and the rest. She had assumed that if such warriors existed they were just a larger than usual group of Sacrifices culled early by one of the other Orders, or even by the palace itself. The orders of Singers and Celebrants, and even some of the larger more powerful noble clans, often chose recruits from among the new Sacrifices while they were still shaking and sweating from their ordeal in Yedade's Box. But the War-Shrikes were not merely a few recruits but a sizable and clearly well-trained fighting force, all posted to a huge fortress she had never heard of . . . in the middle of nowhere. And from a few comments she had overheard, the Legion *Sey-Jok'kochi* was apparently part of something larger—the "Northeastern Host" she had heard it called, another term entirely new to her.

"We are doing the Queen's most important work," was all Scout Rinde would tell her when she asked.

"I have done the Queen's work myself." Nezeru did not like being treated like an ignorant new Sacrifice. "The other Talons and I journeyed farther than this, and risked our lives countless times for the Mother of All—and succeeded at the task she had given us as well. I do not like having things hidden from me."

Rinde had almost smiled, but shook his head. "I admire your bravery, Sacrifice, but trust my words—you do not want to be heard asking questions. Not in Fortress Dark Lantern."

And that had to suffice. Commander Juni'ata might not have formally accused her of being a spy, but Nezeru knew perfectly well that she was being carefully watched.

Soon Saomeji will meet with others of our folk, she consoled herself. *If there are Sacrifices sent to meet them, there will be Echoes among them. Then Juni'ata can learn the truth—that the Queen herself sent us to the mountain, and that the mighty Lord Akhenabi thanked us for the bones of Hakatri when we brought them. Perhaps then they will treat me with some respect.*

But she could not help wondering what had become of Jarnulf. What if he had succeeded in killing the others? Without Saomeji and the captured dragon to confirm her story, Juni'ata might decide Nezeru was simply a deserter, and those who tried to escape their duties with the Order of Sacrifice met very, very bad ends.

Over the days that followed she was allowed to accompany the scouts out on patrol but was never given any responsibility or permitted to stray from Rinde's side. Nezeru was frustrated, having been trained in tracking, but she did her best to remain outwardly calm and do what a good Sacrifice should. The chief scout did not make things too hard on her, but although she admired Rinde's leadership, she could not regard him as an ally. She no longer had any allies, she realized, not even in her own order.

But why did she no longer feel herself completely part of her own people? Was it only that Jarnulf's questions had confused her? She knew now that the mortal had been a traitor, so why had she come to doubt the trustworthiness of almost every one of her leaders except the Queen herself? Whether it had been Jarnulf's words or some deeper cause, her once-unshakeable belief in the Order of Sacrifice had soured. She feared she would never know that confidence again.

Most of the days Nezeru and the scouts did little more than roam the outer boundaries of Fortress Dark Lantern's territory, leagues and leagues of tangled, hilly woodland. A few times they even met and exchanged information with Sacrifice scouts from other forts in the area, such as the small troop from a nearby stronghold called Fortress Deeping who used only hand signs to communicate even when Rinde and his scouts spoke aloud. By the time the two groups parted, Nezeru had begun to wonder if any of the Fortress Deeping scouts *could* speak, and if not, what the advantage might be in assembling a troop of mute soldiers. Rinde told her, "They are silent because they learn to be so and do not speak while they are in service, even when they are away from their charges."

"Charges?"

"The stonechafers they care for at Fortress Deeping are very large and dangerous, with jaws that chew stone. They are also easily startled by noise."

Nezeru had heard the word only a few times before this, but it confirmed her guess about the tunnel excavations—"stonechafer" was an ancient name for the massive cave-borers that lived in Nakkiga's depths.

Nezeru found herself even more disturbed after the scouts encountered mortals one evening, a group of what looked like three or four mortal families, men, women, and children, foraging for nuts and roots on a forested hillside. Since Rinde's troop were shielded by brush and had not been seen, she assumed the Sacrifices would retreat; instead, at a whispered word from their leader, the scouts shook the bows off their shoulders and nocked their arrows. At Rinde's gesture they let fly, and every dart found a target. The surprised and terrified mortals began to flee in all directions. Some charged right toward their attackers without seeing them.

Another flight of arrows felled more of the mortals, then the Sacrifices were running up the hill at what must have seemed terrible speed to the survivors: in a matter of instants the Hikeda'ya were among them, cutting throats. From start to finish the skirmish lasted only a couple of dozen heartbeats.

When silence fell again the scouts stood among the bodies, looking for movement; an old man trying to crawl away was quickly spitted on the end of Rinde's own sword. As Nezeru tried to understand her tangle of feelings— these were enemies, of course, even if they were not warriors, yet the sight of dead women and children lying among them disturbed her—one of the other scouts let out a low whistle.

Far away up the hillside one child was still on its feet, as if it had been returning to the group when the attack began. Nezeru thought it was a female, but the shocked little face was too dirty and the hair too shaggy and unkempt to be sure. The small figure stood for a moment, open-mouthed, then turned and ran.

Rinde lifted his bow and took aim. For a moment Nezeru had the mad thought of trying to discourage him, but kept silent. One of the other scouts murmured something that sparked laughter from the others, then the leader's bowstring sang and the child fell down, limbs thrown all awry. The small body rolled a few paces back down the slope and stopped. A moment later the long summer grass that had been flattened by its fall sprang back.

Why did Rinde not hesitate as I once did? Nezeru was full of both shock and shame. *What is torn or broken inside me that I could not do the same? And given that task again, would I succeed or fail? Any young mortal might grow up to be another slayer of my own people.*

But still, to shoot down a mere child—! She could not make sense of her own feelings and that angered her. *Why has it become so hard to hate our enemies?*

Jarnulf, Saomeji and the helpless Makho spent most of the day descending a long sheet of rock that had been scraped flat by stone and ice in eons long past. The slope was not steep enough to ease Goh Gam Gar's burden, and he had done little all day but groan and complain. When they reached the end of the long, rocky shelf and the giant saw that there was no easy route down to the slope below, he growled so deeply that Jarnulf could feel his own ribs quiver. Then Goh Gam Gar turned loose the sledge and slumped to the ground as though he would never walk another step.

"Get up, beast!" commanded Saomeji. "It is only a little way farther. Must I punish you?"

"You said we meet the rest of your stinking *Higdaja* today," the giant snarled at him between panting breaths. "They can carry the beast down the mountain from this place, because I am finished. Punish me again—kill me. I will not carry it more."

Saomeji's face remained almost expressionless as always, but Jarnulf could tell he was furious. Saomeji raised the red crystal rod and the giant writhed, huge mouth open, great, gray tongue lolling in helpless pain.

"One day old Gam will pull your head off your neck and swallow it," the giant gasped.

Saomeji sent pain crashing through the monster again and again, and Jarnulf thought this time it would actually kill him, but as Goh Gam Gar lay thrashing and bellowing, Saomeji looked down the slope and his odd golden eyes narrowed. Hikeda'ya soldiers were stepping out of the trees beneath the shelf of stone, a few at first, then dozens, all silent as cats. A female Sacrifice wearing the helmet of a war-leader called out. "We are here as promised, Singer."

"You are a welcome sight, Commander," Saomeji called back.

"Punish the giant later," she said. "We have come to help you bring your burden down to our camp."

Saomeji slipped the crystal rod back into his robe, leaving the giant gasping on the ground. As the pale-skinned Sacrifices swarmed up the hillside and went to work, silent as termites, Jarnulf stayed close to the the Singer. Already a good number of the Sacrifice soldiers had noticed him. None had offered him anything worse than stares of contempt, but he did not want to be caught on his own if one of them decided he was a slave in need of being chastised.

With so many warriors, horses, and ropes, the immense bulk of the dragon was soon lowered onto the next slope and moving again. As they reached the bottom of the long shelf of rock Jarnulf could make out the well-hidden outlines of a Hikeda'ya camp nestled in a clearing in the woods; dozens more Sacrifice soldiers waited there. A huge, six-wheeled wagon stood by itself in the center of the clearing, too large to hide. It was painted a red so dark it was almost black, and ornamented with symbols that could only barely be seen in the fading light, at least by Jarnulf with his mortal eyes. A team of eight huge black war-goats stood cropping and chewing disinterestedly at dry grass nearby. Their slotted eyes flicked briefly to the newcomers, but they did not startle even at the trussed dragon as it was dragged to the edge of the clearing.

The wagon's door swung open and a tall figure stepped out into the twilight. Jarnulf knew who it was in an instant. His heart sped and his skin turned cold and clammy as the newcomer turned to Saomeji, his wrinkled mask of dead skin framed by the dark hood. "So you return at last, Acolyte," he said in a voice like a corpse being dragged across gravel.

"I do, great Akhenabi, Lord of Song."

"But you return with fewer members of your Hand than you had at Bitter Moon Castle."

"Our task was a dangerous one, Master." There was a strange note in the halfblood Singer's response, a certain bitterness that even Jarnulf thought out of character for a Hikeda'ya speaking to his superior. "But we succeeded."

"Did you? Then I suppose congratulations are in order. So what have you brought me?" Akhenabi descended the wagon steps and moved toward the captured dragon. "The beast looks as if it is dying. A dead worm is no use to me, Acolyte."

"It is not dying, Master. I have kept it alive through great hardship." Saomeji's voice sounded almost pained. "We captured it high on the mountain and have carried it all this way." The giant Goh Gam Gar snorted at this from the place where he crouched. Saomeji gave him a cold, cold look.

Akhenabi gestured and several hooded Singers sprang forward. "Care for the beast," he told them. "See that it stays alive if you wish to remain that way as well." His eyes narrowed in the eyeholes of his mask as he saw Makho's unmoving form on the sledge. "And what is this?"

"That is Makho, the chieftain of our hand. He was burned with dragon's blood."

This seemed to interest Akhenabi, who approached and studied Makho's ruined face. "Why did you carry him back and risk your mission?" He suddenly noticed Jarnulf lurking behind Saomeji. "And what is *this* creature?" His eyes narrowed into black slits. "Why have you taken on a mortal slave? Where did you find it?"

"This is no ordinary slave, but a Queen's Huntsman," said Saomeji. "Our Echo, Ibi-Khai, was killed by a swarm of *Furi'a* just beyond Bitter Moon Castle, not long after we parted from you. We took the mortal as our guide to help us reach the eastern mountains where the dragons live."

Akhenabi stared at Jarnulf for a long moment, then gestured for him to approach. Jarnulf obeyed as if trapped in a nightmare, knowing that he had no hope of resisting the Lord of Song's power, that within moments his every secret would be revealed.

My death will be unbearably slow . . . unspeakably painful . . .

"Master," said Saomeji. "Please, I beg your patience, but I have one more thing to speak of with you and time is short. The chieftain, Makho—he is dying."

Akhenabi was clearly annoyed by the interruption but for the moment his attention was distracted from Jarnulf. "And what can that mean to me?"

"I brought him back because I thought he might still be useful to us—to you and our queen."

"Useful?" Akhenabi's laugh was like a stick dragged across a paling. "What use could this broken thing possibly be to the Mother of All?"

"Chieftain Makho has been splashed with dragon's blood—you can see how badly—and yet he still lives. He has been a celebrated destroyer of the queen's enemies."

"So?"

"I thought . . ." Now that the moment had come, Saomeji seemed reluctant. "I thought perhaps . . . as another weapon for the queen's vengeance . . ."

"Out with it." Akhenabi's voice was harsh.

Saomeji took a deep breath. "Perhaps the Tebi Pit?"

For a moment the eyes stared blankly from the mask. Then, slowly, the Lord of Song began to nod. "The Tebi Pit . . . !" he rasped. "By the Lost Garden, that *is* an idea. But the Sacrifice chieftain is not dead."

"Would that prevent the Word of Resurrection from fulfilling its purpose?" Saomeji asked, more confident now. "Or might it become even more potent?"

Jarnulf had no idea what they were talking about, but was grateful for anything that took Akhenabi's attention from him; he retreated a few discreet steps toward Saomeji as the Lord of Song moved to Makho and stood over him. "The Word of Resurrection used on a living creature? It will cause him pain that will make what the dragon's blood did to him seem like a festival week."

"Yes," said Saomeji. "I am certain it will, Master. But it was always Makho's greatest wish to serve our queen. We can make him a powerful weapon against her enemies."

Akhenabi nodded again. "The Tebi Pit. It is a clever idea and you have done well, Acolyte Saomeji. I am pleased with you." He called several of his Singers forward and ordered them to carry Makho's litter into his wagon. "And dig a hole," he said. "As wide as the chieftain is tall, and just as deep."

Akhenabi's attention now turned elsewhere, Jarnulf was almost breathless with relief, but could not avoid a twinge of regret for Makho. He would have gladly killed the chieftain himself many times over, but he had seen the horrible agony the dragon's blood had caused, and if this Tebi Pit was worse— well, that was something Jarnulf was not certain he would wish even on his enemies.

All night long he heard disturbing noises from Akhenabi's wagon, gasps and whimpers and even low gulping croaks that might have come from the throats of monstrous frogs. Once he heard a fierce keening like a mountain gale, though no wind blew; later, he thought he heard the sound of leathery wings beating above him in the darkness.

And if I survive all this horror, it will be simply to achieve my own death in the end, he thought, and in that moment it all felt as cold and pointless as the empty light of the distant stars. *But my sacrifice can at least be meaningful, with the Lord's help.* He began to pray. *Please, Lord, let my ending bring good for my people. Please let my death mean something my life never could.*

Because he could not sleep—did not dare sleep—Jarnulf crawled closer to where the giant lay shackled by Akhenabi's minions. He could see the gleam of the creature's eyes and knew Goh Gam Gar was also awake.

"You do not try to run from the Hikeda'ya, do you?" rumbled the giant. "Remember, you owe me two favors, hiding your absence one time, then hiding what you did when we were surrounded by mortals on the hill."

"I am not running," Jarnulf whispered. "And I do not forget. I will honor my word."

"Not like Saomeji the Singer," growled Goh Gam Gar as a ghastly noise floated across the camp. "He said he would keep his chief Makho alive, but listen—!"

"I do not think he breaks his word," said Jarnulf. "But there are worse fates than death, and I suspect Makho is going to learn that."

Another ragged cry split the night. If it was the Sacrifice chieftain who uttered it, he sounded as if he had come back to life only to surrender to utter madness.

"And they call *my* kind beasts," the giant said.

Somewhere in the bleak hours between midnight and dawn Jarnulf was roused out of a shallow doze by the sound of footsteps, something heard so infrequently among the Hikeda'ya that it reached into his uncomfortable dreams and startled him awake.

"They are coming out," said the giant. "Be silent."

Jarnulf rolled over and peered across the camp at the vast black oblong of Akhenabi's wagon. A small group of robed Singers carried a shrouded shape down the steps of the wagon, then across the campsite toward the place where the deep hole had been prepared. For a moment, still half in the grip of sleep, Jarnulf could not help remembering the nights when his Hikeda'ya masters had come to drag the dead slaves out of the barns while the rest slept.

Akhenabi and Saomeji followed the procession, but the younger Singer turned away instead and approached the place where Jarnulf and the giant watched. "We have done it," Saomeji said as he neared them, and the satisfaction in his voice was so obvious it seemed almost childlike. "My master and I have made Makho into something greater than he ever was—a weapon that will make the queen's enemies quail in terror."

Goh Gam Gar watched as the Singers, with Akhenabi's silent supervision, kneeled and began singing quietly over the wrapped body. "It looks as if you killed him once and for all," the giant rumbled.

Saomeji laughed. Between weariness and triumph, he sounded almost drunk. "Makho is alive, but changing. Three days in the ground will change him even more."

"Three days . . . ?" Jarnulf said, nauseated.

"Or at least that is how long it usually takes the Tebi Pit to do its work. The pit and the Word of Resurrection are used to bring life back to a dead body, at least for a little while. The charm has never been tried on one who still lives." Jarnulf could hear the smirk in Saomeji's voice. "I cannot even guess what kind of pain our noble chieftain will suffer—!"

The wrapped figure of Makho suddenly began thrashing and shouting as it was lowered into the pit, though the chieftain's voice was so strangely muffled and distorted that Jarnulf could scarcely hear it from a few paces away. "Why does he sound like that?"

"Because his mouth has been stuffed with yew berries and dried lily flowers and other potent herbs, and his lips have been sewed shut," explained Saomeji with the pleasure of a craftsman describing a skillful piece of work. "His body has been anointed with burning oils until it has become annealed—hardened, as tin hardens copper into sacred bronze. Now it remains only for the dark womb of the earth to finish the task of making him anew. Then Makho will serve our queen as no other creature ever has."

As Akhenabi's helpers continued singing in low, unintelligible voices, they began to fill the hole with dirt, burying Makho alive, though he still struggled even after the soil covered him. It was all Jarnulf could do not to be sick. Goh Gam Gar grumbled in disgust, then turned away and stretched out as if to go back to sleep.

Jarnulf forced himself to remember his great task. All this horror and more would be worth it if he succeeded. "You spoke of the queen, Saomeji," he said. "When will we see her? When will we go to Nakkiga?"

The Singer turned toward him; even in the darkness Jarnulf could feel his suspicious look. "Why do you want to know that?"

"To receive my reward, of course," he said quickly. "Remember, I have helped this great cause of yours in many ways. I wish to be rewarded—and to be recognized by the queen herself. That will be an honor all the other Huntsmen will envy."

"Mortal fool." But Saomeji's mistrust seemed to be allayed. "In any case, we are not going to Nakkiga."

The Singers were tamping the last of the dirt down on the Tebi Pit; there were no longer any signs of movement. In the sudden silence, Jarnulf struggled to hide his shock and dismay. "Not going to Nakkiga—?"

"No, Huntsman." And Saomeji laughed. For the first time since Jarnulf had met him, he seemed full of good cheer. "Because the queen—our holy ruler, the living Garden and the Mother of All—is coming to us instead."

Nezeru found it strange to have the luxury to rest. She did not know what to do with so much time, and found herself falling into lethargy and self-doubt when she took to her bed in the long, empty hours between patrols.

Am I truly as weak as I seem to be? Is my blood so compromised by my mother's race? Or—and this thought was truly terrifying—*did some of the things the mortal said actually pierce me because I recognized he spoke the truth?*

Not his nonsense about Aedon, of course, or any of the other mortal cultishness he had babbled, but the questions he had asked about Nezeru herself: Why *had* she been chosen to come on this mission? She knew there were many other Sacrifices with more experience—there had been much resentment in the ranks when she was chosen to be a Talon and even more when she had been selected to accompany the accomplished and respected Chieftain Makho on an important task for Queen Utuk'ku herself. Nezeru had been a masterly fighter, one of the best of her rank and age, but in her heart of hearts she had always known there were dozens of Sacrifices who could have been chosen in her place. Her family was middling noble and her father was a High Magister, but many other Sacrifices had even stronger claims on the Order's favor.

As she lay preoccupied by disturbing thoughts, she heard a noise and opened her eyes to find Rinde standing over her. For a moment she was confused by the strangely intent look on his face, and wondered if he hoped to couple with her. Nezeru did not know exactly how she felt about the idea—the scout chief was a halfblood and could not force her, but she was still not certain she would send him away.

But he only said, "An expedition, Sacrifice Nezeru. I need you. Come along."

"What is the time?"

"The last lamp of the night watch was lit a short while ago."

She followed him silently toward the fort's front gate and down passageways carved out of stone and those of pressed earth supported by nets of woven spidersilk. They were met in the guardroom by Va'ani and Jhindejo, Rinde's two most trusted underlings, and she felt a moment of pride that he would choose her as the fourth for whatever this task might be. They armed themselves and went out, climbing from the entrance tunnel into the darkness and the long, dewy grass, then made their way silently along invisible tracks the scouts knew. Nezeru moved as quietly and easily as the rest. They followed Rinde for no little time until they reached a spot close to the boundary between Dark Lantern and the nearest fort to the south, a grove of ancient linden trees, leaves withered and almost colorless in the growing dawn light.

"We stop here," said Rinde. "We must wait."

Nezeru looked around but could see nothing out of the ordinary about the grove or what lay beyond. For a moment she feared that Rinde might want her to couple with all of them, although that seemed out of character. After some time had passed without anything unusual happening, she guessed they were meeting scouts or messengers from the nearest fort, and let the sounds and scents of morning's beginning wash over her, a rabbit scuffling in the brush nearby, a starling chattering and whistling in a distant tree, the scent of a million leaves warming as the sun climbed toward the open sky.

"Show me your sword," said Rinde.

The abruptness of his request startled her, but she drew it from its sheath and presented it to him on her palms. He took it and hefted it, closed his hand around the grip and held it with the silver-grey blade pointing up, testing its weight. "A beautiful thing. One of the old witchwood blades, not the crude bronze weapons we scouts must use."

She heard something strange in his voice, something that made her uneasy. "It belonged to Makho, the chieftain of our hand," she said. "It is very old. He says it once belonged to General Suno'ku herself."

"Cold Root," said Rinde, still examining the blade. "Yes, I have heard of it—who has not? But why are *you* carrying it, Sacrifice Nezeru?"

"Makho was badly wounded during our mission for the queen, so he no longer carried the sword. The mortal who stole me from our camp left it with me, though I could not say why. But I have told all this already to Commander Juni'ata. When you speak to my comrades you will learn I told the truth. May I have it back now?"

Rinde shook his head, and in that one movement she saw terrible things. "No, Sacrifice. Our Echoes have now spoken to your people. Your comrades say you lie. They say you stole the sword and deserted."

Her flash of outraged anger was swiftly overwhelmed by a fear that swallowed everything. "No, I do not lie! They must have believed Jarnulf—a mortal, a traitorous mortal! But he lies! He tried to lure me away from my loyalty to our queen, and when he could not do it, he carried me away. I have explained all this!"

But even as she tried to step forward to take back the sword—*her* sword, however it had come to her, the only reward she had received for all her suffering—Rinde's two comrades grabbed her arms from either side, then twisted them behind her back until she was forced down onto her knees.

"I wanted to trust you, Sacrifice Nezeru." Rinde's face had hardened into the grim mask she had seen so many times, on her father as well as her superiors in the Sacrifice order. "I think it is possible you were misled by this mortal. Did he promise you freedom? Affection? But the leader of your Hand has said you are a criminal, and Lord Akhenabi, who is with them, demands your return. Be grateful that I only overheard the orders and was not given them myself."

"Grateful?" Her struggling did nothing except threaten to wrench her shoulders from their sockets. "Grateful for what?" A wild hope was kindled—might Rinde mean to let her escape?

"That I do not release you to the vile torturers of the Order of Song," he said. "They would stretch the span of your agony into years. But I will give you the kindness of a swift death and tell them that you disobeyed me on patrol and I was forced to execute you. Now bend your neck."

Va'ani and Jhindejo pulled her arms further back, forcing her head toward the ground.

"And because Cold Root is so much sharper than my own poor blade," Rinde said, "I will also show you the honor of using blessed Suno'ku's weapon."

Nezeru's thoughts were swarming, darting, flying. She struggled to remember her training, but the pain in her shoulders was dreadful and her face was pressed against grass still wet with dew. She could sense by the tightening grips of the two scouts that Rinde must be raising Makho's sword for the killing stroke. Ignoring the pain, she let herself slump into Jhindejo on her right, pushing toward him hard enough to disrupt his balance. On her other side Va'ani was caught by surprise and did not immediately readjust his grip. As she tumbled into Jhindejo she put all her weight on her right knee and kicked out as hard as she could with her left leg, knowing she would have only one chance to hit her target, and that if she failed, she would not get another chance.

Her swinging kick smashed the toe of her boot into Va'ani's leg behind his knee. He did not howl—he was a scout, and trained to silence—but he gasped, his leg buckled, and he fell. At the same moment she shoved herself into Jhindejo again, trying to keep him off balance and also put him in the way of any possible swordstroke from Rinde. Momentarily shielded from Makho's blade, she wrapped her arms around Jhindejo and brought him down on top of her.

The scouts were all able fighters, but Nezeru had been trained over countless hours in the Blood Reaches to be more than any ordinary Sacrifice. As she grappled with Jhindejo she found the knife on his belt and pulled it free, then drove it upward into his neck. She was halfway under him, so she put her legs up and shoved his bleeding body toward Rinde, who had to dance back to avoid being entangled. From the corner of her eye she saw that Va'ani was clambering unsteadily onto his feet while trying to draw his sword. She had to make a choice, so she kicked Va'ani in his good knee and leaped over him. As he tumbled to the ground making quiet noises of pain she kicked him in the head as hard as she could and yanked the sword from his failing grasp.

Gasping, she stood now with the short bronze blade held before her, facing Rinde.

"You are a fool," she said, her voice so rough with fear and rage she almost could not recognize it. "I am a Queen's Talon. Even if I were guilty of the crimes you falsely lay at my feet, you still could not kill me with such poor efforts." But it was as much bluff as anything else; she was winded, her legs felt like broomstraws, and Rinde had the longer, stronger sword.

"If you are innocent, come with me and face the justice of your people," Rinde said even as he moved slowly toward her. "You will have to answer for poor Jhindejo, but I will tell what happened."

"The justice of my people?" She almost laughed. "Lord Akhenabi wants my head for some reason, that is clear, and Akhenabi does not care about justice, only the Order of Song and his own power." And even as she spoke she could feel the truth in what she said. She did not trust the Lord of Song or anyone else who claimed to serve the queen. She had heard her father tell many ugly tales about Akhenabi, and although she had not wanted to believe them, it had been hard even in those innocent days to think her father a liar.

"I have tried to deal fairly with you—" Rinde began.

"That is what is always said before something terrible is done," she snapped back, still struggling for breath. "And I will not stand talking while the rest of your comrades come looking for us. Defend yourself." She sprang forward, her blade weaving through the flashing figures of the Sacrifice Dance.

Rinde caught her first killing blow on Cold Root's blade, and Nezeru's sword rang in an offkey way, telling her that too many collisions of blade on blade would break Va'ani's bronze sword and leave her helpless. She attacked again, even faster this time, trying to put all her remaining strength into piercing Rinde's guard. She swiped, stabbed, then danced back, slipping his counter-blows, but she knew she could not hold him off for long. The scout chief was a better than average swordsman with a superior blade, and had too much advantage in reach.

As Nezeru slid sideways, pushing his blade away and almost getting her own caught in Cold Root's guard, she felt something against her foot. A glance down showed her that it was Jhindejo's bloody knife; his body was only a short distance away, and Rinde was trying to drive her toward it to entangle her feet.

She had one last gamble available, and she took it almost without thinking, hooking her toe under the knife and then flipping it up to grab it in her free hand. Before Rinde could react, she drove her sword at his face; when he brought up Cold Root to fend off her blow she brought her other hand across and stabbed the knife hard into his leg.

She sprang back, ready to defend herself again, but she had hit something vital and the blood was already sheeting down Rinde's leg. She pressed him again. His movements became more awkward, then gradually he slowed until she could get close enough to end the fight by slamming the side of her blade as hard as she could against his head, dropping him senseless to the ground.

Breathing hard, she pulled Cold Root from Rinde's grasp but could not make herself leave the scout chieftain bleeding to death. Cursing herself, she quickly checked the other two fallen War-Shrikes. Va'ani was insensible but alive. Jhindejo was dead.

You drove me to this, but still I honor you, she thought. *You did what you thought was right. You did what you thought was the Queen's will.*

She pulled off Jhindejo's sword belt and tightened it around Rinde's thigh until the flow of blood slowed.

"You may survive," she said. "If you can hear me, know that I showed you mercy—more than you would have shown me." Then she turned and started away, following the boundary between the two forts as she headed south toward some place where no Sacrifice strongholds lay hidden.

Now I have become the enemy of all, she thought. *Both mortals and Hikeda'ya alike. There is no one in all these lands who does not want me dead.*

25

King of Wolves

Fremur was awakened by the butt end of a spear shoved hard into his stomach. As he lay gasping in the muddy straw of Rudur Redbeard's paddock he was jabbed again. "Get on your feet or I'll have your guts out with the other end, whelp," said the clansman holding the spear.

Fremur pushed it away and sat up. It all came rushing back to him—Unver's capture and his own precarious status—and he realized he no longer cared. Either he had been right to follow the tall man or he had been wrong. But he would not grovel.

He was prodded again. "Take that away from me or I will make you eat it," Fremur said.

The clansman's face writhed into a snarl of anger. He turned the spear to level the iron head at Fremur's belly. "Then I will show you what your guts look like, Thane Mustache."

"Hold," said another voice. "Nothing wrong with a man showing a little fire." The newcomer stepped forward from where he had been overseeing the rousting of the other prisoners. He looked Fremur up and down with amused contempt. "Vybord's right though. A proper thane should have a beard."

"I have not had time to find a bride here at the Thanemoot," Fremur told him. "Rudur's . . . invitation was unexpected."

The man laughed. He was bigger than his underling, brawny, with ritual scars and tattoos covering much of his face. He was also missing half his teeth, so that one cheek sagged a little. "Crane Clan, eh?" he said. "You lake-birds. I know your kind. Good scouts, but when the fighting gets fierce you all take wing."

"Just free my hands and give me my sword and I'll show you fierce." But just looking at the size of this man and the evidence of many combats survived, Fremur knew it was likely a foolish boast.

The other fellow still seemed more amused than angry. "Get up, then, Thane Mustache. I am Odobreg, Thane of the Badger Clan and Rudur's chief bondsman. You have a sharp tongue, pup, but I do not kill men who have been beaten and left in the mud. Get up."

"So Rudur can have me killed instead? I would rather it happen now so I don't have to watch him crow and strut."

"Do not think to know what Rudur wants or what Rudur plans." Odobreg sounded more amused than angry. "He is subtle beyond what any Lake-man can understand. He called you guest and said you would live—it is only that upstart, the half stone-dweller, who has been put outside the fence. And if you get up now, after your clan has bowed to Redbeard I might have use for a man with sharp wits and courage."

Fremur climbed to his feet and stood, hands still tied behind his back, stiff and sore and unsteady as a newborn colt. "And when Unver finally kills Redbeard, Thane Odobreg, I might have use for *you*."

The clansman who had first woken him snarled at this, but Odobreg seemed a man of broader temperament; he threw back his head and laughed. "Good! That is good. Very well, little lake-bird, I offer you a wager. At the end of the day, the one whose chieftain is dead will bow to the other and offer his neck for the sword or the collar."

Fremur could barely hold his temper back at hearing Unver treated so lightly, but these men had not seen what he had. "Very well, then," he said, and let himself be herded toward the paddock gate with the others, "we have a wager."

"Ah, Thane Mustache." Odobreg showed the few front teeth he still owned. "I will enjoy having you bring me *yerut* in my silver cup. You will be like another son for me to cuff into obedience and a respectful tongue."

The crowd that had gathered was even larger than it had been the evening before. Most of the people seemed to have been waiting around Rudur's camp since the sun's first light. Unver's Stallions, Fremur, and his Cranes were marched out to wait in the damp morning until Rudur finally deigned to emerge.

"Has the hour come?" he said loudly, as if this was the first time he had thought about it since rising. "Then we must go and see how the spirits have treated Shan Nobody."

There was laughter, especially from Rudur's own clan, but Fremur thought he saw disapproving faces in the crowd as well, even some unhidden anger. Redbeard had never been popular, but he had made bargains with the stone-dwellers that had kept the city men out of the Thrithings-lands for years. But that had changed of late, and the one thing that all grasslanders shared was resentment of the castle-folk with their cities and walls and weapons. Fremur guessed some among the crowd had also heard that Unver had fulfilled many of the old prophecies, and resented Rudur trying to destroy something that had given them hope.

But though Fremur looked hard at all the faces he passed for signs of Redbeard's weakness or unpopularity, he also knew that none of it would matter if Unver was dead. He might become a figure of future tales, one of the many failed hopes that peopled grassland history, but that would be scant use to those who had cast their lot with him.

If I live after this, it will be as a Black Bear turnspit, he thought with a flame of helpless anger in his belly—*a slave. And poor Hyara will be given to one of Rudur's underlings, someone no better than the brute husband Unver killed.*

The procession led by Rudur and his shaman Volfrag grew even larger as it made its way around the edge of the encampment and headed toward the Spirit Hills. Soon enough they reached the base of the highest of the Spirit Hills, where Rudur's guards were waiting.

"Have you kept the hill safe all night?" Rudur asked them loudly. "Have you left Unver Long Legs alone with the spirits he claims have chosen him?"

"After beating him with the Summer Rose until he was almost dead!" shouted Fremur, but Rudur ignored him. The guards all swore that nothing larger than a mouse had passed them from dusk to dawn.

"Well, then either the spirits came to him in their many forms and worshipped at his feet—or perhaps they came and showed him less kindness." Rudur laughed loudly at his own jest.

Fremur knew that the chances that Unver had survived the night after such a terrible whipping would have been small, but left bound, bloody, and unprotected, he was almost certainly dead. Hunting was forbidden on the sacred hill, and at night the wolves, bears, and sometimes catamounts all roamed the wooded slopes in complete freedom.

Rudur led the crowd upward along the winding trail. Some of them were grave and looked little happier than Fremur, but others clearly found it a merry outing, a bit of fun. But even the noisiest fell silent as they approached the great stone and the wooden post and for the first time caught sight of the figure slumped motionless at its base. Fremur saw how much blood had soaked into the ground around the prisoner's body and felt despair. Unver's chin was on his chest, his legs stretched before him, and every part of him Fremur could see was covered with dried brown blood.

Then Unver lifted his head to look at Rudur, eyes twin gleams under his brow and the bloodied tangle of his hair.

It was not a sudden movement, more like that of a man who has been deep in thought and finally realizes that someone has been speaking to him, but it startled the approaching crowd like a sudden roar of thunder, and transfixed Fremur with sharp, almost painful joy. Unver lived! Many of the clansfolk stopped where they were and cried out, transfixed with superstitious surprise. Even Rudur Redbeard was taken aback: Fremur saw the Thane of Thanes almost stumble before recovering himself. But Rudur was no fool, though he was no doubt cursing himself for not simply taking Unver's head instead of trying to make him an example.

The mood of the crowd had suddenly but definitely changed. Whatever else he might be, Rudur Redbeard was no fool, and Fremur knew that he could sense it too. Against all odds, Unver had survived the night, but for Rudur to accept it and release him would be only to make his legend greater and Redbeard's own reputation smaller.

Rudur waved to Volfrag to follow him. The curious, whispering grasslanders moved forward after them, Fremur and the other prisoners carried forward like chaff on the wind, although fear of Rudur or the spirits of the place caused the crowd to stop a respectful distance from the great stone and the prisoner's bloodied post.

"I see you are stronger than I guessed," Rudur said. "It is unfortunate you are mad—you might have made a good thane to your clan after all. Come, you must be thirsty after your long night, and I am not a cruel man." He gestured, and Volfrag took the top off the carved box he had carried to the hilltop, revealing a golden ewer and two large gold cups.

"Pour the man a cup of wine, Shaman," Rudur said loud enough for much of the crowd to hear. "Let no one say Rudur is not a fair-minded host."

Volfrag, his great bearded face impassive, poured wine from the ewer and then passed the goblet to Rudur. Unver still had not spoken, but only glowered up at the Thane of Thanes, his face a bloody mask.

"Drink it," Rudur said, lowering the cup to Unver's mouth. "There is not much mercy in the world."

"No!" a woman screamed. "Don't touch it! It is poison!"

Fremur saw Unver's mother, Vorzheva, fight her way out of the crowd. Once free of those trying to hold her back she ran across the open ground toward the post, but she was running toward Rudur, not her son, and her fingers were curved like claws. Several of the guards grabbed her, but she nearly managed to slip away from them as well, her hands snatching at the air only a short distance from Redbeard's face.

"By the Midnight Growler," he shouted, "are none of you men, who can keep a woman under control?"

"Coward! Liar!" Vorzheva's face was so full of fury she looked like a madwoman. Her dress was torn at the shoulder, one sleeve left behind in her struggle to reach Redbeard. "Now you would poison him in front of all the clans!"

Rudur's hand snapped out, striking Vorzheva hard enough that she tumbled back into the arms of the men holding her. "Keep that bitch away from me!" He turned to the crowd. "There seems to be no end to the Cranes and Stallions and their lies. You heard this bitch claim I mean to poison him." He held up the cup, then took a long swallow before wiping his mouth with the hand that had just silenced Vorzheva. He lowered the cup to Unver's mouth. "I will not offer it to you again," he warned.

Unver found the strength to kick out with one of his legs and knock the cup from Rudur's hand. Fremur was astonished he could manage it after all he had suffered. The golden cup landed with a dull clink on the stony ground, wine splashing out in a broad half-circle before the cup stopped rolling.

"I am tired of you, Long Legs." Rudur's voice still carried, but there was something in it that Fremur had not heard before—cold hatred. He was perilously close to being made to look a fool and he did not like it. "I am tired of your claims—you, who lets his whore mother fight for him, the woman who took a stone-dweller to be her man. Yes, I know who she is." He gestured to Volfrag. "Pour me another cup, shaman." He took the new cup from Volfrag and held it up. "It is only fair, after all. Unver Long Legs may rest here, but I still have to walk back down." Several of his underlings laughed at this jest as Rudur took a long swallow and smacked his lips. "I am a fool for wasting good Perdruin red on a traitor," he declared.

"He did not waste it—Unver gave it to the spirits!" someone in the crowd shouted.

Rudur turned, glaring, trying to see who had mocked him. "Then the spirits can care for him. He will stay here, tied to this pole, until he dies. I warrant the beasts of this place were put off by all the people tramping across the sacred hills yesterday. This time Unver will remain for three days—and anyone who comes to give him aid will face my anger. He claims to be something greater than a man. Let him prove it."

Rudur waved to his men and was turning to go when Vorzheva, still held by several of them, began to cry out and nod toward the ground. "The spirits *did* come!" she shouted. "Look, all my people! Look at the earth! See for yourselves!"

One of Redbeard's men clapped a hand over her mouth, but the startled crowd was already pushing forward to examine the ground around Rudur, Unver, and the post. At first there was nothing but confusion, because few were close enough to see anything, but then Fremur saw what Vorzheva had noticed and felt his heart swell in his breast. He could not point with his hands tied, but he pulled a little apart from the others and cried, "She's right! She's right! Look at the ground! Look at the tracks! The wolves came in the night!"

And then the crowd shoved forward in earnest, some even falling onto their hands and knees. Those at the front stopped just short of the circle of muddy paw-prints that described a rough half-circle on the stony plateau, a crescent curved around the post where Unver was still tied.

"The wolves came! Just like what I saw in the Lakelands!" Fremur shouted, and though he knew he might be silenced for good with a blow from a sword or ax, he could not stay quiet. "The moon-howlers came to him in the night— the spirits sent them! Unver is the king of wolves!"

"It's true!" someone shouted. "See, the wolves came to him! Just like Edizel the Great!" Some even moved toward the place where Unver still slumped as if to set him free.

Rudur bellowed at his men to push the crowd back, and several of them waded in, not just shoving but swinging swords and axes to drive the people away. The crowd stumbled backward before them, but most of the onlookers were angry now, or at least shaken by what had happened, and those at the back who had not seen and heard were still pushing forward. In a few moments more, Rudur and his men would have to start killing. Redbeard put the Silent One's stone at his back, and his men pulled in tight around him, weapons upraised.

"I will kill anyone who lifts a hand against me," he shouted, staring at the crowd, his eyes bulging, his red beard bristling so that his jaw seemed to have caught fire. "That is a promise, and Rudur Redbeard always keeps his promises . . . always . . ."

His voice, a moment before at a bellowing peak, suddenly became quieter.

"Always . . ." he said, and then stopped to gulp air. "I . . . will . . ." Rudur looked around as though he had forgotten where he was. He blinked twice, lifted his sword once more, and opened his mouth to speak again, then folded to the ground like a dropped saddlebag and lay gasping. He shuddered and fell still.

"It was poisoned wine!" someone shouted. "He has drunk poison that he meant for the Shan!"

For a moment no one else in the crowd said anything, startled and dismayed by the suddenness of Redbeard's collapse. Volfrag the shaman kneeled next to him, looked into his still-open eyes, then felt the veins in his neck before turning to Rudur's bondsmen, who were as stunned as cattle caught out in a sudden thunderstorm.

"He is dead." Volfrag's deep voice carried out across the crowd. The shaman abruptly stood, spreading his arms so that his robes billowed in the breeze, and raised his voice even louder. "Rudur Redbeard is dead! The spirits have spoken! Unver of the Stallion Clan is innocent of all claims laid against him!"

The crowd erupted in a great burst of noise, people shouting, some screaming in superstitious fear, others bellowing with joy. Fights broke out on all sides, and several of Rudur's lieutenants broke and ran, pursued by other clansmen intent on capturing and punishing them. Everywhere people seemed caught up in sudden madness.

"Cut my bonds!" Fremur shouted. "Let me go to Unver! Someone cut my bonds! I must go to him!"

A man Fremur did not know stepped forward and sawed through the thongs with a broad knife. Without waiting for his fellows, Fremur leaped toward the post where Unver was already surrounded by wide-eyed men and women.

"Get back," Fremur cried, pushing his way through. "Let me reach him!"

He called for a knife, then hacked at the thick, knotted cords that held Unver to the post. When he had finally severed them, he and several others helped the prisoner to stand. The tall man left dried blood and tatters of skin stuck to the wood of the execution pole, but he never made a sound of protest. But when Fremur and the others would have lifted him, Unver snarled and swiped at them with an arm still deep-dug with the mark of his bonds.

"I will walk on my own legs," he said, though he barely had the breath for it. His back was a ravaged ruin, and the knife-cuts on his face and chest had opened again, streaming blood, but Unver stood swaying until he felt ready to take a step. Some turned and ran ahead, shouting the news to others in the crowd who could not see what was happening.

"He is alive! And Rudur is dead by his own treachery! The Shan is alive! He has come back to us!"

Unver took a few staggering steps. Fremur tried to convince him to lean on his shoulder if he would not be carried, but Unver would not even look at him. His bloodshot eyes were fixed on something in the distance, his teeth clenched in a mirthless grin of pain. At last Fremur, still weak and aching himself, was pushed aside by others who wanted to touch Unver. Fremur looked around for Vorzheva or Hyara or any of his own Crane clansmen, but the freed prisoner was surrounded by strangers now, folk from all over the Thrithings, some singing old songs, others shouting that the days of prophecy had returned.

As Fremur followed the exulting crowd, a bearded clansmen approached him, face strangely intent. Fremur was too exhausted to fight, and prepared himself for whatever vengeance this stranger wished to carry out: it did not matter now. The Shan had truly returned, and all had seen the proof of what Fremur had said. Nothing could take that from him.

But instead of attacking, the bearded man sank to his knees in front of Fremur, and it was only then that he recognized Odobreg of the Badger Clan.

"What do you want?" Fremur asked.

Odobreg drew his curved sword from its scabbard and offered it up. "Without honor a man is nothing. I made a foolish wager and lost, but the spirits only care that a man is true. I will bow my neck so you can take my head."

Fremur stared down at him and at the gleaming blade, then reached out and gave the man's arm a shove. "Put your sword away. You are a man of honor. Your clan and my clan are one now—we all belong to Unver Shan."

Odobreg looked up at him, his fixed expression now changed to something more doubtful, more fearful. "What has happened here today?" he asked, almost plaintively. "What madness have we all been part of?"

"It is not madness, but destiny." The words seemed the truest Fremur had ever spoken, and at that moment he felt like a shaman, with all the spirits speaking through him. "The world will be ours again, as it once was. We will go out from this empire of grass with our brave horsemen and fight until the entire world bends its knee to the new Shan. And you and I will be at the very heart of it all."

As the madness raged across the Thanemoot, Agvalt and his bandits could do little except post sentries and stay close to the fire in their camp at the end of the lake; Count Eolair, still their prisoner, could do even less. Whatever had occurred on the hill called the Silent One had swept across the camps like the wave that had destroyed ancient Gemmia.

Hours later, as the sun sank and stars began to kindle in the wide sky, Eolair could still hear the sound of chaos everywhere, people rushing back and forth shouting contradictory tales, shrieks of joy and others of agony, people cheering, screaming, arguing, and once the sound of an entire wagon crashing over onto its side not much more than a stone's throw away. Eolair saw flames licking upward in several places beyond the ring of trees in which his bandit captors sheltered, and for the first time was content to be a valued prisoner instead of a free man, because whatever was happening outside their camp sounded like war.

"They have been roused against outsiders by someone," said Hotmer, sharpening his sword with grim attention. "When they find us they will tear us apart."

"Don't be a fool," said Agvalt. "This is not the first time I have heard such madness. Mark me, it is something to do with Redbeard and his hunger to rule them all. Perhaps he has executed the pretender and they are all celebrating."

A screech cut the air, long and ragged—it seemed to come from the spot where the wagon still burned bright against the purple evening sky. The cry rose and rose, then abruptly ended.

"Whatever happened, not everyone is in a celebratory mood, it seems," said Eolair.

"Bah." Agvalt spit into the fire. "You know little of the grasslands, king's man. That is how the free riders make merry. Murder and rape are their favorite pastimes."

A bit too proud, are you not, since you are an outlaw and a clansman yourself? Eolair thought, but kept silent as he stared into the wavering flames. *I never hoped for a quiet life in my later days. I did not think it would happen, nor did I want it to. But by Brynioch and all the gods, I did not want to spend those days in the company of cutthroats and madmen. I do not want to die beside this lake in the middle of the empty grasslands, just to feed the flies.*

"I should learn what is happening out there," he said suddenly. "My king would want to know."

Agvalt looked at him but only spit into the fire again. It landed on a stone and sizzled.

"I only ask that when you go out among them again, you take me," Eolair said. "Tie my legs, tie my arms, I do not care. You said you will ransom me, and I owe a responsibility to the High King and Queen. They will want to know what is happening here."

Agvalt smirked. "We are taking you nowhere, rabbit-eater, so do not try to play the fox. You would be no good to us with your throat slit."

"You said you will ransom me—"

"Piece by piece if you do not shut your mouth." The look in the bandit chieftain's eye was murderous, but Eolair thought it covered fear of the madness that surrounded them. "He will not know you are dead until I send him your head at the last."

Eolair said no more but he was satisfied. He had put the idea in Agvalt's head, like a seed. If he was lucky, it would sprout later when he could actually hope to make use of it.

Shortly, one of the other bandits returned to the campfire. He ignored the questions from the rest of his fellows and sat down next to Agvalt.

"What did you see?" the bandit chief demanded.

"What did I see?" The man shook his head. It took him a moment to find words. "What did I *not* see? They have run wild out there, wild as horses in a fire. Brother fighting brother, clansman fighting clansman. Three times at least I saw men fighting to the death with axes and swords, and none around them were even watching, so busy were they with mischief of their own."

"But what is it *about*, curse it?" Agvalt asked.

"The one called Redbeard is dead. I do not know how—nobody I spoke to knew either—but it is something to do with the one called Unver, who they are already calling *Shan*."

"A pox on them all," said Agvalt. "And if Rudur is dead he deserved it, trying to pull all the clans under his banner while also toadying to the Nabbanai. It makes the wagon folk think things will get better, but it never does."

"But why are they all fighting?" Eolair asked.

Agvalt made a noise of derision. "They're not all fighting. Unver's clan and friends are doubtless celebrating, and their newest allies are busy trying to convince him that they supported him all along." The young bandit chieftain spat again. "What you hear out there is the madness of change—a time to take up old grudges in the old way instead of sober judgments by clan elders. I suppose they think it is freedom." He scowled. "Every time some new upstart declares himself, the wagon-men rouse themselves to a frenzy and make the grasslands unsafe for honest outlaws. Small wonder I left this all behind for a better life." His expression brightened. "Still, if we stay out of their way they are unlikely to seek us out. Tonight they will be more interested in killing their hated brothers-in-law and stealing their neighbors' wives and horses than looking for strangers to mistreat."

Eolair could only admire Agvalt's understanding of the dangers and benefits, but he did not feel reassured. He had seen groups of angry people turn into mobs too many times, and mobs turn into mindless, many-armed beasts, smashing and burning everything they could reach. Drunken clansman might not seek out strangers to kill, but they would probably remember some reason to hate them anyway if they came across Agvalt's band.

"Monstrous," he said quietly.

"Yes. And that is what we all are underneath," said Agvalt. "But there is more than death being given out tonight. There will be many babies born of this when the Green Season rolls around again, and not all of them against the womens' wishes. I said freedom before, and that is the sound you are hearing, Count Stone-Dweller, so remember that when you claim to love it, as most of your kind do. Listen well."

The bandits put out the fire then, preferring darkness to being noticed, and took turns standing sentry. As the night plodded past, Eolair did his best to ignore the cries and screams, the bellows of laughter like the merriment of demons, the horses whinnying and children sobbing.

If I believed in the Aedonite hell, he thought, staring up at the distant, cold stars, *I would swear that I am already in it.*

Porto did not go far afield in his quest to discover what was happening, because the things he saw around him were too frightening and too dangerous. But by the time he returned to the campsite Levias was fighting for his life.

Two clansmen had him backed against a tree. One of them held the horses' reins, as though Levias had caught them horsestealing. Both the bearded men looked and sounded drunk, but they were young and good-sized and clearly were toying with Levias before murdering him.

"You have the look of a spy," one said in halting Westerling. "From Nabban, eh? Did the stone-dweller duke send you here?"

Levias did not waste his breath arguing, but kept his sword raised in front of him to knock aside the half-hearted blows loosed from time to time.

"Not right," said the second clansman, who sounded the drunker of the two. "Not right. Nabban scum." He lunged at Levias, but Levias had shrunk back against the trunk of the tree and just managed to turn the man's thrust aside with his own blade. The curved sword sliced across the sergeant's front and blood began to soak his shirt, black in the dim light of the fire.

Porto cursed, then lifted his sword and ran forward as fast as he could, trying to time his swing.

The less drunk of the two clansmen heard him at the last moment, but turned too slowly and had only a moment to goggle before Porto's sword struck him a fingerspan or two above the collar of his leather armor. Having little else to do in the evenings, Porto had sharpened his blade more than once, and the edge all but took the man's head off with one swing. The grasslander staggered a step to the side and then collapsed.

The other clansman saw his companion fall and managed to spin and block Porto's next attack. As drunk as the fellow was—Porto could smell vomit on his clothes—he was still faster than the old knight: Porto could only pray that Levias would step in so that they would outnumber the clansman. But Levias did not come forward to challenge, and it was all Porto could do to keep the grasslander's curved blade striking him anywhere vital. His opponent had realized that he was the younger one: he intensified his attack. Moving backward, unable to lower his sword and thus unbalanced, Porto stumbled backwards and fell, but still Levias did not come forward to help. In fact, as Porto scrabbled backward on his seat, trying to stay out of the clansman's reach, he saw that Levias, propped against the tree, his shirt quite black with blood, was not moving.

Desperate, Porto grabbed up a handful of dirt as he got to his feet and flung it into his attacker's eyes. The man reeled back, pawing at his face, then abruptly turned and ran stumbling into the trees.

Porto bent his shaking legs until he could kneel beside Levias. "Do you live?" he asked, his voice hoarse. "Oh, sweet God, have they killed you?"

"Not yet," Levias said in hardly more than a whisper. "But not for lack of trying."

Porto cursed, but he also knew he could do nothing about his friend's wounds yet—not here. He looked around for their horses, but they had fled during the fight. "Be brave," he told Levias. "I must move you. Try to hold the wound closed with your hands."

He rolled Levias over on his side as carefully as he could manage, then gripped his companion's armor at the shoulders and began to drag him away from the campsite. There was every chance the Thrithings-man who had run would come back with friends, so despite the burning ache in his own muscles and the hot pincer that seemed to be squeezing his backbone, Porto dragged the gasping, moaning Levias through several stands of trees and across a number of gulleys until he found a deep coomb where he could lay the wounded sergeant down. He covered the space above them with cut branches as quickly as he could, so that no hasty observation would detect it.

"How are you? Can you hear me?" Porto took off his own shirt and poured water onto the cleanest part of it. When he had finally found the wound he saw that it was long and very bloody, but not ragged; his friend's guts were still inside him. That was something to be grateful for, at any rate.

"Will my God take me now?" Levias's eyes were fixed not on his wound but on the leafy darkness overhead. "I am tired—so tired. I am ready."

"Not yet, by the Ransomer. Not yet." Porto began tearing up the shirt and tying the pieces together, trying to make strips long enough to bind around his companion's ample middle. But he stopped, realizing he would need moss to poultice the wound before binding. As the stars wheeled past them in the unseen sky, Porto simply held the edges of his friend's wound together. Over and over, until his words had lost all meaning, even to him, Porto told the wounded man that God would indeed take him when his time came, but swore that time was not now.

Unver's back was such a horror that Hyara could hardly bear to look at it, but her sister Vorzheva kept her in place with a voice as sharp as a snapped bowstring. "Don't be a child. Here, put more honey and beer in that bowl and work it into a paste. I have almost finished cleaning his wounds."

Unver lay face-down on a blanket in the great tent that had belonged to Rudur only hours earlier. Fremur and the others had seized it along with the rest of the camp as the spoils of Redbeard's defeat, since there had not been enough

Black Bear Clan loyalists left to defend it, only women and children and slaves. Outside the camp fences all was chaos, grasslanders of all ages shouting in desperation like beasts in a burning barn, but Vorzheva would not be distracted from her son by any of it. "Here, give that to me. Make more bandages—no, first make pads to put the poultice on, then we will bind them on the wounds afterward."

Fremur came in, still filthy and covered with bloody scratches.

"What do you see out there?" Vorzheva asked without looking up.

"You can hear it for yourself," he said. "Many of our folk believe Unver is the Shan. Others do not. Some are fighting about it. Some are merely taking the chance to steal and ravage."

"All men are fools," said Vorzheva.

"Doubtless," he said. "But there are women with knives out there sawing the rings off dead men's fingers."

Hyara thought Fremur's eyes looked empty. Such a day and night would change anyone, but she wondered if she would ever again see that kindness she had admired, so uncommon among the men she knew. Was that dying too, along with so many grassland folk who would not survive these hours of darkness?

26

A Clumsy Jest

Earl Murdo's castle at Carn Inbarh stood on top of a granite hill, high above a river valley. Standing on the wall of the central keep, Aelin could see miles in all directions, and with unusual clarity. A town's worth of houses crouched along the curving river's banks, and the valley's wooded reaches lay spread before him in a rippling carpet of oak, maple, and beech; clumps of tall pines stood above the rest like arrows in a quiver. The last amber light of day brought out the edges of things, as though everything had been carved in fine detail with a sharp awl; every leaf seemed to stand by itself, even in the middle of countless others. Looking out over the lushly wooded valley, Aelin decided, he could almost understand how the gods must feel when they gazed down on the wide earth with their immortal eyes and saw all its delights at once.

But he had never wanted to leave a place more.

"Will you not come back and have another cup with me, young sir?" Earl Murdo stood in the doorway, arms folded across his chest against the stiff breeze that buffeted the castle's high seat. Aelin had always imagined Tethtain the Great must have looked like Murdo, who was burly and bald on top, with a graying brown beard so thick it seemed to spread from his jaws in all directions. The earl's brows were bushy too, his eyes dark and sharp, and though he was many years past his prime, Aelin still thought he would not like to cross swords with him. But Murdo was a good man, and that was what mattered most in a time when even the royal throne of Hernystir could not be trusted. If Aelin and his kinsman Count Eolair had only one ally left in the world—as it was beginning to seem—then he was grateful it was the Earl of Carn Inbarh.

"Of course, my lord." He turned his back on the day's golden end.

"There is no persuading you, then? I sent my most trusted messenger to Nial, Count of Nad Glehs, who is with us in this. He and his wife Countess Rhona are firm supporters of your uncle Eolair and the High Throne."

"In truth, Eolair is my great uncle, but in many ways more like a father to me than my own, may the gods give that poor man rest." Aelin shook his head. "And I wish you could persuade me not to go, my lord. But though I trust you with my life and the lives of my men without hesitation, I do not trust any single messenger to succeed—not with such grave and timely news."

"But I still do not know how to make myself believe it. That our King Hugh . . . that old King Lluth's grandson should make a pact with the White Foxes—" Murdo shook his head in wonder, his hands clenched into fists.

"If you had spent more time at court, my lord," Aelin told him, "—not that I blame you for keeping your distance—you would know that what is surprising is not the fact of such foolishness or outright evil, but only the magnitude of it. King Hugh has always been changeable, in a roaring, joyful mood one moment and a black rage the next, but lately he has become strange in other ways, too. And that cursed woman—Tylleth, Glenn Orga's widow—has made everything worse."

"I have heard many rumors," Murdo said, leaning forward in his chair to hold his hands near the fire, "but I thought them the sort of thing you hear when a woman with a past, no matter how ordinary, becomes the intimate of a king."

"You are not wrong. Those like you and my great-uncle, who supported Inahwen's right to reign in Lluth's stead, already know what evil talk will follow any woman who dares to walk in the halls of power. But for once the gossips are right. Tylleth is an evil woman, I am convinced, and whether deliberately or accidentally, she has led Hugh into evil practices."

"But worshipping the Crow Mother—!" Murdo sounded pained. "How could anyone forget the foul things her servants did? How could Herynstiri nobles stand by and let it all happen again? Because surely if the king is consorting with the Norns, it is the horror of that filthy old cult that led him there!"

"Again, I think you are right, my lord. When I last saw Count Eolair he was very, very concerned by what he saw and heard at the Taig. In fact, it does not breach my oath to tell you that I saw him when I carried a message to him from the dowager queen Inahwen about how ill things went in Hernysadharc—I know because she told me. And it is perhaps not entirely unrelated to my tale to say that I was nearly killed by a giant on the northern Erkynlandish border on my way to meet him."

Murdo groaned and said, "Brynioch preserve us, a giant so far south? Are those times come again? Is winter to bury us all?"

"I could not say we face the full horrors of the Storm King's deadly weather, but I do know the Norns can still call up a storm when they wish. What I saw on the plain before Dunath Tower stank of dark magicks." Aelin took a sip from his cup. With the warmth of the fire on his legs and the earl's good red wine in his hand, it seemed the easiest thing in the world to find reasons to stay longer. His men were exhausted after being held prisoner, and their long ride to Carn Inbarh. They would need to find new horses, having exhausted theirs in their haste to reach Murdo so that someone would know of King Hugh's treacherous bargain with the Norns.

"At the very least," the earl told him, "you must let me outfit your men and give you supplies, as your uncle requested in his letter to me. All else that he planned for you, I will take as my own duty, passing on his concerns about the king. I will add your story to Eolair's, and tell them I vouch for it. I have known you since childhood, Aelin, but I have never known you to be anything other than a teller of truth."

"I am not as good at telling truth in an artful way as my great uncle," Aelin said, laughing a little. "That is why I knew in my youth that I would never be the minister or envoy that he is—that I would have to find a place for myself where a blunter manner was not such a hindrance."

Murdo clapped him on the shoulder, but his face was sad. "I like a blunt man. Such a fellow saves me much effort picking out what he wants and what he thinks. Take good care of yourself and your men, Sir Aelin. Hernystir needs more like you, especially in these darkening days." He let out a sigh. "I would have sworn such times were over, at least for my lifetime and maybe that of my sons."

"I had hoped that too. But it seems it is not to be."

"Go, then, young man, with the blessings of all the gods. When will you leave?"

"First light, I fear. And now I must tell my men the sad news that after all their suffering, their time of wine and feasting is so soon ended."

"Ended for all of us, it seems," said Murdo, staring into his cup.

The last Yellow Moon had long since waned, and the first Red Moon was fattening: the end of the Thanemoot had come. As Eolair was carried by his bandit captors on the track around the lake toward the great encampment, he could see that many had already left, perhaps as a result of the troubles after Rudur's death, but that many clansmen remained. After years studying the passions of the common people, something often ignored by their rulers, Eolair was uneasy; those who lingered at Blood Lake seemed to have become more excited and warlike, like ships lifted together by a rising tide. They seemed to believe this new leader, this Unver, would lead them in some great enterprise. Eolair could not help fearing terrible ruptures to come, war and death that would afflict all the lands of the High Ward.

Still, perhaps like Rudur, the new leader they called the Shan could be persuaded it was easier to live in peace with stone-dwellers than to make war. Eolair had dark memories of the last Thrithings War, and that had been the work of but a half-dozen western clans, raiding and pillaging along the borders of Erkynland. Even so, King Simon and his knights and men-at-arms had been forced into bitter fighting to quell the uprising. The Thrithings-men did not make war like other armies, with ordered charges and an unequal sacrifice of foot soldiers to prepare the way for their cavalry. Instead they were *all* cavalry, hardened warriors on swift horses, able to shoot their bows from horseback but also deadly at hand to hand combat. He prayed the High Throne would not have to fight them again. It all depended on one question: What kind of man was Unver Shan?

I'll find out soon enough, it seems, for well or ill. Less than a sennight after toppling Rudur Redbeard, the new leader had sent for Agvalt, his crew of bandits, and also their prisoner, Count Eolair.

There were many reasons for Eolair to fear the meeting. This Unver might hate Hernystirmen. He might hate the High King and High Queen. He might simply want a stone-dweller to torture to please his new troops. And there was nothing Eolair could do about it, tied up and riding on the back of Hotmer's saddle like a particularly old and unvalued bride. Not that his bonds mattered: between him and freedom stood Agvalt's bandits, who still hoped to get something for him, and thousands of angry grasslanders. Whatever was about to happen, he knew he was not going to escape it by running.

Rudur's old campsite, now Unver's, was guarded by scarred, painted clansmen who stepped aside to let Agvalt's men through the gate. A few of the sentries led them to an open paddock in front of a large, striped tent that had also once belonged to Redbeard.

Eolair and the bandits waited for no little time, but at last a surprisingly young and slender man wearing the clan badge of the Cranes emerged from the tent.

"I am Fremur, son of Hurvalt," he said. "I am thane of Clan Kragni. Unver Shan is still recovering from the wounds Rudur Redbeard gave him. Any other man would have died, but Unver is very strong. Still, he is not yet healed, so the Shan has given me all his thoughts and bade me to treat with you. Which of you is Agvalt?"

The young outlaw chieftain was no older than this Fremur, and eyed him in a speculative way, perhaps wondering what this youth had done to become a thane and earn the right to speak for the Shan. Eolair understood Agvalt's mistrust: Fremur did not look like he had won his place by force of arms, and he still had the beardless chin of an unmarried man. "I am Agvalt," the bandit said at last. "I bring your Shan my congratulations on his victory over Rudur."

Fremur gave him a cold look. "Unver did not seek the fight. He does not think himself a victor of anything. So is it always with a true Shan. And in any case, you did not come to Unver Shan by your own choice, so let us move past these small words and speak of what brings us here." He waved a hand. On the far side of the paddock, just beyond the fence, a wagon door swung open and a pair of burly clansmen appeared, half-pushing, half-dragging a third man whose hands were bound just like Eolair's. When they reached the group waiting in the paddock the two guards shoved the new prisoner down onto his knees before them.

"Do you recognize this man?" Fremur asked.

Agvalt stared. "I confess I do not. Does he claim to know me?"

Fremur ignored the question. He might be young, but Eolair was beginning to see something stern and determined in him that had not first been apparent, a kind of confidence most commonly seen in the very devout. "This is Ogda Forkbeard, Thane of the Pheasant Clan. It was his men who attacked your troop, Lord Eolair."

"It was not my troop," Eolair said, striving to keep his voice calm and conversational. "It was a company of the High Throne's Erkynguard, on a mission for our king and queen. We never crossed into Thrithings lands, but stayed beside the river you call Umstrejha. The ambush was murder, pure and simple."

"Unver Shan agrees," said Fremur. "And whatever complaints the new Shan may have with the High Ward, the idea that Ogda's Pheasants crossed the border of our lands to attack the king's troops angers him—just as it angers him when the Nabbanai cross into *our* lands and attack *our* people." Fremur gave him a look with generations' worth of hatred in it, and Eolair was again reminded that he was surrounded by countless bitter potential enemies. If he was going to be given the chance to negotiate, he would have to be as cautious as at any royal court. "The Nabbanai do not even have the sense to retreat again when they have done," Fremur continued, his voice growing harder, "but instead stay and build villages on the lands that were given to us by our ancestors."

"Please tell the Shan that the High King and High Queen would agree, were they here, that many of his complaints have merit, and they would hear those grievances with sympathy."

Beside him, Eolair could feel Agvalt getting restless at being excluded from the conversation. He hoped the outlaw's common sense would keep his mouth shut long enough to find out what the Shan wanted. So far they had been extremely lucky, and Eolair hoped to keep it that way.

"Do you offer this Ogda as a trade for Count Eolair, the King's Hand?" Agvalt said loudly, gesturing with contempt toward the dark-bearded man who kneeled before them. "I care nothing about this man. Remember, it was not my people who were attacked. We came in afterward and took Count Eolair as the spoils of an empty battlefield."

"Ah," said Fremur with a smirk. "I forgot that you were not clansmen. You do not care about honor—you want gold." He waved again and this time someone came out of the tent, a tall, long-bearded man in a billowing robe. He walked slowly—like Fremur, he seemed quite certain of his place and privilege—and at last reached the spot they all waited. Now Eolair could see he wore the necklaces and bone jewelry of a Thrithings shaman.

"Volfrag, did you bring the Shan's gift?" Fremur asked.

"Shaman!" said the prisoner Ogda, suddenly and urgently, "tell them I did it at Rudur's bidding. You were the one who gave me his orders!"

"Silence, Forkbeard." Fremur kicked Ogda in the ribs, then kicked him again. The prisoner fell to the ground, groaning.

The shaman did not speak, as though Ogda the Pheasant thane was not worth his words, but held out a single leather bag to Fremur, who took it and turned to Agvalt. "Twenty golden Imperators," he said. "That is what the Shan offers, and it is a generous price. I suggest you take it."

His men murmuring behind him—twenty Imperators was a handsome sum indeed—Agvalt stepped forward to receive the bag, then opened it and peered in. A little buttery light was reflected on the lower part of his face before he closed the bag again, but he showed no expression. "The Shan offers it in exchange for what?"

"For this stone-dweller noble. He is of more use to the Shan than he is to you."

Eolair's heart sped. Did that mean that Unver meant to ransom him to the High Throne? It would not only assure him returning to Erkynland alive, but might even mean the chance to strike other bargains with the new warchieftain of the plains. His diplomat's thoughts were already flitting like bees in clover as he tried to imagine what could be done in this new situation. Of course, he reminded himself, it was still possible that Unver merely wanted to send the king and queen a dead Eolair as a warning to stay out of the Thrithings.

Agvalt was not one to give up so easily, however, even for the princely sum offered. "I could get more out of the High Throne, I think. Why should I give up my prize? And do not offer me that miserable creature on the ground. I told you that he attacked the stone-dwellers, not me. I care nothing for him."

"It is good to hear you say that," said Fremur. "Because Ogda Forkbeard is not a gift to you. The Shan wishes justice to be done. That is what the true Shan brings—justice." The slender clansman suddenly leaned down and grabbed the prisoner by his hair and pulled back his head, exposing a whiskery throat. "Count Eolair, vengeance on this man is yours if you wish it."

Eolair shook his head. "I do not act in that way for my king and queen. Send this murderer back with me to Erkynland . . ."

Fremur smiled as if at a subtle jest. "We are not cold-hearted cowards, we of the clans. Whatever their crimes, we do not send our own away to face judgement by stone-dwellers. Ogda Forkbeard's fate has already been decided by the true Shan." And without another word he drew his own curved sword and hacked off the man's head with one heavy stroke. The prisoner's neck fountained blood for several pulsing heartbeats before his body slowly toppled forward. His head rolled to a halt on the grass a pace away, facing the sky, wide, startled eyes staring up into the sun.

Agvalt pulled at his beard and looked the body up and down, as a man far from shelter might examine a swiftly darkening sky.

"We will accept the Shan's offer," he said.

It took Sir Aelin and his weary men several weeks to cross the great expanse of the Inniscrich plain into northern Erkynland in bad weather, and to ride all the way to the once-mighty River Nartha, now little more than a middling stream winding along the base of the range of hills called the Wealdhelm.

On the thirteenth day of their journey, in late afternoon with the sun hot on their backs, Aelin finally saw the walls of Naglimund standing tall and straight like a jewel in a diadem beneath the crest of the limestone hills. Seeing Prince Josua's Swan banner flying above the towers (though Josua himself had not ruled there in decades) beside the High Throne's twin dragons was an exhilarating, reassuring sight. The whole journey he had been fearful that he might find the castle under siege by the White Foxes.

"We have beaten the Norns here," he said aloud. "Or they have some other destination."

"No army so far from home would be fool enough to leave a manned fortress behind them," said his squire Jarreth with a confidence that made the back of Aelin's neck itch.

"I have heard too many of Count Eolair's stories of the Storm King's War to feel confident of anything about those white-skinned devils," he said.

"But you said yourself for us to remember they were immortal only in age—that they can be killed like any man."

Aelin sighed quietly. "I did not want you to be afraid to cross swords with them, Jarreth. I am not speaking of that now, but of the way they think, the strange tricks they play." He turned to survey the rest of his men and absently counted them, his attention only fixing on it when he realized they were one short. "Where is Evan?"

"Directly behind, Sir Aelin," one of the men at the back called. "Stopped to water his horse at the last stream."

Ever since they had escaped their imprisonment in Dunath Tower, Aelin had a dread of losing track of any of his men, and he was just about to send some of the riders back for Evan when he saw the young soldier riding up the trail. "Do not fall behind," he called as Evan rode up. "Our task is too important."

"Accept my apology, Sir Aelin. I thought I heard something and waited back a bit so I could hear better."

"And what did you think you heard?"

"Not certain, to be truthful," said the youth. "I thought I heard many creatures moving in the trees back there—and not small ones, either, like squirrels."

"It is bright daylight. Is it really surprising to hear animals in the trees?"

"When there are so many and so large, yes."

For a moment Aelin wondered if he was being too careless. "Do you think it might be Norn scouts or spies?"

"Not unless they have taught badgers to climb. The sound was too small for Norns or anything manlike."

Aelin shook his head. "Norns are practiced in stealth, but also, these are wild lands on this side of the river. Few men live here. Who knows what might be found? Come, let us hurry—we can reach the valley long before sunset, and there we will see even Norn-badgers coming a long way off." Evan smiled at his joke, but without much conviction. Aelin raised his voice for the rest to hear. "Hot meals and beds await us! Enough meandering—let's set a pace that will get us to them by nightfall!"

When they reached the closer bank of the Nartha afternoon was fading. The streets of the town were nearly empty as the townsfolk gathered inside for their suppers, but many came to their doors to watch Aelin and his men riding past on their way to the bridge.

Naglimund's great curtain wall dominated the hillside, but up close the castle was not quite the shining ivory object it seemed from a distance. From the valley floor it was possible to spot the places where the wall had been breached during the Storm King's War, the limestone used to rebuild it of a slightly darker cast. It looked, Aelin could not help thinking, like an old scar. Behind it rose the inner wall, and behind that stood the tall, square towers of the castle itself, which Aelin found comfortingly plain and human despite their size.

Evan looked up at the castle with something like awe. "It's so big! I thought the Taig was the biggest in the world when I saw it, but this is twice as high!"

"If we must continue to Erchester, you will see something much bigger than Naglimund before we're finished," Aelin told him.

"But why such a great pile of stones?" His squire Jarreth was frowning at the castle's wall, ten times a man's height or more. "What is there to protect? The river is scarcely a trickle, the city is barely a village, and the only folk who live here are river boatmen, a few herdsman, and sheep farmers."

"Once the river was much wider here," Aelin explained as their horses' hooves rattled on the wooden bridge. "In King Tethtain's day and before, this was a port, and the town was much larger. Many goods traveled up and down the river. So Nagliumd was built atop the ruins of some older fortress to defend the port and its riches. It is a fighting castle, and built for that." He pointed. "See how the great walls slant outward at the bottom? Meant to stand against catapults and great slingstones. Our old Taig back home has not contested a siege in a century or more, but Naglimund has been besieged many times."

"And conquered," said Evan seriously. "By the White Foxes."

"Yes, which is why whoever holds the castle now will want to know of the Norns' coming." Aelin gave his horse a touch of his heels. "Come now," he said as his mount trotted down from the bridge onto the road leading to the castle. "Jarreth, unfurl my banner and lift it as we ride through the town. The sentries on those walls must have already seen us and wondered who we are."

The castle gate was open, and although a large number of Erkynguard troops stood waiting, they let Aelin and his men pass into the courtyard between the inner and outer walls. There they were met by a soldier wearing the crest of an Erkynguard officer on his helm. He took it off, revealing a bearded face so worn by sun and wind that it was hard to guess his age.

"I am Captain Fayn, commander of this garrison," he told Aelin. "What brings you so far east, my lord?" His tone was conversational, but it was plain he was not asking idly.

"I have news for your liegelord. I am Sir Aelin of Nad Mullach, as you see by my banner. Count Eolair, the Hand of the High Throne, is my kinsman. I hope whoever rules here is still a friend to the king and queen and we are welcome."

"That is a strange thing to say," Fayn answered, frowning. "You saw the twin dragons of the king and queen flying from our battlements and towers. We are loyal to our lord and to the High Throne. Why would you wonder?"

"And who is your lord?"

"Raynold, Baron of Uttersall is master here, steward by order of the king and queen in Erchester. I hazard that you will meet him before the evening grows too much older."

"I am glad to hear that. I bear important tidings."

Fayn's creased features grew a little more drawn around the eyes. "I hope not *too* important. Tonight is the Feast of St. Granis and all in the castle are celebrating, including Baron Raynold himself. But come—I can see your horses are lathered and your men not much happier. Come in and let us show you some Erkynlandish hospitality."

Baron Raynold was old but still in good health, thin and active, but he had already had much to drink that evening and did not seem to take Aelin's desire for private conversation very seriously.

"Come, is there an army outside our gates?" Raynold shook his head. "I think not. It is the saint's day. We will save all such dour business for the morrow. Now, come and join us at the table, good travelers!"

"But I bear word from both Count Eolair and Earl Murdo," Aelin protested. "And we have seen things ourselves that must be discussed."

"Then you have my permission to discuss them at table. Come!"

The whole of the baron's small court was in attendance. A fat pig had met its proper ending and the food was excellent. Aelin's men were clearly happy to be under such a formidable roof and so well entertained, but their leader could not enjoy the meal until he had delivered his news.

Maybe when the baron has some food in his stomach he will be a bit more sober, Aelin thought. *I dare not talk about the Norns in front of all, but there may be a moment when I can get Raynold alone. I will ask Fayn to help me.*

But before the pig and its honor guard of baked apples had even been much diminished a commotion started in the entrance hall and the door guards signaled for Captain Fayn. Aelin rose from his seat and moved as inconspicuously as he could to follow the captain, drawn by a fear he tried to keep hidden.

"Well, Cuff, what has you so talkative?" Fayn asked a man who was being restrained by two of the guards, although not in a way that seemed intended to hurt. The stranger was short-legged, broad of shoulder, and long of arm, but had the look of a simpleton. Fayn saw Aelin standing by. "This is Cuff Scaler, who takes the flags up and down on the tower tops," the captain explained. "He cannot count to three but can climb like a round-headed ape. Come, lad, what is troubling you?"

Cuff was doing his best to tell them, but his speech was hard to understand. "He says it's clouds, sir," one of the guards explained. "I can make him out better than most. Known him since we were both boys."

"Clouds?" Baron Raynold had joined them at the doorway, head bent forward like a stork's. "What nonsense is this to bring me when we have guests?"

The baron's appearance only made the bandy-legged man stutter more dreadfully, and Raynold was about to turn back to the table when the guard who understood Cuff best spoke up again. "He says the clouds are on the ground. They're on the ground and they're wrong, he says."

The baron waved a slender hand in dismissal. "Fog on the hills, that is no news. In all honesty, I am out of temper with this afflicted fellow. He is let to come and go too freely. One of these days he will hurt himself or someone else with his frenzies. Come, Sir Aelin. I would hear more news from Hernysadharc. Your tales were a bit lacking in color, so I think we must get more wine into you."

But as Raynold returned to his seat, Aelin gripped Fayn's arm. "I would see what the steeplejack claims to have seen," he told the captain quietly. "Will you take me? Also, I need to speak to you alone because it seems I will not have the baron's attention for a while yet."

Fayn gave him a puzzled look but nodded. Cuff Scaler was set free to lead them to the tower from which he had seen the disturbing clouds, and was so relieved to be able to show someone what had alarmed him that he scampered ahead of them like a dog let out of doors for the first time all day.

After many long hours on horseback there were quite a number of things Aelin would rather have done than climb the hundreds of small, winding steps to the top of the tower, but his heart was not beating fast merely from the hard work of ascending. As they made their way out onto the battlements Cuff pushed his broad upper body through one of the crenellations, leaning out over a long, deadly fall while holding on carelessly with but one strong hand. He pointed out across the valley.

"Clouds," he said, slurring like a drunk. "See good. Cuff see good."

"I see nothing," said Fayn irritably, but Aelin was sharper-eyed and also had an idea of what he was looking for. In the moon-silvered darkness on the far side of the river, beyond the sparse lights of the town, he saw what Cuff Scaler had seen. Aelin's blood seemed to thicken and chill like the life's essence of a dying man.

It was a fog, as Raynold had said, but a fog that never dispersed even along its edges, and it was coming nearer and nearer, creeping across the valley toward Naglimund like a living thing. Aelin felt his skin prickle and his breath grow short. He felt all too sure he knew what that fog was hiding.

"Quickly," he said to Fayn. "I need to talk to the baron alone. There is no time to waste."

Fayn was still staring out across the dark valley. "My eyes are not up to it. What is it you see?"

"Our deaths—and not just our own. I fear that another war is upon us, Captain, one at least as terrible as the last."

"The last. . . . ?" But even as Fayn spoke, Aelin took his arm and steered him back to the stairs. Cuff Scaler still crouched beside the battlement, uncertain whether they were upset with him or with the clouds he had been first to discover.

"I speak of the last war, Captain," Aelin said. "The Storm King's war. There are White Foxes hiding in that mist. That is what I came to warn you about, but I did not dream they would follow so close on our coming here. The murdering Norns who once captured this place and killed all its defenders are before your walls."

"Norns?" Captain Fayn made the Sign of the Tree as he hurried to lead them down the stairs, almost losing his balance in the process. When next he spoke, his voice was different, like that of a man half-dreaming. "Oh, I pray that you are only making a clumsy jest—tell me you are, Sir Aelin, for the love of the Aedon, our sacred Ransomer. Because if not, then God help us. God help us all."

27

The Flowering Hills

Tanahaya set a swift pace. By Morgan's measure they walked a great distance, through stands of stout oak, trembling birch, and smooth-trunked beech, through splashes of shade and bright summer sunshine for hour after birdsong-ringing hour. After so long in the treetops walking felt unfamiliar; Morgan fought a constant worry of being vulnerable to attack. But as the day wore on he began to find the rhythm of a full day's trek again, and was almost able to enjoy himself despite hunger and the constant pang of what he was now willing to admit was homesickness. The memory of Misty Vale still troubled him as well. He had avoided thinking of it during the darkness of the previous night, but now he felt strong enough to face it again.

"What do you think that thing was?" he asked suddenly, out of a long silence. "Ogre, you said. The kind in stories, the kind that eats children?" Tanahaya slowed to hear him, and he hurried to catch up. "Was it a giant like my grandfather fought, just bigger?"

She considered for a moment before answering. "All I have been told is that Misty Vale is a place to avoid at all costs, that old and dangerous things walk there. There are other such places in the world—Nakkiga, Queen Utuk'ku's city in the mountain is another—but the one in the valley is the only one *I* have ever seen, and now I know the *Uro'eni* is something real."

"What is—" He paused, struggling to produce her quicksilver vowels. "—*Uro'eni*? Has anyone seen it?"

"*Ogre*. Giants can grow quite large but not to such an immensity. And even the smallest dragons do not walk upright. What else it might be I do not understand. Master Himano's said only that the ogre is something born out of the deeps of the reckless past, and that the whole of the Vale is forbidden to our folk by the word of Amerasu Ship-Born herself."

Morgan caught a glimpse of Tanahaya's face. It seemed set and hard. For a moment he thought he had done something to anger her.

"Forgive my unhappiness," she said. "We Zida'ya can never forget the queen's cowardly attack that took Amerasu's life," she continued. "We still mourn her. But Amerasu showed rare favor to your grandfather. I am sure you are very proud."

Morgan did feel proud, but also nettled. His grandparents' names seemed to hang over him everywhere he went, like trees blocking the sun from the lesser plants beneath them.

When sunset had turned one end of the sky red as rhubarb stalks they finally stopped. Tanahaya chose another hollow for their camp. A fallen pine made a windbreak behind which they huddled as the breezes quickened in the twilight air.

Nothing came in the night from either within or without to disturb Morgan's slumbers—no enemies, no dreams, no Sithi voices. He fell asleep listening to the night sounds with Tanahaya sitting beside him, and when he woke she was still sitting there, as if she had spent the whole night awake beside him.

Morgan broke his fast with another unsatisfying meal of leaves and petals and one particularly tasteless, chewy root that Tanahaya found for him; by midafternoon, after walking for hours, he was wondering hungrily what sort of table this Lord Himano set. Would he have honey, or cheese, or any of the things Morgan had been craving? *Do the Sithi even eat meat?* He enjoyed a brief daydream about Himano (whom he imagined as a golden-skinned version of his own grandfather) presenting him with a massive haunch of venison, saying, "I know this is what you mortals like. Go to—eat! Enjoy!"

This charming vision was shattered when Tanahaya said, "I wonder if my old teacher is still nimble enough to gather wild apples. I hope so—I would prefer not to go another night with nothing in our stomachs."

This plunged Morgan so deeply into gloom—if her master ate nothing but apples, what was the chance he'd be serving wine?—that he hardly noticed when Tanahaya stopped to look at a small tree growing beside the hill track they were climbing. But when she burst into low but throbbing song, he stopped in surprise.

> *"Ya no-i mamo, ya Mezumiiru shu,*
> *So'e no shunya dao, dao*
> *Isiki sen'sa kahiya yin-te.*
> *Kahiya yin-te!"*

"We have found the outskirts of the Flowering Hills," she said with a smile when she saw his expression.

"What's the song about?"

"Oh, an old tale of the Zida'ya, Mezumiiru and her husband and her dowry—the moon. Look and you will see the reason. Here is the first of Himano's moon trees!"

Morgan stared at what seemed like nothing more than another tree to him, the bark silver-gray, the limbs twisted, the leaves sparse. "Why moon trees?"

"You will discover the answer as we climb. Let us hurry so we can reach the house before dark."

Morgan felt revived by the thought of journey's end, but when they reached a higher part of the hill he was surprised to see what looked like the exact same tree with the exact same array of out-thrust branches growing beside the trail. He stopped in confusion, certain for a moment that they had been going in circles, but Tanahaya laughed and said, "It is not the same tree, though it looks so at first. Every tree is a different mirror, as when we see a different face in our own mirror each day, although it is also always the same face."

Morgan must have looked at her with utter incomprehension, because Tanahaya put on a more serious expression and said, "I will explain later. Now I think you need to eat and rest. But watch the trees as we pass them and you will see what I mean. Each is slightly different, but unquestionably still the same, as the moon itself changes but remains the same."

Tanahaya was right at least about one thing—all Morgan wanted now was to stop walking. When they passed a third seemingly identical tree, he did his best to try to see what might be different, but to him it looked as alike to the previous moon tree as one fly to another.

"It is a shame that we have come in this season," Tanahaya told him in reverent tones. "There is always beauty here, but during the moons of spring the Flowering Hills are covered with all the colors that are, and even some that have no names because they appear nowhere else. The blooms seem to try to out-shout each other, each calling out its hue as loud as it can—'Blue, blue as Nakkiga ice! Red as a dying star! Yellow as a bee's pollen-basket legs . . . !'"

She stopped abruptly. Morgan thought she might raise her voice in song again, but the look on her face did not speak of music. Instead she began walking uphill with determined, swift strides, and Morgan had to hurry just to keep her slender form in sight.

What came over her just then? Was it a bad memory? But she had seemed so eager to come here.

When he caught up to her she was standing silently beside a tree stump, the exposed wood raw and pale. Branches lay scattered around it but the rest of the tree was gone, and now he saw something in her expression that looked like fear.

"What is it?" he asked, his heart suddenly speeding. "What's wrong?"

"I do not know. Perhaps everything. Lord Himano would never take one of the moon trees for wood, and if someone else did, he would have planted another."

"I still don't understand,"

"Nor I, but I sense something very badly amiss. Stay here and do not move or make any noise until I return." Tanahaya turned from the hillside track and stepped noiselessly into the undergrowth, then glided silently up the slope like a shadow. She was gone from his sight within moments, leaving him alone on the track beneath the darkening sky. Suddenly the wooded evening hillside seemed a place where dozens of enemies might wait and watch him. A single thrush cried, and the sound was so forlorn that Morgan immediately started walking up the sloping track despite Tanahaya's warning.

He could see now through breaks in the trees that something was strange about the hilltop. It jutted upward in a pure wedge of limestone as bold as the prow of a ship, though the white stone was streaked with a great vertical smear of black. Could that darkness be some kind of entrance? Perhaps Himano's house was a larger version of the crevice where Morgan and little ReeRee had sheltered, a palatial residence built in a cavern. Certainly the indications he saw around him as he climbed suggested that however much pride this Himano might have about his gardens, they would be difficult if not impossible to see until someone was right on top of them, since they were woven through the substance of the forest.

But as he turned a final bend all these thoughts suddenly flew from his head like bats at sundown. Tanahaya was kneeling by the side of the track just a little way below the hilltop, her posture so slack, so abject that he wondered if she had hurt herself somehow. As he hurried up the path he saw that she was looking down at a bundle of dirty, wind-tattered rags.

"It is Gayali," she told him without looking up. "He came to Himano as a student just before I left."

For a moment Morgan had no idea what she meant, but then he saw the hand protruding from the rags and his stomach lurched. "What . . . what's happened?"

"Terrible things." She picked through the rags until she revealed something that had once had a face. "Here, see. They cut his throat."

He recoiled from the eyeless horror. "But I don't understand—who? The Norns?"

"Yes, the Hikeda'ya, the cursed Hikeda'ya." Tanahaya climbed to her feet with little of her usual grace. "Look." She pointed toward the top of the hill. "Look!"

Just below the very top of the peak, where the track ended between two low cypresses, a doorway and window had been carved directly into the limestone outcrop and fitted with a wooden door and shutters. But the door hung open and crooked, attached solely by its bottom hinge, and it was badly charred. Above the doorway stretched the great smear of blackness he had seen from below, a charcoal-black tongue extending up the limestone wall almost to its peak, left by the fire that had burned fiercely inside the cave.

Tanahaya walked past him, then leaned in to look beyond the door. When she turned, Morgan thought her high-boned face seemed so coldly murderous that he was almost more afraid of her than the situation.

"They have piled his books and scrolls in the middle of the room and burned them," she said in a dreadful, stony voice. "All destroyed. A hundred Great Years of wisdom—twice that!—obliterated in an hour."

"Is . . . is your master . . . ?" He didn't want to finish the thought.

"I do not see him inside, though many things are burned there, and it will not be easy to say for certain until morning light. Perhaps he escaped." But nothing in her posture or voice suggested she believed it. Morgan guessed he was seeing a Sitha in a rage, and his guts pinched him again.

"Why?" she suddenly asked. "Why do such a thing, except to show hatred of knowledge? Do those in Nakkiga no longer value even the purest wisdom—not even the things we learned together in the Garden?" Without another word she left the track and began walking away around the curve of the hill, forcing a path through the trees and shrubbery and rows of stones that looked too natural to be ornamental, but too ornamental to be entirely natural. Morgan was now even less willing to be left behind and scrambled after her.

It was not easy to keep up—Tanahaya had increased her speed, as though she heard a summons he did not, and seemed to float through the dense vegetation like an unsolid spirit. Morgan was less skillful or less fortunate; every branch and thorn seemed to snatch at him, and every root tangled his ankles like a cat eager to be fed. At last he burst out into a little clearing some hundred paces from the front of Himano's burned house and found Tanahaya on her knees once more. This time he could guess what the dark bundle of dusty cloth beside her would turn out to be. When he got close enough he could see a single black arrow sticking up like a burnt reed from the ragged remains.

"It is him," Tanahaya said, and her voice was like a skin of ice hiding deep, dark waters. "They have killed my teacher and left him here without honor. The Hikeda'ya have killed Lord Himano."

Tanahaya remained on her knees for what seemed the best part of an hour in silent prayer or vigil over what was left of her mentor's body. Morgan did not know what to do with himself and was worried that whoever had killed the two Sithi might still be near, so he remained beside her, fear and boredom fighting a strange battle within. A small, selfish part of him could not get over the disappointment of having nothing to eat, but he also knew that these deaths meant much more than that, not just for Tanahaya, but for their safety as well.

"We must bury him," she said at last. "And Gayali, too. He was a good student and loved Himano—I saw that even in our short time together. Dig a grave for him, Morgan. The ground will be soft. I will dig my master's grave beside it." She bent and began to scrape at the dry soil with her bare hands.

"But what about the ones who did this—the Norns? Do you think they were the same soldiers we saw near Misty Vale? Will they come back?"

"I think it was more than three scouts who did this," she said. "But in any case, Himano's killers are long gone. Their footprints are days old. They did what they came to do and left."

When Morgan dug down far enough that he could stand knee-deep in the hole, Tanahaya stopped him. Her anger, if that was what he had seen, had been pushed back inside during her hour of silent mourning; when she spoke she sounded almost ordinary. "I will go and bring Gayali to this place while you finish digging the holes. By rights they should be burned instead—my master would have preferred his ashes thrown to the wind—but even though I think the murderers are long gone, I do not want to show our presence here with fire."

She returned a short time later bearing the remains of Gayali. She set them carefully in the hole Morgan had scraped, then went to gather up what was left of Himano, but when she turned his violated body over, something fell out.

"What is this?" she said, picking up a flattened roll of parchment streaked with dirt and dried blood. "A book? Was he trying to carry it away?"

Morgan stood silently while Tanahaya studied the scroll, then put it to one side before gently bearing Himano forward to the grave. As she covered the two corpses with earth and then stones, Morgan worried he would see those contorted mouths and empty eye sockets in nightmares for the rest of his life.

Tanahaya stood over the two graves. "I did not know you well, Gayali of the Southern Woods," she said quietly. "But I know you loved Lord Himano, and I know you loved learning. Once when I heard you laugh I remembered forgotten joys from my childhood, and that was a gift, because such joys were few. I will tell your story at Year-Dancing Time and so will others. You will be remembered."

When she turned to speak over the second cairn her voice quavered. "There are not enough days in this world to tell all your virtues, Lord Himano of the Flowering Hills, and I am too young to know even half of them. You gave me so many gifts, and I will never forget you, not even when death closes my eyes. You were my family, though you did not share my blood, and my master, though you rejected all titles. You taught me to look, to listen, and to think before speaking, even if only asking a question. You taught me how meaning can hide in places where it seems nothing can be hidden, and how even the plainest revealed truth can be misshapen by hasty consideration.

"I do not know why this terrible thing was done to you, but I pledge to discover the reason. I do not know who did it, but I pledge to hunt them and find them. Some justice will be done, although it will never restore your precious wisdom to your people. The world has lost a great heart here.

"I will tell your story at Year-Dancing Time, and so will others. You will be remembered."

Her last words hung in the air after she spoke, as if some inaudible echo gave them added life. She turned and strode off down the hillside in the evening gloom, and Morgan followed her—a tag-end, an afterthought.

28

Countess Rhona's Tears

Third Day of Anitul, Founding Year 1201

My dear Lord Tiamak,

Greetings from your servant, Etan. I pray that God gives good health to you, your lady, and our king and queen.

Here I will tell you a few of the adventures I have had and the things I have learned since I left Kwanitupul. Since I know you for a supremely busy man, I will preface all by saying that I have discovered nothing that much advances the search for Prince Josua. Whether my quest has so far been completely without useful results, I will leave you to judge.

The voyage from the edge of the Wran to the city of Nabban brought a few unpleasant surprises. All ships stay very close to the shore these days because of the current savagery of the kilpa, so travel is slow.

I told you in my last letter, which I hope you received, that I had seen kilpa for the first time, and of how unpleasant I found them. I have had closer sight of the creatures since then, and it has not improved my opinion. They are very lively this year, the sailors always enjoyed warning me, although I think even they had begun to tire of trying to frighten the monk new to the sea by the time we had the encounter I will describe.

The fishing boat on which Madi the guide had bought our passage lay at anchor one night near Dellis Latia. It was the sort of boat owned by fisher-folk too poor to have a Niskie on board—one of the terrible sea-creatures actually climbed onto the boat in the middle of the night. Madi, his children, and I were all sleeping in a sort of tent the captain had put up for us in the middle of the deck, and we awakened to the sound of shouting and men running up and down the deck with torches.

I did not dare rush out at first, knowing nothing of what was happening, but the shouting suddenly stopped and I could hear the sailors talking in more normal tones again, so I asked Madi to go and see what had happened. He refused, stating his duty to stay near his children, which does not seem to stop him from spending nights in portside taverns and returning only with the dawn's light, so I went myself.

The small crew was gathered at the stern around what, at first, I took for a dead man but soon learned was something quite different. A kilpa had climbed silently up the anchor rope and onto the deck. Luckily for all, the ship's mate had seen the creature and had gone silently for an ax, then came up behind the thing and killed it, staving in its head so deeply that the ax could not be easily pulled out again.

As the men held torches close, making the Sign of the Tree and spitting into their hands—a sailor's custom, I'm told—I took the chance to examine the creature, but only after convincing myself by several hard pokes that it was truly dead. As best I could tell in the dim light it was gray and smooth in some places and knobby in others, like a frog, but its shape was too much like a man for any Godly person's comfort. It smelled of the sea and of corruption. The eyes were black and shiny, and its mouth was like a hole, almost completely round, as if the horrible thing had been surprised by the suddenness of its own death. But one of the sailors leaned in with a boat hook and pulled the mouth open, showing me that inside was a pair of jaws much like a bird's beak, except that both halves of the beak were divided into many sharp, back-curving teeth.

"Get those into you, you'll never get loose," the sailor told me, and it was easy to believe him. I still cannot forget how disturbingly manlike the brutish thing seemed, especially in the shape of its head and the flabby, splayed fingers that looked so much like ours.

We heard many more of the creatures in the water all around the ship that night, honking and hooting and splashing, and so the mate stayed awake on deck with a lantern and the ax that had served him so well, but by God's grace we had no other unwanted guests. I do not know if you have ever heard kilpa, my lord, and I hope you have never heard them in such a situation. The noise they make, I would say, is what you might expect from a goose with a mouthful of water. I do not mean to be flippant, nor to disturb you overmuch with these descriptions, but I know your love of philosophy is wide, my lord, and along with the plants and herbs you love so much, I think you are interested in even the less wholesome parts of God's unfathomable Nature.

The rest of the trip toward the city passed without any great trouble, and at last we came around the Horn of Nabban and reached the city's great harbor and safety, at least from kilpa.

Here in Nabban I have only Josua's distant early days to use as a guide, his years studying with the Usirean Brotherhood and his later time here during the war in which he lost his hand. It was not easy to find anyone who still remembers the prince. I might have had better luck among his fellow nobles, but the city is dangerous now and many of the rich and powerful have fled to their country estates. My best luck came from finding comrades of Josua's from his days among the Usirean Brothers, many of whom are now high officials in the church. A few of these kindly gave me their time but had little to tell about Josua, at least little *of interest to us. The most useful source was Syllaris the Younger (his father was also a paragon of the Church) who exchanged letters with Prince Josua for many years—even after he had taken his family to Kwanitupul at the end of the Storm King's War. But Syllaris had not heard from him or anything about him since the time he left on that fateful journey whose ending we still cannot guess.*

Syllaris did, however, have many letters from Prince Josua that he kindly allowed me to copy. I would never make a writing priest, I fear, and after three days of transcribing them, my arms and hands ached and trembled so that you would have thought me palsied, but I have them with me and if my other tasks permit, will copy them for you as well.

Not a single person of those I spoke to had heard anything about Prince Josua since his great silence began. If anything truly useful is to come of my journey, it will have to be found in Perdruin, his last known destination. But I must confess, my lord, that I am doubtful any trace of him remains there after twenty years and more. Still, my God can work wonders!

May the Good Lord bless you and keep you, Lord Tiamak, and our noble King and Queen as well.

Your humble servant,
Fr. Etan Ercestris

When the rap on the door came, loud and insistent, even the king's servants were confused. Several of them appeared from out of the side rooms connected to the royal bedchamber, none of them completely dressed. Simon was groggy too, but none of the servants were accomplishing anything useful so he pushed past them in his nightshirt and went to the door.

"Who is there? What hour of the clock is it?" he demanded.

"It is Countess Rhona, Majesty. I must talk to you!"

Something in the tone of her voice made Simon open the door without asking first to see if there were guards with her. It was a foolish mistake—he knew even popular monarchs should not be so careless with their safety—but he was alarmed, worrying for all his loved ones, Miri and Morgan and little Lillia, and terrified at the prospect of more bad news.

Rhona stood before a huddle of guards. She was dressed in a white night robe as if she had just come from bed, with only a blanket thrown around her shoulders for warmth against the castle's night draughts; one of her maids stood beside her, similarly attired but without a blanket, young face full of fear. "Oh, Majesty, I am so sorry," said Rhona, and then burst into tears.

As the countess struggled for composure Simon felt a chill of dread creep over him, but the guards were watching and he did not want to show it. "Good God, woman, sorry about what? Tell me! You are frightening everybody. Has something happened to my granddaughter?" Although Rhona's title lifted her far above such tasks and responsibilities, her own kindness of heart had made her one of Lillia's most careful guardians.

"No, no," Rhona managed at last. "Lillia is well so far as I know, all the gods bless her. No, it is my husband. He just rode in and his news . . ." She suddenly became aware of the soldiers staring, their faces pale and ghostly in the dim, lamplit corridor, and took a moment to collect herself. "It was just that his news shocked me. I am sorry to be such a fool, to weep like this. But he is coming directly to speak to you. I am very sorry for the late hour."

Simon heard a clatter on the stairs at the end of the passage, then Rhona's husband Count Nial appeared, still dressed for the road in cloak and high boots. He had clearly not shaved in several days, but it was still easy to see the rivulet of blood on his cheek.

"Are you hurt?" Simon asked.

"No, praise Heaven. Just a branch when I was riding too fast." Nial reached up and dabbed at the blood, then squinted at it briefly. "I must request an audience, Majesty. I am sorry to wake you at such a cruel hour."

"Please, no apologies, my lord." Simon felt a little relieved—it was doubtful Nial would be bringing him news about his wife, so that meant neither Miri nor Lillia were the cause of Rhona's tears. "I can see you have come in haste. Come into my chamber. I will have the servants bring you something to drink and to eat, then we'll hear your news."

The guards, understanding that the moment had passed, and they would have to wait like everyone else to find out what was happening, retreated to their respective posts outside the royal bedchamber. Simon ushered Rhona and her husband in, but the maid lingered in the doorway.

"Rhona?" he asked, indicating the fretful servant.

The countess nodded. "She is trustworthy, Sire. She is my niece from Hernystir. And she has already heard my husband's news when he woke me up."

Simon decided it was better to have the maid inside than outside talking to the soldiers, so he ushered her in, then sent his servants for refreshment for the count.

It was obvious that whatever Nial had to tell was unpleasant: he could barely wait for the food and drink, tapping his foot on the floor. Simon, though, was in no hurry. After so long without dreaming, he was beginning to feel as if his missing dreams had flooded into waking life instead—terrible, mad dreams, like his grandson vanished and his daughter-in-law dead—and he was reluctant to hear what was next.

I never wanted to be a king, he thought as a servant came in and poured wine. He snatched up his own cup and lifted it to his lips. *Never even thought of it. I could barely imagine being a knight. How did this all come to me? And why, if I am only to rule over disaster?*

For a moment he remembered the dull red anger of the Conqueror Star, the flaming comet that had hung over the Hayholt in the earliest days of

Miriamele's father's reign. It had been a warning that bad times were on the way, although King Elias had paid little attention. *But where is my warning?* Simon thought.

He became aware that Nial and Rhona were both waiting for him to say something. He paused, his second cup of wine halfway to his lips. "Please, Count, if you've eaten something, give me your news." He did his best to smile. "I am fortified now."

"We will need a different kind of fortification, I fear, your Majesty." Nial's long face was pinched, and beneath the grime of travel he was clearly distraught. "What good men have long feared has come to pass. An army of Norns have left their mountain and crossed into Erkynland."

"What?" Simon nearly sprang out of his chair in surprise. He folded his long legs under him and perched on the edge of the seat. His hands were shaking, so he clasped them together. "Tell me all."

It did not take long. Nial explained that while in Hernysadharc he had received a private message from Earl Murdo of Carn Inbarh concerning Aelin and Naglimund—a message so shocking and dangerous that it had been committed to memory by a trusted third party instead of written down. Simon listened in amazement coupled with a newer, greater sense of unreality, as if his fantasy about dreams escaping to bedevil his waking life had proved itself true.

"I know Sir Aelin," Simon said at last, struggling to make sense of what he had just heard. "I know he is trustworthy, and not only because he is Eolair's kin." Anger rose in him, a fury he had not felt in a long time. "God's Bloody Tree, what is King Hugh playing at? Is he completely mad? And what do those white goblins want this time? Surely if Aelin is right, the troop he saw crossing Hernystir is too small to attack our cities, even with the Norns' strongest magicks."

"It is hard for me to say, Majesty." Nial looked like a man who had just lost his closest friend. "If this Aelin's report is true, then by all the gods, beyond even the danger it portends, the honor of my country has been thrown down and trampled in the mud! I have never felt ashamed to be a Hernystirman until today."

"You are not to blame for King Hugh's actions, my lord." But God in his Heaven knew that Simon was itching to lash out at someone. The moment Miri had gone the entire world seemed to tumble off its perch. He took a breath. "Eolair had concerns about Hugh the last time we saw him, and then Queen Inahwen wrote to tell that it was worse even than Eolair had thought. But I never suspected Hugh would do this. Nothing like this. Blessed Saint Rhiap, what could have possessed him?"

"Foolishness. Murderous foolishness." Countess Rhona's tears had dried without trace, as if the anger and disgust that twisted her features had boiled them away. "The rumors were true after all. Inahwen said that Hugh and that witch, Lady Tylleth, have revived the secret worship of the Crow Mother—the Morriga. I daresay that has led them to the Norns."

"I wish I had known of this," said Count Nial, his face grim. "Perhaps I could have done something. I heard rumors, but rumors—well, they are as common as flies."

"You could not have done anything," Simon told him. "When a king goes mad, no one person can lead him back. I saw it happen with Miri's father." He stopped to think for a moment. "It was the Norns behind that too, or at least the Storm King."

"Was it not their queen?" Rhona asked. "That dreadful masked witch?"

"Likely. I don't know. It's all going wrong." He was feeling unutterably weary as well as fearful. For long moments he just stared into his wine cup.

"Your Majesty?" said Nial at last.

"I was just thinking. About when I was young. I lived here in the castle, you know. I was a servant, a scullion. Of course you know—that's why they call me the Commoner King."

"It is one of the reasons the people love you and trust you, Majesty," said Rhona.

"But it's not enough. It's never enough." He looked at them both and tried to summon another smile, but this time could not manage. "The thing is, when I was young I heard stories of the Norns and the Sithi, but they both seemed terribly far away, like dragons or witches—things I never expected to see in the world with my own eyes. If someone had told me all that would happen afterward, all the strange sights Miri and I would see, I would have thought myself ungodly lucky. Imagine, a common kitchen boy fighting a dragon—and surviving! And I met the Sithi and even lived with them. But none of it was like the stories. They never tell you that part, you know—the part where you're afraid and you're pissing your pants. They never tell you that these Norns and whatnot live forever and you're never rid of them. That monster of a queen, sitting there in her mountain for centuries like a great spider, and all she ever thinks about is destroying us. And the only ones who could help us, the only other folk who truly understand them, have hidden themselves away. The Sithi are not going to be any help this time, that's as clear as clear. We'll have to face whatever Hugh has unleashed by ourselves." He thought of all those he had learned from and trusted, Morgenes, Geloë, Isgrimnur, Josua. All gone now. "I was lonely as a child, you know," he said.

"I beg your pardon, Majesty?" said Count Nial.

"I had few friends here in the Hayholt. Only Jeremias the chandler's boy, and that was later. When I was little I hardly mixed even with the other servants' children. I lived with the scullions. Most of them were grown men. The chambermaids were my parents, more or less. But I was always lost in my own thoughts. I would be asked to play a game and something would catch my notice, and before I realized it I had wandered off to follow a bird or something. After a while they stopped asking me to play. They called me 'mooncalf.' I suppose I was."

After a stretching silence, he looked up at last to see Rhona and her husband staring at him in a worried way. How long had he been woolgathering? What had he been talking about?

"I know you need rest, Count," he said abruptly.

"But what about my news, Your Majesty? What about the Norns?"

"There is nothing to be done tonight, even if the White Foxes were camped just outside Erchester, pounding their war drums. I will call for Tiamak and Pasevalles and the rest in the morning." He saw they were still regarding him with concern. "I am well, Countess Rhona—don't stare at me that way, if you please. It is just that the late hour and the shock of your husband's message has muddled me. In the meantime, let us say a prayer of thanks for Aelin and Earl Murdo—and you, too, Count Nial—true Hernystirmen all, brave friends who risked much to get us this news. And thanks to your good lady as well, of course." Simon stood. The wine made him sway a little, so that he felt like a tall tree in the wind, roots beginning to work free of the earth. "To bed now, all. We will try to make sense of this bad news when God's sun is back in the sky and the shadows are not so deep."

The count and countess were whispering to each other as they left, perhaps about him, but Simon didn't care. He had never felt so tired and overwhelmed in all his life, and for once his dreamless bed seemed like a refuge.

The news about Hernystir's King Hugh had come to Pasevalles early in the morning, and the king had called for a meeting with all his most important councilors at noon to decide what to do, which left him little time for his errand. But he was unsettled and could not wait.

Pasevalles looked up and down the fourth-floor passage again, then paused to listen but heard nothing. He took a candle from the tray he carried and lit it from a hallway torch before going in.

No footprints showed in the thin layer of dust on the floor, which eased his mind greatly. Hearing Tiamak talk about tunnels and secret entrances had raised his hackles—he had half-expected to find his private sanctum had been discovered. Still, like almost everyone else in the castle, Tiamak and King Simon were busy now considering the news from Hernystir, which meant that the subject of hidden passages beneath the castle would likely be forgotten, at least for a while.

Pasevalles had discovered the hidden door while investigating the passages from John Josua's old workrooms in the Granary Tower. When he realized that the maze of tunnels led not just down to all the mysteries below, but also up to one particular fourth-floor room, he had hastened to make that seldom-used chamber his own secret hideaway. It had been hard to visit the Granary Tower without someone noticing him, since its entrance was outside the residence, against the wall of the Inner Keep, so he welcomed a new entrance to the castle's hidden deeps.

To his relief, he found no signs that anyone had visited the room recently, and no evidence anyone had discovered the secret door or its mechanism. He listened one more time for approaching footsteps, then pulled down on the wall sconce. The secret door, weighted on a pivot at its center, swung wide enough to let him slide through. Just to make certain he would be undisturbed, he barred it from the inside. It was one of the few portals in the whole castle that could be sealed from both directions. Pasevalles suspected the hidden passage might have once allowed Aedonite priests in the time of Tethtain the Usurper to get in and out of the castle without Tethtain's soldiers discovering them.

It was a long way down the hidden stairs from the top of the residence to the bottom, but that was only the beginning of his journey. Holding his candle high and balancing the tray on one arm, he followed the twisting passages and crossings he had traveled so many times that he knew them like the halls of his childhood home, Chasu Metessa. But the corridors of Metessa had not been full of deadly traps like these were.

Pasevalles moved slowly, eyes wide open in the shadowed depths. He came to the end of the last passage, another low corridor cut directly into crude stone that ended in a vertical shaft extending upward to somewhere he could not guess. He did what he always did and stood the candle in the alcove at the end of the passage: the thing that lived here below the castle did not like light. Then he stepped forward until he could sense nothing above his head but an almost palpable darkness and the faint harmonies of moving air.

"I am here," he called, but not too loudly, then listened to the forlorn sound of his voice echoing up the shaft. He waited but did not call again. He had learned that lesson the hard way, when his mysterious benefactor had ignored him for most of a month after he had made too much noise with his summons. Whoever—or whatever—lurked in this shadow-place seemed as averse to sound as to light, and Pasevalles did not wish to lose its favor.

At last, without knowing how he knew it, he discovered that he was no longer alone. A single word floated down to him from some unknown place above, a single whispered syllable as bodiless and inhuman as the wind.

"Speak."

"I need the Witness. I have brought you a tray." He set it down on the uneven stone floor, careful not to knock anything over or raise too much dust.

The voice did not speak again, but he heard stone scraping behind him and knew that the immense door had been lifted, though by what mechanism or magic he still couldn't guess: he had felt the stone door and knew it was huge and heavy. He left his candle burning in the alcove—this was a dance he had performed many times and Pasevalles knew each step by heart—then made his way back down the corridor, trailing his fingers on the wall until he found the open doorway and stepped through. The massive door-stone slid back into place behind him, then another great stone slid upward and the light of the Witness spilled out as the door scraped shut behind him.

For a long time he could only stand and look at the gleaming thing—and no wonder: Pasevalles had never seen anything else like it, and felt certain he never would. He had dreamed of it more nights than he could count. The Witness and the rocky plinth on which it sat were the only two things in the small chamber. The first time he had stood before it he had thought the Witness stone was shapeless, but now it was almost a familiar sight, and he could see that the purple-gray crystal had the form of a cloud scudding along the sky, flat on the bottom but with swirls and peaks like something a baker might whip into being with flour and sugar and eggs. In the center of the object a spherical glow, yellow-white and cold, turned the imperfections in the grayish crystal into dark lines that almost seemed to flow and billow, though he had watched them carefully many times and had never seen them truly move.

Still, it was a beautiful thing, a wondrous thing, an object of astonishing power. Pasevalles moved closer and reached out to put his hands on it, amazed as always that his childhood certainties had proved true, that he truly *was* different than all other men—above them and above their mundane fates as well. What at first felt as cold as ice quickly warmed beneath his fingers until it was hard to tell where his own flesh ended and the Witness began. It seemed as though somehow Pasevalles flowed down into his own arms, and from there into the glowing stone itself. The shadows of the chamber vanished; he was swimming through very different shadows, through darknesses that had length and breadth, that he felt as if he could reach out and touch. But Pasevalles knew better than to try such foolishness, just as he knew better than to move incautiously in these dark subterranean spaces, or to offend the creature, person, or spirit who let him touch this incredible thing and bend it to his own uses.

Did its mysterious guardian ever use the Witness? He doubted he would ever know.

For a long time Pasevalles was oblivious to everything but the not-place in which he floated and the dangers that surrounded him, dangers he could scarcely understand but had to avoid to make the Witness do what he wished. Then, out of the surrounding darkness, he felt something reach out to him and enfold him, holding him as effortlessly as a gnat trapped in a man's closed fist.

Hail to the Lord of Song, Pasevalles said, or thought he said, since words and ideas were strangely interchangeable when he used the Witness.

The presence might have been amused or annoyed. It was so much stronger than he, he would never fully understand it, and even his best guesses sometimes proved utterly mistaken. *What do you want now, mortal?* it asked.

With respect, I wish to know why I was not told of King Hugh's part in this. His soldiers met with the Hikeda'ya, and that meeting was seen by others—others who have spread the word to King Simon and his allies. It has made things much harder for me. He did his best to be measured, calm.

Do you think we owe you something? The presence that held him did not sound amused now. *Do you think all our thought should be shared with you?*

No, no, of course not. But if I am valuable to you, why do you make it difficult for me? Hugh is capricious, even for a mortal. You should not put such trust in him. He has made an arrogant mistake and given the game away.

He could sense the displeasure on the other side of the Witness like a hand squeezing his heart, and for a moment Pasevalles felt himself swooning as the pain grew. Was that all he was to them, he wondered, even as he fought to hold onto himself—a pet? Something to be indulged and then kicked, reward and punishment almost interchangeable?

You have worth to us, the voice on the other end of the Witness told him. *But do not think that worth gives you the right to question the Queen of All and her closest servants.*

No, he said. *Never. But now the people of the Hayholt know that the Hikeda'ya have crossed into mortal lands. They are preparing their defenses. Instead of surprising them, you will have to fight.*

This time the thought came to him with the cold amusement he remembered from previous conversations, an utter certainty of power. It was enough to raise gooseflesh, if he had been able at that moment to feel his own skin.

Has it not occurred to you that we might want them to know? We have suffered long, and we hunger for vengeance. We do not want a bloodless victory. A moment or something like it passed in that timeless place, long enough for Pasevalles to feel a little of the other's thoughts—a blurry, red-lit vision of flames and widespread murder, sudden as the things revealed in a lightning flash. *It is late to be worrying about what will happen, mortal.*

But you will abide by your bargain with me? By the sacred names you swore upon, the Garden and Tzo and Hamakho?

The amusement evaporated in an instant and the cold washed back over his thoughts. *We can do no other. We will give you what we promised. You will stand upon the corpses of your fellow mortals to receive it, but we will give it to you. As to the preparations of those other mortals, they will come to naught. Now, have you any other reason to waste our time?*

Pasevalles, feeling as exhausted now as a bird caught in a gale wind, battered and confused simply by being so close to the voice that spoke for the Queen of Nakkiga, could only form a single negative. *No.*

And then the dark, cold presence was gone, and Pasevalles was back in the chamber, pulling his hands away from the Witness. He was breathing very hard and his knees were weak, so he took a moment to steady himself.

The first time he had been granted use of the Witness, it had been such a profound experience that he had not been able to imagine leaving such an astounding thing behind in the depths. He had even picked it up, heavy as it was, thinking he could carry it away to one of his hidden places in the Hayholt, but a few moments later he had almost fallen to his death down a shaft that opened in the floor of the Witness chamber.

Lesson learned. Pasevalles had realized then that he would have to play by the rules of the stone's mysterious guardian if he wanted to taste such power again.

He moved to the door, empty-handed, as he had been each time since the first. The stone slab scraped quietly upward and he was released into the corridor. He took his candle from the alcove, saw the tray still waiting undisturbed where he had left it, then began his ascent back into the world of light and air and mortal men.

29

The Shore of Corpses

When Tzoja had lived among the Astalines, an older Rimmers-gard woman, a believer in the old religion, had told her of the experience of the departed after death, of their long journey across the fields of ice and stone, of the descent into the Mountain of Tears. There the newly dead had to pass the field of serpents, the giant hound named Hunger, and the River Roaring, which was full of swords and could only be crossed by the Knokkespan, a bone bridge that could not bear the weight of a living man or woman, until they reached the Shore of Corpses, the beginning of the lands of Morthginn, queen of the underworld.

These memories haunted Tzoja like restless spirits as she was led deeper and deeper into Nakkiga by a pair of silent guards, through the nearly light-less corridors of the royal Maze. The palace was an entire world of its own, intricate and insane, or so it seemed to Tzoja's overwhelmed senses, with end-less stairways and confusing passages that curved and re-curved like the nest of burrowing insects. She could hear noises, but so faintly she could not guess whether they were voices or just the whispering air of the deepest pas-sages.

It's the Realm of the Dead, and I'm the dead one, she thought. *The Queen of Dark-ness is alive and waiting for me and I can't turn back.*

Her fear grew, coursing through her like a killing fever, so that it was hard to walk without stumbling. Once or twice her terror grew so great she thought her heart would stop. She prayed that it would, because death was surely better than what awaited her.

She thought of her lover Viyeki, the only one in this great dark mountain who had been kind, and wondered if he would ever know what had happened to her. Would his wife Khimabu inform him out of sheer, hateful joy? Or would she keep it secret and tell him that Tzoja his mortal mistress had run away?

And what of Nezeru? Tzoja could hardly bear to think of her daughter. As it was, her own child had hardly known her. Nezeru had been stolen from her arms at a young age and given over to that cursed box to be judged, then sent to the Order of Sacrifice to be raised as a loveless killer. What would Nezeru know of her mother's end? And would she be sad, or feel only shame?

The journey across the Realm of the Dead seemed as long as a lifetime, or even longer.

It had always been hard for Tzoja to see well in Nakkiga's deep places, where torches and lanterns were few, but her other senses were not diminished. As she was led through yet another empty, featureless corridor of echoing stone she began to sense a change. No longer could she hear the occasional sounds of muffled voices or smell the occasional scents of food or the scented oils that so many of the Hikeda'ya nobles wore. Her guards had not spoken a word, but now she could sense a change in them as well, a slowing of their step, a quickening of their nearly silent breathing.

They were uneasy, she realized. Her guards, the queen's chosen Teeth, were fearful of the places they now walked.

At last a more profound shadow rose before them that Tzoja realized must a doorway. The guards took her arms and, still without speaking, thrust her through it. She stumbled and almost fell. After regaining her balance in the impenetrable black, she almost thought she was floating in a void. Only the stone beneath her feet was real, and the smell of the cold, dry air, and the dim sense of great spaces all around. Then the door behind her closed with a quiet thump. The sound echoed and then died, leaving her alone in the dark heart of the mountain. But she was not alone for long.

Tzoja saw a faint pale shape in the distance, a drifting oval that glowed like marsh-fire. She backed away until she felt the heavy door against her spine. She scrabbled for the latch, but could not find it. The oval floated toward her, more following behind it, two, three, then a half-dozen faintly gleaming shapes that bobbed in mid-air. Only as they wound closer in a sinuous line did she finally understand that the glimmering objects were masks.

As the nearest approached, Tzoja saw that the masks had open mouths and wide eyes, like the moaning faces of suffering victims—but the eyes, she also saw, were only carved surfaces. Whatever these creatures were, they could not see.

Tzoja cried out then, weeping wordlessly as cold hands closed on her arms. The silent shapes lifted her until her feet barely touched the stony floor, then carried her forward. She could see nothing of the bodies beneath the glowing masks but a hint of robes billowing like dark smoke. The scent of ancient, rotting cloth rose and filled her nostrils, and although she could not hear these creatures breathe, she could now feel them singing in her thoughts, a slow, mournful song whose words she couldn't understand and whose melody she had never heard, but still felt she knew.

Her thoughts fell apart as the shadows took her.

★ ★ ★

When she came back to herself, Tzoja was lying on the hard ground in darkness. For a time she did nothing but breathe, because to breathe was to be alive
and she was frankly astonished to find herself still living. Then the singing
began again, this time from all around and even above her; as the strange, almost tuneless melody rose, a light began to kindle. At first it was scarcely
brighter than the sparks that fluttered behind closed eyelids, but it slowly grew
until she could make out a cold blue-tinged brightness with angles and
straight lines.

It was a box. No, she realized with a pang of terror, it was a great stone casket that lay before her, and the light inside it was growing. Now she could get
an impression of what was around her as well, of wide, high spaces mostly
draped in deep shadow. Then the light became bright enough to see what lay
in the casket.

First she caught the glint of the queen's silver mask, then the shapes of
Utuk'ku's white-gloved hands as they reached up and closed on the sides of the
box like the talons of a snow-owl. Tzoja wanted only to get to her feet and run
and run and run, but her legs were useless. She tried to cry out to God, to all
gods, to anyone who might listen, but a great silence lay on her, heavy as the
weight of the mountain itself, and she could not break that silence no matter
how she struggled.

The Queen of the Norns sat up in her oblong box and turned slowly until
the two lightless holes of the silver mask were fixed on Tzoja.

You are the one who lived in the house of Viyeki sey-Enduya. It was not a question,
nor was it spoken aloud. Instead, the words seemed to form in her head like
frost spreading across the surface of a puddle. *You are the one who gave birth to the
halfblood Sacrifice Nezeru.*

Tzoja could not speak or even imagine speaking, could only pray that the
end would be quick. The Queen of the North reached into her thoughts and
began to sift through her memories, pulling them up and spilling them out like
a net full of wriggling fish while Tzoja could do nothing but helplessly suffer
the strange violation. The queen's search was swift and brutal, and if Tzoja had
not been rendered mute by the queen's control, she would have cried out at the
rough cruelty of it.

Then the presence was gone from her mind. The queen sat motionless for a
time, the eyes in the mask still fixed on Tzoja, who sat entranced, like a small furry
thing before a swaying serpent. The glowing masks appeared once more out of the
darkest places at the edge of the chamber and approached the great stone casket.
Silent and graceful as floating goosedown, they helped the queen rise from the
box, then draped the slender shape in a cloak made of what looked and sounded
like the rustling wings of a thousand pale moths. More masked figures appeared
from the darkness and surrounded Tzoja, then bore her up and away.

She was carried out of the chamber and back along lightless, murmuring
tunnels, her feet hardly touching the ground, as helpless in their grasp as a leaf
plucked loose and blown away by a hard, chill wind.

After her defeat of the Sacrifice scouts, Nezeru fled southeast on foot, desperate to escape the Hikeda'ya boundary forts as swiftly as she could. She knew she must be under death sentence for killing one of Rinde's soldiers even without Saomeji's accusation of treachery.

Was this Jarnulf's plan? Did he aim to ruin me? She cursed herself, letting her thoughts snag on something so unanswerable. *Because if I am caught it will be a shameful death for me, far crueler than anything he might do to my comrades.*

Perhaps the only honorable thing to do was to let herself be caught and executed, to go to her death in silence and thwart the mortal's plan. *Otherwise I let the fear of torture—of mere physical pain—prevent me from doing my duty to the Mother of All.*

But what *was* her duty now that she was exiled and disgraced? Nezeru no longer had any idea, and that was the worst thing of all.

Nezeru lay on her belly in a scruff of dry grass and stared out toward the southern horizon. In hope of getting a better idea of where she was, she had climbed a granite outcrop that stood out from the hilly meadowland. Her Sacrifice training had taught her little of these lands, so far beyond her people's territory. She did know, however, that once—before the hateful mortals and their iron weapons came—all this had belonged to the clans of the combined Witchwood Children, both Zida'ya and Hikeda'ya.

The rolling grassland spread before her, but not without limit. To her left, only a few leagues away to the southeast, stood the endless breakfront of the Heartwood, where the Zida'ya still lived. Along its eastern edge she could make out the undulating shapes of the nearest hills, which grew higher and more indistinct as they stretched away toward the south. This was the range her people called the Earth-Drake's Back, *Seku iye-Sama'an.* Mortals called it the Wealdhelm, and it marked the separation between the ancient forest on one side and the mortal land called Erkyland. No matter which side of the *Seku* she chose, she would still be surrounded by deadly enemies.

A dove hooting softly in a tree behind her fell silent, and in that moment of stillness she heard a tiny shower of pebbles somewhere below her and became instantly alert. She crawled to the edge of the outcropping and lay silent and motionless watching the track she had just climbed until she saw something moving that was separate from the wind-swayed grasses.

It was no deer or other grassland animal, she saw with sinking heart, but a Hikeda'ya Sacrifice following her trail up the tall stone. She cursed silently as she saw a second following close behind. Nezeru scuttled like a crab until she could see the entire length of the trail, but saw no more enemies, only two horses waiting at the base of the hilly outcrop.

Still, both her pursuers had bows, and she did not want to wait until they caught up to her, so she drew the polished length of Cold Root from its sheath and crept along the hilltop as noiselessly as she could until she was crouched on all fours some twenty cubits above the track where her first pursuer would pass. At last the low, silent shape came into view. She held her breath, waiting until the angle was just right, then leaped down onto the armored figure.

Nezeru had hoped to kill the first pursuer with that attack—to break their neck or back and then be able to turn her attention to the second before any arrows started flying. But she was not quite that lucky. She struck the Sacrifice only a glancing blow, and the off-center shock of her landing pitched her off the track so that she nearly went tumbling the rest of the way down the steep slope. She managed to catch herself on a well-anchored root, scrambled back onto the track, then caught the Sacrifice struggling up from where Nezeru's sudden attack had flung him. Her foot had struck his shoulder and one of his arms hung limp. Before he could even turn toward her she swung Cold Root with both hands and separated his head from his body.

The second Sacrifice, a female, came into view from below with her bow already in her hands, but although her first arrow scored Nezeru's thigh, she did not get a chance to fire a second. Nezeru had picked up a large stone, and she flung it down the slope at her pursuer, forcing the Sacrifice to leap out of the way. By the time she had squared herself to shoot again, Nezeru was on her, and although the warrior was no weakling, she had not had the vicious instruction that lifted Nezeru out of the ranks of ordinary Sacrifices into the exalted murderousness of a Queen's Talon.

When her second enemy lay dead at her feet, Nezeru looked her over. The corpse wore the emblem of the War-Shrikes. She was surprised and disheartened that they would follow her so far into the wilderness—into what surely must be mortal lands.

She made her way down the granite hill as quickly as she could, wary in case any more pursuers still waited, but she found nothing at the bottom but a single horse: the other had taken fright and bolted. She mourned the loss—she could have taken enough flesh from it to last her for a cycle of the moon or longer—but at least she had gained a mount.

As she climbed into the remaining horse's saddle, she looked out at the great wall of hills and the seemingly endless forest, which looked even more daunting from ground level. Nezeru knew that if she rode into the Heartwood she risked encountering her people's craftiest enemies—their own kin, the Zida'ya. But on the other side of the Earth-Drake's Back a thousand times as many mortals waited. She could not delay her choice: it was clear the pursuit by her own people would not ease, and even now there were doubtless other Sacrifices not much farther behind those she had just killed.

She chose the forest.

Tzoja awakened in utter darkness, half-certain she was still on the journey of the dead. She almost reached down to feel for the birch bark shoes of bleak legend before she realized that though she lay on a cold stone floor, she was wrapped in a blanket that smelled pungently of living bodies, and she could feel her heart beating in her breast.

Even as she sat up, wishing her light-giving *ni-yo* had not been taken from her by the palace guards, along with the rest of her meager possessions, she heard a door open. Light spilled in, a dim radiance that barely gave shape to anything, but suggested she was in a small cell. Tzoja tried to crawl into a corner but was immediately seized by one arm and dragged onto her feet.

They are going to kill me now, she thought. *Or worse.* Her legs felt as though they were made of butter, and she nearly fell back down, but now two large, helmeted shapes stood over her in the tiny cell, one holding each of her arms to keep her upright.

Nezeru, daughter, I did what I could for you. I gave you life. What little else I had, I gave you too.

Tzoja was steered out into the corridor. In the depth of her panic, she found something she had not expected—a place inside her where terror stopped and acceptance began. *Viyeki, I loved you in the best way I could. I sometimes feared you thought of me as little more than a pet, but I gave you my all. If they destroy me now, they cannot take that away. They cannot make it as though it never happened.*

These guards wore the stark white Teeth armor, decorated with the labyrinthine sigil of the queen's Omeiyo Palace. Their sharp-angled faces showing in the slits of their helmets gave nothing away, but they were not unduly cruel in their treatment of her, letting her try to walk when they could more easily have simply dragged her to her fate.

Can they feel pity for a mortal? Or do they simply not care at all?

They guided her a long distance over ancient smooth stones. The corridors were lit only by thin plates in the ceiling of what might have been the same crystal as her lost *ni-yo*. Other than an occasional Hikeda'ya rune carved into the walls at the place where passages crossed, there was nothing to see, nothing to relieve the cold, plodding horror of her predicament.

At last they reached a stairwell that had been worn low in the middle of each step as thousands of feet had climbed and descended over the centuries. At the top was a landing and a great black door with several more guards waiting outside it, all showing the pale, armored sheen of Queen's Teeth.

Her two escorts shared hand-signs with the door guards, then guided her past them into the interior, which in comparison to the dark hallways, dazzled her with its glare. While she was still trying to accustom herself to the new light, the guards let go of her, turned, and left. She heard the great door close behind them with a solid, permanent sound.

The chamber was full of flickering candles—dozens, perhaps hundreds—set in niches and on stands. Tzoja's eyes filled with frightened tears, which blurred the candleflames into hundreds of streaming smears as she slumped to the ground in exhausted surrender. Her moment of calm and bravery was over. She could only crouch and wait for death.

"Face the High Anchoress," said a female voice from the back of the room. "Did you hear me? Lift your head, mortal. Our mistress would see your face."

Tzoja wiped her eyes with the ragged sleeve of her garment, the same she had been wearing since she was dragged from her hiding place by the underground lake. The candles made an aisle of light that led to the far side of the room and a figure seated there on a high-backed chair. For a terrible moment she thought that it was the queen herself, ready now to see her executed, and she almost cried out, but this female shape was more strongly built than the queen, wearing gray beaded robes and a high headdress made from what seemed to be the skull of a huge, horned snake. Her mask, too, was different than the queen's. It had something of the look of the blind servants who had helped the queen rise from her stone sarcophagus, but where their masks had been eyeless, a dark stare glittered in the depths of this one, a gaze that examined Tzoja intently, though the head and its tall headdress never moved.

"Bow to the High Anchoress Enkinu." The speaker stood just behind the figure on the tall chair, her face hidden by a dark, hooded robe. Tzoja lowered her head until her forehead touched the cold stone.

"You may look up, mortal." The new voice was deep and slow and full of the certainty of power. Tzoja obeyed. "So you are the mortal slave who came to live in Viyeki's house," the Anchoress said. "And before that lived in the north, among the mortals who call themselves Astalines."

It was strange beyond belief to hear her past, her personal, unimportant past, being announced as though it were common knowledge. She was too startled to answer at first. "Yes," she finally said.

"Speak more loudly," said the High Anchoress.

"Yes, I am."

"Then you may thank whatever spirits your kind believes in. Because you have been chosen for a high honor."

Among the Hikeda'ya any death for a mortal that did not end with a ruined body being thrown into the Field of the Nameless was considered a gift they did not deserve. Tzoja said nothing, but felt her heart rushing blood through her veins and wondered how much longer she would be able to feel such a simple, reassuring thing.

The masked figure did not move, but the voice took on a tone of mild irritation. "Do you have no words of gratitude?"

"Thank you." And if it truly was to be a painless death, then her gratitude was real. "Thank you, my lady."

"Come closer."

Tzoja tried to stand but her legs still would not support her, so she crawled across the polished stone floor until she kneeled only a few paces from the daïs on which the High Anchoress sat.

"No words said here say may be shared with anyone else, unless one in authority over you asks. Do you understand?"

"Yes."

"Yes, High Anchoress," prompted the figure next to the chair in a tone of irritation.

"Yes, High Anchoress."

"Do not forget this. Those who spread tales about the Queen of the People are sent to the Cold Slow Halls. Their last moments are . . . much prolonged. Do you understand?"

"Yes, High Anchoress." Tzoja felt a moment of ridiculous hope. Did they plan something other than to execute her immediately?

"Listen carefully, for I will only speak to you this once. The queen will soon leave Nakkiga on a grand and holy mission. This has not happened for many Great Years. As she goes out into the world, the Mother of All wishes to have with her at least one person trained in the arts of healing as mortals know it. Our queen knows that there are plants and other simples that her own healing orders no longer understand, so long have we been kept away from the lands your ancestors stole from us. You were taught these arts when you lived among the Astalines, were you not?"

Tzoja drew in a sudden, surprised breath. It was astonishing that the queen meant to leave her mountain, more so that ageless Utuk'ku could want the help of any mortal. And even if the queen had taken the memories of the Astalines and the training they had given her from Tzoja's own thoughts, how had she known to look?

She realized with a stab of terror that she had let the silence hang too long. "Yes, High Anchoress," she said quickly. "Yes. I was trained in the healing arts—in herbs and simples, in the invocations of the body, in the adjustment of humors and the recognition of evil influences on the heart and lungs and stomach. They taught me many useful things." Now that there seemed a chance she might live, the words spilled out of her in a rush of desperate hope.

"Then you will be put under the guidance of the Order of Anchoressess, and you will minister to the Mother of the People as she desires."

"I will do whatever is asked of me, my lady. I will obey in all things." She could not help fearing that both the High Anchoress and her servant must hear the pounding of her heart, loud as a Thrithings funeral drum. She would live! At least for a while longer. But she would live.

"Yes, you will. No mortal has ever been given such an honor—such a position of trust." High Anchoress Enkinu did not sound as though she entirely approved. "If you fail, or if you break faith, your death will be terrible beyond understanding. Do you hear?"

"I do, High Anchoress."

"You may go now, to await a summons. All who wait upon the queen's body must work in darkness, which is what the Mother of All prefers. And they may none of them set eyes upon her form. So tomorrow you will be blinded. Now, rejoice in this honor, but be ever mindful of the trust that has been placed in you, mortal."

"Blinded?" But even as Tzoja blurted it out in shock, she heard the doors open behind her and the whisper-soft footsteps of the guards coming to take her away.

30

The Wheel of Stars

"It is most generous of you to meet with me, Queen Miriamele. I am humbled by your kindness." The astrologer, resplendent in midnight-blue robes covered with silver stars, bowed so deeply that Miri thought an expensive tapestry had been thrown over a footstool. "It is seldom that the importance of our art is fully understood."

"Please rise," she said. "You are welcome, Oppidanis. In truth, it's Duchess Canthia who spoke well of you and asked me to see you."

He nodded rapidly. "The Duke and Duchess—in fact, the entire *Honsa Benidrivis*—have been steadfast patrons of the astrological arts for as long as anyone can remember."

Except for that time Benigaris threw one of your people off the balcony for telling him something he didn't enjoy, Miri thought, but of course did not say. "What can I do for you, sir?"

"Just a little word here and there to help me, Your Majesty. I am constructing a chart of your family and their royal destinies as the stars foretell them, as I already have done for Duchess Canthia. Have you seen the Benidrivine Wheel?"

"I'm sorry, the Benidrivine . . . ?"

"The wheel of stars. Forgive me, sometimes I forget that not everyone I speak to spends his day poring over old histories and such. We call it a 'Wheel' because the stars move in circular motions around the world, which is why their influence is both constant and predictable."

"Ah. No, I'm sorry I haven't seen it. I'm sure it is very fine."

"Modesty forbids me from agreeing, but I can say it is my best work. May I ask you some questions, Majesty?" He lifted the great bag that sat beside him onto his lap, then pulled out rolls of parchment. "I know much of your own family history already, my queen, because of course your mother was born here." He unrolled first one parchment, then another, frowning as he studied them. "But although I know that your husband is himself descended from old Erkynlandish royalty—Eahlstan Fiskerne himself, as all know, the famous Fisher King—I confess that information about that family and its history are in short supply here in Nabban."

Miri shook her head. "I'm afraid you may be digging a dry well, sir. I do not know many details from before my husband's own life began, because he was an orphan. His father was Eahlferend, a fisherman. His mother was a palace servant named Susannah who died giving birth to Simon."

"And your husband's name was originally Seoman, yes?"

"Yes, but most call him Simon, the Westerling version of the name."

"Of course, of course." Oppidanis was busy scratching notes in the margin of his parchment with a lead stylus. His fingers were gray from obviously frequent practice. "But what about the history of Eahlstan the Fisher King himself? There is a famous story that he married some kind of water-witch. Do you know the truth?"

"A water-witch!" Miri could not help laughing. "I have never heard such a thing! Where did you learn that?"

"It is in many old histories," said the astrologer a little stiffly. "We do not make things up, Your Majesty. We strive for accuracy at all times. In fact, it is a famous story, and I am surprised you have not heard it. It tells that Eahlstan met a beautiful woman who was bathing in a lake, and fell in love with her. It was only later that he found out she was the daughter of a river god."

"Please, Oppidanis. I see you wear a jeweled Tree around your neck. You are an Aedonite. Do you also believe in river gods, like your long-ago ancestors?"

"Often there is a germ of truth to be found in even the oldest and most unseemly stories." The astrologer looked like a hurt child, as if he might bundle up his charts and notes and hurry away in tears.

Miri reminded herself she had promised Canthia to give the man an hour. "At least, nobody can say the tale is false," she conceded. "The Hayholt existed in Eahlstan's day, but there were few other settlements in Erkynland bigger than villages, or at least so I have been told. The person you really should speak to is Lord Tiamak, our royal councilor. He has been writing a book about the Hayholt and its history and knows far more about ancient Erkynland than I do."

"Thank you, Your Majesty. I know Lord Tiamak only by reputation. I wrote to him once but received no answer. Perhaps you can put in a good word with me for me . . . ?"

"I would be happy to." *But he probably still won't answer. Tiamak has time for all kinds of scholars, but I do not think he is particularly fond of astrologers.*

She gave Oppidanis the full hour, answering every question to the best of her ability, although she could tell he was frustrated by how little she knew. The Nabbanai had always been far more interested in their ancestors than Erkynlanders, as was obvious in any great noble house in Nabban, where masks and statues of their illustrious dead covered the walls and lined the hallways. And of course, Simon's ancestors, however royal their bloodline, had been unlettered people living a life of hunting and fishing, meeting in loose tribal groups to choose their leaders while the Nabbanai were at the height of their sophistication. Where would Simon's people have hung their ancestors' death-masks? From the trees? Before the church came to take Erkynland back from the pagans, who would have kept records of marriages and births?

Still, when the time was up and Canthia returned to hover politely in the doorway of her own retiring room, Oppidanis seemed satisfied. He bowed deeply before he left, making profuse expressions of gratitude, both to the queen and to his patroness, the duchess.

"Do you see?" Canthia asked Miri when the astrologer was gone. "Is he not a most scholarly and pleasant man?"

"Yes, certainly. I hope I've helped him."

"Ah, but I hope he will help you, too!"

Miri was puzzled. "How so?"

"By telling you what the stars have in store for you and your family, of course. Before my dear little Serasina was born, or before I even knew I was with child, Oppidanis told me, "A great joy will come to you soon."

Not overwhelmingly specific, Miri thought. "How clever of him. Now, is there anything else I must do today? I feel strangely tired. I confess, dear Canthia, that waiting to sign the covenant with Lector Vidian and all the leading families feels like a great burden when I wish very much I could be back in Erkynland at my husband's side. You and the duke have been kind and generous hosts, but I long for home."

"Of course you do, with all that has happened." Canthia tactfully did not mention either Idela's death or Morgan's frightening disappearance, but for a moment an awkward silence hung in the air.

"Just so," Miri said at last. "Ah, it is so warm today! If there is nothing further expected of me today, I would like to rest until the evening meal."

Canthia's sheepish look told Miri that an hour or two of blessed sleep was not going to be the next stop on her pilgrimage. "Oh, forgive me, but I fear there is one more thing."

"Oh, Canthia, not truly, is there? I am hot and I am weary and my temper is as short as a puffin's neck."

"If it had been anyone else, well, be certain I would have said no—"

"Oh, Usires give me strength, is it the lector? I do not know if I can sit still while he goes on again about his gout, or how the Sulian Heresy is running wild in Erchester."

"No, no." But Canthia still did not want to look Miriamele in the eye. "No, I'm afraid it is my husband's brother who wishes to speak with you."

It took her a moment. "Drusis? Earl Drusis has come to speak to me? I thought he went off east again after his wedding."

"He rides back and forth between Chasu Orientis and Dallo's house, like St. Tunato, always moving, never sleeping." The duchess frowned. "But Tunato the Pilgrim was doing God's work. I wish I could say the same for Drusis."

Miriamele sighed loudly. Her ladies were all out trying to find breezes in the shaded garden, and even Canthia's baby was off somewhere with the quiet young Wran nurse, so there was no need to hide her frustration. "Is there no way I can escape this fate?"

Now Canthia looked more like one of Miri's own court ladies when they browbeat her into something—contrite but determined. "I wish there were, Majesty, but I confess I cannot see how it would not be considered an insult. Earl Drusis has waited for no little time already, and he *is* the duke's brother, even if he has now tied his fate to the Ingadarine House instead of his own."

"Very well. I will meet him somewhere a little less womanish than here, however." She saw Canthia's look. "I mean no offense, but I speak from experience. Men like Drusis generally underestimate our sex, think us only fit for babies and sewing. I do not want to make underestimation any easier for him than I need to."

"Saluceris is gone for the day. You can meet Drusis in the throne room or the duke's study."

"Your husband's study sounds like a good choice. The earl's voice is loud, but it will not echo so much there. First, though, I truly, truly must splash some water on my face and tidy up a bit. This heat is dreadful."

Jesa looked both ways down the passage before carrying little Serasina into her room and laying her down on the bed. The child was sleeping, so Jesa set a cushion on either side of her to keep her from rolling.

Jesa had never grown used to having her own bedchamber. For a girl raised in the close quarters of her family house on Red Pig Lagoon, packed with all her brothers and sisters into one small room at night, not to mention the additional, constantly rustling population of insects and mice and snakes who made their homes in the thatch roof, it was sometimes hard to sleep by herself. Still, at times like this she was grateful for the privacy.

Checking Serasina one last time—the little face was pinker than usual on this hot summer's day, but the child did not seem uncomfortable—Jesa took the loaf of bread she had pilfered from the kitchen and wrapped it up in a piece of oilcloth, then pulled out the bag she kept hidden in a chest under her clothes.

A run-away bag, that's what my grandmother called it. A few times every generation great storms swept down on the Wran out of the southern seas, carrying so much rain it sometimes seemed the whole ocean had been blown onto the land. Howling winds threw down the largest and oldest of trees, even the many-rooted mangroves that lined Red Pig Lagoon and, as all Wran-folk knew, it was dangerous to remain anywhere in the storm's path. Houses could not stand against the *bunukta*—the "angry winds" as her people called them—and anyone who stayed would either be crushed in their own collapsing homes or swept away and never seen again, so the Wran folk fled inland toward higher ground and waited for the weather to turn mild once more. Her grandmother had taught the family always to keep a run-away bag filled with food that would not spoil quickly and clean water, usually stored in coconut shells sealed with beeswax, as well as anything the family could not afford to lose, like the small but important funeral stones that memorialized beloved ancestors, or jewelry and other objects of fine workmanship that could not be easily replaced.

But Jesa was not interested in jewelry or even funeral stones. She wanted only food and water. She could not stop thinking about the woman Laliba in the market and the terrifying things she had told her.

"*If you do not listen, it will take you too!*" the old woman had warned her. "*The Great Lodge will burn from the inside. I can see it! Many will die.*"

Jesa knew that many things in the world wished to do ill to people. She had been told since childhood of ghants and water-badgers and river-lurkers, all of which she had actually seen—though only from a distance. But there were spirits and other evil things much harder to see, but whose dangerous hatred of humankind was well known. And it was precisely women like Laliba—the *katulo*, the spirit-knowers—who could sense the presence of such dangers and tell their neighbors when an unhappy ghost was haunting a village, or when a deranged spirit was roaming the swamp, looking for humans foolish enough to go out alone. And at such times people *did* disappear and were never heard from, or their bodies were found in such a horrifying condition that it was whispered about for years or even generations afterward.

Jesa knew better than to doubt the words of a *katulo*, however unexpected the warning might have been. She could read the signs around her as well, see the anger in so many people, the fear. Even in the marketplace she had seen people jump at a sudden loud cry, like a deer startled by a falling branch. Nabban was a city built of stone, but the people in it were not, and they were frightened. And frightened people, Jesa had learned even in her short life, were the same the world over: dangerous. And the great drylander city was full to bursting with frightened people.

As she slipped the last of her purloined supplies into her run-away bag, Serasina woke and gurgled on the bed. The infant tried to roll over but was balked by the cushions and let out a raspy little cry of dismay. Jesa's heart leapt like a fish trying to climb river rapids. What about the child? What about this little one she had spent so much of the last year loving and caring for? How could she leave little Serasina, whose strange, beautiful face was so different from Jesa's own, but still made Jesa's heart beat like a festival drum when she saw her, or when the child's little hand, full of trust and contentment, curled around her own.

Jesa finished and tied the bag shut. It was even bulkier now, and harder to hide in the small chest; it took her long moments to rearrange the clothes over it. She cared for little Blasis too, of course, and her generous friend Canthia, but it was this girl who truly ruled her heart, this child she could not imagine leaving.

I cannot think about it now, she told herself. *And I will not leave Serasina and her mother unless I have no other choice. But I don't want to be caught here, so far from my family and my home, when the angry spirits at last enflame these drylanders into war.*

I don't want to die here in this strange, hard country.

Earl Drusis entered the duke's study with the ease of someone who had grown up in the Sancellan Mahistrevis—which of course he had. He wore armor, although it was obviously ceremonial: his gleaming breastplate had never seen a scratch, and his greaves and other brightly-polished metal fittings looked more like the sort worn by parading imperators than by anyone actually concerned with protecting themselves. Still, the armor and the helmet beneath his arm showed off his handsome face and figure well, as Drusis no doubt already knew. With his sun-browned skin he looked like someone had cast an exaggeratedly heroic military statue of his brother Duke Saluceris in bronze.

His bow to her was swift and short, in the soldier's manner. Miriamele found herself both amused and irritated. "Your Majesty," he said, "I am grateful that you made time to see me."

"My lord, how could I do otherwise?"

"I came because I have not yet had a chance to thank you for your bravery during the wedding. I was not told all of what happened until you returned here to the Sancellan, and then I was called out of the city. But you have my undying gratitude."

Miriamele smiled and nodded, but could not resist poking such a handsome but stiff target. "Have you had any luck yet discovering who would want to do such a thing? Who would dare to send armed men to disrupt a wedding at Count Dallo's own house?"

To his credit, Drusis did not look ashamed or guilty. If, as Miriamele suspected, the whole thing had been arranged by Dallo himself, the earl made a good show of seeming not to know it. "No. But I can promise you that when I find out, someone will be very unhappy that I did."

They made small talk about the man to whom the room had once belonged, the old duke Varellan, father of Drusis and Saluceris. Varellan had been a largely ineffective ruler, only gaining the throne because his older brother Benigaris killed their father and then died a usurper's death himself, so there was not much to say about him and the discussion soon trickled into silence.

"I sense there is something else you want to say to me, my lord," Miri ventured at last. "Please, feel free. Today this room is mine, not your brother's. Everything will be for my own ears and no one else's."

Drusis nodded. "Very well, Majesty. Yes, there is something, but I must say first that I mean it in no other way but as your loyal servant."

"Go on."

He scowled, but Miri knew it was not aimed at her so much as a grimace of general frustration. It was a habitual look of his, as though words were always a poor substitute. "Simply this, Majesty. You must leave Nabban."

"What?"

He shook his head. "It is not a threat, I promise you. You are of our people by blood, but you have been a long time away in the softer, kindlier lands of the north. You do not understand this place."

She could not help smirking slightly at the idea of the north, especially blizzard-scarred Rimmersgard, as soft and kindly. "And what will my lack of understanding cause, my lord?"

"It will cause nothing. It will do nothing. And this idea to have the Ingadarines and the Benidrivines and all the rest come together to sign a pact with the blessings of Lector Vidian will do nothing either. Nothing will change, except that the argument will grow sharper and take longer to be settled."

She gave him a hard look. "It seems to me that it is up to the signatories— and that includes you, Earl Drusis—whether such a pact will work or not. Are you saying that you have already decided not to abide by it?"

"This pact, this . . . covenant . . . is naïve." Color came into his cheeks, turning the sun-browned skin brick red. "It is meddling by outsiders and it will only make things worse."

"Explain, please."

"You and your husband—" he began loudly, then caught himself. "The High Throne believes it can change the nature of men by words. That is foolish, and also dangerous. Here in Nabban we have settled our problems ourselves for centuries. Sometimes those problems were solved by a change of rulers. Other times, by giving more power to the families in the Dominiate, or by taking some away from them—usually the better idea of the two, because that place is full of those who desire success without risk. When my ancestors were shedding blood in Nabban's wars the ancestors of the *Dominiatis Patrisi* were selling faulty goods to the imperatorial throne and starving the troops in the field by failing to deliver what they had promised."

"But we are not making an agreement solely with the Dominiate," she said calmly enough, though she did not at all enjoy being treated like a fool who did not know history. "We are bringing together all the family houses—yours and Dallo's, but also the Claveans, Sulians, Doellenes, and Hermians."

"Nothing good was ever done by talking," Drusis said firmly, "and the only treaties worth signing are written *after* the fighting, when who has won and who has lost is clear. And on top of it all, you are bolstering my brother's hand at a very bad time, when his cowardice is the greatest danger to this country—to your entire High Ward—that there could be."

"You talk of the Thrithings, I assume, but I find it hard to believe that a man who was almost attacked at his own wedding by other Nabbanai could make that claim."

Drusis shook his head and did not speak for some moments as he struggled to contain his frustration. His size and obvious anger made Miriamele wonder whether meeting him in private had been a bad idea. She was not frightened, but she was no longer comfortable.

"Do you remember the last war with the Thrithings?" he demanded.

She looked at him flatly, searching for temperate words, though she was growing angry. "Yes, Earl Drusis, I do. My husband led our armies in that fight, you might remember."

Her unhappiness seemed to escape his notice. "Exactly. The Thrithings-men had spilled over your borders as they currently spill over ours, attacking and pillaging and murdering your citizens. And your husband led an Erkynlandish army—"

"Not just Erkynlandish. The Hernystiri and the Rimmersmen fought beside us."

"Yes, yes," Drusis said, clearly impatient with the interruption. "But when they had finally broken the grasslanders' resistance, instead of going on to solve the problem, they simply turned back home again. Your husband never bothered to make common cause with us, when Nabban would eagerly have undertaken a second attack in the south. Together we could have crushed the horsemen, but instead we let them all ride away again, barely chastened. Which is why we have them on Nabban's doorstep today, in greater force than ever."

Miriamele could feel herself reddening too at hearing a long, painful war described so dismissively. She took a sip of wine before speaking. "First off, my lord, you have made light work of facts. The Thrithings-men that spilled over our borders—some clans warring with old Fikolmij in the High Thrithings—attacked our citizens, slaughtered livestock, burned villages. But here in Nabban you have moved your citizens onto *their* lands—lands that used to belong to the Thrithings-men. That is not the same."

"Pfah. A trick of language."

"I have not finished, sir. You also talk of crushing the horsemen between Nabbanai armies and our own. Where would the rest of the Thrithings-men have gone while this 'crushing' took place? Might war have not spilled out in all directions, destroying much more than the outlaws would ever have done? And what of the grasslanders' women and children, along with the rest of the Thrithings-men who had nothing to do with the fight?"

"You talk as if they were civilized folk," said Drusis, scowling. "They are not. They are vermin, breeding until they are everywhere and then stealing from others to feed their young." He made a visible effort to regain his composure. "Majesty, no matter what you think of me, *we are on the same side.* You have a mission to bring your High Ward and its laws and benefits to all men— why not the Thrithings-folk too? If you worry for them—which I think is foolish, but it shows your womanly heart is kinder than mine—then why not bring them under the sway of the High Ward like you have all the rest of us? Whether *we* wanted it or not."

Miriamele stood. "My lord, you keep talking of things that I know very well, as if I were some innocent girl from the farm country instead of a queen. My grandfather's High Ward came about because he defeated every country that tried to conquer him. Instead of enslaving them, he made them a part of his kingdom. When he defeated Nabban, did he dissolve the Dominiate? Did he destroy the last imperator's family after the Battle of Nearulagh? No, he didn't—because that was *your* family.

"After Ardrivis surrendered, my grandfather, King John, gave rule over Nabban to your great-grandfather Benidrivis under our royal ward. Your people were not enslaved. I daresay most of the ordinary folk, the farmers and shepherds and merchants, noticed no change at all, except perhaps for the better."

She walked toward him. "If the day comes when the choice is between our own freedom and that of the Thrithings-people . . . well, on that day we will talk again, you and I, and perhaps I will agree with you. But not today, Earl Drusis."

He stood his ground, and not only mastered his rage but even looked a little contrite, which surprised her. "Your Majesty," he said, and to her surprise dropped to one knee, "let us not part on these terms. We argue about the words that might be written in a book of history someday, but what happens now is all I truly care about. It is not just Nabban that is in danger if you stay and force this foolish policy on us, these pacts and treaties that cannot survive the way things truly happen here. You put yourself in danger, too. There are currents flowing here you cannot even see, let alone navigate. We have always solved our own problems here. 'Sometimes a family must bleed to live,' is one of our oldest sayings. I beg you, even if you care nothing for anything else I say, believe that my concern is not just selfish."

"I never thought so," she said, but did not find herself entirely convincing.

"An empire must grow or die, even the High Ward. Even now our ships have begun to find ways through the Southern Straits that have been denied us for so many centuries. We may find new lands there, or the people or creatures living there may find us, but either way, things cannot remain the same. Peace never lasts."

"Saying peace never lasts, or that an empire must grow or die, is like saying that only birth and death matter," she told him. "Most of life is what comes between—the simple hard work of living. I think women may understand that better than men." She reached out a hand toward him, bidding him rise. "Know this, my lord Drusis. You have your duty, as you see it, but so do I have mine. Just because it is a woman's heart that beats in my breast does not mean my bravery or my belief is any the less than yours. I will do what I think best for the High Ward and for Nabban. I can do no other."

He rose, kissed her hand quickly, then bowed again, once more as brisk as any field commander after a hasty conversation with a superior officer. "I hope

I never have the opportunity in future to say, 'But I warned you,' Majesty. I bid you good day. Please give my brother and sister-in-law my good wishes."

After Drusis had gone out, she stayed in the duke's retiring room a long time, looking at the paintings hung on the wall, reminders of martial triumph and military splendor. So few of them, she thought, no matter how gory, ever showed the blood of the innocents that was always spilled when men came together to fight over their noble causes.

She rose from her crouch. "Then I shall enlighten you. Even if the Hikeda'ya fail in whatever they plan against us, I fear that one day only mortals will remain in these lands. It would be a shame if no memory of my folk remained." She slid the parchment back into her jacket. "But we will not have your lesson here. I can do my thinking as we travel. Besides, we have another, greater task now."

"Getting back to the Hayholt—to my home."

"No, although I will take you there in time. But first I must tell my people back in H'ran Go-jao what has happened here. That I found you is important, but they already know that. It is more important than you can imagine that I tell them what I have found here."

Morgan was gathering up his few belongings, but paused, a look of confusion on his face. "How could you have told them you found me? When? I thought you couldn't find Himano's mirror-thing. His Witness."

"No, I did not. But when I first came upon your trail back in the forest days ago, and discovered you had taken to the trees, I knew I could not follow you on horseback. I set my mount free to return to my friends and let them know that I had discovered your track in the forest, but going in a different direction than your home."

His look of incomprehension deepened until it became something quite amusing to her, even in the midst of her sorrow. "Can Sithi horses talk? How could it tell them all that?"

Tanahaya laughed, and a small bit of her sadness broke free and took wing, leaving her spirit just that amount lighter. *Thank you, O Life,* she thought. *Thank you for gifting me a memory of what was and what can be again someday.* "No, our horses do not speak. What strange ideas you mortals must have of us! I wrote my words with a burned stick on bark and put it in the saddlebags. Even if they have read my message, though, Jiriki and Aditu do not know that I found you, and the news of Himano's murder will be even more important to my people. My master was one of our greatest and most learned elders, well known even in Nakkiga. The Hikeda'ya who killed him did not wander here by accident. They came on purpose to destroy him."

"But we can't go all the way back to the Sithi camp! You said the Hikeda'ya are all around us!" He struggled for calm but could not entirely manage. "I . . . I miss my home. I want to go there. Please."

She did her best to make her voice reassuring. "I do not plan to go all the way back to H'ran Go-jao. You are correct—it is too far, and the news is too ominous. We must find a Witness and swiftly."

"Why don't *you* have one if they're so important?"

"There are very few left now. Mine, given to me for my embassy to your grandparents, was stolen when I came into your lands and was attacked." She paused because she felt a flicker of unease at being so open, but would not give up honesty now. "And in truth, my leaving this time was even more strongly opposed by the Protector Khendraja'aro and others of my folk, so I was not able to obtain another Witness. But do not despair." She pointed down the hillside, where the deep green of the treetops was still muted by the shadow of the hills. "Down there we will find a stream that winds its way out of the hills and at the bottom joins the great river T'si Suhyasei—I think your people call it 'Aelfwent.' If we then follow it north, within only a day or two we will come to Da'ai Chikiza, my people's ancient city, deserted long ago."

She could see plainly how little Morgan wanted to turn northward. "And you think there will be one of these Witnesses there? But you just said it's deserted."

"Da'ai Chikiza *was* deserted, yes. But after the destruction of Jao é-Tinukai'i and the death of Amerasu during what you call the Storm King's War, some of my people left the Little Boats to return to what they considered the old ways and the old places, saying they wanted nothing more to do with the contending of our two sundered tribes. They called themselves *Jonzao*—"The Pure" would be my best rendering in your tongue—and some of them settled in Da'ai Chikiza. If there is a remaining Witness within a few days' travel of this place, that is where we will find it."

"So you're not even certain they'll have one?"

"The Pure revere our old traditions even more than we do. But, no, Prince Morgan, I am certain of nothing except that each hour the danger grows. The Hikeda'ya are still few and would not wage war so far from home on a whim. Something is happening—something dire. I know it like a mortal can smell a fire burning, or spilled blood."

"But even if these Pure people have a Witness in their city, how are we going to follow a river through this forest on foot? It will take forever!"

This time Tanahaya did laugh, amazed and almost pleased by the complete helplessness of mortals. "Oh, Morgan! Your ancestors came here out of the western seas! Surely you know how to build a boat."

"Not me," he said with more than a touch of sullenness. "They showed me how to fight and do a few sums. I'm a prince."

"Then I will teach you," she said, smiling again, though her heart still ached. "In that way at least I can still honor my lord Himano."

Crickets buzzed in the dry grass as they made their way down the hill, and seeds clung to Morgan's clothing like tiny, desperate refugees. The sun was bright enough that he threw his cloak on and pulled the hood low over his forehead.

The talk of Witnesses had made Morgan think uncomfortably about the things he had kept from Tanahaya. "Can someone talk like you want to do without a Witness?" he asked her. "Perhaps in someone's dreams?"

She gave him an odd look. "It is possible some adepts might do so, especially if they were close to a Master Witness. There have always been questions about the Road of Dreams and whether the messages received there are trustworthy. But I am still a young scholar. I do not know the answer, Morgan."

"I don't understand much of what you're telling me," he admitted. "Witnesses, the Road of Dreams. These are things I've only heard about in stories for children. But there is something I think I should tell you." He took a breath, then another, like a child confessing to a parent. "Your Queen Likimeya spoke to me. In the cave with the butterflies. She spoke *in my head*. I heard her!"

"I know."

He stared back at Tanahaya in honest surprise. "You know?"

"Of course. Something so strange, so unprecedented—did you think Jiriki and Aditu would not tell me when I was recovered from my poison-fever?"

That had not occurred to him. "So you know. But you *can't* know—they don't know—that she still speaks to me. In dreams."

"Likimeya speaks to you in dreams? You are certain it is her?"

"Yes, your queen. But it has been some time since she last did."

Tanahaya shook her head slowly. "She is no queen—she is the Sa'onsera, which is a title far more rare and exalted, but I will not explain now. Tell me what she said to you, quickly."

Morgan related what he could remember, but the dreams and Likimeya's words had been strange and confusing when he first heard them, and most of what she had said was already gone from his memory.

When he had finished his tale, Tanahaya was silent for a long while. "These mysteries are beyond me," she said finally. "They will have to wait until I can speak with others wiser than myself." She let out a fluting sound that might have been a sigh. "But it is growingly obvious to me that you play some important part in all this, Morgan. You have heard the words of the sleeping Sa'onsera, you have seen Misty Vale and met its monstrous guardian and lived—things that almost none of my own people have ever done. The currents of fate have carried you to many places mortals have seldom or never gone. I believe that you—like your grandfather—must have some part to play in the affairs of my people, although what that might be is far beyond my wisdom."

"Some part in *what?*" Whatever sense of being special Tanahaya's words gave him was more than offset by his growing homesickness.

"A part in this struggle that never ends," she said. "In the war between the Zida'ya and Hikeda'ya—the Sithi and the Norns, as you know us. Because it is your fight now, too. The Hikeda'ya have been thwarted too often by mortals. They want your people gone even more than they want my people gone. That means you have little choice—you must prepare to join the fight."

"What fight? I don't understand you."

"Of course you don't. How could you? But you should know the stories, Prince Morgan, especially if one day you will rule over other mortals. If my people are still here when your time comes, you will need to understand us. If we are gone, you will need to learn from our mistakes."

Morgan could only wave his hand in surrender. He knew when someone older than him was going to tell him things, whether he wanted to know them or not. "So you're not just going to teach me how to make a boat, you're going to make me learn history as well?"

She smiled, and the sadness in it was something he recognized. His father had often worn that expression in his last year of life when he left his family to return to the studies that had taken so much of his time.

"I fear I must. And, as I said, at least by teaching I can keep my master Himano alive in my heart—and perhaps yours, though you do not know it."

He sighed. "Go on, then."

"Before you can see and understand Da'ai Chikiza, where we are bound," she began, "you must know how my people came to these lands of exile. Because we began our own journey far away, in another land entirely—Venyha Do'sae, the Garden That Was Lost. If my people existed before the Garden we have no memory of it, no writings or tales. Even the oldest of the Keida'ya could not remember a time before the Garden."

"Kay-die-yah?" He watched a greenfinch hop from branch to branch and wished he was that bird, or at least back in the trees again. Life had been so much simpler there. He had almost enjoyed it.

"Yes, Keida'ya, as we called ourselves in those days. It means 'Witchwood Children.' In the Garden, in the Valley of the Star, beside the great Dreaming Sea, the witchwood trees were the center of our world. At first the trees grew wild on the mountain slopes, but in our earliest remembered days we learned to harvest their seeds and grow witchwood for ourselves; to tend it and shape it and use it not just for its wood but also the bark, the fruit, the leaves. We built our homes around the witchwood orchards, and those homes became our first great city, Tzo—'the Star,' because at night its lights blazed like the constellations of the night sky. We also learned how to cultivate grains and fruits to feed our growing numbers."

Morgan could hear the quiet murmur of a stream below; he hurried to keep up with Tanahaya as she moved confidently down the hill.

"The witchwood gave us tools and building materials," she said, "making us more than we had been. Its fruit gave us life—and not just ordinary life, but life longer than ever it had been before. Its leaves and flowers gave us dreams so that we could understand who we were and where we were going. But those dreams, no matter how dark, never warned us about what was to come, what dark fate we would bring on ourselves."

"What do you mean? What happened?"

"I will explain as much as it can be explained, Morgan. But it is not part of the story yet. Now listen." She stopped, so Morgan stopped too, thinking she had heard someone following, but Tanahaya only went on speaking. "We Keida'ya made the witchwood our own, bending the living world to our will. We thought all was as it should be and would remain so forever. Then the Garden began to struggle against our mastery—though we did not understand that at the time." For a moment she seemed unable to find words. The sun made her golden skin seem almost as smooth and polished as metal. "At first all was mystery and fear. Terrible things came out of the Dreaming Sea, bringing fear to our people. Sea-beasts broke our ships. Strange shapes roamed the darkness where only moonlight and starlight had been before. Dragons—the first ever seen—came up from those deeps and crawled onto the land, destroying all who came against them." She began moving again, leading him downhill toward the sound of moving water.

"Each of my people's Great Years is as long as the life of a mortal, and many Great Years passed in that new, unsettling Garden, a place that had once been all delight, but now contained darkness as well. We fought the great dragons and the other fearsome things that had come from the Dreaming Sea—the sea that we did not yet realize was our enemy, or at least our rival for sovereignty over the Garden. Some among us, like the great warrior Hamakho Worm-slayer, drove the serpents into the highest heights, so that for a while it was as if they had never been, but that respite did not last long. Sa'onsera, Hamakho's mate, who was clear-seeing and thoughtful where her husband was brave and certain, went to the Gatherer's Temple and fasted for many days. At last she dreamed of the Garden as one great thing, and of the Dreaming Sea that sur-rounded it as the greatest part of it, with all of the creatures swimming together harmoniously in its deep and unknown waters. From that dreaming came the Path of the Sa'onserei, something we Zida'ya still strive to honor, but her dream was not welcomed by all who made Tzo their home.

"That was where the fabled Parting of the Norns and the Sithi truly began, Morgan—not here in the lands you know, but in our old home, which none of us but ancient Utuk'ku can now remember. Hamakho Wormslayer's followers believed as he did, that only by destroying that which threatened us could we survive. They could not understand those of Sa'onsera's mind, who argued that we must find a way to live in peace with the world that surrounded us.

"Her followers saw themselves as waiting for a new dawn of understand-ing. Hamakho's followers believed that the blackness of the ocean and what came from it would destroy the light for all the Keida'ya, and that without their strength the race was doomed to utter darkness. Thus, for the first time, they began to call themselves Dawn Children and Cloud Children, and lines of belief were drawn between them. The followers of these two ways lived together still as they always had, and married each other and worked side by side, even among the oldest families, but it was a crack that would widen."

As they reached the bottom of the hill the stream finally came into view, murmuring and singing, surrounded by brown and gray reeds crowding the banks. They rested for a while beside it, or at least Morgan did: Tanahaya re-mained standing, still restless, words spilling out of her.

"But the Garden had not finished surprising us," she went on as though, like the burbling stream, once started she must follow her course to the end. "After many years of war against the dragons and other threats, after many of our people had died—and many dragons and other creatures, too, though they were not so mourned—the Tinukeda'ya themselves appeared in the Garden. Nobody was certain where they came from, though many claimed that like the dragons they emerged from the Dreaming Sea itself, and that is why they were called Ocean Children. At first they did not look much like us, but over time these changelings grew to resemble the Keida'ya more and more, until it was sometimes hard to tell the difference between our two kinds. But though they might look like us, the Tinukeda'ya did not think like us. Some of them founded settlements of their own and did their best to live near us, to tell us what they understood of the Garden and to show us ways to live we had not discovered. But others took on stranger shapes and lived apart from the Keida'ya—some of them seemed little more aware than animals. Soon these more bestial changelings were being forced into what was no better than slavery, doing work we Keida'ya did not wish to do, or could not do. Worse, we bred them as you men breed dogs and horses, to make them what we wished them to be, because the changelings could grow into very different shapes even from one generation to the next, and with practice, we learned to force those shapes to breed true. Carry-men, Niskies, even the hairy things men call giants, all had their first existence in lost Venyha, bred by our hands for our own purposes."

"I know the Niskies," Morgan said, relieved to recognize some part of her tale at last. "And giants, too, of course. The Norns who attacked us on the way back from Rimmersgard had a giant with them. The soldiers and even my grandfather said it was the biggest one they'd ever seen."

"Old then," she said. "They do not stop growing, I am told. Some of the oldest even talk."

"Really?"

"Yes. Because whether you speak of Niskies, or giants, or even those like Carry-men who are treated as beasts of burden, they are all Ocean Children. Whatever their form, they are not animals."

"And that's what you think the Chikri are too? Tinooki . . . that they're changelings as well?"

For a moment she looked puzzled. "'Chikri'—the little tree-folk you traveled with. Yes, I feel certain they too are Tinukeda'ya, although I have never seen that sort before."

They followed the track of the stream, winding down through the golden hills in a burble of bird and insect noises. Tanahaya had been silent for a while, which was a bit of relief for Morgan, overwhelmed by all the names and tales, but a thought suddenly struck him.

"You've talked about your people leaving the Garden," he said. "But why? If it was such a beautiful place, why did they come here?"

"Because in their arrogance the Hamakha made a terrible mistake." She cocked her head, listening. "The river is not much farther now. Perhaps you will even have fish for your supper, Morgan."

Even that mouth-watering prospect could not distract him. "What mistake?"

"In their determination to destroy the dragons and other things birthed by the Dreaming Sea, Hamakho's followers—including his descendant Utuk'ku—began searching for new means to defeat their enemies. And that led them to the discovery of Unbeing."

"*Un*being?" For the first time he doubted Tanahaya's nearly flawless command of Westerling speech. "Are you sure that's right? It doesn't mean anything."

She looked him directly in the eye, and as he saw the sadness in her face he was reminded of her much greater age. "I wish that were true. We call it *A'do-Shao*. In your tongue, 'Unbeing' comes the closest. There are no other words in your tongue that fit it but 'Unbeing.'

"There are some things, mortal prince, that simply should not be—that cannot be. Mere words cannot encompass them, not in your tongue or mine. How can something be both huge and small at the same moment? How can something be both alive and dead? How can anything exist and yet not exist? But that was the secret that the Hamakha uncovered, the secret of Unbeing. It did not merely destroy the things it touched, it made them as if they had never been."

As Morgan tried to make sense of it, they continued down the steep, grassy hillside between tormented-looking oak trees with limbs more twisted than those of the cripples that begged in front of St. Sutrin's Cathedral. Morgan could hear the river below them too—a rumble beneath the splashing music of the nearby stream, a dull roar like a crowd of people all shouting at once a long distance away.

"I don't understand," he admitted at last. "Was it something like the plague? Like the Red Ruin?"

She shook her head. "We know so little about Unbeing now, but it was nothing like even the worst pestilence. Amerasu's mother Senditu, the last Zida'ya alive who remembered Venyha Do'sae, could only say that it spread across the Garden like a storm cloud, and where it touched nothing was left—not grass, not stone, not sky, not even regret. *Nothing.* Unbeing ate everything that was."

"But how did it happen? And how did your people escape?"

"The only thing that saved us was that it began slowly, but once it began it could not be stopped or turned back. How it first came into being, I do not know. The Hamakha philosopher Nerudade who created it—or discovered it—was the first thing it devoured." Words seemed to come only with difficulty now. "They say it was like a black fire nothing could extinguish, although it had no heat and no shape. It was nothing, but it was a nothing that rendered everything else into nothing too."

"But it's not here, is it?" he said anxiously. It was all he could do not to look around for a black fog rolling down the hillside behind them.

"No. The secret of its creation is said to have died with Nerudade. But it is in our people's hearts, nevertheless. Sometimes I fear *that* particular damage is beyond repair." She took a breath. "It hurts to speak of it."

The stream they followed bent one last time, and as they made their way around a drooping stand of willows, Morgan suddenly saw the river's great, shiny back sprawled across the valley's floor below them like a monstrous serpent, its surface undulating in the last of the afternoon sun.

"There," Tanahaya said, and stopped. Then, to Morgan's astonishment, she suddenly gave voice to a peal of song in her own speech, a liquid cadence of words he could not understand in a melody that seemed to rise and dip like something floating on the dark, lively water.

"It is a song about the river T'si Suhyasei," she said when her brief song had ended. "It means, 'Her blood is cool, Her thoughts are green, She is older than Thought, She is wider than Time.' It is a hymn to the great forest and the rivers that are her veins." She spread her arms wide. "It is good to see you again," she cried, as if the river had ears. "It is good." Tanahaya turned to Morgan. A smile curled her lip, giving her for a swift moment the look of a mischievous girl. "Now that we have reached it, can you catch fish? Or would you rather cut reeds?"

"I'm sure I can catch a fish," he said without feeling too confident about it.

"Well, then, you may do so while I begin on the reeds."

"What for?"

"To make a boat, course."

He stared in dismay at the fragile stalks that lined the bank of the stream and clustered even more thickly along the river below them. "We're going to make a boat out of *those?*"

She laughed, a sound he had not heard for a while, as cheering and yet unlike a mortal laugh as a songbird's trill. "Unless you think you can swim all the way to Da'ai Chikiza, then yes, Prince Morgan—that is exactly what we will do."

Binabik sat on a stone at the edge of their campsite and scratched Vaqana behind her ears, which the wolf seemed to enjoy very much, tongue lolling, eyes tight shut. They had lit no fire because of the Norns they had spotted only two short days earlier.

"No, do not bother yet to pack up our few things," Binabik said to Sisqi. "We must have a family council. There is much to discuss."

"Let me go out first," said Qina. "I swear by our ancestors that I can find the track again."

"That is not what today speaks to me," her father said. "No, we must sit and talk as a family."

"This is not Mintahoq," she said in exasperation. "There are no fires to be tended, no chores to be given out. Every moment the sun climbs higher we are falling farther behind."

"Just so," Binabik said. "But he who chases something he cannot see may be caught from behind by something he has not noticed."

"Spare me your old sayings, Father," Qina said sourly. "I have heard them all, I think. Who said those wise words? Your master Ookekuq? Some lowland Scrollbearer?"

"As it happens, my sharp-tongued daughter, the one who told that to me was my own mother—your grandmother—and she was right, because she and my father were both caught in a snowfall and killed. That is why you did not know her or your grandfather—why only your mother's parents are known to you."

She was sorry she had said it, but not entirely chastened. "But why now? Why did we not talk about this at night, when we could not search for Prince Morgan?"

"Because when night was upon us I was thinking about this," her father said. "I thought long while you and Little Snenneq were making enough noises sleeping to frighten away even the bears. And now that I speak of him, where is your betrothed?"

"He went to get some water for washing," said her mother. "He works hard to be a good son-in-law."

"Yes, he does," Binabik said. "And I work hard to be the same sort of father. In truth, I am so old and so full of wisdom sometimes I fear I will burst. But my daughter does not recognize that, and continuously asks me why this and why that." But he did not look put out, only tired, and Qina walked to him and gave his cheek a swift nuzzle.

"I am sorry, my father," she said. "But it is hard to wait, and we have been doing it often these last days."

Snenneq came back to camp, half a dozen bulging skins draped around his neck like saddlebags. "Why is the water never at the top of the hill where we camp?" he asked. "This is a question that torments even the wise. Or why do we not camp down where the water is?"

"Mosquitoes," said Binabik. "And bears coming down to drink in the middle of night. And also River Man waiting to pull you down into his dark lair until your lungs fill with muddy water. But if you wish to sleep down by the side of the stream to make your morning's work easier, you have my permission."

Snenneq let the full bags drop to the ground. Nearby, the rams that would have to carry them snorted and shuffled. "To that I say thank you but no, Master. I am young and handsome still. I do not want my face disfigured by those flying demon blood-drinkers, let alone by bears. Perhaps Qina would not love me anymore."

"I will always love your face, my betrothed," she said. "Especially when your mouth is closed."

"Such a pointed tongue my daughter has!" Binabik said, shaking his head, but he seemed to have enjoyed it more this time.

"Ah! Wounded! I am wounded and near death!" Snenneq sat on the ground near Binabik. "Let me just catch my breath and wet my throat, then we can set out on our way again."

Qina rolled her eyes. "My father wants to talk."

"Good." Snenneq lifted one of the skin bags and took a long swallow. "Let us talk first about where we can find more *kangkang*, because soon I will die from drinking nothing but water. Even croohok beer is better for one's innards. Water is fine for giving to the rams, and when it is cold enough it becomes snow and that is good too, but it makes a poor drink for a Singing Man."

"You are not one yet," said Binabik. "Now, come and join us, my wife. We will help you with those last chores later. You too, daughter of my heart."

Qina moved closer and sat beside Snenneq. She reached up and wiped his broad forehead with her sleeve. "You are not used to summer in these lands," she said quietly.

"Summer? Summer is Blue Mud Lake, where the sun shines *and* the wind blows." He scowled. "Where a man can live without growing scrawny. This is something different." He swiped at his forehead, which was already beaded with sweat again. "This 'summer' as you call it is like what it would feel like to live on a soup stone, spending life at the bottom of a boiling pot. And it is still morning!"

"We will not escape these southern lands for some time," said Binabik, "so you must resign yourself, Snenneq. But we cannot go on as we have been. Each day the signs grow fainter, and each day we hunt for his track, the one we seek increases the distance between us."

"It makes no sense," Snenneq complained. "He has left the trees, or at least we cannot find any trace of the foot-irons I made for him. Why has he become so hard to track? Qina should be finding traces of him on the ground."

"I do not know the reason," said Binabik. "But I know we must do things differently. We were nearly caught by the Hikeda'ya. If not for Sisqi's sharp ears, we might all be dead."

"But they were going the other direction," Qina said. "Surely we do not have to worry about those Norn soldiers again."

"Yes. But it could be they are hunting Morgan too," Sneneq pointed out. "Whatever we will do differently, we must do it soon."

"Yes. So we are turning back toward Erkynland," said Binabik, then lifted his hand as Qina and Little Snenneq immediately began to protest. "We must return to Simon and Miriamele at the Hayholt to tell them what we have learned. It could be they do not even know their grandson Morgan is lost, because we cannot know if the Erkynlandish soldiers found their way home with my message. And if there are Hikeda'ya here in the great wood where they have not roamed freely in centuries, then our friends should know that too."

"But we cannot give up searching for Prince Morgan!" said Qina. "He is not far away—we know that. He has not sprouted wings, unless you have lied to me all my life about what lowlanders can do."

Her father smiled sadly. "I have told you only truth, my little snow cat—or at least as far as I know it, for nobody knows all. But we cannot take any more time here. If we were Sithi, we might use our magical mirrors to talk to our friends far away. If wise Geloë still lived we might use the birds she trained, as the League of the Scroll once conversed with each other. But we have neither, only our own selves, our eyes and tongues, and our friends must be told about the prince. And our friends can send many soldiers to search the forest—enough to deal with Hikeda'ya if they meet them."

"I cannot desert Prince Morgan," declared Snenneq. "He and I share a destiny. I know this to be true."

"Do not talk to me about destiny, please," Binabik said with equal certainty. "The destiny of many peoples is involved here—numbers beyond counting even with every tally-stick from Mintahoq and all our other mountains combined. We must do what is best for the largest number of folk, no matter how painful."

"Then *we* will continue to hunt for him," Qina said. "You and Mother can go to Erkynland and carry the news. Snenneq and I will stay and search. Who knows what dangers Prince Morgan might face in the time it takes for your friends to send soldiers?"

"Do not pull on our hearts, Qina," her mother said. "Simon and Miriamele have lost their grandchild. How could we lose our only daughter, too?"

"You will not lose me," Qina said. "My betrothed often speaks more than he should, but he is smart and strong—and so am I. We are children no longer. You must see that it is the best way, whether you fear it or not."

Her mother and father did not agree, of course, but Qina was stubborn, and Snenneq was wise enough to let her do most of the arguing. They went back and forth for most of an hour, like Blue Mud Lake sparrows fetching sticks to build nests, until both sides had piled their arguments high, but Qina was as much her mother's child as her father's and would not be swayed.

"And if I ordered you, as your father, to come with us?" Binabik said at last.

"Then I would disobey you. Because you did not bring us into this world only to be your eyes and hands, to do only what you wished done. You made us whole, with minds to think for ourselves and hearts to know right from wrong. It is wrong to give up the chance to find Morgan after we have followed his track so long—we might never again be so close to him. Think what will happen if he meets the Hikeda'ya on his own, with no friends to help him."

At last they all fell silent. Her father looked to her mother, and Qina could see from his face that she had won, though it did not feel much like victory.

"I will not order you to come with us against your will," he said at last. "Sisqi, can you see any other way?"

"Unless we tie them both and carry them back to the Hayholt across their saddles, no," she said. "But I am fearful. Qina, my daughter, you are right, you are fully grown. But the world is large and dangerous—more dangerous than ever. Meddling in the affairs of the immortals may bring your deaths. Know that if anything happens to you, my heart will shatter in my breast, as will your father's."

"I will protect her, honored Sisqinanamook," said Snenneq. "Know I will give everything I have to keep her safe."

Qina snorted. "It will be me saving you, if it comes to it." But the small jest did not cover the emptiness she suddenly felt. The argument had been about what might be, but now she had to face the cold fact of parting from her parents in these unknown lands. She took a breath. "We will do our best to stay safe. I still want to see my marriage day. Try not to fear. You two have taught us both long and well." She felt tears come to her eyes and wiped them away with her sleeve. "We will make you proud."

"You have never made us anything but proud." Binabik looked as though he had grown several years older just during the hour they had spent in talk. "Listen to me carefully, before I change my mind and tie you to the saddles, as your mother suggested."

"I did *not* suggest it," Sisqi said sharply.

"I know, my love. Sometimes I joke to keep my own fear away." He frowned, thinking. "The stars that were so untrustworthy where the Sithi make their home have become stretched and strange again here—I cannot guess why—so you may find that the White Bear and the Old Woman are no longer your best guides. But if you continue in the path we have walked the last few days, toward the setting sun, you will certainly at last reach the Wealdhelm Hills. Naglimund Castle, one of Simon's and Miriamele's strongholds, will be on its far side." He took a stick and began scratching a map in the dirt. "In fact, it could be that in a day or two you might find the old Sithi city of Da'ai Chikiza, which lies on the Aelfwent River that runs along this side of the Wealdhelm. From there a path called the Stile will climb the hills and lead you to the castle. You can get help there, and if you find Morgan, you can take him to Naglimund and he will be safe."

"Then why should you two go all the way back to the Hayholt? Why not find this Naglimund place and send a message from there to your friends?"

"Because my heart misgives me, Qina, and I do not trust messengers," her father said. "Too many strange and deadly things have happened of late. Do you remember the Sithi envoy, Tanahaya? She was waylaid in Erchester itself, on her way to Simon and Miriamele, and would have died if not for the luck of being found. Someone did not want her to reach our friends, and that someone has never been discovered. Either the chilly hand of the Norn Queen herself reaches all the way to the Hayholt's gates or else my friends have an enemy closer to them than anyone has dreamed. No, I will trust no more messengers, not with such important news."

"But then you and my mother will be in danger, too!" Qina said. "If some-one can attack the Sitha, they can attack you just as easily to keep you from reaching your friends."

Binabik nodded. "That is the way it must be, when a family is separated. Just as we must fear for you two on your own, you must fear for us. Nothing is given to any of us but our lives and the few hours in which we live them. We must pray to the Daughter of the Mountains that we all find our way together again. Remember our home and have courage."

When the parting came there were tears in all their eyes, even Little Snen-neq's, though he blamed his on dust blown by the summer breeze.

32

The Hole in the Door

Porto managed to keep Sergeant Levias breathing through the first night and through the second day as well. He gave him sips of water from his hand and cleaned and bandaged the wound in the Erkynlander's belly as best he could, but he could see it was a losing struggle, and that was devastating. He had been in a nightmare like this before.

Many years earlier, during the battle for the Nakkiga Gate, a younger Porto had nursed his dying friend Endri until the last moments. But Endri's wound had been made by a poisoned Norn arrow; this one had been made by comparatively clean Thrithings steel, and that was the only thing that gave Porto hope. But it was a long walk to the nearest water, and no matter how hot his companion's skin, how pitiful his calls for something to drink, Porto hated to leave him. It had been while Porto was away from him young Endri had died.

Whatever chaos had gripped the crowds at the Thanemoot seemed to have quieted by the second day. From time to time Porto still heard Thrithings-men shouting outside their hiding place, but the calls and cries no longer sounded like men fighting. Still, he was yoked to a dying man by more than his pride and grief: even if Levias succumbed, it would only release Porto to a long, suffering end of his own. Their horses were gone, and he could not imagine walking all the way back to Erkynland, not even if he were twenty years younger.

But as long as I have my sword and dagger, he told himself, *I will at least have a choice of how I die.*

When Levias began breathing a little more easily in the hours of the second dawn after their fight with the grasslanders, Porto risked carrying him in search of water. He heaved the other man onto his back and then staggered farther away from the Thanemoot and settled his insensible burden by the side of one of the streams that fed Blood Lake. It was shallow this late in the summer, just a thread of water moving between the wide, muddy banks, but the water did move and it tasted sweet to Porto's lips, so he dragged Levias into the shade of the trees and washed out the wounded man's bloody undershirt, then mopped Levias's forehead before trying to clean the wound again. He had seen many such injuries on the battlefield and knew there was small chance the sergeant would survive, but to leave the sergeant to die alone would have been like abandoning poor, lost Endri a second time.

He sat beside Levias all day, moving him now and then to keep the hot sun off his face, cleaning the dark, drying blood off his wound, and giving him water to drink when he seemed thirsty. He could not imagine moving him again any great distance, and could only wait for God to take his friend back. Levias had stopped speaking. Porto had no real company but his own grim thoughts.

A strange noise startled Porto awake from a shallow doze—a scratchy, drawn-out sound like a nail being pulled from old wood. It came from the nearby stream, so after making sure that Levias was still drawing shallow breath, the knight took his sword in his hand and crawled through the undergrowth toward the water until he could get a better look.

At first he thought the stranger must be some kind of giant, because he bulked so large atop his horse, which was drinking from the stream. Then he saw the stranger was truly not so oversized, but only seemed so because he was mounted on the back of a small donkey.

The man turned toward him, though Porto had not made any noise. He gripped his sword hilt tightly, prepared to fight or to lead the stranger away from helpless Levias, but the man on the donkey only nodded his head and then turned away again, as if sword-wielding men crawling through the grass was nothing unusual to him. The stranger was barrel-chested but short of leg, as if one of Prince Morgan's troll friends had grown to man-size, but unlike any of the trolls, he wore a long beard gathered in a single braid. The hair on his cheeks and head seemed to cover most of his face, as though he were part ape or part Hunën, though his features seemed ordinary enough.

"*Vilagum*," the strange called. "*Ves zhu haya.*"

It took a moment for Porto to understand the man's Thrithings words, which were nothing more threatening than "Welcome" and wishing him health.

"*Zhu dankun,*" he answered—*thank you.*

The bearded man recognized that Porto was not a native speaker: when he spoke again it was in good Westerling, though strongly accented, each word as full of sharp bits as an autumn pinecone. "You are not from the great grass, I see. Where do you come?"

"Erkynland, though that was not where I was born."

"Do we muddy the stream, my friend Gildreng and I? Would you have drink? Gildreng is full of his own will, but I think he will move if I make him so."

"I have water in my waterskin," he replied, looking around for the man's friend, wanting to trust but wary of an ambush. "But no food to eat." The last of their supplies had been in the saddlebags and had disappeared with the horses.

Only when he said the words did Porto realize how hungry he was. "My friend is very ill."

The man looked at him carefully, then said, "Come out so I see you, if you please."

Porto crawled out of the long grass and stood. The stranger was a Thrithings-man, he could now see, with a serpent tattoo that began at his right wrist, wound up his arm, then emerged on the other side of his sleeveless shirt and twisted downward to wrap around his left wrist. He also wore a necklace of snake bones.

"What makes your friend sick?" the man asked.

Porto hesitated, but decided that it would be better to be honest, in case the stranger knew someone who could help Levias. "He was stabbed. Here." He pointed to a spot on his own stomach. "We were attacked—we did not seek a fight."

The bearded man nodded, then slipped down off the donkey. He splashed across the shallow stream, leading the donkey up the bank toward Porto.

"I will look," he said. "I have some . . . skill." It took him a moment to find the word, but when he did, he nodded again, as if he had not doubted it would come. "Ruzhvang I am, shaman of the Snake Clan. I know something of healing. How long ago was your friend struck?"

"Two days," Porto said.

Now Ruzhvang's hairy face grew sad, and he shook his head. "Too late, I think. But it could be the Earth Hugger will take pity. What clan is your friend?"

"He is from Erkynland, like me."

Ruzhvang said no more, but followed him back to the hollow where Levias lay hidden. The shaman tied his donkey to a branch and squatted next to sleeping Levias, whose face seemed so pale Porto could not imagine death was far away. The man examined the sergeant's eyes and tongue, then carefully unpeeled Porto's makeshift bandages and looked over the wound, making little clicking noises with his tongue as he did so.

At last he turned back to Porto. "Did you pray for help?" he asked.

Startled, Porto said, "Yes. Of course. To our God."

Ruzhvang waved his hand. "All gods or one god. You must be a man of good deeds for them to hear. We of the Snake Clan are the best healers—it is known."

"Can you help him?"

"I do not say yes, I do not say no. He is very weak." He tied his donkey to a tree branch. "The bad spirits are in the wound and in the blood. Only a gift of strength from the Legless—the Earth Hugger—can help him now. Will you bring him?"

"Bring him where?"

"Follow me. Where the water is deeper."

By the time they stopped, they were close enough to the Thanemoot that

Porto could once more hear voices in the distance. Ruzhvang took a packet wrapped in oilskin from his saddlebag and walked down to the stream again, which was much wider here, and then without any hesitation stripped off his clothes and waded naked out to where the water reached his thighs. He began to wash himself all over, singing quietly in Thrithings words that Porto did not recognize. When he came back, he pulled on his breeches and sat down in the dirt beside Levias. "Build a fire," he said as he began to take things out of his oilskin bag, small earthen jars and leather pouches, then set them before him on the ground. When the fire was going, Ruzhvang sent Porto with a clay bowl to get more water from the river, then crumbled something leafy into it, still singing, and waited for the water to boil. "Now tell me this one's name," he said.

"Levias."

"It is a strange name, but I will try to tell the spirits so they will understand."

By the time the sun had slipped past noon and the shadows had begun to stretch toward the east the shaman had bathed Levias's wound with the herb-water, singing all the while, then covered it with the boiled leaves and bandaged it with long, dried leaves from yet another a bundle in his saddlebag. Then he had Porto fetch more water and boiled this as well, this time with sections of some kind of root or tuber. When the broth had cooled a little, he held it to Levias mouth and poured some in. The Erkynlander's throat moved as he swallowed, but the movements seemed almost accidental; Levias did not look any better at all, at least not that Porto could see.

"Feed him the rest slowly," said Ruzhvang, handing Porto the bowl. "Until the sun is down. The Legless will help him if he is worthy."

"He is worthy," said Porto, thinking of Levias's good humor, his bravery, and his faith.

"Not for us to decide, but the spirits," said Ruzhvang a little sternly. "But now I tell you about Gildreng, my donkey. He is fierce but if you do not put your hand near his mouth, no injury will you suffer."

"Why? Why do I need to know that?"

"Because I leave him for you. I am a long way from my people, and if I must walk now, longer still will I be gone. Six days ago they left the Thanemoot, back to our clan lands in the east."

"You're giving me your donkey?"

"Even if the Earth Hugger spares his life, this one cannot stay here," he said, gesturing toward Levias. "But even with my donkey, you do not carry him so far as Erkynland without him dying." A sudden thought came to him. "But I saw a camp of your people as I came back from trading with shamans of the Sparrowhawk and Bison clans."

"My people?"

"I think it must be Erkynland's flag—two dragons on their banner, and a tree. Do you know it?"

Porto's heart sped. "That is the banner of Erkynland, yes. Did you really see them?"

"It is all the talk of the lands north of here—the clansfolk say the stone-dwellers have come to bargain with the new Shan for an important man that was captured."

"Count Eolair? Could that be the name?"

"I do not know more. A shaman has other thoughts." He shrugged, his braided beard wagging on his chest like the tail of a sitting dog. "They say Unver seeks to trade him, perhaps, or ask something else from the stone-dwellers who rule your Erkynland."

"Do you know where they are keeping this man who was captured?"

Ruzhvang cocked an eyebrow as bristly as a spring caterpillar, and his darkly tanned face showed amusement. "You ask the wrong man. The Serpent gives me strength to heal and no more. But if the new Shan bargains to return him, then the new Shan must have him, do you not think?"

Porto sat back, full of astonishment. Why would a troop of Erkynguards be on the edge of the Thrithings? Even to bargain for Eolair, important as he was? And then he remembered Prince Morgan and the destruction of their mission, and shame stabbed Porto as deeply as the clansman had stabbed Levias. He had failed on all counts. But perhaps if he could find the Erkynlandish camp, he could at least tell them what he knew.

But I cannot leave Levias behind, he realized. *I must stay with him as long . . . as long as he lives.*

"I go now." Ruzhvang lifted the saddlebags from the donkey's back and draped them over his shoulder, making himself look more egg-shaped than ever. "I leave some white currant berries for you and your friend—you see them piled there. You must chew them in your mouth before giving to him."

"But I cannot keep your donkey!"

"You can. You must. So the Earth Hugger tells me and the spirits do not lie. Treat him well and he will bear your friend with care. He is not so evil as he seems, old Gildreng, though he will kick when he is in a foul mood. I will miss him."

And while Porto sat, astonished, Ruzhvang shouldered his burden, stopped to pat the donkey on the nose—Gildreng looked away from him, as if he could not believe he had been given away so easily—and then walked off down the winding path beside the stream. "Remember—keep your hands from his mouth!" he called back, then he was gone into the trees.

Porto spent the rest of the dying afternoon beside Levias, dabbing the sweat from his forehead and giving him little sips of the broth. He was hungry himself, but the smell of it did not tempt him at all, so he ate two of the fruits and found them very satisfying, but not enough to quell his hunger much.

At last, when darkness had come, he fell asleep sitting up, the wet rag of Levias's shirt still clutched in his fingers. When he woke again in the dark hours of the night, certain he had dreamed the whole day, the donkey Gildreng was still tied to the tree nearby and his friend Levias was weakly asking for more broth.

Eolair did not much like that he was still a prisoner, but Unver's people treated him reasonably well. He had been put in one of the many wagons that had once belonged to Rudur Redbeard. Its door was locked from the outside, but the window in the door, although too narrow for him to have crawled through even in his youngest and slenderest days, allowed him to watch a little of the life of the Thrithings camp as the Thanemoot came to a close.

The madness of the first few nights after Rudur's death had ended. Eolair would have been hard-pressed to see any difference between what he saw now and ordinary life at Blood Lake, the women tending fires and cooking, the men bartering animals and engaging in games of chance and strength. But Eolair thought he could see a change in the peoples' spirits, from the aimless excitement of the first days of the Thanemoot to something calmer and more directed. He wondered if that was somehow Unver's doing, or merely what happened each year at the end of the raucous gathering.

The first time grasslanders approached his wagon bringing food, Eolair was amused to see that the man carrying the tray was accompanied by two huge, armed guards.

If they fear an old man like me enough to send three guards, they must think me a very devil, he thought.

But when the man with the tray climbed the steps and came to the door, Eolair saw that the servant was utterly hairless on head and jaw and upper lip. It was uncommon enough on the grasslands, where a man's whiskers told much about him, but as the tray bearer stood before the door, Eolair saw that even the man's eyebrows were hairless, although a stubble grew there that suggested something other than illness had denuded him. Still, Eolair needed information, and even if the man was a foreign slave he might know something. In fact, as Eolair well knew, a slave was often more likely to talk to an outsider. He made sure that the two clansmen guards were standing too far back from the wagon to overhear much.

"*I thank you,*" he said in the Thrithings tongue as the door was unlocked, and he took the tray. "*What is your name, man?*" The smell of warm bread and hot soup made his mouth water. He had not eaten well among Agvalt's bandits: the bandits had not eaten much better themselves.

The man looked at him in mild surprise but said nothing. Up close, Eolair could see that his face and shaved head both were bruised.

"*My people must know the name of the one who serves us or we cannot eat,*" Eolair continued, an improvisation that would have made his fellow Hernystiri nobles laugh uproariously, since few of the richest knew the names of most of their servants. "*Please, tell me, so I may tell my gods.*"

The man shook his head. He would not meet Eolair's gaze. *"I have no name,"* was all he said.

"What? Everyone has a name."

The hairless man shook his head again, but this time he looked up. The hatred and despair in his face almost made Eolair take a step back, and he had trouble holding onto his end of the tray. *"My name has been taken from me,"* the hairless man said, but quietly so the others could not hear. *"I betrayed my clan. I betrayed my people. I no longer have a name."*

"But I must call you something," said Eolair, wondering now at this man's story, *"or the gods will not know who to reward for feeding me."*

A light kindled in the man's eyes. The skin around them was purple with the marks of old blows. *"I told you, I have no name. Now I must go."*

As he let go of the tray and began to turn, Eolair tried once more. *"Just tell me something I can call you."*

The man's hairless brows gave him the look of something unnatural. *"They called me Baldhead."* For a moment his mouth curled in a humorless smirk. *"That can still be my name, as you see. When you speak to your gods, tell them they have made a very poor world."*

The two armed clansmen followed him closely as he walked away, and Eolair realized that he was not the only prisoner in the Shan's camp.

Eolair's second visitor came late that same day, in the dark watches of the evening. He did not hear her coming, nor realize she was there until he heard a voice through the hole in the door.

"Count Eolair, can you hear me?" Whoever it was spoke Westerling, which was a little unexpected, though her accent was barbarous.

He rose from the narrow bed and went to the door. "I hear you," he said. "I speak your tongue, at least somewhat. Would you rather use it?"

The woman standing outside was dark-haired and handsome, but her eyes were wide with unease. By the dim light from the wagon she looked to be just past childbearing age. Something seemed familiar about her features, but he had seen so many Thrithings-folk in the last months that he could not say why. "No!" She looked around and then spoke more quietly. "Better to use these words, though I do not speak them well, in case anyone hears."

He was intrigued, and not just by her admirable face. "Very well, my lady." He could not resist the honorific—she seemed different from the Thrithings-women he had seen, if only in that she spoke another tongue beside her own. "Who are you, if I may ask, and what do you want from me?"

"I am Hyara," she said. "The Shan, as I now must call him, is my nephew."

He was surprised; it took all his practiced skill not to show it. "I am pleased to meet you, Lady Hyara, but I admit I cannot guess why you are here."

"Unver plans to release you—or at least so I am told."

"So he suggested to me, although I am certain there will be a price, and my king and queen may not wish to pay it."

"Unver is no fool. He wants you to go back. He wants you to keep your rulers sweet. He does not want a war with your Erkynland."

"It is not *my* Erkynland, to be truthful, but their interests are mine." He looked her over closely. She looked worried but not frightened, a good sign. Still, he could not help wondering if he was being drawn into some family struggle, or perhaps something even more dangerous. "I ask again—what do you want of me, my lady?"

"I want you to tell your queen and your king that the Thrithings does not want war with your land. Rudur is dead, but Unver is no fool. His anger is pointed at Nabban. Tell that to your masters."

"But Nabban too is part of their kingdom," he pointed out. "They are not king and queen of just Erkynland or my own Hernystir. The High Ward surrounds Nabban as well."

"Then the Nabban-folk must stay in that ward!" she said, and in her flash of anger he saw a strength of will he had not suspected. "They steal our lands, they kill our people, then they blame us. Unver comes from the south, where they must fight the stone-dwellers always. He has a hatred for them that cannot be . . ." She searched for a word, but could not find it. "He hates them," she said finally. "And he will push them back behind their borders again. Blood will spill on the grass and there is no stopping it. But he does not war against the north as well."

"Why would he? Only a fool fights enemies on two different sides." Eolair shook his head. "I will tell my rulers that Unver does not wish to fight them. But they still must watch over Nabban as if it were their own nation. That is what the High Ward means."

"Then they will bring the world into despair," she said flatly. "Widows, orphans, that is all that will remain. Do you know how many men will come from the grasslands to fight? Many of them hated Rudur because he claimed to be the Thane of Thanes and yet did nothing to stop the Nabbanai. They are as ripe for war as fruit hanging on autumn branches."

"Where did you learn to speak our tongue so well?" he asked, distracted despite himself. "Did you live in what you call the stone-dweller lands?"

"No, though others of my family did," she said, but was clearly impatient. "My father was a thane. Many outsiders came to us. I learned because I heard it spoken, and because I wished I could go away to see those lands." She looked around again to make sure they were still alone. "Why do you ask so many questions?"

"Because that is my nature, good lady—and also my trade. Does Unver speak Westerling as well? What is he like? How can I speak to him, to learn what he truly wishes of my masters? I have asked to see him, but no one will bring me to him."

"He was badly hurt by that mad dog, Redbeard," she said. "Unver barely lived after all those torments—only the will of the spirits let him survive. And he is a man, too—he will speak to you when he can do it without looking weak and hurt. But when he is strong again he will also take these clans in his hand like a man with a team of horses, and make them work together, make them go where he wishes. Your masters do not know how strong Unver's will is, how clever he is and how fierce his angers, but I have seen him, and I have seen that the spirits fight for him, too. I saw them send the ravens to destroy his enemy, and that enemy was my husband Gurdig—though I do not mourn him. Your masters must not provoke him!"

Now Eolair felt stung. "The king and queen are not such weaklings or cowards that they will be dictated to, even by this Unver Shan."

"Then we will all see the end of things. I know your people are many and their castles are strong. My people will die too." Her face, so fierce only moments before, now was pale and full of horror, as though she could actually see the terrible things she foretold.

"Lady Hyara, I hear you." Eolair was angry with himself for letting his own feelings leak through. "I do not want war between our peoples, and I know the king and queen do not want it either. Talk to Unver. Tell him to speak to me before he sends a message to them, and together we will find a way to make peace that both peoples can live with."

She shook her head violently. "I cannot speak to him—not about such things. It is not my place, and he would not listen."

"If he is as clever as you say, and loves his own people as much as you say, then he will listen. If he cannot take advice from a woman, perhaps he can take it from an old Hernystirman who has seen many things and many wars." Eolair patted her hand where it clutched the bottom of the window. "The King and Queen of the High Ward have enemies more frightening and more deadly than the clan-folk of the grasslands—believe me. They do not want war with the Thrithings any more than you do. Tell Unver that I will be a go-between. He has treated me fairly so far, so I will see that my masters, as you call them, do the same. Do not despair, my lady. While good people live there is always hope."

"But when the spirits themselves want war, and the people's hearts do too, nothing can stop it." Without another word she turned from the hole in the wagon's door and was gone. When he looked out, Eolair saw only a dark, slim shape flitting away across the grass.

When Hyara returned to the great tent, she found her sister kneeling beside what had once been Rudur's bed; it was rank now with sweat and dried blood. Vorzheva was spooning broth into her son's mouth. Unver's wounds had healed a little, but his face was still disfigured by the cuts and the swollen flesh that surrounded them. Hyara could tell by the way the Shan sat that his flayed back was also still terribly painful, but as usual he kept all sign of discomfort from his face. She knew this sort of strength well from the men in her clan and both admired and detested it. It made all pain, including that of other people, into something to be ignored, something unimportant.

In a month, Unver's torn skin will be only hard white scars, she thought. *But not all wounds heal like flesh.*

Fremur was there too, and he spoke sternly to her. "It is not good for you to walk about so late, Hyara. You are the Shan's kin. Someone might wish to do you harm."

She wondered how much of his concern was really for her, and how much for Unver's dignity. Thrithings-men did not like their women, even older relatives, to walk about freely, to go without suitable escort or without getting permission first. But Hyara had lived with those strictures for so long that she was not willing to be bridled again, especially not by a man ten years or more younger.

And it is not as if he has asked for my bride price, she reminded herself. *Who is he to me, anyway, except the servant of my sister's son? Let him speak for himself if he wants a say in my life.*

"I went out for a walk," she said. "That is all. How is Unver?"

"The Shan is well," said Fremur.

"He is regaining his appetite," her sister said.

"By the Sky-Piercer," Unver growled, pushing the bone spoon aside, "have I died? Do I need a shaman to speak for me, like the spirits of the ancestors?"

Fremur looked pleased, perhaps to hear Unver still swore by the Crane Clan's totem. "Of course not, great Shan."

Unver looked at Hyara. "And what did you see while you walked?"

She hesitated. "Much and nothing, as always." If he asked her what she had done, should she tell him? Nobody had ordered her to stay away from the stone-dweller, Count Eolair, but she sensed that Unver would not like it if he knew, and if he knew she had begged the foreigner to find a way to avoid war he would probably be furious. No man of the grassland clans wanted a woman to speak for him, much less to plead for peace.

Luckily for Hyara, Unver seemed to have his mind on other things.

"The Thanemoot is almost ended." He wiped soup from his lip with a disdainful flip of his fingers. Vorzheva and Hyara had shaved his mustache so they could clean the deep cuts that went down his cheeks and into his upper lip. She was not used to seeing a man of his age with no whiskers. He did not look as bizarre as Fremur's slave, the man once called Gezdahn Baldhead, who now crouched in a corner of the tent staring down at the ground, but it still made Unver seem strange, like something entirely new.

But he is the Shan, she reminded herself. *That is as new and different as any man could be.* Even Edizel from days long past had not had a story as unusual as her nephew's.

For the first time, she thought of Unver's father, Prince Josua. When Josua had first come to the Thrithings, Hyara had been a mere child and had barely seen him or heard him, since he had come as one of his father King John's envoys and met only with Vorzheva's and Hyara's father Fikolmij, thane of the Stallion Clan. When Josua and Vorzheva came back years later, Hyara was old enough to watch and understand. Josua had almost died at the hands of one of her father's minions, but in the end had survived and even triumphed, a humiliation that had burned in her father's heart forever after. But over the years, as Hyara had grown into womanhood, Prince Josua's face had left her memory, though she remembered what he had done very well. It was as though her sister had married a sort of ghost, some kind of supernatural being who could not ever be completely seen.

But now, as she looked at Unver's face, and despite the terrible injuries, she thought she could see things in his hard features that brought back long-buried memories of the prince—the high forehead, the long jaw, the cool gray eyes.

What else has his father given to Unver, the man who will now rule all the grasslands?

She could not ask that question—she was not even certain any of the others would understand it—so instead she said, "You grew up among the stone-dwellers, Unver Shan. What are they like?"

He fixed her with eyes that sometimes seemed impossibly cold and distant, but now looked faintly mistrustful, more like those of a cautious child than the ruler of all the clans. "What do you mean, Hyara?"

"Do not remind him of those bad times." Vorzheva put the empty soup bowl down on the floor so sharply that the spoon rattled and spun. "We were deserted. His father left us. We were alone among people who despised us. How can you ask him to remember such things?"

The faintest shadow of a smile curled Unver's lip, still clotted in several places with dried blood. "Your memories are not mine, my mother. The city beside the marsh was not a hateful place to me, except when I was dragged away from it. I had to hate it then, or I would have hated myself."

Hyara was fascinated. It was the most she had heard him say about his past. "What is Kwanitupul like? I have always wondered. I met a trader once who made it sound like a magical place, full of every kind of person and thing that ever was."

"It was filthy and cramped," said Vorzheva promptly. "I used to stand on the roof of that cursed inn, praying for a change in the wind so that I could smell the clean air of the grasslands and not the stink of the swamps."

Unver did not look at his mother but held Hyara's eye instead, his hint of smile still lingering, although there was something else in his face now too, an anger she did not entirely understand. "A child can make his home anywhere, I think," he said. "If there is something firm on which to stand."

Fremur suddenly stood up and walked across the grass toward the place where the hairless slave crouched. "And you! What are you listening to, you dog? This is not for your ears. This is the Shan that you tried to betray, and yet you sit there like a spy, hearing all. And it is only because Hyara begged for your life that you are not rotting on a stake. Get out of this tent, you wretch, or I will throw you out."

The one called Baldhead did not say a word, but rose and hurried out, head down and shoulders high, as though he expected something to be thrown at him. It was true that Hyara had suggested that Fremur spare him, but not out of sympathy or softness. As someone who had watched her father's way of ruling all her life, she knew that harsh lessons did not breed obedience, only a treacherous silence.

"I should have killed that piece of offal when I meant to," Fremur said, looking at Hyara almost in accusation. "If you spare a dog he will never bite you, but men are not so trustworthy."

"Ho, Fremur, you must have known more loyal dogs than I have," said Unver, laughing a little, though it obviously hurt his healing face. "There is no animal I know—dog or man or horse—who, once injured, will not wish they could return the injury."

"We need fear those injuries and treacheries no longer," Vorzheva said with the crisp certainty of someone who did not entirely believe something, but wanted to. "Now we are the ones who will help those who deserve it, and beat down those who try do us harm."

"And on that, my mother," said Unver, any trace of a smile now gone, "you and I can truly agree."

33

Shadows on the Walls

"Come, High Magister Viyeki," said Prince
Pratiki. "Stand with me and watch our warriors at their brave work."

The prince-templar was resplendent in an ancient suit of witchwood armor
worth more than everything Viyeki owned put together. His hair was bound
into two deliberately hasty war-braids, and his famous sword Moonlight hung
at his waist. But Pratiki was no mere Sacrifice officer: the prince-templar was
a relative of the queen herself, a rank greater than even the High Martial of all
the armies of Nakkiga could hope to achieve. Pratiki had not achieved great-
ness, it was a part of him, a certainty that informed his every breath and
thought. "Please, my lord," he asked Viyeki again, turning this time to look
back. "Come and join me."

Pratiki, Viyeki had come to learn, was surprisingly generous for a Hamakha
noble, courteous with all who served him, even slaves. But as with most born
into great power, he did not understand the obligations even his generosity laid
on those around him.

Viyeki joined the prince and his troop of personal guards at the edge of the
hilltop, though he would rather have stood apart, where he would not need to
hide his occasionally untrustworthy thoughts. The moon had dipped behind
the hills, but even by starlight it was easy to see General Kikiti's army swarming
silently toward the mortal fortress called Naglimund. Viyeki could not help
wondering what it would be like to be a mortal inside those stone walls, to see
so poorly after the sun was gone and then to discover such a great force coming
out of the night to attack.

*The mortals think us demons and monsters. As the war-poet Zinuzo wrote, "The forces
of darkness and death are before us, and they hate what we are. They hate our breath, they
hate our warm blood." But he spoke of the enemies we faced when shadows first crept across
the Garden. Did he ever dream that others might see his own people the same way?*

"Ah," said Pratiki, with the cheerful interest he might display while watching particularly involving game of *shaynat*. "Look! Now the Hammer-wielders
step out. They are proud, everyone tells me. Like your Builders, Viyeki, it is
said they love their tools more than they love their own families. But Hammer-
wielders are so few these days!"

A dozen Hammer-wielders ran uphill through a hail of arrows from the walls, gliding like birds despite the heaviness of the tools they carried. Pratiki was right about their sparse numbers, and already one had fallen, pierced through the chest by a defender's arrow.

"Surely they will never be enough to bring the walls down," said Viyeki. "Why are there not more of them?"

"Because these days our armies are full of halfbloods," Pratiki told him. "Little more than children, most of them. They have not had time to learn the old arts. But do not fear, Magister—Kikiti and the other generals have planned carefully."

The defenders inside the stronghold were swarming onto the walls now, but the weak-eyed mortal archers could scarcely see the Hikeda'ya to aim at them, and though another of the Hammer-wielders fell, the rest of the small company quickly reached the base of the curtain wall. Viyeki knew from other battles that they would swing their great stone-headed mallets with the care of gem-cutters, each striking a single point until the wall quivered like ringing crystal. If enough of them struck, it would set even the thickest stone barrier crumbling. But surely this company of Hammer-wielders was too small!

To Viyeki's astonishment, the first place the attackers struck was not against the great wall itself but at several places on the ground before it. He watched as they spread out even farther and pounded the ground again with their great mallets, soundlessly and with no visible effect.

"What are they doing?" It was all he could manage to keep the agony and confusion from his voice, to maintain the bloodless, placid tones of a Nakkiga noble. "Do you understand what is happening, Prince-Templar?"

Pratiki sounded almost amused. "I told you not to fear, Magister. The wall will come down soon enough—all the walls will come down. But it will take a while before the rest of our attack begins. It is a long way here from their burrows at Fort Deeping."

Viyeki had no idea what Pratiki meant, but he was distracted by the Hammer-wielders. The survivors had spread out far along the curtain wall but now hurried back toward the center of the wall, the fort's main gate. There they gathered, almost shoulder to shoulder, then swung their weapons in unison. This time they did what he had expected all along, slamming their huge mallets into the base of the curtain wall. All of the weapons struck within a few paces of each other, and where they crashed against the mortared stones pale cracks spread across the massive wall like frozen lightning. As the cracks grew longer, Viyeki saw mortals fleeing in panic from the battlements above. The wall beside the gate began to shiver. He felt a little reassured now—this was nearer to what he had expected. Another blow and at least this one narrow section of the curtain wall would collapse. He could already see the pale forms of a few of the warrior-giants as they lumbered up the slope in anticipation.

"See! The mortals cannot stop us, or even slow us greatly," Pratiki declared. "General Kikiti and his troops, with the help of the Northeastern Host, will have taken the fortress before sunrise. Then you and your people will be called on to do your part, High Magister. I am confident you will find success just as our Sacrifices do."

Again Viyeki was a bit confused—he could not remember ever hearing of the Northeastern Host before. But the mention of his own task had reminded him of how little he understood of anything happening here.

"I hope you are right, my lord."

Pratiki gave him a swift glance. "I hear doubt in your voice, noble Viyeki. What troubles you?

Because of the prince-templar's calm, almost gentle way of speaking, it was sometimes difficult to remember how important Pratiki was, and how powerful. "I would be more confident of my order's success, Highness, if I knew exactly what it was my Builders and I were expected to do." As soon as the careless words left his mouth Viyeki regretted them: even the kindest member of the queen's clan might consider them treasonous.

"Do?" The prince-templar looked over to him again. "What do you mean, Magister?"

"I beg your pardon, Serene Highness. Of course I have faith in the mission with which our queen honored me, to find Ruyan Ve's ancient tomb and recover his armor. But I confess I do not understand how any of that will help the queen or her people."

"It is for the Witchwood Crown," said Pratiki, and now his voice was stern. "You know that, High Magister. Everything we do is bent toward recovering the Witchwood Crown."

Relieved that the prince-templar had not immediately denounced him for his doubts, Viyeki hurried to reassure him. "Of course, sire, of course. But before these last days I had heard of this crown only in whispers, my prince, and none of them were from sources I trusted—until now. Although I am certain," he hastened to say, "that my ignorance was necessary." He hesitated, then decided he had stepped too far into the river to turn back; he must wade on, no matter how high the water might prove. "In fact, I confess that I do not even know whether this crown is a palpable thing—"

"Look, look!" Pratiki was distracted again. "Even with so few Hammer-wielders, we begin to have success! The wall beside the gate is crumbling—see there!—and the giants are pushing their way into the fortress." The prince paused, still looking down on the battlefield. The faint chaos-sounds of battle wafted to them across the night air. "You do not know what the Witchwood Crown is, you say?"

"I confess my ignorance, Highness."

A few moments of silence passed before Pratiki spoke again. "It is about the witchwood itself, you see. The last trees are dying."

"So I have heard." It would have been almost impossible not to know that— the subject had been whispered about in the councils of the powerful even before the queen had awakened from her long slumber. "But what *is* this crown, if I may ask? And what will it do?"

"The queen knows," said Pratiki slowly, as if repeating something he had been taught at a young age and had not considered since. "Our blessed Mother of All knows and, as always, she has decided the proper thing to do. She will find a way to bring back the witchwood. For without it, Lord Viyeki, what are we? We lost the Garden—shall we lose the last and most precious remnant of it in these lands as well? Shall we become no different than the hapless, short-lived mortals?"

"Never, my prince." About this, at least, he could speak his mind honestly. "We must do whatever we can to preserve our people."

"Exactly," said Pratiki. "And we must trust our beloved monarch to know the best way to do that."

"Of course, Highness. I hear the queen in your voice."

"Just so." Pratiki grew excited again. "Look now! See what is coming! They have heard the hammers striking—they have come to the summons!"

Viyeki saw the earth bulging in front of the castle's curtain wall in several different places, like the disruption of the soil above tunneling moles—but only if those moles were the size of houses. But Viyeki could not concentrate on what he was seeing, because an astounding idea had seized him.

By the Garden that birthed us, I believe that even Prince Pratiki does not know what the queen seeks! The idea was breathtaking. *Not even a prince of the royal house of Hamakha knows the secret of this Witchwood Crown!*

The sudden appearance of Norn troops outside the walls of Naglimund seemed as unreal as a nightmare. Sir Aelin and Captain Fayn scrambled down the tower steps and ran across the common toward the wall of the inner keep, but by the time they had climbed the battlements a wedge-shaped section of the outer wall had already cracked and collapsed. The shapes of the first besiegers clambered over the rubble into the outer keep—huge, hairy shapes.

"Aedon preserve us," cried Fayn. "Those are giants!"

Aelin watched the monsters pick their way through the ragged hole in the curtain wall and across piles of fallen masonry, but as terrifying as they were, he was most astonished by what they seemed to be carrying.

"Norn soldiers are riding on their shoulders," he said.

"What are you talking about? I see only those white, shaggy hell-beasts. Your eyes are better than mine."

"The giants are carrying Norns with hammers!" Aelin insisted. His great-uncle Eolair had told him that the fairies used magic hammers at Naglimund during the Storm King's War, but he had thought it was the Sithi who had done that, not their Norn cousins.

The sentries on the remaining lengths of the outer wall had regained their feet, and now rushed to either side of the breach and began firing arrows down at the invaders, but although one of the hammer-carriers was hit and knocked off a giant's back, the rest quickly made their way over the broken stones and started up the slope toward the inner keep. Fayn shouted for the castle's defenders to hurry to the battlements, and soon archers stood on either side of him along the wall of the inner keep, loosing their shafts down at the approaching Norns and their hulking, two-legged steeds. At Fayn's next shouted order, a group of pikemen rushed out of the gate to engage with the attackers, but Aelin could see already that the brave defenders were not enough to overcome the giants. Each sweep of a hairy, pale arm sent a mortal soldier flying, and none of them rose after they struck the ground.

"We will need more soldiers!" Aelin called to Captain Fayn.

The cries of defenders and the roars of the shaggy Hunën drifted up from below. The giants had now set down their Norn riders and formed a wide defensive circle around them. Then, as if seized by madness, instead of continuing toward the inner walls, the hammer-wielding Norns began to strike the ground with their long mallets.

"What are they doing?" said Fayn. "Torches! Bring torches here!"

Dozens more of Naglimund's mortal defenders crowded onto the front of the castle wall to stare down at the dead grass and dark earth covering the common below them. Torchlight only made it clearer that the castle's defenders were rapidly being slaughtered by the collared, armor-clad giants.

Fayn too could see the sally had been useless. "Fall back," he shouted to the defenders below. "Men of Naglimund, fall back to protect the keep!"

Even as he said it, the Norns brought their hammers down on the hard ground one more time, then halted. For a moment near-silence fell across the outer keep, and although a few flaming arrows still plummeted to the ground from the castle walls, the Norns and giants seemed not to care.

Aelin could make no sense of it. The hammermen and giants had only created a small breach in the castle's outer curtain wall, but if the gap was big enough for Hunën, then the nimble Norn soldiers should be scrambling through after them like a swarm of white ants. Instead, most of their army still waited outside the wall. As fearful as he already was, Aelin felt an even greater terror beginning.

Why don't the rest attack? By the gods, why? What are those damned White Foxes waiting for?

A low noise like an unending clap of thunder shook the ground, making Aelin's bones shiver and his ears itch. The castle's curtain wall suddenly began to wobble where the first breach had been made; a heartbeat later, huge chunks of stone began to shake loose, then the ragged edges of the breach fell away and the hole in the wall opened even wider—but still the Norns waiting outside did not rush in.

"Fayn!" Aelin called. "Fayn, something evil is happening at the outer wall!"

As he watched, the curtain wall suddenly heaved. A large portion of it on either side of the breach simply crumbled into pieces. Shocked, Aelin could only wonder if the Norns' magic had summoned some invisible giant to join the siege. Then he saw something vast moving toward them, slithering out of the wreckage of the curtain wall.

No, he realized, not something, just the evidence of something—the raised ridge of a vast shape tunneling beneath the ground, impossibly swift and headed toward them. By the immense mass of soil it displaced, tumbling entire houses as it surged toward the inner keep, Aelin knew it must be unimaginably huge.

The giants and the Norn soldiers who had reached the inner keep all scattered as the hidden thing plowed through the spot where their hammers had earlier struck the earth. For a moment its back crested above the roiling earth, a rounded, mud-caked immensity like ship's hull turned upside down. Aelin, full of horror and surprise, thought he recognized its shape.

A cave-borer? But so big! He had seen signs of the many-legged digging beasts in the Grianspog Mountains, and had heard tales of some growing in the depths to the size of prize bulls, but this thing, whatever it was, must be a dozen times larger—as big as a barn.

Then Aelin had no more time to wonder: the hidden shape swam toward them through the soil with horrifying speed until it struck the foundations of the keep's inner gate.

The wall shuddered and swayed beneath Aelin and the rest like a sapling in storm winds. He and Captain Fayn tumbled against the battlements, struggling to stay on their feet, but half a dozen of Fayn's men closer to the impact tumbled screeching off the wall. Then, as those who remained stared down in wide-eyed horror, a shape that seemed possible only in a nightmare burst up through the soil beneath them, its many legs flailing. It was a cave-borer as Aelin had guessed, plated like a woodlouse but impossibly huge. The vast jaws that could crush stone clacked once, then it fell back into its hole and began shoving against the roots of the castle wall again.

"Run!" Aelin shouted. "It is an earth-borer as big as a house. It will eat the walls right from beneath our feet!"

Fayn, to his credit, did not stop to question this impossibility, but bellowed for all his men to follow. They sprinted toward the stairs while the entire battlement rocked beneath them like a ship in a storm. The borer rammed the sunken foundations of the wall over and over. The last thing Aelin saw before he joined the exodus was the rest of the Norn army swarming through the breach in the curtain wall.

Aelin hurried down the steps, certain that they would collapse at any moment. "*Hernystiri!*" he shouted. "Men of Hernystir, where are you? It is Sir Aelin calling you! Come to me! *Come to me!*"

As he reached the bottom of the earth of the inner bailey the entire wall began to sway behind him. Dozens more Erkynlandish soldiers were hurrying

toward them from different parts of the castle, but he and Captain Fayn shouted
at them to stay back. Within moments the part of the battlements where Aelin
and Fayn had just stood sagged, then one of the tower tops crumbled, dumping
chunks of mortared stone as big as wine barrels into the inner keep.

Once they had led the remaining defenders to a safer distance, Fayn bent to
catch his breath, then straightened up, his face almost as pale as a Norn's. "By
the mercy of Elysia, Mother of God. Giants. Digging monsters. Like in the old
stories. What can we do against such things? How can we keep them out?"

"We can do little without numbers," Aelin said, "and I fear it is too late to
defend the walls at all. See, they have more of those great, digging earthwicks—
the walls are beginning to fall in more places now. The White Foxes are breaking their way in on all sides. We can only retreat to the keep."

Fayn shouted to those who could hear him to fall back toward the center of
the fortress. "But what of you and your men?" he asked Aelin. "This is not your
battle."

"It is now. We could not leave you to fight alone."

As he spoke, the wall they had just quitted rumbled once more and slumped
even farther, disgorging huge chunks of stone that crushed both fleeing soldiers
and entire houses with equal ease. As Aelin lunged away from the last few
bounding fragments of mortared wall, he saw that the giants who had brought
in the first Hammer-wielders were now climbing through the gap in the inner
wall, and even as he watched, two of Naglimund's retreating defenders were
obliterated by the swing of a huge war club.

"Haste!" Fayn shouted, voice raw with anger and grief. "Fall back to the
keep, all of you! We cannot stop them here!"

As the captain and Aelin hurried the surviving defenders toward the center
of the fortress, one of the pursuing giants howled at them in what sounded like
mocking triumph, waving the limp corpse of a mortal soldier above its head
like a banner. Aelin felt a flush of shame. He knew he should run, but the sight
of a murdered man being waved like a dirty rag filled him with sudden rage.
He picked up a piece of the wall as big as two fists and hurled it at the giant.
Any stone he could throw was far too small to do any serious damage, but the
missile struck the giant's shaggy leg and the creature barked in pain. It flung
away the guardsman's body, then lurched after Aelin and Fayn.

"By the head of Aedon, now you're done it!" Captain Fayn cried. "Run,
man!"

They were far behind the other survivors, and within a few moments Aelin
could hear the giant growling and panting behind them. He grabbed Fayn's
elbow and yanked him to one side just before a club the size of a tree trunk
smashed down, but he was too late to save the guard captain from a second blow
that came a moment later. It hit with a dreadful muffled smack and flung the
captain two dozen paces or more through the air. Fayn was dead before he
landed, half his head gone and his limbs bent in all wrong directions, like a
shriveled spider in a dusty corner.

Aelin ached to avenge him, but knew that with no weapon but his sword, he stood no chance against the hairy creature. And as long as his men were alive and needed him, he also had no right to toss his own life away.

The giant had almost caught up with him. Aelin dodged into a deserted building and pulled and bolted the door behind him, then realized he had taken refuge in one of the castle's chapels—a place where his own gods might not even see him.

I have been a fool. Aelin cursed himself as he shoved benches in front of the door. His moment of weakness had cost Fayn his life, and lost Naglimund one of its staunchest defenders. *If you can hear me, great gods, I beg your forgiveness.*

The roaring giant outside the chapel seemed to have entirely forgotten the rest of the battle in its furious search for Sir Aelin. As it battered its way through the heavy door, he climbed onto a reliquary and from there to the sill of a side window, then scrambled out and dropped gracelessly to the ground.

As Aelin ran toward the heart of the castle he could see that the inner keep's walls were collapsing on all sides, uprooted by the tunneling of more borers. White-faced Norns seemed to be everywhere, dragging screaming mortals from their hasty hiding places and killing many of them on the spot. They had surrounded the main buildings of the keep as well, and hooting, bellowing giants were busily smashing in the doors.

It is too late, he realized. *We have already lost. Naglimund is doomed.*

Everywhere Cuff looked, manlike, white-faced creatures swarmed through the outer keep, like what happened when he disturbed a rats' nest on his way across the rooftops. The pale things were killing everyone; even as he watched from shadows of a narrow alley, one of them stabbed a priest with a spear then hurried on, uninterested in the holy man's dying moments.

Cuff the Scaler did not always understand what was happening around him, but this time he *did* understand, and it terrified him more than anything ever had: demons were climbing out of Hell to destroy the living. Only demons would hurt priests! Priests were the ones God had sent to care for His people, to keep the bad things away. But now even the priests were helpless. Hell had opened and all the devils were here in Naglimund's keep.

Cuff ran into an alley to hide and crouched shivering behind a pile of stinking rubbish. The terrified shrieks of women and children being slaughtered panicked him into tears. *No! Mustn't cry*, he told himself. *Father Siward said not to!* Only little children cried—Father had told him that many times.

A trio of soldiers backed into the alley. Cuff could tell by the swans on their coats that they were Naglimund-men and he almost called to them, but a moment later a tall demon on horseback rode into view, the horse's hooves clacking on stone. Half a dozen more white-skinned demons followed their mounted leader, blocking the end of the alley. The devils carried axes and long, strange spears and their ghostly faces grinned as if at some terrible joke, but their eyes were black and empty. Cuff wept silently in helpless terror as the demons sprang at the soldiers and swiftly cut them down, hacking them even after they were dead.

The mounted leader peered down the alley; for a moment Cuff was certain the Hell-demon could see him. His heart was beating so hard and so fast he feared it would shake him to pieces. Then the demon rider twitched his reins and turned his horse away. The others followed after him, silent as hunting wolves.

When the screams and other noises of slaughter began to sound farther away, Cuff the Scaler found some of his courage again. He crept out from behind the midden-heap and scurried down the alley between the close-set houses. The streets of the inner keep were full of flickering red and orange light, and fires burned in several of the tall castle buildings as well, hungry tongues of flame licking up from the windows. For Cuff, Naglimund had always seemed as unchanging and immortal as the rocky hills of the Wealdhelm or the great forest itself. Now it was ablaze and bodies lay everywhere. He knew it must be the Day of Weighing Out, the end of all things that the priests had warned him would come to a world full of sinners.

As he stared across the courtyard toward the keep he saw something burst upward through the ground and shake its great, blunt head in the air, scattering stones and dirt. Cuff knew that anything so huge and so terrible must be the Adversary himself, come to take them all. He turned and ran whimpering toward the long wall of the bake house, the closest structure that he could climb. He heard no pursuit, but even as he sank his fingers into the cracks in the plastered wall and began to scramble toward the roof, three or four shapes appeared from the shadows and closed in behind him. He tried to scramble out of their reach, but a moment later a hand closed around his ankle with a grip he could not break. The demons could climb as fast as he could! He looked down and saw a ring of bone-white faces looking up at him, black eyes staring. Cuff the Scaler had time only to let out a wordless, despairing cry before he was yanked from the wall.

Sir Aelin's only duty now was to find any Hernystiri who still lived and get them out of Naglimund, to lead them south to the Hayholt and tell King Simon and Queen Miriamele and his uncle Eolair what had happened here. And all that would happen only if he managed to escape the monster outside and survive the next hour.

This is all your doing, Hugh, he thought as he ran from the chapel, and if the king of Hernystir had stood before him at that moment Aelin would have killed him without hesitation, despite his oath of loyalty. *All tonight's blood is on your hands.* Aelin, who thought so often about what a nobleman should do, tried so hard to live up to his great-uncle's example, was almost in tears at the magnitude of the King Hugh's betrayal, not just of his own subjects, but of all mortal men. *I will see you brought to account for this. I swear on the hazel rod of Brynioch himself!*

The giant had realized he was gone: he could hear it roaring in frustration as it lurched back out of the chapel where he had been hiding, wood splintering and religious treasures being smashed underfoot. Aelin needed to find his men, but it was growing harder every moment to believe that any of them still lived. *Darkness has returned. Nothing left but to fight and die.*

As he neared the residence a silhouette suddenly appeared in front of him, outlined against the climbing fires. To his astonishment, as he raised his sword to defend himself the shadowy figure cried, "No, my lord! It's me!"

"Jarreth? Is that truly you?"

"It is, sir."

"Then hurry. A giant is behind me."

Jarreth fell in beside him, and pointed him toward the stables. "Over there, sir. Maccus and the Aedonite are at the stables getting our horses—if they still live." Aelin heard the raggedness in his squire's voice but could not fault the young man: it was a testament to his bravery that he was able to make sense at all in the midst of so many terrors.

So many of the walls had collapsed that nearly all the torches that had ringed the inner keep were gone. White Foxes seemed to be all around, but Aelin was grateful to see fewer of them than he had first feared. Still, there were hundreds inside Naglimund now, and it took him and Jarreth no little time to make their way past the keep, moving from shadow to shadow. The Norns were already leading prisoners out of the innermost buildings, but they were also killing male prisoners on the spot; it was all Aelin could manage to keep moving. *We can save none of them,* he told himself. *We would simply die ourselves, and then nobody would carry the word away.* But knowing that did not ease the terrible ache. *The High Throne must be told what happened here! These deaths must be avenged.*

With the attention of the Norns on the center of the keep, Aelin and Jarreth managed to reach the stables without having to fight, although several times it was a near thing; once they had to crouch in shadow and watch the corpse-skinned Norns behead several captured Naglimunders, one of them a weeping, struggling woman, and it felt to Aelin as though he had swallowed slow poison.

Inside the stable, Maccus Blackbeard and Evan the Aedonite were saddling and harnessing the horses as fast as they could without giving themselves away to the white-faced warriors ranging the courtyard outside.

"Is this all of us who are left?" Aelin asked. He had brought eight men to Naglimund.

"We saw none of the others," said Maccus. "It's mad out there. Mad!"

"I know. We can only try to escape into the forest. Anywhere else and they'll see us and shoot us down. The White Foxes are fierce bowmen."

"I saddled your horse, Sir Aelin," said Evan.

"You have my thanks." Aelin patted Connach on the withers and the stallion stepped anxiously in place. The smell of smoke and the noises outside had all the animals badly frightened, and Aelin hoped they would be able to control them once they left the stables.

"Lead the horses out and stay away from the main keep," he said. "We don't know what we'll find out there, so don't mount up until I say."

As the only one of noble birth, Aelin insisted on being the first through the door in case the Norns were waiting. Connach balked in the doorway but Aelin gave a firm pull on the reins and leaned in to whisper words of encouragement; after a moment, Connach gave in and followed him.

The borers' attack had collapsed many of the walls around the central keep. Most of the huge beasts seemed to have withdrawn back into the ground afterward, but the gaps in the stonework had been filled with Norn soldiers, so Aelin and the other Hernystiri kept to the shadows as best they could. There were far too many White Foxes to fight against, but Aelin was still surprised he didn't see more.

Still, he thought, *they do not need such numbers as we do—they have their fairy magicks, their great wall-smashing hammers and their digging monsters*. But even as he thought it, he finally understood something that had puzzled him. There had been so few of the hammer-wielding Norns attacking the castle that he hadn't been able to imagine how they would bring the walls down without being shot down by the castle's defenders.

Those hammer-fairies were never meant to bring down all Naglimund's walls, he realized—*only a few, enough to get inside the keep. Then they used the hammers to summon the great digging monsters that could do the task in a few moments.*

Satisfied that there were no Norns immediately outside the stables, he told his men, "Mount up, but pull your hoods down low and perhaps we will pass for Norns. We must head for the eastern wall against the hillside, then find one of the breaches and make our way out. After that it's up the hill and over into the Oldheart Forest on the other side. Now ride!"

They burst out onto the uneven ground of the courtyard and sped past the back of the residence. Capering shadows surrounded it, wildly magnified by the uneven firelight, and he saw Norns in many other places around the inner keep, but for these first few moments at least, Aelin and his men went unnoticed.

They managed to escape the inner keep through a shattered wall, and as they approached the outer wall Aelin saw that it had been breached between the postern and the guard tower at the corner, but that no White Foxes seemed be guarding the gap. A moment later he saw the great cave-borer that had burrowed under the wall and brought it down had collapsed so much of the stone that the massive creature had trapped itself; its blunt upper body swung helplessly from side to side in the middle of the gap, and its legs scratched at the night sky as though it tried to climb to Heaven itself, but the pile of fallen stones held the monster tight. It was a way out, but Aelin could not imagine how to get past the struggling borer without being snatched up in those dark jaws and crushed.

Then Aelin saw a long pike one of the castle's defenders had dropped, and had a sudden idea. "Jarreth," he cried, "hand me that pike. The rest of you—behind me!"

Jarreth clearly did not understand what Aelin planned, but slid out of his saddle and snatched up the pike, twice as long as he was, and carried it to Aelin.

"Now get back on your horse." Aelin did his best to couch the pike in his right arm like a proper jousting lance. Without waiting to see if Jarreth and the others were following him, he spurred Connach forward toward the massive shape of the thrashing, trapped borer.

He could see no eyes—and why would there be on a creature that lived in the blind earth?—so the hooked jaws seemed the most likely place to aim as he spurred up the pile of rubble. He struck, and for an instant he held onto the pike so tightly that the long wooden shaft began to bow, then the iron spearhead popped free and the pike itself snapped back straight and leaped out of his arms. Aelin himself was sprung sideways out of the saddle; he flew a short distance before a painfully hard landing that knocked out his breath.

For a moment the flames and the red-splashed light on the walls seemed to teeter from side to side around him, as though some even greater borer was undermining the entirety of Naglimund. Then Jarreth helped him to sit up and Aelin realized it was only his dizzied brain making everything sway. The great earthwick was still wriggling in the rubble; Aelin's attack had not budged it a hand's breadth.

"It chews through stone," he said out loud.

"What, lord?" asked his squire. "We have to do something—some of the White Foxes have seen us!"

He was right: a group of shapes near the residence had detached themselves from the larger crowd and were hurrying toward them, but Aelin only noted them and turned back toward the borer. "I'm a fool! It chews through stone with that mouth!" he said. "Why did I think I could harm it there?" He scrambled to his feet and went to retrieve the long pike. He was grateful to see that its shaft had not broken. "Tell the others to be ready!" he shouted to Jarreth.

Aelin did not mount his horse again, but climbed up the unsteady pile of stones toward the eyeless monster. This time he did not attack it from the front, but got behind it and shoved the head of his pike in beneath the overlapping armor plates that covered its body, pushing the iron point in until he felt resistance. A moment later the borer felt the attack and heaved its front end upward, jaws clacking. The sudden jerk yanked Aelin from his feet, but he immediately got up and grabbed the pikeshaft, then shoved the point in even deeper. Jarreth and the rest had seen what he was doing now and made their way up the shattered wall as far away from the beast and Aelin as they could manage, Jarreth back on his own horse and leading Aelin's Connach by the bridle.

Aelin began swiveling the shaft from side to side, trying to cut as deeply as he could and inflict as much pain as possible to distract the many-legged monster while his men climbed past. A dozen Norns were running toward them—Aelin knew he had mere moments before he and his men would be caught and killed.

Just as he dug the pike head in again, the great borer made a last effort and heaved itself halfway out of the pile, sending chunks of rubble as big as handbarrows wheeling past him. He heard a cry behind him, but had no time to look because he had shoved the pike in deeper than ever before and the borer was desperately trying to shake it free. The creature reared upward and half a dozen more of its limbs waggled free in the air, each leg a jointed horror nearly as long as Aelin was tall.

Then the whole of the shelled beast swung to one side and tugged the pike shaft from Aelin's hands as easily as a man might snatch a twig from an infant, but in its fierce thrashing the borer struck the postern gatehouse. The stone structure shuddered all the way to its roof, then fell to pieces and collapsed. The borer, still held by its lower half, vanished beneath the stones of the falling structure.

Aelin had no time to gloat: the onrushing Norns had all but closed the distance. Maccus and Evan were already on the other side of the ruined wall, so he turned to take Connach back from Jarreth and saw that only his horse now stood there, eyes wide and legs trembling. A great chunk of postern wall had fallen and Jarreth was gone, nothing left to mark where he had been but one bloody, bootless foot showing beneath the broken stones.

Blinking away tears, Aelin put his foot in the stirrup and swung up into Connach's saddle.

You have stolen from me once again, Hugh Gwythinn's-son, he thought as he rode down off the shattered remains of the wall, then spurred his horse up into the dark hillside. *You have taken a man close to my heart.*

I will see you pay for this. Unless the gods themselves make me a liar, I swear I will take your life for these crimes.

34

Cutting Reeds

Morgan staggered back to the flat spot on the riverbank, lurching through mud almost to his knees. When he got there he dumped the bundle of reeds he had been carrying and groaned. "It's hot. How can there even *be* mud when it's this hot?"

Tanahaya did not look up from her work. "By the time the rains come again it will all be dry. So does the wheel turn." She had assembled several bundles and was lashing them together with rope she had made from other grasses while Morgan had been out sloshing along the river's edge, dulling his sword-edge on the long, waving reeds. "Help me put this up on the logs," she said.

He helped her lift the long, loose bundle of bound reeds. The boat looked as though it would be about twice his own height in length. "Will that hold us both?"

"Since you are always complaining of not having enough to eat," she said without even a trace of a smile, "then I think you will now be light enough for us both to be carried in it at the same time, yes."

Morgan couldn't tell if she was joking or actually unhappy with him. He had done his best not to complain, but hacking at reeds in the bright sun was exhausting work, and he was covered all over with the bites of small winged creatures. He watched as she tightened the ropes that held the bundles together. "But will it be strong enough? The water is fast out in the center of the river."

She gave him another unreadable look, then went back to tying, her fingers nimble as bees humming from flower to flower. "True. There are places where *T'si Suhyasei* moves very swiftly indeed. We will need paddles as well. Perhaps when you are searching for more reeds you could also look for branches that would serve the purpose."

"*More* reeds?"

"Yes, Morgan. But not too many more, I would say. Another bundle of the size you have just brought. Still, there is no hurry—the boat must dry in the sun for at least a day or so before we try to put it in the water."

"Another day?"

Now he could see that she was both amused *and* annoyed. "Yes, Prince of Questions. Unless you would rather try following the river on foot all the way to Da'ai Chikiza. But I think you have learned something of how difficult that is in your search for reeds. Still, as I said, you need not hurry too much. These you have brought will keep me busy for some time. You can go out again when the sun is lower and the air is cooler."

In the first moments after waking, as with every other day, Simon thought he would turn and find Miriamele sleeping beside him, her fair hair disarranged, her breathing so loud he often teased her about it. But even before he rolled onto his side the silence reminded him that she was not there, that she was many, many leagues away.

It was strange to wake each day from his empty, dreamless sleep to the same ache of missing her. It made no sense. They had been separated for months at a time when he was fighting in the Thrithings, and this time she had left for Nabban in Tiyagar-month and it was now nearing the end of Septander. How could he not have grown used to her absence by now?

He sat up and pushed himself back against the pillows and headsheet, then pulled the bed hangings back along the nearest side. Even with her gone such a long time he slept in the same spot every night, just as if she had been there. They had been given the ash wood bed by Isgrimnur and Gutrun at least twenty years ago—or could it be thirty? It was astonishing to consider the swift flight of time. To Simon, who had been raised sleeping on the floor among the other scullions, and had been thrilled the first time he was able to stretch out on his own narrow cot, the gift had felt as if the duke and duchess had given them an entire castle. Sometimes he lay half-awake and looked at the linen curtains and imagined he was in a ship with billowing sails. But now that he was the only passenger it sometimes felt like a ghost ship, doomed to wander the seas forever.

Irritated by his own gloomy thoughts, he sat up and reached for the cup on the small table beside him. As he raised it to his lips a face suddenly appeared over the foot of the bed, startling him so that he spluttered watered wine all over his nightshirt.

"Do you need anything, Majesty?" Young Avel wiped his eyes and tried to look as though he had not awakened only moments earlier. Simon had forgotten about the young servant sleeping on a trundle at the foot of the bed.

"By Saint Rhiap, you startled me, boy." He looked down at his stained shirt. "I need some clothes I haven't covered with wine, that's what I need."

"Yes, Majesty." Avel hurried to the standing dresser and began rummaging through it. "Shall I call for Lord Jeremias, sir? He would be best to help you choose the day's outfit."

Simon sighed. "No, that's not necessary. Just get me something clean and kingly. I have much to do today." And he did, and that was why he felt so little urge to climb out of the high bed-ship and descend to the dry land of duty. He expected a dispatch from Osric on the Thrithings border, and plans had to be made for the visit of Countess Yissola, old Streáwe's daughter, who doubtless planned to scold him over some nonsense stemming from her feud with the Northern Alliance. Simon had never met the woman, and from what he'd heard about her iron will and short temper, he had no urge to.

God, how I wish Miri were here, he thought. *I'd let her deal with this Perdruinese she-wolf.* The queen, he knew, would never let anyone get the best of her, especially not another woman. But Simon knew that he was not good at arguing with the fairer sex, that his worries about being discourteous got him in trouble more often than they did him good.

"How about this, Majesty?" asked Avel, holding up a thick tunic of green velvet.

"For the love of God!" Simon yelped. "I apologize for taking the Holy Name in vain, but what are you thinking, boy? The sun will be hot enough today that even the trees will be looking for shade."

"That's funny, Sire," said Avel. "Trees looking for shade. I'll have to remember it."

Simon grinned and the day felt a tiny bit better. "Old Shem the groom used to say that. Always made me laugh, too. Another one of his was, 'It was so hot I saw two trees fighting over a dog.'"

While the lad puzzled that out, a knock came on the chamber door. A guard stepped in and said, "The Lord Chamberlain."

"I am cheered to see that you're awake," Jeremias told him. He looked to the page, still holding the heavy velvet tunic. "Oh, well-chosen, lad! The green velvet is exactly the right tone to strike, I think. But let me find a jeweled chain to go with it. That heavy silver one should do nicely. Very impressive, very royal."

Simon closed his eyes and silently wished he could go back to bed. But there were things to do, so very many things to do. His people needed him and he was the only High King in the vicinity.

"Well, old friend, what matters of state are before us today?"

The king was trying to sound cheerful, but Tiamak did not like what he saw. Simon, one of the tallest people he knew, slumped in his chair like a man twenty years older, and the dark circles under his eyes told of another night he had not slept well. Tiamak looked briefly to his wife, whom he had brought along for reasons of his own, and saw that Thelía, too, was studying Simon closely. "Much and much, as always," he answered. "First and most important, of course, is reviewing the castle's defenses and the readiness of our soldiers, and Sir Zakiel wishes some of your time for that, but I believe he is planning to come to you after the midday meal. And I am still trying to round up the leaders of the Northern Alliance because they badly want to speak to you before Countess Yissola's visit."

Simon sighed. "Of course they do. Yes, I will certainly see Zakiel. As to the Northern Alliance merchants, I will leave it to you or Pasevalles to arrange things."

Pasevalles, who had been sitting quietly with his lap full of documents, nodded. "As you wish, Your Majesty."

Tiamak was quite willing to pass that chore and most others along to the Lord Chancellor. He had more than enough on his mind. Work on the great library had ceased because of the concerns about the Norns and the bizarre, frightening news from Hernystir. Because of that, Tiamak's and Thelía's chamber was still full almost to overflowing with books that he had hoped could soon be moved to the new building; many more volumes were scattered about the castle in such places of temporary storage as Tiamak had managed to wrestle away from the butlers and chambermaids. The fact that some of those books were hundreds of years old and irreplaceable seemed to make no difference to the castle's servants, who saw greater utility in things like extra brooms and spare wall hangings and sealed barrels of fish sauce that had sat unbreached (but were likely spoiled anyway) since the early days when Simon and Miriamele had been crowned.

Simon waved and one of the pages came to fill his wine cup. This time Tiamak did not look to his wife. "How do you feel, Majesty?" he asked instead.

"Oh, God save me—*Majesty*." The king looked around. "There is no one here but you, me, and Pasevalles. Must you?"

"It makes it easier for me to remember when there are others around. But I will try not to call you 'Majesty' if it displeases you so, Simon."

"And don't scold me for asking, either." He frowned. "It is just that I have had another poor night."

Tiamak saw his opening. "I wish you would let Lady Thelía make you up a sleep draught tonight. My wife is very skilled, as you know."

"It would not be any trouble," she said quickly. "A little melissa, some chamomile perhaps. I could also stuff a cushion for you with peppermint and rose petals, which both help in bringing easeful sleep."

Simon shook his head. "Binabik made me a charm for sleeping and it gave me the most terrible dreams—far worse than no dreams at all. Do you not remember? You were there, Tiamak. I terrified that poor child in old Narvi's castle by walking in my sleep."

Tiamak took a breath for patience's sake. "But, Simon, that was different, from what Binabik told me . . ."

"Charms or medicaments, it makes little difference. There is nothing wrong with me that Miri's return will not mend. I miss her, that's all. But soon she will be back and everything will be well again. No, no charms, no simples."

Tiamak looked to Thelía. He was annoyed that the king considered their application of study and careful experiment no different than the troll's Minta-hoq conjurations, but it was clear that whatever he and Thelía thought, they would get no farther with the idea today. "Well, then," Tiamak said, "what shall we do first of the many things that want your attention?"

"What about this Yissola?" Simon asked. "So she is definitely coming here, is she? Why? What does she hope to accomplish?"

"She is said to be a powerful and persuasive woman, Majesty," Pasevalles offered. "I am not sure it is wise to give her a private audience."

Simon lifted an eyebrow and his weary scowl deepened. "What, Lord Pase-valles, are you like my wife, who does not think I can be in a room with an-other woman without turning into a mooncalf? Do you think she will blink her eyes at me in a wanton way and I will throw over the Northern Alliance for her Perdruinese Syndicate?"

"Of course not, Sire. But these are complicated matters, and although not so pressing as the Norns"—Pasevalles paused to make the Sign of the Tree—"it is still a sort of war. The Sindigato and the Alliance try to block each other from the ports they call their own, and in the neutral ports they are always fighting. Sometimes men die in these brawls. They also kidnap sailors from one another's ships and even engage in acts of piracy, although that they do carefully and selectively."

"Ah, so because it is complicated I need to have you and Tiamak standing over me? The Commoner King might not understand such heady issues?"

Pasevalles showed a hint of strained patience, a look that Tiamak suspected he wore himself from time to time. "No, Majesty. All know and respect your good sense. But these are not the sort of disputes that can be solved without a great deal of study, of contracts and treaties. Surely you do not plan to do all those things by yourself?"

"No, damn it, I don't." Simon's temper was much shorter than usual, Tia-mak could see, and again he desperately wished the king would let him do more to better his health. When Simon lifted his hand to display his frustration, it trembled, although he did not seem to notice. "But I don't think there's any harm in me talking to this Yissola without an entire army of clerks and func-tionaries hanging on our every word. Sometimes people are much simpler than you suppose, Pasevalles. Sometimes they just want to be listened to and heard."

"I'm sure you are right, Majesty." Pasevalles nodded and sat back, but he looked concerned as well, and Tiamak could not help wondering if he needed to work more closely with the acting King's Hand, at least on the matter of the king's ill health. Even without considering his beloved library, Tiamak worried that too many important tasks were still left undone. With the distraction of the Norns and the doubts about King Hugh's loyalties, John Josua and the for-bidden book—as well as the likelihood that Simon's son had explored beneath the Hayholt—had not been discussed for at least a fortnight. Tiamak did not like the idea of trying to defend a castle riddled with underground passages without exploring them carefully, but Simon seemed to find the whole idea too painful, as though he should somehow have guessed his son might find the castle's underground secrets and protected John Josua from them somehow.

Ah, Brother Etan, I sent you away too quickly, Tiamak thought. *I could use another trusted hand in the castle these days!* He remembered that he had not replied to the monk's last letter, which had been sitting on the table in his chamber for days, half-buried under a growing pile of other matters demanding his attention. *I hope you are safe, Brother.*

Still, he thought, *like Simon I must deal now only with what is before me, not what I wish or hope for. It is clear that a storm is coming, though we do not know how big it will be or how hard it will blow. We can only prepare ourselves and pray for luck.*

"What do you think?" Tanahaya asked the young prince. "Is it not a fine boat?"

Morgan looked at it with what she suspected was more than a little distrust. Like most mortals, he wore his feelings like rich clothes, displayed for all to see. "Will it really float?" he asked. "Won't the water come through?"

She let herself laugh, though she did not entirely feel it. "That is why the reeds are tied so tightly together. Now help me carry it down to the water."

The lightness was only in her voice. Inside, Tanahaya was still choked and sickened, as if she had swallowed a hard-shelled nut that had lodged part way down. It was almost impossible to believe that her teacher Himano was truly gone. When she left him to go to Jiriki and Aditu she had known they might never again spend long mornings watching the grasses give their dew to the air and the birds in all their colors darting like glints from a rainbow, but she had not guessed how complete the separation would be.

It was hard not to abandon the present entirely for the happier world of memory. Himano had possessed a way of talking about things that had happened far in the past as though they had happened only yesterday; to be in his company was to be simultaneously in ancient days and in the present moment. "There," he would say. "Such a song that thrush sings, as if it had just thought of it and wanted everyone to hear such cleverness and beauty! Do you know, Vindaomeyo would not begin making an arrow without going out to his garden and thanking the birds for their feathers? He did not care for cities, and lived surrounded by flowers, as we do. He also moved carefully and quietly, so as not to disturb the life around him. Even the songs he wove into his craft were no louder than the buzzing of a single bee."

And so she would sit beside her teacher, watching the hairy bees dart from blossom to blossom, and it was as though Vindaomeyo the Fletcher sat with them.

But the duties of the present could not be ignored for long. With Morgan's help, Tanahaya pushed the boat out into a shallow backwater and then climbed in. She held out her hand to the youth, who took it with a certain hesitancy she did not understand. She was amazed by her own overconfidence of only a few moons past, that she had thought to go to live among mortals as an envoy, to represent her entire people to them, without spending years and years studying them first. It was hard enough to understand this single child, with his moods and misunderstandings.

You were right, Himano, my dear master, when you told me that we learn best only by understanding how little we know.

Morgan climbed in and the boat rocked, but Tanahaya knew she had built it well. He leaned too far to one side and almost lost his balance as it tipped. "Feel its motion," she told him. "Let the movement of boat and water into you, but slowly. Make it part of you."

"I've been in boats before," he said, frowning.

"I meant no insult. But a small boat, especially on a fast moving river, is a different thing. You cannot force it to behave. The water goes where it wants and the boat goes with it. But you can let that movement flow up into you and put yourself at its center."

He looked at her with an expression she hadn't seen from him yet, one that spoke of both annoyance and amusement. "You said you were a scholar, but what you really are is a tutor, I think."

"There is some truth there," she admitted. "My master Himano was both, and he wanted me to be the same. Knowledge—understanding—cannot be hoarded. It must be returned to the world. The story of life and thought, that is everything. And we are all part of that story."

Now Morgan seemed interested. "I was just thinking about that yesterday. That I'm in a story, like my grandparents were. And my grandfather used to say you never know what kind of story it is when you're in the middle of it."

She nodded. "He is wise, then—but it goes further. We are all in a story—existence is a story. What sort of a story, though, is not always clear to those who live inside it. That is what a scholar is, someone who tries to see the shape of all stories, both the small ones that are tales of people or places, and the larger one that we all share, the story of everything that is."

"Now you've lost me." He settled himself in the prow of the little boat.

"I do not fully understand it myself," she said, and allowed the pain inside her to seep closer to the surface. "And now I have lost my teacher, who tried to help me find that understanding. There are times when I wonder how I can live in this story any longer—a story that has so much sorrow in it."

The mortal youth was silent for a long time, thinking. "I don't think any of it has much to do with what we want. I think God puts us in the story that He thinks is right for us, but then leaves it to us to make our way through."

She thought about this. "God" was a word she knew, but it was not a word she used because it was too small, too . . . human. She considered what Morgan had said as though he had named the sun, the sky, the dark and the light—and memory and hope too—and found she could understand the idea better. With that understanding came another. The loss of Himano was indeed part of her story, just as his teaching of her and his death had been parts of his.

"I think your grandparents taught you well," was all she said.

Tanahaya had not been on the river in many years. As they let the current ease them along, helping it here and there with their paddles made from bark and long branches, its beauty helped to ease her sadness at losing Himano. In places the trees crouched and leaned as though hoping to learn some interesting news; in others the banks widened and the shallows were full of nodding reeds where red-winged blackbirds preened, showing their bright epaulets to the world as if hoping for congratulations. And always the river turned and turned again, finding its way—finding the only way—with a perfection that almost left her breathless.

The river is the story but water is the life, she thought. *Water has no artifice, no aim. It goes always where it should, without desire or fear, whether beneath the light of Mother Sun or of the sad, empty house of Father Moon. The river shapes the water, gives it direction, but that direction is not what it truly is. The river is only where it is, when it is, and sometimes how it is.*

This last thought became stronger when they reached the first of the rapids, where T'si Tsuyahsei descended swiftly downward, excited and frothing. They bounced and swerved for a splashing, chaotic time before the danger of over-turning grew too great; then, at Tanahaya's direction, they paddled to the bank and carried the dripping, heavy boat downstream until the water grew calmer again.

She could see that Morgan was thinking about food. It must be painful, she thought, to be unable to ignore such thoughts, to live in a body that was constantly crying for nurture, like a child who had not yet learned to speak. Still, she did not want to stop until they were ready to make camp for the night, but they had nothing to eat unless they caught more fish. She had hoped to sight Da'ai Chikiza before stopping, at least from a distance, but she could tell that would not happen today.

"I'm hungry," said Morgan.

"I know," Tanahaya told him. "We'll stop soon."

"How far away is it?" he asked as he sat in the bow, watching the river roll past them, glassy and serene. "This city we're going to?"

"Many hundreds of years," she said, "—at least in memory. But we should reach it tomorrow."

"And they'll let you use the mirror? The Witness?"

"I do not know for certain that any of my kind still survive there. The Pure have kept themselves separate from the rest of us since Jao é-Tinukai'i was attacked during your grandfather's time there. The loremistress Vinyedu led several of her kin and a few others to Da'ai Chikiza. It could be none of them have survived. But if we do find them, you must let me speak for both of us. The Pure are proud and full of anger toward your kind."

Morgan looked startled. "What do you mean? Are they going to try to kill us?"

"I cannot imagine they have strayed so far from wisdom."

The river bore them on, and for long moments its song was all she heard.

"I couldn't help noticing," Morgan said at last, "that you didn't really answer my question."

"I know. And I would not elect to go there if I had any better choice," was the best she could do.

Morgan hunted for things to eat as carefully as he could, using every bit of woodcraft he had learned from ReeRee and her family, gathering wild currants and digging up a large sheepshead mushroom from the ruin of a rotting log. Thinking about the little creature he had traveled with so long filled him with unexpected sadness. He hoped she was still alive, still with her family.

From ReeRee, his thoughts immediately jumped to his sister Lillia. With her, at least, he did not have to worry quite so much about the danger of snakes and foxes, but he still ached at the thought of her so far away. She didn't even know that her brother was still alive! That made it all the more important that he and the Sitha did what they had to so he could return home to Lillia and the rest of his family.

When he had gathered enough to make the small fish they had caught into a proper meal, Morgan hurried back to their camp beside the river. He knew Tanahaya was in more pain about the death of her teacher than she had showed him, and he wanted to do what he could to make her feel better.

Because the clearing she had chosen for camp was in a hollow concealed between two thickly-forested hills, Tanahaya had made a fire. He took the berries and mushrooms from his bag and crouched down to hand them to her. She looked at them for a long moment, then smiled.

"Thank you, Morgan. It is good to have someone to travel with. To have a friend."

Then, to his astonishment, she reached up and took his head between her cool hands and pulled gently until he bent even closer, then kissed him on the forehead. "You are a kind young man," she said.

He straightened, his cheeks and forehead suddenly warm, as though he had come inside out of a chill wind. "Thank you," he said.

He should have been content with this display of affection, even happy, but it confused him and made him think about the day he had watched her bathe in the river. He had tried to push the memory of her slender, golden form from his mind, but it had never gone very far away. Now it came back as strongly as it ever had, even on the longest, most lonely nights he had spent sleeping near her.

"Give me a few moments to boil the mushrooms, then we will eat," she said. "Meanwhile, sit beside me and warm yourself. Your skin is cold."

During the first hour of darkness the winds rose and a great chill crept down the river valley, silencing the night birds and waking Morgan from sleep. To his surprise, he found Tanahaya curled on the ground beside him with her back toward him, apparently also asleep, something he had seldom seen since they had traveled together. Shivering in the new and deepening cold, he tried to ease back into slumber but could not. The sudden cold reminded him of his grandparents' stories of the days of the Storm King's War, of the winter that had fallen on Erkynland and would not end.

Is it happening again? Are the Norns sending more storms?

Without turning toward him, but as if she had heard his thoughts, Tanahaya said, "It is only the autumn spinning into winter. Do not fear the cold, it is nothing unnatural. Move closer to me if you are too badly chilled."

He did, sliding forward until he was lying just beside her. His sleepy mind wandered over the Sithi and the way they seemed to understand and even control weather and direction, and sometimes even the sun and the lights of Heaven. But if they are so powerful and this Utuk'ku still terrifies them, what can mere mortals hope to do against the Queen of the Norns . . . ?

His anxious thoughts growing disjointed and circular, he drifted back into sleep again.

When he awoke once more it was the darkest part of night. The campfire was scarcely a glow and the chill had grown fierce, so he huddled closer to the warm body beside him. In that moment she seemed little different than the other women he had woken up beside in the years since he had become a man, and he moved closer still, until his face was pressed into her hair, and he could smell the strange, clean scent of her skin.

He remembered the feeling of her cool hands on his cheeks and how she had looked bathing in the river, long, lean legs and back, and wet, shining skin. He felt himself swelling and wanted to move closer still. One of his arms was draped over her, and as he nuzzled her neck and the back of her head, he slid his hand upward to cup the gentle swell of her breast.

An instant later he was on his back, his hand and wrist burning like they were on fire. Tanahaya was crouched over him, her face frighteningly intent in the dim light of the embers. She had bent his fingers back until it seemed they must break.

"What are you doing?" she demanded. Even in his agony, he thought it was the calmest any female had ever sounded when she asked him that question.

"I . . . I was . . . I just . . . I thought . . ." Morgan was so surprised by the sudden change of fortune, so unready to answer questions, that he could only burble like a half-wit. "I mean, I didn't . . ."

The hard look on her face softened a little, and she let go of his hand. He rolled out from under her and sat up, rubbing his wrist until the throbbing began to ease a little. "You must have had a dream," she said. "You must have mistaken me for someone else."

From the way she said it, she was plainly offering him a chance to save face. "I don't know . . ."

"Yes," she said. "That must be it. No undue liberties intended, but only the confusion that sometimes comes with dreams. Let us lie down again. Perhaps it would be better this time for you to lie with your back to me."

Morgan did as he was told. He still was not sure how she had grabbed and bent his hand so quickly, then rolled away and wound up on top of him—it seemed almost like a conjuring trick. He felt her move closer to him. Her warmth was a mixed blessing.

"There," she said. "Are you comfortable? Can you go back to sleep again?"

"I'm certain," he lied.

"Good. Then take your rest. You will need it—we still have far to go tomorrow. But perhaps you should not dream of mortal women while I am trying to keep you warm."

"I'll . . . I'll do my best not to."

"Because in any case, I already have a lover."

Shamed and frustrated, Morgan spent a long time pondering what had just happened, as well as her last statement, before he could finally fall back into sleep.

35

Colors Too Bright

Do not look to war for wisdom,

the poet had written,

> *Death comes to all; seeing more of it brings nothing*
> *But surfeit and sadness.*
> *The sounds too loud, the colors too bright to carry meaning*
> *And sudden death as pointless a lesson*
> *As the rap of an inkstone across the knuckles*
> *Of a dull student.*
> *No, my child,*
> *Do not look to war for wisdom.*

Shun'y'asu's infamous, forbidden lines were as hard to ignore as the stink of death that surrounded them now. Viyeki could only look around him and wonder why he felt no gladness in victory, and why the words of a poem that his masters called treasonous resounded in his head.

Only a short time ago, half a Great Year, the War of Return had ended in failure and humiliation for Viyeki's people. He and his master Yaarike had made their way back to Nakkiga from the mortal lands in the south, harried by vengeful Northmen all the way, a struggle that had ended only when the face of the mountain fell, ending the mortals' siege and burying the great city gate. During that flight and the many skirmishes along the way Viyeki had felt, if not joy, at least a sort of triumph each time the Hikeda'ya had beat back their persecutors. He had rejoiced at every dead mortal as a threat destroyed. But the destruction of Naglimund felt different. During the retreat, the Hikeda'ya had been defending themselves and trying to return home. But the mortals had not come anywhere near Hikeda'ya lands since then: the attack on this mortal fortress was an act of aggression, pure and simple, and Viyeki, though he would never voice his concerns aloud, thought it was both dangerous and foolish for his beleaguered people to anger the mortals again.

He and Pratiki made their way down the hill with the prince-templar's troop of soldiers, steering their horses through the front gate of what had once been a formidable fortress but was now little more than toppled walls and scorched ruins. Viyeki had left his own household guards behind—what was the need when he rode with Pratiki and a half-hundred Hamakha guardsmen? The mortal corpses that lay on all sides, splayed in the gaps in the broken walls or scattered in unrecognizable heaps at the bases of the burned towers, certainly offered little threat.

General Kikiti was waiting on his horse inside the gate, clad in his dress armor, the witchwood polished so that even in twilight it gleamed. Behind him a half-company of Sacrifices stood in perfect order.

"Well done, General." Pratiki might have been congratulating him on a well-laid table or a well-planned entertainment. "What were our losses?"

"Less than a score of Sacrifices, Highness, and some of those are only wounded and will recover. Most of those came because one of the giants was hit in the eye with an arrow and could not be controlled. But all the mortal soldiers and most of the men from the town have been killed—more than four hundred in all. The Garden was good to us."

"Indeed," said Pratiki. "Your Sacrifices have done well. The Mother of All will be pleased. I will be certain she hears of how well you and your order have done here."

"That is kind, Highness, though I do not deserve praise for something the queen herself planned and ordered. It is she who should be exalted."

Pratiki nodded. "You may tell her so yourself. Soon she will be here."

Kikiti was clearly caught by surprise, as was Viyeki, who for a long moment thought he had misheard. "The Mother of All comes *here*, Serenity?" The look on the general's face was something close to worshipful. "Is that true?"

"This was not an idle blow against the mortals," Pratiki said. "And when High Magister Viyeki finishes his work and the queen comes, the War of Return can finally be won."

Viyeki had known he had an important role to play, but he had thought he was merely retrieving an artifact to be taken back to Nakkiga. Never for a moment had he thought that the queen would actually leave the mountain and come to this far-off place. Utuk'ku had not left their mountain stronghold during his entire lifetime. "I . . . I am astonished by this honor," he said weakly. It now seemed all too plain that he would not be seeing Tzoja or his home again for some time, and that thought troubled him more deeply than he would have guessed. "May I ask when the Mother of the People will arrive?"

"Only she knows, High Magister," said Pratiki, but without rancor. "Now, General Kikiti, will you show us the rest of what your Sacrifices have won for us?"

They rode through the outer keep. Sacrifices and low-caste slaves were still dragging mortal bodies away. Instead of being burned, these were thrown into a vast pit in the shadow of the southern outwall.

"I am glad to see you received my message," said Pratiki. "Burning the bodies of the mortals would create even more smoke and increase the speed with which our presence here is discovered. I do not fear any mortal army, but I would not choose another fight before the queen arrives with more of our folk."

"Just as well, Highness," said Kikiti. "The creatures smell even more foul when they are burning."

"And you have been careful to see that none escaped?"

Kikiti hesitated so briefly that it was almost unnoticeable, but Viyeki felt sure the prince-templar saw it. "We think so, but we are still collecting reports. We lost a few Sacrifices on the far side of the castle, and we still do not know all that happened there. A borer was killed by a collapsing wall, along with several of its handlers."

Pratiki seemed only a little interested. "But you have sent patrols onto the hillside and into the forest? We do not want refugees bearing tales."

As they rode toward the ruined gate of the inner keep, a scream slashed the air and a body came plummeting down from above, waving its arms and kicking its legs, to land on the stones at the base of the guard tower with a noise like a dropped egg. Moments later another mortal prisoner was flung off the battlements. This one did not make a sound falling, but the body striking the ground was just as loud.

"Soon there will be none left to bear tales," said Kikiti with a certain amused satisfaction. "But you look unhappy, Magister Viyeki. Does it disturb you to see our enemies—those who stole our land—being given the punishment they deserve? In fact, some might say we are too lenient, their deaths too swift, but we must put efficiency in front of our own pleasures. Do you not agree, Prince-Templar?"

Pratiki smiled absently. He did not appear to mind the screams and the thump of bodies, but he did not seem to relish the sight either. "They are our blood enemies. Given the chance, they would murder the queen and all our folk. There is nothing more to say."

As they rode through the charred remains of the gate, Viyeki saw that those flinging mortals out of the tower were not the only ones dispatching prisoners. A squadron of Night Moth Sacrifices had gathered on the front steps of the mortal church—at least that was what Viyeki thought it by its architecture, though the mortal's Tree symbol had been ripped from its high-peaked roof. The Night Moths, one of the fiercest of the Sacrifice legions, had assembled a crowd of mortal prisoners, not soldiers but women, children, and men too old to have been active defenders of the fort. These prisoners were being taken one at a time to the front of the landing atop the broad staircase, shoved onto their knees, then a Night Moth would step up and cut off the prisoner's head. As Viyeki watched, a woman was forced to the ground, moaning and weeping, and then beheaded. Her head rolled and bounced down the stairs, long hair flailing, until it reached the bottom and came to a stop in the midst of many others. The Sacrifices laughed and talked in quiet voices. Some of them exchanged coins with each other, and Viyeki suddenly realized they were making wagers. He had to close his eyes for a moment as a feeling he did not entirely recognize washed over him. He covered for the failure of nerve by pretending to cough.

They swept past the stairway and rode on toward the main residence, headed for the side of the fortress closest to the hill that towered above Naglimund. Here and there other Sacrifices were dispatching prisoners of their own, but in a more leisurely way, taking a limb off and watching the bleeding creatures as they struggled to escape, then taking off another, trying different combinations.

"Surely that is not a very efficient method," said Pratiki, and for the first time Viyeki thought he heard something like displeasure in the prince-templar's voice.

"No, Highness, it is not. But those Sacrifices are no longer on duty. They are merely amusing themselves. Do not fear, we have already selected the females we will send back to Nakkiga for the slave pens."

Pratiki nodded slowly, displaying no obvious emotion. "Ah. Of course."

Viyeki found himself disturbed by the casual torture. *They are our enemies,* he reminded himself. *Given the chance, they would murder our queen and destroy our entire race. Pity has no place when mortals are involved.* But his disquiet was not so easily allayed.

Several of the largest buildings in the heart of the keep had been smashed to rubble. A few mortal corpses still lay on the ground, a few in armor, most wearing ordinary clothing. But these too were being dragged away by black-armored Hikeda'ya. Many of the corpses were female. Some were children. Even those that were man-sized and clad in battle gear seemed shrunken by death, less like dangerous enemies and more like the frozen birds that sometimes tumbled out of the sky around Nakkiga during a sudden winter storm.

More of Shun'y'asu's words came back to him:

> *I must kill you before you kill me. That is truth.*
> *And you must kill me, or else I will be your death.*
> *Like scorpions in a crystal jar, for one to live the other must die—*
> *But who made the jar?*
> *And who put us in it?*

It was said that those lines alone had been enough for the Maze Palace to ban the great writer's books. Soon afterward, Shun'y'asu himself disappeared. Some claimed the poet had left Nakkiga to find the better world of which he had so often written.

Viyeki thought that might be true, but not in the way that most believers meant it.

As the prince-templar's company turned toward the far side of the residence, Viyeki saw for the first time the tumbled outer wall and the immense bulk of a single dead borer, half-covered by the stones of a collapsed guard tower. A cluster of dark shapes crouched beside it, and for a moment Viyeki thought they had disturbed carrion-eaters feasting on the dead, some sort of huge kites or vultures native to these unfamiliar lands. Then one of the dark shapes straightened and looked to the approaching riders. Even with the dark crimson hood covering her face, Viyeki recognized Sogeyu, the leader of the Singers. She waited for their arrival with the stillness of a serpent watching an unwitting animal approach its den.

When they were only a few dozen paces away, Viyeki abruptly felt the air change. It seemed thicker now, and tasted of lightning. His skin prickled and the hairs on his neck stiffened.

Prince Pratiki noticed it as well and reined up his horse. "What Song is this I smell? Should we continue to approach, Kikiti?"

"Host Singer Sogeyu told us that they have found what we sought," the general said. "She expects us."

Sogeyu detached herself from her Singers and came to greet the prince-templar. She seemed almost to glide, as though her feet did not touch the torn and bloodied ground. "Hail, Prince-Templar, blood of our great mother," she said, dropping to one knee. "May the Hamakha live forever. May the serpent always guard us."

Pratiki nodded. "I thank you for your greeting, Host Singer Sogeyu. General Kikiti tells me that you have succeeded at your task."

Sogeyu pulled back her hood. Her face and shaven head were covered with small, precise brown runes that Viyeki guessed had been painted in dried blood. "We have, Serenity. I see the High Magister of the Builders is with you." She nodded to Viyeki and made a sign of fealty, but he thought he saw something other than welcome in her eyes. "This is good, because we have found Ruyan's tomb."

Viyeki did his best to banish all the unsettling things he had seen from his thoughts. "Is it in the spot your Singers are kneeling?" The ground here was hard-packed, but the frosts were at least a month away and the rain now falling would soften the earth. It should not be a difficult or lengthy task to dig.

Sogeyu shook her head. "No, Magister Viyeki, not precisely. In fact the tomb is deep below the stone building there and encased in even more stone. Basalt blocks would be my guess from the way they echo against our songs . . . but I would not dream of instructing someone like yourself in your own field of knowledge." She did not smile mockingly, but it felt as though she did.

He did not like Sogeyu, and he did not like the task. Still, it was not the place of even a high magister to question the queen's orders. "You said deep, Host Singer. How deep?"

"Again, I cannot pretend to your knowledge, but I would suspect that some twenty cubits of stone lies between the surface and the buried crypt."

"You have a hundred Builders, Magister Viyeki," said Pratiki. "Surely they can breach those depths without trouble. And they must, because the queen herself is coming."

An unexpected chill ran through him. "Our order can achieve anything the queen asks of us," he said. "But numbers and time are always the limiting factors, Serenity. More numbers, less time. I suspect we can manage it, but I would guess it will take until Sky-Singers' Moon has waned."

"That is not acceptable!" declared General Kikiti, barely hiding his anger. "The Mother of All will be here in a matter of days. Do you suppose we can ask her to wait while your Builders meander through their work?"

"A millionweight of stone and soil to shift is not something I think even the Order of Song could manage without considerable time and effort," Viyeki said, keeping his voice as even as he could. "And the great borers are far too clumsy a tool for such delicate, important work. You can give me your Hammer-wielders, General—that will speed the breaking up of the rock. And perhaps the rest of your troops—and your Singers, Host Singer—can help to carry away the rubble while my men dig. Understand, this is earth, not solid stone. Any tunnels must be propped and scaffolded properly, or the mass above will collapse and we will have to start all over. Not to mention that many of my Builders would die."

"Then let them die," said Kikiti. "They live to serve the queen, do they not?"

"So you will give me your Sacrifices to help, General?"

Kikiti seemed perilously close to losing his temper. "Sacrifices are warriors, not . . . not *rodents*. They are trained to fight, not to dig. And our presence here might be discovered at any moment, then the mortals will be upon us. Who will fight if our Sacrifice legions are beneath the ground?"

"Who indeed?" said Viyeki. He had annoyed Kikiti, which was at least a small victory, and it allowed him to do something else—something he had been thinking about since he had entered the vanquished fortress. He turned to Pratiki. "I must have slaves, then, Serenity. Mortal slaves. All those still living must be spared and brought here to work if we wish to reach this tomb or crypt before the queen arrives."

The prince-templar pursed his lips and considered, but Kikiti was again struggling against open, unhidden rage. "It matters little to me that you are the high magister of your order, Lord Viyeki—this is war, and those slaves belong to the Sacrifices! They are ours to do with as the queen bids us, and no one else. You cannot tell me what to do with them."

"I only state what is necessary to achieve the queen's desires, General. For every Builder who is scraping through stone, I need two more folk to carry away the rubble." He turned back to Pratiki. "But I think our esteemed general is wrong, Serenity, at least in part. I suspect that the queen would not have sent one of her own family unless it was with a mandate to make sure things went smoothly and swiftly here before she came. Am I right?"

Sogeyu suddenly bowed. "This conversation does not concern me or my Singers. We are even less fit for heavy labor than Kikiti's Sacrifices. If you will excuse me, Your Serene Highness, I will return to my order now."

Pratiki nodded. Sogeyu turned and headed back to the ring of her kneeling, dark-robed underlings, but not before giving Kikiti a swift look that Viyeki could not entirely read, though he thought he saw a shadow of annoyance on her face.

Whatever Pratiki decides, Viyeki thought, *if I have created a little disagreement between my enemies then I have accomplished at least one useful thing today.*

"Ride with me a little way while I think," the prince-templar told Viyeki. "General, the queen and the Hamakha are pleased with you. Your Sacrifices have made the Mother of All proud."

"Thank you, Your Highness," said Kikiti.

Pratiki guided his horse toward the far wall and reined up a few dozen paces away from the vast carcass of the borer. It did not smell like any ordinary dead thing but had a tang all its own, a stiflingly acrid, almost metallic scent.

The prince-templar stared at the great, mud-colored monstrosity. "There is nothing so big that something else cannot kill it," he said.

Viyeki sensed that no reply was necessary. He waited through the long silence that followed as the prince-templar considered the dead creature.

"Do not create discord between the orders, High Magister," Pratiki said at last. "That will not please me, and it will certainly not please the queen."

"I apologize if I seemed to be doing so, Highness. It was not my intention."

"Of that I am not so sure. And in other circumstances I would not entirely blame you—the Sacrifices and the Singers have long held themselves superior to other orders, and that is sometimes hard to live with. But although I do not agree with your methods, I agree with your conclusion—there is nothing to be gained by killing the rest of the slaves when we need workers. I will tell Kikiti to round up those who live. But I put the responsibility on you, High Magister. You want them, you must feed them and keep them alive and docile. Do you understand?"

"Of course, Highness." But he also understood that he had crossed a line, not just with Pratiki and Kikiti, but in his own heart as well. It would be a long time until he would be able to see all that would come from today's actions. "I hear the queen in your voice."

"Soon enough you will hear the queen's own voice, from the Mother of All herself." Pratiki's face had again become as unrevealing as any of the masks worn by the Eldest.

Viyeki felt a sudden fear at the gamble he was undertaking, bringing mortal prisoners to a task that had not just the queen's eye but the queen's full attention—prisoners who might try to thwart her will even at the expense of their own lives. And he had placed himself in this danger simply because he had felt a moment of pity for the wretched, suffering creatures. For mortal men, the animals who wanted to destroy his people.

"Your mind and attention seem to be wandering, Viyeki Seyt-Enduya," the prince-templar said sternly. "But I urge you to hear me now. If Utuk'ku is not pleased with what you do here, then may the Garden protect you—because nothing else will."

"Why must I come?" Jarnulf did not feel comfortable refusing, but the last thing he wanted was to be marched across the Hikeda'ya campsite by Saomeji.

"Because all during our trip into the eastern mountains you wondered why such honors had been given to me," said the Singer, his unusual golden eyes alight with what looked like fierce joy. "Why one as young as I had been chosen to do the queen's great work. Now you will see and understand."

"You mistake my thoughts," was all he said, but he might as well have been talking to the wind that whistled along the ridgetop.

Saomeji went on as though Jarnulf had not spoken. "Yes, now you will see, mortal. I brought Makho back with us in the hope that my master could do something great with his ruined body. And now you will see it!"

More than ever, Jarnulf wished he could be rid of the Norns and their strange ambitions and treacherous infighting once and for all. *But I have been given a holy task by the Lord my God,* he reminded himself. *Not only will I likely not live past its completion, but it will almost certainly be these Hikeda'ya who take my life when I succeed.* He had done his best to resign himself to that, to put everything in God's hands.

"And soon the queen will be here," said Saomeji. "Utuk'ku herself, praise her name, will see what I have done. She will see what I have helped make for her!"

It was the middle of the night and the camp was largely quiet. The Hikeda'ya seldom slept, but when there was nothing to do—and the Hikeda'ya here had no other task, as far as Jarnulf knew, but to wait for their monarch—they fell into silence and stillness. Only a few sentries watched, expressionless as birds, as Saomeji led him toward the edge of camp.

Akhenabi, the Lord of Song, stood by as three of his hooded underlings excavated the pit where they had buried Makho. Jarnulf had stayed away from the spot during the three days since they had consigned the chieftain's shrouded body to the ground, and had thought about it as little as possible, but it appeared he would be able to avoid their ghastly handiwork no longer.

"Do not stand any closer," Saomeji whispered, though the warning was hardly necessary; as the Singers dug down into the soil, a stench arose that made Jarnulf want to turn and retch. The distinct smell of putrefaction was combined with other, less expected scents—the harsh, salty odor of natron as well as rose petals, beeswax, and the bitter stink of urine.

After a short while they uncovered the shrouded body, now stained with dirt and mold, and heaved it up onto the edge of the pit. Akhenabi, who had watched without speaking, gestured. One of his Singers unwrapped Makho's head.

Jarnulf's first thought when he saw the chieftain's face was that something had gone terribly wrong. Instead of being mended, or at least gifted with some magical improvement of health, the Hikeda'ya chieftain now looked thoroughly dead. His mouth was still sewed shut, and his skin had turned a horrible, hard, wrinkled gray, like the hide of a hairless boar or even a southern cockindrill.

Then Makho's lone eye suddenly opened. It was no longer Hikeda'ya-dark, but bright amber, like a bird's eye. Jarnulf gasped in surprise and took a step backward.

"Did I not tell you?" Even whispering, Saomeji sounded as pleased as a child on St. Tunath's Day.

"Stand him on his feet," Akhenabi ordered. "Cut the threads that seal his mouth."

Makho was dragged upright; he swayed in place like a tree in a gale, held up by two of the Singers. The other Singer reached forward with a knife and grabbed Makho's leathery gray cheek to hold his head steady, then split the threads so that the chieftain's mouth sagged open and crushed herbs dribbled out onto his chin. His orange eye ranged wildly from side to side, as though newly-awakened Makho was eager to find out where he was and who surrounded him, but it never fixed on anything for more than a heartbeat.

"He will not be able to speak for some time," said Akhenabi. "But he can already understand my words, and soon all his strength will return, and more—a might greater than he ever had before. He will bring horror and destruction to our queen's enemies."

"My master is truly great!" cried Saomeji, clapping his hands in pleasure.

Jarnulf turned and stumbled away, unable to bear the sight of Makho's gleaming, deranged stare a moment longer.

Help me to destroy these abominations, my blessed Lord, he prayed, over and over, fighting against the need to be sick. *Let me be your strong right arm. Let me be your cleansing fire.*

When she was taken back to the dark cell, Tzoja sat on the floor and did her best not to weep, but she could not stop herself trembling. Her hands were shaking so badly she had to intertwine her fingers and hold them on her lap. She knew she should pray, knew she should thank all the gods for sparing her eyes, the Aedon and the Grass Thunderer and all of them, but all she wanted to do was stop shaking.

It had been such a near thing. After all the years of living in half-light, of being buried beneath stone like a dead person and only seeing the sun a few times a year, the idea of losing her sight had been too terrible to contemplate. When she heard the dreadful words her bowels had turned to water inside her, and it had been all she could do not to fall down onto the floor before the High

Anchoress and weep for mercy. But in the twenty years that she had been a prisoner in Nakkiga she had learned many things, and one of them was that tears meant less than nothing to the Hikeda'ya. They thought of them as a mortal oddity, like the noises that animals make. Even Viyeki, the kindest of his race she had ever met, had never been moved by weeping, although he had at least tried not to be angry with her when she succumbed. Tzoja had known even as fear gripped her and shook her that the High Anchoress would feel no pity for a distraught slave. So she had used her wits instead.

"But please, High Anchoress," she had said, doing her best to keep her voice steady and respectful, though it felt mad to do so. "Without sight, I will be useless to the Mother of All."

The gray-masked figure stared at her. "Why do you say that, mortal?"

"Because the arts I was taught require gathering herbs and other plants. They must be found before they are prepared. If I am blind I cannot do that."

"There will be Sacrifices and servants who could do it for you."

She tried to make her voice strong, certain, though she felt as if she could not get enough breath into her chest to keep her heart beating. "I cannot teach someone in the time of a turning moon to recognize things it took me years to learn myself. Would you truly risk the queen's health on how well a soldier had learned to recognize the difference between agrimony and meadowsweet? When they are not flowering, they look much alike." Her mind was full of distracting thoughts that flapped and shrieked like birds trying to escape a burning grove, but she did her best to hold down the terror and remember what Valada Roskva had taught her. "Wood agrimony is good for heaviness of the chest and breath. Meadowsweet is not—it can even make breathing more difficult." She struggled with her words, which kept threatening to escape her control, to turn desperate. "Please, High Anchoress, let me keep my eyes so that I can serve the queen to the best of my training."

The stony mask had surveyed her for a moment longer, then the eyes of the Anchoress closed. At first Tzoja thought that perhaps the queen's priestess was merely summoning the energy to have her dragged away by the guards still waiting just inside the door. At last, Tzoja had realized that the Anchoress must be in silent conversation with the queen herself.

The dark eyes had opened again, though the rest of the Anchoress remained as motionless as a statue. "It will be allowed," she pronounced. "But you will be blindfolded and hooded whenever you attend the queen. If you flout this rule you will receive harsh punishment. And if the Mother of the People is displeased in any way by your ministrations, you will be sent to the Cold Slow Halls. By Her hand and Her words this decision is made, and as High Anchoress I witness it."

Tzoja had finally managed to quiet her nerves in the lightless cell. She smoothed herself a place to lie down on what felt like a thin mattress stuffed with straw, damp but not disgusting.

"It's very frightening at first," said a small voice.

Tzoja had thought herself alone, and her heart leapt in fear so suddenly that she thought she could feel it bang against her breastbone.

"Don't be afraid." The voice was female, and though it spoke the Hikeda'ya tongue perfectly, there was something unusual about it. "I am like you— mortal. That is why they put you in my chamber."

"Your chamber?" Tzoja could still feel her pulse beating like a drum. "I did not know. I did not mean to intrude . . ."

"Do not apologize. It is good to have company. May I come nearer? I mean you no harm."

Tzoja heard movement, the sound of soft footfalls, then a moment later someone sat down on the mattress beside her. "My name is Vordis. Who are you?"

"Tzoja."

"That is a Hikeda'ya name, but you are not of their kind."

"My . . . my master gave me that name. Are you truly another mortal? Like me?"

Vordis laughed. She sounded young. Tzoja had not expected to hear the sound of merriment ever again and it cheered her. The stranger took Tzoja's hand in her cool fingers and squeezed it gently before letting go. "May I touch your face?" she asked.

It surprised Tzoja a little, but she could smell the other woman now, ordinary scents of skin and clean hair, a sour tang of clothing that needed to be washed. "If you wish."

"I want to see you." Tzoja felt small hands touch her cheeks. The fingers spread gently across her cheekbones, light as a breeze, and then traced her brows, the arch of her forehead, her nose, her mouth.

"You are pretty," the one called Vordis said, then took Tzoja's hand again. "You may use your hands to see me, too."

Tzoja did, but could make out little more from her exploration than that Vordis was not an old woman—her skin was firm, her jaw taut. She might have been Tzoja's age but she was certainly no older. Tzoja could even feel the other woman's eyes beneath the silky thinness of her eyelids, but no scars, no sign of injury. Why had she not been blinded by the Anchoresses? "How did you come here?"

Vordis laughed again. "I scarcely remember, it seems so long ago. My mother served in the house of the Yansu Clan. When I was very small, one of the female Hikeda'ya picked me up and carried me back to my mother, angry that I had been wandering. While she carried me, I suddenly knew—I could feel it, with my hands—that she had something growing inside her, something ugly and hurtful. I told my mother, who told her mistress. I was right, though nothing could be done, and the one with the bad thing inside her died a few months later. The Hikeda'ya soon discovered that I could feel such things in a way others could not."

"You are a healer."

"No, I cannot heal anything," said Vordis sadly. "I can feel when something is wrong, and often where and how badly. While I was still a child I was brought here to the palace and became one of the queen's Anchoresses. You are only the second mortal that has come to these halls. I am glad. It is . . . sometimes it is lonely."

"But your eyes . . . you still have your eyes." The thought of being blinded, so recently and narrowly avoided, still terrified her.

This time the woman's laugh was quieter. "Yes. That is because my eyes were never of any use. I was born unable to see. Perhaps that is why I can feel things others cannot."

"And do you really wait on the queen herself?"

"Of course. There is no more important task in all of Nakkiga. You should feel honored." But something in her voice, some tiny, discordant note, made Tzoja wonder.

"And what do you do? What will I do here? Is the queen in good health?"

"Oh, yes," said Vordis. "The queen is strong. The queen is very well." But even as she said it, the woman squeezed Tzoja's hand—squeezed it hard. The message was unmistakable: *What I said is not true.*

"That is good," Tzoja said, trying to hide her surprise. "I am pleased to hear that. We owe our lives to her, and it will make my work easier." For a long moment she sat thinking. "And is this place, this cell—are we alone here?"

"The other Anchoresses have their own chambers, their own places. But we are mortals—it is strange to say 'we'!" For a moment the other woman seemed genuinely caught up in the novelty of it. "We are kept to ourselves."

"Does anyone listen to what we say? Can we speak freely here?"

"Oh, of course," said Vordis lightly, but again her hand gripped Tzoja's and squeezed it tight. "Why would anyone bother to listen to two mortal women?"

It was nearly impossible to determine the passage of time in the lightless place where they were kept, but the guards had come in four times to bring them meals and a clean chamber pot, and she and Vordis had slept twice, so Tzoja guessed that two days had passed since she had first been brought to the cell. During that time she and Vordis continued to talk quietly to each other, taking care not to say anything that might alarm anyone listening. Vordis was full of wistful questions about life in Nakkiga, and Tzoja realized that what had been an endless, dull confinement to her must seem like a dream of freedom and excitement to the blind woman. Tzoja was selective with the history she shared, going no further back than her time in Rimmersgard with the Astalines, since it was clear that the Hikeda'ya must already know about that, but she left out any mention of her childhood in Kwanitupul with her father and mother and brother, or the terrible years in her grandfather's camp in the High Thrithings.

In turn, Vordis told her careful stories of her own experiences among the Anchoresses, though living separately from the Hikeda'ya meant she could mostly only talk about what it was like when they were all with the queen. The unspoken knowledge that open speech was not safe meant that Tzoja learned little beyond the routine that would be expected of her.

Tzoja had been prepared to die, or at least she thought she had. Now she had to prepare herself to live the rest of her life in a lightless room, a grim prospect even with a sympathetic cellmate. Thus, when the guards came a fifth time and stood watching them as they ate their meager meal, Tzoja felt a sense of excitement that almost but not quite overcame her apprehension. When the guards silently signaled the two of them to follow, and Vordis took her hand, her legs felt as shaky as a fawn's.

They were led through passages lit only by an occasional torch, but even that dim light seemed glaring to Tzoja after so long with no light at all. The corridors were not crude tunnels but seemed to be part of the huge palace, the floors flat and level, the walls and ceiling finished in stone that had been smoothed like fine silk.

The guards brought them to a door where more guards waited, then ushered them through it and back into complete darkness. Vordis' grip tightened on Tzoja's hand. "Let me lead you," she said. "There are stairs before us—steep stairs."

They made their way down until Tzoja could hear the sound of splashing water and the dull murmur of voices. Damp, warm air rose to meet her, along with the smell of wet stone and other, more complicated fragrances. At the bottom a single *ni'yo* sphere was set on a tripod in a niche, glowing like the first star of evening, and Tzoja could see naked female bodies.

"We bathe here before we wait on the Mother of All," Vordis whispered. "Mortals and immortals alike. All must be pure for the queen."

As she adjusted to the new brightness, Tzoja saw with a thrill of horror that the other Anchoresses had only dark holes where their eyes should be. The immortals were all agelessly beautiful and their faces were calm—some of them talked or even sang in soft, meditative voices—but below the brows of each one were empty sockets, like a room full of living skulls.

Tzoja turned toward Vordis, wondering what damage she might see there, but her companion was not much different than she had guessed, still apparently of childbearing age, though her figure was small and girlish, and with a round face that most would consider pretty. Vordis's eyes did not fix on anything, but compared to the other Anchoresses she looked reassuringly ordinary.

"We bathe in the three pools, one after another," Vordis said. "First take off your clothes."

Almost before Tzoja had finished peeling off her garments, which she had been wearing for more days now than she could count, another female Hikeda'ya, dressed in the dark garb of a palace menial, swept them away. She never saw them again. Then Vordis led her through bathing herself, first in water so hot it made her forehead perspire, then in warm water scented with oils and flower petals, and last in a cold pool. When she and Vordis stood on the other side, shivering a little and with skin needled by chill, another servant handed them loose white gowns.

"Now we go out. Then there will be prayers," Vordis whispered.

A door on the other side of the stone chamber opened without a sound; the Anchoresses, all now dressed in flowing white, walked through it. A Hikeda'ya priestess of some kind waited on the other side, and as she sang the words of some ancient ritual, more servants appeared and gave to each of the Anchoresses a mask, the same eyeless disguises Tzoja had seen before. A servant came to her and with impatient gestures indicated that she should put her hands at her side. When she did, the hard-faced Hikeda'ya tied a cloth around her face, dropping her into darkness again, then pulled some kind of hood over her head and tied one of the heavy masks onto her face.

"Today you will only be in the queen's presence," Vordis whispered. "Do not speak, no matter what you feel or hear. I will explain it all to you when we are home again."

Home. The word seemed to rattle like a dropped spoon, falling from her ears and into her breast. She was more grateful than she could say for Vordis, but the idea that a lightless box of stone would be her home now gave her a pang so painful she could not have spoken if she wanted to.

The rest of the hour was an empty black blur. They were led into a farther chamber, then she heard the other Anchoresses' rustling gowns as they dropped to their knees; Vordis showed her with soft pressure on her arm that she too should kneel. The queen was waiting for them there. Tzoja could not doubt it—she could feel Utuk'ku's presence like an open window on a cold day, a chill that went right through her. She thought of the silver mask and the ageless mystery that must lie beneath it—the oldest living thing in the entire world, an unknowable dark presence that could have her killed with a gesture—and again found it difficult to breathe. Her skin prickled and shifted as if it sought to escape on its own. Perhaps sensing some of this, Vordis squeezed her arm, but then moved away, leaving Tzoja standing by herself in hooded blackness.

A voice floated up from the far side of the room. Someone was singing—someone male. It was a song Tzoja had never heard, in Hikeda'ya words she could not understand except intermittently. It was strange that the sound, after such long silence, did not seem to disturb any of the other Anchoresses; they continued about their invisible business as Tzoja stood, trying not to topple over, until Vordis returned and gave her hand a reassuring squeeze. The singer's voice went on, echoing in the stony chamber, the melody as mournful as a nightingale's.

If the indifference the queen and her Anchoresses showed to the presence of a singer was surprising, Tzoja was even more astonished to discover that the singer was not particularly good, at least not by the standards she had learned in the years she had been captive in Nakkiga. His voice was young and sweet, but he seemed to make mistakes that even she could recognize—a shortness of breath here, a slurring of a sound there, and once or twice even an unsteadily held note. She did not know very much about Hikeda'ya music but she could not believe that the all-powerful queen could not command better entertainment. She had heard better pitch and phrasing from entertainers at the festival celebrations which Viyeki's wife Lady Khimabu had mounted.

At last there came a long silence, and as all the Anchoresses stood motionless, Tzoja could feel the queen's presence diminish and disappear, as though the window to the harsh winter had been closed. The women were led back to the stone chamber and bathed themselves again, this time in reverse order from cold to hot. Tzoja had questions she wanted to ask, but every time she started to speak, Vordis squeezed her hand, silencing her.

When they were at last back in their cell, surrounded by darkness if not by privacy, Tzoja tried to find innocuous words to ask about what had most puzzled her.

"The singer," she said. "He did not seem as . . . as well trained as I would have expected."

"He is very well trained." The other woman's voice held something somber.

"Truly? Perhaps I am more ignorant of the Hikeda'ya than I thought—"

"What he sang was Drukhi's favorite song."

It took a moment for her to understand. "Drukhi, the queen's son? The one that was killed by mortals so long ago?"

"The singer has learned it precisely the way Drukhi sang it to his mother when he was young," Vordis explained carefully. "He learned it from the singer before him, who learned it in turn from the singer who came before, and so on. This one is the third Drukhi-singer since I have been here, but I am told that there have been many, many more over the years. Dozens. Each one learns every note and word and intonation perfectly, so that they can sing to the queen just as her son once did."

Tzoja was so troubled by this that she could summon no other questions. Vordis at last curled up beside her. After a while her breathing became regular, but Tzoja lay awake for a long time, still hearing the haunting, imperfect song even as she finally drifted down into sleep.

36

Storm Winds

Miriamele had never much cared for the Hall of the Dominiate. It had been erected during the First Imperium, and like most public buildings of that time it had been meant not to comfort those who visited it, or to inspire civic pride, but to instill a feeling of awe at the majesty and power of Nabban. As she waited for the ceremony to begin she felt a pang of longing for the Great Hall of the Hayholt, a place that despite its size felt much more homelike, the banners hanging from its roof almost low enough to touch, the walls hung with pictures of people, real people, with faces that told their stories.

The roof of the Dominiate was almost impossibly high, rising to a peak some thirty or forty cubits above the marble floors, and its ceilings were covered with religious paintings too distant and detailed to make out, as though to remind the common people—who almost never saw the inside of the hall in any case— that they could not hope to enter into or even understand the lofty considerations of the mighty.

Risers of splendid Harcha marble lined the hall's two long sides, providing more than enough room for the ruling Fifty Families of Nabban to gather and consider the matters of the day, as they had been doing here for centuries. Miri sat at one end of the hall in the great chair once reserved for the Imperator himself, but which for years had served as the seat for any guest of sufficient importance to warrant it, like Duke Saluceris when he came to speak to (or even occasionally to be lectured by) the *Patrisi*—"the Fathers"—the heads of Nabban's most powerful family houses.

The side of the great hall to Miriamele's right belonged to the supporters of Duke Saluceris, the other side to the coalition led by Dallo Ingadaris, with those who had not chosen one or the other mostly ranged around the center. It was quite obvious to Miri that the number of the holdouts who supported neither Kingfisher nor Stormbird had become shrinkingly small—most of the Dominiate had chosen one party or the other.

On a table before her lay the ceremonial scroll of the new Octander Covenant, the culmination of weeks of labor by clerics and advocates from all the major houses, transcribed into beautifully formed letters by the finest scribes in Nabban. At the bottom of the document was the seal and signature of His

Sacredness, Lector Vidian, who—after a great deal of persuasive effort by the queen—had finally agreed to put his name to the historic pact, beginning what Miriamele hoped would be at least a generation of peace between the leading houses of the Dominiate, and especially between the Benidrivines and the Ingadarines. Although Vidian had declined an invitation to be present, he had sent Escritor Auxis to give the invocation and to witness the signing in his stead.

But Auxis looked unhappy, and even Dallo Ingadaris, waiting in one of the two seats of honor at Miri's left hand, seemed to have lost some of his usual self-satisfaction. The bell had rung the noon hour and all around the hall the *Patrisi* shuffled their feet and leaned close to each other to whisper.

"Surely, Your Majesty, you cannot be happy with such discourtesy," Count Dallo said loudly. "We are all assembled. The Covenant awaits us. But where is the duke?"

"I do not know, my lord," she said. "And, yes, I am unhappy about his absence, but I am concerned as well. Also, I cannot help noticing that your ally, the duke's brother, is not here either."

Dallo's nonchalant look was not convincing. "That is true, but it is hardly to the point, Majesty. Drusis does not sign the Covenant on behalf of House Ingadaris—I do, and I am here. But Duke Saluceris appears to consider the ceremony and the presence of the whole of the Dominiate as well as Escritor Auxis—and of course your royal self—not worth his time."

Miri gave him a flat look. "Now you split hairs, Count Dallo. No, Drusis is not the Patris of House Ingadaris, but it is the rivalry between him and his brother Saluceris that is the reason we drew up the covenant. It is the role of Drusis as your supporter—and you as his—against his brother and his blood that has caused so much of the unhappiness that makes Nabban a dangerous place today."

Dallo waggled his chubby fingers. "If you say so, Majesty." As always, he wore rings on all but the thumb, and on some of his fingers he wore two or even three. She wondered sometimes how he wiped his arse without losing one of the expensive baubles up his own backside.

Has some servant do it for him, most likely, she thought.

"You smile, my queen," Dallo said. "Have you discovered something to enjoy in the situation? I confess I cannot. Perhaps you could share this amusing idea with your servant?"

"Just a passing thought." She saw that Auxis had risen from his seat and was approaching. In his heavy escritorial finery, golden robes stiffly swinging, he looked like a royal treasure ship being eased down the slipway for launching.

"I beg Your Majesty's pardon," the escritor said quietly. All over the hall the members of the Dominiate watched the conversation, not so much in hope that something would change—everyone present could see that the duke was not present—but in the anxious boredom of those who had been waiting for a long time without being able to leave and were desperate for any distraction. "I have come to give the invocation, as you know. Have you heard any word of the duke? Is he coming?"

"Unless the news was brought to me by a tiny fly, Escritor Auxis, I think you would have seen me receive it, since I have been sitting in this same seat in full view since well before the noon bell rang."

Auxis colored a little and Miri was irritated with herself. There was no need to make enemies—she had enough of those in Nabban already. "I ask your forgiveness for a foolish question, Majesty," he said.

"No, rather I should ask yours, Escritor, for my bad temper. Like all the rest of us, I am concerned and disturbed by the duke's absence." She turned to look out at the Kingfisher side of the hall until she spotted Idexes Claves, the lord chancellor. "Patris Claves," she said, "you saw the duke this morning, did you not? Do you know any reason he is not here?"

Idexes, a lean man who seldom smiled, shook his head. "I have dispatched guards to the Sancellan Mahistrevis. I imagine it is some small matter. I know from our talk that he meant to be here, Your Majesty."

"Then why isn't he?" shouted one of the other *Patrisi*, a plump elder of the Larexean House, from the midst of the Stormbird side of the hall. "And where is Earl Drusis? Has he been dragged to one of the duke's dungeons while our attention was here? Is he even now being tortured?"

"Shut your mouth, Flavis," said Idexes, "or I will come over there and shut it for you, you traitorous pig. We all know perfectly well who arranged that charade at the wedding, and you were in the middle of it all!"

More shouting erupted from both sides, until Miriamele had to order the guards ranged along the back wall to step forward and stamp the butts of their long spears against the floor, which only diminished the uproar but did not silence it. She signaled again and the soldiers banged their spears against their shields until the sheer din overwhelmed everything else. Miri saw that Sir Jurgen had gathered her own Erkynguard around him, prepared to charge in and protect her, and that even Count Froye, veteran of Nabbanai political squabbling, had moved closer to her chair in fear of a general riot.

"Is this the great legacy of the imperators?" she demanded of the now quiet hall. "Of the Dominiate, which once ruled the world? Nothing has even *happened*, for the love of all the saints. All this is because of what has *not* happened. No, the duke is not here, and we do not know the reason why. And his brother Drusis is absent too. But that is all we know, and it may well come to nothing in the end. In fact, it almost certainly will. And yet you act like children when their parents are gone. I am ashamed of my Nabbanai blood today, and I never thought I would say that."

"Your Majesty," said Rillian Albias, rising like one of the orators of old, his face grave. "May I say something?"

"No." Miriamele stood, and Rillian stared at her in wonderment for a moment, then looked to his colleagues, who gazed back helplessly. At last he lowered himself into his seat once more. "I mean no insult, Patris Albias, to you or any of the others, but the time for speeches is past. It is time to swear allegiance not to one family or another, not to this house or that, but to Nabban as a whole, under the High Ward. If we cannot do it without Duke Saluceris, there is no point in all of you men of affairs sitting here through the long afternoon. We are ready, but we lack our principals. As the ruling power here, in the name of my husband, myself, and the High Throne to which you are all sworn, I am ending this day's business now. We will find the duke and his brother, and we will meet here tomorrow, at noon, to finish what we have begun. I will hear of nothing else. This is too important for argument."

A collective groan arose from the gathered nobles. Many of them were only in the capital for the day and had other plans before they returned to their houses in the provinces, but if they were willing to show defiance toward the Nabbanai opposition and even offer violence, none were so bold as to contest the will of the queen. Miri gestured to Froye and Sir Jurgen, then marched her small company out of the Hall of the Dominiate. The *Patrisi* watched, some— she thought—in outright displeasure, others with a kind of admiration she thought was more in response to her bold show of power than what she had chosen to do with it.

"You have not made anyone happy here," said Froye quietly as they walked out between the ranks of Dominiate guards. "I apologize for saying so, Your Majesty, but you have always told me you wanted me to speak what is true, not what is convenient."

"To be honest, Count," she said through clenched teeth, "I am no longer much interested in making anyone in this poisonous, backbiting city happy. I am concerned only to let them know that the High Throne will not put up with their foolish squabbling, this constant endangering of the peace my grandfather brought them."

Froye made a strange face. "You share their blood, Majesty. You of all people should know that what the Nabbanai most want is not peace, but their neighbors' riches. It has always been that way."

"Then it is my duty to change that," she said, but even as she spoke she felt the hollowness of her words. "At the moment, though, all I want to know is where in God's holy name Duke Saluceris has gone."

"And his brother," added Froye.

"I care less about that," she said. "As far as I'm concerned, Drusis and Dallo can both go to the Devil, and I will gladly pay their passage myself."

Brother Etan watched as the peak of Sta Mirore grew taller and taller, filling the sky. The mountain dominated Perdruin like a roast boar on a serving tray, the island's busy harbor located in a pocket bay where an apple would be wedged into the boar's open jaws. He was glad to be out of Nabban, but the sight of another strange country coming into view from a boat filled him with melancholy.

Lord Tiamak had said that it was good for a man to see the world, and Etan had seen a great deal of it on this trip, from the watery, steaming swamps of the Wran to the rolling, desolate dunes of the southern deserts. He had eaten things he had never imagined that people woould even put in their mouths, including crispy fried locusts on the wooden walkways of Kwanitupul, as well as the face of a goat presented to him with great reverence by a trader from the edge of the Nascadu barrens when Etan traveled on his scow. He had resisted eating the goat's eyes, though the trader had not understood how he could turn down this greatest delicacy, but he had explained that his religious calling prevented it (though he would have been hard-pressed to find anywhere in the Book of Aedon where goats' eyes were even mentioned). He had not wanted to insult the man, who had been otherwise a very kind and generous host, but his new-found worldliness simply would not stretch quite that far.

The latest passage Madi had arranged for him was not as hospitable, a small coastal trader whose captain had been as anxious to get out of Nabban as Etan had been, and had been quite willing to take the monk's silver to make up for the profits he had been unable to secure in the city. The great markets had been closed by order of the Sancellan Mahistrevis after fights between the ruling factions had in some cases turned to all-out battles, with trading pavilions set on fire and dying men left bleeding on the cobbles. The streets were no safer than the markets, full of roving gangs who used the excuse of public strife to create mischief of their own, robbing travelers and sometimes killing them for what seemed no more than sport. After discovering what he could about Prince Josua's days with the Usirean Brothers, Etan had spent only a few more nights at the run-down inn near the harbor before deciding it would be better to move on. Queen Miriamele would be safe up on the Mahistrevine Hill with her guards and the duke's army, but a humble monk had no such protection, even if he was a royal envoy of sorts.

But in the midst of all this chaos, in places that made Etan fear for his life hourly, Madi and his two young children always seemed as happy as pigs in a world made entirely of mud and manure. As Etan's funds had grown short—and as he had also learned to immediately halve any sum Madi requested of him before beginning to bargain with his servant and guide—young Parlippa and Plekto had taken it upon themselves to swell the family coffers with various thefts and cheats of their own, from stealing purses to pretending to be crippled beggars. After the pair of small villains had received charity from, then robbed a man of local importance in the town of Rasina, Etan and their father had been seized by local watchmen and almost hung as criminals. It had taken a large amount of Etan's remaining coins to buy off the local officials. In truth, the family had left a trail of dubious behavior all along the route of Brother Etan's voyage, but their conduct in Nabban had been nothing short of scandalous.

One day Etan had even returned to their inn to find the children hiding some-one's horse in his room, which was on the highest of three floors. He still had no idea how they had managed to sneak it past the innkeeper, but Plip and Plek, as their father fondly called them, not only wouldn't tell Etan where it had come from, they pretended to have no idea how the horse had wound up in the small rented room.

Thus, though he understood much better now what Lord Tiamak had meant about a man growing by seeing more of the world, the main emotion Etan felt as he watched Perdruin's great central mountain slide into view was that of homesickness.

Exhaustion was a close second.

Even after all these years Etan could still see many marks of the fire that had destroyed the neighborhood where the Scrollbearer Lady Faiera once lived, part of a crowded dockside *settro* the locals called the Cauldron. Most of the houses had been rebuilt long ago, but the church that had once been the tallest thing in the area was only tumbled stones half buried by earth that still made the rough outline of a Holy Tree. All that still stood was the steeple wall that had been its entrance, half-fallen and showing signs of the burning even after de-cades of rain and wind.

"I was the sacristan here," said someone behind him in excellent Westerling. "We passed buckets up the hill from the harbor, but we could do nothing to stop the flames."

Etan turned. The man who stood there was bent and old, but his eyes were unfilmed and his expression suggested he still had his wits; Etan felt a moment of quickening hope. He had spoken to many of the nearby residents, but no-body recognized Faiera's name, let alone anything about a visit from the former Prince Josua. "You lived here?"

"What kind of a sacristan would I be if I didn't? In those days we lived and died serving a single church." He shook his head and pulled meditatively at the end of his substantial nose. "Not like today, where they wander like beggars, trying to find the best posting, always greedy for more."

Etan nodded, not so much in agreement as to keep him talking. "What was it like here before the fire?"

The erstwhile servant of the church looked him up and down, clearly taking note of his monkish robes, worn and dirty now after all his travels. "Like most places, I expect. Full of sinners and fools. If not for Mother Church, the Lord would have burned all the world by now like He burned these houses. Like He burned our church." He did not sound as if he had entirely forgiven God.

"Do you remember a woman who used to live here? She was named Faiera—Lady Faiera."

The man actually started and took a step back. "The witch?" He made the Sign of the Tree on his breast, and for a moment looked as though he might actually flee.

"Is that what people called her?"

"What else should they call her?" Curiosity seemed to be fighting with disquiet, and it resulted in the old man swaying in place like a windblown sapling. "A great house full of pagan books, visitors coming from strange places at all hours—even on holy days when they should have been on their knees at prayer!" He made the Sign of the Tree again. "You are a man of God, are you not, sir? One of the traveling orders, doing the Lord's good work—or are you one of those other kind, the ones who wear the cowl but are no better than they should be? Why would you want to ask about such a woman, or even know of her?"

"Tell me your name, sir, for the love of Usires and His Sacred Father, and I will tell you mine and answer your questions."

The old man squinted, clearly torn. "Bardo. Bardo of St. Cusimo's, they called me then," he said at last. "Many still do, though the church has been a ruin for long, long years."

"May God grant you a long, healthy life, good Bardo. I am Brother Etan, and I will tell you a secret." He remembered something Tiamak had said once about catching fish, an occupation that seemed to have taken up much of the Wrannaman's childhood and youth. *"When it nibbles on the bait, that is the time you must be most still,"* he had told Etan. *"That is the time when any too-sudden movement can send it speeding away, never to return to your hook."*

Etan carefully took the letter from inside his cassock. He had carried it so long and so far that it didn't look like a scroll, but more like a Thrithings-man's meat cured between saddle and horse. He had to unroll it slowly so it would not tear—the parchment had been flattened until he could barely pry it open. Finished, he held it under the man's nose. "Can you read that?"

"I . . . my eyes are not good. I was never much for reading anyway," Bardo added a little defiantly.

"But you see the seal, do you not? That is the royal seal of the High Ward in Erkynland. The king and queen themselves sent me to find this Faiera if she lived and ask her questions. I assure you my purposes are only godly."

The old man scowled as he leaned close to the parchment, but it seemed more a reflex than anything else. He looked up. "And what would you know, Brother Etan?" he said at last. "What can old Bardo tell you? Yes, I knew the witch back in those days—or the *lady*, if you'll have it thus."

Etan sized up the old man's thin wrists, unshaven cheeks, and ragged cloak, worn even on this hot summer day and likely to conceal even more ragged garments beneath. "I tell you, sir, I have been walking all morning and I have a fierce hunger. Is there anywhere nearby where we could have a bite to eat—and perhaps a bowl of ale, too?"

Bardo hesitated.

"Surely you would not deny me a chance to spend a little of the High Throne's money on your comfort?" Etan said.

Bardo licked his lips. "As a matter of fact, Brother, there is a tavern just down the hill where I sometimes take my custom. The owner will likely have a few plump quail on the spit." He rubbed his mouth with the back of his hand. "And the ale—the ale there is not bad, either."

On that long-ago day, Jesa and one of her older brothers had stood before the entrance to a cavern that burrowed into a rocky hill, both rare things in the flat, swampy Wran. She had been small then, and had accompanied Hoto without knowing what he wanted to show her or why he was being so secretive about it. But as they reached the dark hole into the earth, the gray sky hot and wet above the trees, she had become frightened, and Hoto had clutched her arm hard to keep her from running away. The cavern opening looked like a mouth, and it was not hard for her to imagine it opening to swallow her down, like the maw one of the Wran's great crocodiles. She struggled, but he only tightened his grip.

"Don't be stupid," he told her. "I just want to show you something. Now watch." One hand still firmly gripping her arm, he took a chunk of stone that had rolled down from the hill and tossed it into the gaping blackness.

An instant later they were surrounded by shrilling, rustling shadows, a storm of small shapes so thick that for long moments Jesa could see no light at all. Wings slapped at her hair and face and shoulders. She had no idea what was happening, only that the world had turned dark and burst into twittering pieces. She tried to throw herself to the ground but her brother held her up, and it was only long moments later, when the storm cloud of wings had dispersed, that she realized she was still shrieking with terror.

Hoto slapped her on the top of her head and let go of her arm. "Stop screaming! Mother will hear you!"

But she could not stop, so he hit her again. At last, angry and ashamed, he picked her up—her screams had finally turned to whimpers—and carried her back to their house. There was no hiding her terror, and her mother was furious with Hoto, who kept saying over and over, "But I only wanted to show her where the bats live!"

That was what the Sancellan Mahistrevis felt like to her in this dreadful moment, with people running everywhere, shouting that the duke was gone, that someone had taken him or killed him. It was all Jesa could do not to begin screaming again, just as she had on that day so long ago. Only the baby in her arms helped her keep her head, and she clung to little Serasina like a charm, but her heart sped on and on until she was dizzy.

"How could this be?" Duchess Canthia asked yet again. She was weeping, her face wet and red, but she swatted angrily every time one of her ladies tried to wipe away her tears. "Where is my husband? A hundred guards and nobody saw him? What madness is this?"

Jesa crouched in a corner of the chamber and rocked Serasina in her arms. The wet nurse had tried to feed her, but even an infant could feel the wrongness, could hear the cries of alarm and the sound of running feet, and she had refused the breast. Now Jesa clutched the small, silky-soft head against her bosom and crooned wordless tunes and snatches of things that had been sung to her when she was young and frightened.

> *Storm winds blow, blow, blow*
> *But our house is strong, strong, strong*
> *Rain falls down, down, down*
> *But our roof is high, high, high . . .*

Queen Miriamele came and sat beside Canthia. She said little to soothe the duchess, but held her hand. As always, Jesa marveled at the queen's calm strength. Her face gave away almost nothing, only a little annoyance when one of the maids shrieked or burst into tears.

"Enough of that," the queen told one serving girl, a helplessly talkative idiot Jesa often thought would not survive an hour in the Wran, but would immediately wander into a ghant nest or a crocodile's mouth. "The duchess needs your help, child, not your blubbering." She looked to Jesa and the baby before turning back to the girl. "Where is young Blasis?"

The maid's face was as shapeless with fear as a dollop of swamp yam paste. "He is . . . he is with his tutor," she said, struggling for words. "It is his . . . his day for lessons. He hates them, but the duke insists . . ." At the thought of the duke, her mouth writhed as though she would weep again.

"Go and get him," said the queen, making her words hard as the ring of a jeweler's hammer. "Bring the tutor as well. They can continue their lessons here."

The maid performed a shaky courtesy and scurried toward the door.

"You go with her," the queen told another maid, one who at least was not screaming or crying. "Find the duke's heir and bring him back here."

"But what could have happened?" Canthia asked again. One of her ladies brought her a cup of wine. She accepted it without looking and drank it straight down. The queen shook her head when one was offered to her. "Where could Saluceris be?"

"He will be found," said Queen Miriamele. "You will see. But remember, you are the duchess—you are the heart of Nabban. Do you want your husband's enemies to say you fell to pieces at the first sign of trouble?"

"First sign!" Outrage and anger crackled in Canthia's voice, and for a moment Jesa was fearful that the duchess actually might strike the queen. "First sign? There has been nothing but trouble for months! It's Drusis, that cursed, damned traitor, stirring up the people! And that poisonous toad, Count Dallo . . ." Canthia's voice had risen so that every eye in the room turned toward her. She finally realized it and stopped, breathing heavily. "Someone tries to destroy us," she said more quietly. "And now they have taken my husband . . . !" Again tears overspilled her eyes and coursed down her cheeks.

At that moment the door of the retiring room swung open and Countess Alurea, the wife of Count Rillian, burst into the room with several confused guards in her wake who were clearly not sure they had done the right thing in letting her pass. The sight of Alurea's face, almost death-white, her eyes as wide as a startled owl's, sent a cold shock of fear all the way down into Jesa's innards, a clutch so hard and so sudden that she almost lost her grip on the baby.

"Sweet Usires save us!" the countess cried, as unsteady as if she stood on the deck of a foundering ship. "He is dead! They found him dead in the chapel! Oh, by our Lady and the child of her holy womb, they slit his throat! They will kill us all!"

"God save me!" screamed Canthia. "Saluceris!" The duchess rose halfway to her feet, then her face went whiter than Alurea's, and she tumbled to the floor. The queen had clutched at her hand but could not keep her from falling.

"The duchess has swooned," said the queen, and though she kept her voice level, Jesa thought she could see fear even in Miriamele's face. "Someone go and get the hartshorn salts." She turned to the countess, still standing in the doorway like an apparition from a mummer's play. "Stop shouting like a fishwife, Countess. What has happened? Who is dead? Is it the duke?"

For a long instant Alurea stared at her as though the queen spoke some tongue she had never heard before. Then, just as the countess opened her mouth to reply, shouting and the clanking of weapons and armor echoed in the corridor outside. Without thinking, Jesa grabbed Serasina and got down on the floor to hide behind a wooden chest, but before she had even reached it she heard a familiar voice.

"Great Hell, what goes on here? Did nobody even notice I was gone? What sort of fools serve me?"

Duke Saluceris stood in the door, surrounded by more guards. "Canthia!" he cried in alarm when he saw his wife. "What has happened to her? What madness is this?"

"She is well," said the queen. "Only swooned. I am glad to see you well, my lord duke. But now I think we must hear what Countess Alurea has to say."

The noblewoman seemed hardly to notice the duke's presence, though he stood just behind her. She was still pale, and as she spoke her hands trembled. "It is Drusis," she said. "Earl Drusis. He . . . oh, by the Tree, I can hardly say it . . . !"

"Out with it," barked Saluceris.

Startled, the countess turned. "Oh, my lord! Oh, my lord! Your brother . . . he is dead!"

"Dead? That cannot be." Saluceris looked to his soldiers as though one of them might be able to solve this puzzle. "What do you mean, dead?"

"In the chapel at Dallo's townhouse. They found him. He was stabbed and his throat was slit—the whole of the court is full of the news." She lifted her hands in the air as though to protect herself. "The Stormbirds carry his body through the streets, and they have set fire to the docks, too. They are attacking any who wear the Kingfisher badge—many people are dead already. Oh, God is punishing us all, punishing us—!"

"You have told us your news, Countess," said the queen, cutting across her with a voice grim as Fate itself. "Thank you. Now it is time for you to keep silent."

"But how could this be?" asked Saluceris, and Jesa thought he seemed genuinely mystified. "How did it happen?"

"That is not the question we must ask now," said Miriamele, rising from her chair. "Instead, we must decide what we will do to prepare."

"Prepare . . . ?"

Queen Miriamele took the jar of hartshorn salts from the maid who had just returned, then spread her wide skirts and crouched beside the duchess. She held the jar beneath Canthia's nose until the duchess coughed and groaned and her eyes fluttered. "Yes, Duke," the queen said as she helped Canthia sit upright. "Prepare for the storm that is coming. Because otherwise we may all be swept away."

PART THREE

Winter's Bite

Hear the drums!
Hear the drums!
Beast or brother, I must end you
My queen has spoken. Her words are my thoughts
Brother or beast, it is all the same
Without my queen I have no eyes, no arms, no legs
No spirit
What use a blind soldier? What use a limbless ghost?
Hear the drums!
Hear the drums!
I must fight you whether you are beast or brother
Brother or beast
Or else betray myself
And go nameless into the long shadow

—ZINUZO OF QUAVERING REACH

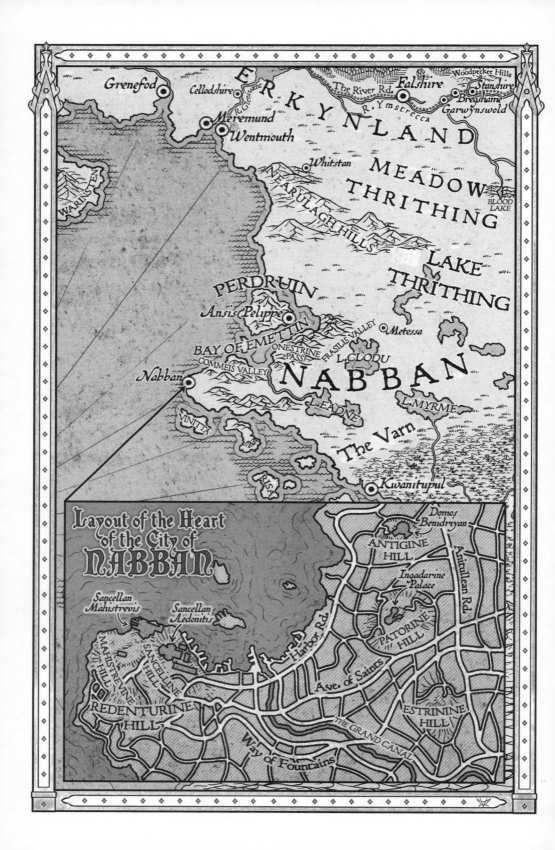

37

Snakes on the Path

Whatever healing arts the shaman Ruzhvang had employed on Levias seemed to be working. The guard sergeant's fever was mostly gone, though he was still fearfully weak, and the jostling as he sat in front of Porto on the donkey—or rather leaned, with Porto holding him as upright as possible—continually opened up his wound to fresh bleeding. But neither blood nor wound had the terrible stench of the first days, which made it easier for Porto to live with phantom memories of his friend Endri, whom he had carried before him in the same way, so many years ago, but had not been able to save.

The donkey stopped again, looking with distrust at a crooked stick that lay before him. "Curse you, you foolish beast!" Porto said. "That is no serpent! It is a piece of wood."

Gildreng looked at the stick and made a noise of disagreement.

Sighing, he propped Levias carefully against the animal's neck and dismounted. His own long legs almost touched the ground when they rode, so it was no trouble to slide himself backward off the donkey's hind end. He picked up the stick and tossed it into the deep undergrowth.

"There. Stick is gone. Are you happy now?"

The donkey showed him teeth and made a noise that suggested happiness was not a likely prospect, but that he would settle for no sticks. Porto awkwardly climbed on again and shoved himself forward until he could support Levias properly. His wounded friend stirred and said, "You put too much salt in the bread, Gran."

"I know," said Porto. "You've told me already."

"I'm hungry, Gran," Levias said. "Hurry."

"We're hurrying."

They had been traveling for three days since the fateful meeting with the shaman. Gildreng might not be an adequate replacement for the beautiful horse that Lord Pasevalles had given Porto, lost back at Blood Lake, but the balking, single-minded creature was certainly better than making the journey on foot, especially with a companion as large as Levias who could not stand, let alone walk.

I will remember you for your kindness, Ruzhvang, Porto promised. *And if there is a way to pay you back someday, I will do so. This I swear on my God and my family honor.*

The land along the Erkynlandish border was hilly, forested here and there with copses of beech and stony oak. It was also scant of game, but Porto had encountered several streams of clean, running water along the way, which every soldier knew were gifts from God to be accepted with gratitude. He gave Levias as much to drink as the man could take, did his best to keep the wound clean as Ruzhvang had directed, and when they stopped, tethered the donkey on whatever grass he could find. He and Levias did not have such easy access to food, since he did not like leaving the sergeant alone to go foraging, but Porto did his best to make the bits of dried meat the shaman had given them last, chewing Levias' small portions until the ailing man could swallow them.

He grows stronger, Porto told himself. *It will not be as it was with Endri. If there is anything I can do to make it so, he will live.*

Still, even seeing Levias move a short distance out of the shadow of Death did not silence all Porto's dark thoughts. He and the rest of the prince's protectors had been ambushed and slaughtered on the High Thrithing, which was not his fault, but he had also singularly failed in the task the troll Binabik had given him, to find Count Eolair and free him from his captors. In fact, if Ruzhvang was right about Eolair being sold to the new Thrithings chieftain, this Unver Shan fellow, then all he and Levias had accomplished by their search was losing both their mounts. *Lord Pasevalles will be angry,* Porto thought. *I would be angry if I were him. All that gold—and that lovely horse—!*

As if to underscore the difference between his old steed and his current one, Gildreng the donkey suddenly stopped in the middle of a dale and would not move. Heavy oaks surrounded them, their twisted branches nearly blotting out the afternoon sky, and at first Porto thought the beast had heard some large animal. He drew his sword and sat for some time, but decided at last it was just more of Gildreng's bad behavior and kicked his heels against the creature's bony sides.

"Go on, you. Go on!" A phrase from his childhood came to him, something his father used to say to crooked nails or recalcitrant tools. "By all the Heavenly saints, did God make you just to spite me?"

The donkey grunted and moved ahead a few more paces, then stopped again. Porto dismounted and tried to pull the donkey into movement, but Gildreng only leaned backward against the tug of the reins, hooves firmly planted in the mulch and head turned away from Porto as though he smelled something foul.

"You will be the death of us," Porto told him angrily, though he had discovered days earlier the donkey could not be shamed.

As the last word left his lips, something whirred past him, so close that Porto raised his hand to slap at it, thinking it a stinging insect. Then he saw the arrow stuck deep in the earth not two paces from where he stood and his heart clambered up toward his throat.

He spun, trying to see where the shaft had come from, but the glade was empty. Then he heard another snap of air and a second arrow bloomed beside the first.

Porto raised his hands, still clutching his sword. *"Kill us not!"* he called loudly in the Thrithings tongue. *"Not enemies."* He could not remember the word for wounded. *"My friend sick! No gold have!"*

Heart thumping, he waited for a long silent moment. When the voice came, it was from above. "By the many, many saints!" it said in Westerling. "Nobody can speak the grassland tongue well because it is a barbarous mumble—but old Porto makes it even worse!"

He peered up into the trees to find its source. "If you are a friend, come down. If you are not, come take what you want but let me tend to my wounded friend in peace. We mean no harm."

"You mean nothing useful at all, I wager," said the voice, then something moved in the high branches of one of the oak trees at the edge of the clearing. A moment later Porto was looking in astonishment at Sir Astrian dangling from the tree's lowest branch by one hand, still holding his bow in the other. He let go and dropped to the ground, landing with the grace of a cat, and bowed. "It is a surprise to see you here, old fellow. Did you have to come so far to avoid our company? As you can see, you have failed in your aim. Olveris! Come down. It is the world's most ancient warrior, and by the look of it, his dead enemy is a fat Thrithings-man whose heart may have burst while they fought."

Olveris appeared on a lower limb of a nearby tree. "I wish I had seen it. Fat against old. A brave combat."

Porto clambered down from the donkey and pulled Levias off its back. Wheezing, he set his wounded friend down on the ground, then stumbled forward to grasp Astrian in an embrace that the younger knight suffered for only a few moments before disengaging. "Now, now, Uncle Porto," he said with a waspish smile. "Too much sentiment, especially from someone as dirty as you are at the moment, is not to my liking. How come you here?"

Olveris had climbed down and now stood examining Levias. "And where did you get this fellow? You did a poor job killing him. He's still breathing."

Startled, overwhelmed, his pulse still racing, Porto was nevertheless plunged back into his old and confusing friendship with these two. And as always, he was never certain when they were jesting with him. "He is my friend and he has been badly wounded by a Thrithings clansman. You know him, I think—Levias, sergeant of the Erkynguard."

"Levias?" said Astrian. "The one who frowns on dicing and the company of women?"

"He is a devout man, that is all," Porto said. "A good man. He needs rest, and to be off this wretched donkey, who bumps and stops like a wagon with a loose wheel. Can one of you carry him on your horse?" A sudden thought occurred to him. "By all that's holy, what are you two doing here in the middle of nowhere?"

"Shooting arrows at old men," said Olveris. "An amusing pastime."

"Somewhere is nowhere only when there are no interesting people," said Astrian. "We are here, so it stands as truth that this cannot be 'nowhere'."

"Nevertheless, I did not expect to see you two again, let alone here."

"We are with Duke Osric, the stubbornest man ever to put on a suit of armor," Astrian explained. "He is camped across the river from the excitable Bison Clan, which is like laying your sleeping blanket on a nest of scorpions." He shook his head. "And Olveris and I are meant to save old Count Eolair and young Prince Morgan from the Thrithings barbarians. But it has taken days for His Grace to set us free to do what we were sent by the king himself to do."

Porto shook his head, his relief and joy at seeing familiar faces suddenly darkened. "Count Eolair you may find—I can tell you something of that. But the Thrithings-men did not take Morgan. He ran for the forest."

Astrian stared at Porto for a long moment, then exchanged a look with Olveris, whose face as always showed no more expression than the blade of a shovel. "That is rather poor news you bring us. Tell us all."

Porto shook his head again. "First we must get Levias to the duke's camp. Please, Astrian, take him on your horse."

The knight's nostrils wrinkled in dismay. "No. Olveris, that is your task. You are large enough. If this great lump falls on me, he will knock me from the saddle."

Olveris did not argue, but the look he gave Astrian spoke for him. Still, he walked from the clearing and appeared a little time later with two fine coursers. Porto looked at them with sadness and envy, keenly aware of what he had lost by his ill luck.

"Don't just stand there," Olveris said as he led one of the horses up beside the donkey. "Help shift him." Together he and Porto managed to wrestle Levias up into the horse's saddle, then Olveris climbed on behind him. "What is the fool babbling about?" Olveris asked. "He keeps talking about wanting more porridge."

Porto caught up the donkey's reins and walked toward Astrian, who had mounted his own horse. When he made it plain he meant to climb into the saddle behind him, Astrian looked at him as though he had started to drip spittle like a mad dog. "No, no," he said. "That will not happen. Look at you, old man, smeared in blood and only the blessed Usires knows what else, and stinking like a herring that has fallen off the table and down behind the bed. No, you have your own mount, Porto. I think it is more than fit for your purposes. If you are truly so worried for your friend, this guardsman who hates joy and thinks gambling the Devil's pastime, I suggest you spur your brave steed smartly to keep up."

And then the two turned and rode out of the clearing, leaving Porto to scramble back onto the donkey. Gildreng, as usual, did not seem to approve of his given role, and followed the two knights on their horses like a man on his way to the gibbet.

Baldhead had brought his evening meal as usual, but Eolair thought the grass-lander seemed restless. The hairless man kept looking over his shoulder at the two bearded guards, who for their part seemed to have decided the count was no great danger, especially with the wagon's heavy door between themselves and the aged, unarmed diplomat. As Eolair took the tray, Baldhead leaned close. His voice was a whisper and the count could barely hear him. "I have something to tell you."

"Tell, then."

Another quick glance over his shoulder, then he continued. "Unver is not to be trusted. Nor especially you cannot trust his helper, Fremur of the Crane Clan. They will betray anyone, as they betrayed their own thanes and then blamed me."

Eolair tried not to lean away from the man, whose strange, shaved features did not make him any more likeable. "What do you mean, do not trust Unver? I am a prisoner. It is not up to me to trust anyone."

"But your king will trust him, and that will be bad for you and all the other stone-dwellers." Baldhead looked behind him again, but the two guards were no longer even facing the wagon. "Tell your king that Unver must be destroyed. He plans to burn your cities. He will lie that he wants peace, but I know he already musters the clans to make war against your folk."

Eolair could not discount what the man said, however much he did not trust him. "And why is that?"

Baldhead looked frustrated. "Because he wants more power! He believes he is the Shan, and the Shan is a leader in war—not against other clans, but to lead the clans against outsiders. That is always the way!"

"I will tell my king and queen what you have said."

The man dropped his voice even lower, until Eolair had to lean his face against the cold iron bars to hear. "When they send for you, when they pay for your freedom, take me with you! I will tell your rulers all I know. I will help them fight Unver." Baldhead stared straight into Eolair's eyes, and the count thought he could see something dark and squirming beneath the man's features—fear? Hatred? But that did not disprove what he was saying.

"It will not be up to me to grant your freedom, but I will do my best to let my masters know what you said, and to have them help you if I can." Eolair had decided that the man was most likely trying to sell information he did not have in order to escape his life of servitude, but wars had been won with uglier bargains, and the count was a practical man.

Baldhead's lip curled. "You do not believe me."

"I believe nothing without proof," Eolair said. "But I do not disbelieve you, either. That you can trust. I will think on what you said. And do not underestimate the wisdom of our High King and High Queen."

The slave made a noise of disgust. "Oh, yes, I understand. You want the information first, then if you still wish you will help me." He let go of the tray. "It will be your mistake to think so. You are wrong. Your cities will burn because you thought me a liar."

Eolair could think of nothing to say, but it did not matter. Baldhead had already descended the wagon's steps and returned to the two guards, who did not even look at him as they led him away.

But as Eolair stared through the barred window of the wagon's door, still holding the tray with his meal of cooling mutton stew, he saw something else that pushed Baldhead's warnings out of his head entirely. A woman wrapped in a heavy cloak was walking across the paddock through the failing twilight. It was her short hair that caught his attention first. He was certain it was Prince Josua's wife Vorzheva, or at least the same woman he had seen before when the bandits had first brought him to the Thanemoot. The light was poor, but she was only thirty or forty paces away.

"Vorzheva!" he shouted. "It is me, Eolair—Josua's friend!"

She looked up at his first cry, but when she saw where the sound came from, she quickly looked down again. Eolair felt sure it was not mere shyness, or even fear of a foreign prisoner, and the way she hurried her steps to the tent did not change his mind.

What is she doing here, if that truly is her? Why would she be part of Unver's company? She was Stallion Clan and Unver is Crane Clan, as many have told me.

Was Vorzheva a prisoner of the new Shan? No, for she seemed to walk free, without guards or protectors of any kind. Perhaps she was now the woman of one of Unver's supporters.

He watched as she vanished from his view, but he could not see where she went. At last he left the window and sat down to eat his supper, though his restless thoughts would not settle.

Porto found Duke Osric's war camp a strange place. As the barber-surgeon stitched Levias' wound, and then saw to Porto's own, much lesser injuries, the talk he heard from the soldiers was of Prince Morgan and their fixed idea that he was being held prisoner by the Thrithings clansmen, that he had been kidnapped by the chieftain called Unver and that it was part of some strategy to bedevil Erkynland. Porto knew from what Binabik and the trolls had told him that Morgan had escaped into the forest, and from what he had heard during his time at Blood Lake, none of the clansmen even seemed aware that the heir to the High Throne had been anywhere nearby.

"I must talk to Duke Osric," he told Astrian and Olveris. "He needs to hear what I have seen. The troll Binabik sent a message to the king and queen—did they not get it?"

"Message?" said Astrian. "I seem to remember that Ordwine was carrying some such thing when he died."

"Ordwine is dead?" Porto had liked the impious young guardsman. "God rest his soul. How did it happen?"

"It might have had something to do with all the Thrithings arrows in him," Astrian said, sharpening his knife on a whetstone.

"If the troll's message got through, then why is everyone saying that the clansmen have Prince Morgan? They don't. I told you, he ran back into the forest. His tracks showed it."

"Ah, well, then," said Astrian. "If his tracks showed it, it must be true. And when did you become so canny about the spoor of princes?"

Porto shook his head. "Just take me to the duke, I beg you. This is no time for jokes."

"Here," said Olveris, handing him a wineskin. "What time is it, old fellow? Is it time for this?"

Porto gave him a hurt look, but accepted it and took a long draught. He had drunk nothing but foul Thrithings drippings for a fortnight, since his own wine had run out—some dreadful thing called *yerut*, sour as vinegar and as thick as whey—and he could not resist a proper beverage, no matter his hurry. "Thanks for that," he said, wiping his lips. "Now, please—take me to Osric."

Astrian shrugged. "As you wish. But speak carefully when you speak of his grandson. He is in a fearful temper about Morgan, and he hates the Thrithings-men."

"You ask me to take the word of those little troll savages?" Duke Osric said, scowling so fiercely that Porto could almost feel it. "Because one of them saw footprints, I should apologize to the barbarian horse-men and head back to Erkynland, leaving them free to do what they please?"

Porto had never seen Osric so distracted—the man could hardly look in one direction for more than a few moments. "Please, Your Grace, I only tell you what I know, what I saw, what I heard. The trolls are wonderful trackers, and the one called Binabik showed me where the footprints of Prince Morgan and Count Eolair came out of the forest to the battlefield, then Morgan's footprints returned to the trees. When Levias of the Erkynguard recovers, he can tell you—"

"He can tell me what? That he too believes in this fairytale? No, any fool can see what happened. Why would the clansmen attack a company of armed Erkynguard without a purpose? They came to take hostages. And what better prize than the heir to the throne?" In the firelight Osric seemed like some fierce old god of the north, long-bearded, his brow as menacing as a thunderhead.

"But Morgan was not with the rest of the company when the clansmen attacked," Porto said. It was hard to look at the duke when disagreeing with him. "The prince and Eolair had gone with the Sithi, as they were sent to do. The attack happened while they were away. What Binabik said made good sense— that they returned when the battle was already almost over—"

"Then why flee back to the forest?" Osric rubbed both hands over his bald head as if to chase away distracting ideas. The weather had turned cold and the duke wore a fur mantle on his shoulders, which made him look more than a little like one of the Thrithings thanes. "Why would my grandson run away if the battle was over?"

Porto did his best not to show frustration. "Because, Your Grace, the battle was over but the battlefield was not empty. We found signs of another struggle, and Eolair's torn cloak was found nearby."

"*Pfah.*" Osric spat into the fire. "Stories. Ideas. Signs! The king wants me to deal kindly with these murdering horsemen, so I have sent their chieftain, this Unver, a message telling him to bring me my grandson and he will be rewarded. And Count Eolair, the Hand of the Throne, too," he added as if to ward off any more comments from Porto. "And that is all I am going to speak of my charge to you, sir. You did what you could. The king and queen will hear of that, never fear." The duke still could barely keep his gaze on Porto, his eyes roving as if the tent was filled with dozens of other people instead of only the two of them and Osric's silent page, who moved only to tend the fire. "Now go. If this Unver Shan will not treat with me as he should then I will have to find other means to get my grandson back. I cannot waste my time arguing over shadows and smoke and what-might-have-beens."

Outside, Porto found his two friends waiting for him. Astrian wore a sour, knowing grin. "So you see, old bag of bones, Duke Osric does not need to be told anything by you. He already knows all he needs to know."

"Surely he is not going to war over this—Morgan is not even there!"

Astrian laughed. "Men do not need reasons to go to war—not good ones, anyway. But you are not being ignored completely. In fact, we want you to tell us everything you remember about the Thrithings' encampment—especially the part where this Unver Shan has his stronghold."

"It is no stronghold," said Porto testily. "It is a group of tents in a paddock. They are not preparing to make war, or even to defend themselves."

"All the better," said Astrian. "Because if Olveris and myself can quietly make our way into the place and remove Count Eolair from the clansmen, and if Morgan is truly somewhere else as you say, there will be no need for war at all."

Porto felt a momentary surge of hope. He had seen more than enough of blood lately. "Perhaps you are right."

Astrian bowed. "When have I ever been wrong?"

Olveris snorted. "Every time you call yourself a swordsman. Or a ladies' man."

"I like you better when you are silent, sir," Astrian told him. "In truth, everybody likes you better when you are silent."

38

Two Offered Bargains

"**Don't climb** on that, Lillia."

"Why not? It's not alive, silly. There aren't any dragons anymore."

"I don't care. For one thing, it's very heavy. It might fall over and hurt you."

"It's not heavy, Grandfather! Look, it doesn't fall over even when I do *this*—"

"Lillia!" The king's voice had the sound that meant "I'm about to be angry." Reluctantly, she climbed down from the chair made of dragon's bones. "Then can I sit in your lap?" she asked.

"For a moment only. I have many things to do today. Why aren't you upstairs doing . . . something? Something else."

She climbed up, using the arms of his chair and also his leg, which made her grandfather grunt. She knew she hadn't hurt him, though, because King Grandfather Simon was very big and couldn't be hurt by anything. That's how he had killed the dragon that was now a throne. She was quite certain of that, because one of her nurses had told her. "I'm not upstairs because it's terrible, terrible boring," she explained. "Auntie Rhoner's never around anymore and the nurses are all mean. Nurse Loes has a big red face and she shouts. And Aedonita and Elyweld went back to the country with their mama and there's nobody to play with except some stupid boys and all they want to do is pretend to be knights."

Her grandfather looked at her for a moment. "Don't you ever pretend to be a knight? I thought I saw you galloping around the Monk's Walking Hall the other day with your wooden horse and a lance."

"I wasn't pretending to be *that* kind of knight, the kind they always want to be. I was being a hero."

"Ah, well. That's all right, then." But she could tell he was thinking of something else and it annoyed her.

"Why won't Auntie Rhoner play with me?"

"Because there are some very important things happening just now, and she and her husband are helping me." He looked around. "Where is Tiamak?"

"Important things are stupid," was Lillia's opinion. "When's Grandmother Miri coming back? I miss her."

The king's smile was sad. "I miss her too. She had to stay longer in Nabban because there are still things she has to do there. What about your other grandmother? Doesn't she want to spend time with you?"

"All Grandmother Nelda ever does is pray. And she tries to make me pray, and I do, but then I start thinking about other things and I forget the words. She gets grumpy and tells me I have to pray for Grandfather Osric and Morgan. Why do I have to pray for them? I do it at night every night already."

The king looked grumpy. "Is that what she tells you? Well, Grandfather Osric has gone out to bring back Morgan."

"Why? Did he get lost?"

Her grandfather took a long breath. "Not really. But he's out in the Thrithings—that's the grasslands on the far side of the Gleniwent River."

"I know the Gleniwent. We went on it when Mama took me to Meremund once." She remembered something that made her frown. "It made my stomach sick." She decided not to think about that. "Why is Morgan in the Ridings?"

"He was on his way to visit the Sithi. I told you about all this. As to why he's in the Thrithings—well, it's a long story. But your grandfather Duke Osric went to get him. Grandmother Nelda worries a lot. Just pray with her when she asks you. It will make her feel better, because she's also missing your other grandfather."

Lillia had finally found a comfortable spot halfway up King Grandfather Simon's leg just above his knee. His leg was a little bony, but not too bad because he had on woolen hose. Her feet didn't quite touch the ground, so she swung her legs like she did on the high garden benches.

"Oh," said her grandfather and made a face. "Lilly, you're getting too big to do that. You're going to break my leg."

She laughed at his joke. "When will Morgan be back? I miss him, too. He promised to take me down to the Kynslagh to see the heron nests, but then he went away again and I still haven't seen them." Another thought occurred to her. "Do you think my mama is in Heaven yet?"

"I'm fairly certain she is. And likely she's keeping an eye you. So you'd better not do anything you shouldn't, especially with all the rest of us too busy to watch you properly."

For the moment, the thought that all the grownups were too busy to watch her properly washed over her like a very cool breeze on a hot day, both exciting and chilling. "Really?" she said.

"Really what?"

"Never mind." She slid down from his lap. "So Morgan and Grandmother Miri are coming back soon? How soon?"

"I didn't say 'soon,' but I hope so, yes. I don't know—they're both a long way away and—" For a moment the king seemed to lose his voice. When he spoke again, his words sounded a little raggedy at the edges. "Don't forget to pray for them. And Grandfather Osric. And your mother, of course."

"But Mama's in Heaven with God. So I don't need to pray for her."

Her grandfather smiled, a small, gentle one this time. "You might as well, young Lilly. It couldn't hurt."

The chambers given to Aengas as First Factor of the Northern Alliance were large but unfortunately dark, because of their position facing the eastern wall of the Inner Bailey. Not even the window looking out over the courtyard below brought in much light, so the main room was full of candles. Surrounded by flickering flames, Tiamak felt as though he sat once more on the roof of his long-lost hut back in the Wran as stars warmed into light in the evening sky.

Tiamak sighed. "I have failed my two greatest trusts," he said as Aengas's cook Brannan set a cup of wine down before him on a table otherwise buried under books and parchments. The Herynsitiri wine was sour to Tiamak's taste, but a few sips helped to ease his racing mind.

"Well, there lies a grand and self-absorbed statement, my dear little man," Aengas said with a mocking smile. "But if you feel the need to unburden yourself, well, of course you must. I am here to listen, and to agree with you out of pure loyalty that you are one of the great villains of the age." He made a show of settling himself comfortably in his large wooden chair, a process that, due to his limited range of movement, mostly consisted of craning his neck toward Tiamak and resetting his hands in his lap. "Proceed, my dear. How have you failed so dismally?"

Tiamak could not even muster a smile of his own. "You jest, but the truth is evident. It is my task to foresee problems and try to solve them without unduly troubling the High Throne. Norns, missing heirs, attempted murders and sudden deaths—I have solved none of them."

"And do not forget that my Northern Alliance is at war with the she-wolf Countess Yissola and her Perdruinese shipping syndicate," Aengas declared with a certain satisfaction. "That clearly counts as a failure of yours as well. Even worse, she is coming *here* to plead her case to the king and you did not stop her. Also, my dear, the weather has been a bit dry this year as well, and you have done nothing whatsoever about improving it."

"I am beyond amusement, Aengas. And, yes, the shipping conflict *is* a failure of mine, because at a time when we might have been solving that disagreement—"

"Disagreement? With that grasping, cold-blooded bitch?"

"—*At a time when we might have been solving that disagreement,*" Tiamak continued, more loudly, "we were caught up in other things, some of them that now seem so unimportant to me I could weep. But my greatest failings have been to the League."

"Do you mean my Northern Alliance? Because while you have not done as much for us as you should, I would hardly call your failings worse there than with other things."

"Aengas, I told you I am not in the mood. I am genuinely unhappy. Also, I am getting to something, but with your continual mockery I will never arrive. I am talking about the League of the Scroll."

"Goodness! I have not heard you mention that name in a long time."

"And that, sadly, shows the depth of my failure. When Doctor Morgenes died, the League was left with no leader, no guiding force to hold us together. It could have been Prince Josua, but he was new to our ranks then and resisted any kind of responsibility as a matter of course. It could have been Binabik the troll, but he lives far away, and with Geloë gone, as her trained birds aged and died, we had nothing to replace them, and communication became ever more difficult. It takes the best part of half a year or more now to send a message to Mintahoq."

"Where is that? On the moon?"

Tiamak frowned. "It might as well be. So if responsibility for the Scroll League belonged to anyone, it was to me. But there was so much to do here, especially in those first years after the Storm King's War. So much rebuilding! So many people without homes, without food, the toll of that terrible, evil winter. I spent every moment trying to put the High Throne's plans to work, and trying to make plans of my own. There are so many things we could have made better if we had only had the time . . . and the gold—"

"And there is the difference between us in a nutshell, as we Hernsmen say." Aengas cleared his throat and waved for Brannan to bring him his cup again. "Gods, I am dry. My friend, your work is so careful and rigorous in both your studies and your writings, my sweet fellow—thank you, Brannan, now why don't you go and see if you can find something Lord Tiamak can eat since he looks so thin and drawn?—but your ideas are so large and unworkable. I am the opposite. My scholarship is a horror to those who love rigor, but I know human beings so much better than you. My faith in humanity was lost long before my legs, but you still imagine people to be creatures who can be made perfect and perfectly happy."

"That is one reason I wished to talk to you today—" Tiamak said, but Aengas was in full flow.

"You fault yourself for what others do not do, but your fellow men will always fail you. If not individually, then they will manage it as a group. That is almost the same fallacy as that of the Aedonites, the idea of a single, perfect God who somehow contrived to make humanity so utterly imperfect. Was it a jest on some scale we cannot conceive? Do they think their God so bored that only the hapless flailings of His creatures can entertain Him, or did He really set them a series of tasks that none of them could ever fulfill? Cruelty, my friend from the swamps—I call such an idea pure cruelty."

Tiamak took a breath, then another. "Perhaps I take too much on myself, as you say, Aengas. Perhaps the fraying and unraveling of the League was inevitable during long years of peace, since we were always so few and so separated by distance. But the fact remains, at a point when we are most needed, when wisdom and scholarship are the only things that might help us, the League of the Scroll has fallen to pieces. In plain fact there are but two of us now, Binabik and myself. Josua is long gone and so is Faiera, if she even lives. Perhaps Etan will bring us back some word of her, but I doubt it, for why would she not have made herself known if she lived?"

"Is all this because we have had so little luck finding evidence of what 'Witchwood Crown' might mean?" Aengas waved his hand at the books and scrolls. "It is obvious that it has many meanings to the Hikeda'ya and the Zida'ya both. We have found at least half a dozen mentions since we have been searching, almost all of them different. A prize, a funerary token, a strategy for a Sithi pastime . . . and what if the whole thing is only some misdirection or a trick, like the nature of the swords collected during the Storm King's War?"

"Anything is possible," Tiamak admitted. "The immortals, especially the Norn Queen, play a long game and we cannot guess all their ends or means. But the fact is, when the League is most needed again, it is a broken thing. And much of that is my fault."

"Well, I cannot provide several more Scrollbearers for you out of thin air," said Aengas pettishly. "I can feed you and listen to your complaints. I can sympathize with your fears—I share many of them. But reforming the League is beyond my powers, especially since I am not even a member."

Tiamak hesitated. "Well, to be honest, that is why I wished to speak to you."

Aengas stared at him for a long moment, then blinked as slowly and deliberately as a frog on a half-sunken tree. "It is?"

"You said it yourself—you see things differently than I do. Our experiences, our lives, have been completely different. Yet you have one of the most cunning minds I know, and a skill at seeing things I do not. Your scholarship is, as you said yourself, not the most rigorous—in truth, you let yourself be led astray by every new idea that catches your fancy—"

"Not just ideas," said Aengas as his cook appeared with a tray of leeks, bread, and cheese. "An attractive face or figure can do the same for me, though there is damnably little I can do beside look, curse the Heavens." He pointed at the table. "Put it down and then go away for a little, while we talk—will you, Brannan?" Aengas sighed. "He is quite handsome, isn't he? But though he has left the priesthood, he has taken their cursed ideas of asceticism with him. Another reason for me to despise the Aedonites." He reached awkwardly for a piece of cheese. "I apologize for the interruption. You were talking some nonsense about the League of the Scroll, I believe—about to ask me to become a member, if I guess your drift correctly. Have I?"

Tiamak nodded. "You have. Because there is little sense now in mourning for what should have been done. But we can remedy that failure, even if it turns out to be too late. I will rebuild the League, and I would like you to join me." He looked his friend and colleague in the eye. "Will you?"

Aengas shook his head. "May the gods love you and watch over you, my darling—no, no, a hundred times no. I have far too much to do and far too little time as it is. I have spent nearly a quarter of a year here in Erchester, trying to help you with this witchwood business and Bishop Fortis's nasty book, while leaving my duties as a factor almost completely ignored. I will likely be sitting here in a dark chamber as Yissola is bending King Simon to her will, securing special treaties and arrangements for her cursed Sindigato while I squint at ancient texts—but you want me to become even more deeply involved with your League? No, my Wrannaman friend with the still-wet feet, it is quite impossible. My allies are furious with me as it is."

Tiamak's heart grew heavy. "Please, Aengas. I do not ask this lightly, you must know that."

"What good to have three instead of two, and one of those three crippled as I am, unable to go anywhere or do anything without being carried around like Lector Vidian in his sacred litter—although never, I hasten to say, wearing such ridiculous hats—?"

"We will not stop at three. I have long groomed Brother Etan. I wish you could have met him, but you have heard his letters."

"The one who is currently being bilked by your Hyrka friend?"

"Etan is not wise in the ways of the world, but his mind is sharp and his heart is good. Yes, Brother Etan. And there is also my wife. Thelía knows far more than I do about many things, and like you does not suffer fools gladly. She is a bit more courteous than you, though."

Aengas laughed harshly. "Ah, and so I can join you, your wife, and an Aedonite monk against the coming of the final catastrophe. How could anyone say no?"

"You can say whatever you like, of course. But I ask you because I need you, Aengas. Even if we survive whatever is coming, we will need to do better in days to come so we can prevent something worse next time. I will not die with the League of Scrolls still in disarray. I cannot."

Aengas looked at him for some time and not with his most kindly expression. He managed to get his cup to his mouth with some difficulty, hands shaking, and took a long sip. "A bargain," he said at last. "I offer you a bargain, Lord Tiamak, my friend. I have neglected my duties to the Alliance terribly while helping you in your search for the meaning of 'Witchwood Crown,' and that means something to me, even if not to you. Months have passed while we have pored through countless old tomes like Usirean priests trying to find a loophole for self-abuse, and my colleagues are justly furious with me." Aengas set the cup down on the broad arm of his chair. It threatened to tip, and Tiamak leaped up to set it farther from the edge, ignoring the pang in his sore leg at the sudden movement.

"Bargain?" he asked. "What sort of bargain?"

"Countess Yissola will arrive from Perdruin in two days, I am told. There will be public receptions, of course, but the king has agreed to meet with her to discuss her complaints and demands in private."

"Of course."

"Well, then. If you will ensure that I can have a report of exactly what is said between them in that discussion, I will join your league."

Tiamak stared, half-certain he had misheard. "Do you mean her private conversations with the king? But that is impossible!"

"Do not fear that you have to hide me and my chair somewhere in the throne hall!" Aengas showed a crooked smile. "Young Brannan is as slim as a cowslip and writes a fair hand—he is my secretary as well as my cook, you know. He can be secreted in some place where he can listen without being seen and take it all down for me. That way I can serve the needs of my Alliance colleagues and will not feel so bad about giving them short measure of my time while embroiling myself in your League of Scrolls."

Tiamak shook his head. He felt cold and sick. "No. No, Aengas, that is impossible. I could not betray my king's trust. I am shocked that you would even ask me. It would be a crime against everything I hold most dear." He rose. "Forgive me. I must go now. I am sorry to have taken so much of your time."

As he walked back down the hall, heading for his own chambers, Tiamak was disturbed to find his eyes filling with tears. He blinked them away as best he could, then dabbed with his sleeve so that by the time he reached his own door the evidence was gone.

Thelía still knew something was wrong, but after a few curt answers made it clear he did not want to talk, she found an errand that needed attention and left him alone to work through his unhappiness. He sat and tried to read, but could not make his eyes fix on the words. He felt as though he had been suddenly attacked by something he had not seen or even suspected, as though some bandit had run up behind and hit him in the head with a club.

How could I have been so wrong? was all he could think. The words sounded in his head over and over, unceasingly, like a bell rung by a madman.

An hour later someone knocked on Tiamak's chamber door. Young Brannan looked stern, like the parent of a child attacked by one of his playmates. "This is for you, my lord," he said, and handed Tiamak a letter stamped with the factor's seal. "I am surprised at both of you."

Tiamak carried the letter back inside with shaking hands.

My dearest Wrannaman,

Let me not waste time in unnecessary formalities. You were right. It was a dishonorable bargain that I offered you, and I regretted it immediately after you left, although it took me a while to sift the chaff of my own bad temper from the grain of our disagreement. In all honesty, I would have been disappointed in you if you had agreed. There is a part of me that sometimes longs to prove others as venal as I suspect them to be, but that is not a part of myself that I love well.

I am glad you are as pure of heart as I often suspected, although I fear for you in this dangerous world. I let my cynic heart get the better of me and thereby harmed our friendship, which is worth more to me than any Alliance or League. I hope you will forgive me, or if not, that you will provide me with some method by which I can one day earn that forgiveness.

Of course I will join your league of scholars if you will still have me. I am not completely selfish, and I see the same evil signs you do. Like you, I fear the days ahead. Of course men of good will and brave heart must do what they can to make things better, but so must those of us whose characters are weaker, for we are far more numerous than your sort.

Let me know if we can speak again. I have wronged you, and for that I will never entirely forgive myself. You must think of what I did as a weak man having a moment of greater than ordinary weakness.

Your ally always, even if I am no longer your friend,
Aengas ec-Carpilbin

When Thelía returned in the early evening, she could see that Tiamak's mood had improved, but she sensed that something more than ordinary frustrations had perturbed him, so she kept her talk light, speaking of what was flowering in the gardens and what birds she had seen. He accepted her gift gratefully, and after a meal of cold meats and bread, they retired early and spent a peaceful night.

Simon looked around the small gathering. His head felt heavy, and he wanted nothing so much as to go back to bed, though it did not much feel like a place of refuge without Miri. "Count Nial and Countess Rhona, I thank you," he said. "You know Sir Zakiel and the lords Pasevalles and Tiamak, of course." He paused, momentarily lost. "Ah. And we have Lord Duglan, our envoy to the Taig, who has returned to bring us King Hugh's response." Duglan, a lean, balding Erkynlander with Hernystiri blood, looked grim. Simon had already heard his news and thought it an appropriate expression. "Go, then—tell us what the king of Hernystir has to say, my lord."

"He says, with apologies, that he has not enough men under arms now to send to you." Lord Duglan took a breath. "He will not beat the Cauldron. He will not summon his people to war. He does not think the threat as great as we have made it to be—claims that if Norns were truly seen, they are just a raiding party who will break against the defenses of Hernystir and Erkynland like a wave upon a rocky cliff."

"Liar!" said Captain Zakiel, then looked around. Of all present, he was the least exalted, and he seemed to feel it then. "I apologize for my strong words, Majesty. I know Hugh is your brother monarch—"

"I never much liked that expression," said Simon. "And at this moment I do not like the king of Hernystir much at all, so do not worry too much about curbing your tongue. Does Hugh call Eolair's nephew a liar, then? Does he think Aelin made up his story of a great Norn army?"

Duglan frowned. "He does not say so outright, but he talked much of Aelin being under Count Eolair's spell, as he put it. He claims that young Sir Aelin has been somehow convinced by his uncle of threats that do not truly exist."

Simon sat back against the throne, trying hard to keep his temper. "He might as well call me a liar to my face as to speak against Eolair, perhaps the most cautious, sensible man I have ever met."

"All who support Hugh—and it is most of the court—spout such nonsense these days," said Count Nial. "It makes my heart sick to say it, but I think it is clear that he intends to let you spend your strength against the Norns, leaving him free to pick up whatever pieces remain. At the very least, I think he hopes for a Hernystir no longer tributary to the High Throne."

"Then he is a cursed traitor to his own people!" Simon banged his fist on the arm of his chair. "Does he not understand that the Norns are no mortals' friends? Does he truly think they would destroy Erkynland but leave him free to do what he wants?"

"The real question is not whether he believes such a thing or not," said Tiamak, "but why? History shows that the Sithi and Hernystir were allies. The only mortal with whom the Norns made compact was King Elias, and they betrayed him in the end."

"It is this mad Morriga-worship," said Rhona. "It has addled Hugh's mind, and the minds of many at his court."

Lord Duglan nodded. "What the countess says is true—and it has grown worse. Just in the month passed, with the claim of renewing faith in the gods of Hernystir, the king and Lady Tylleth had a shrine erected to the Dark Mother in the Taig itself."

"Brynioch's chariot!" Count Nial turned toward him as if he might grab Duglan by the shoulders. "Is this true? Tell me I misheard you."

"I cannot. They said it was a shrine to Talamh, claiming she has been neglected, but Talamh of the Land was always just another name for the three-faced goddess of war and death. That is why she is no longer worshipped—or has not been, until now." Duglan turned to Simon. "To be honest, Majesty, I will of course go wherever you bid me, but my heart does not want to return there. Hernysadharc has become a strange place—a dark place, or so it seems to me."

"Oh! My heart is breaking," cried Rhona. "I never thought my countrymen would wander into shadow this way, so quickly, so heedlessly. The Morriga!"

Pasevalles cleared his throat. "I understand the concerns here, and I lament how far from decency King Hugh seems to have fallen, but none of this solves our problem, Your Majesty. If the king of Hernystir will not help us, where will we find men and arms enough to protect us if the Norns come against Erchester? Duke Osric has taken many of our knights and a thousand foot-soldiers to the borderlands of the Thrithings in search of your grandson."

"Have we heard anything from Duke Grimbrand in Rimmersgard?"

Pasevalles nodded. "Isgrimnur's son at least remains a firm ally, but the duke has problems of his own. More Norns than ever have been traveling the Re-farslod, the Foxes' Road, and they have pillaged farms and estates along its length, killing many and terrifying the people. Duke Grimbrand also worries that Hugh has designs on the lands in the south and west of Rimmersgard. Already there are more Hernystiri troops in the border forts Hugh controls than they have seen in years."

"God's Bloody Tree," Simon swore loudly. "Does this pup thinks he's an-other Tethtain? Does Hugh plan to move into the Hayholt and sit on the High Throne? If we didn't have problems on every side of us, I'd ride to Hernysad-harc myself and teach him a lesson!" He mastered his anger, though it was not easy. "Forgive me, Pasevalles. What can Grimbrand send us?"

"He thinks he might find a thousand foot soldiers and a hundred knights, but he said he dares not strip his cupboard bare." Pasevalles smiled sadly. "He says he begs you not to think him a shirker. He will send what he can, but warns that they may not arrive for some long time, especially if there are Norns barring their way in the north of Erkynland."

Simon let his breath out in a great, flat hiss. "Well, this is a pretty puzzle. And what of Duke Saluceris? What does Froye write from Nabban?"

Pasevalles shrugged. "Much the same as Grimbrand, though Duke Saluce-ris's problems come from within the Nabbanai borders—his brother and Dallo Ingadaris, and all of the Fifty Families who would rather go to war against the Thrithings for their own gain than send troops here to defend against a threat they do not entirely believe exists."

"Do they truly think we have invented the Norns? Do they not remember a mere thirty years ago when the White Foxes nearly destroyed us all?" Simon could feel his face getting hot. Tiamak was looking at him with concern, which only made him angrier. "So when we need them most, our allies are all too busy with their own troubles!"

But the Wrannaman's expression had changed to something more thought-ful. "It does seem that the times have conspired to make us weaker than we would ordinarily be, doesn't it? That when Queen Utuk'ku sends troops against mortal lands, one of our allies suddenly takes up an old religion that worships a dark goddess? That the Sithi send us an envoy who is shot down with arrows that might belong to Thrithings-men?"

"I have not heard this about the arrows," said Simon. "You mean the Sitha-woman who was shot in the Kynswood? Why was I not told about Thrithings arrows?"

"Because I had no proof and still do not. Just because they were fletched with feathers that Thrithings-men use does not mean they were shot by Thrithings-men. But it is interesting that the grasslanders are also the cause of several of our other problems, an excuse for the Nabbanai to hold back on sending men—and, of course, the possible kidnapping of your grandson, Prince Morgan."

Simon's head was swimming. "I don't think I understand you—are you saying that someone in the Thrithings might be behind all this? I thought our enemy was the Norn Queen."

Tiamak frowned. "She is our most fearful enemy, there is no question. I must think about this, Majesty—write it all down so I can see it more plainly. I do not know how the immortals would make trouble for us in Nabban without anyone knowing, but the rest is certainly within their power—especially if they had help from . . . from our own kind."

"From our own kind?" Simon could not make sense of this. "From the Thrithings-men, you mean? Or do you suggest something closer? We know Hernystir is not trustworthy, but . . ." He looked to Nial and Rhona. "I mean that swine Hugh, of course, not the good people like yourselves."

Count Nial waved away his apology. "Please, Majesty. I myself am so angry with what Hugh has done that only the common need—and the greater danger—keeps me here. Otherwise, I would ride to Herynsadharc today and denounce him for the criminal he has become."

"You would not," said Countess Rhona. "They would kill you, and then I would die myself."

"Please, everyone, please." Simon waved his hands. "Nobody is riding anywhere. We have much to think about, but we have even more to do. With or without our allies, we must face the likelihood that the Norns are within the borders of Erkynland. We need to know where they are and what they're doing. Captain Zakiel, now it is your turn. Tell me what scouts we can send. Tell me what the news is from Naglimund and Leymund and the other northern border forts."

But though he wanted very much to hear what Sir Zakiel had to say, Simon found himself struggling to think of anything but his own memories of the Norns, of those white, inhuman faces that had haunted his dreams for so many years.

My worst dreams have become real. No, not the very worst, he reminded himself, and made the Sign of the Tree to keep ill fortune at bay. *Miri and Morgan are still alive. They will come back to me.*

It was all Pasevalles could do to keep his face expressionless as he bade goodbye to the king and others and left the throne hall. It felt as though a great, pulsing fire was burning in his spine and boiling his brains, and he could barely keep his hands from twitching.

Resist the anger, he told himself. *It will not serve you well.* He wanted the clarity of high places, of a Godlike view. He was furious and frightened by what Tiamak had said, how close to the mark the little man had come. The Wranna-man had all but told the king and other nobles that someone inside the Hayholt must be helping their enemies.

He walked for a short time on the castle walls, using the pretense of inspecting the fortifications, but even that high vantage point could not ease his restless, unhappy thoughts. He was so close to victory—so close! And yet each hour that brought him nearer to his goal also left him more exposed. A failure at any point in the chain and he would stand revealed. The thought of punishment did not frighten him, but the idea of failure, of revenge uncompleted, burned and burned until he wanted to cry out. He abandoned the walls to return to his working chamber in the Chancelry.

As he approached it, though, one of his pages ran out to tell him that Father Boez was waiting to speak with him. Pasevalles instantly turned away and headed toward the residence instead, wanting nothing to do with the priest, who seemed obsessed with the smallest details of the castle's financing since he had replaced Gervis, and had more discomforting questions than a centipede had legs.

It was Tiamak, though, who filled his thoughts. If the little man were not so close to the king he might have removed him long ago, but there had always been too many obstacles, not least of which was the Wrannaman's own caution. He considered briefly whether Lady Thelía might be an easier target, but could not convince himself that it would not cause more harm than help. A widowed Tiamak would have even less to lose, and might give more of his thought to uncovering the traitor he had clearly begun to suspect.

Pasevalles even contemplated simply going to their chambers one night and removing both of them from the game board once and for all, but knew that was his frustration speaking. He had not come so far only to fail because of obvious mistakes. He had spent two decades making himself both indispensable and above suspicion.

As he made his way toward his own chambers, he came upon a young maid on the landing of the stairs. A large basket of clothes sat on the floor before her as she sat with her hands on her knees, catching her breath. When she saw him her reddened face colored even more deeply, and she leaped up and made a clumsy courtesy.

"Oh, my lord! Forgive me!"

"Are you unwell, my dear?"

"No. It's just that the basket is so heavy. I was only resting for a moment." She grabbed at the handles and began to lift it.

"Stop, young lady, you will harm yourself." He paused, considering. The last people who had passed him on the stairs as he climbed were long gone and there was no one else in sight. "I will offer you a bargain. First, what is your name?"

"Tabata, my lord, and it please you," she said and made another courtesy, this one a bit more steady. Her face was round but pretty beneath the flush.

"Well, Tabata, here is my bargain. I need your help with something upstairs. If you will lend me a few moments' assistance, afterward I will carry that heavy basket for you wherever it needs to go."

"No, my lord, I couldn't let you!"

"Of course you could. Favor for favor—that's fair, isn't it?"

Her look became a bit more guarded. "What sort of help do you want from such as me?"

"Nothing difficult, my dear. You may even find it a pleasant diversion from your ordinary work—you work hard, don't you?"

"Oh, yes, though I shouldn't say it. The Mistress of Chambermaids works us terrible hard sometimes, especially when the weather is hot like this." She swept a damp lock of hair from her forehead.

"Then leave the washing here and come with me. No, I have something I must quickly do first. Go on up to the top floor and wait for me. Go on, child, hurry. I am a busy man, and I don't have the whole day."

Still looking a little uncertain, Tabata made her way up the stairs. Pasevalles waited until she had reached the next floor, then bent and picked up the basket and carried it downstairs. He left it on the first floor near a doorway that opened out onto the gardens, then made his way back up. As he had hoped, his thoughts were already cooling, the rage that had blasted his composure almost gone. It happened sometimes. No great work could be achieved without the occasional moment of relaxation and release.

She was waiting in the hall on the top floor, looking around as though she had never seen it before.

"Has anyone else come up?" he asked in the tone of one who doesn't much care.

"No, my lord. Just you."

Pasevalles reached up to light the torch he had brought from downstairs at the wall sconce. "Ah. Well, I wanted to show you this room at the end. It is a dusty fright, and with Countess Yissola bringing only Heaven knows how many servitors from Perdruin, we will need all our rooms ready." He opened the door for her, then closed it behind them.

Despite being a chambermaid, Tabata seemed a little surprised to be asked to do chambermaid work, but she did her best to seem willing. "Oh, it is not too bad, my lord. I could do this all for you within the hour."

"I want to show you something else first—have you been in this room before?"

"Once or twice to clean when I first came."

"Well, I wager you haven't seen this." He went to the hidden door beside the fireplace, pulled down the sconce, then gave a push. The door swung open almost silently despite its great weight, revealing the darkness beyond. He turned and saw her staring, eyes and mouth both open wide, her pink flush gone and her skin suddenly pale.

"By our Lady, what is that?" she said.

"Come and see." When she did not move, Pasevalles went toward her, still smiling. "It is truly most interesting, Tabata. You would never guess what's down at the end of this passage."

"No, I can't do it, my lord—they make me terribly frightened, places like that. I just can't."

"Oh, yes, my dear." His thoughts were clear now, clear as air, clear as ice. He could see everything—imagine everything, his plan laid out before him like a palace of transparent, shining adamant. "Yes, you can." And with that, he grasped her arm and covered her mouth and dragged her toward the waiting dark.

39

The Place of Voices

"I know this stretch of water," said Tanahaya. "We have almost reached the first gate." It was the first time she had spoken to Morgan in hours.

He had been silent too. He was still full of shame about the night before, and every time he opened his mouth to say something, the memory of his foolishness leaped up to mock him. "Gate?" he said after a few moments. "On a river?"

"In a sense." She seemed determined to act as though his mistake had not happened, but that only made Morgan feel worse, as though he were a child or some animal that did not know better. "In truth, the gates are bridges over T'si Suhyasei—roads once rang along both its banks—but those who came to Da'ai Chikiza on boats called them gates. The first one we will see will be the Gate of Cranes."

Morgan watched the trees slip by on either bank. As the sun neared noon the light plunged between the trunks all the way to the forest floor: they seemed to be traveling through a vast, columned church without walls. Other than the vigorous splashing of the river, Morgan could hear only birdsong and scolding squirrels, and that was good. He could think of nothing to say that seemed worth saying, and nothing that Tanahaya might say that would make him feel any less of a fool.

From the position of the sun, Morgan guessed it was an hour or so after midday when they finally reached a slender, curved bridge of translucent stone netted in ivy and the branches of thicker plants, its carvings almost obliterated by time and weather. A large stone bird stared down blindly at them from the span's highest point above the river. The Sitha might have called it the Gate of Cranes, but the bird's long beak and the spreading wings had long since worn away; Morgan thought it looked more like a lump of clay waiting to be shaped by a potter's hands into something finer.

They passed beneath several more of these stone bridges, not one exactly the same as another. Tanahaya recited their names in turn—Tortoise, Rooster, Wolf, Raven, and Stag, though the Gate of Stags was now only a tumble of ruined stones on either bank, and the Gate of Wolves had lost enough stones that it looked as though it would soon follow the Stags into the river.

Morgan had lost count of how many gates they had seen when they reached a bridge whose tan, blue-seamed stones must have been harder than those of the others. The details had not been worn away by water and wind: the sharp little beak of the carved bird atop the bridge was open in song, its edges well defined, even the round eye clearly visible.

He turned to Tanahaya to ask her if this one was newer than the rest, but was stopped by her expression: her angular face and half-lidded eyes made her look like someone asleep and dreaming. Suddenly she began to sing, an odd, almost haunting melody with words he could not understand and a tune that went in circles, wandering back across itself with only slight differences, over and over.

Then, as suddenly as she had begun she fell silent and steered their little boat toward a cracked stone pier that jutted out at a bend in the river.

"We will leave the boat here," she said. "Be cautious. The landing is old, as old as the bridges. Test it carefully before you put your full weight on it."

"That song you were singing," he asked as he carefully climbed out onto the stone platform and from there to the overgrown bank, thick with bracken and wild strawberry. "What was it?"

"It was a song about Jenjiyana of the Nightingales—the gate brought it to my mind. Queen Utuk'ku's son Drukhi was killed by mortals. His wife was Nenais'u, Jenjiyana's daughter, and Jenjiyana mourned the loss of her child no less fiercely than Utuk'ku mourned hers, but without anger. Jenjiyana lived long at Tumet'ai in the north, until the ice and snow came and devoured that city and the Zida'ya left it behind. But always afterward she dressed in the heavy gown she had worn in that cold place, as if time for her had stopped when her daughter died. The song says:

> *Dressed in billows,*
> *Mournful white cloud*
> *Soft without rain*
> *But still it weeps*
>
> *Mournful white cloud*
> *Carried by the wind*
> *Carried by grief*
> *Where will you wander?*

She made a gesture, the fingers of both hands spread with her thumbs touching. "It is only a small part of a longer whole. I cannot make it sing in your tongue. That is my fault, not yours. Follow me now. You will see something worth seeing."

She led him around the bend. Although the riverbank seemed a little flatter in places, as though there might once have been a path, most was so overgrown with knot-rooted trees and thick underbrush that he hardly paid any attention to where he was being led until Tanahaya stopped him with a hand on his arm and said, "Look! You have come to the Tree of the Singing Wind. Very few mortals can say that."

Ahead of him the river bent away to the right, its banks thick with buckram and bluebell and gently waving ferns, then vanished down a tunnel of close-leaning alders. But on the side of the river where they stood the forest did not grow so close to the bank, and the trees and plants took on strange, angular shapes. He stared for long moments before he realized he was looking not just at crowding trees and thickly twining ivy, but at a crumbling city that the wood had all but swallowed.

Shapes now became visible all along the bank as his eye separated them from the engulfing forest—sections of roofless buildings, solitary doorways stitched with vines, and more ruined walls than he could hope to count. Here and there on the ground glints of pale stone peeked through dense mats of moss and fern. The city stretched far back into the forest, where he could make out the crumbling remains of slender towers. In places the spires still seemed to stand tall, though so enmeshed in ivy and snapdragons and vines that the underlying stone might have disappeared long ago, leaving only the leafy ghosts of the towers behind.

"This . . . this . . . ?"

"Is what remains of Da'ai Chikiza. One of our old cities—one of the Nine Cities of lore. After Tumet'ai vanished beneath the ice, this was considered the most beautiful dwelling of our people—lovely beyond even Enki e-Shao'saye in the eastern forest."

"What happened to it?" He felt a weight on his chest, as though the age of the place was squeezing out his breath, forcing his heart to race simply to keep him standing. "Where did they go? Why did your people leave?"

Tanahaya shook her head. "It happened before I was born, but our chronicles say that something happened to T'si Suhyasei—to the river." She gestured to the wide waterway. "It was the city's life—that is why this place was named "Her Cool Blood," after the river and the forest. But something happened near the time my people fled Asu'a, when the Storm King murdered his father and then died fighting the mortal Northmen. Many Zida'ya had retreated here, but the river suddenly ceased to flow. Then one day the river suddenly returned, swollen and raging, and flooded the city. Many of my people died, many more lost everything they had brought out of Asu'a or had saved from Tumet'ai. Most fled farther into the forest, vowing not to build anything again that they could not take down and carry with them. But as I said, all that was before my time."

"How old are you?"

She looked at him carefully. To his immense gratitude, she did not smile. "Not so old by the standards of my people, although none of us live so long now that the witchwood is lost."

"That's another question you didn't quite answer."

She was silent for a moment. "I am a child of our Second Exile. I was born after my folk left Asu'a and the rest of our cities behind. But I was alive when your grandfather's many-times-great grandfather Eahlstan Fiskerne first came with his river-wife to the castle in which you were born. Do you need to know more?"

For the moment, Morgan was overwhelmed. The ancient, ruined city was daunting enough, but the idea that this young, womanly creature beside him was centuries old was even harder to compass.

As they walked across the uneven ground toward the overgrown walls and empty doorways, Morgan caught his foot and fell into a patch of ferns. By the time he clambered upright again his fingers were sticky.

"You must be cautious here," said Tanahaya. "If you look where the undergrowth is not so thick, you can see remnants of what was here." She pointed down to a place where he could see dull colors through the moss. She pulled loose a handful of vegetation and brushed away dirt to reveal broken tiles caught in a net of roots. Morgan could see bits of color, but could make out nothing of the faded figures or designs.

"This was the Place of Sharing Out," Tanahaya said. "The people of Da'ai Chikiza would gather here where the boats came in off the river, or sometimes to make festival. At Year-Dancing time the whole of this place would be lit with lamps of many colors, and boats on the river carried lanterns too. My master Himano told me once that it seemed to him what it might feel like to stand high in the sky among the stars themselves."

Her voice had changed as she spoke, growing more distant, as though she spoke more to herself than to Morgan. When she looked at him again she smiled, but it seemed an expression more of weariness and self-deprecation than of pleasure. "It will soon be Year-Dancing again, but I wonder if the Zida'ya will come together this time. Jao é-Tinukai'i, our last gathering place for the whole of the House of Year-Dancing, is gone now. The witchwood is gone too. And our people are fewer now, and more scattered than ever."

Tanahaya led him deeper into the forested ruins, until the afternoon light was almost entirely filtered by greenery and the noise of the river faded to a distant murmur. Since so much of the city was in ruins, it was hard to tell whether the streets of Da'ai Chikiza had been broad, or simply that so many of the buildings had been pulled to pieces by time and storms and the marching forest. Morgan could make little sense of it as a city—nothing seemed to be set at a right-angle to anything else, and very large ruins stood next to some structures no bigger than a crofter's hut.

As they moved deeper, what seemed at first a clearing in the forest revealed itself to Morgan as an open space with ruined buildings on three sides, like the square in front of St. Sutrin's cathedral in Erchester. In places tree roots had pushed up the ground, revealing fragments of broken tiles under the dirt and plants.

"This was another gathering place," she said. "It was called the Place of Voices, because the people would—"

If she finished what she was saying, Morgan never heard it: at that moment, something struck him on the head—not a killing blow or even a vicious one, but hard enough to disorient him for a moment, so that he lost his balance and fell to his knees. As he was shaking his head and wondering what had happened, he realized that he and Tanahaya were both covered in a thick net of woven vines.

"What . . . ?" He barely finished the word before he saw white shapes running at them from all directions, bursting out of the forest and from behind ruined walls, moving with the terrifying, silent speed of phantoms. He began to struggle, but the vines were thick and heavy.

"Morgan, do not fight!" Tanahaya said sharply. There was a tone of uncertainty in her voice as well as something he hadn't heard before, and it scared him badly. "We cannot escape. Do not tempt them to kill us."

Vaqana was off hunting, and Sisqi's ram was cropping sedge at the edge of the clearing. Binabik had taken off his jacket and thin shirt to enjoy the warm night, and now patted his bulging stomach fondly. "We have had many hardships on this journey," he said, "but at least you must admit that the birds of this part of the forest are toothsome in the extreme. That grouse—wonderful!"

Sisqi would not smile. "They seem a little dry to me—none of the lovely oil of a ptarmigan. Perhaps because you have spent more time in these southern lands you have developed a fondness for them."

He laughed. "You are a terrible liar, my beloved. I know how much you look forward each year to Blue Mud Lake and the birds and other delicacies there. 'Lovely oil', indeed. Do I not remember you saying that ptarmigan tasted like an old snowshoe?"

She poked at the fire. "Perhaps. Once, long ago. But do not think you will so easily cheer me out of my worry for our daughter."

His face grew more serious. "That was not my intent. I fear for them too. But our Qina is the cleverest young person I know, and even Snenneq—though he has a few awkward qualities—is a resourceful young man. They are on their nuptial walk, after all—it is only fitting that they do some of it on their own."

"Nowhere in the words of the ancestors is it said that a nuptial walk should be taken in a place where enemies will try to murder you." She poked the fire harder, so that the flames sprang up and for a moment bathed the ceiling of trees with yellow light.

"I did not mean that," he said. "And there are few places any of the Yiqanuc can go, in our own mountains or here in these lands, where someone or something will not try to harm us."

"I know, husband."

"It is so warm," he said after a while. "Why do you not take off your jacket so that you can be more comfortable? Summer is gone. Soon the cold will come again, and you have been complaining of the heat since we left Rimmersgard."

"I do not like the warmth of these southern lands," she admitted. "And I do not like sweltering in these heavy clothes. But I like the bites of midges even less. They are worse here than at Blue Mud Lake, I swear! Why do you think I keep poking the fire? The smoke helps to keep them away. At least a little bit."

Binabik nodded. "Then perhaps a distraction is in order. Come, lie with me and we will rub faces. After that, we can see what happens."

Sisqi gave him a look. "With me full of worry about my only child, and these bloodthirsty creatures hovering all around us? No, my husband, we will not be shaking the tent tonight."

"May I point out that we have no tent?" He patted the blanket. "Only the trees and sky for a roof. Our children are not here. We are alone."

"You know what I meant," she said. "I am not in the mood for lovemaking, in any case. Perhaps later, if we find a place where the swarms of midges are not thicker than the smoke of our fire."

Binabik swatted at something on his chest, lifted it on his finger to examine it, and seemed about to comment on its size and fierceness before reconsidering. "Ah, well," he said instead. "If you are certain, my dear one. I have had to travel without you enough that I have learned to live with loneliness."

She gave him another look, this one even more sour than the first. "Such foolishness did not work on me even when I was young, Binbinaqegabenik of Mintahoq."

"It must have worked a little," he said. "Because we married and made a child."

She almost smiled. "Here is something to consider," she said after a moment. "Instead of sitting on our blanket, let us roll ourselves in it as protection from these biting things. Then, when we are forced into such close proximity—well, perhaps we will see what happens, as you said."

"An excellent idea," he said, grinning. "Poke that fire again. Fill the woods with smoke until the midges all flee. Then we will begin this plan of yours."

"You do love to talk, my husband," she said as she rose and shook out the bearskin blanket. "Most of it is foolish, but at least you make me laugh."

Morning found them climbing a series of hills. Binabik was not riding Vaqana because he was looking closely for signs of other travelers, but he kept the wolf close by. Twice since they had left the younger Qanuc and turned southward they had almost stumbled into Norn soldiers. Only Vaqana's sense of smell had warned them early enough for them to hide.

"It concerns me," Binabik said now, breaking a long silence. "It makes no sense to me. Why would the Norns come so far from their home—and for

what? Do they seek to destroy the Sithi? But after such a terrible defeat in the
Storm King's War, how could they be strong enough?"

"Perhaps as you said before, they are on their way somewhere else." Sisqi
guided her ram Ooki around a cluster of low-hanging branches. Her mount was
almost tireless, but did not always pay attention to the rider's well-being.

"That was when I thought there were but a few of them," he said. Vaqana
paused, shaggy white head erect, and Binabik stopped too. Sisqi pulled back
on her ram's harness and together they waited silently until Vaqana trotted
forward once more. "Now I wonder," Binabik said, but more quietly than
before, "whether something else is not underway, some grand design of the
Norn Queen's—especially this Witchwood Crown, which we still do not understand. Is it a thing, a weapon, a treasure? Is it a plan?"

They were nearing the crest of the hill. "I smell water," Sisqi said.

"Yes, I do too. That means we are close to Geloë's lake now."

Sisqi made an unhappy face. "Lakes mean midges. And flies. And only the
ancestors know what other kind of biting thing."

"As long as there are no Norns, I will be content, my beloved. Besides, if her
hut still stands perhaps we can shelter in it tonight. That will be an answer to
those midges."

Once upon the hilltop they made their way through a crowning stand of
birches and emerged at last where they could finally see for a distance in front
of them. They stood atop one of a ring of tree-blanketed hills that surrounded
a dark green bowl of a valley with a mirror-flat lake at its bottom. A bittern
lifted its honking call, then the valley fell silent once more.

"Geloë's house was there," Binabik said, pointing. "There along the water's
edge."

"I don't see any house."

"We cannot see it from here. It is behind those trees. But we will reach it
long before the sun sets." He stood, listening. "Quiet—this was always a quiet
place. But the Norns are a very quiet race, especially when they make war, so
let us stay vigilant."

Sisqi nodded. "No fear that I will be anything else. I have never much
trusted these lands, and the White Foxes terrify me."

They followed a dry streambed down the hill, then Binabik led them cross-
wise along the slope into a thick grove of alders. When the trees finally fell
away it was because they had stepped out onto the edge of a muddy shore. The
trunks of other trees, long dead, loomed from the water like crippled beggars
washing their limbs in a holy fountain.

"I fear I have made a mistake," said Binabik, looking around. "I would have
wagered my best knucklebones that this was the spot where Geloë's hut stood,
but look! Not a board, not a stick. I do not understand. Wait for me." Despite
Sisqi's protests, he took off his boots and waded out into the lake until it almost
reached his waist, then moved along the shore until he had disappeared from

her view behind a drooping line of silvery willows. A little while later he emerged again and sloshed his way back to shore.

"It can be nowhere else. This was the spot, but everything is gone. How could that be? Even after all this time there would be some sign, surely, but look—nothing."

"I am sorry we will have no door to shut against the insects," said Sisqi, "but I do not know why you were so anxious to find it, anyway. Geloë herself has been dead for a very long time. What could be so interesting about her empty hut?"

"Likely nothing after all the years it would have been deserted. But she was uncommonly wise, and I had hoped—only a little, it is true—that there might be some of her books left, anything that might help to explain the Witchwood Crown, or at least shed some light on what the queen of the Norns might be planning." He frowned and poked at the ground with his walking stick. Somewhere nearby Vaqana was crashing through the undergrowth in pursuit of some small, unhappy animal.

"A long throw, it seems to me," she said. "Did you really think there would be anything of use left after all this time?"

"I should have come years ago," Binabik conceded. "Geloë was never like anyone else. Part Tinukeda'ya, some claimed. I do not know if that is true, but she had rare gifts and I hoped for a stroke of fortune." He sighed. "I suppose we should make camp. I do not like to make a fire so close to the edge of the lake, where anyone on the other side could see us—"

"What is that?" asked Sisqi. "Out there in the middle of the lake?"

Binabik squinted. "I do not have such sharp eyes as you, my beloved. What is it?"

"There, look—do you really not see it? I thought at first it was a log, but it has a more regular shape, like the roof of a cabin or hut—just the angled top, sticking up above the surface of the lake. Could that be Geloë's hut, all the way out there? Could it have fallen into the lake and drifted out there?"

Binabik looked out across the dark waters for no little time. "I think I see it. You may be right."

"But I have never heard of such a thing," Sisqi said. "How could her hut have ended in the middle of the lake? What could have swept it there without destroying it?"

"It is another puzzle." It seemed for a moment like he might say more, and Sisqi watched him closely. "Much that has to do with Valada Geloë we will likely never know," he told her at last. "But I confess it makes me uneasy, although I could not easily say why. Let us find a more sheltered place to make our fire, then tomorrow we will leave this place and its mysteries behind. After all, our destination is still far, far away and the days rush on toward winter."

In the first moment, as the net fell on them, Tanahaya thought they had been caught by the Hikeda'ya and a cold fear seized her. But as she struggled without success to loose herself, she recognized the weave of the vines and a different kind of fear took its place.

Who could have guessed so many of the Pure are still here, she thought. "Brothers and sisters," she cried. "What are you doing? I am one of your kin!"

But the white-clad figures did not respond. The net was pulled around her and the mortal prince and more coils of rope were looped over it and then yanked tight. Something struck at her legs, not hard enough to cripple her, but hard enough to sting, until she understood what was wanted and struggled back to her feet.

"Get up, Morgan," she said in Westerling. *"Do not resist them. Let me do what I must."*

"Who are they? What's going on?"

Something struck him. She could not see, but she heard the blow and then heard him groan.

"Leave him be," she said loudly in her native tongue. "He is no enemy. Punish me if you must—I brought him here." Her captors still did not respond; when the boy had clambered awkwardly to his feet they were both forced to march across the Place of Voices. Each stumble by Morgan was rewarded with a retaliatory strike from one of the long, flexible rods the Pure carried, rune-scribed branches of hardened willow. Tanahaya protested each time they struck him, but many of their captors also carried swords, so she did not fight back.

The prisoners were goaded down a long, crumbling flight of stairs into darkness, their captors poking and prodding so that even Tanahaya found it hard to keep her balance. She kept one hand tightly clutching Morgan's shirt, helping him stay on his feet. She was stunned by the savagery she was being shown by her own people.

At last she and Morgan, still wrapped in the net, were led out into a wider space, polished stone beneath their feet and lights sparkling here and there, dim as the last stars at dawn. They were forced to the ground, then in a matter of a few heartbeats the ropes were loosened and the net roughly pulled away.

What had been the open peak of the circular room's wide ceiling was covered with a densely woven mat of sticks and branches so that very little light could enter, but she knew the place now, and the empty plinth at the center left her with no doubt. They were in Da'ai Chikiza's Dawnstone Chamber, surrounded by armed, white-clad figures. Most wore horizontal stripes of gray paint or ash across their faces, but their golden skin and eyes proved they were all Zida'ya like herself. Beside the plinth stood a tall female Sitha with the ageless, weathered features of someone who had lived a very long time.

"Mistress Vinyedu," she said to the imposing figure. "I am Tanahaya of Shisae'ron."

"I know who you are." Vinyedu stared at her with obvious distaste. "You are Himano's acolyte and thus at least as much of a fool as he is. What I do not know is what you are doing here, or what madness has seized you that you should bring a mortal to Da'ai Chikiza, of all places."

"The mortal is innocent. I brought him—"

"No mortals are innocent," said Vinyedu with cold certainty. "Mortals killed Nenais'u, the Nightingale's daughter. Mortals killed Amerasu Ship-Born. Saying that you brought this one here does not excuse the mortal—it only makes you his accomplice."

40

The Blood of Her Enemies

Nezeru had heard tales of Oldheart all her short life. She had often wondered if one day she might see the Mother of Forests for herself, but she had never imagined that she would first encounter it as a fugitive, pursued by her own people. Still, even knowing that Sacrifice soldiers must be less than a day behind her, she could not help reining up when she first entered under the eaves of the great wood.

So many kinds of trees! The forests she knew around the great mountain Nakkiga were composed almost entirely of pines, firs, and a few hardy birches. They reminded her of the Hikeda'ya themselves, slender, pale survivors that thrived where others would perish. Here on the northern edge of the great forest there were also evergreens, but they were far from alone: oaks, beeches, hornbeams, lindens, and countless others she could not recognize crowded as thickly as slaves in a barn, and a thousand other green things grew beneath them. Birds sang everywhere, fluting, whistling, chirping, so different than the forests of her home, in which the only birdcall to be heard was the harsh rasping of crows. She found the scented air equally overwhelming, perfumed by so many kinds of bark, by the sweet rot of fallen limbs turning slowly into earth, the tang of moss and fungus, even the warm fragrance of the earth itself as it digested all that fell and renewed it—soil so alive and so full of change that it made her light-headed.

As Nezeru rode her pilfered horse deeper into the trees, with the first moonlight striking through the tangled branches like long, silver spears, it was hard to keep her mind on the enemies that followed her. She wondered if the magnificence of the forest would catch them too. Surely even the most hardened Sacrifice would slow in stunned amazement as she had when faced by this onslaught of life.

But Nezeru could not count on that. Many of her pursuers were not crippled as she was by mortal blood. They had not lived for half a year in the confusion she had experienced, where all that she thought right seemed suspect, where those that should have been her dire enemies spared her life when they could easily have taken it.

She cursed silently to herself and ducked her head. Thinking of Jarnulf again, she had almost run into a low hanging branch. Why could she not shed herself of that treacherous creature even in the privacy of her own thought?

She discovered that her hand had drifted down to Cold Root's hilt, as if Jarnulf had appeared before her in the forest. If the Garden was good to her, she promised herself, one day she would have a reckoning with the so-called Queen's Huntsman. And before he died she would make him tell her why he had cursed her this way, wring an explanation from him before relishing his dying breath. She would not be haunted forever by the madness of one mortal.

As she rode deeper into the wood Nezeru could see the spoor of many different animals, deer, foxes, even the broad, deep hoofprints of something bigger than her horse, perhaps a bison. But either the animals were avoiding her or something else had come through this part of the forest recently and frightened them off. The reason mattered little, though. What mattered was her hunger. She had finished off the last of her food four days earlier, and had gone nearly twice that many days without sleep or even rest, which made it harder to ignore hunger's ache. It would do her no good to race on ahead of her pursuers only to fall from her saddle in a swoon of starvation.

She had been taught to feed herself from the land around her, and these fertile green halls carpeted in fallen leaves and branches should have made it easy; her failure to catch even a squirrel made her wonder whether she had lost more than simply her place in the Order of Sacrifice. It almost seemed she had lost her Hikeda'ya skill and strength as well, that she could only wander the forest like one of the hapless mortals who could not live without a roof above them and a fire to warm them, who had to live off food they had gathered and put away during the warm months. The thought infuriated her, but by the end of her first full day in Aldheorte it had become as impossible to ignore as her bitter hatred of Jarnulf.

Nezeru began to wonder whether she was losing her wits.

Perhaps the farther I get from Nakkiga, the less of me remains, she thought. *Is that what happened to our people in the War of Return? Did all that makes us what we are, brave and true, the queen's sworn servants, just sift out of us like sand in an hourglass as we entered the mortal lands, until we were left weak and empty?*

Then, as she rode down a long slope thick with wild arum, ugly thoughts flitting through her head like biting flies, she smelled smoke.

She reined up, pulse beating in her temple and her skin prickly. For a moment she thought it was her pursuers, much closer than she would have guessed, but a little consideration told her that was unlikely: the Hikeda'ya seldom made fires even in the coldest weather, and never when they were tracking. Her heart slowed a little and she gave the stolen horse the lightest of taps with her heels to set it moving again. Her nose told her the fire was linden wood, which didn't burn well, as Jarnulf had taught her when they had been skirting the southern Dimmerskog, and she wondered that anyone would use it when the surrounding forest was full of ash and birch.

A little farther down the slope she reined up again in surprise. Drifting in and out through the smell of burning wood was the scent of something being cooked, and while it made her mouth water, it also made her heart beat fast again. It was a fungus that she knew well, called Dead Fingers, and despite the unpleasant name it was a delicacy in Nakkiga. By reassuring herself that Hikeda'ya seldom lit fires, she might have made a fatal mistake.

But after she sat motionless long enough for birdsong to fill the air again, she realized she could also hear voices, so faint that she could barely separate them from the wind in the high branches above her. To her surprise and relief, though, the words she could hear were not Hikda'yas speech.

She silently dismounted, looped the horse's reins around a stout branch, then began to make her way through the undergrowth toward the smoke and murmuring voices. Soon she was close enough to see the dark cloaks the strangers were wearing. Her mouth was watering from the smell of the roasting fungus, but she remained cautious. She crawled even closer, until she could see the faces of those gathered around the fire. She was relieved that they were not Hikeda'ya, but they were not mortals either. Their spidery fingers and huge heads seemed straight out of childhood tales her mother had told her, and for a moment Nezeru could almost believe she had stumbled onto a pack of forest goblins. Then, with a start of surprise, she recognized them.

Delvers. The dozen or so creatures were Tinukeda'ya, and although this kind of Changeling was now rare in Nakkiga, their imprint was on most of the city inside the mountain. Delvers were gifted beyond understanding at digging and shaping stone. Most of the great cities of the Keida'ya had been built with their help—or rather with their forced labor. But thousands of them had died from fevers that had swept through the Tinukeda'ya of Nakkiga, and few still lived in the mountain. A company of them in the middle of Oldheart Forest was as unexpected a sight as a living dragon.

But I've seen those, too.

The breeze shifted direction and wafted the smell of the roasting fungus into her nostrils, driving other thoughts from her mind. Her stomach clenched painfully and her mouth watered. She climbed to her feet, drew Cold Root from its scabbard, and pushed her way through the bracken.

All of the Delvers looked up as she entered the clearing, large heads swinging around on their slender necks like flowers swiveling to the sun. Their pit-dark eyes widened with terror, and a few of the creatures farthest from her got up and ran clumsily into the forest, but the rest only cringed and stared. As she had guessed, these were not the sort of creatures that would fight back.

"Give me some food," she said in her native tongue, but none of them moved. "I know you can understand me. I am also from Nakkiga. I have not eaten in many days. Give me food." She pointed at the campfire, where bundles of Dead Fingers wrapped in leaves were cooking in the embers at the edge of the fire.

"I speak your tongue," said one of them, a female, after a long silence. "Do not hurt us. We will give you some of our food. Go—take what you want." She pointed a long, trembling finger at the hissing bundles. Nezeru leaned forward and snatched one from the ashes, burning her hand a little but not caring, then retreated to the edge of the clearing. She laid her sword across her lap, then used her knife to poke open the leaves and let out the steam. As she blew on the roasted fungus to cool it, the Delvers who had fled at her appearance came back to stand at the edge of the trees and watch her.

The fungus was bland, with none of the usual seasonings, but after days with no more than an occasional handful of berries it was like devouring pure bliss. It was still very hot, and her lips and tongue and the insides of her mouth suffered for it, but she could not stop until she had bolted the whole thing. She sniffed the fire-wilted leaves it had cooked in, then brushed off the ashes and ate those too.

"Do not hurt us," the female Delver repeated. She had gray hair, sparse as spider moss on a rock, and looked to Nezeru like nothing so much as a wrinkled and particularly scrawny child grown to adult size. But her hands, like those of her fellows, were big as platters, the fingers almost impossibly long. "Eat all you want."

"Who are you?" Nezeru asked, still chewing the last of the leaves.

"Zin-Seyvu am I," said the speaker. "And these my fellows are. We mean you no harm."

"I have little fear of that. Why are you here?"

Zin-Seyvu turned and murmured to the others. As they carried on their quiet conversation, Nezeru returned to the fire and took another packet of fungus, watching the Delvers all the while for any hint of treachery. The Changelings, though, seemed unwilling to do anything but watch her, and she saw no evidence of swords, knives, or bows.

What kind of foolish creatures stumble through the great forest without weapons?

"We are Tinukeda'ya," said Zin-Seyvu finally. "As you must know if you are Hikeda'ya. We come from the mountains called Clouds' Rest."

Clouds' Rest was the range far to the northwest of the forest, home to the great city of Hikehikayo, once one of the greatest homes of her people but now empty as an abandoned rabbit warren.

"Truly, we mean no harm to you or any others," the Delver said, perhaps fearful of Nezeru's silence. "We wish only to go our way in peace."

"You keep saying that." She swallowed a last mouthful of fungus. Her hunger had eased enough for her to mourn the absence of some *puju* to make the meal more palatable. Still, beggars could not call for salt, as the old saying went, and if Nezeru was not a beggar, she was certainly not the founder of this particular feast. "But whatever mountains you come from, you obviously don't belong here. What are you doing in the middle of the Oldheart?"

Again a whispered colloquy. "We are here because we have been called," Zin-Seyvu answered. One of her fellows said something that sounded angry, but the speaker shook her head. "No, there is no point in hiding it. This soldier has a sword. We have none. There is no need to hide the truth of the voices that summon us." She looked at Nezeru, her huge, heavy-lidded eyes so imploring they seemed on the verge of tears. "You do not bear us ill-will, do you, brave Hikeda'ya? You need not harm us. We will give you whatever you want."

Nezeru was gratified that there seemed little chance of a fight, but she was obscurely irritated by the Delvers' unwillingness to defend themselves. All through her childhood she had been told that the enslavement of the Tinukeda'ya was itself enough to prove they deserved no better. *"They did not even fight to save their own people,"* one of her superiors had told her when she lived in the Sacrifice order-house. *"Creatures so weak and cowardly not only deserve to be enslaved, slavery is doubtless all that has kept them alive."* The way these Tinukeda'ya had given in so easily, despite their greater numbers, seemed to prove those words beyond doubt. Once again she felt a pang of angry sadness for all that she had lost since leaving Nakkiga—her people, the comfort of her past, everything. Her first meal after a long time of hunger was scant recompense.

The rain returned now, pelting down on the clearing and dripping from the leaves all around. The Delvers huddled together, their large heads like so many mushroom caps. The worst of her hunger sated, Nezeru knew she had to move on. Her pursuers would not be sitting and listening to woeful stories—they would be hurrying after her.

On his way back into camp Jarnulf stopped to watch Goh Gam Gar helping to assemble the monstrous wagon that would carry the dragon back to Nakkiga. Its wooden wheels were almost as tall as the giant himself, and it took six Sacrifice engineers to hold one in place while the giant lifted the wagon to raise the axle to the necessary height. The wagon was so heavy that Goh Gam Gar groaned aloud as he held it while the Sacrifice engineers used cloth-wrapped hammers to ease the wheel onto the axle.

At last the giant was allowed to set the wagon down again. Still groaning, he staggered into the shade of broad yew tree, though the autumn day was not terribly warm.

Still, thought Jarnulf. *All that hair.*

Jarnulf had a brace of rabbits in one hand and a fat goose he had caught rising too slowly from a pond. He handed them to one of the slaves at the cook tent before wandering over to Goh Gam Gar.

The giant watched him from behind half-lowered lids. As Jarnulf sat down on the ground a few paces from the tree, the giant settled back against the broad trunk of the yew, which creaked like a ship's mast in a storm but held, though the whole crown of the tree quivered and needles fluttered down like gray-green snowflakes.

"You are not much in the camp these days," the giant said. "You go out in the morning light, you come back late."

"If I had wanted a wife I would have taken one," Jarnulf replied, untying his jacket. "And I suspect I could have found one less ugly."

The giant curled his lip, showing his yellow, finger-length fangs. "I say only what *Higdaja* must notice also, mortal man."

"I go out hunting. A man can only eat so much fungus, so much sour mushroom broth, so many creatures with an excess of legs."

"And yet for the time he is gone, great hunter Jarnulf brings back a poor bag. Goose and two rabbits? That will not even feed old Gam one meal."

He glared at the giant. "I don't hunt for you, I hunt for myself, and that fat goose will keep me happy for several days."

If the giant had been a mortal man, Jarnulf might have thought the expression on his leathery face was one of amusement. "Why are you angry? You can leave this place if you want. For me . . ." Goh Gam Gar reached up and fingered his heavy collar, thick enough to bow the head of an ox. ". . . not so lucky."

"We are both slaves. I am of a different kind, that is all."

"If you were a slave, you would run if you could." The giant looked out across the camp, then turned his huge, lambent eyes back to Jarnulf. "Why are you still here, mortal man? Don't you know who comes?"

"I know." And that was the true reason he remained, of course. But he did not trust the giant much more than he trusted the Hikeda'ya. "Let us say I wish to see the Queen Who Never Dies. I have heard of her since I was a child, but I have never seen her in the flesh."

"I have," said Goh Gam Gar, and from the way he said it, Jarnulf could not be certain whether he meant something more than just stating a fact.

Jarnulf stood up. "Even though you insulted my skills, Master Giant, later I will bring you a rabbit roasted in goose fat, and I doubt you will turn it down."

Goh Gam Gar showed his teeth again. "Come too close and I will have your arm as well. That would taste good with goose fat too, I am thinking."

"You make me sorry that neither you nor I will get to try such a delicacy," said Jarnulf, and executed a mocking bow before walking away. "But I still have some use for my arms!" he called over his shoulder. "Both of them!"

The giant's words troubled him more than he wanted to admit. Had the Hikeda'ya indeed begun to notice his long absences? A worrisome thought, but things were going to happen soon that would change everything. Jarnulf had no idea whether he would succeed or fail, but either way, there was almost no chance he would survive.

As he settled himself into his customary resting spot at the edge of camp, Jarnulf looked around to see if anyone was watching him. He spotted Saomeji soon enough, pacing back and forth beside the cart where the dragon was being force-fed. The Singer spent a great deal of time making certain everyone knew that he was the one who had captured the prize the queen had demanded—as if the giant and Nezeru and Jarnulf himself, those who worked hardest to bring the creature down the mountain, had simply ceased to exist. But that did not

surprise him. Even mortal men in the slave pens of Nakkiga fought to ingrati-
ate themselves with their masters, informing on other slaves, sometimes even
making up lies that would mean execution for others, simply to keep themselves alive and fed. Why should it be different among the rigid, militant
Hikeda'ya, with their fanatical loyalty to their queen? They were as dangerous
and untrustworthy as wasps. Some of that rigidity worked to his advantage, of
course. Jarnulf had come to this place with Saomeji, and as long as Saomeji was
considered to have achieved a great feat, the Hikeda'ya were willing to over-
look the presence of someone they considered little more than a beast, as Jarnulf's own people might think someone's hunting hound to be beneath their
notice.

And by the time I have changed their opinion, he told himself, *it will be too late for
them to correct their mistake.*

The truth was that during the last fortnight the Hikeda'ya had been in this
camp, Jarnulf had spent only a fraction of his time actually hunting. The rest of
those hours he had put into refining a certain set of skills—skills that, though
considerable by most standards, were not to a point where he felt confident of
success. He knew he would only get one chance to act, most likely in very the
hour of Queen Utuk'ku's arrival, when all was in confusion and all eyes were
fixed on the Mother of the People.

His eyes, still roving around the camp, fixed on a pale, unmoving shape in
front of Akhenabi's wagon. It was Makho, or at least the thing that had once
been Makho. The hand chieftain scarcely moved most days, often spending all
the hours of light and long into the night sitting motionless in the same place,
the twisted, dead gray face empty of any recognizable emotion, the bright
hawk's eye fixed on nothing obvious. The Hikeda'ya were a famously patient
race, but this was something different. It was not weakness: he had seen the
reborn Makho performing exercises with the heavy sword he had been given
to replace Cold Root, acting out the Dance of Sacrifice with terrifying grace
and speed.

Jarnulf turned back to the dragon, now moving its head fitfully as it tried to
escape its handlers, unable to take in any more food. Saomeji and the Sacrifices
under his direction removed the funnel and sack of mashed meat and bone,
then tightened the straps around the beast's mouth once more. It was clear that
the meal had revived the dragon's strength: it struggled against its chains and
groaned in frustration until Saomeji blew a handful of dust into its snout and
the thing finally quieted. For a moment, Jarnulf could not help sympathizing
with the imprisoned brute, but then another thought occurred to him.

Even small things can defeat the largest and most powerful enemies. After all, had
not he and a few Hikeda'ya captured that immense monster? He thought instead of the queen in the silver mask, as powerful as a goddess, as dangerous as
any dragon. But even she could be defeated with the right tools—or at least so
he hoped and prayed. *Wits. Planning. Surprise,* he told himself. *Those are the tools*

by which the small can defeat even the greatest enemies. But only with your help, of course, my great Lord, my God.

Jarnulf knew he was not ready. He also knew he did not have much time. But whatever happened when the moment came, he was unlikely to survive it. There was a kind of terrible comfort in that.

Nezeru woke when water splashed onto her head, startling and frightening her. She leaped to her feet brandishing Cold Root, poised to defend herself, but she saw nothing except the Delvers watching her in sudden fear. A moment later she realized it had only been a broad leaf on the tree just above her that had filled with rainwater, then folded beneath the weight and dumped its contents on her.

She was horrified to realize she had fallen asleep sitting up, leaving herself defenseless, though it seemed as if it had only been for a few heartbeats. Despite all her years of training, her weariness had been so great that with a little food in her stomach she had simply dozed, like any ordinary creature—like a helpless mortal. She sheathed the blade, disgusted with herself. In any case, it was time to be moving: the pursuing Hikeda'ya were likely only a few hours behind her.

Her horse was cropping at the greenery where she had tied it. *This creature is tired too*, she told herself. *Days on end without stopping.*

Reins in hand, she led her mount across the clearing to the place the Delvers huddled. "I am sorry I ate all your food," she said to Zin-Seyvu. "I have not eaten in a long time. I am being hunted. I will leave now, and then you can go on your way."

Zin-Seyvu spread her long hands. "We cannot fight you," she said mournfully. "We are grateful you wished to take nothing else from us. We will find more food."

Nezeru pulled up the hood of her cloak and began scraping mud from her boots with a stick before climbing into the saddle. "Where are you and your people going?"

"We do not know. We only know what we have seen."

"Seen?"

"In our dreams. She speaks to us in our dreams. She called us in our tunnels beneath the city of Cloud Castle—called us to come here."

Nezeru was confused. She tossed the stick aside. "You come from Hike-hikayo itself? The old city? But who is this 'she' who called you? Queen Utuk'ku?"

"We do not know, but her voice was strong and we could not ignore it. We had to obey." Zin-Seyvu turned and said something to her fellows that Nezeru could not understand, but several of them nodded and began rocking back and forth where they sat. A few even set up a soft hooting that she realized after a moment was singing. "She calls us every night when we lie in darkness. She says, 'Come. I need you. I need all the Ocean Children.' Sometimes we see visions of a shadowed vale, and a dark figure as big as a mountain. We only know it lies before us, somewhere in this forest." Zin-Seyvu's face took on an expression of desperation. "You cannot understand, warrior. These dreams and these calls haunt us. Some of us have been driven mad by it. We could ignore the summons no longer. We set out from the Cloud Castle with twice these numbers. The road has been hard and several have perished. But the call continues, night after night. Like you, we cannot stop, cannot take any comfort. Like you, we must keep moving. But you are being pursued. We are being summoned."

Nezeru was intrigued but decided it would have to remain a mystery. *What was it Jarnulf said about stories? That all thinking creatures have one that is theirs alone? So my story has met theirs, but neither of us will ever know how the other's story ends.*

She tilted her head under a dripping branch and took a last drink of water, but before she had even finished swallowing, several of the Delvers suddenly cried out, and she heard Zin-Seyvu coming toward her from behind. Cursing herself for being too trusting, she grabbed at her sword hilt and turned to face what she felt sure was treachery, but the female Delver had stopped a few paces away and was swaying, one great starfish of a hand held out toward Nezeru as if to beg some boon. Then Zin-Seyvu crumpled to the ground and pitched forward onto her face, a long black shaft sticking out of her back. In the split-second it took her to collapse, another of the Delvers was knocked from his place on the log as if slapped by some powerful, invisible spirit. Blood pumped from his long neck around the long, quivering shaft of an arrow. *Black feathers*, she saw with a sinking heart. *Hikeda'ya.*

Her pursuers had been closer than she had guessed, but she had no time to curse. herself for overconfidence. Several more arrows snapped past her as she leaped onto the horse's back and leaned low against its neck, gouging at the beast's side with her heels. She could hear thin, whistling cries of despair from the Delvers behind her as her mount plunged out of the clearing and into the trees, but she could do nothing for them.

Another arrow missed her by a finger's breadth and smacked into the trunk of a tree as she raced past it. Her horse, at least, needed no coaxing to run as fast as it could, making dizzying leaps over fallen logs, crashing through chest-high undergrowth. Nezeru could hear her attackers calling to each other through the trees—as much to frighten her, she knew, as to communicate with each other.

She set her teeth. *But I am no ordinary fugitive,* she thought, and for a moment something burned hot in her breast. *I am a Queen's Talon.*

But even as she clung to the horse's back, fixed on this moment and escape, she was also aware she was being driven south by her pursuers, deeper and deeper into the ancient forest, a place she did not know, a place with many more things to fear in it than simply the Sacrifices chasing her. *Perhaps I should turn and fight . . .*

No, she told herself, and laid her head on her mount's shoulder just in time to avoid being clubbed by a heavy, dripping branch that jutted across her path. *I must try to outrun them . . . try to live. And if I cannot, then I will try make a good ending.* Her Hikeda'ya horse came upon a gully at a speed too great to stop, and leaped. As they descended Nezeru felt herself rising out the saddle, and was almost jarred off completely as they landed with a violent impact on the far side. Only her knees digging into the horse's flanks and her fingers entwined in the mane kept her on its back. They raced on and the trees rushed past her, close enough to touch.

And when my ending does come, I promise I will pass over to the Garden with the blood of many enemies on my sword.

41

A Heart of Ashes

"After all the years that my family and I have been loyal to the crown of Erkynland, Your Majesty, I am disheartened you do not believe me!" Duke Saluceris did not sound disheartened, he sounded furious. The Sancellan's council chamber was full of people—Duchess Canthia, the duke's uncle Envalles, and several others—but Saluceris had not sat once, instead pacing back and forth around the table at the room's center, weaving between the assembled courtiers.

"I do not disbelieve you, Your Grace." It was hard for Miriamele to keep frustration and anger from her voice. "Please do not put words in my mouth. I asked you to tell me again what happened so I can understand."

"More idle talk when my brother has been murdered!"

"The streets are full of rioters. On every corner of the city Ingadarines accuse you of the killing. This is not 'idle talk,' Duke." She turned to Envalles. "My lord, help your nephew to hear me, please."

The older man nodded. "The queen is not your foe, Saluceris. None of us are."

The duke stopped pacing for a moment and looked around the room, as though to make certain that his uncle spoke the truth. "Nevertheless, there is conspiracy afoot here. Someone tries to make me responsible for my brother's murder—my own brother! But I am innocent, and may God strike me down if I lie!"

"I do not doubt you," Miri said again. "Now, please, tell me what happened. You said you received a message."

"From Drusis, yes. It was his written in his hand—would I not know my brother's hand?"

"How did it come to you?"

"I told this already. It was put under my door in the middle of the night. A servant found it and brought it to me. Here, see for yourself." He took out the folded parchment and waved it, then opened it up and read. "You and I must speak, Brother. There are things you do not know. We have a mutual enemy. Meet me at the tenth hour in the Dead House." Saluceris had calmed himself a little, but his face was still flushed and agitated. "That is the name Drusis and I called the Benidrivine mausoleum when we were young. You remember that, Envalles, don't you?"

His uncle nodded and showed the ghost of a smile. "It is familiar, yes. Your mother thought it a terrible sacrilege and forbade you to play there."

"Just so. Who else but Drusis would have known that? And see, the letters are just like his!"

"I see," said Miri. "And what did you do? Tell me again."

"I am no fool. I did not go alone. I do not trust Drusis *that* far. I took three of my most trustworthy guards. We made our way through the gardens and out toward the park. I saw Uncle Envalles sleeping in a chair in the Orangery Garden." He turned to the old man. "Sleeping when he should have been preparing for us to go to the Dominiate."

"I was waiting for you," said Envalles simply.

"In any case, you can pledge that you saw me go past with my guards."

"If you claim that I was asleep, how can I pledge anything about what you were doing?" Envalles replied crossly.

"Enough," said Miriamele. "Speak on, Your Grace. You went through the park to the family mausoleum?"

"Yes. No one was there—not Drusis nor anyone else. The guards will all testify to what I say."

Of course they will, thought Miriamele. *But they would do the same if they helped you murder your brother.* Still, at this point she was inclined to believe Saluceris. It was not just the genuine confusion he had shown when he returned to the palace; if his red-rimmed eyes and air of stunned indignation were play-acting, the duke was one of the most gifted mummers she had ever met.

"I went in first—with one of the soldiers, of course. He went before me. I do not know if you have been in the Benidrivine crypt, Majesty, but it is very large, a veritable catacomb. We found no one waiting there but the dead." He paused again, disturbed by his own words. His mouth twisted in what might have been anger again or something sadder, but he shook it off and resumed his story. "The other two guards, fools that they were, came in behind us to help look. While we were searching the place, someone pushed the great door closed—we did not even hear it. We only discovered that we were locked in when we tried to leave again."

"And that is where you were the whole time, while the rest of us were at the Hall of the Dominiate? Until you appeared here?"

"Yes, and may the Holy Aedon blast me if I tell a single untrue word. We broke open the door at last. It had been barred with a piece of wood from one of the forcing-houses on the slope above the mausoleum. I returned to find all *this* . . . this madness."

At last, as if he had emptied himself like a storm cloud, Saluceris fell into a chair beside his wife. She clutched at his hand. He tried to resist at first, but Canthia would not let go. Her face, Miriamele thought, was that of someone trapped in a nightmare.

Miri felt a little the same.

"And while you were locked in the crypt, Drusis was murdered in his own chapel," she said. "One person could not manage both acts—the Ingadarine estate is too far away, even by horse, for one man to do both. If everything you have told us is true, Saluceris, then this was a conspiracy."

"Of course it's true!"

"I do not mean you have lied, Your Grace. Calm yourself. I mean only if your memories of time and circumstance are correct." She took a moment to look at the others gathered in the chamber. None looked any different than she imagined innocent folk would, all fearful but doing their best to contain it. She looked to Canthia, still doggedly clutching her husband's hand. "Duchess, I will say it again—I think you should take your children and leave the city."

Canthia was startled. "I will not go to Domos Benidriyan and leave my husband here alone. My place is at his side. After all, I am not just his wife, I am the duchess!"

"And your children are the heirs," said Envalles. "The queen is right, Madam. Who knows what will happen if Dallo whips his supporters into a frenzy?"

"You truly think Canthia should leave?" Saluceris seemed bewildered, as though only now realizing how bad things could be. "How can I protect her at Domos Benidriyan? There are only a few dozen guards there—we have hundreds here in the Sancellan."

"I do not mean your city-house," Miriamele said. "That is far too close to the troubles and too hard to defend on top of it. No, I think your wife and children should go as far away as they can. Ardivalis in the north is the Benidrivine heartland. Send her to your family lands there."

"No!" said Canthia. "I will not go! Even the High Ward cannot force me to leave my husband."

"Then you are a fool," said Miriamele, and her harsh words sent a shock through the whole gathering. "And so is your husband if he lets you sway him." She stared at the duke. "Do you not see that whatever happened was no chance attack? This was a plan, carried out by more than one person. We cannot say who would be willing to murder Drusis—not yet—then try to make it seem as though it was done by your hand, but it was clearly part of a larger plan. And as long as you stay here with your children, not just your dukedom is in danger, but the survival of your house."

"What do you mean we cannot say who the murderer is?" said Saluceris. "How can you call me a fool and then pretend it is not obvious to all who is behind this? Dallo! Dallo Ingadaris, that fat spider!"

"Perhaps," said Miri. "But Drusis had only been married to Dallo's niece for scarcely a month and a half. It seems a bit risky for Dallo to give up his best claim to the dukedom so easily."

"But, Your Majesty," said Count Matreu, "who else would benefit from the death of Earl Drusis?"

"Many, perhaps." Miriamele shook her head, suddenly so weary she wished she could get up and go immediately to her bedchamber. She was aching for her husband—for dear Simon, who might not know the answer to any of these questions, but would calm her by his mere presence while she struggled to sort it out. "And that is one of the things we must discover. Duchess Canthia, it might be in my power to force you out of the city against your will, but it is not my wish. I am first and foremost your friend. For the sake of your children, for young Blasis and little Serasina, I beg you to heed me."

Canthia did not reply but only looked back defiantly, though her eyes were wet with tears.

"Be certain that the guard officers in charge are those you most trust, Your Grace," Miri told the duke. "And for the love of Elysia, Mother of God, tell them not to fight back against the people unless it is to save their own lives! Nabban is full of wild rumors and angry citizens—terrified citizens as well, who wonder what has happened, why thirty years of peace has so quickly disappeared. I doubt any of us will sleep much tonight because of the unrest and the earl's murder, but that is all the more reason for the Sancellan Mahistrevis not to make things worse. Anything can happen, but let us not put a torch to our own roof."

Nineteenth Day of Anitul, Founding Year 1201

My good Lord Tiamak,

I send you greetings and trust I find you still under God's loving protection. I have astounding news for you. I have found Lady Faiera alive!

I will not delay by telling of my continuing problems with your friend Madi and his dreadsome offspring, the small criminals who have beggared me and twice forced me to leave a lodging just ahead of being brought to assizes by the innkeepers. That said, I would vastly appreciate it if you would send a decent sum of money no smaller than two gold pieces to the proprietor of the tavern called Li Campino as soon as you receive this, or I may spend the rest of my life in Perdruin, locked in one of Countess Yissola's prisons.

That said, I move to the purpose of this letter.

I learned from someone who knew Faiera that she was thought to still be alive, but that she had left Ansis Pellipé some years before and moved to a mountain village called Piga Fonto on the far side of Sta Mirore, so I hired a mule and rode there, leaving Madi and his bandit offspring behind. This was a mistake, I discovered later, hence the sudden need for two gold pieces, but I will not let that slow my story.

Faiera did not live in Piga Fonto, and nobody there recognized her name, but I was told of a woman named Grandi—some said a "witch woman"—who lived in a hut high on a crag and eked out a living growing vegetables and herbs and concocting healing draughts for those who wished them. So I climbed back on my mule and made my way farther up the mountain until I came upon a tumble-down cottage with a garden full of plants I recognized—and you and your wife would recognize as well—such as Hyssop and Motherwort.

She stood in the doorway of the hut, watching as his mule trudged up the winding path. Her unbound hair was long and gray and fluttered like a cloud being shredded by the swift autumn wind. Her expression was hard and suspicious, but he saw none of the fear he might have expected from an old woman facing a male stranger in her dooryard.

"Are you the one the folk down in the village call Grandi?" he asked.

"They call me many things in the Piga Fonto. 'Grandi' is one of them." Despite the sour flatness of her tone, her words were well formed: she spoke much better Westerling than most he had met in these parts. Away from Ansis Pellipé and its harbors, few bothered to learn another language so well.

"Then I bid you good day. My name is Brother Etan of Erchester. I would have speech with you. I have money and can make it worth your time." He did not have much, though, and he hoped that if this turned out to be another path leading nowhere, he would at least only have to pay her according to local standards. The city and its expensive bribes had all but flattened his purse.

"You might be a handsome young fellow under that idiot's tonsure," she said. "But I am still not in the habit of inviting strangers into my house." She pointed to a log half swallowed by wild thyme. "You may sit on my bench, and we will look over the gardens together as we speak."

This dour jest made Etan's heart quicken a little. "You are too kind, my lady."

She gave him a crooked look. "So. I have little to offer you, Brother, but I always try to show courtesy to God's messengers, even when they arrive by mule. Will you have a little burdock wine?"

"I will, thank you. The weather is cooling now that autumn is here, but it was still a hot ride up the mountain under the sun."

She disappeared into the tiny hut as Etan tethered his mule and cleared a place for himself on the log. She returned with two clay mugs and handed one to him, then returned to her doorway with the other. "Forgive me if I do not sit," she said. "It is pleasant while I am doing so, but it is painful when the time comes to stand again." She took a sip. When she looked up, her expression had sharpened. "Now, what brings a traveling monk to Grandi's door?"

"To be honest, my lady, it is not Grandi with whom I would speak." He took a draught from his cup, wondering only when it was in his mouth whether this might be some mad old woman who poisoned travelers and robbed them. It gave the burdock wine a sour flavor, but he bravely swallowed it down. God would not bring him so far, he reassured himself, simply to let him die here on a hill in Perdruin. "I am looking for Lady Faiera."

To his surprise, the old woman laughed, a deep, throaty sound that went on for some time. It lasted so long that by the time she finished she was wiping her eyes.

"So it is you, after all these years," she said, then laughed again, but it only lasted a moment. "You."

"I beg your pardon? Have we met?"

"No, no. But I knew someone would come. I just did not expect it would take so long—or that the messenger, when he arrived, would be . . . someone like you."

Etan's annoyance at what felt like an insult was pushed aside by the swell of triumph. "So it is you, then, truly? You are Lady Faiera? You do not know how long I have looked for you or how far I have come."

"You have come from Erkynland," she said. "And while you yourself have not been searching for twenty years, I would wager that whoever sent you has been looking for me that long." She shrugged, amusement long gone. "But it does not matter much. Twenty years ago, today—the story is much the same. I will not go anywhere with you, so if that is your intention, put it from your mind. And do not think to force me." For a moment he saw something strong in her face, strong and angry. "I plan to die here. Alone, if I am lucky. But I will not be taken from this place by anyone. Here I have found the closest thing to peace that I will know until God takes me."

"I did not come to destroy anyone's peace, but to bring some peace to others—those who would know what happened to Prince Josua."

"Ha. Of course. I should have known that it would not be my well-being that troubled the minds of anyone in Erkynland."

Etan did not like the look on her face much. "You wrong my friends, Lady. They also have looked for you, and for a long time, as you guessed. But no one knew what happened to you. I have been here in Perdruin a fortnight at least, searching, but I was lucky enough to meet someone who had heard tales of you."

Faiera did not seem interested in that. "And who is left of the old League? For they must be the ones who sent you. The priest Strangyeard, perhaps, since you are both religious men?"

"Father Strangyeard died some years ago from a fever. It was Lord Tiamak who sent me."

This time her laugh was a little less bitter, but still Etan heard pain. "*Lord* Tiamak? My, the swamp scholar has come up in the world. And he sent you? Who else lives? The little troll? I have forgotten his name."

"Binabik of Mintahoq. Yes, he still lives."

"I met the troll long ago, when I met Josua." She sipped from her cup. "Do you truly want to hear my tale? I warn you, it will not lead you to the prince."

Etan swallowed disappointment, although he had not let himself hope too much. "Tell me what you know, please, my lady."

"Very well. But it is a tawdry story—you will not leave here with your faith in God renewed, or anything like it."

"I will treat with my own faith, Lady Faiera, you may rest assured."

"I sense a little steel under that dirty cassock. What did you say your name was—Etan? Very well, Brother Etan. As I said, I met Binabik when I met Prince Josua, although Josua had long since renounced his royal heritage. In my earliest days as a member of the League of the Scroll, Josua invited the Scroll-bearers of the time to the place where he lived in Kwanitupul. Why he should choose such a backwater to make his home I still cannot understand, but he and his wife owned an inn called Pelippa's Bowl." As she spoke, she refilled her cup from a pitcher. "But to speak of Pelippa's Bowl runs wide of what you wish to hear. Still, if you are going to understand, I must start the story even earlier in my life—if you are not in too much hurry."

"Whatever time you can give me, I will take, with thanks. I am your servant, Lady."

"Hah! It has been long since anyone was my servant. Still, I will take you at your word. I was not born in a hovel like this, I will have you know. I was born the daughter and only child of Baron Amando, a Perdruinese noble of some little wealth. As his only child and his heiress I was much sought after, if I say so myself. I danced at the court when I was young, and had many suitors, though you would not credit it now."

A little life had come back to her, and for a moment Etan could see beyond the ravaged, weathered face, past the wrinkles and dirt and all the years, and could very much imagine her as a young woman worth courting.

"Count Streáwe himself was very taken by me, but nothing came of that. Still, my parents did not lack for eligible suitors, though I was not interested. Already I had grown fascinated by books, by poetry, and by natural philosophy, and could not imagine being married to someone who would cage me and show me off like a pretty bird. It would have turned into anger in the end. My father wanted me to marry and birth a boy to take the family name, but both my parents died of the Red Ruin when it ravaged Ansis Pellipe at the end of the Storm King's War. I sold the family land and bought a fine house near the ocean. I made the place a haven for artists, bards, and poets, and answered to no one. I became a scholar of sorts, in part because, with the money I had inherited, I could afford to buy any books I wished, even those that many would have guessed had vanished from the knowledge of mankind. I had friends and intimates—lovers—but learning became my deepest love, particularly the recovery of old, lost knowledge.

"One day I received a letter from Josua, onetime prince of Erkynland. I had heard of him, of course, but did not know he had lived beyond the war. He had learned my name from some of his friends in the Usirean Brothers—the circle of those who buy and study rare books is a small one, so I knew several of them—and he had some questions for me about one of the subjects that interested me most, divination as practiced by the ancient Sithi. We wrote back and forth—so many letters!—and if he was impressed by my knowledge and interest, I was even more impressed by him. After a year or two of such correspondence he asked me if I might have interest in joining the League of the Scroll. I knew of the League and a little of its role in the Storm King's War, and was very much interested, but I was more interested in Josua himself, who even in his letters was like no man I had ever met. So I said yes.

"A few years later he invited the members to come to his inn at Kwanitupul, which is where I met Binabik the troll, the Wrannaman Tiamak, and Father Strangyeard, who seemed at first out of his depth but soon showed that he had depths of his own, as well as a breadth of knowledge unlike anyone else's. But it was Josua who most impressed me, of course." She fell silent, then leaned back, eyes closed, and for a moment Etan wondered whether she would stop talking entirely.

"You would not understand," she said at last, eyes still firmly shut, "what it was like to meet him for the first time. I had formed such a picture of him, of his kindness and his wide wisdom, that I thought that seeing him in the flesh would be a disappointment—but it was not. He was a handsome man, of course. His brother Elias was too, it is said, but his heart was weak and he fell into corruption. Josua was like a saint stepped off a statue, tall and calm, with gray eyes so full of kindness that it was easy to forget how clever he was. Even the hand he had lost only made him seem more tragic, more heroic. I think I fell in love with him then, though I might have been a little in love with him before I ever reached Pelippa's Bowl, just from the letters we had exchanged over the years. Not that he was ever anything but a colleague in those letters. A colleague and a friend. But I had come to want something more. I was not much past thirty years, and my heart was still young.

"His wife Vorzheva was there, of course. She was beautiful in a terrible, dark way, the daughter of a barbarian chief, as full of anger and life as a thunderstorm. She did not like me from the first—women see things in other women that men do not always see, and I am sure she could sense a rival. All through the time we Scrollbearers stayed at the inn, through our long nights of talk and our ramblings across the city—which is one of the strangest in the world—she hovered at Josua's elbow, claiming his attention whenever she could, so that I came to resent her as much as she resented me."

Faiera poured a little more from the pitcher. "Yes, I know," she said. "What right did I have to resent his lawful wife, who only fought to defend what was hers? But I was lonely, not simply for the fleshly part of love, but for the meeting of two minds, two souls, which I had never really known. Josua seemed like the perfect man to me." She laughed harshly. "He still does. Is that not sad?"

When Etan said nothing, but only got up and refilled his own cup with burdock wine from her pitcher, she shook her head. "You do not have to speak. Your judgment is plain on your face. Did you lead a man's life before you became a monk? Did you love someone you could not have? No? Then you will not fully understand, no matter what you have been taught.

"In any case, I did nothing to show how I felt, and when the others went away again I went too, back to my house in Perdruin. Despite the troops of guests and all the servants, it seemed quite empty. I decided that if I could not have Josua I could at least show him that I was someone to be reckoned with, offer him little gifts of my scholarship—something his grasslander wife could never match. So I threw myself even deeper into my studies. The Storm King's War had ravaged the nations and done terrible damage, but the fact that men fought beside the immortals for the first time in centuries brought much learning into the world as well. Some like your King Simon actually lived among them and even became friends with them—or at least so I have heard. It was a wonderful time for those who studied Sithi lore.

"At the same time, Josua's letters to me, which still came frequently, and which I treasured as dearly as if they spoke of love instead of learning, began to have a troubled tone. He had been in correspondence, it seemed, with a young scholar who was following many of the paths I was treading myself. But this was no ordinary cleric or young noble. This scholar was Prince John Josua, King Simon's son, the heir to the High Throne of all Osten Ard."

Startled, Etan made the sign of the Tree. "Prince John Josua? What year was this? How long ago?"

Faiera frowned and brushed her wind-tossed hair away from her face. "I'm not certain. Things changed for me very soon after. But John Josua was very young then—perhaps only twelve or thirteen years. He was a clever, inward-looking child who had found his direction very early, or so I remember being told. He had been named in part after Josua, his great-uncle, and so it was only sensible he would share his fledgling discoveries with him. But young John Josua was already wandering into territory that worried the older Josua—I almost said 'my Josua'—a great deal. I do not remember the details, but the young prince had found certain books or documents in the Hayholt that dealt with the ancient scrying arts of the Sithi, and Josua was frightened for him. *'That is how Pryrates was ensnared,'* Josua wrote, and it was enough to frighten me, too. Pryrates had also been a member of the League, before evil thoughts and evil magic cankered his soul."

"I know," said Etan. "But I am still surprised to hear John Josua was involved in such things at such a young age."

She shrugged. "I do not know much. I remember only what Josua told me.

I wanted to help him, of course—I would have done almost anything for his good opinion—but I was a little afraid as well. In any case, over the year that followed Josua became more and more concerned about what the young prince was doing, what he was reading, what he was thinking.

"I was still very interested in all these matters myself because of my own studies. One day a trader who often found obscure books for me, and occasionally stranger articles, sent me a message. He had found something not just unusual but surpassingly rare, and knew I would be his most likely customer. What he had found truly was astounding, and though it cost me a pretty price—five gold Imperators, if my old memory still serves me—he was right. It was an amazing find and worth every cintis-piece I paid."

"But what was it?" A thought occurred to him. "Was it a book?"

She shook her head. "I will explain soon enough, Brother. The night I brought my new prize back to my house, I had a letter from Josua. He wrote that he was traveling to Erkynland to see his grand-nephew the prince, but that he hoped to stop in Perdruin along the way to visit me and have my advice, because scrying and other forms of divination were my chief study. I was thrilled—more than thrilled—and wrote back at once, telling him he would be most welcome. A part of me was excited simply to have Josua to myself, since his wife and family would not be accompanying him, but I also thought to surprise him and impress him with my find, so I said nothing of it in the letter.

"So it was that he came at last to Perdruin. I had sent away my guests, though 'guests' is not precisely the word—most of them were all but living there and had been for years, feeding off my wealth. I had become disenchanted with them anyway as I grew more and more intent on scholarship. Josua was a little surprised to find the large house empty of everyone but me and the servants, but still we had a merry first evening, talking of many things and staying away from the subject of Prince John Josua, since I could see it troubled him and I wanted nothing to mar our first time together since we had met in Kwanitupul.

"That first night I was so happy—! If Heaven is not just like that, I will be disappointed, because I can think of nothing better. And in truth, I think Josua did care for me more than a little. At the time, it felt like something much larger than that, but we had drunk a great deal of wine. It was hours past midnight when we both stumbled off to our separate chambers, and I remember praying that he would come to me—yes, sacrilegious, I know—but it did not happen."

"I do not judge you, my lady," said Etan, though he was not certain it was true. "But it is clear you judge yourself."

"You cannot possibly guess." Her anger had returned, like an ember fanned by a sudden breeze. "In any case, the next night over supper we returned to the subject we had carefully avoided—young Prince John Josua and his dangerous, foolish explorations."

"And what were those?"

She waved her hand impatiently. "I have already told you what I remember. He was fascinated by the Sithi's art of talking over long distances. He had been searching the castle for old books and had discovered things—not just books, but something else as well, though Josua did not give me details—that worried his great-uncle badly."

"Did he speak of a book called 'A Treatise on the Aetheric Whispers'?"

"The lost book of Fortis?" Faiera gave him a sudden, sharp look. "No, I do not think that was mentioned. I would have remembered, despite all else that happened."

"Please go on, then."

"I was conscious that my time with Josua was limited—that he meant to leave the next day and continue on to Erchester and the Hayholt. It made me a little frantic, I think, to spend so much time talking about such faraway things, about the prince and about the long-dead Sithi, when Josua was sitting there with me. So I told him I had something to show him and brought out my new and expensive purchase—a Sithi scrying-glass."

"A scrying-glass?" Etan did not immediately recognize what she meant.

"A mirror—but a special kind of mirror, made from the scale of a dragon, or so the stories are told. The Sithi used them to talk to each other over great distances. They called them Witnesses."

"A Witness!" said Etan. "Ah! Now I see. Of course." He had never seen one himself, but they were mentioned several times in Fortis's *Treatise* and he had heard Tiamak speak of them as well. "I am told King Simon once had one. But you had one too!"

Faiera's face was grim. "Yes, I did—for a little while. I thought Josua would be delighted by it. Such things are so rare, like finding a piece of the Execution Tree, or a shard of the actual bowl with which Pelippa gave water to the Ransomer. I suppose I even thought of it as a sort of love-gift, to share it with him. Instead, he was horrified."

"Why?"

"He said it was dangerous—unspeakably dangerous. He talked of Pryrates and even of Fortis the Recluse, who wrote the book you spoke of earlier. Josua said that many thought Fortis had found one himself, and that using it had exposed him to the terrible, mysterious fate that had taken him."

"I have never heard that before," said Etan, more than a little disturbed. "What happened then?"

She showed him a sour smile. "Do not think that I will say Josua took it from me, or that we used it and he vanished. My story is not that sort. I argued with him—I could not understand his unwillingness to even look at it, and it hurt me. I had offered him the finest gift I could, and he threw it back in my face, or at least that was how it felt. The argument grew heated, though not angry— Josua was not that sort—and I suddenly realized that instead of drawing him closer to me, as I had hoped, I was pushing him away. That is when I made my terrible mistake."

Again she fell silent, this time looking at her callused hands as she rubbed them together. Some time passed in silence before Etan's patience began to unravel. "Your mistake, Lady?"

"Do they no longer teach Senigo? Senigo of Khand?" she asked, still looking at her hands.

"Of course I know him."

"Then you should remember what he said about truth. *'It is like the foxglove. In proper measure it is the most sovereign of medicines. Too much, though, brings suffering and even death.'* And he was right."

Etan could not help shaking his head. "I'm afraid I don't understand, Lady Faiera. What did you tell Josua?"

"Are you even listening, monk, or are you a fool?" For a moment, in the flash of her temper, Etan could see the noblewoman she had once been, proud, full of her own importance and her own woes. "Do you know nothing of women or men? I told him the truth, and by doing so cursed myself. I told him how I felt— that I loved him." As she fought against a powerful sorrow, her face seemed a mask of something suffering its final throes. Etan could not think of anything to say. When she spoke again, her voice was raw. "With those few words I destroyed all the happiness of my life." She finished her cup in a long swallow and then poured herself another with such haste and inattention that half of it spilled onto the ground beside the log. "What could he do but turn away from me?"

After another silence, Etan at last ventured a question. "What did Josua say when you had told him?"

She looked at him with reddened eyes. "All the expected things. That he cared for me. That I meant much to him. But he had a wife, and he loved her." Her lips writhed like those of a baby about to cry. "I was furious, so hurt that I could barely take a breath. Instead of taking what I offered, a life of two kindred minds, he chose instead to chain himself to that . . . barbarian woman, that jealous savage who did not understand him. But the worst thing of all was his kindness. Even as I raged at him, as I slandered his wife and called him a fool, he never lost his temper with me. I still wake in the middle of the night remembering his sad face, those terrible words that he spoke so gently that I finally fell silent to hear him. He said, 'I want to remain your colleague and dear friend, Faiera. Do not make me choose between our friendship and the marriage I have pledged.' By my God and His Sacred Son, monk, I wish he would have hit me instead of saying that—I wish he would have stabbed me through the heart. No, he *did* stab me through the heart, but he did it with words, and with perfect, knightly kindness. Then he left. Left me in that huge, empty house. I had sent the downstairs servants away after supper so we could have the evening to ourselves. He took his belongings and went, apologizing all the time, as though the fault was his.

"But the fault was that I was a fool. The fault was that I could not force him to love me. The fault was that I had lived with my feelings for Josua so long I could not believe he did not share them, at least a little."

This time Etan did not speak. Faiera stared across her dooryard at the wooded hillside beyond her little plot of land like some battered bird of prey just escaped from a terrible storm.

"I went a little mad, I think," she said at last. "I drank wine and walked back and forth, back and forth. I could not rest. I wanted to see Josua again, to take it all back, to tell him I had made it all up as a strange jest—anything to undo the terrible, final way he had left me. And in that madness, I picked up the Sithi glass. All I could think was that I wanted to see his face, see his expression. Was he sad? Had he at least cared for me a little? Or would I see nothing but scorn? I stared into the scrying glass, the Witness, and thought of him with all the bitterness and hope that swirled within me. And after a while, the reflection began to change. Something was there—but it was not Josua."

"What did you see?"

She waved her hand again, but with the weariness of a dying person. "I don't remember. I remember very little. I was drunk, and mad with grief and love. Something was there, and it spoke to me, though I did not hear words, and I do not remember now what it said. But it pulled me along and I fell in."

"Fell in? Fell into the mirror?"

"There are no words, monk. Fell in, fell through, went beyond . . . I don't remember. I recall very little, as I said. Sometime later I was walking through the house, feeling as cold and solid and empty of life as a stone statue, and I was putting a torch to the hangings, the furniture, my bed. Soon everything was burning. Then I was outside, watching it all as though someone else had done it." She was breathing hard now, the sharp collarbones rising and falling above the bodice of her tattered dress. "There is little else to say. I went mad.

"I lived in darkness for longer than I can remember—like an animal. At last some kind people found me and brought me to the Pellipan Sisters, who took me in and cared for me as best they could. Years went by, and little by little my wits returned. When I was something like my old self again I left the abbey and went back into the world, but there was nothing there for me anymore. My house was gone, I was thought dead, and in truth I *felt* dead. Later I learned that Josua had disappeared after that night, and I wondered if somehow the thing in the mirror had harmed him, or worse, had let *me* harm him." She was wringing her hands again in a curious, unthinking way. "Monk, if you had the eyes of God himself and could look into my breast, you would see a heart of ashes. But this body of mine did not die, and I must live in it until my Ransomer takes me. I have made a life for myself the best I could. My learning, at least, has left me with some use as a maker of potions, a healer. I have lived by myself for a long time. I have thought of these things often. Still, I wish you had not come today."

Faiera pushed herself away from the doorframe, not without effort. He could see her legs trembling. She turned to him and her eyes were now cold and distant. "I know nothing of what happened to Josua, except that the last moments he was with me will haunt me until I die, and maybe longer. I doubt you will find him. Either he is dead or he does not wish to be found. And now, Brother Etan of Erchester, I think it is time for you to go."

42

A Single Arrow

Fremur and Unver were the last two to arrive at the great stone called the Silent One. Fremur thought the scene of the Shan's torture an ill-chosen spot to hold this gathering, but Unver had insisted.

Fremur moved to help Unver down from his horse. The Shan's wounds had healed to deep, blue-purple lines on his face, chest, and back, but he still limped badly.

"If you offer me that arm again where anyone can see, I will cut it off," Unver said. "Many of these men are the same who called me a halfbreed weakling, and who laughed when I was whipped with the Summer Rose. I will not show them any weakness."

He swung himself down from the saddle and began to walk up the hill, hiding his limp with what must have been sheer will. Two dozen men representing a wide range of mostly western and southern clans waited for him beside Spirit Rock—Fremur saw the thanes of Wood Duck and Dragonfly, Adder, Fox, and Lynx. Most of them watched with carefully empty expressions but others showed open suspicion. Only Odobreg and the tall, long-bearded shaman Volfrag seemed completely at ease.

To the obvious surprise of those waiting Unver walked past them to the tall stone, still flecked with spots of his own dried blood. When he reached it he turned and lowered himself to the ground, sitting cross-legged against the pole with the Silent One looming behind him like the tall throne of some stone-dweller king. Fremur seated himself on Unver's right, then Odobreg came to sit on his left. The others joined, facing the Shan in a broad crescent. Fremur could not help looking at the thanes and remembering the tracks of the wolf-pack that had sat in just this way during Unver's long night—like subjects before a great lord. He hoped the others remembered that, too.

The afternoon sun was already slipping toward the horizon and its slanting rays painted the crests of the Spirit Hills with a glow that was almost unearthly, but as the thanes sat in silence, all eyes on him, Unver did something very ordinary. He took off his skin bag and took a drink of it, then passed it to Fremur, who downed a swallow of the sour, fiery *yerut* before passing it to the next man, Anbalt, thane of the Adder Clan from the lakelands.

As the bag moved from one man to the next, Fremur could feel the thanes lose a little of their stiffness. Sharing the *yerut* was not the gesture of some would-be monarch, but of an old grassland chieftain, someone first among equals. By the time the skin had made its way around the circle to Odobreg, who tipped it up and squeezed out the last of the thick, fiery drink, the thanes were looking at Unver differently.

Volfrag began to intone a prayer, but Unver raised his hand. "The spirits spared me and saved me here," he said. "We do not need to ask their permission. I would not be alive if they begrudged me this place."

The shaman's bearded face showed nothing. "As you wish, Unver Shan."

"And if I am the Shan, it was not by my choosing." Some of the chieftains stirred and shared covert glances. "But since the guardian spirits of all the clans have put their trust in me, I cannot turn away. I pledge my life to our clans. I pledge my life to you, the chieftains of those clans." He paused, and it seemed that he would next ask them to pledge their lives to him in turn, but instead he said, "Who is with us, Odobreg?"

"All that you see here," said the Badger Clan thane. "And many others who have left Blood Lake with their people because the First Red Moon waxes and they have far to go. But not all are with you. Antelope Clan and Pheasant Clan refused to swear their allegiance. The thanes of Otter, Wild Horse, and Kunret White-Beard of the Vulture Clan all made excuses, but they are small-hearted and will crawl back to you if you stay strong."

"And what does that word mean—*strong*?" Unver set his hands on his knees, his back straight as a spear against the blood-spattered post. "Does it mean protecting our people and our lands? Then I will be strong. Does it mean waging wars that will do us more harm than good? Perhaps I will disappoint some of you."

"We cannot be disappointed in the choice of the spirits," said Etvin, thane of the Wood Ducks, one of the youngest present. "We all saw what happened. You are the Shan."

"Then tell me what the people need."

Etvin hesitated, unready to be asked to speak so openly. "They need . . . we need . . . to defend our land from the Nabban-men. Every year they take more of the Lakelands. Every year we are forced farther out into bare, rocky lands while they build their houses and castles beside our rivers."

"Unver knows of this," said Fremur. "We are Cranes, remember? We have fought the stone-dwellers for years all up and down the edge of the marshy Varn."

"I am no longer a Crane," said Unver, not in anger but with grim finality. "Nor am I a Stallion, though my mother and grandfather were. If I am Shan, I am Shan of all the clans. But I do not forget that I *was* a Crane. Fremur speaks rightly. I do not ignore what the Nabban-men are doing, and Etvin speaks rightly too. If we are men, we will put an end to such thievery. If they reach toward our cookfire, we must send them away with burned fingers."

"Send them away with no fingers!" said Anbalt of the Adders.

Unver smiled. "It is a way of speaking, only. I am not feared to shed blood. Any who know me can give witness."

"I saw Unver Shan kill many stonedwellers," said Fremur. "Many. He saved a dozen of our kinsmen when armored Nabban-men had trapped them. He fought like Tasdar of the Iron Arm himself." He was suddenly shamed by his own eager words—he was the youngest thane present and did not want to seem it. "He defeated my brother Odrig, who was bigger than any man here, even though Unver was already tired and hurt from another fight."

"We all know he is strong—that he can fight," said one of the other thanes. "We have all heard the stories and we saw him survive what no one else could at Redbeard's hands." He turned toward Unver. "But will you fight against your own people? Your father's people?"

Several of the men stirred, and a few even dropped their hands to their weapons in anticipation of violence.

"That is an ugly question," said Volfrag, and for the first time Fremur saw a little emotion from the shaman, a spark of anger. Fremur still did not trust the man entirely—Volfrag had moved his wagon very quickly out of Rudur's paddock, as the old saying went, but he was the most revered of all the grassland shamans; his support of Rudur had been a large part of what had made Redbeard a man to be feared and respected in the first place.

"Peace, Volfrag." Unver did not seem offended. "The stone-dwellers are not my people," he said calmly. "I have not lived among them since I was a child. My father, may his name be cursed—I will not utter it—and may the buzzards pick his bones, left our family behind without a word of warning or apology. I owe him and his world nothing." He held up his hand to forestall anyone else speaking. "But I know the stone-dweller world better than the rest of you. There are more of them than of us, and their castles are not built just to keep out the rain and wind. They have set all those stones together to protect themselves from each other—and from us. Their strong places are strong indeed. Even a great collection of clans would dash themselves against those stone walls in vain."

"So we should sit like helpless wild dogs while the wolves of Nabban bite away our land, piece by piece?" Etvin of the Wood Ducks spoke with real fury, his voice shaking. "I was born beside Shallow Lake. My family's grazing land, the place my father tied his horses and built his first wagon, now belongs to a Nabban noble. He chased us away from our own lands like we were rats in a midden."

"Do not think we will sit helplessly," said Unver. "But when we strike back at the Nabban-men—and we *will* strike back, I swear by the Sky-Piercer and the Grass-Thunderer—then the stone-dwellers will send their armored knights and foot soldiers numerous as ants against us. We cannot fight them in the old ways—if we could, why did High King Simon and his men defeat us so easily twenty summers ago, though we had three times their numbers?"

The gathered thanes looked at each other, angry and shamefaced. The memory of that lost war was still painful, even for those who had not fought.

"Because we fought the old way," continued Unver. "Each man his own thane, with none listening to any other. That is how we were pushed to these empty lands in the long ago, and that is why we will be pushed and pushed farther east by the stone-dwellers of Nabban. Unless we learn to fight back in a different way. Unless we fight as a nation of warriors, not a collection of clans who come together only when they must."

Several of the thanes gave nods of approval, but others looked doubtful.

"You speak of the High King," said Anbalt. "Even now, he sits at the gate of our paddock, making demands. It is said you bargain with him, but it is not only the Nabban-men who steal our lands. All along the Umstrejha the Erkynlanders have begun pushing their way into our pastures, our hunting lands. We can scarcely water our horses without having to fight our way through them. And their stone city they call Gadrinsett is growing like a boil. Yet you have said nothing about them."

All eyes turned to Unver.

"This is what I speak of," he said. "We men of the grasslands, we are like children, our attention taken by each new thing that happens, forgetting what went before. The High King's men have come to our lands because they barter with us for one of their nobles. He is an old friend of the king and the queen. They are willing to pay much for him."

"How much?" asked one of the northern thanes. "And if they pay in gold, how will it be shared? Who captured him?"

Unver stared at him until the man looked down. "Gold? What will gold bring us? Where will we spend it? In the markets of the stone-dwellers, of course, as we always do. No. I want no gold from the High King."

"Horses?" said another.

"Hah," said Odobreg. "Horses from Erkynland? I would rather ride sheep like the snow-trolls do than one of those sway-backed, heavy-footed things."

Unver shook his head. "Not gold, not horses. What we will receive from the High Throne for the return of their valued friend will be agreements. Treaties. We will make them affirm that everything below the Umstrejha is ours."

Now several of the thanes reacted with open dismay, and Fremur caught Odobreg's eye, letting him know to be ready in case trouble broke out. "We had treaties after the last war!" Anbalt cried. "Nabban gave us treaties and broke them all!"

"But the High Throne did not," Unver said. "The king and queen have kept their words." He laughed, but anger coiled beneath it. "Do not act like fools! Do not think I trust the Erkynlanders to leave us alone forever. Eventually their people will need more room and whether the High Throne wills it or not, the stone-dwellers of Erkynland will turn to our lands. But that will give us time—time to learn to fight against them. And while we have peace with the High Throne, we will make war against the scum of Nabban who think to steal our land without a fight. Would you rather have war at both ends of the Thrithings, north and south? Or would you prefer to be able to fight back against our greater enemies now, and deal with the northern foes later?"

This said, Unver let the thanes murmur among themselves as he stared out into the middle distance. The sun was all but gone now, but its light lingered all along the western horizon like blood seeping into water.

"Here is my word," he said at last, and the bearded men grew silent, watching him now with something like superstitious awe. Fremur saw that he had done something more than incite them—Unver had made them think. "As of this hour, all private feuds between clans must end. Those who cannot settle them peacefully will bring them to me—to all of us—and a settlement will be reached. We waste no more strength fighting among ourselves."

"Bring them where?" asked Etvin. "Will you rule from the Crane camp in the south, Unver Shan, or in the north with the Stallions?"

"I will remain here," Unver said, so calmly it was clear he had already decided. His words sent another stir through the thanes. "This place is sacred to all of us. It is here the spirits chose me. And it is in the center of all our lands—I will not rule as a man of the High Thrithings or any other, but as Shan, and the Spirit Hills will be my clan ground. This stone, the Silent One, will be my seat."

"I hear the spirits speak through your mouth," said Volfrag solemnly.

"And I hear hunger growling in my belly," said Unver. The tall shaman looked offended, but the many of the thanes laughed.

"Come, there is food for you at my camp for all of you—a feast," Unver said. "My mother herself oversaw the preparations, and if you think *I* am a frightening enemy, you will not want to offend her hospitality. Let us make our way down the hill and celebrate a new day for the grasslands." He rose to his feet so easily that anyone but Fremur would have found it impossible to believe how hard it had been for him simply to walk up the hill an hour before.

The thanes, who had waited for him with the faces of men to whom he owed gambling debts, now surrounded him, all seeming eager to walk beside the Shan.

Fremur was willing to give up his place for now. He let himself fall into the rear of the crowd as they walked down the ancient path to where the horses were tethered. He had followed Unver since the first—he had no need to prove anything. And from now on, someone would always have to be watching the Shan's back.

Eolair had only one light in the cramped confines of the wagon, a small oil lamp, but he had nothing to read so it mattered little.

The fortnight he had been Unver's captive had passed very slowly. He had written letters to his sister at Nad Mullach and to Inahwen in Hernysadharc—

that missive had been kept cautiously free of anything that might excite King Hugh's distrust—but of course had no way to send them. They waited in his purse, and if things went as well as he hoped, he would be free to hand them over to the High Throne's royal post himself before too long.

Outside, daylight was fading fast—the bit of sky he could see had turned the purple of ripe grapes—and Eolair was wondering when his evening meal would come when he heard noises outside, grunts and even what sounded like a low cry of pain. He went to the barred opening in the door and looked out, but could see nothing outside but grass and the distant line of the paddock fence. He had just returned to his seat when something thumped hard against the side of the wagon near the door, making him jump in surprise.

He turned, expecting the door to open, but it didn't happen. He got up again and went quietly toward it. As he reached it, a face suddenly appeared in the opening, bearded and grimacing, flecked with blood, startling him so badly that he stumbled backward and almost fell. The face hung there for a moment, pressed against the bars, then the eyes rolled up until they were only crescents of white and the face fell away.

Eolair stared at the door, heart speeding, as another shape appeared at the barred window, a man-shape that he could not quite make out. The door opened and the slave called Baldhead stepped through into the wagon and pushed the door shut behind him. As he came toward Eolair and the light of the lamp fell on him, the count could see that Baldhead's hairless face and rough garment of sacking were dotted with blood.

"What is happening?" Eolair did not like the look Baldhead wore, his mouth pulled tight in a grin. "Who was that man whose face I saw at the door?"

"One of the guards." Baldhead held up a large hunting knife, a formidable blade half a cubit long and smeared with red. "I gutted the first before he knew what was happening, but that second one gave me a bit of a fight before I slit his throat. They forgot that Gezdahn was only a slave for a little while. Before that I was a warrior." His grin widened. "I still *am* a warrior. They can tell that to the other men in the lands beyond who I have sent to death over the years."

Eolair had very little room to maneuver. He backed away until he stood at the far end of the wagon, beside the flimsy cot on which he had sat and the shelf with the small lamp. "Gezdahn? Is that your real name?"

"It does not matter," the bloody man said. "Not to you, Herynstirman. You can call me what you like . . . when you reach the other side." Baldhead lifted the knife and held it before him. Eolair had nothing with which to defend himself except his trembling fists.

If you remember nothing else from the days when you took lives, he told himself, *remember not to be frightened.*

He briefly considered throwing the lamp, hoping the oil was hot enough to burn his enemy, but evening had fallen outside and the idea of fighting an armed man in a dark wagon did not appeal. Instead he began grabbing for whatever might come to hand, but the wagon had been stripped to make it a cell for him, and all his hands closed on was his threadbare blanket. He wrapped it around his forearm just as Baldhead lunged, and the first thrust tore through the blanket. Eolair felt a hot-cold sting along his skin but he had kept the blade away from his body. He did not think he could manage to do it much longer—Baldhead was bigger and younger than he was.

"Why are you doing this?" Eolair cried, more to distract his enemy than out of actual curiosity—the light of madness was in the man's eyes. "I have done nothing to you." He managed to work the cot away from the wall with his foot, and now shoved it between the two of them. "Unver will kill you if you harm me."

"I will not be here for that mongrel to kill." Baldhead made a lazy swipe with the knife toward Eolair's face. "But when you die, your king will blame him, and will make war on him. The stone-dwellers will come to avenge you, then Unver and his motherless followers will die as well."

Eolair saw blood was dripping from beneath the blanket on his arm. He shoved the bed hard against the other man's knees, making his enemy stumble backward a step, but he was still trapped against the wall and Baldhead recovered quickly.

One of the women had left a broom in a corner when cleaning the wagon, and though it was a poor thing made of sticks, Eolair snatched it up and jabbed at Baldhead's eyes, hoping to confuse him long enough to get around him and make a dash for the door. But the Thrithings-man was an experienced fighter and guessed what he planned; he ignored the broom and took a step to the side to block Eolair's escape. "Enough," Baldhead said. "Enough playing. You waste my time, old man." He reached down and grabbed the cot, then flipped it at Eolair, who was hit across the mouth by one of the legs and fell backward with the cot on top of him.

Brynioch of the Skies, forgive your erring son, was his only thought.

Muddled by the blow to his face, he heard something crash and thought Baldhead had kicked the bed away, but then realized he was still caught beneath it. When the fatal blow did not fall, he began kicking his way loose, certain each moment that he would feel the knife enter his flesh. When he was free he looked up from the floor and saw Baldhead was no longer looking at him. The door of the wagon was open and a figure stood there, dimly illuminated by the dancing, windblown flame of the lamp.

"For the love of God," the newcomer said, "the hairless fellow only has a knife. Olveris, throw him your sword."

Another figure now climbed the steps to the doorway behind him, looming a good head higher than the first. "Go fuck yourself, Astrian." He saw Eolair where he crouched on the floor in the splayed wreckage of the cot. "My apologies, Count. *Futústite,* Astrian. I'm not giving some grass-eater my sword."

"Then it will have to be knives," said the short man with a sigh; he sheathed his own long blade before drawing a dirk from his sleeve. Eolair could only stare at this madness, half-certain the fall had disordered his wits, but Baldhead let out an angry growl and leaped toward the short one, the big knife flashing in the lamplight.

As swiftly as a frog catching a fly, Astrian's hand snapped out as the hunting knife came down, and his dagger pierced the Thrithings-man's wrist. Baldhead let out a high-pitched shriek of pain, but managed to hit out with his other hand and connect with his enemy's face, making Astrian stumble backward. Baldhead stood, panting, clutching his wrist as it bubbled blood between his fingers.

"Stone-dweller pigs!" he snarled.

"Try to make it a fair fight, what do I get? Insults." Astrian kicked out and caught the Thrithings-man in the knee, then ducked a flailing swipe of the long knife and drove hard into the man's body, pushing Baldhead back against the wall so that the whole wagon shook. When he stepped back, Baldhead dropped his knife and looked down at the wound in his stomach, which was only beginning to drizzle red, then he slid down the wall to sit on the floor, still staring at his own belly as the light went out of his eyes.

"Much help you were," said Astrian to his tall companion.

"You wanted to make it a fair fight."

"What are you doing here?" Eolair demanded, struggling to his feet. "I know you—I've seen you both at the Hayholt. But what in the name of Rhynn's shining daughter are you doing *here?"*

"Not exactly falling over himself to thank us, is he?" Astrian said. "We are here to save you, Count Eolair. Sir Olveris and I apologize if we interrupted you in the middle of something more important."

Eolair looked down at the dead Thrithings-man. "Leave me your knife and get out of here. I'll tell Unver I did it myself. He wants to negotiate with the High Throne and if you are caught here it will ruin everything!"

Astrian pursed his lips. "I think it is a bit late for that, Your Lordship. You might explain the dead man in here, but there are two more dead men and a spilled supper tray outside. No, you must come with us—we are rescuing you whether you want it or not. When we all get back to camp you will see things differently."

"Are you mad? Unver had agreed to barter me back. He wants peace." Eolair shook his head angrily. "He *did* want peace. Only the gods know what he will want now. Who sent you?"

"Duke Osric," said Astrian. "And you may argue the merits of all this with His Grace. But if you do not come with us peacefully, my lord, I am afraid we will have to tie you up and take you unwilling."

"Ask him about the prince," said Olveris, who seemed to be a man of many fewer words than his companion.

"Ah, yes. Is it true that Prince Morgan is not here with the Thrithings-men? Or was that doddering fool Porto wrong about that, too? He managed to send us a league out of our way as it was."

Eolair still could not believe this was happening—it felt like a fever dream.

"I have no idea what you're talking about, but Morgan was never here. He escaped back into the forest before I was taken."

"Ah. Too bad." Astrian gestured to the door. "Shall we go?"

Eolair allowed himself to be led out of the wagon. The short one was right—it would be hard to explain the two dead guards outside the wagon to a crowd of Thrithings-men already full of hate toward outsiders. Even if Unver believed his story, the Shan might find it hard to convince his underlings. Besides, there was still something Eolair could do that might make all this bloody mess worthwhile.

As soon as he stepped off the stairs and over the body of the guard Baldhead had killed, Eolair immediately headed toward the tents at the other side of the compound. A second body lay not far away, another bearded corpse. This one had fallen with the prisoner's supper tray still in his hand.

"Hai, where are you going, my lord?" Astrian asked, as if Eolair was a wayward child. "Our horses are over there, in the trees."

"If you interfere with me, sir, you will have to kill me. And the king and queen will have your skins. I know what I'm doing. Either follow and keep your mouths shut or start a fight and have grasslanders all over us in an instant." He looked around. "Where have they all gone?"

Astrian hurried his pace to keep up. "They are putting on some kind of feast in the *setta* over there. That is why we thought the time is good. And many of the men are gone somewhere."

"We are going the wrong direction," said Olveris, who had not sped his pace and was falling farther behind.

Eolair ignored them both and hurried across the grass toward the great tent. He could hear voices from within, and when he pushed his way through he saw a large group of women and a few old men, all busy preparing food and drink to be carried out to the field. In the center, with the clear look of a commanding officer, stood the short-haired figure of Vorzheva, Prince Josua's wife, just as he had hoped. Eolair hurried toward her.

"Vorzheva!" he cried. "Lady Vorzheva!"

One of the other women let out a cry and dropped a serving tray—Hyara, whom he had not seen in his first look. "Eolair?" she said. "By the Grass Thunderer, what are you doing here? You are bloody!"

He did not look at her, but went right to Vorzheva, who was shaking her head as if she thought she dreamed. "Lady Vorzheva," he said, "I know you know me. I am Count Eolair of Nad Mullach, and I was one of your husband's close allies. Simon and Miriamele, the high king and high queen, have been searching for you for years. Come with me. Your friends have been looking for you—and for Josua, too. Where is he?"

Her eyes widened and her nostrils flared. She threw her own tray on the floor with a loud crash. "Know you? I know you are one of them. I know you are one of those who tried to take him away. Get out of here. I would never go with you. I spit on your king and queen."

"She doesn't seem to want to come," said Astrian. "Did you notice that?"

Some of the others in the tent had run out, one of the women bumping into Olveris who had just arrived, surprising both. Eolair knew it was only moments before she or someone else summoned help. "Please, Vorzheva. I have been looking for you since I was brought here. Just come and speak to the king and queen. They will honor you! They will send you back here with gifts—they only want to speak to you!"

Vorzheva turned and snatched a knife up from the table, not as long as Bald-head's had been but still a wicked blade, something meant to cut meat. "I will stab you if you touch me. Go on, city-man, run away before my son comes to kill you."

Eolair was desperate now; he took another step toward her, never taking his eye off the knife. Vorzheva was thin but not frail, and he wondered whether he could twist the knife away before she could do him any real harm.

"Perhaps put your thoughts in a letter, instead, my lord," said Astrian, but the alarm in his voice was clear. "I think I hear people shouting."

Eolair lunged forward, hoping to catch Vorzheva's arm before she could cut him badly, then wrestle her out of the tent, but she had already reacted, darting the long blade toward the count's midsection. Something moved suddenly between them.

"No!" Hyara cried as she pushed her way between them. "Vorzheva, don't!"

It was too late—the blade had already plunged into flesh, taking Hyara high on the chest. She took another step, then stumbled and fell to the floor, blood darkening the front of her dress.

A hand closed on Eolair's arm and yanked him backward. Vorzheva threw herself on her knees at Hyara's side, weeping and shrieking with rage, calling down vengeance in the Thrithings-tongue in a voice too maddened for Eolair to understand.

"We must run, now," Astrian said as he shoved Eolair toward the door of the tent.

"Hyara!" Vorzheva shrieked. "No! I will kill them all!"

Olveris was already outside, waving them on. Now Eolair could hear noises from all directions. He realized what he had done and his knees went weak, but Astrian held him up until Olveris could help take his weight, then they hurried him across the paddock toward the dark shadow of the trees.

"You saved me." Levias tried to sit up, but it was still painful for him and he slumped back onto his pallet. "God be praised—and may He preserve you especially, Porto. You saved my life."

"To be fair, it was a Thrithings-man who saved your life—a shaman fellow called Ruzhvang. Do you remember him?"

Levias shook his head. "No, but I bless him too. And your friends. I remember them."

Porto remembered riding the balking mule back to camp behind Astrian and Olveris, both on horseback. "Yes," he said a little sourly. "God bless them too."

"Our Lord Usires has a plan for me—I feel it." Levias reached out and took Porto's hand. "And for you, too, my friend. That is why He spared our lives when we were among the grasslanders. God the Father has work in store for us both, holy work. I will spread His name with joy and thankfulness."

Porto nodded. "God was good to us both. It is surprising, because I have not been His most dutiful son."

"He forgives all," Levias said, then yawned. "He wants you back, as all fathers want their sons back."

Porto thought of his own father, a good man despite his faults. "I can believe that. I want to believe that."

"That is all you have to do." Levias yawned again. "Our time on earth is short, but our time in the hereafter is long. Do you want to spend it in God's loving presence or in a darker place?"

"I have kept you awake too long," Porto said. "I am so happy to see you recovering, but I'm being selfish. You need to rest."

"Never selfish, my friend." Levias squeezed his hand. "What you have done for me I will never forget. Neither will God."

Porto wandered through the camp, waving to those soldiers who hailed him. His return with Levias had been a subject of much talk, and his first nights back he had been given drinks at many campfires, then woke with an aching head and unfamiliar regrets. Was Levias right? Was God trying to tell him that it was time to quit his drunkard's ways and prepare himself for Heaven? Would he see his dead wife and child again there? And poor Endri, his friend who had died so horribly in the Nornlands?

Astrian and Olveris had vanished again, which meant that he had something like a choice of whether to indulge himself or not, and tonight, after talking to Levias, he was not feeling the urge in quite the same way he ordinarily did. It was still there, of course, the sweet song of wine, the invitation to darkness and oblivion, or at least moderate, thoughtless happiness, but his days trying to get his wounded friend away from the Thrithings encampment had made it all seem different. He could not help remembering the night when Rudur Redbeard had died and the grasslanders had gone mad. Men fighting and killing each other, women dragged into the woods and raped, old blood feuds suddenly sprung to deadly life. It had been like some vision of Hell, like the heedless damned tormenting each other—the Adversary's demons were not even necessary.

We make our own Hell on Earth, he thought. But the difference was, death would end *this* Hell. The other one, though, the one that waited for unshriven sinners, not just for murderers but for drunkards and thieves as well, both of which Porto had been—that Hell awaited. And in that Hell, the bleak, terrifying night in the Thrithings camp would last forever.

Porto realized he had wandered near to the edge of the camp, where the Erkynguard had built bulwarks on the banks above the Laestfinger. On the far side of the wide river lay the shadowed, flat emptiness of the High Thrithings. But it was only empty of trees and mountains. Even as he walked along the edge of the barriers he could see grasslanders of the Bison Clan on the far side of the river, carrying torches, hooting and taunting the Erkynguard, sometimes throwing spears that splashed into the river. Once or twice one of them even got off a throw so powerful that a long spear crunched into the sandy bank on the near side of the river.

Somebody hailed him from one of the guard posts and he walked over. The nearest Erkynguardsman offered him a wineskin. The night was cold so Porto took a swig, but the next time it was offered him he waved it off. He could not stop thinking about what Levias had said.

"God's mercy, here's that big one again," said one of the guards. Porto looked up and saw they were all peering over the barrier, across the river. A large shape, monstrously malformed by the flickering light of windblown torches, was loping toward the far side of the river. The spear in his hand disappeared as he threw it, sailing invisibly through the blackness, then it landed with a loud *kritch* in the sand of the nearer bank.

"He's going to get one in here before too long, you mark my words," another soldier said.

"Well, keep your heads down then," said the sergeant. "Bloody fools."

But one of the other guards had stood, drawing his bow.

"Hi, there, what are you up to?" the sergeant said. "Put that away or I'll have you whipped. You want to start something with these mad clansmen?"

"Just wishing I could let him have one," said the soldier, sighting down his arrow. "Tch! There he is! I'd love to give the big hairy bastard one in the belly."

"He's at it again," someone else said. "Get your heads down!"

Porto was peering between two of the huge logs of the barricades, and saw the giant Thrithings-man had been given another spear, and was starting a run to the edge of the water. A dozen or more other grasslanders trotted beside him, waving torches and bellowing their approval. The big man took a last step, but jerked and stumbled as he released his spear, which wobbled only a short distance and disappeared into the gurgling river. The man who had thrown it took another wobbling step, then slumped to his knees. As the other Thrithings-men gathered around him with their torches, Porto saw a long, feathered shaft sticking out of his belly.

The Erkynguard sergeant had seen it too, and his voice rose to a panicked rasp. "Bloody Tree of the Aedon, Renward, what did you do?"

"It wasn't me!" the soldier said. "See, it's still on the string!" He brandished his bow and unshot arrow, as if that would make what had happened go away.

"Sweet Usires, *someone* did it!" cried the sergeant. "Now we're in the shit and that's certain!"

The slain spear-thrower had collapsed to the ground with his comrades milling around him. One of them let out a high-pitched howl of rage that seemed barely human, then waded into the river, spear in one hand, ax in the other, still screaming his anger. The rest of the grasslanders followed him. Within the space of a few dozen heartbeats they had splashed their way across and were running up the bank toward the Erkynlanders' barricades, waving their torches and shrieking like the tortured souls Porto had been imagining just a short while before.

"Someone blow a horn, for the love of Heaven!" the sergeant shouted. "Raise the alarm! We're under attack!"

Porto heard the sputtering wail of a horn climb into the air. Within moments it was answered all along the edge of the camp by more horns and the shouts of startled Erkynguards.

"They're coming! The grasslanders are coming! Every man forward! To arms!"

43

Something for the Poor

The wafting smoke of torches and incense filled the Cathedral of Saint Granis, a murk that hovered like a cloud above the heads of the mourners, obscuring the stained glass images of the saint and the Ransomer's other acolytes. Miri stared at the windows, hoping to glimpse some sunlight or at least some color through the pall.

She definitely did not want to look at the corpse of Drusis in its casket, resting on a bier in front of the high altar. It was not because the body was horrible to look at—the funeral priests had done their work well, and the wounds that had killed him were hidden. Earl Drusis, hands folded across his sword, looked as if he was merely resting before rising to lead Nabban against barbarian invaders. But Miriamele had never been so fearful about her mother's country before, and the dead man was at the heart of that fear.

Who had killed him, and why? She stole a discreet glance at Duke Saluceris, who had decided to attend his brother's funeral despite Miriamele's cautions. Of all in Nabban, it seemed that Saluceris had the most to gain from the death, and she did not doubt many if not most of those present at the funeral mass believed the duke was guilty, especially with his strange story of having been tricked and then locked into the family burial vault while the murder took place. But it was precisely the ludicrous nature of the story that made Miriamele doubt Saluceris had been involved. The most powerful man in Nabban could easily have arranged for his brother to be killed in a way that made him look less culpable.

Still, it was hard to imagine who else would benefit. Dallo Ingadaris, sitting grim-faced a few seats away from Saluceris, had lost his best tool for opposing the ruling family. Yes, it made Saluceris's position shakier, but that seemed like a poor trade for Dallo to make. His niece had only been married to Drusis for the shortest period of time—why would Dallo act to destroy that?

Miri could not make much of the expression Turia wore, because her face was hidden behind a dark veil, but it was not hard to guess: the girl was a mere thirteen years old and already a widow. Miri had no doubt that Dallo would be marrying her off again soon to the next suitor who could bring him some advantage in the dogfight of Nabbanai family politics. She seemed to be handling the situation bravely—Miri had not seen a shudder or sign of despair from her once during the long funeral *mansa*—but she must be frightened at how quickly her life had changed.

Escritor Auxis finally began the last stages of the *Mansa séa Cuelossan*. Miri shifted in her seat, fighting the ache of sitting too long in one place. Lector Vidian had conveniently decamped to his winter palace in Sina Gavi—conveniently for him, at least—leaving Auxis to carry the flag of Mother Church. If there had been any doubt that the escritor was Vidian's heir-apparent, it was gone now. For a brief instant Miri wondered if Auxis might be the one manipulating things, but although she did not like the man, she had seen nothing in his character or acts to suggest he might actually murder an important noble to further his own ambitions.

Sweet Mother Elysia, save me from this madness! she prayed. *I suspect everyone of everything.* When she had agreed to come back to Nabban she had feared that the violent bitterness of the age-old struggle for power here might pull her into ugly situations; that fear had been proven horrifyingly real.

The Octander Covenant is as good as dead now. I will try one last time to force Dallo Ingadaris and Saluceris to sign, but Dallo knows the advantage has shifted to him, as well as the sympathy of the people. Would that have been enough to lead Dallo to kill Drusis? She could not make it work out. Drusis was a much more useful player alive, as an unspoken alternative to his brother. Now Dallo was the leader of the opposition, and though the fat little man was vain, he was also clever enough to know he was not liked or trusted even by his allies.

As Auxis began the final blessing and everyone rose, Duke Saluceris made the Sign of the Tree and then, with his guards, moved toward the back of the cathedral so they could leave ahead of the procession that would carry Drusis's body back to the palace to be entombed in the family vault. Miri approved of the duke's caution. The streets were full of angry people, and they would be even angrier when the body of Earl Drusis was brought out.

As she looked up, a thin shaft of sunlight stabbed through the nave, illuminating for just a moment the glass window of Saint Granis himself above the high altar. The saint was praying at the base of the Execution Tree, hands raised in woe and supplication before the writhing, inverted figure of Usires. The only other figure in that momentary illumination was humble Saint Yistrin, his shovel lying on the ground beside him. Yistrin's Day had just passed—Simon's birth-day—and Miri was suddenly pierced by a pang of love and regret. She missed her husband and felt shamed that she had not written to him in days, despite all that had happened—all that he needed to know. She resolved to prepare a letter that evening, so it could go with the packet ship on the morning tide.

Escritor Auxis had finished. The bearers of the casket had stepped forward to move it to the wagon that would carry it to the Benidrivine vault. Miri rose, assured Count Froye and Captain Jurgen she was well, and then waited for the crowd to file out. She was going to break tradition by walking at the back of the funeral procession instead of leading it, which would have been the normal protocol, but she felt it important at this moment to try to separate the High Throne from the local passions that had turned so murderous.

The morning sunshine vanished as the clouds blew in from the sea; the mourners were lashed by rain as they climbed the Mahistrevine Hill behind the earl's casket, from Saint Granis' Cathedral to the Benidrivine family mausoleum, but the procession halted before continuing into the ducal palace.

"What is this?" said Sir Jurgen. "Why have we stopped?"

"Has someone attacked us?" asked Froye, nervously fingering the Tree that hung on his breast.

"It feels too orderly to be an attack," Miri said.

"Let us go around, then," Jurgen said. "We will force our way through to the palace."

"Do not let your men draw weapons unless we are truly threatened," she warned him. "That is an order. I will not be the cause of a riot. Not today."

When they had forced their way around the edge of the crowd, swollen now with many who had not been in the church but had waited outside, she could see that the wagon bearing Drusis had stopped before the gates of the Sancellan Mahistrevis. It was not hard even in the rain to see faces in the palace windows, and Miri felt certain that one of them would be that of the duke, since he had left early and his troops were now lining the walls in full armor. She could breathe a little easier now—at least Saluceris and his family were safe. But why had the funeral procession stopped? What was Dallo doing?

The answer came quickly enough. A portly shape, aided by soldiers wearing the Ingadarine Albatross, clambered up onto the open wagon to stand over the casket. As the sun found a chink in the heavy clouds, Count Dallo pulled back his hood and looked down on the mourners, who had begun crowding even closer when the funeral procession stopped.

"Today is a day of sorrow for us all!" cried Dallo in a voice loud enough for even those far from the wagon to hear him. "Drusis, Earl of Trevinta and Eadne, lies here in his coffin, struck down by vile murderers in the chapel of my own house. Twelve wounds his murderers gave him—twelve times they struck with their cruel knives, and left him dying on the floor. Murderers who still walk among us!"

The crowd's murmur rose to a growl of anger.

"For the love of our Ransomer, what is he doing?" asked Froye. "Does he mean to whip them into attacking the palace?"

"No," Miri said. "His tricks are always more subtle than that. Jurgen, keep that sword sheathed. We are guests in Nabban."

"I will not let anyone harm you, Your Majesty."

"Nobody has offered me harm—not yet."

As Dallo continued to declaim about the murder, Miri looked at those who had been closest to the wagon and saw Lady Turia immediately behind it, her veil thrown back, watching her uncle with a blank, pale face. What must she be thinking? Miri's heart ached that a girl so young should be dragged into such events, as she herself was when her father had gone mad. But whatever else Dallo planned by this display, she felt certain he would not want any harm to come to his own niece, the dead man's grieving widow.

"And the last of them struck at his heart—his lion's heart, that beat only for Nabban and his people!" Dallo had been enumerating the wounds of Drusis. "Only then did he cease fighting his cruel attackers. Only then, with his noble blood soaking the stones of the chapel, did he give up his struggle. They killed a great man."

The crowd's roars took on a hungry note, a sound of need, of violence barely restrained. Miri suddenly wondered whether Dallo really might intend to try to rouse them to attack the Sancellan Mahistrevis.

"We stand before the palace of our leaders," said Dallo. "We stand before the heart of our nation, and I ask Duke Saluceris, *where are the murderers of your brother Drusis?* Does someone hide them? Why have they not been brought to justice?"

Miri could hear the cries of some of those nearby. One man screamed, *"Burn it down!"* and Jurgen moved his men in more tightly around the queen, Count Froye, and the other courtiers, who looked terrified. Miriamele could also see the danger, and was just considering having Jurgen and the other soldiers force a way through the crowd when Dallo abruptly held up his hands.

"But this is not merely a day to mourn," he cried. "This is also a day to celebrate the life of Drusis, who cared for his people more than he cared for himself. For not only did Earl Drusis fight for Nabban against the barbarians of the grasslands, and against all traitors and dishonest men here in our great city, but he made a will to share his wealth with *you*, the people, whom he loved best." Dallo gave a sign to his soldiers and a couple of them climbed up onto the wagon with him, bearing a wooden chest that even the pair of them struggled to lift. Dallo threw back the lid and reached in, then withdrew his hand and showed it to the crowd. Even beneath gray skies and slanting rain, the gleam of gold was compellingly bright. "Drusis said, 'If I should die untimely, give my gold to the people!' And I cannot but honor his wishes." So saying, Dallo threw a handful of golden and silver coins into the crowd. Some were caught in mid-air, but many more fell at the feet of the mourners, who threw themselves down like otters chasing a fish, shouting and struggling to snatch the rolling coins.

"Do not fight! Drusis would not want that! There is enough to share for all who loved him!" Dallo reached down for another handful to fling into a different part of the crowd. "Drusis said *'Give the people my gold!'*" he shouted.

As the coins flew glinting through the air like burning bits of the sun and stars, some snatched by grasping hands, others splashing into puddles so that men and women wrestled for them in the mud, Miri stood dumbfounded.

Count Dallo was clearly enjoying himself, death of an ally or not, flinging coins far out into the throng and watching the convulsions where they landed.

"We must go, Highness," said Froye in a panicky voice. "Even if they do not mean to storm the palace, Ingadaris will make a riot here. We are not safe. *You* are not safe."

But as Jurgen and the rest forced a path to the gates through the surging throng, Miri could not help looking back, wondering what Dallo hoped to accomplish by this bizarre spectacle. He had all but suggested the dead man's brother was hiding the killers, but instead of fanning those flames into an inferno of anger, he had turned the mournful procession into a festival of mud and gold.

The people had crowded close to the funeral wagon now, despite the best efforts of Dallo's Albatross guards. Many who pushed toward it were beggars who could not hope to win out in a physical struggle for what Dallo was distributing, and so besieged the wagon instead, a garden of waving, grasping hands all around Dallo Ingadaris and the earl's casket. A few of them even made it past the guards and began to climb the wagon itself, which rolled a little bit from one side to another as the soldiers dragged them back off again.

Then, as Miriamele watched, one determined beggar in a tattered cloak made it onto the wagon and crawled along the side of the coffin to Dallo's feet, but instead of snatching gold from the chest or raising his hands to plead like the others, the cloaked figure grabbed at Dallo's legs. While the count swayed and tried to pry him loose, the beggar swung his arm at the count's stomach, as if trying to shove him away while still clinging to him, then abruptly let go and rolled off the wagon and disappeared into the frenzied crowd. Dallo stood up straight, watching where the tattered figure had gone, then looked down at himself and slowly raised his hands toward his face.

For a moment, because of the rain and dim light, Miri thought the dark stuff on Dallo's fingers was something else—mud, perhaps—but then the count swayed and took a step and fell full-length across Drusis's casket, smearing it with blood. The guards kneeled beside him, and the mourners nearest the wagon let out screams of horror and alarm.

"Mother of God preserve us!" Miri cried. "Dallo has been attacked! Hurry, Jurgen. We must get away from here now!"

Like salmon swimming up the Gratuvask rapids, the queen and her party forced their way through the tide of humanity pressing forward to see what had happened. The moment of stunned near-silence had given way to shrieks of terror and bellows of despair. One of the guards pushed his way onto the driver's bench of the funeral wagon and whipped the horses forward while the other cradled Count Dallo. Many could not get out of the way fast enough, and were trampled beneath the hooves of the horses or ground beneath the wagon's huge wheels.

"Hurry," she said. "Hurry! We must reach the palace or be killed here!"

The sun had vanished behind the clouds again; the day had gone dark. The rain began to pour down, and the crowd around them was all wide, white-rimmed eyes and screaming mouths.

Jesa was back in her family's hut in Red Pig Lagoon. The ladder was creaking. The wind wailed outside and rain battered the thatch roof, but she still could hear the ladder going *eek-eek-eek* as someone climbed it.

Now she was standing before the doorway. The house was empty and she was alone, but someone was coming up the ladder. She saw the face first, the handsome, full-lipped face beneath curly hair matted by rainwater. She tried to tell Lord Drusis that he did not want her—that he was in the wrong place—but could not make words come out of her mouth. Something had put a spell of silence on her, and she could only back away from the door, helplessly lifting her hands.

As he climbed higher, she saw that Drusis wore a white winding sheet marked in many places by the blood of his wounds. This did not seem unusual, although the emptiness of his face frightened her. But as the figure made its way onto the floor of the hut and straightened up, she could see that the earl's arms were backward, the elbows toward her, the hands facing away. He was a *dhoota*, an angry, hungry ghost. She tried to scream, but her voice was still sealed in her throat. Drusis took a step toward her, then another, each one louder, louder . . .

Jesa woke up gasping, to the sound of thunder booming in the night sky.

She rolled off her bed onto the floor, then crouched on her hands and knees as her heart struggled to escape her breast like a trapped bird. As soon as she could breathe again she scrambled across the room, still on all fours, and looked into Serasina's cradle, but the child was sleeping peacefully on her stomach with her head on one side, her fat cheeks squeezed by the bed so that she looked like a lump of bread dough. Jesa sat down on the floor beside the cradle and wept a little.

It was not the first time she had dreamed that terrible dream. Her mother had once told her of how her own uncle Jaraweg, taken by a crocodile, had come to her in a dream as a ghost with arms on backward, and had chased her through the swamps, crying out that he was cold from sleeping so long in the depths of the lagoon. The story had terrified Jesa as a child, and even though she had never seen her mother's uncle and had no idea what he looked like, he had come to her in many nightmares.

Now the ghost had a new face.

Jesa said a prayer to He Who Always Steps On Sand and She Who Waits To Take All Back over the sleeping baby.

Guide her safely, she begged. *And do not take her before her time. Let her live to know life. Let her escape these terrible days.*

Outside lightning flashed. Moments later, as she finished her prayer, thunder boomed like an angry crocodile.

What will become of us? she thought. *First the duke's brother, now Count Dallo. Is the drylander God killing the duke's enemies? Or does he mean to kill us all, one by one?*

"The Great Lodge will burn from the inside." The voice of the old Wran-woman at the market came back to her again, each word icy and painful as a knife-slash. *"Many will die."*

She could not stay here in this doomed place a moment longer, but she could not leave little Serasina behind, either. Jesa went to her chest and dug down until she found her run-away bag, packed and ready. Her heart ached at the thought of how frightened the duchess would be if Jesa took the baby away to safety, but she told herself Canthia would thank her later for saving her daughter. How could any of them not see that their God—that all the gods—must be angry? That something even more terrible was about to happen?

As she opened the sack she heard a noise behind her and turned. A shape stood in the doorway, all blowing white, and Jesa let out a strangled scream.

"Oh!" said the duchess. "Oh, I didn't mean to scare you, but I'm so worried. I couldn't sleep. I wanted to hold my little one."

Jesa could only stare at her mistress, suddenly as unable to speak as in her dream. Canthia walked across the room and lifted Serasina from the cradle. The baby complained sleepily but did not wake.

"Come with us," said the duchess. "Come and get into the bed with us, dear Jesa. My husband is downstairs—he will not sleep tonight either. He and his advisers are trying . . . trying . . ." She trailed off, suddenly as wordless as Jesa, and walked out of the room with the baby clutched to her bosom. Jesa let out her breath and tucked the bag back into the depths of the chest, then followed.

It was one of those increasingly rare things, a day of clear skies, though the air had a chill bite to it. Miriamele had taken her ladies walking in the gardens, but if she hoped to cheer them with a promenade among the now leafless fruit trees she had failed. All the women could talk of was danger and doom, the curfew, the deaths of Drusis and Dallo, the perilous streets of Nabban that they dared not walk even with the duke's soldiers out in force.

Miri had just decided it was past time to send them all back to Erkynland, even if she could not allow herself to leave yet, when a messenger came from the duke asking her to come to the throne room.

Saluceris, his uncle Envalles, and several more members of the duke's inner circle were all waiting there. Most of them wore their swords in acknowledgment of the dangerous times. They all bowed as Miri came in with her guards, although she thought she saw hints of resentment on more than a few faces, including that of Duke Saluceris himself, and she felt a moment of anger. Did they think that all this was her fault? That things would have somehow gone better if the High Throne had not been in Nabban during these dark days?

"We have had a response from Sallin Ingadaris, Dallo's son," Saluceris told her. "I thought you might like to read it."

She took it from the duke's hand. *"If I cannot even give my father a proper funeral,"* Sallin had written, *"I can hardly be expected to sign a treaty that gives away the rights and privileges of my house. The duke's troops bar me from the streets of my own city . . ."* She looked up. "I have the gist of it. Am I the only one who also sees that Sallin, that great lump, did not write this?"

"It does not matter who wrote it," said old Envalles. "Sallin signed it, and he now speaks for Honsa Ingadaris."

"It's full of lies," said Saluceris. "He is not banned from giving his father a funeral. He is banned from giving his father a public funeral."

"For the Ingadarines, those are the same thing," said Lord Chancellor Idexes.

Miriamele knew that in this at least, Envalles was right—it did not matter who had authored the letter, Sallin the count's unfortunate son, who cared only for hunting and drinking, or some family adviser. The Octander Covenant, which Lector Vidian had only signed after near-blackmail, was no more. "They have nothing left," she said in irritation. "Whatever the cause and whoever the fault, the brains in that family are gone. Why will they not make peace?"

"Anger," said Saluceris. "Dallo had a plan to snatch the throne, or at least to snatch at power to match mine. Now they have nothing." He looked at Miri. "Will you stay, Majesty?"

"I suppose not. But if a new pact can be negotiated, I will return." She sighed, but tried to hide it with a movement toward the door. "Lord Envalles, I wonder if you would grant me a little of your time?"

The duke's uncle rose from his stool. "Of course, Majesty. You honor me."

She led him out. "Sir Jurgen, come along," she told her guard captain. "Bring a pair of your men. I will have some work for you later."

When they reached her chambers, she left Jurgen and his men outside. "Lord Envalles, will you take a cup of *Cudomani* with me?" she asked.

"I will, thank you," he said. "You are very generous, Majesty."

"Generous with someone else's cellar. It's not quite the same thing."

When her maid had served them both and retired to the bedchamber, Miri sipped her apple brandy and looked the older man over. In tribute to the martial spirit, Envalles too had donned a sword. He was still a trim figure for his age, and she did not doubt he could wield the weapon to some effect if it was necessary, but she could also see more than a little anxiousness in his posture.

"How may I help you, Majesty?"

"I've been wondering about Saluceris being lured away, and I was hoping you might be able to lend me your thoughts. First off, it seems unlikely that letter was written by Drusis himself, don't you agree? From what we've heard, Drusis must have been dead since early in the morning. Even on foot, a messenger could make it from Domo Ingadaris to the Sancellan in a matter of a half hour. Yet the letter only came here at ten of the clock."

Envalles tugged at his beard. "I suppose you are right, unless Drusis wrote it and asked for the letter to be delivered later in the morning."

Miri nodded. "Perhaps. But why would Drusis want to meet on Saluceris' home ground, and so soon before the ceremony to sign the pact at the Dominiate? And how would the duke even reach the mausoleum without coming through the main gates of the Sancellan Mahistrevis? I've had my men search— there is no easy way over the walls into the graveyard."

"Hmmm, yes." Envalles looked disturbed. "You raise a good point, Majesty."

"But if the letter did not come from Drusis, then from whom? Who would know enough to mimic his hand so aptly? And who would know that the mausoleum was once a meeting place for them when they were young—a place that Saluceris believed only Drusis would know?"

"I'm afraid I cannot help you, Majesty," Envalles said. "These matters are too deep for me."

"Are they? Because it occurred to me that you, Envalles, are one of the only people left in this Sancellan who saw the boys grow up, who knows Drusis well enough and long enough to perhaps be able to forge his hand in a letter."

A faint gleam of perspiration now became apparent on Envalles' brow. "I . . . I don't . . ." He licked dry lips. "Are you accusing me, Your Majesty?"

"Of killing Drusis and Dallo? No, no. Of writing a letter and helping to make sure the duke could not establish his innocence during the time of Drusis's murder? Yes. Yes, Lord Envalles, I think I am." She swallowed the last of her brandy, then rose and walked around the room as she continued. "Saluceris saw you sleeping in the garden. Or he thought you were sleeping. But it would have been easy enough to deliver that letter in the dark of night, then wait in the garden until the time came."

"This is sheer madness, Majesty. I have been one of the Benidrivine House's most loyal members—!"

"Interestingly enough," she continued as if he hadn't spoken, "while they were looking for ways into the cemetery from outside the palace, my soldiers found an old gate, half-hidden by ivy, which leads from the orangery, where Saluceris saw you sleeping, to a path that leads to the cemetery and the Benidrivine vault. It would have been easy enough for you to follow the duke and his guards, wait until they were inside, and then bar the door shut."

"Were you not my queen, I would demand satisfaction for my honor!" Envalles' face was red, but Miri did not find his show of indignation convincing. "You have no proof for any of this . . . this . . . wild fancy."

"I have gathered that Saluceris has some very painful ways of getting proof out of those he deems criminals," she said. "I would hope you would confess now, so that we can find out who put you up to it—who is really behind all this—without having to resort to such methods."

"I have done nothing! This is preposterous!"

"Sir Jurgen!" Miri shouted. An instant later the door opened and the guard captain came in with his men. "Lord Envalles will be confined to his room, and that room will be locked. If any of the duke's men try to stop you, here is my signet." She handed him the ring. "I will discuss my reasons with Duke Saluceris."

Envalles was still protesting his innocence and making vague threats as Jurgen led him away, but Miri thought—not without a little satisfaction—that the prisoner did it without much real conviction.

In the two days that followed Miri noticed a definite chill in the Sancellan Mahistrevis, much of it directed at her, if only by looks and whispers. Saluceris himself had barely been dissuaded from freeing Envalles immediately, and the rest of his advisers were aghast. Only Duchess Canthia spoke up in Miri's defense.

"Envalles has always resented you," she told her husband. "He was quiet about it, and I did not think it would ever go so far as treachery, but it is true nonetheless."

"What are you talking about?" Saluceris demanded.

"When your father died and the High Throne made you duke, he was very angry. He thought you were too young, and that as oldest male of the household he should have been named regent until you were of age. He said that to many people. Some of them have told me over the years."

"Who? Who said this?"

"It doesn't matter, Your Grace," said Miri. "And I do not suggest Envalles had an active hand in your brother's death. We know he did not leave the Sancellan that night or that morning. He may even have thought he was delivering a note that Drusis wanted but did not dare write himself."

"That makes no sense," said Saluceris angrily, but was distracted by the arrival of one of the heralds, resplendent in sky blue tabard emblazoned with the golden Benidrivine kingfisher. "What do you want, man?"

The herald, mindful of protocol, bowed deeply to the queen and then to his master and the duchess. "At the gate, Your Grace. Lady Turia Ingadaris—with six armed men wearing the Ingadarine albatross. Your brother's widow desires an audience."

"What is that child doing here? And why would I see her, especially when she brings soldiers with her?"

"A mere half a dozen," Miri pointed out. "The smallest possible amount any noblewoman of standing would take with her for protection these days. She has not come to attack us. Perhaps she wishes a parley."

"Why would I parley with a child?" said Saluceris, scowling. "Very well, bring her in. But her men will be disarmed. If she does not trust me that far, she has her own house to go to—although it is short of menfolk these days, even if you count that muttonhead Sallin."

A very short time passed before the herald returned. He stopped in the doorway of the throne room and announced, "Lady Turia Ingadaris, Countess of Eadne and Drina."

The girl was dressed all in black, wearing a hooded cloak against the rain, but Miri could still see that her mourning clothes were of exquisite make, Khandian silk with ilenite threads gleaming in the subtle embroidery. Turia stopped just inside the doorway and made a courtesy toward Miriamele, then straightened. "Your herald is wrong." Her voice was small and high, but somehow it carried. "I am the widow of the duke's brother. I am called Turia Benidrivis."

Saluceris did his best to hide his annoyance. "Our apologies, sister-in-law. And we extend you our sympathies on the death of your uncle."

Turia showed him a swift smile with no life in it. "On behalf of Count Dallo's family, I thank you. And now, since the curfew you have instituted is but an hour or so away and I would not want to be arrested by your soldiers, Duke Saluceris, I wish to have an audience—"

"I am very busy, Lady Turia," the duke said hurriedly. "I can make a little time for my brother's widow, of course—"

"You did not let me finish." This time she put a bit of a sting in her words. The courtiers grew wide-eyed and began to whisper among themselves. "I do not seek an audience with you, but with Her Majesty, Queen Miriamele. A privy meeting, away from other eyes and ears."

Miri was surprised but did her best not to show it. "Certainly, my lady. If the duke does not grudge it to me, I can meet with you in his study." She turned to Saluceris. "Would that be agreeable to you, Duke?"

Saluceris was as startled as she was, and more than a little offended—the color in his cheeks emphasized the lightness of his whiskers and the white hairs so newly visible in them. After a moment, he waved his hand, almost violently. "As you wish, Majesty. But for your safety, I will post guards outside the door."

Miri frowned. "I do not think that necessary, Duke Saluceris. Not while I have a conversation with this bereaved young woman, just the two of us."

The duke gave in with poor grace, shrugging his assent. As Miri and Lady Turia walked out, he started a conversation with Idexes Claves. Miri heard them laughing loudly as she left the throne room.

Once in the duke's study, with faithful Jurgen standing guard outside, Miri seated herself and gestured Turia to an embroidered bench. "Will you take some wine?" she asked.

Turia shook her head. "No, Your Majesty. I will not stay long. I have only a brief message for you, though it is an important one." Raindrops still sparkled on the fur lining of her hood. Real diamonds sparkled in her black hair, a slender circlet of gems that Miri guessed could pay for a small country estate. But she could not read the expression on Turia's face. Placid, at least at first seeming, but with something working beneath. Anger? Unhappiness? "Please, then," she said. "Share your message with me."

"It is a simple one," the girl said. "It is time for you to leave Nabban."

She spoke in such a matter-of-fact way that for a long moment what she said did not sink in. When it finally became clear that she had heard exactly what she had heard, Miri did her best to compose herself. "Is that a piece of advice, Lady Turia, or a warning? Or is it a threat?"

"The first two, certainly." The girl's dark eyes now met hers and held her gaze for so long that Miriamele was the first to look away. "When we first met, Your Majesty, I told you that I respected and admired you. That was true and still is. But you are in a place you no longer understand, if you ever did. And if you do not leave, I cannot promise you will be safe."

Miriamele fought against rising outrage—was the child mad? Had grief at losing husband and uncle so closely together damaged her wits? "Pardon me, but did you just tell the High Queen of all Osten Ard that *you* cannot guarantee *my* safety? To be honest, I do not know what to say to such an affront, Lady Turia."

"Then do not think of it as an affront." The girl smiled again, a swift, thin sliver of white, like bone revealed by a butcher's knife. "Think of it as a warning, sincerely given. You do not understand Nabban, Queen Miriamele. This place is in your veins, perhaps, but not in your heart. You do not understand *vindissa*."

Beneath Miri's anger something else was stirring, incredulity turning slowly to something a little like fear, but when she spoke it was with heat in her words. "Do you mean I do not understand vengeance, my lady? Or that I do not understand the Nabbanai word?"

"You do not understand the idea, I fear, and what it means here. In Nabban, we do not wait for kings and queens to solve our problems. When blood has been spilled—family blood—we take revenge. My husband was murdered. I will have *vindissa* for that. Even if it brings God Himself down in fury—even if the whole city must burn—I will see the murderer of Drusis punished."

She said it with such flat certainty that Miri found it hard to respond at first. "These are terrible things to say, Turia. You are full of grief and anger—"

"No. I am not."

"—But you do not understand what you say. I cannot leave, even if I wished to. This city and this country are balanced on a knife's edge. I will stay here until I see peace return. Do you not think I want to go back to my home, my husband, my grandchildren?" She thought of lost Morgan and felt a sudden stab of fear she could not entirely hide, a shortness of breath that took a moment to pass. "No, Turia. This overwhelming anger is not the way. We do not know who killed your husband."

"I know." She spoke with utter sincerity. "I know all that I need. And I will make his murderer pay."

"And what of your uncle? He too was killed. Will you find his murderer too and have your *vindissa* there as well? Must all of Nabban watch the blood-feud rage on and on, watch murder after murder, all for this vengeance you think is so important?"

Turia laughed. It was an astonishing sound in the circumstances, a girlish trill that Miri would have expected from a child dancing around the Yrmansol tree at a jolly festival gathering—but Turia's dark stare was flat, empty. "Vengeance is not something I choose, any more than I choose to breathe. It has been chosen for me. And you are not the only one who does not understand it. You speak of my uncle's death. He tried to tell me that my vengeance for Drusis's death was a small need, that it must wait until this and such was accomplished, that if I could but be patient—on and on, blowing like a bellows, saying nothing.

"I will not need to take *vindissa* for my uncle's death, Queen Miriamele, because it was my doing. He tried to forbid me my vengeance. If you seek to do the same . . . well, it will not go well, not for you, not for the High Throne. I make no threats, Your Majesty." This time the smile was almost shy; Miriamele could still not entirely believe the words she heard were coming from this pretty, rosy-cheeked girl. "As I said, I admire you. I also have no desire to start a fight with the High Throne. But Nabban is mine. Proving that may take months or years, but I am young and patient. If you stay here it will not slow my work by even a day, but it will make things more difficult for everyone. And it will put you in harm's way."

Turia abruptly rose and made another courtesy, even as Miri struggled to make sense of all she had just heard. "*You* had Count Dallo killed?"

She gave a sort of shrug. "He tried to tell me what I could and could not do. But if you tell the duke or any of his courtiers, I will deny I said it, of course. And even if they believe you and try to hold me here, by tomorrow the supporters of my house will pull down the very walls of the Sancellan to free me, and more people than just the murderer Saluceris will die—many more. I do not wish that. It is unnecessary."

"*Unnecessary?*"

"Yes. I do not claim *vindissa* against any but those who have wronged me. But it will be difficult to achieve it without many deaths, and the longer I am forced to wait, the greater those losses will be. Anger runs high in this city, my queen—anger my uncle fed for a long time, and his foolish son, my cousin Sallin, now thinks to use for his own gain. *He* thinks House Ingadaris is his now. He is wrong and will find it out soon enough."

"Stop!" Miriamele got to her feet. "This is madness, Turia. My heart aches for you, raised in such a household. I can see now that Dallo has poisoned your understanding, darkened your heart . . ."

"Dallo taught me many things I needed to know. But he also lacked resolve." She nodded her head, then pulled up her hood. "I came here to give you fair warning, Your Majesty. My vengeance will not wait. Leave this place before Nabban kills you. Leave it to those of us who understand its ways."

Turia opened the door and went out. For a moment Miri considered ordering Jurgen to stop her, to hold the girl so that she could make her listen to reason. For a moment Miri told herself that she could talk Turia into something like sense, that the terrible things she had said could be unmade or changed. But when she remembered Turia's cold eyes, her tuneful laugh as she talked about murders done and murders to come, Miri knew she was lying to herself.

"I have made a mistake," she said out loud, though there was no one else in the room to hear her. She stared at the door that had closed behind Lady Turia. "I have made a terrible, terrible mistake."

44

Departure

Tzoja found herself thanking all the gods she could remember—the martyred Aedon, the Grass Thunderer of the Stallion Clan, even the Hidden God of the Astalines—for saving her eyes. Even if she were to be blinded tomorrow, she would remember this moment forever. She was trembling so badly that she had to clutch at the carriage's windowsill to keep her feet. Surely nobody, not even the longest-lived of the Hikeda'ya, had ever seen anything like this.

Queen Utuk'ku was leaving Nakkiga.

Tzoja leaned out the window of the wagon, breathless and frightened. The procession stretched far ahead of her vantage point, to where the first of the Sacrifice legions had already reached the distant gate, while Tzoja and Vordis and the rest still waited on the Field of Banners beneath the shadow of the mountain. All along the ancient Royal Way the denizens of Nakkiga stood dozens deep, waiting for a glimpse of their godlike queen. Many had not seen the sun in years. They moaned and wept and cried out, exhilarated but also terrified by this unprecedented event.

Hundreds of Sacrifice riders on powerful black horses rode behind the foot soldiers, and behind them rumbled the first of the train of immense wagons full of Hikeda'ya nobility. Their carriages were like great houses, each wagon pulled by a dozen shaggy Nakkiga goats with oddly shaped, powerful legs. The queen's train stood waiting behind the courtiers' wagons. Utuk'ku's wheeled palace, made of half a dozen even larger wagons, the whole assembly as long as a merchant ship, now began to creak as the goats, a full half-dozen yoked teams, pulled against their harnesses. As the carriages rolled forward the wheels of the heavy carts cracked the already ruined stones. A few bystanders, mostly human chattel, were jostled helplessly forward by the huge crowd until they fell beneath those mighty wheels, but the wagons did not slow. Slaves trudged after with long, hooked sticks to drag away the mangled bodies.

At last the leading section of the great parade was coaxed through the old gates on the outskirts of Nakkiga-That-Was. The crowded wagon that held Tzoja, Vordis, and a half-dozen other mortal slaves now began to move, rocking and lurching as it slowly rolled past the hills of rubble that had been stacked after the siege and the mountain's collapse. Tzoja heard the cracking of drover's whips and shouted curses, then almost fell when the cart lurched into a rut of collapsed paving stones, though they were only halted for an instant. Drums beat and more whips cracked. Slaves strained against heavy ropes and sang songs of mortification and despair as the wagon began rolling forward again.

"What do you see?" asked Vordis from the floor where she sat with the other captive mortals.

"Everything."

"Tell me, please."

Tzoja did her best to describe the procession, which now stretched all the way into the wild lands outside Nakkiga-That-Was, but was distracted when the throng gathered beside the road began to shriek and wail in frenzy.

"What is that?" Vordis asked, frightened by the tumult.

"I'm not certain. I . . ." Tzoja fell silent, staring.

Rumors had passed even among the slaves that the queen was not inside her great train of carriages, but Tzoja had assumed the Mother of All would enter them when it was time to for the procession to depart. But now, as she looked back along the line of wagons, she saw an astonishing immensity emerge from the darkness of the mountain. It was Queen Utuk'ku, mounted on the most bizarre and frightening beast Tzoja had ever seen, a creature beyond imagining.

One of the Astalines had told her a story once of a legendary empress of Khandia, who rode out once a year on a great beast called an Ebur, an animal three times as tall as a man, with a snake for a nose and wings for ears. Tzoja had doubted such a monster could exist, but the queen of the Norns had just emerged from Nakkiga into the dull sunlight riding the back of a monster that beggared any Ebur that might ever have lived.

The thing looked like a cousin to the borers of the lightless Nakkiga depths, armored like them in a segmented, dark-gleaming shell, but this creature was much longer than any borer, and had countless pairs of legs. Its front end was blunt, but many eyes glittered there, and its mouth was an abomination of twitching parts that might have been jaws or simply more legs. The queen, as well as several nobles and a handful of Queen's Teeth guards, were mounted atop it in a sort of pavilion secured behind the immense thing's head. As the vast beast crawled out into the light onlookers began to scream. It was hard to know whether they were more frightened by Utuk'ku's monstrous mount or the unprecedented prospect of the queen's departure.

A low-caste Hikeda'ya woman held her child up as the many-legged beast approached, perhaps hoping for a blessing from the queen. Instead, the great, blunt head lashed to one side, and she and the child were snatched up and swallowed. Those around her tangled in shrieking chaos, trying to escape a similar fate, but the drovers walking beside the creature poked at its eyes with long spears that smoldered red-hot at one end. The many-legged thing flinched away and took no more onlookers.

"Why do they scream?" Vordis asked. "What is happening?"

"It is the queen," said Tzoja, but words still failed her. "The queen is leaving the mountain."

Days passed as the great royal progress moved south and east, not as swiftly as it had marched out of Nakkiga, but still moving with surprising speed, the teams of black goats replaced at intervals with fresh ones so that those who had been pulling could walk unencumbered until they were rested. The massive train of the queen's carriages never stopped moving for long.

Queen Utuk'ku abandoned the pavilion on the back of the many-legged thing once they were past the outer wall of fortresses that surrounded the heart of Hikeda'ya lands and from that point rode in her train of carriages. For a day or so the monster's handlers kept the great beast walking behind them, then the first snow flurries of the coming winter began to fill the sky and the great crawling thing slowed until it could not keep up. The last Tzoja saw of it, as she and Vordis were being brought to the queen's carriages in a smaller wagon, the massive beast lay dead or dying on the road behind them, curled and motionless as a discarded ribbon, snow piling in the crevices between its segments. Its purpose of spectacle served, the royal progress soon left it behind.

Several times Tzoja was summoned with Vordis and the rest of the Anchoresses to Utuk'ku's great, linked carriages, but each time Tzoja was left with other body-slaves instead of attending the queen. She began to wonder why she had been plucked from her hiding place and spared the death she had thought certain, only to be ignored.

Then came a day when Tzoja alone was summoned.

"What will I do if you are not there?" she asked Vordis. "What if I cannot understand the queen's words? I do not speak *Hikeda'yasao* as well as you."

Vordis touched her face with a cool hand. "Do not fear, dear friend. The Mother of the People will make her wishes known. Wait until you are instructed and do only what you have been told. It is frightening, but you are clever and brave."

Tzoja did not think of herself as particularly clever, and she knew she was not brave, but she also knew that she had no choice. She allowed the expressionless Hikeda'ya guard to lift her from the running board of their carriage onto his saddle. The horse was large and heavily muscled beneath the thick black hair. It had been years since she had been on a horse, since her days in the Astaline settlement when she had sometimes ridden a swaybacked old mare out into the birch woods in search of useful herbs for the founder, Valada Roskva. Feeling this much larger mount beneath her only reminded her of how much of her life had been taken from her. Every time she had found peace—during her childhood in Kwanitupul, her brief time in Erkynland after escaping from the Thrithings, or the dream of contentment that had been her time among the Astalines, even during the unexpected moments of comparative comfort with Viykei in Nakkiga—someone had snatched it all away again.

Why have you chosen this path for me? She did not know who she was asking, did not know if she prayed to anything at all, but the question still burned. *Why am I allowed no happiness?*

She was handed from one guard to another at the rear of the queen's train of wagons, then delivered to a group of Anchoresses who silently washed her and prepared her for the queen. After she had been anointed and dressed in a clean robe, the blindfold and mask were put in place, then she was taken by one of the Anchoresses into the next wagon, a place of moisture and warmth and silence. No voice of Drukhi sang this time. She could hear no other sound of breathing or movement in the room, so she thought she must be alone.

Come closer, said a warmth-less voice that seemed to come from everywhere at once. Tzoja flinched and almost fell back against the door. *Come closer,* the voice said again; she heard it everywhere but in her ears. She had no idea where it came from, or where she was supposed to go, but when she had regained control of her shaking legs she took a step away from the doorway.

Here.

Light-headed, her heart speeding like a bumblebee's wings, Tzoja took a step, then another, her hands reaching to feel for obstacles. After a moment she touched something hard and solid. She stopped and let her fingers move carefully across it and realized it was a sort of raised bed or table.

Do not fear, mortal creature. I did not bring you here to harm you.

The source of the words seemed no closer, but Tzoja could sense something just beyond her fingertips, and she hesitated. "I do not know what to do, O Great Queen," she said in a voice she could barely control. "I do not know how to serve you."

I suffer. The words entered Tzoja's thoughts as though she had conceived them herself, but the strength, the potency of them were nothing of hers. *I am in pain. My healers cannot help me. Do what your folk have taught you to do. If you succeed, you will be rewarded.*

At that moment, the only reward that would have meant anything would have been to be set free to go and hide in the carriage with Vordis and the other slaves and never have to come so near to this overwhelming, frightening creature again, but she could not say that. She could barely think. "Then I . . . then I must touch you, Great Queen," she finally answered. "I cannot know anything without searching for signs of your illness on your body." Even as she spoke, she felt a sudden moment of hope, for surely the Mother of All would never allow herself to be touched by a mortal's hands.

Do what you must.

Tzoja swallowed, then swallowed again. She cautiously reached forward until her fingertips encountered the almost intangible barrier of a spidersilk blanket that covered the chilly length of the queen: Utuk'ku was lying on her back like a corpse being prepared for burial. For the first time, Tzoja was truly grateful for the blindfold—she did not think she could have looked into the queen's eyes so closely without her heart stopping.

She let her fingers drift along the royal body, but kept them outside the blanket. With her hands on the narrow ribcage she could feel the slow move-ment of the queen's breath, one inhalation for every half dozen of her own. She found the testing spot at the side of the queen's neck, just beneath the cold metal of her mask, and felt for the heartbeat. At first, frightened and ashamed, she was certain she had done something wrong because she could detect noth-ing. It came at last—*tum-tum*. Relieved, she waited for it to return, and counted many of her own hurrying beats before she felt it again. *Tum-tum*. Slow, so slow! But how was she to know what was right for someone so impossibly old? She could not even guess at the queen's age—from what she had been told, Utuk'ku might be a thousand years old or ten thousand.

For a moment Tzoja paused, overwhelmed by the hopelessness of the task. How could she, a mere mortal, hope to help this ageless creature? But if she did not, she was only another useless slave, and Viyeki had told her many times about the Fields of the Nameless.

She traced down the length of the queen's hip. It was unutterably strange to realize that the Mother of All was no larger than Tzoja herself—a little taller, perhaps, but more slender, with fine bones that might have belonged to some soaring bird of the air.

At last she put her hands under the covering, struggling hard to keep from shaking as she touched the queen's skin. She did not know what to expect and half-feared to discover something terrible, scales like a serpent or the damp stickiness of an earthworm, but instead she felt nothing stranger than a woman's body, thin but not fleshless, the skin dry and cool. She put her fingers against the stomach and pressed gently, searching for inflamed organs, but found noth-ing she could call unusual, and the queen did not seem to feel pain at any of her probing.

"I . . . I do not find anything clearly wrong," she said at last. "And in any case, I must gather herbs before I can help you, Great Queen. I had no physic garden in Nakkiga—it has been long since I practiced any healing—and it is late in the year, but there are still things I might find that could help ease your pain."

You have permission. The second thought was sharper. *You will be accompanied by a guard at all times.*

"And there are . . . other things I need too." Tzoja's heart was still rabbiting. She could not have imagined this day, this moment, even in her maddest dreams. "I need fluids of the body, to examine." She swallowed. "Fluids of your body, Majesty."

My Anchoresses will provide them to you. Help me and you will be rewarded. Fail me and you will be a long time in sorrow.

Tzoja jerked her hand away as though it had been burned, then forced herself to reach back toward the queen's body again, willing her hands to stop trem-bling, wondering if the queen could glimpse her every thought. *Like God* she thought. *As they say about God, that He sees everything, knows everything . . .*

"I have it!" said a voice just behind her, speaking out loud, frightening Tzoja so badly she almost fell forward against the queen. "It has ripened! Oh, see it! Great-Great-Grandmother will be so pleased, she will surely give me more—"

Jijibo! Silence! The queen's angry thought crashed through Tzoja's head like a clap of thunder, dropping her onto her knees, her skull throbbing.

"But you cannot be wrathful with your dutiful grandchild!" the newcomer burbled. "Look, the last one has ripened! It is as beautiful as blood!"

Out, mortal. There was no question this was meant for her. Tzoja scrambled to her feet, desperately trying to remember where the door of the wagon was. She felt someone brush past her and smelled the strangest combination of scents she could remember, peach blossoms and spoiled meat and the sour tang of blood, all suffused with a cloying perfume that would not have been out of place on a slave-whore chosen from the lowest pens. *Jijibo*, she finally realized, her thoughts chaotic and slow. The new arrival must be the queen's descendant, the one that the Hidden had told her was their savior, or at least their master, the Dreaming Lord.

Fumbling, she found her way to the door only to be met there by another body, an Anchoress who must have come at the queen's silent call. For a moment they tangled in the doorway and Tzoja's mask was knocked askew. The Anchoress roughly pushed her through the door; as she stumbled over the high threshold the mask fell off, tugging the blindfold down far enough that one of Tzoja's eye was uncovered. She fell to her knees again, scrabbling on the floor of the wagon for the mask, her thoughts full of terror. She found it and lifted it to her face, but as she did a sound made her turn.

The door had been left open, and a lurch of the wagon had made it swing wider. For an instant Tzoja saw the inner room whole, frozen in a single moment, like one of the religious paintings she had seen in northern churches.

A blind, masked Anchoress was helping the queen to sit up on her cot, Utuk'ku wound in her sheet like a corpse, all of her hidden but the masked head. A strange, tatterdemalion figure was on its knees beside her, holding out something that gleamed pink-orange like a sunset sky. It was a fruit, round and scarcely larger than a fat plum, and it seemed to glow with a light of its own.

Tzoja pulled the mask back over her face, then turned and crawled as swiftly as she could away from the queen's retiring room and down the passage that ran the length of the wagon, feeling the great wheels bumping below her, grinding everything beneath them as they turned. Another Anchoress lifted her to her feet and led her away, and it was all gone again as swiftly as a dream.

Cuff the Scaler spent his days dragging heavy broken stones across the ruins of Naglimund and his nights in a muddy pit with the rest of the slaves. It was hard to sleep while the dying moaned and the living wept, but every night his exhaustion quickly dragged him down into slumber.

And every night he dreamed.

Ever since his foundling childhood, the only thing Cuff could do better than anyone else had been to climb. His legs were short but strong and his arms were as long and powerful as those of Brother Aart, the abbey's blacksmith. As a child, when Cuff made mistakes and people grew angry with him, he would run away and climb to the rooftops. Later, as he grew bigger, he would climb the guard towers, or even onto the high walls of the keep. Sometimes he would linger in the high places for hours while the priests or others he had offended followed him from building to building, shouting up at him to come down and be punished. At last kind Father Siward had recognized that Cuff's exceptional skill was God's gift—"a gift to someone who has not many others" the priest said—and urged people to give the young man tasks that suited his abilities. Soon Cuff was fixing roof tiles on the fortress or thatches in the town below, ringing the bells in St. Cuthbert's steeple, and chasing pigeons and rooks from the statues of the saints that decorated the outside of the church. "Scaler," the people began to call him, and every time he heard that name it made him proud, just as Brother Aart the smith was proud, or Brother Girth the wheel-wright: it meant he had work of his own, that he was doing what God meant him to do.

Cuff was strong, too, with hands toughened by his climbing and fingers that could grasp a branch or the edge of a roof like an owl's claws and not let go. Sometimes the soldiers in the fortress towers would give him a walnut so he could crack it between his thumb and one finger. They even made wagers with other soldiers who had never seen the trick. Cuff worried a little that making wagers might be against God, so he didn't tell Father Siward about it, but he was always pleased to show what he could do. It was good to have friends, even if they teased him sometimes and called him names when he did something wrong. He did not blame them for getting angry. He knew his thoughts were slow and his tongue did not always work the way it should. He had been named after the abbey when he was a foundling; Father Siward always said the name was inspired because Cuthbert was the patron of the lame and the halt. But even when he grew, Cuff could never say the saint's name properly, though it was his own name, too. He pronounced it as "Cuffer" because his mouth wouldn't make all the sounds, and "Cuff" was even easier.

Cuff had not always been happy, but his life had seemed useful. He had be-lieved he understood what God wanted of him, and that he could do it, and even be welcomed into Heaven someday. He had believed all these things . . . until the demons with white faces had attacked his home, killed his friends, and made him a slave.

And every night as he slept shivering on the damp ground, he dreamed—but not of happier times, which would at least have been a kind of escape. Instead he dreamed that someone was calling him—summoning him. The dreams had begun before Naglimund fell, but now, like a river that had overflowed its banks, the dreams had become a roaring flood from the moment his eyes closed until they opened again. And they were always much the same—a voice out of darkness, a woman's voice, calling him to come, begging him to come to her. *"You are needed,"* she told him, night after night. *"We are waiting for you."* But day after day he woke in a muddy pit, still a prisoner of the white-faced demons, unable to go anywhere except back and forth between the ruined church and the growing mountain of rubble he and the others had hauled away. But the dreams never left him now, even when he was awake, and though Cuff thought slowly, when he began to think of something, it was hard for him to stop.

Could it be holy Mother Elysia he heard, calling him to Heaven? Cuff told the other slaves about his dreams, begged them to explain what the voice meant, but no one could tell him. Some only stared at him, and some were angry. They were all slowly dying, beaten, overworked, and starving, enslaved by the heartless creatures who had destroyed their homes and murdered their kin. Many of them would have given much to dream Cuff's dreams—to have any hope at all.

It seemed there was no escaping Shun'y'asu, Viyeki admitted to himself. The poet of Blue Spirit Peak had written:

> *Be wary of charity*
> *If you give a starving child a crust of bread*
> *Soon you may feel pity for the servants who fail*
> *To remember the scented oils for your bath.*
> *You may stop beating your slaves*
> *When they look on you without love.*
> *All that is good will totter and fall*
> *Because of a crust*

He had always assumed the short poem to be merely ironic: Shun'y'asu's sympathy for Nakkiga's lower castes was one of the foremost reasons that his work had been forbidden by the Hamakha Clan. But now Viyeki thought perhaps there was more truth to the poet's words than he had ever guessed. *Because once an exception is allowed,* he thought, *how can the others be kept out? How can you ever stop?*

Viyeki suppressed an unmagisterial sigh and raised his hand. "Nonao," he told his secretary, "tell the foreman to stop beating that mortal slave."

Nonao shouted the command and the Builder foreman turned with a look of anger on his face, but as soon as he saw the High Magister watching from the stairs the foreman dropped the rod and fell to his knees, pressing his forehead against the damp ground.

Viyeki made his way down, moving at a pace commensurate with his station. The first part of the work had gone swiftly, the engineers needing less than two days with their hammers and grapples to bring down the shell of the mortal temple, which now lay in mounds of scattered rubble. But Viyeki knew that clearing it away would not go as swiftly, and all the stone would have to be removed before his Builders could begin digging down to the old structure beneath the ground. Even the addition of a few hundred mortal slaves could only speed things so much—most of them were women, children, or old men— and Viyeki could feel the queen's impending arrival with the same trepidation as a farmer before harvest watching an approaching storm.

But it must be done. The Mother of All does not share Shun'y'asu's sympathies. She will not hesitate to execute us all if she is displeased.

He reached the place where the foreman still kneeled. The slave he had been beating was a male, apparently healthy and strong, though he cowered now with his hands over his head. Few mortal males of any age were still alive, and Viyeki thought it would be a shame to lose another. "What happened here?" he asked.

The foreman rose to a crouch but would not meet the High Magister's eye. "A thousand apologies, my lord, but this one, this slave, he talks to the others. He distracts them, and for all I know he incites them against us."

"Do not let them kill him, great lord!" begged one of the other slaves, a woman. *"He does not understand, that is all. He is simple-minded."*

Viyeki's command of the mortal tongue was not good enough to understand all her pleading, but he recognized the words "understand" and "simple" and reasoned out the rest. He looked down on the slave who had been beaten, who was now peering up at him between his fingers.

"What is his name?" he asked the woman.

"Cuff, my lord. That is what everyone calls him. He is simple-minded. He means no harm."

Viyeki waved away the explanation and examined the huddled figure. The slave had long, strong arms, but as he slowly lowered his hands, Viyeki could see the shape of his face and his confused look, and knew he had understood the woman rightly.

"Cuff," said Viyeki. "That is your name?"

The slave nodded his head rapidly, his overstretched smile revealing several missing teeth. "Cuff," he repeated. His tongue was too large for his mouth, his speech slurred and awkward. "Cuff the Scaler. That's true! Cuff is a good boy." And then suddenly, before Viyeki, his secretary, or the foreman could do anything to stop him, the slave scrambled over and threw his arms around Viyeki's legs, prostrating himself at the magister's feet. "Don't hurt Cuff. I work hard! Hard!"

The foreman hurried over to drag the slave off him, but it was too late— Viyeki's magisterial robes were smeared with mud. The foreman dragged the offender away and threw him to the ground. The slave lay on his back, weeping now, arms and legs curled protectively above him like a dying insect. The foreman pulled a sharp-bladed adze from his belt and looked to the high magister for permission to dispatch him.

"Work hard!" the slave cried in a long, agonized whine.

For thousands of years the Hikeda'ya had routinely disposed of such misfits whenever they were born, defending the queen's sacred blood and the purity of their race as it had come out of the Garden. But now they lived in a different age—Hikeda'ya nobles were encouraged to mate with mortals, and halfbloods like Viyeki's own daughter were to be the salvation of the people. The great certainties with which he had been raised were tottering, just as Shun'y'asu had said, and Viyeki knew that he was one of those who had helped weaken the foundations. Perhaps the poet, for all the talk of his treasonous sympathies with outcasts, had seen truths that had eluded the Hamakha nobles themselves— even the queen. Once the gate of pity had been opened, no matter how narrowly, it could not easily be closed again.

Where will it end? Viyeki could not imagine. But he also knew he had only a short time until the queen herself would come, and he needed every slave he had been able to save from the vengeance of Kikiti's Sacrifices.

"We must keep healthy, strong slaves like this one when we can," he told the foreman. "Let him work by himself, where his babble will not distract the others." The foreman looked at him in surprise for a single unguarded moment, but quickly composed his face to reflect only obedience.

"As you say, High Magister." The foreman tucked the long-handled adze back into his belt, then grabbed the slave roughly by the arm and led him away to a pile of rubble far from where the other mortals were working. He indicated by gestures and slaps to the slave's head and shoulders what he was to do.

"The mortals are animals," said Nonao as the other slaves turned back to their work. "Worse than animals. Look, the creature has covered your gown with dirt, my lord."

"We must all make sacrifices for the greater good," said Viyeki. "For the race. For the Garden that birthed us."

"I hear the queen in your voice," his secretary replied, but he did not sound entirely convinced.

Because of a crust, Viyeki thought, and cursed poetry.

After the terrible day when her blindfold slipped, Tzoja's sleep was fitful and filled with nightmares, but time passed and the queen did not summon her again. Either the Hikeda'ya did not know what she had seen or they did not care.

The only advantage of being a slave, she thought. *Not important enough to notice.* She prayed it would continue that way.

She had not even told Vordis what had occurred, but her friend had sensed her fear when she returned and had comforted her. "We all are frightened when we first wait upon the Mother of All," the blind woman said. "Do not let it haunt you. It will pass. Soon it will be second nature."

Tzoja could not imagine such a thing ever being second nature, but she was content to have fallen away from the queen's notice. She would have been happy to be forgotten entirely. That did not happen, however.

On perhaps the fourth or fifth day after she had attended the queen, one of the Queen's Teeth appeared at the wagon and made it known by signs that he had come only for Tzoja. Frightened, not certain whether she was being taken back to the queen or for summary execution, she moved as helplessly as in one of her evil dreams, letting herself be lifted onto the hard saddle of the guard's horse like a bundle of rags. The sky was high and bright, with a stiff breeze blowing, and as the guard shook the reins and the horse started away Tzoja looked all around, wondering if this would be the last time she would see the sky. The snow had stopped falling, though the mountains looming in the northeast were capped in white, and she wondered without really caring where they were now. They must have crossed over into the lands of mortal men by now—that seemed obvious—but where? How far away was the place where Valada Roskva and the Astalines had taken her in, half a lifetime ago? Had any of those women survived? Perhaps they had rebuilt the settlement after the Skalijar left. She hoped so, fervently. It would make it a little easier to die if she could think that somewhere Roskva's followers still lived, still worked and laughed and shared what they had.

She was terrified at the prospect of seeing the queen again, but when the guard steered his horse away from the great train of wagons, a colder feeling stole over her. So it was to be death, then. She was to be taken out and killed. Back in Nakkiga they would have thrown her into the Fields of the Nameless. Out here her bones would be gnawed by animals, lashed by rain, and scattered over the cold ground until nothing was left but white shards.

The silent guard rode until the wagons were only a distant line of oblong shapes behind them. When they reached a stand of birches, the horse was reined to a halt and the guard dismounted. He lifted her from the saddle and set her down, then pointed at the ground. For a brief, almost giddy moment she thought about trying to run. Surely her executioner would find it hard to chase her in that white-enameled witchwood armor! But the breeze changed direction, and the chill blast brought a flurry of white petals skipping across the ground before her. *Windflowers*, she thought. She could smell the musky leaves.

I will not run, she decided.

The guard pointed again. She got down on her knees and began to pray. The smell of the windflower leaves and the rattling of the birch trees over her head so filled her in what she thought was her final moment that when something gently touched the back of her neck, she did not move, but waited calmly for the blow to fall.

She was touched again, more firmly this time. Tzoja looked up to see the guard staring down at her, confusion visible on what she could see of his face through the slot of the helmet. He pointed to the ground again, then at the trees, then spread his hands wide before pointing to Tzoja herself. His sword was still in its scabbard.

She understood then. He had brought her out at the queen's orders, to forage for herbs and wild plants.

Tzoja had time for one more prayer before she rose on unsteady legs and walked into the grove of slender white trees.

I have begun too late in the year, she thought mournfully as she looked down at what she had been able to collect—mullein leaves, purple elderberries, and two roots of bistort, as well as a rootstock of Rhiappa's Bells, a useful remedy for women's pains, although who could know what would work on the ageless Queen of the Norns? It was a meager collection. No healer could find even a fraction of the things she needed as late in the year as the Fire-Knight Moon.

No, she corrected herself. *I am no longer in Nakkiga. I can call it what my mother's people call it, the Third Red Moon. Or even what my poor lost father called it—Novander. I am in the world of men once more.* She looked around, and though she still felt some of the curious dreaminess that had come over her when she had been sure she would die, she also felt a fierce joy at feeling the sun, at the wind chafing her face. Nakkiga was a world away. There was sky overhead— sky!

It was perhaps the strangest feeling at the strangest time that she had ever experienced, but Tzoja realized that at that precise moment, she was happier than she had been for a very long while.

Even such a small bit of freedom was heady, but the days were shortening now with autumn fading and sooner than she would have liked the sun began to set. Wolves howled in the nearby hills, and it did not take the guard's summoning gestures to convince her it was time to go.

The great train of wagons had stopped to change the teams of goats and let those released from their harnesses drink their fill at a nearby stream, so she and the guard did not have to ride far to catch up. To her surprise, though, her escort rode past the end of the procession where the slave wagons stood and continued forward. For a dark moment she thought she was being taken to the queen, but the guard stopped beside one of the other wagons in Utuk'ku's train. He reined up at the steps below the wagon's door, then sat unmoving. Tzoja waited too, uncertain of what was happening, but the guard did not respond even when she carefully tapped his witchwood-plated arm.

He will not move until I release him, a voice said, speaking inside her head as the queen did, startling her so that she felt a sudden chill all over. The voice was not the queen's but something stranger, something colder, a sighing whisper that echoed as though it traveled a long, lonely distance before it reached Tzoja. *I have frozen his thought like a beetle beneath a drift of snow. When I am done, I will warm him back to life again. Come inside. Come to me.* It was not a request but a command. Tzoja slid clumsily down from the saddle, her earlier dreamy contentment suddenly torn to tatters. She made her way up the wagon steps, but could not bear to touch the door. That did not matter, because it opened of its own accord.

Heat and scented smoke engulfed her as she stepped inside. The interior of the large carriage was windowless, the blackness streaked with red, the only light she could see from a tray of coals smoldering on the floor. Behind the tray, seated cross-legged like a mendicant, was a shape that made Tzoja's indrawn breath stop partway between her mouth and her suddenly straining lungs.

The apparition was manlike and wrapped in a hooded cloak, as though even in this steamy compartment it huddled against the cold. Where she could see beneath the cloak, the shape was shrouded in cloth like a body readied for burial—old bandages, charred along the edges, with red light gleaming through the worn spots. The only other thing she could see were its eyes, but Tzoja could not look at those twin, burning points for more than an instant before turning away in quivering fear. She stared at the pan of coals instead and tried not to swoon. If she could have made her legs work she would have run, but they were as lifeless as sticks.

So here you are. The voice rustled in her head like wind in standing reeds, like the rattle of dead leaves chasing each other down an empty street. Just hearing it made her want to weep like a child. *I have wanted to see you in flesh, as more than the knot in the tapestry that you represent. This mortal form I wear is burning away, and soon I will not be able to see what is on this side of the door.*

Tzoja could no longer support herself. For the second time that day she kneeled, surrendering her doom to a greater force.

So my triad-sister has gathered you to her. I am not surprised.

"Who . . . who are you?" Tzoja finally managed to stammer. She could barely recognize her own words.

You are not the only unusual traveler in the queen's company, the faraway voice said. *I am one who has been beyond the door. One of the Three, whose shaping will bring the final answers. I am the one who goes beyond and returns. There is another who stands in the doorway, and one who will not cross. We are the triad, and we will end things. You see, mortal child of stone and grass, there is an order that shapes all—an order only those who have stood outside the walls of death can understand.*

Tzoja could not bear to look into the smoldering red emptiness staring at her from the shadowed hood, but when she looked down, she saw that the cloaked and bandaged thing floated a hand's breadth above the wagon's floor like a wisp of burning ash. She closed her eyes.

"But why did you call me here?" she whispered, weeping now. "What do you want from someone like *me?*"

The words came to her across some inconceivable distance. *Because you and yours are wound through all that will happen. Even with all I have seen, through the time-less shadows in which I have existed, I still feel something like curiosity. Your blood is a singular scarlet thread that crosses the great picture we three are weaving. The dead cannot lie, and I tell you this—your line has a destiny that even I cannot see in its fullness.*

Go now. We will meet again before the end. That I promise you, child of mortal man and mortal woman.

The embers sputtered and faded. Smoke rose up from the tray of coals and shrouded the figure in swirling darkness, so that only a few glints of scarlet showed it was still there. Suddenly mistress of her own limbs again, Tzoja turned and stumbled out of the wagon.

Outside, the guardsman of the Queen's Teeth waited on his horse, both rider and beast still motionless. Tzoja took a few moments to regain her breath and slow her speeding heart, but the knowledge that the floating thing remained just on the far side of the wagon door was too much to bear. She clambered up into the saddle behind the guard, thinking she might slap him awake; a moment later, as if nothing had happened, he shook the reins and turned the horse back toward the rear of the train. The drovers were getting ready to whip the great black goats into motion once more. As they rode past, and as the whips sang and the goats bleated in angry distress, Tzoja's womb ached and her stomach churned with the knowledge that she had given birth—that she had brought a child into this world of unending horror.

When the guard had helped her down from the saddle, he handed her the sack of plants she had collected, then rode away, stiff, straight, and silent.

Tzoja bent over and was violently sick, spattering the meager contents of her stomach over the steps of the wagon and the ground below.

45

The Dust of
Ancient Thoughts

Morgan had been told all his life to sit still and wait to speak until it was his turn—and he had always hated it. It was all he could do to watch silently now as Tanahaya argued with the leader of the angry, white-clad Sithi who had captured them—the Pure, as they called themselves. But he had learned at least one thing in the months since he had first met the Fair Folk: there were many things he didn't understand about the world, and sometimes it was better to keep his mouth closed until he learned more. He clenched his teeth until his jaws hurt and kept his hand away from Snake-splitter's hilt. His life was in someone else's hands—or, to be more precise, hung on someone else's words. Since he could not understand the argument that flew back and forth between the two women in their swift, liquid Sithi tongue, his heart was beating very fast indeed.

Tanahaya must have seen it on his face. "Do not be fearful," she told him. "It will do us no good." Then she turned back to Vinyedu and the Pure, but to Morgan's surprise, this time she spoke Westerling. "All scholars know that the last time Amerasu Ship-Born spoke in the Yásira, she used the tongue of mortals because of the presence of Seoman Snowlock, whom she held in high esteem."

Vinyedu said something in her own tongue. It did not sound like any kind of agreement.

"Because this mortal who stands before you, Morgan of Erchester, is the grandson of that same Seoman," Tanahaya answered, and though there was no widening of eyes or gasps of surprise, Morgan could feel the change in the way Vinyedu and her followers looked at him. For the first time he sensed almost as much curiosity as outright dislike. "He has the right to hear what is said about him . . . and against him," Tanahaya continued. "The Sa'onsera of Year-Dancing House, the greatest of us in these lands, decreed that was true for his grandfather. Would the Pure deny Amerasu's wisdom?"

As Vinyedu stood, silently thinking, the other Pure stared at Morgan in a way that made him tremble with the effort of staying silent, but Tanahaya's face spoke clearly to him without words: *This is dangerous. Do not interfere.* At last Vinyedu turned back toward them.

"I will not forgive you for using my reverence for our First Grandmother against me this way, Tanahaya of Shisae'ron." Her words were measured and careful, and she spoke some of them strangely, but Morgan was still surprised by how well she used his tongue. "In respect of Amerasu's memory I will speak so he can understand, but I care nothing for mortal kings or crowns. The presence of this child's grandfather in Jao é-Tinukai'i brought us nothing but death and destruction."

"It was not the presence of Seoman Snowlock that brought death to our home, Vinyedu," said Tanahaya. "It was the treachery of Queen Utuk'ku and the Hikeda'ya—something you know as well as me."

"All the same," Vinyedu said. "I am not swayed. I will speak the animal tongue of the Sudhoda'ya, but that does not mean we will excuse this trespass. We *Jonzao* have broken with all who have turned their back on the old ways. We reject any alliances between our people and the mortals. And if we are dissatisfied with your answers, Tanahaya, you will still be driven out into the forest, and as for the mortal youth . . ."—she gave Morgan a significant look that started his heart rabbiting once more ". . . we may still destroy him, as a matter of principle."

"Then you will have to destroy me as well," Tanahaya said calmly.

"I can think of things I would regret far more than that," Vinyedu replied. "Why are you here? Why did you seek us out?"

"I sought you out in desperation. Out of fear for all our people, not just myself. The Hikeda'ya are everywhere in the forest, even along the boundaries of Misty Vale."

"This is known to us," said Vinyedu.

"Then did you also know that Hikeda'ya Sacrifices killed my master Himano and burned his house in the Flowering Hills?"

Vinyedu fell silent, and although Morgan could never tell for certain with the stone-faced immortals, he thought she was surprised. Some of the other Sithi in the chamber spoke to her, and she replied rapidly in their tongue before turning back. "How do you know it was Hikeda'ya?" she asked Tanahaya.

"Their marks were everywhere. And do you truly think even an army of mortals could have caught my teacher unaware?"

"How long ago did this happen?"

"I cannot say. Perhaps as much as a moon cycle, but certainly no longer. I studied his body and that of his current student before I buried them."

Vinyedu sank down to her haunches and for a time did not speak. *"Tsi anh pra Venhya!"* she said at last, with real feeling. "It is no secret that Himano and I did not agree on many things, but I still mourn his death. The Hikeda'ya have lost all sense—they are more lost than even the most foolish of our own tribe."

She narrowed her eyes. "That still does not tell why you are here, though. Or traveling with a mortal, no matter his ancestry."

Tanahaya quickly told the story of all that had happened to her since she had last been in H'ran Go-jao. Vinyedu repeated her words in their own tongue for the crowd of Sithi who had gathered to watch and listen—they now numbered something close to three dozen. Surrounded by the sea of impassive faces and golden-eyed stares, Morgan felt as if he hardly dared breathe.

After passing on the last of Tanahaya's words, Vinyedu turned back toward them. To his surprise, Morgan saw the ghost of a smile curling the edges of her thin mouth. "And did you truly say that to Khendraja'aro, or do you exaggerate to make the story better?"

Tanahaya's words were cold. "I am a scholar and historian, like you, Lady Vinyedu, and like your admirable sister. I tell what I experienced as truthfully as I am able."

The smile disappeared. "Do not throw my sister in my face. Zinjadu chose her own course. She went with the others to aid the mortals—this whelp's grandfather—and met her death because of it." Vinyedu paused; when she spoke again it was without any expression Morgan could detect. "So you came here to find a Witness so you could tell Likemeya's son and daughter what has happened. That makes a sort of sense, but Jiriki and Aditu mean little to us. They have chosen to flout the old ways. We have purified ourselves of all that."

"Can you purify yourself of the Hikeda'ya and their mad queen?" Tanahaya asked.

"We do not need to answer to you, young one." Vinyedu now rose. "You are not one of the Pure. In that way, you are no different than Utuk'ku, who sent a mortal to kill Amerasu—a *mortal*!"

"Do not poison our talk with such foolishness. I am *very* different," Tanahaya said. "Whatever you may think, I still believe we are one people, one blood. You suggest there is no difference between the Hikeda'ya and the rest of the Zida'ya. But Utuk'ku's Norns see no difference between you and us—and they intend the same thing for you that they plan for both the mortals *and* the Sithi, which is destruction. Utuk'ku will not permit any of the old Keida'ya to survive unless they worship her."

Vinyedu shook her head. "Words."

"Yes, but words are what we use to build the world." Tanahaya reached into her jacket, but stopped as several of the white-clad folk around her raised their bows. Morgan found himself clenching his hands into fists. "I draw no weapon," Tanahaya said evenly. "You spoke of words, Lore-Mistress Vinyedu. Let me show you some." She drew a flattened roll of parchment out of her jacket, which Morgan recognized as the writings she had taken from beneath Himano's body.

Vinyedu stared. "What is it? You said nothing about this before."

"I had not had the chance, with the constant threats of death and banishment and assertions that there is no difference between my kind and the Hikeda'ya."

She passed it to Vinyedu. "This was beneath Himano when he fell, pierced with arrows and left to die like a dog beside the road."

Vinyedu carefully opened the parchment. "There is very little blood on it."

"The more fortunate for us. But the runes are the old writing of the Hikeda'ya, and I am not enough of a scholar to read it with full understanding—only a word, an idea, here and there."

"I will study this," Vinyedu said slowly, "and see if I can find a reason that Himano might have tried to escape with it." She looked around. "But we cannot remain here in the Place of Voices. We know as well as you that the Hikeda'ya have grown bold, and though they have not yet dared to enter our city, that does not mean they might not come close enough to loose arrows, especially if they hear us. We will go to the archives." As she spoke the Sithi surrounding them began to move out of the chamber, quiet as stalking cats. "But you are still our prisoners," Vinyedu added. "Forget that at your peril."

The undergrowth was so thick with hazel, bracken, and firethorn that after an hour of hacking at it with his ax but making scant progress, Little Snenneq's palms and fingers were bloody.

"You will ruin yourself," Qina told him. "Come here and let me bind those hands. The daylight will be gone soon—no point in trying to go farther today."

Snenneq made a face, but allowed her to clean his hands and rub leaves out of her bag over his many scratches and gouges. As she wrapped them in the clean linen brought from Erkynland, he stared over her shoulder.

"But the river must be close!" he said in frustration. "I can smell it! Almost hear it!"

"I can smell it too," she said. "But the rams are tired and so are you." She looked to their two mounts, Snenneq's Falku and her Ooki, chewing shoots of dry autumn grass in their annoyed-looking, sideways manner. "We have a pair of birds left from your excellent hunting yesterday. Let us make a fire. You rest while it burns down to coals. I will wrap them in some wood garlic leaves. That will give you something to smell that will not frustrate you."

Snenneq smiled, then kissed her nose and stood. "I agree with your plan. But first I will do one thing. I will climb that high tree and see how much of this foul thorn and bracken lies between us and the river. Perhaps there is an easier way to get through it."

"You should not be climbing trees while your hands are still bleeding," she scolded him. "If you tear loose those bandages I will not do my work all over again. And if the smell of your blood calls some hungry animal, I will not lift a finger to save you."

Snenneq pounded his chest with his fist. "I hear you, Grandchild of the Herder and Huntress! I will be most carefully careful of my bandages. And in case some fierce beast should scent me on the wind and think me supper, I will carry my ax in my belt, and if attacked I will use it to dissuade my attacker from such foolishness."

"You'd better sharpen it first," she said. "You've been hacking at the bushes so long it's probably as dull as your tongue."

He raised an eyebrow. "It could never be as sharp as yours, my betrothed." But he took out his whetstone and brought the blade back to a keen edge before he started climbing.

Qina could hear him rattling in the branches high above, noisy as a weasel trapped in a basket. She leaned closer to the fire and poked the pieces of wood apart so they would burn down more quickly. "Are you well?" she called. "Do you see anything?"

"Leaves!" he cried. "More filthy leaves than you can imagine. But if I get a little higher, I think I will be above them and then can . . ." He fell silent again, or at least his voice did, but she could hear the rattling as he clambered higher. "Hah!" Triumph was plain in his voice. "Now I can see the river in truth! It is not far away, and I see also that we can find a better path through this hateful undergrowth."

She sighed and leaned away from the fire, which was making her sweat. "Is there perhaps not a way we could walk around it instead?" She heard a loud rustle above her. "Snenneq?"

"What? Daughter of the Mountains, woman, I am trying to do what you asked!"

Something still rustled in a treetop above her, but it was not the same tree that Snenneq had climbed. "There is something else in the trees!" she cried. "Snneneq, be wary!"

"What did you say? I cannot hear you. Are you shaking the tree? Do you want me to fall and break all my most useful parts?"

"It is not me! Something is in one of the other trees—something big!" She paused and now could see leaves trembling near the tree's crown. A moment later something large clambered from one tree to the next, and now was in the one next to Snenneq's. "Come down at once! Something is coming toward you!"

"What do you mean? What is coming?"

The branches were swaying, but the thick foliage of the new tree, a buckthorn, made it hard for Qina to see anything but the movement. Before she could shout another warning, whatever it was slipped from the rustling, rattling crown of one tree and into the foliage where Snenneq sat hidden. "Get out of the tree!" she cried.

She got no reply. A moment later the entire upper section of the Snenneq's tree began shifting, the branches wagging as something heavy moved through them. She heard a cry of surprise from Snenneq, then he cursed loudly. Qina grabbed a smoldering branch from the fire and picked up the knife she had been using to split the birds, then ran to the base of the tree.

"Snenneq! What is it?" she cried. "I'm here! I'm coming up!"

"*No!*" he shouted, and his voice was ragged with fear. More commotion, more rattling, then she heard sound of tree limbs breaking. Her betrothed gave a loud cry and an instant later something came crashing down through the branches. It struck first one branch, then another, bending the large ones and snapping the smaller. She leaped out of the way as it struck one last branch nearly a dozen feet from the ground, hung there for a moment, then slid off and crashed to the mossy ground with a muffled thump.

"Snenneq!" she cried, hurrying to him. His eyes opened. There was blood on his face. "Are you alive? Oh, by the ancestors, do not be dead!"

He stared at her, then over his shoulder. His eyes widened. He grabbed her and wrestled her to one side, rolling half on top of her, as something large came skittering headfirst down the trunk of the tree and sprang onto the ground. Groaning at the effort, Snenneq dragged her backward, away from the knotted roots.

The thing rose onto its back legs until it stood twice her height, as big as a flatlander man, and Qina felt her heart smack against her ribs in fear. She had never seen anything like it. It was man-shaped, but nothing like a man, with dull, shiny skin of several colors, muddy gray, brown, and green. Its face was a rigid horror of black, bulbous eyes and quivering mouth parts at the end of the blunt snout. It raised its front limbs—its arms—and she saw that each one ended in weird, clawed paws halfway between human hands and the flattened feet of some climbing lizard.

Then it lunged toward them and there was no more time to think. It grabbed at Qina first, but Snenneq had his ax in his hands, though he had no time to grasp it properly and only managed to strike the thing with the back of his ax-head. He hit it squarely and one plated arm dropped to the thing's side, apparently useless, but the clawed hand of the other arm closed on Qina's hair and began pulling her. It was too strong for her to resist, so she lifted the smoldering brand and pushed it into the twitching mouth as hard as she could. The stick hissed and steamed and the thing let go of her with a terrible whistling shriek.

Now Snenneq had his ax the right way around. He leaped on the creature, hammering it over and over around the head and neck while it buzzed and clicked and frothed from its wounded muzzle. His relentless blows cut the armored body, but did not seem to do much real damage.

"Go and get . . . !" he shouted, but Qina was already scrambling back toward the fire on her hands and knees to find her Huntress spear. The creature had a squeezing claw around Snenneq's neck when she returned. She dared not attack its midsection for fear of hurting her beloved, so she aimed at the back of the thing's neck and used both hands to plunge the spear into the leathery tissue between the armored head and the shell-like back. The sharp stone spearhead smashed out through the front of the creature's neck in a fizz of pale fluid. Qina pulled back on the spear, yanking the flailing creature off of Snenneq. It writhed and fought so hard that it pulled the spear from her hands, but Snenneq was finally free. He stumbled to the place where he had been cutting brush and came back with a large stone, which he lifted just as the creature was trying to right itself, then crushed the horror's head like an egg. It collapsed, nothing left above its shoulders but a sticky ruin. Its jointed legs thrashed for a moment, then gradually went still.

Qina and Snenneq both crouched on hands and knees like sick dogs, gasping for air. At last she stood up and went on shaking legs to her beloved. "Are you badly hurt?"

"I have bruises I will feel for some days," he said, "but nothing worse. And you, my so-brave *nukapika?*"

"My neck is scratched," she said. "I will not be able to rest until I clean it. What was that foul horror?"

Snenneq rose and scraped the worst of the mud and leaves from his clothes. "I do not know." He went to the dead thing and poked it with his booted foot.

"It looks as though it is plated like a crab," she said. "Or a beetle."

"A ghant," he said, almost in wonderment, as though he had seen a new star in the sky. "Hearts of our Ancestors, I swear it is a ghant. But not like any I have ever heard about. And what is it doing here, in the Aldheorte?"

"But they are creatures of the southern swamps, are they not? I have heard my father speak of them."

"There never have been any so far north," Snenneq agreed. "Not in the tales of any of the learned folk I have studied. But Queen Miriamele and others fought them in the Wran during the Storm King's War—Miriamele and Duke Isgrminur even went into a ghants' nest to rescue Lord Tiamak when the creatures had captured him. But those ghants were nothing so manlike as this—and nothing so large, either. This one is nearly twice the ordinary size." He took the still-smoldering brand from her and tipped the wreckage of the thing's head so they could see what remained of its face. "See, the eyes are in front, like a man's. And look—those are so much like hands, but true ghants are said to have claws like an insect." He stared at it, frowning. "I would like to study it more carefully, but I think we do not want this dead thing near our campsite. Let us carry it away some distance."

"I'm not touching it," Qina said firmly. "I'll gather some branches and we'll weave them together and roll it onto that." She bent closer to look at it but could not stand the sight of its smashed, gaping face. "Did you hear the noise it made? As though it was trying to talk—to use words like a man."

"Do not say such things, even if they are true," said Snenneq. "It will be hard enough for us to sleep tonight. I think I may have lost my appetite."

"You truly *are* upset."

Snenneq detached her spear from the slimy ruin and wiped it on the ground. "By Kikkasut the Winged Father, I am!" He handed her the spear. "You fought well, my wife-to-be, but by all the sacred mountains of Yiqanuc, I am glad we have nearly reached the river, if such things climb in these trees. What is a swamp-demon like this doing here in the middle of the forest?"

There was far more to Da'ai Chikiza, Morgan was now learning, than even the extensive ruins he had already seen. Vinyedu led them into the city's depths, and as they descended to the lower levels he saw they were riddled with underground chambers and passages, not the hasty work of mortal miners nor the braced tunnels of siege engineers but continuations of the buildings above and created with the same care. Though the walls of these new passages were often covered in moss and black lichen, in places Morgan could see the stone beneath them, which had been protected from the elements even as the surfaces beside them slowly wore away like a marchpane sweet melting in the sun. Here the carvings were still hard-edged, as fresh as if they had been crafted only yesterday; Morgan saw bits of hands, faces, leaves and flowers, as well as dozens other things too shrouded by moss and dirt to recognize.

These glimpsed details, so beautiful and yet so inhuman, filled him with the most powerful homesickness he had known in months. It seemed likely no other mortals had ever seen them, and that should have filled him with wonder, but instead it made him feel small. The weight of all this ancient, abandoned grandeur turned his own life—perhaps even the whole history of his mortal kind—into something fleeting, the glint of dragonfly wings in summer sunshine, the brief flash of something born only to die.

At last they reached a wide underground chamber almost as large as the Place of Voices, though the roof was comparatively low, only three times Morgan's height above them. The walls here were also meticulously carved, but the lichen and moss had been removed or kept away, and the dozens of lamps set in niches along the walls shed enough light that he could have studied the ancient carvings instead of guessing at them. His attention was caught instead by more than a hundred Sithi ranged about the broad chamber, silent as deer. Many of them looked up as Vinyedu led them in, and he could almost imagine them all startling at an unexpected noise and running away.

Seeing the immortals in such numbers of course reminded him of Aditu's and Jiriki's camp at H'ran Go-jao, but those Sithi had been busy with the daily life of their settlement, working, dancing, laughing; these Pure seemed half-asleep. A few stood or sat in small groups around the archive chamber, but he saw no sign of conversation between them. Others sang quietly by themselves or in small gatherings, but where the music of the other Sithi camp had touched his heart with joy, the melodies he heard here seemed more like the keening of mourners.

"What are they all doing here?" he whispered to Tanahaya.

"There are many more living here in Da'ai Chikiza than I suspected," she said. "In evil times, even my people can be convinced to reject history, though they claim to embrace it."

Most of the Sithi faces looked hard, cold, and unwelcoming, so it was a relief when Vinyedu announced, still in Westerling speech, "We will draw apart from the others so that I can read Himano's parchment." She gestured for Morgan and Tanahaya to follow her.

"They don't seem very pleased to see us," Morgan said, but the jest sounded hollow even to him.

"Nearly everyone here would be happier if we both were dead," said Tanahaya. "But the most dangerous enemies are often those who do not make their hatred of you plain to see."

He tried to take comfort from his father's sword bumping at his hip, but it did not much help. He had seen how fast the Sithi moved when they wished, and he did not think the legendary Sir Camaris himself could have defeated so many of them at once; Morgan knew he was only a mortal princeling who had spent far too much of his training time bending an elbow with Astrian and Olveris in *The Quarely Maid*.

All the dozen or so Sithi in the smaller chamber looked up as they entered, but after seeing Vinyedu they returned to their reading. Morgan and the others had entered what he guessed must be the heart of the archive, the walls honeycombed with alcoves containing rolls of parchment. Some contained several such scrolls, but the largest number of alcoves were empty or held only scatters of dust.

The dust of ideas, Morgan thought, and it gave him a peculiar, skin-creeping feeling. *The dust of ideas from long, long ago that nobody remembers anymore, not even the Sithi.* Where had they gone, the ones who wrote all those things—thought all those thoughts?

It doesn't matter, he told himself, almost in anger. *They're not here. They're not alive. I'm alive. And I want to stay that way.*

Vinyedu went to a flat table, an abbreviated column made of shiny gray stone unlike anything Morgan had seen in the city so far. She took the parchment Tanahaya had given her and spread it out, weighting it with two rounded stones that looked like they had been gathered from a riverbed. "I cannot speak the mortal language and also read the secret tongue of old Nakkiga," she said, "so I will be silent for a time. But I will have one of my people bring you something to eat and drink. Is there anything that would be poisonous to mortals?"

Morgan was not certain whether she was speaking in jest. "I'm not certain I should tell you that."

Vinyedu actually smiled, though it was little more than a tightening of the lips with a slight pull on each end toward her sharp cheekbones. "I meant only that we should avoid giving you such things. I will guess that water, bread, and honey will not harm you."

"Do you have any wine?"

The smile went slack. "None that I would give to you, mortal child." She made a gesture to one of the silent Sitha, who turned and glided from the room like a sailing ship on a freshening wind.

★   ★   ★

It was surpassingly strange that Morgan had gone in the matter of a few hours from fearing for his life to utter boredom, but that was exactly what had happened.

He still did not trust the Sithi, or at least this particular frowning variety dressed in white, but the simple fact of a full stomach had gone some way to calming him. Since eating, he had sat with nothing to do but watch Tanahaya and the one called Vinyedu as they took dusty scrolls out of dusty alcoves, read and discussed them in the liquid Sithi tongue, then put them away again.

At least Tanahaya is enjoying herself, he thought. She had called herself a scholar many times, but during their time together she had been consumed with the business of staying alive—or at least with keeping *him* alive, if Morgan was honest about it. Now he could see her doing what she most cared about, and it was like watching a warrior finally able to draw a sword and put enemies to flight. She moved with such confidence in an unfamiliar place that he thought even Vinyedu had noticed. Morgan did not pretend to understand the immortals, but it looked like the older Sitha had stopped treating Tanahaya like an enemy and had begun to give her the courtesy due a near equal. Certainly when some of their discussions grew heated, at least by the reserved standards of the immortals, Vinyedu no longer seemed merely scornful.

Morgan could only hope this meant the Pure were less likely to execute him: Vinyedu was clearly one of their leaders, and her opinion might make the difference between life and death. Because he was in favor of not dying, Morgan had sat quietly all this long time, not even asking permission to walk outside the archive chamber.

"Ai!" said Vinyedu suddenly and loudly. The pitch of her voice was enough to make Morgan sit up. Tanahaya gave him a quick look—a warning? Hadn't she noticed how careful and quiet he had been?

"What did you find, *S'huesae?*" Tanahaya asked in Westerling.

The silver-haired Sitha looked up and for a moment seemed startled, as though she had forgotten a mortal was in the archive. "The answer, it seems. As I said, it is a court cypher from the era of the Tenth Celebrant, but it was not one I had seen. But here it is." Vinyedu gestured to the parchment she had unrolled on the stone table.

Bored with sitting in one place, Morgan rose and made his way to the table, being careful not to stand too close.

"The more fortunate for us," Tanaheya said. "But the runes are old. The Hermit Ibis cypher? I have not heard of it."

"Nor would most scholars—only a few records remain. At a time of great discord among the Hikeda'ya, when secret messages were common, it was devised by the infamous philosopher Yedade." Vinyedu began to run her long fingers along the row of what to Morgan were incomprehensible symbols, more like stylized pictures of insects than proper runes. "It is not derived from the words themselves, but from the . . . I have forgotten the word—by the

Garden, must I speak everything so this mortal child can understand? From the *kayute*."

"Brush strokes?"

"Yes, from the number of brush strokes with which each rune is created—from "*A*" with but one to "*HIN*" with thirteen. But enough of this. Let us see what we can make of Himano's parchment. I will cypher the runes and you write them down."

It took no little time, but both of the Sithi worked with a newfound interest. Morgan walked slowly back and forth behind them, wondering whether it would turn out to be anything in the end. Perhaps the parchment was only what Tanahaya's master had been reading at the time of his death, and he had simply fled from his enemies without dropping it. And even if it was something more, what difference could it make? It would not bring Tanahaya's teacher back to life, and neither would it change Morgan's own situation, still deep in the forest and far from his home and family.

"Now read it," said Vinyedu when she had finished.

As Tanahaya looked over what she had written her face changed, eyes widening just a little, but to Morgan, at the end of long hours of nothing happening, it seemed like a shout. "Did you find something?" he asked, then closed his mouth and bit his lip when Vinyedu gave him a hard, chilly look.

"It is a chronicler's tale of the founding of Asu'a," said Tanahaya slowly, reading back over the document. "The place you were born, Prince Morgan, that mortals call the Hayholt."

"But the Hayholt is hundreds of years old."

"And I told you that we built Asu'a there—our greatest city—before you mortals came to these lands. Now be silent and listen—you and Eolair spoke with Jiriki—it is about that thing." As Morgan struggled to remember, Tanahaya slowly read it out in the original language, then translated into Westerling so he could understand.

" '*But in those days a great enmity had grown between the two—*' " Tanahaya paused. "I do not know a word to fit your tongue, but I will say 'respected' or 'mighty'—'*between the two mightiest clans of the Keida'ya, that of Hamakho Wormslayer and that of his wife, Sa'onsera the Preserver. Great Hamakho did not live to see the new world, and his body was consumed by Unbeing when the Garden fell, but from his crypt his descendants had brought the crown of witchwood which had been entombed with him. Now, in secret, the Hamakha buried that crown beneath the keystone of Asu'a even as the great palace was being built, and with it they laid a dozen seeds of the witchwood brought from the Garden itself, that no catastrophe might ever leave the People without the sacred fruit, the sacred leaves, the tree of our people, nurtured in the soil of the place that gave our race birth.*' "

"The Witchwood Crown," Morgan said, remembering. "That was what my grandparents and Eolair and all the others kept going on about. The Witchwood Crown!" All their talk, months behind him, now came flooding back. "We had a message from someone who was traveling with the White Foxes—a mortal." He let the thoughts sift. "He said the Norns wanted to take back the Witchwood Crown. Does that mean this is the crown they were talking about?"

Vinyedu was staring at the runes as though something else was still hidden there, but Tanahaya turned to Morgan; he saw something in her face that chilled him. "I fear it can mean nothing else," she said. "Why else would my teacher Himano have tried to escape with this piece of old writing? He must have discovered it and understood what it meant, but somehow the Hikeda'ya found out. They killed him to silence him. They murdered him to hide what they truly seek." Tanahaya was finding it hard to hold in her anger, but Morgan could see fear as well. "Queen Utuk'ku seeks the witchwood seeds buried with Hamakho's crown, because those seeds must now be the only living witchwood seeds remaining. If they can make the witchwood grow once more, it will give Utuk'ku and her most powerful followers back their ageless, timeless strength. And now we know where they seek them. The crown and those last seeds from the Garden are buried beneath the castle of your birth, Morgan—beneath the Hayholt."

46

The Bishop's Worries

Pasevalles was halfway down the stairs beyond the secret door when he realized he was not wearing his thick leather gloves. He set the tray down and took them from his belt. It was always a bad idea to forget precautions, but especially in the deep places that belonged to the red thing. He had no guarantees that it would not start placing poisoned sewing needles and house nails once more in places where they could scratch an unwary visitor. He and the lurker had a truce of sorts, and Pasevalles had lived up to his end of it by bringing offerings of meals, as he did today, as well as the occasional young woman, but he was not entirely certain that the red thing was a human creature—he was not even entirely sure that it was a living thing. Who was to say when it might grow tired of their bargain?

Gloves donned, he carried the tray down to the place where, by tradition, he always left it. There was no sign of the chambermaid he had carried down days earlier, but he had not expected to find any. Whatever the red thing did with the young women he brought, it never left anything behind to suggest their ultimate fate.

As he set down the tray he thought he heard a quiet noise from the cob-webbed heights above him, like a rat skittering across one of the fallen beams.

"Is that you?" he asked, expecting no answer and receiving none. "I brought you something from the kitchens. Meat. I pray you will enjoy it." He settled himself on a fallen cornice that had tumbled from atop a wide doorway. The dark places beyond it were largely blocked by fallen timbers and masonry. This part of the underground castle lay between the deepest levels of the mortal buildings and the beginnings of the old Sithi ruins, so it was a strange mixture of the ancient cellars and remnants of the far more ancient palace called Asu'a. Pasevalles had explored as far as the red thing had allowed him, but he did not much like the deep ruins. He always felt watched there, even when he could tell that his hidden host was occupied elsewhere. He heard unintelligible voices and felt currents of air where there should be none, and encountered scents he never smelled in the living buildings above.

"I've been wondering about you again," he said to the darkness above him.

"What you are. Who you are. How you came to be here. No, do not fear! I
have no desire to end our . . . friendship by trying to seek you out. Everyone
has things to hide. Everyone has the right to keep to the shadows if they choose.

"But it is a game of thought for me—an exercise. I would not want you to
tell me even if I guessed correctly. Still, my mind plays with it like a tongue
probing in the hole where a rotted tooth once sat.

"You wear red and you are particularly protective of Pryrates' tower, especially the depths beneath it. But many people saw the priest die, burnt to ashes
by his onetime master, the Storm King. Still, if any mortal could survive such
a thing, it would be the Red Priest. But would he hide? That does not seem
likely to me.

"Perhaps you are Cadrach the monk, the queen's friend. His body was
never found after Green Angel Tower fell—but of course, many bodies
were never found, though several died in the tower on that last day. The deep
hole left behind by its collapse was simply filled in with stones and earth and
covered over, then a *mansa* said over the rubble.

"Or are you something else? Did Pryrates open a door to some other place
and release you? Did his death leave you trapped in a world unfamiliar to you?
That is possible too—I have learned much about the Red Priest's explorations,
though I can only understand a little of what he did."

He sat for a while, enjoying the quiet. Even the red thing, if it still listened,
had gone utterly silent.

"You see, I have been thinking about many things," he went on at last.
"Things that, as always, I keep from all the others above. Like you, I must
hide the greatest part of me. You use darkness and the depths as your cloak—
I use a fair face and fair words and unending caution to keep my secrets. But
it becomes tiresome, always dissembling. As there is a part of you driven to
see the light, even if only the light from the stars—yes, I know that you have
found a way up through the stones of Hjeldin's Tower to the roof—I sometimes long to share what I am thinking. It is tiring to speak the truth only to
oneself.

"You see, I have been considering the throne—the High Throne. For long
I thought only of bringing down those unworthy creatures who were given
that seat, of slowly undermining their rule just as you have somehow moved
heavy stones to give yourself the freedom of Hjeldin's Tower. For years I could
think of nothing else but taking away everything that God had given to the
Commoner King and his hard-faced wife, the Mad King's daughter. My father
and my uncle died so those two could rule. I was driven in disgrace from my
own house and forced to walk the streets as a beggar and cutpurse while they
sat in comfort on the throne of all Osten Ard.

"It seemed enough at first to begin to pull their empire apart and to see how
the loss of their son tormented them. But when they made their grandson heir,
it came to me that if I played the game with courage and daring, I could

someday rule through him. Oh, I thought that would be a wonderful jest, the grandson of my enemies dancing to my tune. A drunken fool for my puppet, who would do what I told him as long as he was left to dissipate himself.

"But now, my silent friend, I have begun to think I might have set my aim too low. The king and queen have never been strong in their rule, always too quick to forgive their enemies, to placate those who are hardest to satisfy— especially Simon, that creature of low birth, whatever lies they might have invented about descent from King Eahlstan. He and his wife have always sowed the seeds of their own failure. But then some grasslander fools attacked the troop accompanying Morgan and threw my plans into chaos. What good to be a trusted counselor with no trusting ear to listen? What good to make a puppet of a prince if he dies before he can take the throne?

"But, like you, my secretive friend, I do not surrender easily. I never wanted merely to destroy them. That would be too simple. Anyone can kill a king or a queen. The trick is to ruin them slowly, so that they see it happening. To take their precious High Ward apart piece by piece so they must mourn each part as it is lost, and to destroy their family and allies, death upon death. I thought to end it with their own ends, leaving myself as Morgan's only trusted advisor when he became king, but now Morgan is gone and even I do not know where he is, or if he even lives."

For a moment he fell into another silence, this one full of fury he could barely suppress. If he had before him now the barbarians who had caused so much trouble, he would take them to pieces and savor every whimper, every scream. That such foolish animals should thwart years of intricate plan- ning . . . !

He closed his eyes until the rage cooled a little, then took a deep breath. "Ah, but that is when it came to me, you see. Why should I mourn the loss of my puppet? Because if the king and queen fail, or die, someone must still sit upon the High Throne. Someone must replace them when the day comes.

"Why not me?"

He stood. "Know this—I ask nothing from you. I will not expose you. Even if I win my way onto the Dragonbone Chair—and I promise you, I have no childish qualms about sitting on that particular throne—I will not drag you from your hiding place or even reveal your existence. You have helped me in my task. I am grateful. These speculations of mine are only amusements. I do not care if you are the deathless spirit of Pryrates himself or merely a beggar who found his way into the ruins beneath the Hayholt. I do not want or need to know your secrets. We have an arrangement I would not change, the things I bring to you in exchange for letting me use the Mooncloud—the Master Wit- ness. And I have kept all my promises—remember that. Without me you would have to go hunting for the things you need, and risk being captured and dragged into the light.

"We are allies. I remind you of that. I want nothing else from you today.

Enjoy what I have brought you. I promise there will be more. If you stay true to me, there will always be more."

For a moment he thought he saw the glint of an eye in the shadows of the overhead beams, but it might have been a trick of his own guttering torch. Pasevalles bowed toward the place where he thought the red thing crouched, then turned to find his way back out of the depths.

Tiamak met his wife on the stairs. He was going, she was returning.

"Do not disappear," she said. "I have a question for you—and a message."

He waited, not without impatience. "They are busy moving books for me," he explained. "I dread to think what they will do with some of the older volumes if I am not there to watch over them."

"Moving them where? I thought the library building was stopped for the present."

"It is, my lady. But Lord Jeremias is in a passion because we need more rooms for Countess Yissola's entourage, so my books must be moved from the places I have been storing them. But they must be protected, not left in leaky cupboards, and I am the only one who will make sure that doesn't happen. Surely you don't think I'd trust Jeremias and his minions with that." He paused. "I thought you had a message for me."

Thelía gave him a dubious look. "You remembered that, but not the question I said I had? I mentioned the question first."

"Well, then. The question first."

"Good. How does your bread oven work?"

He stared at her in confusion. "My what?"

"You know, the thing you call your bread oven. Your alchemical furnace, the one in the forcing shed."

"The athanor? What on earth do you want with that, wife? I thought your religion prejudiced you against all such foolery?"

"Enough of your jibes. I do not want to do alchemy, I simply want to try to learn something. I found the bedclothes, you see."

"Now I am confounded all over again. What bedclothes?"

"Those that were on the bed when the Sitha-woman was brought into the residence back in Marris-month. One of the chambermaids found them at the bottom of one of the linen chests. She was about to wash them when I heard of it. I only managed to save them."

"Save them why?"

She narrowed her eyes. "Are you truly so distracted, husband? Where is that very sharp wit of yours? We never found the arrows that almost killed the Sitha woman. We still have no idea of what poison was used on them. But on the bedclothes there are black stains—stains of the poison, I would guess, from when Etan took the broken arrows from her poor body. The arrows vanished and someone left the sheets in an out of the way place. Perhaps one of the maids was too lazy to try to clean them, and thought to hide the evidence."

"Or feared the poison, as any sensible person would. Yet you are going to handle it?"

"Carefully, of course. You did not marry a fool." She almost smiled. "But I do not know how to fire your silly oven, and I need proper heat for what I wish to attempt. How do I do it?"

Tiamak did his best to reassemble his now utterly scattered thoughts. "Brother Theobalt, Etan's less than adequate replacement, can show you how to do it, although he must be watched at all times lest he burn down the forcing shed. But will you please be careful, my dear one? Whatever poison was used on the Sitha is nothing to trifle with."

"I already told you I would be careful. I have handled at least as many poisons in my life as you have. Now run along to watch over your books and I'll find Theobalt."

"Now you are the one teasing me, Thelía. You spoke of a message for me . . . ?"

"Ah, yes. It came to me in a very roundabout way, I must say. I think Bishop Boez wishes it kept secret. He would not put it on paper, but entrusted it to one of his servants to whisper it in my ear."

"Whisper?"

"I exaggerate, but not greatly. Bishop Boez requests an audience with you at your earliest possible convenience—but in the Almonry, not here."

Tiamak sighed. "He Who Always Steps On Sand, give me patience. And I suppose 'earliest convenience' means "even as clumsy workmen are mishandling a collection of writings beyond price or replacement."

"Do not drag me into this. But I think Boez is a good man and would not ask for you over nothing."

Tiamak stood on his toes to kiss her cheek. "I promise I will go see him as soon as I make certain they are not setting some priceless volume of Senigo on fire. And speaking of setting things on fire . . ."

"I will keep a close eye on Brother Theobalt, yes. Go, then. Go to your precious books."

"None so precious to me as you are, my wife."

She made a face.

When the counting-priest showed him into the back room of the Almonry, Boez stood to greet him. "Forgive my sending you such an unorthodox message, Lord Tiamak. Will you take some refreshment?" He looked around the table and its mounds of records as though an ewer of wine and plate of cakes might be hidden among them. "I can call for some," he said after a moment.

"Please, do not trouble anyone."

Boez came around the edge of the desk, polishing his spectacle-glasses on his surplice before setting them back on his thin nose. He had a slight squint, and the habit of bobbing his head forward as if for a closer look, which made it seem as though he wasn't quite sure who was on the other end of the conversation. "Well, then," he said. "We will get straight to the matter at hand, my lord. Will you walk with me?" The priest had the air of someone who had recently been told a dozen or more important things and was trying to keep them all in his head but failing, and was feeling dreadful about it. In that way, at least, he reminded Tiamak a bit of his old friend Father Strangyeard. Tiamak did not know Boez well, but for that alone he rather liked him.

"I have not had a chance to congratulate you on your . . . elevation, Bishop, if that is the proper term," he said. "Blame my heathen upbringing if I have it wrong."

Boez waved his hand dismissively. "Ordination, we say. It was Archbishop Gervis's doing, to tell the truth. He could not bear the thought of his place being taken by a mere priest. I certainly don't think the king cared. In any event, thus I became a bishop." He stopped, as if he had lost track of what he was doing, then took his spectacles off his nose and polished them again. "Where . . . ? Ah, yes. Will you walk with me in the Archbishop's Garden? Well, Gervis is an escritor now, if we are to worry about titles and such. Will you join me in the Escritor's Garden, Lord Tiamak?"

The day was gray and cold, but the rain had held off. Tiamak wrapped his cloak tighter and tried to match his limping steps to the bishop's rather brisk ones, without luck. Boez at last noticed and slowed down, bubbling with apologies.

"It is nothing," Tiamak said. "An old injury. More troubling when the weather turns cold, that is all." He looked around at the thick hedges, at the trees waving in the wind. "What troubles you, Your Excellency?"

Boez stopped dead in the middle of the path. "I shall never grow used to being anyone's 'Excellency.'" he said.

Tiamak laughed. "It has been many years and I still haven't grown used to my own title either. Never fear. Titles and honors do not change us. Only believing that they are truly deserved will do so—and then generally for the worse."

The bishop smiled, but it was a small, worried expression. "I am glad you came, my lord. I do not dare speak to anyone else except perhaps the king himself, but he is so beset with problems these days . . ." He cleared his throat. "You see, I am taking a risk even talking to you, I suppose, but of all those who might . . . well, of those who could . . ." He gave his spectacles yet another furious polishing. "Forgive me. I have muddled things already."

"Start from the beginning," Tiamak suggested.

"Yes. Of course. I have, as you can imagine, been much engaged in the last months with trying to make sense of Archbishop—*pft,* I have done it again!—with Escritor Gervis's books of accounts. It is not so much that he and the priests under him did not keep adequate records. In fact, they kept everything, not just the records of income and expenditure, but countless small messages about this and that in explanation of various things. And their organization was . . . eccentric. Gervis left the work to a succession of counting-priests, and to be perfectly honest, they did not always seem to talk to each other, let alone create an order they all might share. So my work has been slow. And somewhat frustrating."

"I can see how that would be."

Boez nodded. The wind had freshened, and it ruffled the short hair on his head. "I should have worn a hat," he said, then contemplated that omission until Tiamak could not stand to wait any longer.

"The records of the Almonry?"

"Yes. Of course. As I have worked, it has become more and more clear to me that there are certain . . . discrepancies. Allowing for the eccentricity of some of the record keeping, I did not speak of it at first, but now I can no longer deny what I have found. And everyone I could speak to—even you, my lord, if you will forgive me for saying so—fall within the circle of those who . . . well, you understand . . ."

"I understand very little, Bishop. What have you found?"

Boez seemed to steel himself, like a man about to jump from a high place to an uncertain landing. "Money, my lord. Money gone and not accounted for."

Tiamak resisted the impulse to make a sour face. It was almost impossible for money not to be misdirected, and even in the heart of the High Ward there were greedy people who would try to take advantage, but it was not really the cause for such upset. He was beginning to wish he had remained with his beloved books. "I am sorry to hear it, Bishop Boez. How much money, and do you know where it has gone?"

"My latest count is a discrepancy adding up to some two thousand gold Thrones. Give or take a few dozen."

A moment before Tiamak had been irritated. Now he felt as if he had been struck by lightning. "Two thousand! But that is a monstrous sum! They Who Watch and Shape, how could such a great amount disappear?"

"It did not all go at once," said Boez. "That would have been very difficult to hide. And as I said, I am still trying to make sense of the records. But there has been a steady diminishment at orderly intervals for some time, from many, many sources—twenty gold pieces paid here, fifty there. I only noticed at all because there seemed too many round sums." Boez took his eyeglasses off once more, but this time only held them for a few moments, then fitted them back on his nose, their brief excursion over. "In any case, you can imagine it is difficult to learn the truth of every purchase or grant, especially over a matter of some years. Thousands of records. But now that I have seen the pattern it is hard to miss. Would you like me to explain the pattern, and how the disbursements were falsified?" He sounded almost hopeful.

"No, thank you, Bishop. Later. Though it sounds fascinating." Tiamak stopped walking and peered around the deserted garden to make sure they were not being overheard. "Tell me the truth. Do you think it could have been Gervis?"

Boez looked pained. "By our merciful God, I hope not! But I cannot say, Lord Tiamak. To be completely truthful, it could be you, though I doubt it so strongly that I have trusted you and no one else with this news."

"Why are you so certain it was *not* me?" Tiamak asked, darkly amused even in the midst of his shock at the theft. "I am a pagan, a foreigner—more or less a savage—who has been given unprecedented powers by the king and queen. Most would think me a likely candidate, if not the most likely."

Boez frowned, but it was one of concentration. "I know little about any of the things you mentioned, but to begin with, you are known for living very frugally. It is a bit of a scandal in some circles, to be truthful. You dress like a monk, you and your wife live in a single set of chambers here in the Hayholt when your title guarantees you land and healthy income, but neither of you have ever shown any interest in those things."

"Money—particularly large sums such as these—need not be used solely for adornment and land," Tiamak reminded him. "They can buy other things. Influence. Power."

"I know. And if I have guessed wrongly, then I suppose you will have to kill me in some heathenish Wrannaman way for stumbling upon your secret." Boez gave him an almost defiant squint. "But I had to trust someone."

"Why not trust the king? He is the only one above suspicion. There is no reason the Throne should steal from itself."

The defiance of a moment before suddenly turned to something like embarrassment, and the new bishop did not answer immediately. "Because, in all truth, my lord, I do not trust the king, either. No!" he said as Tiamak began an angry reply, "I do not mean that as you think I do. I mean that King Simon is so . . . consumed with current problems—and also sometimes quick to temper because of it, poor man—that I do not trust him to stay quiet about this. Someone who has been so careful will not be so easily tricked into revealing himself. Also, everyone knows the king is swift to choler, but just as swift to return to forgiveness. This is not a situation that suits either impulse. Someone has been stealing from the High Throne for several years—immense sums. None of those with the freedom of the exchequer have been grandiose in their spending, so it must be for something else, to keep and to hide, or to use some for some purpose we cannot yet understand. My lord, I think we must learn who did this and why before we reveal that we know anything about it at all."

Tiamak found himself admiring Boez all over again. "I cannot fault your reasoning, although I think the king must be told at some near time."

"Yes, agreed. But first . . . well, to be honest, I do not know what should be done first."

"More study, that is certain. But that is my answer to everything, as the king and others will happily tell you." Tiamak was not very amused by his own joke, but Boez attempted to smile. "Who else has access to the High Throne's power of disbursement?"

Boez began walking again, forgetting Tiamak's limp, but Tiamak gritted his teeth and hurried along beside him. "Well, I do, for one. And Count Eolair, as Lord Steward, and Lord Pasevalles as Lord Chancellor. And of course Escritor Gervis."

"So have more of these thefts happened since Gervis and Eolair have been gone from the castle?"

"Sadly, no. That would make it easier to narrow down who might be responsible. But I have not named all who might have done it, or even half. The king and queen themselves, of course, although neither you nor I would imagine them guilty." He pondered. "Duke Osric as Lord Constable handled a great deal of money, though it would have been harder to hide his hand if it had strayed. I think he would have needed an associate within either the Chancelry or the Almonry. And of course, anyone like Sir Zakiel who oversees the pay for the Erkynguard and other expenses on Osric's behalf. Lord Jeremias in his role as Lord Chamberlain also has a budget, and access to many places and things. Then there are the masters of Horse, the Lord Marine, and the Keeper of the Privy Seal." After more thought, Boez went on to name half a dozen more who might possibly be able to drain gold from the royal coffers. "And there could also be someone more lowly-placed in the Chancelry or Almonry who does not have the right to disburse moneys but has access to the records, and might have done this for themselves or for almost anyone outside the castle. In fact, if he had a confederate on the inside, the true perpetrator would not even have to be in Erkynland."

Tiamak clutched at Boez's elbow. "Slow down, please. I am out of breath."

"Oh! Forgive me, Lord Tiamak. I have trouble thinking of one thing while I am thinking of another. Your pardon, please. Here, let us sit on this bench."

"So any of more than a dozen might be doing this," Tiamak said when he had taken the weight off his aching leg. "Do you know whether any of them have recently spent a large amount of money?" He frowned, considering. "We should also find out if any of them are known to gamble. Osric does, a little, but I have never heard of him playing for stakes so high that he would need such sums to pay his debts."

"Nor I. And none of them have spent money in any obvious way. None are quite as frugal in their lives as you, my lord, but Pasevalles's estate is run by a castellain and he has not visited it in a year and a half, nor have any alterations been made or any new land purchased. Gervis—well, it is perhaps a little hard to believe of someone who enjoys his escritorial finery so much, but our former archbishop was not known for profligacy either. I have looked into these things already and found no obvious spending to suggest guilt."

"Which is alarming," Tiamak said, rubbing his calf through his robe. "Because if whoever is robbing the treasury does not use the money for their own private pleasures, what *are* they using it for?"

"That is my concern also, my lord, and that is why I asked you to come to me. It is not a burden I want to carry alone, not any longer."

But it is another burden I must carry now, Tiamak thought. *Another fear. Another secret.*

He watched as the wind swept the last few yellow leaves from a skeletal hazel tree and whirled them through the air before discarding them on the stones of the path.

Guide me now, if you ever did, he prayed to his gods. *Help me to find sand beneath my feet, for I trust none of the ways I see before me.*

The throne hall of the Hayholt was packed with courtiers, all in their most expensive finery.

Rowson the Inevitable was there, of course, looking every inch the wealthy dullard that he was, with a fashionable new floppy hat that looked like a chair cushion, and a gold medallion the size of a warming pan dangling on his chest. Duchess Nelda, fretful because of her husband Osric's dangerous mission to the grasslands, had managed to swallow her grief long enough to appear in an elaborate dress covered in pearls and a crescent headdress that looked disturbingly like cow's horns.

Simon wondered whether they were all merely curious to see Countess Yissola of Perdruin, or had crowded in because they had enjoyed so few chances in the last grim months for ordinary court life. Escritor Gervis, the bishops Putnam and the newly elevated Boez, the lords Tostig, Duglan, and Evoric—nearly all of the court's other leading lights were present. Even Pasevalles, who usually favored somber clothing, no matter how well made, wore a coat of rich sea-green. All seemed determined to remind the southern visitors that Erchester might not be the largest or the richest city in the world, but because the High Throne was there, it was the most important.

Jeremias plucked at the sleeve of Simon's new boldcoat, trying to get it to hang just right. The king put up with it as long as he could before finally reaching over with his free hand and gently but firmly pushing Jeremias's fingers away.

"These sleeves are ridiculous, and no amount of fidgeting with them will change that," he told the Lord Chamberlain.

"The boldcoat is what everyone wears in Perdruin," Jeremias said in a disapproving tone.

"Did you not tell me only weeks ago that everyone in Perdruin was wearing some sort of mock fish-scales? You had all those little pieces of metal sewed on my doublets. I looked like a bag of cintis-pieces."

"That was more than a year past, Majesty." Jeremias started to reach out toward Simon's sleeve again, then thought better of it. "Almost two years! Fashions change."

"Well, I don't."

Tiamak appeared on Simon's other side, along with Lady Thelía. Simon was glad to see they both wore sensible gowns without unnecessary frippery. "Good afternoon, Majesty. Is all well?"

Simon decided not to mention his irritation about the boldcoat. "Well enough, I suppose. But I could wish—"

He did not finish, because a noise arose outside the throne hall and three solemn knocks sounded. Simon lifted his hand and the guards opened the great doors.

Sir Zakiel came first with an escort of Erkynguards, looking so handsome and martial in their green livery that even Simon felt a swelling of pride. They were followed by a swirl of Perdruinese courtiers, perhaps a dozen in all, many dressed in parti-colored boldcoats of mixed blues and greens and yellows. For a moment it was impossible to tell who was who, but as they made their way through the doorway the guards withdrew to either side and the mass of well-dressed folk fell into a kind of order, leaving one figure standing in the middle of the doorway.

"Her Excellency Yissola, Countess of Perdruin," cried the herald.

"Is that her?" Simon said in a whisper louder than he had intended. "Merciful Rhiap, Jeremias, why didn't you tell me she was so young? How can that be?"

If he doubted her identity, the way that Yissola looked up to meet his eye convinced him: she seemed no more daunted by the High King than at meeting a beggar in the road. She wore a dress of black slashed with scarlet; the hood of her mantle, which she now threw back on her shoulders, was of fur dyed to match the black of her dress. Already the courtiers were whispering around him at the boldness of her costume.

She could not have much more than thirty years, Simon thought in wonder, looking at the long, shapely line of her neck and her firm jaw. Yissola did not wear a hat or even the newly fashionable headstall. Instead, her golden brown hair was bound in a simple braid down her back and constrained only by a thin silver circlet around her head. Her nose was strong and her face was slender and oval-shaped. Her large eyes reminded him for a moment of Aditu's.

"Majesty," said Jeremias anxiously. "She is waiting. Everyone is waiting."

He remembered himself and extended a hand. "Countess. We greet you."

She came toward him then, tall and regal. When she reached the foot of the daïs she executed a graceful courtesy, then lifted her hand. Simon walked down to take it, and lifted it to his lips.

"My lady, you are very welcome here."

"I thank you, Your Majesty, for your kind greeting," said the countess. "I bring you the greetings of your Perdruinese subjects." Her words had no discernible trace of an accent, but Simon was not surprised by that—the Perdruinese were famous for how well they spoke the languages of their more powerful neighbors.

Taken aback by her youth and grace, Simon had forgotten almost everything he was supposed to say. "I trust your voyage was good?" was all he could summon.

"Middling, but that is no fault of the captain or the crew," she said. "I did not know you had so many kilpa in the north these days. Did you know, three of them actually came on board my ship at night as we neared Wentmouth? The crew fought them off, so all was well, but I thought we only had to worry about such things in southern waters."

Simon frowned. "I do not like to hear that. It appears they are spreading." He had again forgotten what he was supposed to say. "Well, we can thank God that you and your people were not harmed."

"Indeed, we prayed and prayed," she said. "We huddled in our cabins together until the sailors told us it was safe again."

Simon was not entirely certain he believed that the countess had been as daunted as she suggested. Despite her slender frame, he thought she looked like the sort of woman who might take up a cudgel to lend the sailors a hand. "In any case, you are welcome in Erchester and the Hayholt," he told her. "Please, let the Lord Chamberlain lead you and your fellow nobles to your chambers. I hope you will be able to join us for this evening's meal. The cooks have laid on something special, I'm told—is that not right, Jeremias?"

His old friend winced a little at being called by his first name in front of visiting nobility, but gamely stepped forward and performed an intricate bow. "His Majesty speaks the truth, Countess. The kitchen has produced a catalog of wonders!"

"Thank you," she said. "I do hope it is not all fish, though. I have had my fill of that on the voyage."

The Lord Chamberlain's smile faded, but he rallied himself and bowed again. "I am certain you will not be disappointed, Countess. Please follow me . . ."

As the Perdruinese courtiers came forward to join their mistress, Jeremias turned to one of his servants and told him in a piercing whisper that the kitchen had better provide something other than seafood for the night's meal, then replaced his smile and led the guests toward the residence.

"And you and I will have a chance to talk soon, I hope," Yissola said to Simon. "On our own, of course, without all the trouble of crowds and advisors and other such busybodies. That is not too much to ask, Your Majesty, is it?"

"Not at all," he said, so quickly that he could almost feel Tiamak's disapproving stare. "I'll make sure such a meeting is arranged."

"I am very, very sorry that Queen Miriamele could not be here," Yissola added. Simon thought her voice was a very pleasant instrument indeed. "I have admired her since I was a child."

"I am sorry too," he said, "but as you know, the situation in Nabban is quite complicated just now." Simon felt the need to add something more. "She would have been most pleased to meet you, Countess."

It was the first thing he had said that afternoon that did not feel entirely truthful.

47

A Duty to Die Well

"It is the duty of every nobleman to show lesser men how to meet Death," Aelin's father had often said. These words were very much on Aelin's mind as he and his companions made their way down the hill on the far side from Naglimund, pursued by White Foxes, demons out of old stories.

His father Aerell had not been allowed a glorious death—he had been taken by flux and had died voiding himself from every orifice. But even so, he had done his best to live up to his own credo, refusing anything but water and sending away the priests of Dun who had come to sing prayers over him and daub his face with woad.

"If the gods recognized me in this life, they will not need my face painted blue to know me when my time comes!" he had declared. A fierce man, Aerell had refused to unbend even as death came, and at the end had sent even young Aelin and his mother away because their weeping disturbed him.

Now Aelin had the chance his father had been denied, to die bravely in battle as a lesson for lesser men—but very few lesser men remained. With his squire Jarreth dead in the rubble of Naglimund's outwall, Aelin had only two companions, Evan the Aedonite and Maccus Blackbeard. The Norn enemies who had followed them out through the shattered wall were close behind, spread out and calling to each other across the hillside with strange, birdlike cries. Only the thickness of the trees prevented the Norns from feathering them with arrows. Evan had already been struck just above the shoulder blade. Maccus had pulled the shaft out again but the youth was bleeding steadily and barely able to stay in his saddle. Aelin knew that soon he and his men would be driven into an open place and then slaughtered.

Through a break in the close-leaning trees below he caught sight of a broken stone tower looming between the trees, and thought he could see tumbled stone walls beyond it. Aelin knew from his great-uncle's travel tales that ancient ruins lay on the far side of the hills from Naglimund, though he had never seen them; he felt a momentary pulse of hope. If they could find their way through the knotted undergrowth and close-crowding trees they might be able to find somewhere among the broken walls they could make a stand.

"Down there!" he said in an urgent whisper, pointing. "Out of your saddles. Lead your horses and head for the broken stones."

"That is a heathen place," said Evan weakly. "An old, Godless place. There is evil there."

"There is evil behind us," Aelin reminded him. "And *that* evil has arrows. I'll take the ruins. Haste!"

He helped the youth down and took the blood-slicked reins of Evan's horse. The Hernystirmen stumbled over roots, crashed through blackberry brambles that tore their clothes and skin, and ducked beneath branches that swiped at their faces like witches' fingers. Aelin could hear cries along the hillside as the Norns hurried to flank them. He led his men and the horses past a wall and into the bracken-choked remnants of an enclosed courtyard, only to discover half a dozen hooded figures waiting for them there with drawn bows.

"Throw down weapons!" said the tallest of these. His Westerling was crude but still understandable, his voice strangely hushed.

Aelin readied himself to charge, but young Evan, weak with loss of blood, swayed and then collapsed to the ground beside him. Maccus, seeing it was hopeless, bent over and gasped for breath, his sword-point drooping toward the damp ground.

"Throw down weapons," the leader said, more harshly. "And quiet."

The birdlike calls passed by in the near distance. A few heartbeats later, Aelin heard answering calls, but these came from even farther down the hillside; they became fainter even as he listened.

He was not certain what was happening. He looked at Maccus, then at Evan where he lay senseless on the ground, rain running down his pale face. "Very well," he said, and dropped his blade. "Spare my men and you may do as you wish with me."

"We will do what we wish to all of you," the tall one said. "The decision is not yours to make." He threw back his hood to reveal the narrow, high-boned face and uptilted eyes of one of the immortals, though his skin did not have the corpselike pallor that Aelin had expected: this was not a Norn, but a Sitha. His face was hard, his mouth tight-lipped like a carved figure of one of Hernystir's old, grim gods, and his short hair was speckled white and black. "But our task is not to harm you. Rather, we must bring you to our mistress. She was told by our scouts that mortals were pursued by Hikeda'ya." Their captor tapped himself on the chest. "I am called Liko the Starling. You are prisoners, now. If you make noise or try to run, it will go badly for you."

Aelin was confounded. "It seems we have no choice. But who is your mistress, that she cares what happens to mortals like us?"

"It is not for me to say what her cares might be," the Sitha with white and black hair replied. "All I know is that the mistress of high and ancient Anvijanya told me to find you and bring you to her. Save your questions, mortal. I will not answer them."

The river was full of Thrithings-men, howling like wolves as they splashed toward the Erkynguard camp. Some of them had brought their horses and used them to keep from being swept away by the sluggish but strong current. The swiftest of the grasslanders had already reached the pits and sharpened stakes that served as the camp's outermost barrier, and were hacking their way through the stakes with their axes.

All over the camp the alarm was spreading. Erkynlandish soldiers came running, most without armor, or with only a helmet, some not even carrying weapons but only what they had been able to snatch up when they heard the sentries' cries—sticks, stones, even iron spits from the camp cookfires.

Porto was terrified for Levias, but before he could turn back toward the tent where his wounded friend was recovering, a bearded clansman came shouting over the low wall, quickly followed by several more. Several Erkynlanders beside Porto were still fitting arrows on bowstrings and were unprepared to defend themselves. Porto was grateful he had been wearing his sword, but did not think he could do much except be hacked to pieces trying to protect his fellows.

Too old, too tired, too many days in the wilderness, he thought, but managed to sink his first two-handed swipe into the leg of a grasslander who was doing his best to murder the guard sergeant. The Thrithings-man, who had pinned the sergeant's sword with his hilt, now turned on Porto, his paint-daubed face stretched in a terrible mask of pain and fury. As he lifted an ax to strike back, the guard sergeant finally managed to draw his poniard and shove it into the man's side, then stabbed him twice more in the ribs as the grasslander staggered and dropped to his knees.

The sergeant kicked the man in the head with a muddy boot and the Thrithings-man fell to the ground and lay still.

"We need more men!" the sergeant said. "They are climbing over their own dead to get across the wall here."

Porto was already out of breath, but he could see that the sergeant was right: the fence of stout logs had been built around a great chunk of stone in the riverbank, a slab of rock bigger than a wagon bed, and because they could not dig through it or set fence posts in it, the engineers had left an inward angle in the barrier. The guards on either side had moved in to defend that angle, but the grasslanders had recognized a weak spot and were beginning to swarm toward it in numbers. But that was not the only danger. The barbarians coming up out of the river were loosing arrows and spears. Even as Porto looked to either side to see where help might come from, one of the guards beside him fell back with an arrow in his face, shrieking like a scalded child.

"Here, men!" shouted the sergeant. "Erkynlanders, to me! Here, and push the bastards back!"

Those who could hear him rallied to the wall. Porto did not have time now to think about his aching limbs, about Levias helpless in the tent, about lost Prince Morgan or anything else. Bulky shapes in animal skins clambered over the barrier, bearded faces that screeched like demons swarming toward him out of the darkness and rain. He set his shoulder against the sergeant's and did what he had to do.

Time passed for the aged knight, not as in a nightmare, but as in a fever dream, a great sliding jumble of confused impressions. The grinning, painted faces seemed endless—surely every Thrithings-man in the north was attacking the camp! For a little while the attacking grasslanders flowed over the wall like a wave overtopping a dyke, and Porto was separated from the sergeant and all those on his right side. He heard a chorus of shouting behind him, though he did not dare look to see what was happening; moments later the Thrithings-men who had forced their way past him came staggering back, tripping over each other as they retreated. Porto stabbed one in the side with the point of his sword but the bearded wild man seemed barely to notice, because a great shoving mass of armored Erkynlanders was forcing the invaders back against the barrier. A moment finally came when Porto could look up as these new troops hacked their way through the barbarians, and what he saw gladdened his heart.

It was Duke Osric himself leading a crowd of new Erkynguards wielding long pikes. Most of the Thrithings-men had thrown their spears already; few of them could stand against the surging mass of helmeted soldiers. Osric stood tall in their midst, though he alone was not wearing a helmet. The duke's hair was flattened against the sides of his head by the rain, his bald crown gleaming wet. He jabbed his spear over and over into the mass of retreating Thrithings-men, who were being pushed back against their own fellow warriors; every time he pulled it away, blood ran black from the leaf-shaped spearhead. Osric's face was a mask of pure fury, his eyes so wide Porto could see the whites of them even through the rain and darkness.

He looked, Porto thought, like one of the old gods of the past, before the Aedon came to make mankind gentle. A warrior god who would punish all who came against his people with blood and fire. It was only later, when he had time to consider it, that Porto thought there had been more than anger in the duke's face. There had been a kind of madness there, too, one that would not be quenched by a single battle.

The attack failed at last. Once the Erkynguards were roused they were too many for the grasslanders, who fell back and ran toward the river. Several floundered and were shot down, but the rest fled back across the night-dark grasses toward the trees and their camp.

The fighting finally over, Porto drank water until he thought he might be sick, then went to find Levias. His friend was safe and had slept through it all, thinking it another fever dream. Together they offered God their thanks, then Porto went out again, so weary he could barely stand.

As the first of dawn's light turned the horizon first a smoky violet, then pink, and the sky began to whiten, Porto trudged across the camp. The rains had finally ended. Water ran everywhere in muddy rivulets, making wider and wider flows as they joined and continued toward the river below, so that in a few places Porto had to wade through ankle-high streams to make his way. Bodies were already being dragged from the places of fighting beside the fence, some of them so trampled in black muck that they did not look human. He was told that perhaps four score of dead Thrithings-men remained in the camp, but that not even a quarter that many Erkynguardsmen had fallen. The soldiers who gave him this news seemed to think this something to celebrate, but Porto knew otherwise. The grasslanders who had attacked the camp had not been prepared for war. Few of the mounted ones had even reached the walls, so the barbarians had mostly been fighting on foot, and almost none of the corpses wore armor. Yes, the Erkynguard had repelled the attack, but it had been a chance battle, not real warfare, and Porto's side had been in a fortified position on the high ground.

They do not understand the savagery of these folk, he thought. *They do not guess at the numbers of them who live on these wild plains.* His mood was dark. *Perhaps I am too old for fighting*, he thought. *Perhaps I am just too old.*

Near the center of the camp he found Duke Osric and his knight-officers in counsel beside a high, roaring fire. Someone recognized Porto as having been close to the spot where the attack began, and he was called over to tell his story. But when he told of the arrow that had flown from somewhere in the camp— the arrow that had started the battle—Osric seemed to dismiss it as of little account.

"Daily the barbarians have thrown spears and flown arrows against our bar- ricades," the duke said, then drank deeply from the goblet in his hand. He still wore his armor, which was heroically bespattered in blood and mud. "As if it were some festival." He spat. "It was only a matter of time until someone re- turned the favor. These folk are savages, and savages only understand one thing—a fist of iron." He lifted his own gauntleted hand as if to demonstrate, then brought it down hard on the log he had chosen as his seat. "We came in peace, as the king ordered. Now we will show them what it means to bargain in bad faith." Duke Osric's cheeks were full of color, though the battle had ended at least an hour earlier. Porto, who had swallowed nothing but water, could not help thinking the duke was more than a little drunk.

Walking along the perimeter of the camp, watching men putting things to right after the battle and the heavy rains, he saw a group of guardsmen gathered around a pair of new arrivals at the gate opposite the river. He was still a good distance away when he recognized the short one on horseback.

Astrian sat high in the saddle like a triumphant general accepting accolades from his men. Olveris stood beside his own horse, but that was because another man was in his saddle, a thin figure in torn, soiled clothes.

"Ho, look, it is our old friend!" Astrian cried as Porto approached. "We hear you have won a fierce battle here, but we ourselves have not been idle! See, we have brought someone to the feast you might recognize—Count Eolair, the High Throne's lord steward!"

The slumped, frail-seeming figure was indeed Eolair, Porto saw, but thought the count did not look as much like a rescued man as like someone who was still a prisoner. The Hernystirman's gaunt face was days unshaven and his dark-circled eyes had the stare of someone who no longer cared where he was or where he was going.

"Astrian did it all by himself," said Olveris with heavy mockery. "Ask him. I do not think I was even in the same country."

"And Porto fought in a war!" Astrian's good cheer was undaunted. "I am sure that just like you, my terse friend, he acquitted himself bravely from a safe place in the rear guard."

"You see, he does not change," said Olveris, but Porto could not take his eyes from the count. Eolair was at least as old as Porto, and every line in his face showed it. He looked as though he could barely sit straight and his stare was fixed on nothing, as though he had seen too much of the world and its ways.

"I am glad you two have returned," Porto said. "And you, my lord Eolair. We all give thanks to God for your safe return." He bowed to the count, then turned and began walking away toward the tent where Levias waited.

"Stop!" said Astrian. "We have much celebrating to do! We will open a jug of the duke's brandy. Where do you go?"

"To my bed," he said without turning. "Usires Aedon give you all health."

Dismayed in ways he could not fully understand, Porto made his way back across the camp, walking slowly, feeling every ache now that his blood had calmed. When he reached the tent he found the wounded knight was asleep again, resting peacefully, a Tree on a leather cord clutched in his fist. Porto curled his long limbs so that he could lie down across the base of Levias' pallet. As soon as he put his head on his arm, sleep took him suddenly and utterly, like a river pike swallowing an unsuspecting fish.

Fremur stared down at Hyara's face. It was pale as eggshells, pale as boiled bones. An hour before she had been flushed with fever, turning, panting for breath. Now she was as white and clammy as the woman Fremur had once seen pulled from the waters of a deep pool in the Varn, a sodden corpse the color of a fish's belly. Only the slow movement of Hyara's breast as it rose and fell kept rage from utterly consuming him.

"How does she fare?" Unver's face as always gave little away, but his clenched fists showed white at the knuckles. "Can you save her, Volfrag?"

The shaman spread his thick hands in a show of blamelessness, though the turn of his mouth seemed to show a dislike of being questioned even by his master. "It is up to the spirits, Great Shan. The wound to her chest has let in evil essences, and she fights for her life against them. Only the Ones Above can help her now. I have prayed to them all, especially the Grass Thunderer, spirit of her clan."

"Pray harder. And say a prayer for whoever did this as well," Unver said.

Hyara's sister, Unver's mother Vorzheva, gave Volfrag a look that had little sympathy or approval in it. She had sent all but a few of her female servants away and taken charge of her sister's healing, guarding Hyara like a mother fox standing over a wounded cub. "It was Eolair and the treacherous stone-dwellers," she said. "I told you. I would not let them take me, then Hyara was stabbed instead when she tried to protect me."

Unver gave her a curiously dispassionate look. "If they were trying to take you to their king and queen, as you say, why would they strike at you with a knife?"

Vorzheva did not look up, wiping moisture from her sister's brow. "How should I know? They are mad, all of them. Eolair and his soldiers tried to steal me away. Only a madman would do that. Why would they want an old woman as a prisoner?"

Fremur felt sure he knew. "To make the Shan helpless," he said. "The count thought to hold you prisoner, then force us to do as the stone-dwellers wished."

"Perhaps." Unver did not seem interested in more talk. He nodded briefly toward his mother, then rose. Volfrag remained, praying over Hyara, but Fremur followed him out of the tent. *It is strange*, he thought, *that the Shan does not call Vorzheva 'mother,' and seldom even by her name. The woman who birthed him!* Vorzheva was the daughter of a powerful thane, even if Fikolmij had been much disliked, and she had also been the wife of a powerful stone-dweller prince, which surely lessened the shame of Unver's mixed blood. Yet still there was some uncrossable distance between the two of them that Fremur could not understand. Unver showed Vorzheva respect—he had given her servants and everything else she might desire—but he never seemed comfortable with her.

"What do we do?" Fremur asked as they walked.

"Talk to the other thanes. Have you forgotten they are waiting for us?"

"No. But I do not know what there is to talk about. Your mother's sister was attacked and lies near death! Have you no feeling?"

Unver walked on for several paces before speaking. "What feeling should I have? Anger? I have that in plenty. I thought Eolair different from other stone-dwellers. My father talked of him when I was a child, and once told me, 'There is no man I would trust beyond Count Eolair.' But he has betrayed all trust."

"Then let us punish him! Let us punish all the stone-dwellers. Even now their king has sent his men to sit on the edge of our lands and dictate terms to us, as if we were children, even while he schemed to rob us of our honorable ransom. Let us go and take iron and fire to their camp. Let us show them what true men are like."

Again Unver was silent for a time. Fremur could now see Odobreg and the other thanes waiting for the Shan, all of them standing around a great fire which had been built against the chill of the gray morning.

"You seem much concerned with the life of my mother's sister, Fremur," Unver said at last. "Is this all to honor me? Or is there something else behind it?"

Fremur felt himself flush, and hoped his already wind-burned cheeks did not show it. "Should I not fear for the loss of your mother's sister at the hands of the city-men?"

Unver only raised an eyebrow, then looked out toward the campfire.

"Very well, I will say it," Fremur finally said. He did not know why it seemed so hard, but he had to swallow before he spoke. "She is a good woman and did not deserve this."

"I agree," said Unver, still staring fixedly ahead. "But still I think you hold back some truth."

"I care for her. Is that what you wish to hear? I care for Hyara. I planned to ask you to give her to me . . . I mean in honorable marriage," he added hurriedly. "By the Sky-Piercer, you cannot believe I would mean it any other way."

For a moment, Unver's stern mouth showed a trace of amusement. "I thought nothing else. But she is much older than you, Fremur. Nearly twice your age. She is not likely to give you sons—or even daughters."

"I care not." And it was true, he realized. So many years under his brother's unpleasant rule, and all that time he had wanted only escape from Odrig's heavy hand. But suddenly the world seemed full of other possibilities. What mattered sons of his own when the Crane Clan was his? When soon the Children of the Grass would take back the lands they had been driven from in the distant, dark past? What need would he have for sons when all would remember his name—Fremur, the great lieutenant of Unver Shan?

As if he had guessed at the grandness of Fremur's thoughts Unver shook his head, but said only, "You speak truth. She is a good woman. And if you wish to make her your wife, and she will have you, I will grant it."

Fremur almost asked why what Hyara wanted should come into it, then remembered how his brother Odrig had given his sister Kulva—Unver's love—to another man. It was a wound that had still not healed, Fremur sensed, and kept his peace.

If only Hyara lives! he thought. *Then my happiness will be complete.* But it did not heal the cold, heavy place in his stomach, the knot of fear that she would die.

The thanes had been watching their approach, and now came forward to greet them.

"How is your mother's sister," asked Odobreg. "Does she live?"

"Yes," Unver answered.

"No thanks to the stone-dwellers," Fremur added. "How can they call themselves men, who would strike a helpless woman with a knife?"

"Especially with my mother's own knife," said Unver, but so quietly only

Fremur seemed to hear him. Not certain what the Shan meant, he could only wonder if he had heard him correctly.

"And what will we do?" asked Etvin, thane of the Wood Ducks. "They have sent armed men not just across the river, but all the way to Blood Lake. They have struck at our heart. Only the spirits can now prevent it from being the most treacherous murder ever done."

"She will live," said Fremur, surprised to hear the sudden anger in his own voice. "She will live."

As some of the thanes looked at him warily, Unver motioned them all to sit around the fire.

"Let us talk now of the things we must," he said. "Let us talk of insults, of blood, and of vengeance."

Despite his hard words, Fremur thought Unver showed a strange reluctance to ride against the stone-dwellers. He did not want to question the Shan at such a time, but the other thanes more than made up for Fremur's silence.

"Surely Odobreg is right," said Anbalt now. "At the least, we must catch this Eolair before he is able to return in triumph to the Erkynlanders camp beside the *Fingerlest*."

Unver looked at him, eyes half-closed as though he had grown weary of all the talk. "Do you think I did not send men after them as soon as I heard?" he asked. "Do you think I am a fool?"

"No, Great Shan." Anbalt would not meet his eye. "Never."

"Then know that I sent Wymunt of the Bustard Clan and a dozen of his riders after them. For all we know, they may have caught the stone-dwellers already. That is one reason I feel no haste to decide. If they return with him, things are much the same as they were."

"Except that he tried to kill your aunt!" said Fremur.

Unver looked at him impatiently. "There are still things I do not know, and this is no mere grassland feud . . ."

"Who is that?" said one of the thanes, staring out across the northern plain. "Look! A rider comes."

They all rose to look. Fremur, who was the youngest and proud of his eyes, said, "He wears tipped feathers."

"One of Wymunt's troop," said Odobreg. "Perhaps they have caught the stone-dwellers."

They stood and watched horse and man grow larger, until at last he could be seen clearly.

"That is young Harat," said Odobreg. "Hard to say who looks wearier, him or the horse."

The rider reached them and swung out of the saddle, landing on both feet. "Hail, Unver Shan!" he said. "Wymunt sent me because I am the fastest rider."

"Your horse is the fastest," said Odobreg. "I should know—I sold him to you."

Harat frowned at him but would not be distracted. "The Erkynlanders have attacked the Bison at the Fingerlest River," he said. "They have killed two hundred of the clansmen, it is said."

The thanes all burst into talk at the same time, angrily demanding details and cursing the stone-dwellers. "I do not think there are two hundred men in all the Bison clan," said Unver, but Fremur could hear a deep anger beneath his words.

The youth was not cowed. "There were Sparrowhawk and Whipsnake clansmen camped with them, someone said, bartering for brides. Perhaps some of those were killed as well. I tell you only what Thane Wymunt bid me tell you, Great Shan."

"How did it happen?" Unver demanded.

"I did not hear the full tale told, but what I heard from others is that the Bisons were testing their arms, throwing spears and shooting arrows toward the stone-dwellers' camp. It was in fun, and it had been going on for days. Then the soldiers shot several of them dead. The rest of the men charged the camp and there was much fighting."

"Did they drive the Erkynlanders back from the river?" asked one thane eagerly.

Harat gave him a pitying look. "They were thousands. Against them, only a few hundred Bisons."

"Of which nearly every one was killed?" asked Unver.

The young man shrugged. "All I know is that the thane of the Bison Clan has lost two sons and he is full of rage. Thane Wymunt sends to ask what you will do, Great Shan. Because if you will not come to the Bisons' aid, their thane says he will pursue his vengeance alone."

"It is not meet that a single thane should dictate to the Shan," said Odobreg, but Unver raised a hand to still him.

"Call the thanes, all that are in a day or two's journeying," he said. "Bring them here. We will ride to the Fingerlest. If the stone-dwellers have indeed done this, then it will go badly for them."

"Why do you say 'if'?" Fremur demanded, and then saw the eyes of the others, shocked that he would question his lord. "I am sorry if I speak out of turn, Unver Shan, but what more do you need to hear? Your mother's sister stabbed, your prisoner stolen before he can be ransomed—and now this? The king of Erkynland laughs at us."

For a moment Fremur thought that the look on Unver's face was meant for him, and felt his blood curdle in his veins. To his relief, he realized a moment later that he was wrong, that the ferocious scowl betokened something else entirely. "Does he? Then we will see if he still laughs when the bodies of the Erkynlandish dead lie piled as high as their stone houses." He turned to the other thanes and threw off his cloak, revealing his armored shirt of leather and steel. Fremur thought the large, square plates looked like the scaly back of a

Varn crocodile. *The stone-dwellers have wakened a monster,* he thought, but instead of triumph he felt a sudden uneasiness.

"If the city-men think to treat us like animals, then they will feel our teeth." Unver's eyes had narrowed to slits and his long, scarred face was terrible to see. He pulled his curved sword from its scabbard, then held it up against the pale sky. "Bring me my battle paint," he cried in a voice as chill and fierce as the worst night of winter. "Bring all the horses and call the thanes together! We have been attacked. Now the men of the grassland empire will go to war!"

48

The Courtyard

Miriamele watched as the servants and squires fitted the
last pieces of the duke's gold-inlaid armor and then began to buckle his cuirass.
"For the last time, Saluceris," she said, "I beg you not to go outside." She could
scarcely hear herself for the noise made by praying priests, but even the continuous murmur of old Nabbanai could not cover the sound of shouting from
outside the walls, a dull rumble like the sea pounding against the rocks. A
scream of rage from outside overtopped everything for an instant, piercing as
the cry of a gull, then faded beneath the murmurs of the priests once more.

The palace had been surrounded for two days by angry citizens, whipped
into a frenzy by the idea that Saluceris had murdered both his brother and
Count Dallo. The duke, his wife and children, even Miri herself, were all but
prisoners.

The duke lifted his helmet and paused. "Some of them have already made
their way inside, Majesty. They are tearing up Canthia's gardens. Soon they
will be at the door of our palace."

"That is because the Sancellan Mahistrevis was never built for siege," Miri
said angrily. "It was foolish to stay here. It is foolish now to go out. If anyone
should go and speak to the people, I should. I am still the queen. They will
listen." But even as she said it she heard the hollowness of her words.

Saluceris shook his head. "I will not let you risk your life, Majesty. Those
brutes outside are not our people—not the true folk of Nabban, my subjects.
This is a mob paid by Sallin Ingadaris, cowards and criminals and the worst
scum from the docks. They understand nothing but strength."

She stared at the duke's armor, her stomach knotted and heavy. "Tell me that
at least you will not wear that helm, my lord. The crest will mark you out from
half a league away."

He ruffled the blue kingfisher feathers with his finger. "Yes. And it will
remind those who have been led to this madness what they are truly doing."

"By Elysia, God's mother, why are you such a stubborn man?" She could not
sit still, and rose from her stool to stand before him. "Think of your wife,
Saluceris—your children! Stay here and protect them. Let us wait until the
mob's temper cools. If they are maintained only by Honsa Ingadaris, the money

will run out. They are here to riot and be paid for it, not to overthrow a royal house."

"All the more reason to show them some steel," he said. "You have been too long away, Majesty. You do not know the true nature of my people. Their hearts will rise to a brave show. They know their duke. They know what I have done for them."

Miriamele was tired of people telling her what they thought she didn't know. "They think what you have done is kill your brother," she said. "Ah, if only you had listened to me this would not be happening."

Saluceris looked at her carefully. His face seemed older by years than when she had first arrived, cheeks sunken, eyes peering from dark hollows. Even his whiskers seemed to have lost their color and were more gray now than golden. At last he nodded. "That could be true," he said after some moments. The priests finished a passage and were silent for a moment, then began once more. "But whatever mistakes I have made, I dedicate them to God's mercy. I have never claimed to be infallible. But what I will not have said of me is that when the darkest hour was upon him, Saluceris, Duke of Nabban, hid in his palace in fear of a crowd of peasants. How could I stand here, surrounded by the monuments of my ancestors, and do nothing?"

Before she could say anything else, he kneeled before her.

"Give me your blessing, Majesty, before I go out. Whatever else you may think of me, I swear to you that I did not murder my brother—nor Dallo, though I will never shed a tear or say a prayer for his blighted soul."

"I know." She had wrestled with the possibility that Envalles might have been acting on the duke's instruction when he locked Saluceris and his guards away, but it did not pass the test of good sense. It was far too complicated a ruse when the duke could have achieved a much more convincing effect merely by going to the Dominiate and waiting, surrounded by witnesses, for his brother to arrive. And although she had not told Saluceris or anyone else for fear the duke would do something to make things worse, she already knew who had ordered the death of Dallo Ingadaris. "I know you are blameless in these things," she said.

"Then give me your blessing, Queen Miriamele." He bowed his bare head.

She touched his forehead, then made the Sign of the Tree. "Of course. I give it whole-heartedly, Duke Saluceris. May the Lord God and Usires our Ransomer watch over you and keep you safe."

Saluceris made the Sign of the Tree over his shining breastplate. "And I beg you, Your Majesty, keep my wife and children safe, whatever happens."

You trusting fool, she thought, angry yet also on the verge of tears. *If there is fighting and the mob gets past your soldiers, there is little I or anyone else will be able to do to stop them. Save myself? Perhaps. But save the duke and his family . . . ?*

The thought was too dreadful to finish. She watched as Saluceris sent his lieutenant into the antechamber—the noise of prayers washed in, louder than ever—to form up the ducal guard. Saluceris put on his helmet as he walked, the tall blue plume nodding. His squires followed him. Two of them pulled the throne room door closed behind them, and several of the guards who still remained hurried to lower the bar across it.

May God keep you, Saluceris, she thought, *you brave but foolish man. For only He can save you now.*

Sir Jurgen met her on the stairs. "Your carriage is ready, Majesty. That is the only way out. Very few of the crowd are at the eastern end of the palace where the gate from the carriage house lets out. A dozen of my men are waiting there to protect you when it opens. Your team has been chosen from the best grasslander horses in all Nabban. No one will be able to catch us once we are through the gate."

"Thank you," she said, "but there is still business to be done. Come with me."

"But Majesty . . . !"

"Come with me."

She made her way up to the third floor of the Sancellan's residence, site of the duke's apartments as well as those of the rest of his close family and advisors.

"Do you mean to take Duchess Canthia with you?" Jurgen said, a little out of breath from climbing in his heavy armor.

"Perhaps. But there is another matter to be seen to first." She led him down the corridor and stopped in front of a door. "I wish to enter."

"But the door is locked and I have no key," said Jurgen. Outside the crowd seemed to have grown louder: she could hear screams of rage wafting in through the narrow windows at the end of the hallway. They sounded like nothing human.

"Then I suggest you improvise," she said.

Jurgen stared at the door for a moment, then began kicking it with the flat of his boot. A moment later Miri heard someone shouting in alarm inside, but she only waved to Jurgen to keep at it. After half a dozen kicks the lock gave and the door sagged inward a short distance, showing a gap along the frame where the latch had been.

"I wish to go inside," she said. "Or to bring someone out, at least. There will be scant use for that door soon, or I badly miss my guess. Break it in."

Several more hard kicks from Jurgen and the door at last lurched and crookedly swung open, like a bird's broken wing. Miri saw Lord Envalles huddled in the corner of his bedchamber, eyes wide with terror.

"Majesty!" he said, half fearful, half relieved. "What is it? What do you want with me?"

"To show you something," she said. "Jurgen, bring him out here."

The guard captain grabbed the old man by the elbow and forced him out into the passage. Miri was already on her way to the window at the end. "Here, kind old Uncle Envalles. Have a look at what you have done."

"Do not throw me down, Majesty!" Envalles was weeping now as Jurgen wrestled him toward the glass. "I only tried to do what was best for Nabban!"

"You are not even a good liar," she said, and grabbed the back of his neck, which was cold and damp with perspiration. "Look at what you've done, old man. Look!"

And as she held his head before the window, Miriamele also saw what was happening below, and her heart seemed to freeze solid in her chest. The outer walls, built largely for show, had been breached. Some in the crowd had brought ladders and had clearly climbed the walls in too many places at once for the duke and his men to stop them. The gardens were full of people, many carrying torches, almost all carrying wooden clubs or hay forks or other make-shift weapons, but she saw that the leaders who were shouting them on were better armed, many with swords and battle axes that no ordinary villain would own. To her momentary relief, she saw Saluceris' blue plume still waving. He and his men had put their backs to the gate that led to the inner courtyard, but they were only a hundred or so, struggling to keep a much larger throng at bay.

"Oh my sweet Aedon, save us!" cried Envalles. "What is happening?"

"That is your nephew out there, fighting for his life. Because of you. But you did not do this on your own, did you?"

"I did nothing!" Envalles nearly shrieked. "Only what I was told! I had no idea, no notion . . . !" He was panting like a terrified dog.

"Then who did? Who told you to lock Saluceris in the crypt? Answer me, or by God I *will* throw you out this window. And the fall will not be enough to kill you, unless you are lucky. You will lie there helpless, with your bones broken, until the mob notices you."

"I did not know anyone would die! He told me it was only to keep one side from gaining an advantage!" Envalles turned toward her, eyes red. "He said it was necessary!"

"Who? *Who said that?*"

"*Lord Pasevalles!*" He burst into tears again, jaw trembling. "Please do not kill me, Majesty. I thought I was—"

"Pasevalles?" The cold heaviness in her chest became something else, an icy abyss that seemed to have no bottom. "Do you mean the Lord Chancellor of the High Throne?"

"God save me, I did not know! I thought I was doing what was wanted—I was to be rewarded, given my due . . . !"

Sickened and terrified, Miriamele let go of his neck and stumbled back from the window.

"Majesty?" Sir Jurgen said in a voice ragged with shock. "Is it . . . does he speak the truth?"

Miriamele could only press her hands to her temples. Her thoughts stampeded through her head, running into one another until she could scarcely think. Why? Pasevalles? Could it be true? Why would he do such a thing?

And what else has he done? The new thought was like icy water splashed over her. *Oh, sweet Ransomer, what terrible serpent have we held in our bosom?*

She was light-headed, and did not speak until the worst of the dizziness had passed. "Hold him," she told Jurgen. "Hold him here. I will be back."

"But Majesty, you must get out of this place!" Jurgen reached out a hand as if to restrain her but she slapped it away.

"I know! And I will. But if this poison came from our court, I have to do what I can to keep it from spreading."

She turned and hurried back up the corridor, passing Envalles's shattered door, then raced to the end of the hall where she turned again, counting the doors until she reached the ducal bedchamber. The door was locked, so she pounded on it and shouted, *"Open! It is the queen! Canthia, open the door!"*

It was not the duchess who came at last but the young Wrannawoman, Canthia's companion and nurse. She fell back from the doorway murmuring apologies as Miriamele entered, but Miri ignored her and hurried through the anteroom to the chamber beyond. Canthia sat on the bed, her infant daughter clutched in her arms. The little boy, Blasis, was stretched on the floor at her feet, looking at a richly illustrated copy of the Book of Aedon. He glanced up in curiosity at Miri's entrance, and for a moment she thought she had walked out of a dream and back into a world that made sense. But she knew this dream of normality was not hers, nor was it one that could be trusted.

"Go!" she cried. "Down to the stables, now. Take only what you are wearing."

"Majesty, what do you mean?" Instead of rising, Canthia leaned away, shielding little Serasina as though it were Miriamele who was the threat.

"Do you not hear me? Get up and hurry down to the stables. By Elysia, Mother of God, we have no time, Canthia. If you want to save your children's lives, get up!"

"But my husband—"

"The duke's fate is in God's hands." Miri took the baby from Canthia—the duchess resisted only a little, but she seemed unable to understand what was happening. The nurse had followed her into the bedchamber, so Miri handed her the baby, who was awake and beginning to cry at the sudden noise. "Jesa— that is your name, am I right? Take the infant and hurry. Do you know where the stables are?" The girl nodded. "Wait for the duchess—she is coming, too, with the little boy. Then down the stairs and do not pause."

The dark-skinned girl turned, taking time only to pick up a sack that lay behind the door, then hastened from the bedchamber with the baby in her arms. Miri pulled at one of the little boy's arms until he got to his feet, then pushed him after the nurse. "Go, Blasis. Follow your sister." As he went, Miri turned back to the duchess. "How many times must I say this? Get up! You will have to join me in my coach."

Canthia was still staring at her, as though Miri spoke a language she had never heard. "We must wait for Saluceris—"

Her patience strained beyond all reason, Miri slapped her face. Canthia's head swung back, then she lifted her hand to her cheek and stared at the queen, wide eyes filling with tears. "You cannot wait a moment longer, woman." Miri grabbed her wrist, set her feet, and pulled until Canthia had to rise or be yanked to the floor. Miri got behind her and pushed her out into the anteroom, where the nurse waited with Blasis and the baby. The little boy looked fiercely at Miri.

"Where is Papa?" he demanded.

"He is coming when he can. For now, you must protect your mama and your little sister. That is your duty, Blasis. That is what a knight would do."

Miri turned to Canthia. "I am coming after you, Duchess. If we are separated, you must take my carriage and leave. The driver will carry you to Erkynland. You will be safe there. Tell my husband—and *only* my husband, do you hear me—that I said Pasevalles is a traitor. He must be arrested immediately." But if they were separated and Miri herself was not there to affirm Canthia's words, Pasevalles might be able to convince Simon that the duchess was mistaken, or even that she had lost her mind and made up the accusation out of her own fancy.

Oh, husband, if only I could talk to you now as the Sithi talk, heart to heart despite the distance!

An idea came to her: she took her golden wedding ring from her finger and pressed it into Canthia's palm. "Keep this safe. When you see the king, give this to him and tell him what I said about Pasevalles."

The duchess stared at the ring, then up at Miri. "But you are coming with us!"

"I have one more thing to do before I join you. They are setting fire to the palace, Canthia. There is no time for talk now."

She closed the woman's fingers around the ring, then hurried them all ahead of her into the passage and down to the stairwell, where she sent them on their way.

"Tell the carriage driver to prepare to leave at any moment!" she shouted after them.

Miri turned and ran back down the passage and out to the hallway where she had left Sir Jurgen and Envalles. To her surprise, she found the old man stretched on his belly across the floor, paddling like a drowning swimmer and calling for help, with Jurgen sitting on top of him.

"He tried to escape," the guard captain explained. "I was getting tired of trying to hold him."

"Bring him with us. He can tell his story to my husband, then we will hang the cursed traitor who gave him his orders."

As Jurgen dragged the weeping prisoner back onto his feet, finally having to resort to a drawn dagger pressed against the old man's ribs to get his attention, Miri hurried to the window. What she saw below was almost enough to make her legs fail beneath her. The mob had pushed in past the inner gate and was swarming through the courtyard below the window, so close now that she could see individual faces. A few of the duke's soldiers had made a stand in front of the residence gates, but several of the maddened citizens had already broken into one of the Sancellan's wings. Others were pouring in after them. Smoke drifted from the windows, and she could see flames licking upward inside. She could see no sign of the duke's kingfisher-feather crest.

Then, just as she was about to turn from the window, she saw Saluceris. His helmet was gone, but she could make out his bright armor, now dinted and stained with blood. He was being dragged by a crowd of men toward the statue of his ancestor, Benidrivis the Great, founder of the Third Imperium. Even as Miri watched in open-mouthed horror, someone produced a rope and flung it over the statue's outstretched arm.

For a moment the roil of the crowd around the statue's base was so great that she could see little of what was happening, but then several men pulled on the rope and Saluceris was jerked up into the air with the other end of the rope knotted around his neck. As the crowd screamed and jeered the duke kicked and thrashed just above their heads. Several hands reached out to pull down on his legs, but his death-struggles were too violent and they could not hold him.

Her own eyes suddenly blurry with tears, Miri turned and ran until she caught up with Jurgen, but she could not speak and did not answer his questions.

The main rooms of the palace were full of courtiers running, servants crying, some just kneeling on the floor and praying. No one seemed to notice Miri or her companions, and they were halfway across the great entrance hall, heading toward the rear courtyard, when someone stepped out before them.

"Heavens be praised, Your Majesty! I am heartily glad to see you!" Count Matreu briefly bent his knee, then straightened. "Where are the duchess and her children? I have been looking for them everywhere!"

Miriamele instantly felt mistrust—if he had been looking for them so assiduously, why had she not met him in the upper floors of the residence? "I do not know," she said. "You should look to the duke's chambers."

"I went there earlier," he said. "I knocked and knocked, and called that it was me, but nobody answered."

Miri was torn. She did not know whether to believe him or not, but she was certain she did not want him to know where Canthia and the children were. "Then you must save yourself, and trust God to protect the innocents," she said.

Matreu looked at Envalles, slumped at Sir Jurgen's side, before turning back to Miri. "And what of you, Majesty? The people are drunk with disorder and blood. This is no place for you."

"I have my own protection, my own plan of escape," she said, but even as she said it she knew it might not be enough to dislodge him. "Instead, I give you a royal command—a task that will bind you to me and the High Throne by our gratitude. Take this whining cur, Envalles. Get him to safety, but do not release him. He has played a grave part in all this and must answer for his crimes. Do you hear me? He must live, but I cannot take him with me. Will you lead him out of this place, Count Matreu, before it is too late?"

She could see thoughts jump like sparks behind Matreu's eyes, but he did not hesitate for more than a heartbeat or two. "Of course, Majesty. I will get him safe from here. He will be prisoner in my father's house. Are you certain you do not need me for aught else?"

"I am certain."

"Then God protect you, Majesty."

"Thank you, Count," she said. "And God protect every true, loyal soul from the terrors of this day."

Jurgen passed the unresisting Envalles into Matreu's care, then Miri and the guard captain hurried across the wide, echoing room, heading for the door at the far end that led down to the stables. Already she could smell smoke from the west wing and hear people shouting that a fire had broken out. She did not want to look back for fear Matreu would be following them, but when she finally weakened and peered over her shoulder, he and Envalles were gone.

The stables were a madhouse. Miri's guards fought to hold back members of the duke's household, servants and nobles both, who were trying to make their way to the gate and escape, screaming and shoving until the soldiers could hardly hold them. Smelling smoke, horses pranced and whickered in their stalls. The stable doors had been flung wide; the royal coach stood waiting, the team harnessed, the driver and three Erkynguards all in their places. Miri could see the back of Canthia's head through the tiny window at the rear, as well as a bit of the baby's blanket. She finally let out the breath she had been holding since she and Jurgen had first come down the stairs. The duchess and the children were safe, or as safe as they could be.

Before she could take a step toward the waiting carriage, Miri heard a loud clanking of chains and the creak of wooden wheels. The outer gate began to swing open.

"What are they doing?" she cried. "Have they lost their minds?"

Jurgen grabbed her and pulled her to one side as a group of palace residents finally forced their way past the Erkynguards who were trying to hold them back, then spread out through the stable even as the gate continued to open. A moment later, as the gate swung wide, Miri saw that the winches were being worked not by the gatehouse guards but by an outshoot of the mob that was already laying waste to the courtyard and the eastern wing. The bodies of several guards lay motionless and bloody where they had been flung down from the top of the gatehouse onto the cobbles, and intruders were swarming through the open gate with torches and shovels and mattocks, screaming "Murder!" and "Drusis!"

The horses harnessed to the royal coach reared and shrilled at this, hooves flailing the air as the crowd eddied around them. Some tried to grab at their harnesses, but the Erkynguardsmen on the carriage cut at the attackers' hands until they fell back and went looking for easier prey. But the horses had panicked and could not be held back; an instant later, one of them broke forward, yanking his harness mate along, and then they were all plunging through the crowd so swiftly that the carriage, dragged helplessly behind, wobbled on its wheels and threatened to overspill. It stayed upright and hurtled out of the stable toward the gate, crushing many of the crowd beneath its wheels as it went, while the driver swung his whip wildly and uselessly, barely able to hang onto his seat.

As Miri watched in numb astonishment the carriage crashed out through the open gate at speed, tilting so badly as it turned onto the road that it almost overtipped again, then sped along until it vanished behind the palace wall, leaving only a cloud of dust and a few writhing bodies behind it.

"Onto my horse, Majesty," said Sir Jurgen, his face quite white. "Orn is faster than anything in Nabban, I trow, even with two people on his back. None of them will catch us." He pulled his sword from its scabbard and then led her toward the stall, clearing the way before him with swipes of his blade, no longer caring whether it was groom, ducal soldier, or angry peasant that he struck. His big gray courser, eyes rolling, quieted a little when he grabbed its harness and put his face close to speak a few soothing words. He clambered into the saddle and reached down for Miri.

"Here, let me help you, Majesty." Jurgen had lost his helmet somewhere between the stairs and this moment; as she took his hand and let him hoist her up onto the saddle, she could not help marveling how young he was, this guard captain. *I was already a grown woman before he was born,* she thought. *And now he saves me. I will see him made a lord for this.*

Then something came hurtling from the side and struck Jurgen in the head, knocking him out of the saddle. Miriamele was almost torn from Orn's back by the knight's fall. When she looked down she saw that he had been hit by a shoeing hammer, which now lay in the straw beside him. She could not tell if Jurgen was alive or dead, but a deep dint in his forehead oozed blood, and she knew she could not possibly lift him up into the saddle before she was pulled down herself by the crowds streaming in through the open gate.

She slid down from the skittish horse just long enough to yank Jurgen's sword from its scabbard, then clambered back into the saddle, pulling her skirts up until she could straddle it, though her feet did not quite reach the stirrups. She kicked with her heels as hard as she could and the gray horse sprang forward, shoving open the unlatched stall and heading for the open stable doors.

Faces loomed before her, and hands tried to grab at the reins, but she hacked at them all with the heavy sword and then clung to the horse's neck as they burst out into the thickest part of the crowd. Some of the intruders tried to get out of the way and were run down, others flung themselves aside. By the time the gray horse reached the gate and burst out into the road, most of the folk that had forced the gate were already behind them.

God rest you, Sir Jurgen, was all she could think. She clung to Orn's neck as a few rocks flew past her, thrown by members of the mob—one even struck the horse's flank and made him dance for a moment, but Orn found his stride again and galloped on. Half the west wing was now afire, flames climbing from the tops of the windows, reaching greedily for parts unburned, and the east wing was beginning to burn as well. She could see men on the palace roof above the main residence tipping statues from their niches down to the courtyard below, dancing on the roof tiles and exulting like demons.

God rest you, Jurgen, she thought again. *Without you I would be dead and Simon a widower. God protect the duchess and her children. And God's mercy on this ungodly hell called Nabban.*

49

Gatherers' Way

Jarnulf had been in his eyrie since the hour before dawn, poised to deal or receive death, perhaps both; his nerves were tightened to such a pitch that he felt if someone touched him he might hum like the strings of a lute.

He had spent weeks preparing for this day. He had prayed to God over and over for strength, for sureness of touch, for the eye to see and the mind to understand, so that he would not waste what he felt sure would be his single chance.

The doubly curved shape of his bow came from the Thrithings-men, who often fought from horseback; Jarnulf had purchased his from a bowyer in Erkynland who had learned the trick of making them from the grasslanders themselves. It had cost him quite a few silver quintis-pieces but he had never regretted it.

Even with such a powerful bow, he knew he would have to make a long, long shot from a place far outside the camp, so he had built himself a platform in the trees high on the hillside, working silently for only an hour at a time so he could still bring back enough game to lull any suspicion about his absences. When the platform was finished and tied securely into place, he took countless practice shots—always away from the camp—to learn how the winds and height and surrounding vegetation affected the arrows' flight, then climbed down and laboriously gathered the flown arrows. He knew he would have to draw the bow to its outermost limits, as well as his own, but after all his preparations he felt sure he could manage one accurate shot. He had never heard any tale of Queen Utuk'ku wearing armor, and though she would be surrounded by armed, lightning-swift Queen's Teeth guards, Jarnulf felt certain he could put an iron-tipped arrow into her heart before any of them even grasped what had happened.

His bow now lay on the platform beside him, still wrapped in the cloth that kept it, and the arrows, and the coiled bowstring, dry and warm. When the time came he would add his finishing touch to the chosen arrowhead, then stake everything on a single shot.

And if God is good and my heart is pure, the bitch queen will die. My oath to Father and to the Lord of this world will be fulfilled. The Hikeda'ya may catch me and kill me, but it will not matter. I will have a certain welcome in Heaven.

★   ★   ★

It was past noon when the camp suddenly stirred into greater life. Jarnulf sat up, rubbing his hands to warm them, and watched as the Hikeda'ya warriors and others swarmed over the clearing, busy as ants. Clearly something was happening, and it seemed equally clear that it must be the queen's arrival driving them all into such a frenzy.

He took the bow from its protective cloth and looped the bowstring over one end, then used his foot to brace it as he bent the bow back to receive the other loop. He had done this over and over in recent days, and had thought through each step so many times that he felt now as if he moved in a dream.

The bow strung, he watched the excitement far below as his hand lit on his chosen arrow. He would not wipe the dragon's blood onto the arrowhead until just before he was ready to fire, because he knew that the corrosive blood would eat away the iron if he left it on too long, but he kept the clay jar ready, as well as the splinter of stone he would use to spread the black, sticky stuff when the moment came.

But as he watched, Jarnulf suddenly felt uncertain. If the Norn troops were preparing for the queen's arrival, why were they taking down the tents of Akhenabi and the other officers and nobles? Would they not even stay here long enough for the queen's company to water their horses and rest before marching out?

A good-sized group of Sacrifice soldiers were hitching a team of eight horses to the front of the great cart that carried the bound, sleeping dragon. As Jarnulf watched, a figure in white that he knew must be Saomeji led the giant Goh Gam Gar to the back of the immense cart, where a large wooden yoke was lowered onto the giant and locked in place, then chained to the cart's back end. The giant did not resist, which showed that Saomeji must be using the crystal rod that controlled him.

Jarnulf saw that Goh Gam Gar was going to be used to push the wagon through mud and wheel ruts that the horses could not overcome by themselves. That meant the Hikeda'ya were not just taking down the camp, they were preparing to move out, and soon. But he saw no sign of the queen's caravan or of Akhenabi and the others waiting for her arrival. In fact, some of the Sacrifices had already formed into lines and were beginning to march silently away from camp toward the southeast, farther into mortal Erkynland.

He could not wait any longer to find out what was happening. Jarnulf left his bow and everything else on the platform and swung himself down from limb to limb until he dropped to the ground, then hurried downhill toward the camp.

As he made his way through the milling Hikeda'ya, most of whom did not bother to look at him, Goh Gam Gar spotted him.

"Ho, little mortal!" the monster bellowed. "There is still room for you. Perhaps they find a yoke small enough for your shoulders and you help old Gam push this lizard to Naglimund."

Naglimund! Jarnulf knew the name, though he could not guess why the giant had spoken it. The castle had been the site of a horrific battle during the War of Return, taken by the Hikeda'ya and then eventually retaken by the mortals. It still had an evil name to many, though it was only a mortal fortress now.

He saw Saomeji instructing a half-dozen Singers as they removed books, chests, and sacks from Akhenabi's carriage and packed them onto a baggage wagon. Jarnulf could not help wondering how many deaths were contained in that collection, how many plagues, how many poisons, how many spells to maim and kill. The thing that had been Makho stood near Saomeji, watching, his single eye dull and showing scant sign of life. Jarnulf had stayed away from the onetime Sacrifice since Akhenabi had revived him, but he could not afford that now—he needed to find out what had happened during the morning.

"My lord Saomeji," he said as he approached, then remembered to bow: Saomeji had conducted himself like a member of the nobility since they had returned with the dragon. "I see much activity. Will you tell me what happens here?"

Robed in white, and with skin scarcely darker, Saomeji's eyes seemed to glow like little suns as he turned to Jarnulf.

"We are leaving."

"But why? I thought we waited for the queen and her forces?"

"What right do you have to know the movements of the Mother of All?"

"None, Lord Saomeji. But I had hoped to be rewarded for the help I gave you and Chieftain Makho."

"Hah." Saomeji's mouth curled in a malicious smile as he looked over to the unmoving Sacrifice. "Chieftain Makho. He is less than that now—and more, too. But the queen does not stop here. We are to meet her elsewhere. Time is fleeting, so plans have changed."

"You are to meet her at Naglimund?"

Saomeji's expression closed like a shuttered window. "Where did you hear that?"

"The giant shouted it at me. But I do not know where that is," he lied.

"The giant thinks himself necessary—but he will not be so for much longer." Saomeji pursed his lips in barely hidden annoyance. "Yes, we go to the place the mortals call Naglimund. If you still hope for some reward from the palace, saddle and prepare to ride."

Jarnulf's thoughts were racing. It had been a risk waiting here for the queen, one that could have ended in his death at any time if Saomeji or Akhenabi had decided they had no further use for him. He had already wondered several times why he had been allowed to stay with the Hikeda'ya so long. And who was to say this group of Sacrifices would even see the queen, let alone be allowed near enough for Jarnulf to do what he planned? No, if he was to complete his sworn mission and fulfill his oath, he would have to find another way—another opportunity.

"In truth," he said at last, "I do not wish to go any farther into mortal lands. I have done my duty to the queen, but I have left my other tasks unfulfilled for too long."

This caught Saomeji's attention. The Singer looked at him carefully, as if, like his master Akhenabi, he could discern the thoughts behind a man's face. "So just like that, you will go back to being a Queen's Huntsman?"

"It is the task for which I was trained. And it is a task I have always done well." But if he wanted to keep the imposture believable, he had one more thing to do. "But before I go, there is the matter of . . . silver."

"Silver?"

"Makho agreed to pay me a silver drop for every day I guided your Talons. Even if you would be a miser and only pay me for the trip to Urmsheim, that is still the matter of many silver drops—but I would hope you would pay me also for each day I helped you bring it down the mountain. I did what I promised and more. You, Lord Saomeji, will present the beast to the queen, and receive praise and no doubt advancement. I ask only my due."

"I do not seek advancement," Saomeji said, but there was an odd edge to his words, almost more wistful than angry. "I seek only recognition for my loyalty."

"And I am sure you will receive it, my lord. But I wish to return to a quieter life, tracking and capturing fleeing slaves. Will you honor Makho's bargain?"

Saomeji seemed about to say something, but whatever he was thinking was hidden again behind the stony seeming that the Hikeda'ya showed to the world. He motioned to one of his servants and made a series of gestures, Order of Song sign-talk that Jarnulf did not understand. The servant bowed and went off.

"He will bring back your silver, mortal, one drop for each day of your labors. And when you are among the other Huntsmen again and bragging of your riches, tell them also that their Hikeda'ya masters keep their word, even to mortal slaves. The Mother of All is generous."

"I have never doubted the queen's goodness, my lord," Jarnulf said.

For Nezeru, it was a day full of surprises.

The first came just before sunrise, while she was waiting for her pursuers. Her stolen horse had been running for several days with hardly any rest and was exhausted. She had seen enough of the current troop of Sacrifices following her to know that they numbered half a dozen, and she knew even with her Talon training she could not hope to beat so many Hikeda'ya in open combat, so she left her horse higher up the hill, found a great shelf of reddish granite that stuck out like a snake's tongue from a heather-mantled hillside, then hid herself on top of the slab and waited for her enemies.

Yes, enemies, she thought, full of bitterness. *But not by my choice. Because of*

Jarnulf. Because my own people believed him over me. And because Saomeji, another halfbreed like me, called me a traitor and set the War-Shrikes on me. I owe the Singer for that. But since she doubted she would survive to see sunrise, she could not make herself believe she would ever have a chance to exact revenge.

She lay tight against the shelf of rock, peering down at the rainy forest. Already she could see a hint of movement in the darkness, shivering branches, the hint of hooves against the damp ground. For the dozenth time, she wished she had a bow and enough arrows to send her pursuers to the Garden, but she had nothing except Makho's sword and the knives at the back of her belt.

Not just Makho's sword—Suno'ku's sword, she reminded herself. *One of the greatest of our people, she who broke the Northmen's lines and rescued hundreds.*

But Suno'ku had died. That was the end of the hero's story. The general had been crushed beneath the falling mountain at the gates of Nakkiga, and all the songs of praise, all the flowers placed before her grave at the Iyora Clan's vault did not make brave Suno'ku any less dead.

And in any case, there will be no songs for me—who honors a traitor? If I die here, I will never be anything else in my people's memory. Saomeji and the mortal Jarnulf had stolen from her something far more important than her life.

Now, as she stared through the dim light at the forest below her, Nezeru saw the first of her pursuers and received her first surprise. They were Hikeda'ya Sacrifices, there was no doubt of that—she could see the pale smear of their faces before she could see anything else of them—but as they moved through a gap in the tree cover, she saw the insignia on the arms of their dark coats.

They were not War-Shrikes.

Instead, they wore on their arms the rune that stood for the sound *"Zo"*. They were of the Legion Zosho, named after the gyrfalcons that ruled over all the birds of Lake Rumiya on Nakkiga Mountain's broad skirts.

So more than one legion of Hikeda'ya were chasing her. No wonder her pursuer's horses always seemed fresh. But how could that be, unless they came from some other fort even nearer than the War-Shrikes'? How many Sacrifice fortresses had been built in what she had always been told were lands that the mortals had stolen long ago? And why would so many Sacrifices be sent after Nezeru, one lone Sacrifice, even if they thought her a traitor?

She never discovered whether the hunters had already caught her scent, or if she had given herself away in some other manner, but within moments after she spotted them the Gyrfalcons dismounted, left their horses in the cover of the trees, and began making their way up the slope where she had hidden. She could see they had more in mind than simply getting to a high place: they moved like spies, staying close to the ground and using the dark, brushy heather for cover. They did not know she had neither bow nor arrows, so they were taking no chances. She almost laughed.

Some of them may be many Great Years older than I am, yet they chase me like I was the most dangerous beast in the woods.

She could not help wondering whether she could help bear out their caution. Thinking of Suno'ku made her remember not just the great general's death, but also a deadly trick the Hikeda'ya had played on the mortals during the long retreat to Nakkiga after the failure of the War of Return. She rolled over and began to look around the shelf of stone and on the hillside above her, but there were no stones small enough for her to work loose that would be do any real damage to her pursuers. The moment of hope guttered and died.

It would be sword-work, then, though Nezeru had little doubt how it would end. She only hoped she earned an honorable death while wielding Sunoku's blade.

Silently, she repeated her death-song while she listened to the almost noiseless approach of the Gyrfalcons. She slid forward again to check their numbers, and counted five, which meant one had probably stayed behind with the horses.

If I cannot be a hero, I might settle for being an infamous terror. It is too bad I will not live long enough to become that kind of story, either. They would tell the young Sacrifice acolytes, "Never leave your bed at night, or Nezeru the Treacherous will take you—"

She was distracted by a thin cry from below. For a moment she thought it was her pursuers' call to attack and readied herself to spring to her feet and fight, but as she peered down she saw one of the Gyrfalcon soldiers rolling back down the slope. It seemed impossible—no trained Sacrifice would lose their footing so easily—but then another of the Gyrfalcons staggered to one side. Nezeru saw him clutch at his ribs, where blood was already draining from him. Arrows! But from where?

The other Gyrfalcons retreated into the nearest stand of trees, taking their own bows from their shoulders. When they loosed their shafts it was not toward Nezeru's position atop the stone but at something lower down the hillside.

As she watched in astonishment and with extremely mixed feelings, the Gyrfalcons traded arrows with an invisible enemy. The only sound she heard was the hum of insects and, once every long while, the buzz of an arrow.

At last, when it had been a hundred heartbeats or more since the last arrow flew, she decided she should try to escape while the stalemate continued. She crouched, prepared to run up the slope to where her horse was tethered, but a sudden movement below her caught her attention: several shapes had burst from the thickly wooded base of the slope and were running toward the tangle of pines where the Gyrfalcons were hiding.

Zida'ya, she thought, amazed and confused. *Those warriors are Zida'ya!*

The Gyrfalcons did not wait for the Dawn Children to reach them, but spilled out of the trees with loud cries meant to imitate the voices of hunting birds. The Zida'ya moved swiftly but silently toward them along the hillside. Neither side carried bows; Nezeru guessed they had both exhausted their supply of arrows.

The Hikeda'ya soldiers were outnumbered—she counted only four of them now. Two had swords, and the other pair carried the hand-axes known as *xari*—scorpions—because of their hooked blades. The seven Zida'ya had swords and short spears.

Nezeru's next surprise followed quickly. The Hikeda'ya might have been wearied after pursuing her since late the previous night, but they were all death-sung Sacrifices, and she expected them to fight off even a greater force of Zida'ya easily. All her life she had been taught that their forest-dwelling kin were weak and cowardly, that the Hikeda'ya had stayed strong while their soft relatives had surrendered to the corrupt world outside Nakkiga.

But these Zida'ya didn't fight that way.

Even in the first, faint light of day it was easy for her to follow the struggle. The Gyrfalcons were uniformed in the dark colors of their legion, but the Zida'ya wore at least a half-dozen different shades of browns, grays, and greens, and even their hair colors were individual. The only thing the Dawn Children shared was a glinting brooch they wore on their shoulders; even Nezeru's sharp eyes could not make out the insignia from such a distance.

The Zida'ya did not stand back and rely on their superior numbers, but came leaping along the slope. They threw themselves at the Hikeda'ya almost care-lessly, as though rushing to meet a lover long missed. The knot of fighters tightened; she saw the dull gleam of weapons and heard them clicking as the two sides clashed, then the Hikeda'ya fell back to a higher spot, leaving one of their number motionless on the rocky hillside. The Zida'ya leaped after them. The Gyrfalcons had stopped shouting, and the two groups came together again in silence, then whirled and fell away into several separate struggles. It quickly became clear that the Gyrfalcon Sacrifices were being surrounded and dis-patched, and even in her astonishment at this unforeseen result, Nezeru realized that when the Zida'ya finished with her pursuers they would see her as just another enemy. She turned and began scrambling back along the stone ledge, then headed up the hill, trying to stay low and quiet, hoping she could reach her horse unseen by the fighters below.

It didn't work. *"Hike!"* someone cried from below her—"Cloud!" The Zida'ya had seen her and recognized her as one of their foes.

Nezeru reached her horse, unspeakably grateful that none of those below had any arrows left. The Nakkiga steed made no sound as she vaulted onto its back. She would have to run again, and hope that the Gyrfalcons still fighting for their lives could at least delay the Zida'ya.

By the Garden, I saw it with my own eyes—the Dawn Children's warriors are as fierce as any Sacrifices! She urged the horse over the crest of the hill and down into the thickly forested valley below. Were they some special troop, like the Talons or the Queen's Teeth of Nakkiga? Or was what she had been taught about the Zida'ya a lie all along?

She thought of Jarnulf, who had tried so hard to destroy her faith in her queen and people, to make her believe that her lifelong truths were lies. She felt poisoned by the cruel things he had told her.

But what if he had been right?

★   ★   ★

Nezeru's flight led her ever deeper into the forest. She had no idea where the Zida'ya had appeared from, but she knew where her Hikeda'ya pursuers did, so she rode south through the night, letting the horse find its way through the trees. Sometime past midnight she heard the distant sounds of pursuit, hoof-beats echoing dully through the damp air. The Zida'ya must have finished with the Gyrfalcons and recovered their horses. She had to assume their mounts were fresher than hers.

Just as the moon was disappearing, Nezeru stumbled on what she at first thought was an animal track. It was full of obstacles, low-hanging branches and trees growing in the center of the uneven path, but it was much less densely forested than the surroundings and she could ride more swiftly. Unfortunately for her, those pursuing her would have the same benefit.

As she leaned low and sped along, desperate to stay ahead of the hunters as long as possible, she decided that the track she traveled was too long and well-defined to be merely a path made by deer or bison. It had to be an old road, a very old road, and she wracked her memory trying to make sense of it.

Like most of her order, Nezeru had not much studied the things that clerics and chroniclers learned. History had been taught to her only as a series of wars and battles, victories and retreats. But as she coursed down the ancient road with rain whipping her face and the sounds of hoofbeats behind her drawing steadily closer, she knew she had found something old. A snatch of poem her father had taught her when she was very young rose up from her memory.

"*In the Old Heart, behind the hills . . .*"

The track, which had meandered along hillsides and down through dells for at least two leagues, now became straight. The trees on either side seemed re-luctant to grow upon it, though their branches hung over and mingled to form a tunnel of darkness.

"*In the Old Heart, behind the hills and shielded from wind and sun, lies . . .*"

And suddenly she could see pillars of weathered stone looming through the greenery before her. She had to hold tight to her horse as it leaped over a shat-tered arch which lay across the ancient road. She slowed without thinking. The central piece of the arch was a circle with coiling rays, like a sun, like a flower, like . . . a star.

The Gate of the Star, she realized. The track she was following must be Gath-erers' Way, the great avenue that had once led into the city from the north. The memory came to back to her in a single piece—she could hear her father's voice, hear the words from her childhood.

"*In the Old Heart, behind the hills and shielded from wind and sun, lies the ruin of The Tree of the Singing Wind, one of the Nine Cities of our people.*"

This must be Da'ai Chikiza, the City of Refuge. She had never for a moment guessed she might see it someday, never imagined she would travel so far from the dark familiarity of Nakkiga. Now here she was, and by the sounds of the nearing pursuit, it also seemed that she would fight the last battle of her life amidst its crumbling walls and toppled towers.

Tzoja had not been called to the queen again since Jijibo had come to Utuk'ku with his strange, glowing fruit. She did not regret that. Simply being in the ancient queen's presence was like nothing she had ever experienced, as terrifying as being locked in a lightless cage with a deadly beast.

As the days passed, she continued to go out and gather herbs when the great procession paused, always in the company of one of the silent Queen's Teeth. Each time the wagons stopped, the country around her had changed. Though winter was coming on, they were traveling south, exchanging the chilly plain beside snowy mountains for rainy hills and woods of gold and dark green.

If Tzoja was not being called to the queen's side during those days, as Sky-Singer's Moon waxed and then waned, Vordis still was. She brought back many tales, mostly things she had gleaned from listening to the Hikeda'ya women talking.

"We are near the end of our journey," she said. "We are far into the lands of men now, on the Frostmarch, crossing into Erkynland."

"But how can that be?" Tzoja asked. "Why aren't the mortals fighting against us? I have lived with those people. They hate the Hikeda'ya and call them demons. Why would they let such a great company ride into Erkynland?"

Vordis shook her head. "I don't know, Tzoja. Perhaps there is peace now between the mortals and our masters."

Tzoja strongly doubted that, but she was conscious that no words were safe. "I was not always named Tzoja, you know," she said instead. "That is the name that Magister Viyeki gave me when he first took me from the slave pens. I was born Derra." She laughed a little. "It is funny. They both mean 'star.'"

"Then 'Star' must be your true name," said Vordis, smiling. "Even in Nakkiga, someone recognized it."

Tzoja felt oddly soothed by this, and by the simple fact of Vordis's presence; for the first time since she had been summoned to the Norn Queen, the sensation of impending disaster eased. The blind girl was the first mortal she had befriended since being stolen from the Astaline settlement so many years ago, and she had not understood how much she had missed that companionship. There had been no room in the slave pens for loyalty and friendship, and the mortal slaves she had known after being taken into Viyeki's house had envied her, or even hated her, for her privileged position.

Tzoja's attention was abruptly seized by a red glow she saw in the window of their wagon. "The sky," she said. "Something is burning."

Vordis was obviously confused by this sudden change of subject, but Tzoja did not stop to explain before climbing to her feet and hurrying to the window.

For long moments she could only stare ahead, up the line of the wagons, toward the reddish glare in the distance.

"Where are we bound?" she asked in a dry-throated voice.

"A place called *Ujin é-da Sikhunae*, the Anchoresses said," Vordis answered, "—'The Hunter's Trap'. I have not heard of it before. The mortals call it Naglimund."

Tzoja knew that name well, as did everyone she had ever met in the mortal towns of the north when she lived there. It had been the site of a terrible battle between the Hikeda'ya and the mortals, a place of dark magicks and death, but the mortals had reclaimed it long before Tzoja had come to Erkynland.

As she looked out of the window, craning her neck, she saw that they were moving through a river valley. On the far side of the water a line of hills rose up tall and dark against the twilight stars. Between river and hills stood a set of shattered walls, like a skull's gap-toothed grimace, and from those broken battlements and the fortress beyond them came the wavering red light of hundreds of fires—beacons and torches. A dark pall of smoke or dust hovered over the ruins, and the reflected light of the flames played along the bottom of the cloud like crimson lightning.

Hell, she thought, remembering Aedonite tales about the fate of sinners. *Surely that is Hell, not Naglimund.*

The infamous fortress was a vision of war and destruction, but the destruction seemed new-minted, as if only moments, not decades, had passed here in this valley since the Storm King's War. Tzoja stared, unable to look away, and her heart was cold and anxious. It seemed to her that Time, like the serpent-symbol of the Hamakha clan, had swallowed its own tail. Naglimund was in flames, and the past had returned to devour the present.

50

A Powder of
Dragon's Bones

Not even Simon, who had been born within the walls of
the Hayholt, knew why half the rooms were named as they were. Din's Passage,
the Blue Knight's Pantry, and the Chaplain's Walking Hall had all been named
long before anyone alive could remember. As he watched Countess Yissola
explore the Bishop's Reflection Room, a high-ceilinged chamber above the
royal chapel, he wondered idly who the bishop had been, and what had re-
quired his reflection so much that a large chamber had been named for it. The
chamber overlooked the Small Pleasance, a walled garden deep near the heart
of the keep, and was visited almost solely by gardeners and the occasional pair
of lovers seeking privacy, though none of either type were in view just now.

The countess examined the walls, hung with religious pictures and portraits
of religious men, then paused for a last look at the garden, which was not its
best in autumn, the trees mostly leafless, the hedges brown and shrunken-
looking. "Every year, I think that the winter takes a little more than it did the
year before," Yissola said. "That in the long battle, life is losing."

"But there is always more life, surely."

"Is there?" She turned from the window and made her way to the table. A
servant came forward to hold her chair, then slid back into the shadow of the
doorway. "I suppose so. But increasingly it seems to be a world I do not know."

Simon snorted. "Forgive me, my lady, but you are a good length younger
than me. Shouldn't I be the one saying such things?"

She gave him a smile both pretty and sad. "Perhaps. Or perhaps it is the difference in our situation. You have an heir, your grandson, as well as your delightful granddaughter. She could rule as well, you know."

"I certainly do. And God help you all if you got on the wrong side of her.
She is as fierce as a grassland widow, that one." He said it in the tone of a jest,
but his heart had clutched at the mention of Morgan, still lost somewhere along
the Erkynlandish frontier. He wondered how much Yissola already knew—the
Perdruinese were famous for their spycraft—but decided not to press for an

answer. "Why, if I may be so bold, have you never yourself married, Countess?" he asked instead. "You mourn the lack of an heir, but it is my guess that there are dozens—nay, hundreds—of men of station and wealth who would gladly husband you."

She lifted her hand and waved away all those suitors with a flick of her long fingers. "There are, of course, Your Majesty. Were I broad as an ox and with a face like a monkfish, I would have suitors. Perdruin's throne is a prize that many desire. But I have different wants. I have no desire to become the consort of an ambitious man," she said, and her handsome face took on sterner lines. "I have worked too hard for my people, suffered loneliness and the scorn of small minds, simply to give over my power to a husband and become a brood mare to future generations."

There were depths of anger in her voice that Simon had not guessed from her outer semblance. "You are much like your father Streáwe, then. He did not allow anyone to dictate to him. He would have bargained with the Devil himself, and won."

"As you have likely guessed, I was the child of his old age," she said. "What you may not know is that my mother was only one of several women that he kept. Some even gave birth to sons. But one reason he did not marry any of them was that my father liked having only illegitimate children—an entire falcon mews of bastards, and none could be his heir unless he chose them. None of his male children were what he sought, but he saw something of himself in me—as you just did—so I became his successor."

"And the others? Were you not afraid that one of them would rise against you?"

"A few did," she said. "The fact that you do not know that shows you that the challenges did not last long. But do not think I killed them all!" For a moment she opened her eyes wide, looking so much the innocent young woman that it was easy to forget they were talking of the eradication of rivals. "My nearest half-brother, Costante—the best of an indifferent lot, I must say—was sent away on a voyage to the unknown south before my father named me his choice. Costante never came back." She smiled, and Simon thought it looked like genuine sadness. "I miss him, God defend his soul. We were close friends in our childhood."

The territory of heirs safely negotiated, Simon said, "Obviously your father chose well. The people of Perdruin are prosperous and at peace."

"We are *always* at peace," she said, amused. "How could we prosper, as you put it, if we took sides?"

"I am corrected." Suddenly, despite the allure of the handsome woman before him, Simon felt deeply weary. "So tell me, Countess, what brings you to Erkynland, then? Why did you wish to speak to me?"

"Because you have done the people of Perdruin a wrong, King Simon."

"Have I, Countess? And what wrong is that?"

"You are the master of the High Ward, Majesty. Please do me the courtesy of not pretending you do not know. Your Royal Establishment was signed only one year ago."

Now that he had seen her show scorn, Simon was even more impressed. Not even Miri at her most withering could achieve such quiet fury. "I am only half of the High Ward, as you know, but I don't think Queen Miriamele would do something as important as you seem to make this—whatever it is—without my knowing." Even as he spoke, though, he felt a moment of worry: Miri had told him many times he did not pay enough attention to the small matters of statecraft, leaving them to her. Still, she always brought him anything of import. He could not believe that had changed.

"I speak of your own neutral ports here in Erkynland—Grenefod, Laestmouth, Meremund, among others. Do I refresh your memory?"

"I must confess you haven't."

She rose so swiftly that he thought she might throw something at him. One of the armed guards even took a step forward from his place by the door, but Simon lifted his hand to keep him back. Yissola turned, gown swirling, and went to the window. She stared down. "Perdruin is an island country, Majesty. We survive on our wits, on the speed of our ships and the mastery of their captains. We have never asked for favors, only measure given for measure. But this law of yours—it is a blow at our heart."

"I swear I do not know the law you speak of, Countess. Tell me what angers you, and I will discover what I can."

She turned, and for a moment she looked at him with incredulity. Gradually the anger left her features. "Is it possible? Very well," she said. "The Royal Establishment on Sea Ports, signed and sealed by your hand—*yours*, Majesty, not the queen's nor any lesser noble's. It purports to set laws for the neutral ports, but underneath the flowering language it festers with unpleasant intent. Everything that could be done to undercut the freedom of the Sindigato lurks in those words. You have stripped us of any right to sell our goods north of the Nabbanai border, and harmed your own citizens by allowing the Northern Alliance a monopoly. Without having to compete, they can set any price they wish."

Simon could only shake his head. "I swear to you, if I signed such a law, I did so without proper knowledge of what it said."

"A poor apology for a monarch to make," she said with more than a touch of bitterness.

"What do you want?" His weariness had turned to anger—it was all he could do not to upend the table and send the wine and bread and cups crashing to the floor. "What do you want of me, Countess? I can only tell you what I know, and I know nothing of this. The fault may be mine—by the Bloody Tree, my wife says often enough that I do not hear all I should!—but that does not make what I am saying false. *I do not know of this!*" He stared at her, but her return gaze was not what he expected. Instead of fear or anger, he saw something else, although her expression—a narrowing of the eyes, a flush in the cheeks, mouth half-open in surprise—could have been either. But her next words proved he had guessed correctly.

"So the Commoner King is indeed swift to passion." She returned to her chair. The servants, still cowering in the doorway after Simon's shouting, did not spring forward this time to help her. "I will not apologize, Your Majesty, for what I said was true. But perhaps you do not know everything that is done in your name."

He scowled. "I fear that may be the case, more than I ever guessed. And I will find out what happened, this I promise. I will find out the truth of this law." He saw that his fists were tightly clenched on the tabletop and eased them. "Let me bring in all my councillors. We will get to the bottom of this."

"I doubt they will tell you the truth—some of them, in any case—if I am here." She rose. "But I look forward to another meeting between us, King Simon, and I look forward to learning what you discover." She drifted toward the door, suddenly as light and unperturbed as a sailboat catching the morning breeze. Then she turned. "Ah! I have forgotten! I beg your pardon, Majesty, after you have given me so much time and have let me speak so frankly, but may I presume on you a few moments longer?"

He was calmer now and did his best to be expansive. "Of course, Countess. And any more time in your company will be a pleasant burden to bear."

She made a mocking little courtesy, smiling. "But it is not I who needs your time, it is one of those who came with me. He has been waiting outside, craving a moment of speech with you—a swift moment only, he swears."

Simon wondered why any of the other Perdruinese would want to speak to him. "He has been waiting all this time?"

"He comes from a patient race," she said. "Shall I send him in as I go?"

Taken aback and not certain what he had let himself in for, he nodded. "Of course, my lady."

"You are very kind, King Simon. I think the Commoner King could teach some of supposedly nobler blood a few lessons in manners." And with that she made a full courtesy, then swept out.

In the moment of silence that followed Simon again felt the tug of exhaustion. It seemed sometimes that he was back in the Aldheorte Forest of his youth, stumbling through snow, hungry, weary, and without hope. So many things to do, and none of them what he really wanted—to have Miri back, to have a quiet kingdom to govern, to know that his family and his people were safe.

The door opened. In the first moments, as he stared at the hooded stranger, Simon felt a shock of superstitious fear. Then the visitor threw back the hood and Simon was even more surprised. "By Rhiap," he said, "—you're a Niskie!"

The stranger bowed his head in acknowledgement. His color was a bit like Tiamak's, but the large, wide-set eyes and the roughness of the skin on his cheeks and neck marked him out. "I am, yes, Seoman King."

Simon laughed in surprise. "Very few people call me by that name, and almost all of them are Sithi. Who are you?"

"Tey Seiso is my name, and I am the sea-watcher of Countess Yissola's ship *Li Fosena* . . . but I myself am not important. I bear a message for you from the Spar."

Simon was feeling overwhelmed by all the things he did not know. "And what is that?"

"The council of elders of my people, the Tinukeda'ya of Nabban. They have entrusted me with words for you alone. Not even my mistress, Countess Yissola, knows what I will tell you." He cast a sideways glance at the servants. "I must speak so only you can hear."

Simon looked the messenger over carefully. Tey Seiso was small but also wiry, with the long, strong arms of his folk. *By the Tree*, Simon chided himself, *if I do not trust myself alone with a little fellow like this I might as well just take to my bed and never get up again.* He sent away the servants and all but two door guards. "Well, then," he said when they were gone. "It is just you and me, sir. What is this secret dispatch?"

The Niskie bowed his head in acknowledgement. "We are tied to your house by our love for your wife. She came and spoke to our elders in Nabban, because they had concerns to share with her—but those concerns are not the reason for my commission." He blinked hugely, like a frog. "The sea-watchers of Perdruin and Nabban are of the same people. Borders mean little to us. In the ports of Ansis Pellipé we hear news from our southern brothers and sisters every day as they arrive. My commission was given to me by Gan Lagi herself, one of the chief servants of the Spar, and it is to tell you that Nabban is in a grave state and Queen Miriamele is in danger if she stays."

Simon's breath caught in his throat. "What do you mean? What danger?"

"Drusis, the Earl of Trevinta and Eadne, the duke's brother, is dead. Murdered."

It was all Simon could do not to lean across and grab the Niskie to drag him closer. "Dead? How? When did this happen?"

"A fortnight ago. He was stabbed to death while at chapel in Count Dallo's house. Many people blame his brother the duke for his murder, and there are riots and fires across the city. Niskie-town, as some call the district near the old docks, has suffered particularly badly, as it always does in times of unrest, but that is beside the point. This anger is being steered, the Spar believes, perhaps by House Ingadaris."

Simon was trying to make sense of it all, but he was terrified for his wife. "Then she must leave. Miri must leave! Why is she still there?"

Tey Seiso gave strange, wriggling shrug, like an eel sliding out of grasping fingers. "We do not know much of what goes on in the Sancellan Mahistrevis, we know only what happens on the ships of Nabban. You must ask someone else why the queen lingers, but the elders of the Spar are concerned for her."

"Nabban is weeks away, even if I had soldiers on ships already."

"We do not seek to counsel you, Seoman King, but my people had this news first and believed that you should have it too. Nabban is afire, and very few think matters there will end well."

His embassy finished, the Niskie bowed and went out. Simon paced back and forth across the Bishop's Reflection Room until a knock at the door reminded him he had forgotten to summon back the guards and servants. When he opened the door, he told them to call for Tiamak, Pasevalles, Sir Zakiel, and the rest of the Lords Military and that he wanted them there on the instant.

Although the news was dire, Tiamak was heartened to see the king returned to something like his old vigor. Simon did not wait a moment before demanding to know how soon soldiers could be sent to Nabban.

"We are not like the Nabbanai or the Pedruinese," said Colfrid, the Lord Marine. "We do not have ships ready for war, Your Majesty."

"And most of our able guardsmen are already on the border with His Grace, the duke," added Lord Zakiel, recently granted a baron's title to reflect his growing importance in Osric's absence.

"I *know* that," the king said, giving the two lords a look that few had seen from their monarch, and which even fewer would have wanted to see again. "By God's Bloody Tree, I want to know how long it will take to put soldiers on cogs and get them there. Can nobody answer a simple question?"

"We will have to seize merchant ships and refit them," offered Pasevalles. "The guilds will not like it, nor will the Northern Alliance."

"The guilds can go straight to Hell," Simon said. "We are talking about the queen's safety. We are talking about my wife, curse it!" He turned to Tiamak. "As for the Alliance, is not one of their most important factors living here under my roof, eating my venison and roast capon and drinking my wine?"

Tiamak might have smiled, but he thought the king might kick him if he did. "You mean Aengas ec-Carpilbin, Majesty. Yes, he is here."

"By God, that name is a chewy mouthful! Tell him I want his help and I want it now. Tell him that the Alliance must give me their aid if they hope to ever again have a sympathetic ear in this court."

Tiamak promised he would do it as soon as the Inner Council was dismissed. "I am certain he will help, Majesty. Aengas is a good man."

"I don't want good men, I want men with ships. I want soldiers. I want my wife out of that cursed nest of vipers before Saluceris loses control of things completely." Simon stared around the table as if hoping someone would dare disagree.

"I will be honored to lead the rescue party as captain," said Earl Rowson, and before Tiamak could intervene, Simon turned on him.

"*You?* Do you think I would send you with my wife's safety in question, Rowson? You have not done any fighting since the Thrithings days, and you have grown fat and soft."

"Your Majesty, that is unfair—" the nobleman began.

"Silence! And if you speak again before I ask you, our flagship will sail to Nabban with your head nailed to the bow!"

Rowson turned white. His mouth opened, and it seemed he might test the king's threat then and there. Instead, he swept his velvet hat from the table and then turned and walked out of the throne hall.

"That might have been done more . . . kindly, Majesty," said Tiamak quietly.

Simon looked at him. The king's face was red, and he had disarranged his hair by clutching at it until he looked a little mad. "I do not care what Rowson thinks. The man is a fool, and I will not pamper a fool when Miri is in danger."

"Nobody expected you actually to *send* him, Simon—" Tiamak began but did not get the chance to finish.

"Good. Because I would rather send the most dimwitted stable boy to Nabban than him." He turned back to the rest of the table, where his councillors were looking at him with more than a little alarm. "What do you all wait for?" Simon demanded. "The heir has been kidnapped by Thrithings-men, Norns roam the north of Erkynland, and your queen is in danger. Go! Find me ships and men! I will announce a captain soon. God, but I wish I could go myself—I would gladly cut Dallo Ingadaris into small pieces with my own hands and feed them to the gulls. Go, all of you! Go and see to what needs doing!"

Tiamak dutifully delivered the king's message to Aengas, who had the sense not to ask too many questions, since Tiamak warned him that the king was in a shouting mood. After his friend had promised to contact the local Alliance merchants immediately, Tiamak made his way back to his rooms, wondering at what terrible news might next be delivered.

I was right that day back in the snows of the Frostmarch, he thought. *My gods sent me a sign of evil times ahead. But I could never have imagined the dangers to be so many and so widespread!*

When he reached his chambers he found his wife holding a glass beaker so she could examine its contents against the flame of an oil lamp.

"How went the council meeting?" she asked without looking up. "Was I missed? Did you give the king my apologies? I was at a most delicate moment in my investigation."

"To be honest, dear wife, the king did not notice your absence. Simon is in high dudgeon. He insulted Earl Rowson and all but threw him out of the throne room."

"*Tch*." She shook the beaker, squinted. "Rowson is a famous idiot."

"Do not shake it so!" It was all Tiamak could do not to snatch the vessel from her hand. "Those were made by the finest craftsmen in Ansis Pellipé! They are ungodly dear, and I fear it would take half a year or more to replace one."

"Calm down, husband. I promise you I will not damage it. I have already done the worst." She finally looked at him. "You look grim."

"Nothing you have not heard," he said, then gave her a summary of the Inner Council's arguments and Simon's impatience. "Now," he said when he had finished, "let me put aside these grim matters of state for a moment, dear wife. What exactly have you been doing with my best glassware?"

"Ah!" Her face suddenly lit with pleasure. "I have made a rare find, I think. Even you will not fail to marvel, husband. Do you recall that I found the pitchy stains of the poison that felled the Sitha-woman on some bedsheets?"

"I recall that you found some soiled bedsheets," he said drily. "Everything else was conjecture. That is my memory."

"Like all your heathen kind, you ask for proof when you should have faith," Thelía said, as fondly as if she spoke to a beloved but troublesome pet. "Meanwhile, I have let my faith lead me to discovery!"

"And that is?"

"Look. Hold this beaker up to the lamp's flame and look, Tiamak."

He set down his wine, already half-finished, then took the vessel from her and angled it in front of the light. "It is cloudy," he said.

"Because you have shaken it," she told him. "Wait for it to settle. That is the ash left after I subjected the poison to the heat of your bread-oven for more than an hour. Nothing was left but the gray powder you see swirling there."

He was about to ask her what property of wet ash could be so important when everything around them was under threat but held his tongue. Simon might get away with berating people—he was the king. But within this household of two, Tiamak was in no way the ruler.

In fact, I am lucky if my voice counts as equal measure, he thought, then was arrested by what he saw at the bottom of the beaker. "Pass me my seeing glass, please."

She put it in his hand so quickly he did not doubt she had been using it herself. "What do you see?" she asked, sounding almost childlike with anticipation.

"You sound like young Lillia," he told her, but he was squinting at the particles floating in the bottom of the beaker. "Crystals," he said at last. "Though I have seen none quite like them." He moved the seeing glass back and forth until he could make them out clearly. "Long and strangely-shaped. You say these were left in the ash of the burning?"

"Yes." She moved around the table and brought back another beaker. "Now look at this."

"Two of my best beakers? Two?"

"Quiet. Look carefully."

He did. The murk in the bottom of the second beaker gradually resolved itself; at the bottom, just as with the first, he saw a few long crystals, smaller than a grain of southern island millet. "I see them. What are they? Is this a second batch of your bread-oven poison?"

"No." She came and took the second beaker back. "No, my husband. As to what they are, I cannot tell you, but I can tell you with great certainty where this second batch came from."

"Would you make me guess? From the moon? Did you build a long ladder this afternoon and climb to the sky?"

"Don't be foolish. Beside, the answer is even stranger. In both cases—both your beloved glass beakers—what sifts to the bottom is what remains after burning dragon bones."

Tiamak stared at her. "What are you saying? How could you know? You said only that it was a dark poison, black and pasty."

"That was the smears taken on the Sitha's bedsheets. But the second sample— well, that I know for a fact was once the bones of a dragon."

"But how could that be?"

"Because I took some so I could compare. The first was the poison. The second was dragon's bone."

"Where would you find . . . ?" But even as he said it, Tiamak suddenly saw the whole thing clear. "Oh, my wife, you didn't!"

She made a dismissive face. "The back of the throne is riddled with cracks and fissures. Goodness, Tiamak, the king and queen do not even use it!"

"You broke off a piece of the Dragonbone Chair?"

"Scraped a little bit from a hole in the back." She was clearly not in the least ashamed. "But you are missing the point, husband. I had read in one of your own books that the residue of dragon's bone contains small, angular crystals. When I saw what the burnt poison yielded—well, what else could I have done? I needed something to compare it to."

Tiamak did not know whether to laugh or to cry out in horror. "So you carved a piece out of the most sacred object of Prester John's High Ward." But now another, much more disturbing thought was beginning to make its way up from the darkest parts of his memory.

Thelía was pleased with herself. She poured herself a cup of wine and drank the first few sips with hearty enjoyment. "You are not the only one gifted in natural philosophy, Lord Tiamak of the Wran." She saw his expression. "Why are you so horrified? Surely you do not think the king will be angry I scraped off a bit of the throne."

"No." He tried to smile, but could not. "No, I suspect that as far as Simon is concerned, you could go at the thing with a battle ax and he would not turn a hair. But if what you have discovered is true—that there is dragon's blood in the poison used on the Sithi woman—then I have new terrors to add to those I already had."

"Tiamak, what is it? You look quite ill."

He shook his head, cursing himself for having drunk so much of the under-watered wine at a time when he wished badly for a clear head. "I told you that we found a book the priest Pryrates had owned, and showed you also the box of John Josua's prizes, the things I thought had been made by the Sithi."

"The beads, the mirror frame—yes, I remember."

"And that I suspected they might have come from the tunnels beneath the castle—or even from Hjeldin's Tower itself."

"That last seems unlikely, since the red priest's tower was sealed and filled with stones. But I still do not understand what has upset you so about my dragon's blood crystals."

Tiamak let himself drop onto the bench that sat beside the table. His legs felt quite weak. "Then listen. Long ago, during the Storm King's War, Simon was trapped for a while in Hjeldin's Tower."

Thelía's eyes widened. "By Pryrates?"

"No, not then. But while Simon roamed the tower, looking for a way out, he told me he saw something that I have never forgotten. Pryrates had a great cauldron in one room with a fire burning beneath it. In it he was boiling the bones of some huge beast. Simon said he thought they could only be dragon's bones, and I think he was right."

She shook her head. "I still do not understand."

"Prince John Josua, Simon's son, likely also roamed those passages beneath the castle. He died from an illness I did not recognize, but now that I think back on it, the signs were not so different from what the wounded Sitha woman showed, though its course with her was much slower. It comes to me now that John Josua might have come across some of that poison down there in those terrible deeps."

She let out a breath. "That is horrible, husband! But that was seven years ago now—."

"Everything we heard about the Sitha's wounds suggested the arrows were Thrithings-make, and not something the Norns would use. And that makes me wonder—and worry as I have not worried before. Because if the poison is made from dragon's bones, it means someone else has been beneath the castle since John Josua's death."

She looked at him with dawning understanding. "You think the poison might have come . . . ?"

He did feel ill now, as though he had swallowed some of Thelía's delicate crystals himself, but he knew it was fear, not poison, that gripped him. "Yes. I think it is a possibility we ignore at our peril. The poison that almost killed the Sithi envoy may have come from inside this very castle, the remnants of some ghastly spell of the red priest's. But Pryrates is long dead, so if the poison was made in the Hayholt, it is possible we have a traitor in our midst."

"But Grandmother Nelda, I'm *tired* of praying! I just want to know when Morgan's coming back."

"Saying that you're tired of praying is like saying that you're tired of being good, Lillia."

The other court ladies in the duchess' chambers all looked at each other. Some shook their heads. No sooner had Nelda arrived then all the grumpiest, oldest ladies of the court had gathered around the duchess like honeybees around their queen, and had not left her since. They did nothing but sew and complain about the servants and the way some of the other court ladies dressed.

"I didn't say I was tired of God, Grandmother. That's not fair. That's not what I said!"

The duchess set down her embroidery hoop and gave Lillia a stern look. Some of the other ladies whispered to each other over their sewing. Most of them were stitching words from the book of Aedon, but all Grandmother Nelda ever seemed to do was to embroider flowers—lush, velvety things that looked more like face cloths than anything Lillia had ever seen in the gardens. "You want to be a good girl, don't you?" Nelda asked. "You want God to take care of Morgan and your Grandfather Osric, don't you?"

She turned away so the duchess wouldn't see her scowl, since that was another thing that Grandmother Nelda didn't like, as Lillia had been told many times. "But I just want to know when my brother will be back! I pray all the time, but I don't know!"

"We all want them to come back. Don't you think I want your grandfather back safe? Don't be a selfish girl."

The other ladies made sniffing noises. One even quietly said, "So selfish."

"Come now, my dear," the duchess said. "You know you want to be a good girl."

Lillia knew there was no winning one of these disagreements. If there was anyone in the castle as stubborn as Lillia herself, it was Grandmother Nelda.

Outside, thunder rumbled again. Lillia put down her book of saints and walked to the window to look out. The rain was coming down hard and straight out of a sky the color of stone. She could see it running off the tower roofs in little waterfalls, and gurgling from the mouths of gargoyles. She had wanted to go out in the garden that morning, and Auntie Rhoner had told her, before she left to do some boring grown-up thing, that Lillia could go outside when the sun came out. She had eaten her supper an hour ago, but she had not seen sunlight all afternoon, and the darkening sky made it clear that she would not see it again before tomorrow. Maybe not even then.

Watching the raindrops bouncing on the rooftops and drizzling out of the mouths of the statues on Holy Tree Tower made her wonder again about ghosts. Did they get wet when it rained?

"Grandmother, is my mother really watching over me?"

"Oh, child, what a thing to say! Of course she is. Don't go on, you'll make me weep."

"If she's watching me, maybe she'll come to me and tell me when Morgan will come back."

"Don't be silly. She's watching you from Heaven, and that's a long way away." The duchess shook her head. "My poor Idela. She was too young—too young! I can scarcely bear to think about it, and you are wicked to remind me."

"But if she's up in Heaven and it's so far, how does she watch me? What if I'm inside somewhere? And I don't go near a window? How can she see me from up there?"

"Now you're being foolish, child. She's with God. She can see anything God wants her to see, and God lets her watch over you."

But Lillia had discovered the flaw in that argument long ago, though she knew better than to say anything about it. God might be able to see the very fledgling when it first stretched its infant wings, new-warmed by the sun, like the Book of Aedon said, but the sacred book never said anything about dead people seeing anything. Not unless they were saints, some of whom could even run after the Imperator's soldiers had cut their legs off. She had learned that grisly fact from the life of Saint Endrais, one of the few stories in her book that she had actually enjoyed. But ghosts were different. They were always around, just out of sight. Lillia knew a lot about ghosts because the serving girls and nurses told her. Tabata, the maid who ran away, had seen a ghost leading a ghost-horse on the road one evening when she was a little girl. Tabata had said she knew they were ghosts because she could see the trees through them, and she had run away as quickly as she could. And even Auntie Rhoner had told her the story of Prince Sinnach, whose phantom sometimes appeared on a hill above the battlefield where he had died, blowing a ghostly horn. So Lillia was fairly certain that while the saints in her books might stand next to God in heaven, many of the dead people stayed on the earth for reasons of their own. One of the youngest grooms, a strange boy with a cast in one eye, had told her once that the Hayholt was full of ghosts. "And not just ones of people, neither," he had whispered.

So if her mother was watching over her, as everyone promised, it stood to reason she must be in the castle somewhere. Did ghosts have places they stayed? Did her mother watch over her all night as she slept? That didn't seem right. Her mother had always been in a hurry to say goodnight, to see Lillia in bed because she had things to do, people she wanted to visit with. No, if her mother's spirit was in the castle to watch over her, she must have a place she stayed in so that not everyone would see her. That was another thing Tabata had assured her—ghosts didn't like to be seen.

She thought about this for a long time, until thunder boomed again, startling her a little.

"Come away from that window, child," her grandmother said. "You'll be struck by lightning."

Lillia sighed and came back to sit on the floor beside her grandmother. Outside the thunder grumbled and the rain kept falling. Lillia stared at her book, but she was not looking at the pictures of saints anymore. She was thinking very carefully about hiding-places. She was thinking about where the castle ghosts, especially her mother's, might be lurking.

51

A Web Across the Sky

The tale told by the Nakkiga parchment of witchwood seeds hidden beneath old Asu'a seemed something far away but closing fast—a storm that no one but Tanahaya could see coming, though its arrival would affect everything.

The witchwood? She could scarcely believe it. *Is that what has caused this new conflict—the sacred wood, the last seeds of the Garden? Would Utuk'ku truly make war against the entire mortal world simply to live longer?*

Of course she would, she realized a moment later. *The Hamakha witch is trapped in times and grievances long gone, full of hate for mortals and even for her own kin. She cannot die until she has her revenge, but without the witchwood even her long life must end. Of course she will go to any lengths to find the last seeds.*

Jiriki and Aditu must know of this quickly. They must tell the other Zida'ya clans about Utuk'ku's cruel plan—my word alone does not have enough weight to convince Khendraja'aro or the defenders of Anvijanya and Vhinansu. She turned to Vinyedu. "Do you have a Witness? I must let the Sa'onserei know of our discovery."

"Look here!" said Vinyedu as if she had not heard Tanahaya's words. "The page is marked with the old Hamakha Seal—the queen's own rune. This parchment was not merely copied, it was stolen from the archives of Nakkiga. Who could accomplish such a thing?"

An ornate rune had been stamped in white ink on a shield of black at the bottom of the unfolded parchment. Tanahaya had noticed it, but had not realized it meant that Utuk'ku herself had touched the document. A shiver of foreboding went through her. "Are you certain, S'huesa?"

"That is the queen's own sigil, not that of one of her ministers."

Now that Vinyedu had pointed it out, the import was clear. Still, something about the chronicler's name and the mark above it tugged at Tanahaya's attention, though she could not say why. "And who is that—the one who made this chronicle? I do not recognize the name—'Nijin'."

"Nijin was one of Utuk'ku's court historians before the Parting," Vinyedu said. "It is the first time I have seen an actual document with his name upon it. He died in the days of the Tenth Celebrant."

Something about the parchment still puzzled Tanahaya, but the frightened voices in her head would not be ignored any longer. A wildfire was now burning across the land, that seemed clear, and every moment that it blazed unchecked would make it harder to extinguish—if it was not already too late. "I asked before, I ask again," she said, "do you have a Witness here, Mistress? It is why I came to this place. Whatever you may think of them, the House of Year-Dancing must be informed of this."

"The enemy of my enemy must be my friend, is that it?" Vinyedu's face was sour. "The Pure must bend so as not to inconvenience those who have already cast their lot with the mortals?"

"No, you Pure must realize that you are Zida'ya by blood and heritage—the armies of Nakkiga will not see a difference between your folk and mine. Utuk'ku is mad and cares for nothing but herself. She will destroy us all without discrimination." She saw Morgan watching their angry words. *"Do not fear,"* she told him in his own tongue. *"We have learned something important today—something that may help everyone, especially your own people. Be of strong heart."*

"Even in the midst of argument, you take time to coddle a mortal," Vinyedu said with bitter satisfaction.

"As I would any innocent trapped among people he did not know who were speaking a language he did not understand. Let go of your hatreds, at least for this moment, Vinyedu. I bear you no ill-will—nor, I think, do Jiriki and Aditu of the Sa'onserei."

"Fair words that hide a foul history."

"I think instead that your hatred of mortals blinds you to the crimes of Utuk'ku. She is the enemy, not Year-Dancing House."

"Perhaps. But you are just as blinded by your own connection to the Sudhoda'ya. Why should there be some secret conspiracy to regain the witch-wood seeds buried beneath Asu'a? Only a few seasons ago the Hikeda'ya all but owned it. The mortal priest Pryrates gave the Hikeda'ya freedom to roam the whole of old Asu'a. Why did Utuk'ku's people not secure the witchwood seeds then?"

"Perhaps because the crisis was not so great then," said Tanahaya. "When they fought what they call the War of Return, Utuk'ku and her Hikeda'ya still had their witchwood groves beneath the mountain, mirror-fed and secure. The line of the Garden-Root had not yet begun to fail."

"What you say is not without sense," Vinyedu conceded. "But Witnesses are nearly as hard to find in these terrible days as witchwood, yet you demand to use ours. You say you must warn the Sa'onserei, but is this not exactly how disaster came to Jao é-Tinukai'i? Jiriki brought a mortal there—this child's grandfather, to make the folly even more pointed!—which led Utuk'ku's destroyers down on them all."

"That is not true!" Tanahaya said. "The Hikeda'ya attacked Jao é-Tinukai'i to silence wise Amerasu. This child's grandfather was not to blame, and Morgan is not to blame now. And it is precisely because Utuk'ku wants her plans to remain a secret that Jiriki and the others must be told now."

Vinyedu seemed about to respond with even more anger, but instead held up her hand, her lips pressed tightly together. After a long silence, she said, "I cannot consider what I must do and argue with you at the same time. You and your mortal ward remain here. I will return after I have had time and peace to think." And with that, she turned and left the archive chamber. The other Pure watched her go, then turned their golden stares to Morgan and Tanahaya for a few moments, silent as flowers following the sun, before resuming their reading.

"Is she going to have us killed?" Morgan asked.

Tanahaya looked up from Himano's parchment. "I do not know, to tell you the whole truth. The Pure have so removed themselves from the world I know that it is hard to say what they will think or do." She saw his look. "I am sorry I have put you in danger, Morgan—but you are a prince, grandson of monarchs. You should know that sometimes the danger to all outweighs the danger to a few."

He nodded, but looked distinctly unhappy about it.

The door to the archive silently swung open. It was Vinyedu, and she was not alone—half a dozen white-clad Pure, armed with bows and spears, stood behind her. Full of anger and regret, Tanahaya lifted her hands, determined not to sell her life cheaply.

"Do not fear," said Vinyedu. "They are with me only for our protection as we cross to the Place of Silence. The sentries on the outskirts have sent word that Hikeda'ya are in the woods just outside the city. That is nothing unusual, but I will not take chances this day."

"Tanahaya, what's happening?" Morgan stood poised to run or fight.

"Forgive me," said Vinyedu in Westerling. "I forgot I that I am to speak the mortal tongue for the benefit of the mortal youth." She came forward, but the armed Pure remained in the outer chamber. "I have thought and thought. I do not agree with much of what you say, Tanahaya, but I am not so selfish that I wish to keep what we have learned from the scholars among your kind."

"They are your kind too, Mistress."

"Perhaps, but I am weary of that conversation. I have come to tell you that you may use the Witness—but only to speak to the Sa'onserei."

Relief washed through Tanahaya. "Thank you, Mistress Vinyedu. I praise your wisdom and your generosity."

"I still doubt it is wisdom, and it is most particularly not generosity." Vinyedu had slipped into Zida'ya speech again. She made the sign called the Garden Endures. "I pray it is not foolishness either. Know this, though. You will only use the Witness with me watching, and you will cease the moment I say so, no matter what else is happening. Only with these promises will I let you touch it."

Tanahaya looked to Morgan, who was still clearly disturbed by what must have seemed the threat of a deadly fight. "Do not fear, Prince Morgan," she told him. "Much smoke but little fire. Good will come of all this, I promise."

"Do not be so quick to promise what you cannot be certain to give,"

Vinyedu told her, this time remembering to speak so Morgan could understand. "Come with me to the Place of Silence. But the young mortal cannot roam unwatched. He must accompany us."

Morgan looked more than ready to escape the confines of the archive; he followed them without a word.

"It will be fastest to pass through Sky-Watching," Vinyedu explained as she led them toward the surface, the half-dozen armed Pure surrounding them. "In a better time we could have used the Hall of Memory to reach it, but that collapsed long before our return. We will have to go up before we can go down."

Tanahaya was trying to order her thoughts. She had not spoken to Jiriki or Aditu for two moons, and suddenly realized how many things she needed to tell them. She did not even know if her horse had made it back to H'ran Go-jao with the message that she was following Morgan.

As they reached ground level and mounted into the Place of Sky-Watching, rain fell on them through the ruined dome, spattering across the cracked, bare stone of the floor and making the ferns bow and dance. Once there had been nothing to see beyond the dome but sky, but over the years Oldheart had grown so close and high around the city that now all but the area directly above the roof was crowded with thick greenery. Tanahaya looked up at the hemispherical lattice of stone, crumbling in more than a few places but still stretched above the great chamber like a fishing net or a web, and wished keenly that she could have seen it in better days. Behind her, Morgan had stopped to stare upward as rain fell on his shoulders and matted his hair.

"Once the framework you see was filled with panes of crystal called Summer Ice," Tanahaya told him. "We have lost the wisdom of its making now."

"Speak for yourselves, you and the rest of the Zida'ya," said Vinyedu from the top of the stairwell that led down below the chamber. "We Pure have found the secret again. One day we will have what is needed to rebuild it—to bring Da'ai Chikiza back to life."

Tanahaya watched her vanish into a stairwell hidden behind part of the great frieze that covered the circular chamber from the floor to the bottom of the webbed dome. Stone representations of the moon calendar spanned the chamber, many carved as if in violent motion, each creature devouring the next— Lynx swallowing Crane as Crane in turn devoured Tortoise and Tortoise consumed Rooster, an endless cycle that represented the procession of seasons and years.

Morgan was still staring upward, but Tanahaya could see that the armed guards were growing impatient.

"Swiftly, please," she told him. "I do not want Vinyedu to change her mind."

"I thought I saw people in the trees," the young mortal said. "Up there."

Tanahaya looked, but saw nothing in the thick, intertwined boughs that loomed over the dome. "Did you hear her say there are Norns out in the forest? The Pure are warlike, as you have already seen, so do not fear—or at least do not fear a few Norn soldiers."

Morgan only shook his head, but let her lead him across the uneven floor of the ancient chamber to the stairs.

As they entered the wide chamber, their escort of Pure warriors fanned out on either side of the doorway. Tanahaya barely noticed them as she took in her new surroundings. The Place of Sky-Watching had been a gaudy shambles open to the forest and the weather, but the Place of Silence was its opposite, a windowless, almost featureless circular chamber of stone lit only by the glow of a few lamps. Instead of the carved stone creatures that paraded around the walls of the domed chamber, the only decoration here were concentric horizontal lines that climbed the cylindrical walls to its low roof, as if she and Morgan now stood inside some mighty stone beehive. Large vertical alcoves with empty shelves, were carved directly into the wall of the chamber at intervals, thirteen in all, each with its own empty bench before it, but though all the benches faced the center of the room, nothing stood in the chamber's center but bare dirt and a broken stone plinth, half of it standing, half lying on the floor.

"Is that—?" Tanahaya began, but Vinyedu did not let her finish.

"The seat of the Dawnstone. Yes, it was." The mistress of the Pure did not bother to hide her painful feelings. "Da'ai Chikiza's Master Witness. It vanished when the floods came and all the people fled the city. Some say it was swept away and lost. All we know for certain is that it is gone from our knowledge and from our hands, like the Green Column of Jhiná-T'seneí or the Speakfire, lost in the collapse of Hikehikayo."

"We all know these tragedies," Tanahaya said. "Nobody grieved more deeply for these losses than my master, Himano. But I do not need a Master Witness. One of the lesser ones will do for my purposes."

Vinyedu surprised her then by reaching into her robe and withdrawing an object the size of two open palms, the largest Witness-mirror Tanahaya had seen. The dragon scale of which it had been made was intact, polished to a glassy sheen, and couched in a frame of age-darkened witchwood.

"It is very old," Tanahaya said reverently.

"One of the first made in these lands of Exile." Vinyedu held the mirror out to her. "Take it," she said. "Use it. But remember my strictures."

Tanahaya weighed it in her hands; the mirror was heavy, and seemed as full of potential as a living thing. "This will not be swift," she told Morgan. "Sit quietly, please. No harm will come to you."

His look suggested he was less confident about that than she was, but he found a space along the wall that was free of tumbled rocks and slumped to the ground to wait.

Studying the Witness, Tanahaya could not help wondering about the monstrous creature of whose body the polished scale had once been part. The dragon scale had a burnished silvery sheen over layers of reflection and refraction, so that her own image seemed that of a phantom. She held it up and stared into it as she chanted the Words of Joining—silently, because her master Himano had taught her that when she used a Witness she was not singing to anyone but herself. She did her best to order her thoughts and her needing heart so that she could reach out to that which she so deeply needed to find.

The scale's shimmering surface seemed to have moving depths beneath it, like water. She let herself slide down through the levels and currents until she found the deeps that lay behind it all, the dark but clear place where only thoughts moved.

Jiriki of the Sa'onserei, she called, or she might have sung it—the words were no longer just words, but something less easily defined. *Jiriki, can you feel me? I have need of you now. Join with me.* But nothing came back to her except silence and emptiness. She tried to make her thought even more pure, as sharp as a blade. *Willow-Switch! My need is great. If you have any power to answer, join me!*

Then she felt it—a warming, then something emerging, small at first, but growing until it seemed to fill all the empty place. And at the center of it, *he* was.

Spark? Is that you? My heart fills with joy to feel your thoughts again. Are you well?

A surge of joy swept through her. *In body, yes, dear friend, but troubled and full of news you must hear.* She could not keep the jaggedness from her thoughts, though she feared they must be uncomfortable for him. *I am in The Tree of Singing Wind, with the Pure. The mortal youth Morgan, grandchild of your friend Seoman Snowlock, is with me. He is alive and, for the moment, also safe.*

That is welcome news indeed, Spark. She could feel his sudden pleasure and relief, like buds bursting from a naked bough.

But there is more you must know, and it is fearful.

Speak, then, and I will listen. But I wish there was no need for haste. You have been missed.

My teacher Himano is dead. She waited for his wordless rush of sympathy and surprise. *Killed by the Cloud Children. He was trying to escape them with a parchment written in their ancient tongue—trying to hide it from them, I believe, but they caught him and cruelly ended him.*

Utuk'ku's crimes are unending, Spark. I am full of sorrow.

Master Himano is beyond this world's pain now, but your mortal friends are not. The parchment says that the Witchwood Crown Utuk'ku seeks—a dozen seeds buried with Hamakho's crown—was hidden long ago beneath the castle of the mortals, in old Asu'a.

She could feel his surprise deepen, and with it a creeping frost of worry. *Are you certain?*

As carefully as she could, Tanahaya shared what she and Vinyedu had learned. For long moments afterward the course between them was silent, empty. Then she felt him again, but now his thoughts seemed to come like echoes down a long valley, faint and indistinct.

. . . Grim, but we cannot be . . .

Jiriki? Willow-Switch? I could not understand you. . . . At once. We feared something . . .

Then she could not feel him at all, only the emptiness that yawned between them. Tanahaya spoke the Words of Joining again, wondering what she had done wrong. Nothing came back to her, as though the scale had suddenly lost its potency, though she had never heard of such a thing happening.

And even as she wondered at this a new force intruded abruptly into her thoughts, something she could almost see and could certainly feel. Strands of nothingness that somehow had substance were stretching across the empty places where the Witness had brought her, filling the darkness and twining about her own thoughts until she felt caught like a bird on a limed twig. The strands suddenly seemed to be everywhere, closing off the space that only moments earlier had seemed almost limitless. Frightened, Tanahaya tried to let go and return to the world, but she could no longer feel her hands or the Witness she held, could no longer see, though her eyes were open.

The strands grew together into a single mass, the shape of a mask like a gloating face, its empty mouth and eyes agleam with scarlet light.

A new and unfamiliar voice pushed into her thoughts then.

So. Tanahaya, is it? Himano's little pupil. It is a great pity you were not with him in his last moments. Does that grieve you? Would it have been worth it, to suffer as he suffered and to die at his side?

The only remnant of her body she could feel was her heart, pounding faster and faster as the cold thing enveloped her in hopelessness.

Begone! she said, though her thoughts were so weak she felt as if she murmured against a thunderstorm. *You are not wanted here. You will fail. Nakkiga has fallen under shadow, but shadows can be driven away.*

The thing laughed, and she thought its disgusting enjoyment might drive her mad. *And what do you know of shadows, young scholar? What do you know of any darkness but your own ignorance? Come, and I will show you things Himano never dreamed of. Come to me and be my pupil instead. You will learn that the darkness goes on and on forever—it has lessons for you that you cannot even imagine!*

The presence on the other side of the Witness was far too strong for her: Tanahaya could feel it pulling her out of herself and deeper into the cold that lay behind its fiery laughter—the cold of death, the cold of emptiness unending. Her racing heartbeat was now a single overwhelming and continuous thunder, like many drums pounding at once with no silence between beats. She could feel herself diminishing, stretching, being pulled ever closer toward a place of return.

Then something snapped that pull like a cut thread. The darkness flew to pieces and light flooded in, a bright, blinding glare that she slowly recognized as the few small lamps that lit the Place of Silence, achingly bright compared to the darkness that had nearly swallowed her.

Tanahaya was on her hands and knees, head ringing and body shocked, as if she had fallen a long distance to the stone floor. The blurry form in front of her became Vinyedu. Someone else was crouching beside her, trying to lift her.

"No." Her own voice sounded like something dying. "I will rise when I am ready." She realized it was Morgan trying to help her, and felt a moment of unexpected affection for him. *"Do not fear,"* she told him between gasping breaths. *"I will be well again."*

When she could finally climb into a crouch, she saw that Vinyedu was again holding the Witness. "I had to pull it from your hands," she told Tanahaya. "Something had you."

"Yes, it did. Something dark. I think it might have been Akhenabi of the Stolen Face. It felt like what I know of him—arrogant and cruel."

"Arrogant, cruel, and very powerful," Vinyedu said. "He bears no weapon of witchwood or bronze, but he is Utuk'ku's greatest servant. You are fortunate I was here, but I have done myself no favors in breaking your bond with the Witness. I hurt all over, as though I have been burned." Vinyedu sighed, and for the first time Tanahaya heard real fear in her voice. "We have learned a terrible lesson today. The Witnesses are no longer safe—" Vinyedu began, but she never finished. Someone was calling from the Place of Sky-Watching in the hall above them—a voice tinged with alarm.

"Cloud Children! There are Cloud Children in the city! There is fighting in the passages!"

Vinyedu gave Tanahaya a savage look. "Your great need to speak to the Sa'onserei has revealed us to our enemies."

"No," Tanahaya cried. "That can't be! Even Akhenabi could not find us so quickly!" She turned to Morgan. *"Unsheathe your sword and stay with me. Do not leave my side, no matter what happens."* And so saying, she drew her blade and guided him to the stairs that led upward to the rain and the city.

Rain was falling hard now, rattling the leaves above their heads, and the wind made the trees thrash as the Sithi named Liko led Aelin and his men deeper into the ancient forest.

The immortals had taken their horses—several of Liko's followers were riding ahead of them through the dark, wet wood. The rest of the Sithi led Aelin, Maccus, and wounded Evan swiftly across high, slippery places and along hillsides dense with bracken, forcing the captives to leap over new-formed streams that raced down the muddy slopes into the dells below. Thunder growled and threatened, and from time to time a flash lit the sky beyond the trees, as though some impossibly vast creature was searching for them with a lantern.

At last, about half way across a long slope, in a spot thick with trees and dotted with rocky outcroppings, Liko the leader slowed to let the rest of the company catch up. Aelin was grateful for the chance to catch his breath—the immortals seemed able to run forever without wearying.

"Be quiet. Now we go into lodge," Liko told them, his face stern. "I go first.

Follow without noise. You understand?" Apparently satisfied, the Sitha made a sound like the cry of a bird; an instant later, the ground itself lifted up. Startled and fearful, Aelin almost fell before he saw that the opening into the earth had been covered by a sort of wooden screen disguised on top with dirt and leaves, and had been lifted by a Sitha beneath it, who now climbed up to hold it ajar.

"By Cuamh himself," breathed Maccus Blackbeard. "Would have walked past that a dozen times and never guessed."

Liko abruptly struck Maccus on the back of the head, not hard enough to injure him, but enough to freeze the Hernystirmen with surprise. Again the leader of the Sithi brushed his mouth with his fingertips, then pointed to the hole.

They were surrounded by armed Sithi, their weapons and horses gone, and even more dangerous enemies were lurking in the forest. *As Uncle Eolair would say,* Aelin told himself, *when you are given only bad choices, choose the least dreadful.* He took a shaky breath, then lowered himself feet-first into the darkness.

The tunnel was steep but short: Aelin managed to slither down and land with no injuries except to his dignity. Maccus and Evan were coming down behind him, so he crawled forward, then suddenly light burst out before him. The glare came from a shining round stone set on a wooden tripod, and though it was not as bright as it had first seemed when he came out of the dark tunnel, it was enough to show that the lodge, as Liko had called it, was a long, low, angular cavern inside a great mass of ancient limestone. He heard his two men emerge behind him from the base of the tunnel, but Aelin did not look back, overwhelmed by what was in front of him. He could not see how far the cave extended, but the part he could see was full of Sithi. Some were sharpening their swords—not made of proper metal, but a substance that looked more like stone or polished wood—while others fletched arrows, or sat alone or by themselves or in unspeaking groups. The silence of so many felt unnatural, and made Aelin's heart beat faster.

Liko the Shrike had left them without a word, and now Aelin saw him talking to a hooded figure on the other side of the cavern. He then bowed and disappeared deeper into the cavern, out of Aelin's sight.

"Evan's bleeding quite a bit, sir," Maccus said. Aelin turned to see that the young Aedonite's face was white and he was shivering, his eyes unfixed. Aelin rose to look for something to bandage the wound, and almost stumbled into the hooded figure with whom Liko had spoken. This figure threw back the hood to reveal another handsome Sitha face, this one female.

"Your companion looks to have lost much blood," she said. "My grandson should have told me." She spoke with slow care, but her command of Westerling seemed nearly flawless, much better than Liko's. She turned and called softly, then another Sitha rose from where he had been grinding something in a mortar and came toward them. The female Sitha spoke to him for a moment in their tongue, then with her help he removed Evan's mail shirt. After a moment trying to unknot the wet cords of the shirt beneath shirt, the Sitha drew a small, thin knife from his sleeve. Maccus made a noise of surprise and reached for his own weapon.

"Stop," said Aelin. "Be still. He means Evan no harm. He is only cutting away the lad's shirt."

"You are correct." The Sitha woman had hair as white as a sun-bleached linen, which gave her a look of age, but her angular face seemed to Aelin like that of someone still capable of bearing a child. "We will not harm your friend." She looked on as the Sitha she had summoned pulled the shirt back. Evan's back was smeared with blood, but the wound did not look too deep. "Good. There is no sign of poison," she said.

"Are we prisoners?" Aelin asked as he watched.

"No," she said. "I do not think so—but not precisely guests, either." She gave him a strange look; Aelin did not think it looked friendly. "My grandson did right to bring you here—these hills are not a good place for mortals. The long shadow war we have fought here against our own kind has become deadly."

"Your own kind? The Norns?"

She nodded. "As you call them, yes. And you, mortal man—who are you and why are you here? Liko feared you might be sent to spy on us, but I think the Hikeda'ya would not bother with observers who were so obviously out of place."

Aelin fought against rising anger. "Spies? The Hikeda'ya slaughtered my men, and hundreds more of my kind at Naglimund, only a league away on the other side of the hill. You are not the only one at war with them, my lady."

Her lips twitched in what might have been a smile, but it did not touch her hard stare. "Perhaps. But you still have not told me your name, mortal knight."

"I am Sir Aelin of Nad Mullach," he said. "And who are you?" He nodded toward Evan, whose wound was being cleaned by the other Sitha. "At the very least, I owe you thanks for helping my man and giving us shelter." He spread his hands. "Forgive me if I speak clumsily—I have never met one of your kind before today."

"My mother named me Ayaminu," she told him. "And I know your mortal kind better than I might wish, Sir Aelin."

52

The Crypt

Viyeki already had a thousand problems to distract him
as he drove his Builders and the mortal slaves through the backbreaking, dangerous work of pulling down the mortal temple and digging away the stone and
hard-packed earth beneath its cellar. Then he received a visit from Pratiki, the
Prince-Templar.

"I apologize for not having spoken to you lately, High Magister," Pratiki
began as he entered Viyeki's makeshift quarters in the residence, which had
been the chambers of one of Naglimund's lesser nobles. "I have had much to
do mediating between the Orders of Sacrifice and Song. Both are fiercely loyal
to our beloved queen, and both are eager to take the lead in this affair, since
they know how close it is to her heart."

Viyeki nodded and did his best to look sympathetic, though the prince-
templar's visit worried him. "It must be very difficult, Serenity, since we are
now poised between the most important work of the Sacrifices and the Singers.
But my Builders still have much to do."

"And that is what I wish to speak to you about now." Pratiki lifted a slender
hand. "No, I have no complaints or criticisms. You have done an admirable job
under difficult circumstances, High Magister."

"Thank you, my lord." Viyeki was not so alienated from his masters that he
disliked praise. "I have done my best to do the queen's bidding as efficiently as
possible."

"You are planning to lift the stone lid of the Navigator's crypt soon, I think."

"Yes, Prince-Templar. Tomorrow morning, if all goes well today."

"Your timing could not be better. The queen herself will arrive the day after
that. We have received word."

Viyeki still found it astonishing that Queen Utuk'ku had left Nakkiga after
countless centuries. It seemed like something that would happen in a dream,
then dissolve with the return of waking life. "We are honored beyond any of
our ancestors that she will come to us. It is historic."

"Yes, but it is also very, very important that all goes well, as I am sure you
understand. The Mother of All does not wish to wait. That means all must be
in readiness, and all must be . . ." Again he paused to search for a word, which

always meant that a sensitive moment had arrived. Pratiki had not lived so long in the viper's nest of the Hamakha court without a facility for knowing where danger lay. "All must be *orderly.*"

"Does this mean you wish the slaves hidden?" Although most of their work was done, Viyeki dared not reveal his extreme reluctance to execute the captive mortals, who were mostly women, children, and old men. Pratiki might be largely uninterested in violent retribution against mortals, but he was still Hamakha.

"No, Magister. My concerns lie elsewhere. I have seen the great crane you use to lift heavy pieces of stone and brickwork. I take it you will use it to remove the lid of the crypt as well."

"I had planned to, yes. Otherwise we must break up the crypt's stone cover and risk damaging the queen's prize within."

"Just so. But currently you are using Tinukeda'ya Carry-men to power the wheel."

"Their strength is vital, yes. They turn the drum, which allows the crane to lift great weights. Best of all, they do not complain."

Pratiki shook his head. "But I cannot promise you that will continue. In fact, I think we dare not use the Carry-men to lift the slab off the crypt."

Viyeki was startled. "My lord, what do you mean? Those eight Carry-men do the work of dozens of ordinary workers. How could we replace them?"

"I'm afraid that is something you must decide for yourself. High Magister. But we cannot use them to lift the slab atop Ruyan's tomb."

His mind racing, already wondering how he might compensate for losing the single most important element of this final step, Viyeki could only ask, "Why, my lord? Why?"

"Because they are Tinukeda'ya," Pratiki said. "And this spot has long been sacred to their kind. To them, Ruyan the Navigator represents almost what our queen means for us—the embodiment of their race, the touchstone of their beliefs."

"But the Carry-men are witless! They are docile—less intelligent than oxen or dray-goats."

"In any other year, I would agree with you, High Magister." Pratiki motioned to his cleric and guards to wait outside the shelter. When they had gone the Prince-Templar leaned forward, his face carefully expressionless. "But the truth is, Magister Viyeki, that something strange is happening to all the Tinukeda'ya. In Nakkiga, many have become restless and badly behaved. Before I left the city, several went mad and had to be destroyed. Many of those who could speak, delvers and house-slaves, talked of a great day coming. Others said the opposite—that they had dreamed of the destruction of their race. Several of the other nobles asked for an audience with the queen to talk of this unrest among the Changelings, but Her Majesty only sent word that it was 'to be expected.'"

"What could that mean?"

Pratiki shook his head. "I do not know, but when the queen has spoken—

well, then it is for lesser folk to determine how to deal with *a problem that is not*." He spoke the phrase with a certain archness. The words struck a chord of familiarity, but Viyeki was too overwhelmed by Pratiki's declaration to ponder it.

"So you worry that something similar might happen here? That the Carrymen might run mad?" It was a frightening thought. They were as large as the hairy giants, but even stronger. If one of them suddenly went mad, the carnage would be terrible. And if it happened in the presence of the Queen herself . . . Viyeki shuddered.

"What matters," the prince-templar said, "—especially knowing how much importance the Mother of All places on our success here—is that we dare not risk such a thing. The Carry-men and any other Changelings must be kept away from Ruyan's tomb when it is opened."

"But how are we to replace them? It would take several dozen Sacrifices to match their strength, but there is no room for so many in the drum!"

Pratiki's mouth curled in distaste. "By the Dreaming Sea, Magister, do not even think of asking for Sacrifices. I cannot imagine trying to convince Kikiti to let his warriors take the place of Changeling slaves. He would assassinate me and then kill himself to avoid the dishonor, as he would see it. No, somehow you must get your mortal prisoners to manage it."

"Women and children! And weakened by hunger and hard labor." Viyeki forced himself to take a breath. "And I must do all this in one day?" He was staggered, and becoming more fearful by the moment. It would require rebuilding the great crane and its windlass drum, something that had taken several days to construct even with his engineers working in shifts from dawn to dawn.

"I am sorry I could not bring this to you sooner, High Magister. I have the needs of many to reconcile." Pratiki stood and laid a hand on Viyeki's shoulder, a very unusual gesture for a noble of his stature. "I understand that I have presented you with a terrible task. If you can accomplish it and the queen is satisfied with our labors here, I will not forget your loyalty."

And if we don't accomplish it, Viyeki thought, *then the queen will doubtless have me killed. And you may not have a happy reunion with Her Majesty, either, Prince-Templar. You may even join me in the Fields of the Nameless.* But knowing that one of the Hamakha might share his ugly fate did not make Viyeki feel a great deal better.

Viyeki called in his engineers, and as midnight came silently to the ruins of Naglimund after hours of desperate work, they hit on an idea that might allow them to finish on time. The great hollow wheel of the windlass which, when turned, lifted any weight the crane carried in ratched steps, had been built for Carry-men and so was not wide enough to hold the dozens of mortals who would have to replace the monstrous Tinukeda'ya slaves in turning it. But after many calculations, Viyeki decided that if he built a second wheel inside the first, this one a much longer cylinder, and buttressed both wheel and crane with additional support on either side, they could accomodate the greater number of bodies needed to turn the wheel. He put several dozen Builders to work on it immediately. They would have to take the crane out of operation for that time, but human slaves could continue clearing the dirt and rubble from on top of the crypt.

Viyeki and his foremen labored desperately all through the night and into the morning, but as the hidden sun climbed to midday behind threatening gray clouds, the great windlass was again ready for use.

Only a few hours late, Viyeki thought. *If I have not managed to save my life, it is because I have been given an impossible task.* That was faint comfort, though, and as he checked his engineers' final calculations and his workers finished bracing the tall crane, he found himself thinking of all he loved that he might never see again if the new drum and buttresses could not handle lifting the great weight of the slab.

Nezeru, my daughter, he thought, *I hope your successes will make you safe even if I fail.* Pratiki had told him in secret some days earlier that his daughter had been part of a group of Queen's Talons who had accomplished great things. Viyeki longed to hear the story from his child's own mouth, but had no idea where she was or when he might see her again. *And Tzoja too—my dear Tzoja,* he thought sadly. *I hope your daughter's triumphs will bring you security as well. I had hoped I could always protect you, but now—who can say?*

Rain began to fall as the crane's massive ropes, each as thick as Viyeki's arm, were secured in the notches the masons had carved in the side of the thick stone slab that covered the grave. Almost all the Builders not actually engaged in the project had gathered around the edge of the great pit, and quite a few of General Kikiti's Sacrifice troops were watching as well. Only Sogeyu's Singers, whose great work was still to come, stayed away.

At Viyeki's signal the chief foreman shouted a command and the slaves who had been chosen to move the wheel began to walk forward inside the longer inner wheel. Each time they managed to turn it far enough, winding up a few measures of the crane's ropes, a tooth of the mechanism fell into place and kept the wheel from spinning backward. The ropes tightened, creaking in a loud and worrisome manner, but they held, and the slaves, under the direction of several Builders with whips, kept the wheel slowly turning. The tension in the ropes grew greater until at last the great slab began to lift away from the crypt. Several of the watching Builders cheered, but Viyeki was busily praying that everything would hold during the next and most delicate part of the operation, the moment when his work and life were most endangered.

Now that the walls of the crypt no longer supported the immense weight of the slab, the great crane, built on a swiveling base with a monstrous counterweight of gathered stone, had to be turned so the slab could be lowered again to one side, exposing the sarcophagus beneath. At any moment the immense weight of the unsupported slab might cause the whole thing to shatter, dropping pieces of stone a cubit thick and as wide as the foundation of a small house on those below, killing dozens of Builders and—even more horribly—burying the crypt again under rubble they would never be able to clear before the queen's arrival. Worst of all, it might destroy the contents of Ruyan's tomb. Viyeki watched with his fists clenched so tightly his nails scored the skin of his hands as the Builders pushed and pulled and the vast mechanism slowly rotated.

Another cheer went up as the inside of the crypt was exposed. Viyeki and waited impatiently while boards were laid across the top of the tomb so that they could inspect it from close up, but even from a distance he could see something inside gleaming wetly under the bouncing rain drops.

"Cover that!" he shouted, then clambered down a ladder into the pit. He waited for Pratiki, then the two of them went cautiously over the rain-slicked boards until they could look down into the tomb.

Several Builders pulled back the heavy cloth they had spread over the sarcophagus to protect its contents. Viyeki squatted at the edge of the board, mindful not to block Pratiki's view. For a moment, he was fearful at what he saw, that all their work might have been for naught. "Is this what you hoped to see, Prince-Templar?"

Pratiki spoke in words that seemed almost reverent. "It is. The armor of Ruyan Vé. It has not been seen for many Great Years. We are blessed. And the queen has blessed us with this great task."

Viyeki could now see the outlines of the armor amid the rubble of smashed or deteriorated grave goods, though it was covered in drifts of dust that the rain was rapidly turning into mud. The armor was flattened, and he could see no sign of the legendary Navigator's body inside it, but it unquestionably had the shape of something with two arms and two legs. As more of the dust washed away under the splashing rain Viyeki could see that the entire suit of armor was made, not from witchwood or metal, but from scales of some transparent crystalline material held together tightly with golden wire, which shone as if it had been placed there only yesterday. The helm, which had slid forward as though Ruyan had put his chin on his chest to sleep, was a golden cylinder decorated with dirt-caked shapes Viyeki could not easily make out, and from what he could see, the eye holes were filled with the same crystal as the rest of the armor.

"I have never seen anything like it," he said with a shiver of superstitious awe. He had never experienced a feeling quite like it, had never felt the past so strongly, not even in the presence of deathless Utuk'ku herself. "So this is what remains of the great Navigator."

"When the queen arrives," said Pratiki, "I would suggest you refer to him only as 'the Great Traitor.'"

"But is it truly Ruyan Vé? Where is his fleshly body?" Viyeki asked.

"Gone to dust, no doubt," the prince-templar said. "Eventually we all come to the same end, the greatest and the worst, mortals and those called immortal, too."

"Except the Mother of All," said Viyeki dutifully, staring at the mounded dust, now darkening as raindrops struck it.

"Except the Mother of All, of course," Pratiki agreed.

Cuff had slept very badly the night before. He could not remember much about his dreams except that he had awakened several times during the night with his heart beating fast and tears coursing down his cheeks.

Now, as all the other mortal survivors of Naglimund stood beside the far wall of the slave pit, trying to make out what the Norns were doing with their great lifting engine in the wreckage of what had once been St. Cuthbert's church, more or less his home, Cuff the Scaler sat by himself on the far side of the enclosure feeling sick and frightened.

"Not right," Cuff said over and over, though nobody was listening. "Not right, knock down the church, dig it up. Shouldn't do it. Father Siward would say so." But Father Siward was gone like so many others, burned, buried, or killed during the madness on the night Naglimund fell.

Still, though his desperation at being alone again had caused him many miserable nights, that was not why he sat by himself now, long arms around his knees, rocking back and forth on the muddy ground as the rain soaked his tattered garments. Instead it was the feeling that had gripped him all day that frightened him so—a feeling no one else seemed to have, despite the fear and hunger they all felt. And now it was getting worse.

As the other slaves stared sullenly, watching white-skinned Norns scuttling over the ruins of the church like maggots in spoiled meat, Cuff felt his fear growing until he could think of nothing else. It seemed as if something was lifting the top off his head, pulling open his skull to expose him to the sullen thunderclouds—as if something invisible could see him, even see his thoughts. He felt as though someone or something was staring at every private, shameful thought he had ever had—and whatever it was, that something did not like Cuff the Scaler at all. It thought he was an insect. It thought he was a worm.

But even this was not the worst.

Because as the other slaves murmured, some holding their thin, ragged children on their shoulders as though to watch a passing saint's parade, Cuff felt the air tighten around him until his chest ached and his ears were filled with stabbing pain. Something was coming, though he did not know what it could be. Something was being born—a thing that should not exist. He could feel it in every limb of his body, every pore of his skin, and it was all he could do not to throw himself face down in the mud and beg for someone to kill him.

It's a sin, I know it's a sin, Father—but I hurt! I hurt so much!

Then the other slaves let out a dull cry as something happened that Cuff could not see and did not care about, because at that precise moment the top of his head finally came off, or felt as if it did. Suddenly he was naked and unprotected beneath an angry, hating sky. A great black funnel reached down from a place beyond the clouds and pulled all the things out of him that made Cuff who he was, then scattered them to the winds. He felt himself come apart, and all the bits of him were swept helplessly through a terrible rushing blackness.

"It's coming!" he shrieked, but there was no one to hear him, nothing around him but the hideous, endless roaring of the wind from nowhere. "They want me! They want me! The Mother wants me! The Three!" He did not know what he was saying, but he could not stop, even as he flew up and out in a thousand pieces, blind and unknowing. He could hear himself crying, "The Three!" over and over, as if he had left his own body behind.

Then something came to him that was different from the howling black. It had the shape of a person, but it shone like the flames of many candles, like the chapel during *mansa* when their familiar glow lit the altar, flickering before the great picture of Usires on the Day of Weighing Out.

As it floated toward him, he saw that this figure was garbed, not in clothes or even the heavenly robes Cuff had seen in church paintings, but in a suit made of stars, countless diamond-bright points of light.

"We are not finished—not yet," the figure told him, and he heard it with his heart, not his ears. *"Our race has not ended."*

And then Cuff was himself again, lying on the wet ground. He could hear people talking above him.

"He's had one of his fits," one said.

"Poor thing won't last much longer," said another. "None of us will."

Cuff opened his eyes. For a moment he thought they might be angels—angels covered in mud. Then he saw that it was only a man and a woman, two of his fellow slaves. "D-d-don't be afraid," he told them, rubbing at his cold wet face, tasting gritty dirt between his teeth. "The angel made of stars is coming."

"Poor thing," said the woman. Together they lifted him back into a sitting position, then left him there in the mud and the rain and went back to join the other slaves.

"It's coming," Cuff said once more, though there was no longer anyone to hear him.

Viyeki was struggling with something more vexing than even the most difficult engineering calculation of unequal weights at unequal distances, and this problem carried a penalty for failure perhaps even more frightening than a miscalculation about heavy stone.

To Lady Khimabu of the Enduya,

My good wife, mistress of my household, I greet you and hope this finds you in sound health. I write in a place far from Nakkiga, but my thoughts are ever there, with you and all those who serve us.

He stared with dissatisfaction at what he had written. It was not the runes that displeased the high magister: they had been drawn with his usual care, each line crisp and economical, as he had been taught during his childhood in the Builder's Order-house. Rather, it was the obvious flatness of the sentiments. If even he found fault with them, how much more would Khimabu, daughter of a grand old family, raised on courtly conversation? But Viyeki had no poetry in him at this moment. He had no news to share—none that he was allowed to relate, at least—and he really wanted was to ask Khimabu of news about his mistress Tzoja and his daughter Nezeru, but he dared not ask his wife such things. Tzoja's desperate fear of Khimabu had troubled his thoughts, though he had dismissed it at the time. He did not want to give his wife more reasons to resent the mortal woman.

He had even considered writing a letter just to Tzoja herself, but did not trust it would reach her without Khimabu discovering it, and a secret message to his mistress would be even more certain to infuriate his wife.

Khimabu's last letter, written back in the hot days of the Stone-Listener's Moon, had conspicuously failed to mention Nezeru at all, let alone her mortal mother. It had been full of petty complaints about the servants and how Khimabu felt she was being treated badly by other noblewomen of the court. The veiled implication, only slightly hidden by dutiful language, had been that Viyeki himself was somehow to blame for all of these things. But his irritation was leavened now by the knowledge that he was now swimming in very deep waters indeed, responsible for a project that was important to the queen, although he had been given little authority to make it happen. If there was ever a time he might need the good will of his wife's rich and ancient family, fierce supporters of the Hamakha since the Garden, that time was the present.

Beguile her, he told himself. *It should not be difficult—she is already your wife. The poetry of our people is full of easeful words. Find some that will soothe her.*

But the distance between Viyeki and his wife seemed greater than merely the leagues that separated them. He was surprised, even disturbed, by how little he thought about Khimabu these days, and how much he thought instead about his mortal mistress.

It is Tzoja I truly miss, he realized with a mixture of surprise and shame. *I am lonely here in these strange mortal lands. I was often lonely in the Enduya Clan House as well, but being with Tzoja always eased my heart.*

Fool, he cursed himself. *Find words that will sing to Khimabu for you, then your half-hearted voice will not be a problem.*

For a moment he even considered asking Pratiki for advice—the prince-templar was a well-known patron and student of the poetic arts, after all. But showing weakness before a Hamakha noble, whether in war or in a dynastic marriage, could have many unforeseen consequences and almost none of them were good.

A memory of something Pratiki had said earlier came back to him—"a problem that is *not.*" That line was from a poem, Viyeki felt sure, though he could not recall its author. For some reason it had struck him oddly at the time, and it had stuck in his mind like a burr, but he still could not say why.

As he pondered, he became aware of a presence waiting just outside the door of his makeshift chambers. "Is that you, Nonao? Come in. I am not resting, but trying to write something."

"I am glad, High Magister, because a force of Sacrifices and a train of wagons have just arrived from the north."

All thoughts of letter-writing vanished in an instant as Viyeki leaped to his feet. "What? The queen here already? She was not expected until much later today!" His heart was beating swiftly. "It is a blessing from the Garden that we managed to lift the slab on our first try."

Nonao frowned politely. "This worthless observer thinks that perhaps the newly arrived company is too small to be the queen's. Someone also suggested that the runes on the largest of the wagons indicate it belongs to Lord Akhenabi."

Viyeki's heart slowed a little but his stomach felt sour. "Ah. How fortunate for all of us. The Lord of Song has come, no doubt, to make sure all is ready for the Mother of All."

"No doubt."

Viyeki rolled up his parchment and put it away in his writing box. "Come," he said. "Help me put on my ceremonial robes. I must greet the queen's favorite."

Only a small company made their way across the ruined fortress to the broken gates where the Lord of Song waited—Pratiki and his guards, Viyeki, and General Kikiti with a few soldiers of his own. Akhenabi, who knew Viyeki well, gave him only the briefest acceptable bow when Pratiki introduced them, but Viyeki thought that the halfblood Singer who accompanied Akhenabi looked almost startled when he heard Viyeki's name, though the high magister could not imagine why.

Not all the greetings were so cursory. The Lord of Song and Prince-Templar Pratiki enacted a brief war of propriety, trading empty compliments with deft precision, fulsomely acknowledging each other's value to the queen and importance to the Hikeda'ya people with laudatory phrases and an impressive array of gracious gestures. But for any observer with eyes and ears—and Viyeki had two of each—the obviousness of their mutual dislike was laughable. Or would have been, had not both possessed the power to destroy even a High Magister like Viyeki at a whim.

Queen's close relative and queen's conjuror, Viyeki thought. *I know which one I trust more, but good sense tells me to trust neither.*

Akhenabi's patience ran out before Pratiki's and the great Singer abruptly ended the ritual greetings. "Take me to the crypt now, Prince-Templar." His voice was like a shovel digging gravel. "We must make preparations for the arrival of the Mother of All."

Sogeyu and her robed Singers met them at the crypt. Akhenabi left the lesser arrangements to his halfblood lieutenant while he spoke to Sogeyu in whispers and hand-signs only Singers could recognize. A swarm of the Akhenabi's dark-cloaked servitors, with scarves over their faces and thick leather gloves on their hands, swarmed into the crypt and began to remove Ruyan's crystalline armor from its sarcophagus.

Pratiki stood a little way apart from it all, at the very edge of the cloth tent that had been erected over the hole. The moon had long set. Rainclouds streamed overhead in the strong wind, shrouding the stars, so that Viyeki could barely make out the Prince-Templar's face, but what he saw of Pratiki's expression did not look like joy to him, but something altogether more troubled. And with that sight, the words he had not been able to remember finally came back to him.

> *When those who love their people must go in silent fear*
> *When honesty sees a grave problem, but power says it does not exist,*
> *Those who would keep honor in their hearts must ignore the lies*
> *And move to solve the problem that is not.*

It was no poem, but the words of the Exile's Letter, written by Xaniko sey-Hamakha when he left Nakkiga, and—though the queen and her clan had done their best to eradicate all memory of it—it was still repeated in whispers in the present day, albeit very, very quiet whispers. The Exile's Letter was an infamous, treasonous document, Viyeki realized, one he only knew about himself because his own master Yaarike had once taught it to him—by memory only, since nobody after Xaniko's departure had dared to keep it written down.

Why would Pratiki say such a thing? First he quotes Shun'y'asu to me, and now this? Is he really so confident that his high birth protects him? Does he suspect me of being a traitor and hopes to trick me into revealing myself? Or is something deeper in play?

Viyeki was so stunned by this realization that he had scarcely noticed Sogeyu's Singers at their task. They had removed the individual pieces of armor from the tomb, and as he watched they shook the dust out of them—the dust that had once been the body of Ruyan the Navigator, greatest of the Tinukeda'ya, dust which now sifted to the ground and disappeared into the rivulets of rainwater.

Emboldened a little, but still cautious, Viyeki said to the prince-templar, "The Singers are careless with Ruyan's remains. Do they not fear his spirit might want vengeance?"

"The queen fears nothing, least of all the spirit of Ruyan," said Pratiki flatly.

"As for me, I fear I still understand very little," Viyeki admitted. "How can Ruyan's empty armor be useful to our queen?"

"You will see, High Magister." Pratiki's words remained devoid of feeling. "With it, our great queen will bring Hakatri, brother of Ineluki the Storm-King, back into the world, and thus make herself victorious over all. No greater feat of resurrection has ever been performed, not even when the Mother of All brought back Ineluki himself, for the Storm King's spirit was still prisoned in the Well beneath Nakkiga, and thus the mortals could still thwart his full return and banish him back to the darkness. Now our queen will raise an ally who can go wherever our monarch commands, dealing horror and death to the mortals who seek to destroy us."

"But why Hakatri?" Viyeki knew he was asking too many questions, but he wanted to take advantage of the prince-templar's strange, detached mood. "Hakatri was Zida'ya, not Hikeda'ya like us, and he left these lands long before his brother Ineluki was killed by mortals. What purpose will he serve for the queen?"

"He will help us capture the Witchwood Crown," said Pratiki. "That is all I know—and all I *need* to know, High Magister."

His last words had such a sound of finality that Viyeki dared not ask anything further, but he already had much to consider. He stood in silence beside the prince-templar while the gloved and masked Singers gathered the pieces of armor and placed them carefully on a litter, then, at the Lord of Song's direction, carried them away through the rain toward Akhenabi's wagon.

53

Smoke

Her feet did not reach the stirrups of Jurgen's horse, so at first all
Miriamele could do was cling as it careened down the Mahistrevine Hill.
Orn's hooves pounded against the cobbles, jolting her like a beating from a
bailiff's staff. The roads were all but empty, though everywhere she passed
people were standing on roofs or leaning out of windows, staring up toward
the crest of the Mahistrevine Hill. At intervals, as the road circled downward,
she could see what they saw—the fire at the Sancellan Mahistrevis belching
black smoke into the sky. Too many people had already seen her for Miriamele's
comfort, so she guided the horse off the wide Way of the Fountains and rode
on back streets through the capital until she had escaped the heart of the city,
then made her way across to the Anitullean Road and followed it north.

As the first rush of terror began to recede, Miri began to think about her
circumstances. She could see no obvious signs of pursuit, but the winding
curves blocked many parts of the road behind her. Still, she slowed Orn to a
trot, if only to give herself a few moments of rest without the immediate threat
of being thrown from the saddle.

I must get out of this city. She had a nightmare vision of being caught and
dragged in front of Turia Ingadaris. The idea of being delivered to that cream-
faced little witch, a child younger than Miriamele's grandson, was infuriating
and terrifying.

Riding steadily, she reached the outskirts of the capital near dark. She was
already wondering whether she dared try to find a ship to carry her to Wentmouth where she would be on Erkynlandish soil, but she did not like the idea
of stopping anywhere that agents of the Ingadarines might be watching for her.
Miriamele had a new and fearful respect for Turia: she thought it entirely possible that the Ingadarines might have sent word ahead to their agents to watch
out for those escaping the destruction at the Sancellan Mahistrevis. She could
only pray that Duchess Canthia and the children had enough of a head start to
make it all the way to the northern border without being overtaken.

Her other alternative was to ride all the way north by herself. She knew it
would take well over a fortnight to cover the distance—perhaps as much as a

month if the weather was bad or she had to evade searchers—but she would not have to risk being trapped in one of the Nabbanai ports.

She decided to wait and see what happened. She still had several days' riding ahead of her just to cross the peninsula, and she was determined to do it as swiftly as possible, to stay ahead of any news that had not been sent before the Sancellan fell. She hoped Jurgen's courser was as able as the knight had claimed.

Thinking of her guard captain brought a clutch of despair, swiftly followed by a blaze of anger. *You owe me for Jurgen, little Turia. And you owe me for all the innocent lives lost while you pursued your games of power. A queen does not forget that.*

By sundown, Miri was well outside the city walls. She had been noticed a few times by guards, but since nobody expected the queen of the High Ward to be riding alone, no one had recognized her, although a few asked whether she was certain she wished to be out in the countryside after dark. A league or so outside the city proper she found a vintner's barn and spent the night there. The tang of fermenting grapes was very strong, and Miri felt sure she would never smell anything like it again without thinking of this desperate ride, but she was too weary to let it keep her awake. The vintner's horses had been put up for the night, so she stole an armload of hay out of the stalls and gave it to Orn as a reward for his hard work, then curled herself up in a pile of straw and fell asleep.

Noises woke her just before dawn, but it was only Orn stirring and pacing at the end of his tether. She led him out, alert for any sign of being watched, but did not see anything except the vintner's house at the top of the hill, a single lamp in the kitchen suggesting that the household's earliest risers were beginning their day. She walked the courser until they reached the road, then climbed on. The saddle was too big and too hard—she felt like she was sitting on the keel of an upturned boat—but it was safer than riding bareback.

By morning the Anitullean Road seemed almost as it would on an ordinary day, with farm wagons blocking the way at inopportune times and hundreds of people on foot, priests, peasants, and peddlers, all going about their business, though only a few leagues away the sky was still clotted with the smoke of the Sancellan Mahistrevis.

Did they not know? Or were the necessitudes of daily life simply more important? Miri supposed that if she had children to feed or a crop that had to reach market before it went bad, she too might be trudging along that road, ignoring even the horrors of civil war.

She had found a little food in Jurgen's saddle bag, stale bread and a rind of cheese hard as Orn's saddle. She chewed and swallowed them as she rode through the countryside. She could see the full panoply of Nabbanai dwellings alongside the ancient Anitullean Road, from the hovels of the poor to the estates of the wealthy looking down on them from the hills. Miri could not help wondering how many members of the Dominiate had elected to leave the city and might be watching the Queen of the High Ward ride past without realizing it. Surely some of them would be sympathetic—the duke's party had made up more than half the Fifty Families, after all. If she chose correctly, she would be welcomed in, given food and shelter, and no doubt helped in her flight back to Erkynland. But it was an impossible risk. Even those most loyal to Saluceris must have seen the blaze atop the high Mahistrevine Hill and would think twice about sheltering an enemy of the Ingadarines, even if that enemy were the queen herself.

By midday Miri was hungry again. She knew she could not reach the nearest safe seaport without a little money, so she stopped in a good-sized market town called Arbris Sacra and made her way to the street near the square where gems and jewelry were sold. She chose an establishment that looked prosperous but also somewhat discreet, a shop beneath a family dwelling, and tied Orn outside.

The owner, a small, round man with dark jowls, inspected her carefully as she entered. He clearly decided that the tattered hem of her dress and the disarray of her hair was less important than the quality of her gown, and treated her with cautious courtesy.

She put her items on a table—an enameled brooch in the shape of a Holy Tree, studded with polished emeralds, and beside it one of her remaining rings, a small circlet of chased gold. An interval of bargaining ensued that, though perfectly ordinary, seemed to Miriamele to last hours. She knew it was not impossible that even this far outside the city someone would recognize her, and the longer she stayed in one place the more likely that became.

At last, and with a great show of magnanimity, the jeweler acceded to her price. Miri was hungry, but as soon as the jeweler had paid her and she was back in the saddle she decided she would spend the money elsewhere. The town of Bellidan was only a short ride away, and Miriamele wanted to travel faster than any news about strange noblewomen; she could ignore her stomach for a while longer. As she guided Orn out of town it felt as though hostile faces watched her from every doorway and window.

At last, in the middle of an overcast gray day, hot and moist, she reached Bellidan, a good-sized settlement she had visited in her youth. She bought a dark blue hooded cloak at the market and as much food as she could expect to eat before any of it went bad, then returned to the road again.

Last time I was here, she thought as she left the town gates behind, *I was with Father Dinivan and Cadrach. Both dead now.* An impossible yearning flooded through her. *Ah, Elysia God's gentle mother, how I wish I were back in Erkynland right now. How I wish I were in my bed with Simon. How I wish . . . !*

But wishes were pointless things. Prayers might be answered, though, so she offered fervent entreaties to Elysia, God's mother, and also to Elysia's son, the Sacred Ransomer.

Let me reach my home and my family, O Lord. Help me find my way out of this terrible danger.

★   ★   ★

Several more days riding, several more nights snatching sleep in unguarded barns or in hillside copses, only her cloak for a blanket against the chilly autumn air, found Miriamele in the hills of northeastern Nabban. She knew that soon she would reach the place where the broad Vea Petranis crossed the Anitullean Road and she would have to decide whether to head west toward the coast and a ship that might take her to Erkynland, or continue to ride north.

As Orn carried her up the winding road into the hills she stopped from time to time in high places to observe the lands around her. During one such halt, she spotted something on the road she had traveled that, though distant, made the hairs stand up on her neck. A large party of riders had joined the Anitullean Road, perhaps two dozen in all, though she could only guess from this distance. She felt sure that they had been sent by Turia or someone else, and that their quarry was either Miriamele herself, Duchess Canthia, or both. She had never caught a glimpse of the royal carriage since fleeing the Sancellan Mahistrevis, and could only hope that the duchess and her children were far, far ahead and nearing the Erkynlandish border. Miriamele, on the other hand, was scarcely half a league ahead of the mounted company she had spotted, and she had been riding for days. Orn was weary; it was hard to make him gallop for more than a short distance.

Just ahead she saw a road that she knew had once led east to the Vea Orentem, an old thoroughfare considered less safe in these days of violent conflict with the Thrithings-men, but which still would eventually bring her to the North Coast Road on the other side of the Commeis Valley. She had only a short while to think before she reached the crossroads nestled between the hills. Since the riders she had seen were coming from the south, there seemed little chance they would be indifferent to her, and she knew she had little hope of outrunning them all the way to the border, even with a horse as strong as poor Jurgen's.

She guided her mount onto the road leading east, which once had been a fine, wide thoroughfare, but now was little more than a dirt track incised with wheel-ruts, surrounded on both sides by encroaching trees and brush. *A good place to be unnoticed,* she thought, *but also a good spot for an ambush.* The sky was darkening and she thought she could hear a purr of thunder in the distance. She pulled up her hood and urged her horse onward.

She was right to worry about an ambush, but wrong about the place.

Miri reached the Vea Orentem by mid-afternoon and turned onto the old track, once one of the chief avenues of the old imperial system, now little more than a trade road winding along the outskirts of the Lake Thrithing. She passed a few wagons and folk traveling on foot, but otherwise it seemed as if she had left the world of cities and people entirely. The old road followed the eastern slope of the Commeian Hills, and was set high above the plain because of the flooding that inundated it during rainy years. As the road climbed higher and the trees changed from oaks to pine, she could look down across the vastness of the grasslands below her.

Hard to believe so much trouble could be caused over this place, she thought as she nibbled on a piece of dried mutton. *This part of the Thrithings looks as empty as the surface of the ocean.* It had a strange beauty, the leagues of grass gone to gold, the distant waterways and lakes gleaming silver in the slanting light as the sun moved across the sky toward the top of the hills.

The sun at last dipped behind the hills. The air was still hot and damp with the feel of an approaching storm, the sky a uniform stony gray. As she neared the summit, where a small forest of pine and rosemary filled the air with their tangy scents, the bandits were waiting.

She saw them step out of the trees as she approached, and as quickly as she realized what was happening and started to pull on Orn's reins to turn him, several more men stepped out from their hiding places behind her, cutting off her escape. These were not the riders she had seen following on the Anitullean Road, at least—they were too few, too ill-armed, and without horses. Ordinary bandits, she decided, criminals who had fled justice for a lawless life in the wild. Half a dozen of them had now blocked the road ahead of her, several holding bows. She let Orn pace to a halt a few yards from the one who seemed to be the leader. He was a tall fellow wearing a makeshift mask, a cloth tied over his face with holes for his eyes. He had an arrow on his bowstring and was pointing it at her.

"What do you want?" she demanded in Nabbanai.

"What do you think?" the man with the mask and bow said. "Get down. Give over your purse."

They looked a ragged lot, and Miri tried to calm her racing heartbeat to consider the situation. She did not dismount, but urged Orn forward a few steps, though he did not like the smell of the bandits and shied a little before obeying. "You may have my purse," she told them. There was not much left in it, but the idea still made her very angry indeed. "If you get out of my way, I will throw it to you."

The man in the mask laughed. A couple of his fellows joined him, though a moment later. "Do you think we are fools, m'lady? You will get off the horse. We are taking him too. He looks a good piece of horseflesh."

Miri did not dare to give up Jurgen's horse, not here so far from home. And that was if they did no worse than rob her. She looked around the desolate hillside, the clumps of wind-stunted trees and knew that nothing whatsoever could keep these men from raping her and murdering her if they chose.

"You would not harm a woman, would you?" She made her voice small and fearful, which was not that far from how she actually felt. "A lone traveler, with no protection but God's?"

"God sent you on the wrong road, woman," the leader said. "Now get down before we kill you where you sit."

Instead, Miri threw herself against the horse's neck and shouted, "Orn—

forward!" kicking at his flanks with her heels. He reared, and his iron-shod forefoot took the leader in the chest. The man's arrow flew up into the air as he fell back, then Orn was trampling him underfoot as he bolted through the bandits and up the road with Miri hanging on for dear life.

Arrows flew past them as Orn charged toward the top of the hill, one buzzing through her cloak and scraping her arm, but within a few moments they were clear and galloping full out. They reached the crest and started down the other side, Miri still clinging to the horse's mane, the reins bunched uselessly in her fist. She had gambled that if the bandits had horses of their own, they had left them some distance away. When she looked back she seemed to have guessed correctly: there was no sign of pursuit. Still, she dared not ease off, even when she slid into a better position on the saddle: she kept her heels drumming against Orn's ribs as he raced down the winding hill road. Thunder cracked overhead and a few drops of warm rain began to fall.

Only after a very long time with no sign of pursuit did Miri dare to pull up on the reins and let Orn drop into a walk. The rain was falling harder now, making dark spots on the dirt of the road that overlapped in places to form small puddles. She turned in the saddle and looked behind her, examining as much of the hillside as she could see, as well as the empty curve of the road, but saw no sign of pursuit. Orn was exhausted, she could tell, almost staggering beneath her, and she knew she must find a place soon to hide and let him rest.

Just before she turned back, though, she saw something else. A drizzle of something wet had left a broken line on the road behind her, something more regular than the rain drops. The nearest streaks were bright red.

Her throat suddenly tight with fear, she reined up and clambered down from the saddle as fast as she could, holding tight to the reins. An arrow dangled loosely in Orn's belly just behind the stirrup, and he was streaming blood. Miri was horrified—how far had she ridden, how fast had she driven him with a wound like that? Would he even survive it? As she stared in shock, the horse suddenly stumbled a few steps toward the outside of the path and the steep slope below it. Miri tried to let go of the reins, but they had become wound around her wrist and she could not free herself.

An instant later Orn took another step and then, with a rattling groan, slipped off the path and over the edge. Before she knew what was happening, Miri was yanked off her feet.

Orn's huge, tumbling weight whipped her back and forth like hammer blows until her hand finally slid free of the reins. They slid into a copse of pines. The horse struck the trees like a catapult stone, then Miri was rolling free, brown and green flashing past her like a lightning storm, as she bounced and skidded through grass and stones and underbrush. She struck her head, once, twice, and then hardest of all a third time, like the blow of an angry giant.

"All will be well," Duchess Canthia kept saying, and even though she was only trying to calm young Blasis, who cried because he wanted to go home, hearing her say it over and over made Jesa want to scream with rage. All would *not* be well. Everything the old Wran woman had said had come true. The palace was in flames and its people, servants and nobles alike, had been killed. Jesa could only clutch little Serasina in her arms as the carriage jolted and bounced over the cobblestones at terrifying speed, and pray to He Who Always Steps On Sand not to let it overturn.

I do not want to die here, was all she could think. *I should have listened to the* katulo-*woman. I should have run away!*

But she would have had to leave the baby in her arms behind. How could she have done that? The little one was not to blame, no more than Jesa herself.

"By Usires and all the saints," the duchess said, "I pray that Queen Miri-amele will be well."

"No one will hurt her," said Jesa. "No one would hurt the queen."

Canthia shook her head, clinging to the handle of the carriage door with one hand as the coach rattled around a turn of the road. "I thought no one would harm us, either. I do not know what has happened. They were like animals!"

Men are *like animals,* Jesa thought but didn't say, knowing it would only make things worse. *It only takes a little for them to turn on each other, to bite and claw like beasts.* She had seen it during the terrible floods when she was a child, had watched a man in a boat push away drowning swimmers with his oar, and had seen another man kill a woman with a hand ax for trying to steal some of the food he had hoarded. Jesa knew that men were only as good as the world allowed them to be. *But we have guards and a driver,* she told herself. *They are sworn to the duke and his family. They will protect us from the worst of the others.* All the same, she held Serasina so closely that the child moaned a little in her arms.

They had no choice but to take the Anitullean Road—no other would have been wide enough for the royal carriage. Canthia did not seem to mind, but it made Jesa feel like a frog cowering beneath the shadow of a black kite. The road was so open, and though traffic in this autumn rain was light, there were still riders, walkers, and wagon drivers passing them many times in each hour. Almost all of them moved off the road to let the great carriage pass, and most removed their hats or at least bowed their heads, but Jesa felt certain that more than a few of them were wondering what a carriage with the royal arms of Erkynland's High Throne was doing so far south of that land's borders.

Still, two more days passed without incident, and most of a third. Darkness was falling, and the coach driver had just told them that they had only a short way to go before reaching Chasu Rutilli, where they could stop for the night. Even Jesa was beginning to think that they truly might have escaped the disaster that had taken the Sancellan Mahistrevis, when one of the guards on the back of the carriage began pounding on the roof with his fist, startling Canthia out of a doze and making little Serasina wail.

"What?" shouted the driver. "Who is making that noise?"

"Riders!" cried the guard. "Behind us!"

Jesa could not see out the back window of the carriage, which was covered with oiled parchment to let more light into the dark interior, but she handed the baby to the duchess and clambered up onto her seat so that she could put her head out the window.

A good-sized troop of men on horses were following them, perhaps half a league behind, mounting the base of the hill the royal carriage was climbing. When she told the duchess, Canthia cried out to the coach driver, "We are being pursued! Drive faster!"

The driver cursed, but Jesa heard him plying the whip; the horses surged forward, though the weight of the coach and the uphill slope meant they did not move a great deal faster. The sudden movement bounced Blasis against the seat and he slid onto the floor of the carriage, where he lay complaining loudly, still only half-awake.

As they neared the top of the hill the carriage swayed dangerously at each curve of the road. A man walking with a donkey barely had time to leap aside—Jesa saw him flail past the window, his donkey scrambling away up the hillside. Jesa took Serasina back from her mother so the duchess could pull Blasis up from where he had tumbled. Canthia got him back onto the padded bench and set him between herself and the outer wall of the carriage so he would not fall again.

Time seemed to pass with nightmarish slowness as the driver whipped the horses on toward the hilltop. With Serasina clutched tightly against her chest, Jesa finally risked another look out the window. She could see only a little of the road behind her where it curved, but the nearest of the riders was close enough now for her to see him clearly, a bearded man in hides waving a curved sword.

"Grass-men are chasing us!" she told the duchess. "Men from the grass-lands!"

"Thrithings-men?" Canthia sounded terrified, as if one group of men hunting them could be worse than another. "Faster!" she shouted to the carriage driver. "They will kill us all!"

Either the carriage driver did not hear her or he was already coaxing all that he could from his team. They reached the top of the hill and for a few moments raced across almost level ground. Something thumped against the back of the carriage; Jesa heard one of the guards cry out. When she leaned out again she saw him lying in the road, an arrow in his back, and now there were at least half a dozen of the riders in sight, loosing arrows at the carriage. Several of them carried torches, and in the growing darkness the horsemen seemed to float above the road in a ball of flame-colored light, like thunder demons.

A foot pushed through the parchmented window at the back of the carriage.

It was the other guard trying to climb up to a safer place, but even as she stared in astonishment Jesa heard him grunt, then he slid back past torn window cover and fell away.

Something bright and hissing burst through the back window and smacked into the front carriage wall, streaming flames. It was a burning arrow, and fire quickly raced up the coach's padded wall. The painted roof began to turn black above it. Canthia screamed.

"Stop!" she cried. "It is on fire! The carriage is on fire!"

But the driver did not stop. They crossed the top of the hill and sped downward. Jesa could hear the cries of their pursuers, harsh shouts that sounded like joy. Another blazing arrow crashed through the back wall but stopped partway through, still blazing. The front wall of the carriage was engulfed in flames now. Smoke was everywhere.

Someone else was scrambling across the roof of the carriage, but this time going from front to back. She felt the wheels dip as whoever it was leaped off. She could not help looking out again, and saw that fully a dozen or more riders were now just behind them. Even as she watched, the lone remaining guard who had just jumped down from the carriage in a fit of madness or bravery climbed to his feet, but before he could even lift his sword the bearded horsemen ran him down.

The coach hit a stone or some other obstacle and the wheels on one side leaped high in the air before crashing down again. Jesa fell back, clutching baby Serasina. The duchess lay crumpled on the floor, and by the light of the flames that were now devouring the roof of the carriage as well as the walls, Jesa could see a bloody mark on Canthia's head. Little Blasis screamed and pulled at his mother's arm. At that moment a dark shape pulled abreast of the carriage on the outside, then an arm rattling with bone ornaments and metal bangles reached in through the window, grabbed the boy by his collar, and jerked him out into the darkness like a snake taking a baby bird from a nest.

The coach hit something else and tilted high, then plunged downward. Jesa heard a terrible crunch, and suddenly the coach lurched off-balance, leaning to one side, making a rasping, dragging noise as it tipped ever farther. A wheel had come off. Jesa had no time to think, but clutched Serasina against her breasts and clambered to the window, then pushed her upper body through until she hung in blackness and rushing shadows. Before she could decide to jump, the coach lurched again and sent her spinning through the air.

The child! Save Serasina! was her only thought. She landed in a crackling pile of underbrush, poked and scratched as she rolled through it, clinging to the baby as though nothing else in the world mattered—and at that moment, for Jesa, nothing else did.

She came to a stop at last, so deep in prickling branches that she could not move. Serasina stirred against her, somehow still alive, and Jesa heard the infant take in a breath that would surely end in a howl of outrage. She put her hand over the child's mouth and pulled her close so that she could whisper in her little ear. *"Don't cry. Don't cry. You are with me. Don't cry."* Her own body hurt in so many places she could barely tell one from the other, but she heard the drumming of hooves on the road only a few paces away and was terrified to move for fear of making noise.

She stayed silent and motionless in the brambles for what felt like an hour, smelling smoke and seeing orange, flickering light through the branches, listening to the incomprehensible shouting of the Thrithings-men riding back and forth as they searched for anyone who might have escaped.

She Who Waits, Jesa prayed over and over, *do not come for me yet! Let me keep this little child safe. Let me keep her from these evil creatures.* And, as if touched by the gentle hand of a kindly god, Serasina did at last fall back into squirming, uncomfortable sleep.

The noises ranged all around Jesa in the darkness. Once she heard heavy footfalls just a few steps from where she lay hidden, but she stayed as still as any rabbit or mouse until the footsteps moved away. At last, after what seemed like hours, she heard the men ride away, but she still did not dare fight her way out of the undergrowth. She hid on the cold ground until the first light of dawn showed her it was safe to emerge.

With Serasina still clutched against her belly and beginning to stir again, Jesa crawled out through the scratching twigs until she stood on the road once more. Something small and limp lay in the middle of the road behind her, and she trudged toward the spot until she was close enough to recognize the tunic Blasis had been wearing. The boy's head was flung back and his eyes were open, his limbs tangled as though he had been flung aside like an apple core. His throat had been cut down to the bone.

Her eyes dry, but her heart so filled with horror that she could barely breathe, Jesa turned and walked forward along the road until she found the royal carriage, or what was left of it. It had run against a tree, and lay on its side by the road. The two wheels still on the axles were broken and scorched, the body of the carriage a smoldering, blackened shell with spots of glowing red like dying stars. She looked into the wreckage only long enough to see the charred thing that had once been Duchess Canthia, but then had to turn and be sick.

Afterward, she wiped her mouth with her tattered, filthy sleeve, then made her way down the hillside and through the trees with Serasina still held tightly at her breast. The baby was hungry and complaining about it. Jesa did not know where they were or where they were going, but she wanted nothing more to do with roads.

54

Dead Birds

Tzoja knew that they had entered the fortress called Naglimund and had been waiting inside the gates for several hours, but from inside
the wagon she could discern little else. The shutters had been pulled and secured before they passed through the gate: other than the acrid scent of recent
fires and the occasional birdlike calls of Hikeda'ya sentries, she could not guess
what was happening outside.

"Why are we here so far from Hikeda'ya lands?" she asked Vordis. "Did any
of the Anchoresses tell you why we came here?"

"If they know, they said nothing. There was a battle. But it seems the queen
and her armies have been victorious. A great triumph." There was an odd flatness to her words.

Tzoja had no such divided loyalties, although she knew better than to say so.
When she thought about the mortals who must have been slaughtered she could
not forget they were her own people. But more than anything else, she was
frightened that her daughter Nezeru might have been involved in the fighting—
might even now be wounded, or worse, while her mother was kept in darkness
and ignorance.

Keep her safe, all you gods, she prayed. *And protect Viyeki too, wherever he may
be.* She wondered then whether her master and lover and might be here in
Naglimund—she had never been told where the queen had sent him—but that
possibility only added to her fear.

As the two women sat, ordinary conversation exhausted after so long in
captivity together, Tzoja heard a strange sound from outside the wagon. At first
she thought it was the wind, which had been fierce, but the noise seemed too
deep for that—a single peal of distant thunder that would not end. She could
feel it in her body as well as hear it, a rumble like the hoofbeats of many horses
galloping and galloping but never passing by. She heard a second sound then,
the squeaking of heavy wheels, and moved to the wagon's single window. The
wooden shutter had been tied closed from the outside, but when she pushed it
the shutter moved a little, and she could see purple evening sky around the
edges. She went back and picked up her wooden supper bowl.

"What are you doing, Tzoja?"

"Seeing what I can see." Back at the window, she pushed against the shutter until she had opened it as far as she could manage, then wedged the bowl into the gap to hold it open.

"Be careful!" said Vordis. "We will be punished if we are caught!"

"I know." She looked quickly from side to side through the narrow space to make certain none of the guards were standing close by, but it was hard to be certain: something blocked most of her view, a large gray shape like a stone wall, but it was slowly moving past them. Then an immense wheel rotated into view—for a moment the squeak of its axle was almost as loud as the rumble— and she pressed her eye against the gap.

"Something's out there!" she whispered. "Something big!"

She could feel Vordis standing behind her now, clutching her arm. As the great wheel circled past Tzoja saw that something long was tied to the wagon bed—the gray wall she had first seen. It tapered down as it passed, from an obstruction higher than the window where she stood to a massive shape like a monstrous snake.

Her heart fluttered as she realized that what she was seeing was a vast *tail*. A moment later, when the rest of the wagon had passed, she saw the creature that was pushing at the back of the wagon behind the monstrous tail—a manlike shape, but far bigger than any man. It turned its huge, hairy face toward her, and for a moment the gleaming, yellow-green eyes caught her own. The giant bared its teeth in a snarl and Tzoja's legs gave out from under her.

Vordis kneeled above her, chafing her wrists. "Tzoja! Tzoja, what happened? What did you see?"

She tried to explain but could only summon fragments. "There were monsters," she said at last. "One pushing another on a great wagon. Monsters."

"But why are they here?" Vordis asked in an ecstasy of fear. "And why did they bring us here? With such creatures?"

Tzoja felt empty and cold. Her own words seemed to come out of someone else's mouth, someone who had stopped feeling. "All the world is full of monsters now," she said. "Everywhere."

Jarnulf looked down at the splayed bodies of the two Sacrifices, their blood turning transparent as rain washed it away. He had spent so many years killing Hikeda'ya soldiers that it had become hard to think of them as anything but bundles of cooling meat. He had killed both of these with arrows, one shot in the neck and the other in the heart when he came to his fellow's aid, but all Jarnulf really wanted was the armor and cloak from one of the corpses. After he had pulled it off, he dragged the two bodies deeper into the forest and rolled them into a ravine, then wiped the blood off his hands with the fronds of some ferns.

He still had to be cautious. Far more Hikeda'ya were roaming the forest than he had suspected: from his hiding place in the treetops he had counted Sacrifices from at least three companies whose insignia he did not recognize. Even more strangely, he had seen some of them days earlier, but the queen's party had only just arrived today at Naglimund on the other side of the hill. Something was going on here in the forest his old masters called Oldheart—something unusual. At any other time Jarnulf would have felt compelled to investigate, but now his task was narrower and much more important. He meant to kill the queen of the Norns.

Jarnulf still did not know what had brought ancient Utuk'ku out of the mountain on a long journey to the mortal fortress, although he felt sure it had something to do with the dragon he had helped her Talons to capture. The blood of dragons was rare, but useful in many ways, both in the spells of the Order of Song as well as for its more immediately dangerous qualities. Jarnulf still had his own small pot of the stuff scraped from the mummified worm's claw on the mountainside, and he intended to put it to use. But before Jarnulf took her away from the rest of her kind, Nezeru had also let something slip—this Queen's Hand, the one she was part of, had recovered the bones of the Storm King's brother Hakatri from a northern island at Utuk'ku's order. What the Hikeda'ya might want with a bundle of ancient bones was beyond him, as it had been beyond Nezeru when he had asked her.

"The queen and Lord Akhenabi do not open their thoughts to Sacrifices like me," Nezeru had told him, and he had not doubted her ignorance, but the bones and the captive dragon had both been handed over to the Lord of Song, and now he and the queen were both here at Naglimund. Was that why there were so many other Hikeda'ya soldiers roaming the forest? Was Naglimund to be the launching-point of some invasion into the mortal lands to the south?

Jarnulf pushed these questions from his mind. His own course was set. If he succeeded, all speculation became pointless because everything would change. He had to wait until he found a chance to put an arrow into the deathless queen, then he had to make his shot count—likely the only shot he would get. If he worried only about that one thing, the world became a very simple place.

Even with his hood pulled low over his face, Jarnulf knew he did not look much like a real Sacrifice. He had rubbed his skin with white clay from a streambed to make it pale, and could imitate at least a little the liquid, gliding movements of a trained Hikeda'ya warrior, but he knew the imposture would not fool any true Hikeda'ya who came closer than a dozen yards. He not only had to find a spot that would provide him a clear shot, he had to manage it while remaining hidden from the sentries who would be walking the walls.

Though light or dark did not make much difference to the immortals because their sight was so much better than his own, Jarnulf still waited until twilight began to dim the sky before approaching the ruined fortress from the forested hillside. Rain was falling hard now and wind tormented the trees. He was pleased to see that one of the square guard towers in Naglimund's devastated curtain wall still stood, though its battlements had been badly damaged by fire. Sentries patrolled the walls on either side, but the tower itself seemed unguarded. Jarnulf kept downwind from any sentries he could see, and stayed close to the ground where he was shielded by thick undergrowth. He watched their movements for no little time until he was certain they were not entering the tower itself, then he crawled downhill through brambles and creepers toward the base of the curtain wall.

Both the tower and the walls on either side of it were cracked from the siege that had overthrown Naglimund, and gaps in the stone offered Jarnulf comparatively easy handholds, but the height and the wet walls still made climbing difficult. Halfway up, the wind rose in pitch and strength until he could feel it pushing him. He clung in place and waited for the storm to die down, but it quickly became clear to him that he would have a long wait. He resumed his ascent instead, more slowly now, and was buoyed by a sudden, hopeful thought.

If You have sent this storm to make it harder for the Hikeda'ya to hear me coming, O Lord, I thank You. For a moment, just a moment, he felt protected, God-armored, and it made his heart swell, until the wind almost swept him again from the damp, slippery wall.

He stopped just below the battlements and pressed himself tightly against the stones, waiting for the sentries to complete another circuit of the walls and turn away. When he saw their backs he sent up another silent prayer of gratitude, then scrambled up the last few cubits of the tower. But when he pulled himself over the scorched battlement he discovered that the center of the tower's wooden roof had mostly burned away, and that he was dangling headfirst over a long drop onto broken spars and sharp stones in the gutted interior. At last he found beams that would support his weight and made his way around to the inner side of the tower where he could peer down into the fortress.

Jarnulf had never seen the interior of Naglimund, but he doubted it had ever looked as devastated as it did now. Many sections of its great outwall had been thrown down and the inner wall that surrounded the keep had been even more thoroughly demolished. Most of the tall buildings at the center of the fortress were also little more than ruins, a graveyard of doorways and chimneys and rubble.

How did the Hikeda'ya manage so much destruction? he wondered. *Is the Lord of Song really so powerful?* But it seemed obvious that far more than even Akhenabi's formidable skills had been involved in the destruction. The Sacrifice troop that had come to meet Saomeji and his captured dragon had numbered fewer than a hundred fighters, but Jarnulf could see many more soldiers than that just in the courtyard below him, waiting in serried ranks beneath the heavy rain as though something important was about to happen. They stood in rigid silence around a cloth tent that looked more practical than ceremonial, a great expanse of dark fabric bulging and billowing in the strong winds. From what Jarnulf could see, the tent covered the ruins of more than half an Aedonite church, although the destruction had not extended to the steeple, which seemed strange to him. Why bother to tear down the enemy's church and leave the towering steeple with its golden Tree untouched?

Jarnulf made the holy sign on his breast and mumbled another prayer. *For this and the desecration of so many of Your houses, Lord, lend me strength to avenge You.*

A sudden rattling from below startled him; Jarnulf crouched down before recognizing the sound as a muster-drum. Something was going on where the Sacrifices had gathered below, but most of it was hidden from his sight beneath the great, rippling tent.

The drum sounded again, but this time the noise was swallowed by a peal of thunder that seemed to come from right above Jarnulf's head. Black storm clouds were writhing above the keep like worms, but as hard as the wind blew, the clouds did not disperse. Instead, they seemed to draw closer together into a great and growing ink-black knot.

A movement near the inner keep drew his gaze down from the ugliness of the sky. Something large was rolling across the commons toward the tent and the waiting soldiers. The cart's driver and the waiting Hikeda'ya seemed as minute as flies to him, but Jarnulf had no trouble recognizing the monstrous thing strapped to the bed of the long wagon, nor the hairy, manlike creature laboring along behind it, pushing the cart while a team of war-goats pulled from the front. Even Goh Gam Gar appeared childlike in comparison with the serpentine beast on the cart, though Jarnulf knew the giant's true size.

Then he saw the wagons following the dragon-cart across the castle commons, all headed toward the great, billowing tent. All other thoughts flew from his mind as if the moaning wind had snatched them away, because the first and largest wagon bore the sacred Hamakha serpent crest.

Jarnulf lifted his bow from his back and took the string in its oilskin wrap out of his purse. He had practiced stringing the bow hundreds of times, and it was a matter of only a few heartbeats before he finished. The wind was a horror, gusting from different directions, but there were also moments of calm; he prayed God would send him one at the time he needed it. He took out the arrow with a cropped feather and the pot containing a small amount of dragon's blood and set them beside him on the burnt boards, then took out a second arrow and set it close beside them just in case the first arrow broke, but he did not think he would have enough time to use it. One failed shot at the queen and she would be surrounded by her guards.

Finished with his preparations, he lifted his head and saw that something was happening at the edge of the tent—a struggle between the dragon, which seemed to be trying to break free of its bonds, and the giant Goh Gam Gar. The door of the queen's wagon was open, and Jarnulf saw a flash of her silver mask as she moved into the doorway. He snatched up his bow, heart rabbiting. All the time he had prepared, all the years he had lived with his hatred, and now the moment had finally come.

But even as he set his arrow on the string and reached for the pot of dragon's blood, which he hoped would be poisonous enough to undo even Utuk'ku the

Deathless, the queen's guards, alarmed by the dragon's ferocity, fell back around the steps of the wagon and drew their white shields together into a single over-lapping wall in front of the queen, like a flower closing its petals at sunset. Jarnulf lowered the bow and crouched behind the parapet again, waiting.

It took no little time for them to subdue the dragon, and Jarnulf did his best to slow his racing pulse. When all seemed calm again, he dipped his arrowhead into the pot of black blood, trying to think only of that brief, fatal instant when he would see the queen revealed, and then dipped the point of the second arrow in and laid it on the beam where he could reach it swiftly if he was in need.

The heads of both arrows were well-wrought iron, but within moments they were giving off thin wisps of smoke. Thunder cracked and rolled across the sky; lightning flared across the whole of the horizon, turning the night sky a glow-ing white. Jarnulf prayed that the Queen's Teeth would choose that moment to unlock their shields, but instead they began to march from the wagon toward the tent, the queen still hidden in their midst, and Jarnulf could only murmur whispered curses.

I will wait, then, he told himself. *I will wait until she comes out from beneath the covering again. There will be a moment. God will give me a moment.*

But if God wanted Jarnulf to succeed, He seemed uninterested in bending the weather to His will. The winds grew even fiercer and the thunder bayed louder, ever louder, until the very tower beneath him seemed to shake in fear.

It will be a very long shot, he told himself. *The wind will make it very difficult. But this may be the only shot I am ever given and I must not miss. Strengthen my arm, I beg you, O Lord. Strengthen my eye.*

But even as he waited, unable to see what was happening beneath the great tent, Jarnulf could feel the very air around him grow prickly, as though a thousand tiny thorns pierced his flesh. It was all he could do not to scratch at himself; his arms trembled as he held the bowstring taut. *Sorcery*, he thought, hackles rising. *Protect me from the Singers' dark tricks, O Lord. Give me the strength and courage to do Your will.*

Then he felt something abruptly change, like a window thrown open in the middle of a freezing storm. A great cold swept through him and into him, a deadening frost that suddenly turned his innards to ice. It did not come from any single direction, like the wind, but from everywhere at once, and it clutched at him and squeezed until he lost track of the difference between up and down, between standing and falling. Jarnulf grabbed at the parapet, swaying, light-headed, and looked in alarm to see whether his movements had attracted atten-tion, but the sentries on the walls were all staring down toward the hidden ceremony beneath the tent, motionless as statues.

Jarnulf's sensation of cold horror grew stronger and stronger. It felt as though something was trying to pull him apart, to crawl inside him. The great knot of clouds above the fortress was crow-black now, and its outer strands lashed like the legs of some terrible, legendary sea creature. He did his best to lift his bow, to train the arrow on the spot where the queen and her guards would appear, but blood was pounding in his temples so powerfully that he could hardly see. Spots of light danced before his eyes, seeming to match the prickling of his skin, but it was the sense of dreadful, endless spaces yawning before him that pushed everything else aside.

God save me! He heard his own voice screaming, but he could not tell whether it was out loud or inside his own head. *God save us all, they have opened up Hell itself!*

And then he found himself scrambling over the edge of the tower, not toward his target but away, away from the gaping hole in the world, away from the breathing heart of darkness the queen and her minions had flung open. He could make sense only of instants, cracks in the tower wall, bright white cracks across the sky, howling wind and horizontal rain. He fell the last dozen feet to the hard earth, then he crawled, bruised and gasping, into the underbrush at the base of the hill, aware only of his consuming need to escape that awful, life-devouring nothingness.

When he came back to himself Jarnulf was lying on his side in a stand of bracken, panting like a dying buck. Every muscle ached as though he had been beaten with cudgels. His bow was nowhere to be seen—in his unreasoning horror, he had left it on the tower top. His hand still clutched the arrow, but all that remained of the iron arrowhead intended for the queen's heart was a smoking black sliver.

I have failed—failed You, my God, and myself. He was empty, strengthless, beyond any feeling but despair. *I have failed all the world.*

It had been fearful enough back on that day in the Chamber of the Well when the queen had summoned Ommu of the Red Hand back to life and the world. But Viyeki found it even more dismaying to feel something like that happening under open skies in the middle of the mortal lands.

Queen Utuk'ku's great train of wagons and soldiers reached the ruined fortress just before the middle of the night, climbing slowly under lowering skies up the steep switchbacks from the river valley. As soon as the queen's massive carriage passed through the gates, the winds began to blow harder and harder, howling like all the souls swallowed by Unbeing when the Garden disappeared.

The team of black goats pulled Utuk'ku's wagon across the great open space of the commons, then halted at last before the tumbled gatehouse of what had once been the castle's great hall. Viyeki, standing beside Pratiki in the inner keep, surrounded by the prince-templar's guards, expected that the queen would soon emerge. His heart was beating so swiftly that he felt short of breath, but as the winds rose to a painful pitch and tattered clouds raced across the sky in front of the descending moon, Utuk'ku did not appear. Even the shaggy black goats seemed preternaturally still, their yellow eyes empty, only an occasional movement of their jaws or flick of their ears showing that they were not made of stone.

Viyeki and the rest waited. The air had become oppressively close now, like the tunnels in Nakkiga's hot depths, and for the first time in his life he felt himself utterly dislocated from his blood, from the world into which he had been born and had lived all his life. In a barely-contained panic he did not entirely understand, he asked Pratiki, "Why does the queen not come out? Is she ill?"

"May the Garden forbid it," said the prince-templar quietly. "But I think she waits for an auspicious hour. When the moon has set, perhaps, or at the moment of middle-night."

Viyeki looked quickly from side to side, but other than Pratiki's guards, none of the other Hikeda'ya were close enough to hear them. "But why? I still do not understand, Serenity. What was the purpose of coming here? Of Ruyan's armor and the dragon?"

"I do not pretend to understand all," said the prince-templar, his pale features composed to show no expression. "It is the queen's desire. It is some cleverness of Akhenabi's, I do not doubt."

In that moment, Viyeki thought he heard a faint, almost imperceptible sound of distaste in Pratiki's words. *Even the prince-templar distrusts the Lord of Song,* he realized, and suddenly many things seemed clearer to him. *Is that why Pratiki was sent here? Not because of what the queen wants him to do, but because some in the court do not want him, a well-loved figure who is one of the queen's closest relatives, to remain behind in Nakkiga with Utuk'ku gone?*

Does Akhenabi fear Pratiki? Then another, even stranger thought came to him, one that for a moment made him forget the sky, the broken walls, even the royal wagon waiting silently only a few paces away. *Does the Mother of All fear Pratiki, too?*

He could not consider that, not without risking thoughts that might lead to his own execution if the queen somehow overheard them.

She is the Mother of the People, he thought, trying to bury his treacherous musings. *I praise her. I must praise her. She is our soul and our salvation.* It had not been so long ago that he had believed it utterly, but now he felt as though he were coming apart inside.

Another hour passed. The winds rose to a shrieking pitch and rain beat down on the ground, spattering mud against the ruined walls of the fortress. At last, just when Viyeki thought his fearful anticipation might make him swoon or cry out in despair, he heard the creaking of huge wooden wheels. These wheels did not belong to the queen's wagon, though, which remained shuttered and silent before the gate of the inner keep: another wagon was rolling forward from the great mass of vehicles arrayed just inside the fortress walls. This wagon was as long as the queen's, but open like a farmer's oxcart. It was also perhaps the strangest thing Viyeki had ever seen.

The cart was pulled by more of the great, black goats, creatures bigger even than war horses, but it was also pushed from behind by the largest giant Viyeki had ever seen, a huge, dirty gray creature twice the height of the tallest Sacrifice soldier, with arms like tree trunks and eyes that gleamed foxfire-bright by starlight. But even this creature was as nothing compared to the thing that lay trussed on the cart—a dragon. A *living* dragon, Viyeki saw as its tail writhed beneath the restraining ropes. He had thought he was beyond astonishment, but here was a living dragon, captured and bound, being pushed slowly across the uneven ground of the mortal keep. He could hear the monstrous creature rumbling like an earth tremor, its growl so deep it was hard to separate it from the swelling thunder.

The dragon-cart squeaked slowly past the gatehouse and continued toward Ruyan's tomb where it lay beneath the wind-strummed tent on the side of the fortress nearest the great hill.

"Stay, Magister," Pratiki told him quietly, though Viyeki had not considered moving, had barely realized he had a body that could move. "We wait for the queen."

"It is alive," was all Viyeki could think of to say.

"An astounding feat, capturing such a beast without killing it," Pratiki replied. "I was told that it was . . ." The prince-templar stopped abruptly. Viyeki waited for him to finish, but it quickly became clear that His Serene Highness would not say more.

After the dragon-cart had trundled past, half of the Queen's Teeth waiting beside her wagon formed up into new lines in front of it. A single drum began to pound; the white-armored guards began to march after the dragon. The driver of Queen Utuk'ku's wagon, who had been motionless for so long that Viyeki had forgotten he was there, unfurled his whip and snapped it, and the silent black goats began to move. Their traces pulled taut, then the great wheels of the queen's wagon turned and the carriage made its way slowly after the marching Teeth as the rest of her guards fell in behind her.

"And now we follow, too," Pratiki said. "Wear your most devout face, High Magister. We are in foreign lands."

Pratiki strode out, followed by his guards. Viyeki hurried after him, still trying to make sense of the prince-templar's words.

Lord Akhenabi himself, as well as General Kikiti, High Singer Sogeyu, and many other high members of their respective orders, had all been waiting beneath the tented roof since the queen's arrival. Now the driver of the dragon-cart, with help from the groaning, yoked giant, brought the long wagon to a halt beside the open crypt as well. Viyeki did not much wish to join Kikiti and the others, and was relieved when Pratiki stopped and took up a position at the outer edge of the billowing nettle-cloth roof. Viyeki had no idea what was going to happen and wished he could ask, but he stayed silent. Did no one else feel what he did, that a door was about to be opened and something extraordinary and horrible was about to be released? Did that feeling not trouble any of them? His growing sense of dread was so strong it was all he could do not to turn and walk away.

Even the captive dragon seemed to sense it. Now that he could see it more fully, Viyeki could not take his eyes off the imprisoned beast. It was moving against its restraints, though it was still tightly bound. The tip of its tail had pulled free and wriggled like some monstrous earth-crawling worm. Its jaws were wrapped in heavy rope, but its eyes, the dazzling color of a sunset, had snapped open, and the oddly jagged black pupils swiveled to watch every nearby movement.

Now the Queen's Teeth and the queen's wagon at last reached the tent. At the noise of their approach the dragon began to squirm even harder beneath the many thick ropes that held it. As the queen's wagon rolled to a halt the Teeth guards divided themselves into two lines, making an aisle that led from the wagon's steps to the covering over the crypt. Another thunderburst rolled across the sky as the door above the steps opened.

Utuk'ku herself appeared in the doorway, a small, slender figure robed all in white, like a mourner or a corpse. She did not step forward at first, only stood looking out at the great pit from behind her mask, at the waiting Sacrifices and Singers and the bound dragon. Then she began to walk down the steps, and though she moved carefully, she seemed so much stronger and more sure in her movements than the last time Viyeki had seen her, when she had brought Ommu back from the dead lands, that for a brief instant Viyeki almost believed that it must be some impostor instead of Utuk'ku herself. Then her voice rolled through his thoughts with a force that almost drove him to his knees, and all doubt disappeared.

Take me to the traitor's tomb, the queen's voice said. *Let us do what we have come to do. What we have waited so long to do.*

It was plain from the expressions of even the most stolid Sacrifices that everyone present had heard her words and felt their power. Even Sogeyu the Singer lifted a trembling hand to her forehead, as though the queen's voice had pierced her like a blade. Only Akhenabi seemed unmoved. The Lord of Song stepped forward as the queen reached the bottom of the stairs and spread his arms in ceremonial welcome, sleeves whipping in the wind like pennants.

Then, with a crack like the splitting of a rock face, one of the ropes that bound the dragon's tail snapped; a moment later the entire bottom half of its coiling tail was free. It lashed back and forth, swinging so close to the giant's face that the huge, manlike beast let go of the wagon and stumbled a step backward before reaching the end of the chains that kept him yoked to the wagon's huge bed. Akhenabi's halfblood servant rushed forward, waving a crystal rod at the giant, but the dragon's tail swept out again and struck the halfblood, who tumbled head over heels, the goad flying into the darkness to land somewhere on the muddy ground. Lightning flashed again as the dragon strained against the restraints around its upper body and neck. Another of the massive ropes snapped with a crack that could be heard even above the rolling thunder. The dragon's head lifted a full cubit off the wagon bed, stretching the bonds even farther.

Then Akhenabi strode forward. The lightning flashed once more, and his mask of flesh seemed the face of a moving corpse, slack and lifeless, but with terrible, bright eyes. He lifted his arms and spoke a single word that Viyeki could not hear or understand. The giant, who had been crouched at the end of his chains, out of reach of the bludgeoning tail, let out a horrid screech and fell to the ground, rolling, hands on its huge, misshapen head.

"Get up, monster!" shouted the Lord of Song.

The giant staggered to its feet, still clutching its head, and then took a stumbling step forward and grabbed at the dragon's flailing tail. For a moment the giant was thrown off-balance and nearly lost its grip, but the shaggy, manlike beast held on, yellow teeth clenched, and then let one hand go to grab at the wagon wheel. The giant let out another inhuman bellow, then Akhenabi shouted again and a dozen Sacrifices and a pair of Singers rushed forward to aid it. As the giant clung desperately to the dragon's immense, muscular tail the Sacrifices grabbed at it as well, and the two Singers hurriedly draped a cloth over the dragon's head. Viyeki guessed it was soaked in *kei-vishaa*, because within a few heartbeats the dragon's struggles began to slow; after a short time it stopped moving entirely but for the gradual heaving of its vast chest. More Sacrifices hurried forward with ropes, and soon they had the dragon's tail and neck tightly bound to the cart once more.

Only then did Viyeki look toward the queen, but he could not see her. The stairs of her wagon were surrounded by her Teeth, more than a dozen guards, and their white shields had been lifted and locked around her as if in imitation of the dragon's own scales.

"If the beast does not survive because of your carelessness, giant," said Akhenabi loudly, "I will take off your wretched skin, piece by piece."

The giant, still shackled to the back of the cart, fell onto all fours, groaning.

The shields of the queen's guards now folded back and the slender, pale form of Utuk'ku stepped out. The guards quickly fell into place around her once more and escorted her beneath the great tent roof. Though she took only two dozen steps, it seemed clear to Viyeki that something had put strength back into those ageless limbs.

"Swiftly now!" cried Akhenabi in his deep, rasping voice. "It is time, and past time. The hour when the world changes! Swiftly!"

And as Viyeki watched, Singers in their redblack cloaks began to scurry out of the depths of the rippling tent like agitated beetles. Four of them appeared with a litter on which was stretched what Viyeki took at first for a body, but a white glare of lightning across the sky revealed the fine gold wires and crystal scales of Ruyan Ve's armor, cleaned and polished. Only as the bearers set it down before the queen—far more reverently than when they had poured out Ruyan's dust onto the wet ground—could Viyeki see the brown skull that now sat in the open gorget.

But Ruyan was dust, he realized. *They have clothed Hakatri's bones in the Changeling's armor.*

A fifth Singer walked close behind the litter, solemnly carrying Ruyan's cylindrical helm. The weird, masklike face on the helmet seemed to stare back at those watching, its eyes and mouth round with surprise. Viyeki looked at Pratiki, and thought he saw a shadow of unhappiness in the set of the prince-templar's lips, but he no longer trusted his own impressions.

Several more Singers now clustered around the dragon. Three of them wrestled an ornamental urn of witchwood into place beneath the sleeping monster's head, while another stepped forward holding something shiny in a gloved hand. Viyeki thought this one might be Sogeyu herself, but the cloth mask wrapped around her face made it hard to be certain. She placed the shiny thing—a large, sharp, and apparently hollow silver spike—against the dragon's throat just beneath the jaw. Another Singer approached with a hammer. It was no ceremonial instrument, but a brutal-looking maul that had seen much use, and as Sogeyu held the spike in place, the maul swung and thumped home, forcing the spike into the dragon's throat. A shudder ran through the creature from head to tail, but the ropes held and the *kei-vishaa* kept the prisoned beast insensible. An instant later a jet of steaming black blood spurted from the hollow spike to splatter against the rim of the urn; many of those watching gasped or groaned at the sight. Other Singers, also masked and gloved, hurried to tip the urn to a better angle to catch the pulsing blood as it gushed in great, gleaming arcs. Within moments the Singers and the dragon's head had vanished in a growing cloud of vapor. The great beast did not move again.

Dragon's blood. The bones of a dead Zida'ya prince. The armor of the great lord of the Changeling folk. Viyeki felt not just fearful but actually ill. The Singers ranged beneath the tent now raised their voices in a harsh, sharp-edged chant that briefly outshouted the thunder. *Such a dark, ugly song*, he thought. *Such dark old magicks. What good can come from any of this?*

As if she had heard his disloyal thoughts, Utuk'ku's silver mask swiveled across those watching, freezing Viyeki like a startled animal. She raised her hand, and for a moment he thought she was about to single him out for some terrible punishment, but instead Akhenabi glided toward her and kneeled at her feet.

Now the Opening of the Mouth and the Song of Resurrection.

The queen's thought was still echoing in Viyeki's head like the tolling of a great stone bell as Akhenabi rose and made his way to the urn. Only a few black drops now trickled from the spike in the dragon's neck. The great beast seemed to have settled lower in death, flattening like a bellows that had lost its air. One of Akhenabi's Singers gave the Lord of Song a witchwood ladle, which he dipped into the urn to draw out a pitchy spoonful of blood. He carried the smoking stuff to the litter, which had been lifted by two more Singers at a steep angle, until it almost looked as though Ruyan's armor stood waiting. Akhenabi pried open the mouth of the yellowed skull—for an instant Viyeki caught sight of the golden wires that held it to the neck bones inside the armor—then poured the contents of the ladle into the mouth as the skull disappeared within a cloud of steam.

Akhenabi stepped back. Another Singer hurried forward with the masklike helmet, which the Lord of Song then placed over the skull until the bottom sat squarely on the high gorget. The wind, which had slowed for a moment, now rose to a shrieking pitch once more; the tent roof bulged upward in some places, while in others it pressed down as though a giant hand was feeling for those beneath. The guy-ropes that held the great cloth swayed and sang under the wind's rough handling, and it seemed at any moment the whole covering might fly away. Viyeki heard the queen's voice chanting in his head, echoed by Akhenabi and Sogeyu and the Singers, but it was impossible to separate out their words (if that rhythmic, vengeful-sounding song contained any words at all) from the storm winds and the continuing thunder.

The door of a wagon that he had not noticed, which had been pulled to only a short distance from where the queen herself stood, now swung open. Red light spilled out of the doorway. With it came a feeling of such immense emptiness that Viyeki shook all over and had to struggle to stay on his feet. An imprecise figure took shape in the wagon's doorway, a thing of fluttering bandages and fiery light.

Ommu the Whisperer had joined her power to the queen's.

Viyeki's head was empty of everything but the shrieking wind and the now constant bellowing of thunder. He could not stand to look at Ommu for more than an instant, but everywhere else he turned his gaze he saw chaos. Some of the Singers were now leaping and twitching in fits. Many Sacrifices had fallen to the ground, dropping their weapons, their helmets rolling loose like severed heads. Even as he felt the great hole that had been opened into the very substance of the world, he could also feel that whatever was on the other side was fighting not to be drawn through. The air had grown thick and moist, nearly impossible to breathe: Viyeki saw his people shrieking and clutching their heads, but still the moaning song went on and on and the sky flashed light and bellowed like an angry beast.

Darkness swallowed everything.

For a long moment after sight and thought came back to him, Viyeki believed the entire world had been turned sideways. Then he realized he had fallen to the ground. Laboriously, he levered himself onto his hands and knees. The thunder had ended but the rain still poured down. The wind had pulled the huge tented roof to tatters, and Viyeki was crouching in a cold puddle.

Something moved, catching his eye. The crystal-plated armor of Ruyan Vé stood upright by itself now, arms slowly spreading as if in astonishment, gloved fingers clawing the air. The Singers who had held the litter lay face-down on the ground beside it, either dead, senseless, or prostrated by awe and terror. The armored thing took a step, swayed, took another step. It looked up at a sky full of thunderheads, then turned to look at the queen, one of the few figures still standing upright.

For the moment the two empty faces simply stared at each other, the queen's expressionless silver mask and the crystal-eyed helmet of Ruyan.

You have come back to us, Hakatri of the Sa'onserei, the queen said. *Now you will do what must be done. Now we will end the cursed mortals.*

Hakatri, if it was indeed him, seemed to look at her for a long moment, then threw back his head and raised his hands toward the hidden stars. He screamed— not just in thought, like Utuk'ku's words, but in sound as well, a cry so loud and terrible that it echoed from every stone of the fallen castle and all along the hillside above, a cry so full of anguish and rage and desperation that all those climbing to their feet dropped back onto their knees. Viyeki's very thoughts seemed to catch fire and burn, blazing and then turning to ash, floating away, even as the awful cry went on and on.

Dark shapes began to fall from the clouded night sky, pattering to the ground all across the courtyard. Viyeki looked down and saw a dead bird lying beside him, but could not understand why it was there. Though the ruined fortress had now gone silent but for the wind and the moans of those who could not rise, Sacrifices and Singers alike scattered on the muddy ground like the bleeding survivors of a dreadful battle, Viyeki could still hear Hakatri's scream echoing in his mind. He knew with terrible certainty that he would never be free of it, no matter how long he lived.

55

My Enemy

As she led Morgan up the stairs into the ruined splendor of the Place of Sky-Watching, Tanahaya saw with a sinking heart that Hikeda'ya soldiers had already fought their way inside the great chamber. Perhaps a dozen of the Pure were fighting hand to hand against them, but they were outnumbered by more than two to one, white robes almost swallowed up by the dark garb of the Norn attackers.

"Morgan, stay!" she called, but the mortal youth came leaping up the stairs behind her, so that she had to put out her arm to keep him from charging into the midst of the fray. Something was amiss here and she needed a moment to understand it.

The attackers were not just ordinary Hikeda'ya Sacrifices, she saw: they wore dark, hooded cloaks, but although rain was falling through the ancient stone web of the domed ceiling, the Sacrifices were famously contemptuous of weather. These warriors must be cloaked for concealment and stealth, she decided, and that was a mark of the Talons, Queen Utuk'ku's elite fighters and spies. These were not the ordinary soldiers she had seen in the forest—these had come specifically to attack Da'ai Chikiza and the Pure. Why?

As she hesitated, Vinyedu and other Pure poured out of the stairwell, then pushed past her and threw themselves against the Hikeda'ya. The rest of Da'ai Chikiza's defenders were falling back—several of the Pure had already fallen—and Tanahaya knew she should carry her blade to the fight, but she could not help hearing the words of her master Himano: *"When something seems not to fit, look for a missing piece."* If her use of the Witness had touched off this attack, how had it begun so quickly? Why would the Queen's Talons have been waiting for this very moment to strike when Vinyedu had said that the Hikeda'ya had been lurking on the edges of Da'ai Chikiza for several moons?

Tanahaya could not hold Morgan back any longer, nor could she leave the others to fight alone, but she knew something was very wrong and that she would regret not giving it proper thought. "Forward, then," she told Morgan. "But stay behind me no matter what happens. No, behind me! We are fighting the Norn Queen's elite warriors."

She could almost smell his anger at her warning, but Tanahaya could not imagine letting the young prince die under her protection, not after she had just told Jiriki and Aditu that he was alive. She led him through toppled and unbalanced pillars toward the place where the Pure were trying to defend the eastern portal of the great sky-chamber.

"We must keep them here until the rest of our people in the city can come to our aid," Vinyedu called to Tanahaya. The invading Hikeda'ya seemed content for the moment merely to push the Pure farther away from the center of the chamber and thus limit their movements, but Tanahay knew that Sacrifice archers would soon join the rest of their foes and then the fight here would become hopeless. Still, a desperate question was burning in her thoughts, and she had only this one moment to ask it.

"Vinyedu, has that happened before? Have Akhenabi or some other powers among the Hikeda'ya taken control of the Witness?"

"What are you talking about?" Vinyedu avoided a Hikeda'ya sword-thrust, knocking it aside with her own blade; while the Talon fighter was off-balance, one of the other Pure drove a spear through his neck and he fell to the stone floor, coughing out blood. *"They have never wrested it from me, though I have used it many times. Now stop wasting breath. We must hold this door until more of my people can come to help us."*

Tanahaya knew that she was not wrong in her concern, but also realized that death would silence her inquiries forever, so she gave her attention to keeping herself and the mortal prince alive.

One of the Talons suddenly leaped onto the top of a broken pillar and crouched above the fighting for a moment, like a hawk ready to stoop. An instant later he flung himself down, cloak billowing, and landed on his feet behind Tanahaya. Nothing stood between him and Morgan, and though the mortal youth did his best to defend himself he was badly overmatched; he could only struggle to keep his blade up as he stumbled backward toward the wall. Tanahaya knew that was what the attacker wanted, that when the youth had run out of room to retreat he would be quickly skewered, but she was too far away to reach them before the fight was over.

She bent to snatch up a chunk of stone that had fallen from one of the columns and threw it at the Hikeda'ya, who was intent only on the mortal boy. The Garden favored her aim: Tanahaya saw it crunch against the attacker's neck and knock him staggering. As the Talon lowered his sword to try to regain his balance, Morgan saw the chance and thrust his sword into the attacker's side, a lucky blow between two pieces of the witchwood armor; when he yanked his blade away again a great freshet of blood followed. The Talon took a few steps in a bewildered circle before dropping to his knees, hands cupping the pulsing hole beneath his bottom rib. Tanahaya stabbed him in the neck and kicked him to the floor.

"That was luck—for both of us!" she shouted at Morgan. "Now stay close to me!"

But as she turned back to the fighting it was clear that the dispatch of the

Talon had only been a moment's respite. Other dark shapes were now swarming into the chamber from other entrances, and Tanahaya knew that even if she and the city's white-clad defenders fought to the last breath, there were not enough of them to hold the attackers at bay more than a short while. Where were the rest of the Pure? Or were they already under attack in other parts of Da'ai Chikiza?

Shisae'ron, Shisae'ron, she sang silently to herself, and in that instant could hear her mother's voice across the years, as if even now she sat beside her. *Land of beautiful water. Land of soft grass. I will never see you again, but in my heart you live forever.* Tanahaya thought it strange that the story of her life would end here, beneath a gray, rainy sky in the ruins of a city she had never lived in, and even stranger that the life of a scholar should end on the point of a kinsman's sword.

As she stepped up to stand shoulder to shoulder with the remaining Pure once more, her eye briefly swept across the decrepit stone of the roof canopy and the columns that time and earth movement had slowly begun to pull into pieces. A memory struck her. Her mother's most beloved songs had been those of Benhaya, the ancient warrior-poet. One of his famous *numi* had a favorite of Himano's as well:

> *Find the melody of the conflict—find its rhythm.*
> *Change that rhythm.*
> *Introduce new melodies that unravel your opponent's song and make it anew.*
> *Thus will seeming defeat be turned into something useful, even beautiful.*

Himano had quoted it in discussions of scholarly argument and the search for truth, but at the moment the only thing that mattered was keeping herself and Morgan alive. *Blessings on your memory, Mother,* she thought. *Blessings on your memory, Himano my teacher. You have given me the gift of hope.*

She had no time to explain her idea to Morgan, but did her best to stay between him and the worst of the fighting as she threw down her pack and began to dig inside it. Hikeda'ya archers were pushing in at the far side of the chamber; already black shafts were leaping across the wide room so swiftly that she could not see them in the shadows but could only hear them as they passed. She found her coil of rope and yanked it free of the pack, then quickly tied one end around the hilt of her dagger. "Stay behind the others!" she told Morgan, then sank her fingers into the cracks of the nearest pillar and began climbing. The top of the column had long since fallen away, but the shaft still stretched up almost three times her own height. She tried to keep the uneven cylinder of weather-pitted stone between her and the Hikeda'ya arrows as she climbed. The pillar been made in pieces that had originally been stacked together in perfect symmetry, but centuries of neglect had created many places where she could catch a broad gap and swiftly pull herself upward.

At the top of the broken pillar, still trying to stay hidden from the enemy archers, Tanahaya swung the weighted length of rope in a broad circle before letting it go, so that the dagger at the end drew it upward toward the immense stone spider's web—all that remained of the Place of Sky-Watching's once-famous ceiling. The first cast missed, but she spun the rope harder the next time and saw the knife sail up and over a branch of the arched stone lattice. She slackened the rope to let it drop down, then found a boss of stone where she could tie the loop tightly in place, linking the pillar on which she clung to the cracked web of the ceiling.

"Morgan!" she called when the rope was tied. "Move back to the doorway—now!"

A couple of the Pure glanced up at what she was doing, but they were pressed hard from several sides by black-cloaked Talons. Another arrow flew past her, buzzing like a wasp, but she ignored it and grabbed at a crack in the pillar with one hand, then bent herself backward until she could touch the wall behind her with her other hand. Next she put her feet against the pillar and extended herself between it and the nearby wall, then moved her other hand to the wall as well, so that she stretched between wall and pillar. Struggling to keep her back rigid, she straightened her legs and began to push at the great cylinder of stone.

The section of column she was pushing gave a little, but the scrape of stone was so small it was lost in the noisy clash of witchwood and bronze weapons. Tanahaya did not dare look down to see where Morgan was—everything depended on the next few seconds. She set her feet more squarely and pushed until she was almost horizontal between pillar and wall, but though the piece of column slid again it was only a little way, and she was unable to make it topple.

Something struck her then, a blow that almost knocked her from her dangerous, upside-down position, followed by a sensation of weakness and cold. An arrow stood quivering in her shoulder. Dizziness swam up her spine and into her skull, but she dared not let anything stop her. She was already beginning to believe her effort was pointless—she was simply not strong enough to make even a half-crumbled stone pillar collapse—but she had to try.

"*Shisae'ron,*" she sang, in part to distract herself from the pain of her wound, and this time the words came from her mouth as well as her thoughts—breathless and shaky, but something to hang onto in that moment of last effort. "*Shisae'ron, my heart . . . !*"

And then she could hear, feel, sense someone just below her, also pushing. She looked down and saw that Vinyedu the mistress of the Pure had taken up a position below her between the column and the wall but the reverse of Tanahaya's, Vinyedu's feet against the wall and her hands against the column.

"*For Kementari!*" Vinyedu cried through clenched teeth, her face a mask of effort, her eyes so wide the whites showed at the bottom. "*Kementari, may memory never fade!*"

And suddenly, with a long, scraping sound like the hiss of a giant serpent, the piece of column beneath her feet lurched forward, and she and Vinyedu both tumbled to the floor. The upper part of the pillar wobbled, but for a

moment it seemed nothing else would happen. Tanahaya lay half on top of
Vinyedu at the pillar's base, sick with hopelessness at her failure.

Then the top of the pillar slowly tipped out and downward. The rope went
taut and yanked loose a section of the ceiling's web of stone. Tanahaya heard a
loud cracking, as if the ice on a frozen lake was parting, then more shards of
stone began to fall from the ceiling.

She had only a few moments to huddle over Vinyedu, who had struck her
head in the fall and lay senseless. More deep groans and cracks came from above
her. For an instant, the entire chamber seemed to shiver, then the massive stony
filigree broke apart and began to fall, some of the chunks as large as banquet
tables. Above the sound of shearing stone she heard screams of agony from the
Hikeda'ya, and some that might have been the Pure as well. For a brief moment
it seemed some massive creature had lifted the Place of Sky-Watching like a
child's toy and begun to shake it into pieces. Then something struck her and
wiped away her entire world in a single burst of silent whiteness.

Qina hacked at the reeds with her knife, reflecting for perhaps the hundredth
time on how small and inadequate the blade was for such a chore.

"For a fellow who loves to slide on thin ice above freezing water," she said,
"I would think my beloved would not have such a problem with boats."

Snenneq, who because of his bulk was following her, smacked at a few reeds
with an impatient wave of his hand. "They are doubtful things, boats. One
moment you are upon the water and life is good. Next moment you are under
it, and life is less so."

"So it is better to trudge and slash our way alongside the stream, enjoying
all of the biting insects and none of the swift travel?"

Snenneq gave her a sorrowful look. His insistence on approaching the ancient Sithi city on foot had been the source of discord for several days. "Which
would you rather have, my bride-to-be, a swift trip or a happy Snenneq?"

"That is not a question whose answer you wish to hear, I think."

She could not understand him sometimes. So brave and full of confidence
when he was climbing a dangerous cliffside or sliding on ice, he became a child
at the mere thought of traveling on water, or of getting into it at all. In all their
summers together at Blue Mud Lake she had never seen him even wade in the
shallows. He had always told her that he had other, more important things to
do, but now she knew the truth. "A Singing Man cannot turn away from ex-
periencing things," she told him grumpily. "My father often says that."

"Your father is a wise man, but he cannot tame my fearful heart like he
tames wild wolves. It does no good to shame me, Qina. There is no help for it.
The thought of boats turns my heart to something tiny and chill."

It was not as though they were avoiding getting wet by sticking to the riverbanks, she reflected sourly. It had rained on and off for several days—not the warm rains they had felt earlier in the year, but the cold, heavy rains of winter—and despite her oiled leathers she felt sodden and unhappy. Little prickly things had worked their way into every crevice beneath her clothing. She could only hope they were bits of river plants and reeds and not crawling things that would bite her all night, but she was fairly certain they would prove to be the latter.

"May we at least find a place to stop and perhaps clean ourselves and sleep?" she asked. "We have seen no sign of your stone gates yet, or bridges, or whatever it is you look for, and the sun is almost gone."

"You are right about that," he said. "Look, there is Sedda in the sky, waiting for the dark to fall so she can shine." He pointed at the ghostly white moon where it hung against the deepening blue of the afternoon. "Perhaps it is time to look for somewhere we—"

Qina made the sign for silence. For once—perhaps because he was tired and short of breath—Snenneq did not need to be told twice. He moved up behind her and waited.

"What do you hear?" he whispered at last, so close to her ear that she could feel his warm breath despite the cold breeze blowing down the river valley.

She shook her head. She was not entirely certain, but thought she had heard a splashing that seemed out of keeping with the general noises of the river. These shadowy backwaters surrounded by waving reeds were exactly the sorts of places where voracious Qallipuk often lay in wait, though they had not seen one since the outward journey with Morgan.

After standing some long moments in silence, Qina still had not heard a repetition of the noise that had startled her, and was just about to continue when she heard it again—a series of splashes, each like a fish breaking water to take a fly, but too numerous to be fish this early in the afternoon. She turned to see if Snenneq had heard it too, and could tell by his wide eyes that he had. The noise was definitely coming from the river, perhaps less than a stone's throw from where they were now crouching in the reeds.

"Are we being followed?" he whispered.

"Who would walk in the water to follow us?" she murmured. "Let us move a little closer."

They went forward slowly on hands and knees. The liquid burble of the Aelfwent grew louder as they carefully parted the reeds and crawled toward the river at an inchworm pace that made Qina's heart beat fast. *We are like beetles, hugging the ground,* she thought. *If something moves above us, one of those ghants in the trees, it will be on us before we know.*

Qina only kept from flinching by her determination to stay ready to flee if necessary. She edged forward until the river's confident, gurgling voice sounded just before her. She waited until Snenneq crawled up beside her, then cautiously spread the last curtain of reeds so she could see the river.

Something was thrashing its way down the water just a few paces out from the bank. For an instant she thought it was another of the hideous ghants and her heart seemed to force its way up into her mouth, but this thing was different, with longer arms and a more manlike shape, although she could see in the very first moments that it was no man.

A moment later she saw that it was not alone, either. Another long-limbed shape was pushing through the deeper water at the center of the river, not walking but swimming. And behind it came a third. The trailing two were smaller than the first, but all had the same half-shiny gray skin, lumpy as a frog's, and they all moved through the water with weird confidence—any normal creature in the same situation would be thrashing and fighting to stay afloat in the swift, deep river.

Snenneq took a deep, surprised breath. The leading creature seemed to hear him, and stopped to look around, standing tall against the river current with an economy of movement that was startling. It turned in their direction, looking for the source of the sound, and for a moment Qina felt sure she was seeing some terrible demon, something that her great-grandmother might have told her about during a long winter's night. Its face was nightmarish, a pair of bulging, shiny black eyes and then a noseless expanse of gray skin. The mouth was almost circular and red against the otherwise gray skin like a bloody wound. The thing stared toward the reeds where they hid and let out a strange wet hooting noise, like an owl drowning in a rain barrel. Then it turned back against the current and began half-swimming, half walking along the bottom again, leading the two smaller creatures forward until they all vanished from sight around a bend in the river.

Qina was shaking so that she could barely support herself, even on hands and knees.

"Daughter of the Mountains watch over us!" Snenneq said quietly, half in fright, half in amazement, after some time had passed. "Those were kilpa or I am a *croohok*!"

"Kilpa?" Qina could only shake her head. "I have not traveled or read as much as you, beloved, but kilpa are creatures of the southern oceans. How could they be here, in the north—and in a river?"

"I do not know," Snenneq said. "But I have seen pictures in your father's scrolls and read the tales of many travelers. I know what I know." A little of his stubbornness had returned. "Those were kilpa. They should not be here, like the ghant should not have been here. But that does not change what is."

"But why? What is happening that these things are leaving their homes and coming here?"

"I do not know." Snenneq let out a long breath. "I cannot even make a guess, my only love. But it is clear we must be careful every step of the way, and even within the ruined Sithi city itself. Only the ancestors can guess what other horrors we will encounter."

"I am shaking," she said. "I want to find a safe place—far from here, at least for the night. I cannot go farther, and I do not want to face darkness beside this river."

"Neither do I, my beloved," Snenneq said. He gave her a sickly smile. "Perhaps now my dislike of the water does not seem quite so foolish, eh?"

She had no answer to that.

In the first instants, as he saw Tanahaya scramble up the column and throw her rope over the stone web that was all that remained of the domed ceiling, Morgan was horrified, thinking she meant to escape and leave him behind. Then, when she began to climb back down again, he thought she was going to take him with her after all, and he felt a momentary flush of hope. Then she began tying off the rope and hope disappeared in a cloud of utter confusion.

By the time he understood what his companion was actually trying to do, it was too late to help her: the other Sitha, the grim mistress of the Pure, had seen Tanahaya's purpose and climbed up to add her strength. All Morgan could do was stand in the rainy chaos of the Place of Sky-Watching, wondering what would happen next as Sithi and Norns fought and died all around him.

And then it happened.

At first only a few pieces of the roof fell, though they were all large enough to cause serious harm. Morgan pushed himself back against the curving walls of the great chamber and watched in fearful astonishment as the entire complicated stone web of the domed ceiling rippled like a bedcover being shaken out by Hayholt chambermaids. The middle of the ceiling shuddered as a vast, slow wave passed through the whole thing. The center drooped, then the whole branching structure came down with a noise like the end of the world, crushing or tipping the columns beneath, obliterating the ferns and small trees that had grown beneath the broken dome, stones piling on top of each other as they collapsed. Morgan did not even hear the cries of those caught beneath it because the noise of the roof falling was like the continuous roar of a giant.

A single piece of stone bigger than a fist spun out of the falling stones and hit him in the chest, knocking him back against the wall and dropping him to his hands and knees. He fought for breath, blackness closing around him for long moments. When he could see again, it was over.

The great room was as silent as if a spell had been cast over it. All but a few of the torches in the chamber had blown out at once. The lattice of stone that only moments before had curved overhead had now tumbled in shards of angled stone, most of them bigger than he was. At first he could see no living thing anywhere, and could not even guess where in the wreckage Tanahaya might lie buried, but then he saw half a dozen more dark shapes slipping into the great room on the far side of the massive pile of rubble. He dragged himself to his feet and staggered as quickly as he was able through the unblocked door behind him.

Every childhood aspiration to heroism, every impulse of bravery, urged him to go back and find Tanahaya, but with all that stone fallen on her Morgan knew she must be dead. He could hear the voices of the Norns rising, their language as liquidly unintelligible as the Sithi's speech but full of hisses and sounds sharp as knives. Terror overwhelmed him. He was alone again. The only person who had cared for him was gone. His only choice was to run from those soulless, white-skinned *things*.

A few torches still remained in their sconces, illuminating the curving hall-way. He came to a place where the passages split, and for a moment thought to take the one that seemed more level, thinking he could find his way out of the city and into the forest. But he could hear the White Foxes calling to each other from in front now as well as behind, so he plunged down the sloping track that led into the deeper reaches of the city. His eyes were dry, but a powerful despair had gripped him; his legs felt weak as if he were stumbling through a foul dream.

Another crossing appeared before him, then another, and each time he could only choose and hurry on, with no way to guess where he was going and no hope but to find somewhere to hide from the pursuing Norns. In the upper part of the city the walls had all been carved in fine detail, but now the passages were little more than rocky gouges, and instead of stunning animal shapes the walls were decorated with grotesqueries, crude things with no faces, faces with no eyes, as though he was fleeing from sense into madness. As the tunnels twined and turned, it almost seemed he was being carried helplessly through the interminable gut of some great serpent.

Swallowed, he thought, and it echoed over and over in his head. *Swallowed. Eaten.*

Midway down a corridor he thought he heard new voices just ahead of him, though the air currents were strange in the forking tunnels and he could not be sure. Still, he stopped and turned back, then picked a cross-corridor that seemed to lead away from the harsh whispers. But a moment later he heard a soft sound, a patter so faint that it might have been falling leaves, if leaves fell beneath the ground, and he stopped short, his sword Snakesplitter wavering in his hand as he tried to decide what to do.

A moment later a cloaked shape came around a bend in the corridor—one of the Norns, holding a strange bronze sword with a serrated edge like the teeth of a wolf. It was too late to run: Morgan could only shrink back against the wall and lift Snakesplitter in front of him. He could see the pale face and the empty black eyes in the depths of the hood as the Norn soldier saw him and hurried forward, drawing back his blade, and Morgan prepared for a fight to the death, most likely his own. But in that moment, as silent prayers of regret for all his foolish mistakes fluttered through his head, Morgan's attacker abruptly stag-gered to a halt and dropped his sword. The Norn reached up with suddenly clumsy arms, trying to dislodge something from the back of his neck, his pale face a mask of bewilderment, then he sank to his knees, blood drooling from his lips.

Morgan did not wait to learn what had happened, but turned and dashed back up the corridor. Before he could reach the cross-passage something struck the back of his head, filling his skull with sparking fire, and he fell.

Morgan did not wake so much as float up from dark emptiness into confusion. It was too dark to see anything, but he could feel hard stone against his shoulder on one side. He was leaning back against something complicated that was more yielding than stone, but his head was throbbing and he could only lie helplessly in place, trying to find his thoughts again to reassemble them in some meaningful order.

Something cold slipped against his throat just below his jaw and pressed until he could feel how sharp it was. Morgan let out a little grunt of astonishment and pain. The blade at his neck pressed even tighter.

"Do not speak," said a voice in his ear, cold and harsh and very oddly accented. "Others coming."

He heard voices above and outside the place where he lay, and realized he was in a sort of narrow cave or crevice. Soft footfalls echoed mere inches away, and Morgan thought that if he had been sitting upright he could have reached out and grabbed at the ankles of whoever was passing this hiding-spot, but instead he lay as still as he could manage until the steps faded again—quickly, because they had been so quiet to begin with.

Whatever was happening, at least the one with a blade at his throat hadn't killed him outright. "I won't give you away," Morgan whispered.

"Silence," was the only reply. The blade stayed snug against his throat.

More time passed. He could tell now that he was half-sitting on whoever held him captive, and that his captor was no bigger than he was. "Who are you?" he asked at last. "What do you want of me?"

He could feel warm breath against his cheek. "I am Nezeru, once a Sacrifice." It was a woman's voice, but even as he realized it he understood that she was also a Norn, and his heart flopped in despair like a dying fish. "Now Hikeda'ya hunt me. Zida'ya hunt me. All want me dead."

"But I'm not either of those," he told her. "I'm a mortal."

"That is why you live," she said, and pushed the knife against his throat until he felt its bite again. "All want me dead. Hikeda'ya—my enemies. Zida'ya—my enemies. And you will be . . ." She went silent for a moment, searching for a word.

"Your ally?"

"No. Shield." She kept the knife against the base of his jaw as she moved out from under him, then dragged him away from the opening with surprising strength, pulling him deeper into the blackness of her hiding place. "To kill me, first they must kill you. That way I take more with me before I die."

Afterword

Sir Zakiel of Garwynswold was a hard man. The lines of his stern face might have been sculpted from dense stone. His bearing was always rigid and his eyes were always clear. But now, Tiamak thought, the acting constable looked as though something had eroded him from within. His skin looked almost gray, and his eyes were red around the lids.

"It is as we feared, my lord," Zakiel told him. "The report from the garrison on the Nabban border has been confirmed. And they sent this as proof."

For a long moment Tiamak could only stare at the object in Zakiel's palm, wondering where such a thing as that gray velvet bag might have come from, the fabric smoothed shiny in many places by handling. Had one of the soldiers carried it as a reminder of a dead mother or sweetheart? Or was it something familar Zakiel himself had dug out of his own possessions in an attempt to make the horror less?

He accepted the bag, feeling the small, hard thing through the velvet. It weighed less than he had expected, but the burden of it seemed heavy as a gravestone. Tiamak's hands were shaking.

"Shall I go in with you, my lord?"

He shook his head. "Thank you, Constable. I have known him longer than anyone here. I think it must be me. I wish by all the gods of my homeland it was not, but I think it must be me."

Zakiel nodded and made the Sign of the Tree. "God's mercy, then. On us all."

After the constable had left Tiamak stood outside the throne hall door for no little time, trying to decide what to say and how to say it. His stomach felt as if it wanted to squirm its way out of his body. The last month had been a growing storm of terrible news, and now this, the worst of all. First they had heard of the terrible events in Nabban, including the disappearance of Queen Miriamele. Then had come the tidings from the Laestfinger River that Duke Osric and his men had not only been attacked by Thrithings-men, but had been driven back by an astonishingly large army of grasslanders and forced to take refuge in Fellmere Castle some miles inside the border, whence the duke had called for reinforcements. No sooner had soldiers been sent than news had drifted in of the capture of Naglimund by the White Foxes, and the presumed death of all its citizens and defenders. Erkynland was besieged from two sides, and murderous chaos seemed to have taken root everywhere.

And now this, Tiamak thought again. It seemed to spin through his head like a thrown ax; it whirled around and around, but its power would only be felt when it finally struck its target. *And now this.*

King Simon was in the throne hall, sprawled on one of the ordinary council benches as his granddaughter Lillia clambered on him, trying to pull his beard while Simon, somewhat wearily, entertained her by resisting. The Dragonbone Chair stood on the daïs behind them, flanked by the almost invisible black statues of earlier kings; the great reptilian skull that canopied the chair loomed through the shadows like a vengeful spirit. Simon had always disliked the throne. For the first time he could remember, Tiamak wondered if the king might have been right after all—if the grim thing had been a harbinger of disaster all along.

Simon must have recognized Tiamak's expression, or perhaps his slumping, overburdened posture, because as soon as he entered the hall the king lifted his granddaughter under her arms and set her down on the floor. Laughing, Lillia tried to climb back onto his lap, but Simon would not let her.

"Quiet now, child. Time to go back to your chambers so that I can talk to Tiamak."

One leg already up on the bench, clutching at Simon's clothing, she turned to the new arrival. "Uncle Timo, he's trying to make me go! Tell him you want me to stay."

"I can't, my dear. He's right. He and I have important matters to discuss. And you should be helping your grandmother the duchess to pack, in any case."

Lillia gave him a fiercely disappointed look, a look of betrayal. "No, don't say that! I don't want to go to the country. I want to stay here until Morgan and Grandmother Miriamele come back."

"Go along, Lillia," Tiamak said. His heart was so heavy it was all he could do not to burst into tears at the sight of her angry, innocent little face. "Be a good girl."

Outflanked and unsupported, she slid off the bench onto the floor and made her way toward the door of the throne hall with the sullen defiance of a drunkard thrown out of a tavern. "I'm going to tell Auntie Tia-Lia that you're the meanest man who ever lived in the Wran."

Tiamak did not have the heart for teasing today. "Go on, my dear. You and I can talk later, I promise."

He watched her out the door. When she was gone, Tiamak could feel Simon's eyes on him even before he turned.

"Well? More of it? All bad, I presume?" But the look on the king's face made a mockery of the lightness of his tone. He looked like someone ready to be slapped.

"I'm afraid so, Majesty. Simon." Tiamak could barely control his voice. "We had more news from the commander of the Suthmark garrison." His stomach was so roiled that Tiamak wanted nothing more at that moment than to go somewhere and be sick, but he pressed his hands against his stomach and continued. "Nabban is in a shambles, and the commanders of their northern forts are uncertain of what to do, suspicious of foreigners. But finally some of our men managed to reach the site and confirmed that they found the wreckage of the royal carriage. The queen's carriage."

"Tell me everything." Simon's face was rigid.

"It seems to have been a Thrithings attack, by the signs and the arrows they found. The coach was struck with several flaming arrows and was almost completely consumed. It seems that several Erkynguards were killed defending it, but no one can say for certain because animals have dragged the bodies away."

"But no sign of Miri, is that right?" Simon seemed to be struggling inside himself. "She will have gotten away. She is fierce and clever, my Miri."

Tiamak wanted to blurt it all out, just to end the torment he felt, but could not do that to his old friend, the king. "There was a body in the carriage. Badly burned. The Suthmark soldiers said they thought it was a woman."

Simon's face was losing its solidity and growing more pale by the instant. "But that could be anyone—one of her ladies. We still do not know where half of them are—!"

Tiamak swallowed, then held out the gray velvet bag. "The garrison commander sent this. He said they found it on the dead woman's hand."

Simon stared at the bag as if it were a coiled adder, but took it at last. He shook the shining thing out onto his hand and stared in utter silence.

"Oh, my God, my merciful God, how could this happen?" he finally asked. "Not . . . it couldn't . . ."

The ring dropped from his hand and bounced once on the floor with a loud *clink*, then bounced again and began to roll past Tiamak. Without thinking, he bent to snatch it up before it vanished under the benches or one of the hangings. As he stared at the twin dragons, entwining face to face, ruby eyes staring into eyes of diamond, the coils of the long bodies wrapped so tightly around each other as to make a single circlet of gold, he heard a tremendous crash. Shards and chunks of wood danced past him.

Simon picked up the largest remaining piece of the bench he had just smashed to the stone floor and hammered it against the stone flags, breaking it into even smaller pieces, his face transformed in an instant from death pale to the scarlet of rage. With his height and his full beard, he looked like a towering prophet from the Book of the Aedon—a prophet of death and loss.

"*No!*" Simon shouted, so loudly and brokenly that the guards outside the throne hall peered in through the doorway to see what was happening. "No! No! No!" But already the fury was dying like a smothered flame, and by the last negative the king was weeping. He fell to his knees. "It cannot be," he said in a broken voice. Tiamak was weeping now too. "Not my Miri," the king said, his voice halting and raw. "Not my happiness. Not my *beloved . . . !*"

Tiamak could only go to him and put a useless hand on Simon's shoulder. The king pressed his forehead down against the stone and wept and wept.

Appendix

PEOPLE

ERKYNLANDERS

Aart, Brother—St. Cuthbert Abbey's blacksmith

Abigal, Mistress—Mistress of Chambermaids of the Hayholt

Aedonita—playmate of Princess Lillia

Aldyn, Sir—Kenrick's lieutenant in the Erkynguard

Avel—a young servant

Boez, Bishop—recently elevated Chief Almoner of the Hayholt

Colfrid, Earl—Erkynland's Lord Marine

Cuff—a young man of Naglimund, known as "Cuff Scaler"; real name "Cuthbert"

Denah—a woman in Queen Miriamele's retinue

Duglan, Lord—a noble; envoy to Hernystir

Eahlferend—a fisherman; King Simon's father

Eahlstan Fiskerne, St.—King Simon's ancestor and founder of the League of the Scroll; sixth king of the Hayholt; called the "Fisher King"

Ealmer, Baron—lord of Grafton, known as "Ealmer the Large"

Elias, King—former High King; Queen Miriamele's father, killed in the Storm King's War

Elyweld—Lillia's playmate; Aedonita's sister

Enok—Captain Zakiel's young son

Etan, Brother—an Aedonite monk, also known as "Etan Fratilis Ercestris"

Evoric, Baron—baron of Haestall; Earl Rowson's ally

Fayn, Captain—guard captain of Naglimund

Firman—soldier of the Erkynguard

Gervis, Escritor—the highest religious authority in Erkynland; Lord Treasurer of the Hayholt

Girth, Brother—wheelwright at St. Cuthbert's Abbey

Ham—a boy aboard the *Hylissa*

Herwald—a fur merchant

Idela, Princess—recently deceased widow of Prince John Josua; daughter of Duke Osric

Jack Mundwode—a mythical forest bandit

Jeremias, Lord—Lord Chamberlain of the Hayholt

John Josua, Prince—dead son of King Simon and Queen Miriamele; Prince Morgan and Princess Lillia's father

John Presbyter, King—former High King; Queen Miriamele's grandfather, called Prester John

Josua, Prince—King Elias' brother; Queen Miriamele's uncle, who disappeared twenty years ago

Jurgen of Sturmstad, Sir—Night Captain of the Erkynguard; Queen Miriamele's protector

Kenrick, Sir—a young Captain Marshal of the Erkynguard; former drinking companion to Prince Morgan, now member of Duke Osric's host

Leola—wife of Herwald

Levias, Sergeant—officer of the Erkynguard

Lillia, Princess—granddaughter of King Simon and Queen Miriamele; Morgan's sister; called Lilly by her grandfather

Loes—a nurse, one of Princess Lillia's minders

Melkin—Prince Morgan's squire

Miriamele, Queen—High Queen of Osten Ard; wife of King Simon

Morgan, Prince—heir to the High Throne; son of Prince John Josua and Princess Idela

Morgenes, Doctor—deceased Scrollbearer; young Simon's friend and mentor

Nelda, Duchess—wife of Duke Osric; Princess Idela's mother

Ordwine—soldier of the Erkynguard, from Westworth

Osric, Duke—Lord Constable and Duke of Falshire and Wentmouth; Princess Idela's father

Putnam, Bishop—a cleric of the Hayholt

Rachel—Mistress of Chambermaids of the Hayholt during King Simon's youth; also known as "The Dragon"

Raynold—Baron of Uttersall

Renward—an Erkynguard bowman in Duke Osric's troop

Rowson, Earl—a nobleman of Glenwick

Shulamit, Lady—one of Queen Miriamele's court ladies

Shem Horsegroom—groom at the Hayholt during King Simon's youth

Simon, King—High King of Osten Ard and husband of Queen Miriamele; also known by his birth name, "Seoman"; sometimes called "Snowlock"

Siward, Father—a priest at Naglimund; Cuff's mentor

Strangyeard, Father—deceased Scrollbearer and former royal chaplain of the Hayholt

Susannah—former servant of the Hayholt; King Simon's mother who died in childbirth

Sutrin, St.—an Aedonite saint, also known as Sutrines

Tabata—resident chambermaid of the Hayholt

Theobalt, Brother—a monk, Brother Etan's "less than adequate replacement" per Tiamak

Thomas Oystercatcher—mayor of Erchester

Tostig, Baron– a wool merchant

Tzoja—Lord Viyeki's mistress; mother of Sacrifice Nezeru; daughter of Prince Josua and Lady Vorzheva; Unver's twin sister, called Derra by her parents

Zakiel of Garwynswold, Sir—Captain of the Erkynguard; Sir Kenrick's commander

HERNYSTIRI

Aelin, Sir—grand-nephew of Count Eolair

Aengas ec-Carpilbin of Ban Farrig—a merchant and scholar of ancient books

Aerell—Sir Aelin's father; husband of Elatha, Count Eolair's sister

Bagba—a cattle god

Brannan—former monk, cook to Aengas

Brynioch of the Skies—sky god, called "Skyfather"

Cadrach ec-Crannhyr—deceased monk of indeterminate order; travel companion of Miriamele during the Storm King's War

Cuamh Earthdog—an earth god

Curudan, Baron—Commander of the Silver Stags

Dun—a god of death

Eolair, Count—Count of Nad Mullach and Hand of the Throne

Evan—one of Sir Aelin's men

Fintan—an Aedonite soldier of the Silver Stags

Flann—leader of Flann's Crows; a legendary bandit king

Gwythinn, Prince—King Hugh's father, killed in the Storm King's War

Hern, King—legendary founder of Hernystir

Hugh ubh-Gwythinn, King—ruler of Hernystir

Inahwen—Dowager Queen of Hernystir; last wife of King Lluth, Hugh's grandfather

Jarreth—Sir Aelin's squire

Lluth, King—former ruler of Hernystir; father of Maegwin and Gwythinn; killed at the Battle of the Inniscritch

Maccus Blackbeard—a soldier; one of Sir Aelin's companions

Morriga—the Maker of Orphans, the Crow Mother; an ancient war goddess

Murdo, Earl—a powerful noble; ally of Count Eolair and Sir Aelin

Murhagh One-Arm—a war god

Nial, Count—a nobleman of Nad Glehs; Countess Rhona's husband

Rhona, Countess—noblewoman of Nad Glehs; friend to Queen Miriamele; guardian of Princess Lillia, who calls her "Auntie Rhoner"

Rhynn of the Cauldron—a god

Samreas, Sir—Baron Curudan's hawk-faced lieutenant; a Silver Stag

Sinnach, Prince—historic prince of Hernystir, also known as "The Red Fox"

Silver Stags—a Hernystiri elite troop; members are hand-picked by King Hugh

Talamh of the Land—an ancient goddess of war and territory

Tethtain, King—fifth king of the Hayholt; called the "Holly King" and "Tethtain the Usurper"

Tylleth, Lady—widow of the Earl of Glen Orrga; betrothed to King Hugh

RIMMERSFOLK

Agnida—a woman among the Astaline Sisters

Dror the Thunderer—storm god

Dyrmundur—a chieftain of the Skalijar; Jarnulf's former companion

Einskaldir—companion of late Duke Isgrimnur, killed in the Storm King's War

Grimbrand of Elvritshalla, Duke—ruler of Rimmersgard; Duke Isgrimnur's son

Gutrun, Duchess—Duke Grimbrand's late mother

Hjeldin, King—second ruler of the Hayholt; King Fingil's son, called the "Mad King"

Isgrimnur of Elvritshalla, Duke—Duke Grimbrand's late father

Jarngrimnur—Jarnulf's deceased brother

Jarnulf Godtru—a man of unclear allegiance, self-proclaimed Queen's Huntsman in Nakkiga; accidental companion and guide to Makho's Talon

Morthginn—ancient queen of the underworld

Narvi, Thane—a nobleman of Tach Bredan

Roskva—a leader of the Astaline Sisters; Tzoja's surrogate mother, called "Valada"

Skalijar—an organized troop of brigands in northern Rimmersgard

Vordis—a woman born to slavery in Nakkiga

QANUC

Binabik (Binbiniqegabenik)—Scrollbearer; Singing Man of the Qanuc; dear friend to King Simon

Kikkasut—legendary king of birds

Little Snenneq—Qina's betrothed

Qina (Qinananamookta)—daughter of Binabik and Sisqi

Ookekuq—former Scrollbearer; Binibik's master, killed on the Road of Dreams during the Storm King's War

Sedda—moon goddess, also known as "Moon-Mother"

Sisqi (Sisqinanamook)—daughter of the Herder and Huntress (rulers of Mintahoq Mountain); Binabik's wife

THRITHINGS-FOLK

Agvalt—a young bandit leader

Anbalt, Thane—leader of the Adders Clan; from the Lake Thrithings

Earth Hugger—the totem spirit of the Snake Clan spirit; called "the Legless"

Edizel Shan—the most recent Shan, a legendary hero and leader of the Thri–things

Etvin, Thane—leader of the Wood Duck Clan; born by Shallow Lake

Fikolmij—former March-thane of the Stallion Clan and the High Thrithings; Vorzheva's father, recently killed by her

Forest Growler—the totem spirit of the Bear Clan

Fremur, Thane—interim leader of the Crane clan; Unver's first follower and closest friend

Gezdahn Baldhead—a Crane Clan rider

Grass Thunderer—the totem spirit of the Stallion Clan

Gurdig—former thane of the Stallion Clan; husband of Hyara; recently killed by Unver

Harat—a member of the Bustard Clan

Hotmer—a bandit; son of Hotvig

Hotvig—a Stallion Clan ally of Prince Josua during the Storm King's War

Hurvalt—former thane of the Crane Clan; Fremur's father

Hurza—a bandit

Hyara—Vorzheva's sister; Unver's aunt

Kulva—Fremur's late sister; Unver's love

Kunret White-Beard, Thane—leader of the Vulture Clan

Night Eater—a mythical creature/demon

Odobreg, Thane—leader of the Badger Clan

Ogda Forkbeard, Thane—leader of the Pheasant Clan

Rudur Redbeard, Thane—leader of Black Bear Clan; March-thane of the Meadow Thrithings; self-proclaimed "thane of thanes"

Ruzhvang—a shaman of the Snake Clan

Sky-Piercer—the totem spirit of the Crane clan

Tasdar of the Iron Arm—a Thrithings tutelary spirit; a metal-working deity worshipped by all the grassland clans, also called Tasdar the Anvil Smasher

Unver—"Nobody", new Thane of the Stallion Clan; son of Prince Josua and Lady Vorzheva; Tzoja's twin brother, called Deornoth by his parents

Volfrag—Rudur Redbeard's chief shaman

Vorzheva—Unver's mother; Prince Josua's wife; daughter of Fikolmij; sister of Hyara

Vybord—a man of the Badger Clan

Wymunt, Thane—leader of the Bustard Clan

NABBANAI

Abbess of Latria—the leader of a religious order; Lady Thelía's friend

Albian House—one of the fifty noble families

Alurea, Countess—wife of Count Rillian

Anitulles the Great—a historic Imperator

Ardrivis—the last Imperator, defeated at Nearulagh by King John

Argenian—a historic Imperator

Aspitis Preves, Earl—an ally of King Elias during the Storm King's War

Asta of Turonis—historic noblewoman who founded the Astaline order two hundred years ago

Astrian, Sir—a member of the Erkyguard and former drinking companion of Prince Morgan, now part of Duke Osric's host

Auxis, Escritor—an envoy of the Sancellan Aedonitis to the High Throne

Benedrivine House—the ruling family in Nabban for the last two hundred years; emblem is the Kingfisher

Benidrivis—first Duke of Nabban under King John Presbyter; father of Camaris, great grandfather of Duke Saluceris

Benidrivis the Great—founder of the Third Nabbani Imperium, ancestor of Camaris, Saluceris, Drusis, and many others

Benigaris, Duke—former ruler of Nabban; uncle of Saluceris, killed in the Storm King's War

Blasis—son of Duchess Canthia and Duke Saluceris

Brindalles—Pasevalles' father, killed during the Storm King's War

Caias Hermis—Earl of Vissa

Camaris-sá-Vinitta, Sir—King John's greatest knight, also known as "Camaris Benidrivis"; disappeared at the end of the Storm King's War

Canthia, Duchess—wife of Duke Saluceris; mother of Blasis and Serasina

Clavean House—one of the fifty noble families

Crexis the Goat—a historic Imperator

Dallo Ingadaris, Count—Queen Miriamele's cousin and opponent to Duke Saluceris; ally of the Duke's brother Drusis

Dinivan, Father—former Scrollbearer and secretary to Lector Ranessin; killed in the Sancellan Aedonitis during the Storm King's War

Doellene House—one of the fifty noble families

Dominiate—ruling council of Nabban, consisting primarily of the fifty noble families

Drusis, Earl—Earl of Trevinta and Eadne; Duke Saluceris' brother and rival

Endrais, St.—an Aedonite martyr

Envalles, Marquis—counselor to and uncle of Duke Saluceris

Elysia—mother of Usires Aedon; called "Mother of God"

Fifty Families—Nabbanai noble houses

Fino, Father—Lector Vidian's servant

Flavis—a Patris of the Larexean House

Fluiren, Sir—a storied knight of the disgraced Sulian House

Granis, St.—an Aedonite saint

Hermian—one of the fifty noble families

Idexes Claves, Count—Lord Chancellor of Nabban

Ingadarine House—one of the fifty noble families; in opposition to the current Duke. Emblem is the Albatross

Kingfisher Guard—the Duke of Nabban's private guard

Larexean House—one of the fifty noble families

Matreu, Viscount—son of the ruler of Spenit Island

Metessan House—one of the fifty noble families; Lord Pasevalles is a member. Emblem is the Blue Crane

Mindia, Lady—one of Duchess Canthia's ladies-in-waiting

Nessalanta, Duchess—former duchess of Nabban; Saluceris' grandmother; died near the end of the Storm King's War

Nulles, Father—royal chaplain of the Hayholt

Oliveris, Sir—a knight; former drinking companion of Prince Morgan, now member of Duke Osric's host

Oppidanis—court astrologer

Pasevalles, Lord—Lord Chancellor to the High Throne

Pelippa, St.—Aedonite saint, called "Pelippa of the Island"

Pyrates—priest, alchemist, and wizard; King Elias' counselor, presumed dead during the fall of Green Angel Tower at the end of the Storm King's War

Rhiappa, St.—Aedonite saint, called "Rhiap" in Erkynland

Rillian Albias, Count—the Solicitor General of Nabban; head of Albian House

Sallin Ingadaris—Count Dallo's son

Saluceris, Duke—ruler of Nabban

Serasina—infant daughter of Duchess Canthia and Duke Saluceris

Sessian, Baron—Lady Mindia's uncle

Stormbirds—supporters of Dallo Ingardaris; the Albatross is their sign

Thelía, Lady—a versed herbalist and also Lord Tiamak's wife; called "Tia-Lia" by Princess Lillia

Sulian House—one of the fifty noble families

Syllaris the Younger—a church official and Usirean Brother

Tiyagaris—a historic Imperator

Tiyanis Sulis—a nobleman and ally of the Ingadarines

Tunath, St.—Aedonite saint, also called Tunato the Pilgrim

Turia Ingadaris, Lady—Count Dallo's niece; bride of Earl Drusis

Usires Aedon—Aedonite Son of God; also called "the Ransomer" and "the Redeemer"

Varellan, Duke—Duke Saluceris' deceased father; younger brother of Benigaris who became ruler after the Storm King's War

Vellia Hermis—wife of Imperator Argenian

Velthir, St.—a holy prophet from the southern islands; a prominent figure in the Aedonite Book of Prophets

Vidian II, Lector—Head of the Aedonite Church

Xaxina—semi-mythic widow of an Imperator, fought to protect Nabban

Yuvis—called "the tailor's son"

PERDRUINESE

Amando, Baron—father of Lady Faiera

Bardo—former sexton of St. Cusimo's church on Almond Tree Hill in Perdruin

Costante—son of Count Streáwe of Perdruin; Yissola's half-brother

Endri—a soldier and friend of Sir Porto's; killed in the Nornfells in the Storm King's War

Faiera, Lady—Scrollbearer; disappeared

Felisso—captain of Erkynlandish ship *Hylissa*

Froye, Count—Ambassador of the High Throne to Nabban

Grandi—an old woman in Perdruin

Honora, St.—an Aedonite saint

Porto, Sir—a hero of the Battles of Nakkiga; one of Prince Morgan's former drinking companions, now member of Duke Osric's host

Sindigato Perdruine—a trade organization, also called the Perdruinese Syndicate

Streáwe, Count—former ruler of Perdruin, deceased

Yistrin, St.—an Aedonite saint

Yissola, Countess—ruler of Perdruin; daughter of Count Streáwe

WRANNA-FOLK

He Who Always Steps on Sand—a god

Hoto—Jesa's older brother

Jaraweg—Jesa's late great-uncle

Jesa—nurse to Duke Saluceris' infant daughter Serasina; named "Green Honeybird" by her elders

Green Honeybird—mythical Wranna spirit; Jesa's namesake

Laliba—a cloth seller in Nabban

Old Gorahok—a blind denizen of Red Pig Lagoon

She Who Birthed Mankind—a goddess

She Who Waits to Take All Back—a death goddess

They Who Watch and Shape—gods

Tiamak, Lord—Scrollbearer; scholar and close friend of King Simon and Queen Miriamele; called "Uncle Timo" by Princess Lillia

SITHI (ZIDA'YA)

Aditu no'e-Sa'onserei—daughter of Likimeya; Jiriki's sister

Amerasu y-Senditu no'e-Sa'onserei—mother of Ineluki and Hakatri; called "First Grandmother," also known as "Amerasu Ship-Born", killed during the Storm King's War

Ayaminu—mistress of Anvijanya

Dunao the Rider—a supporter of Khendraja'aro

Gayali—apprentice to Himano, from the "Southern Woods"

Hakatri—historic figure; Amerasu's son who vanished into the West, his bones were recently retrieved by Makho's Talon

Himano of the Flowering Hills—a scholar; Tanahaya's teacher; sometimes called "Master" or "Lord"

Ineluki—Amerasu's son; called the "Storm King", deceased

Jenjiyana of the Nightingales—historic figure; mother of Nenais'u

Jiriki i-Sa'onserei—son of Likimeya; brother of Aditu

Jonzao–"the Pure", a faction with a strictly traditional lifestyle

Khendraja'aro—Likimeya's half-brother; uncle of Jiriki and Aditu; self-styled "Protector" of House of Year-Dancing

Kira'athu—a healer who cured Tanahaya

Kiushapo—friend and ally of Jiriki and Aditu

Likimeya y-Briseyu no'e-Sa'onserei—the Sa'onsera; mother of Jiriki and Aditu

Liko the Starling—a Sitha of Anvijanya

Mezumiiru—Sithi moon goddess

Nenais'u—historic figure; wife of Drukhi; daughter of Jenjiyana

S'aonsera the Preserver—historic figure; wife of Hamakho Wormslayer; founding-mother of House of Year-Dancing

Sa'onsera, the—title of the female leader of House of Year Dancing

Sa'onserei—Clan of Jiriki and Aditu; also called House of Year-Dancing

Senditu—mother of Amerasu

Shima'onari—father of Jiriki and Aditu; killed during the Storm King's War

Spark—Jiriki and Aditu's pet name for Tanahaya

Tanahaya of Shisae'ron—a Sithi scholar; envoy to the Hayholt

Vindaomeyo the Fletcher—historic arrow-maker of Tumet'ai

Vinyedu—leader of the Pure; sister of Zinjadu

Yeja'aro of the Forbidden Hills—Khendraja'aro's nephew

Zinjadu—lore-mistress of Kementari; sister of Vinyedu; killed during the Storm King's War

NORNS (HIKEDA'YA)

Akhenabi, Lord—High Magister of the Order of Song, also called "Lord of Song"

Anchoress—title of Queen Utuk'ku's female body-slaves

Denabi sey-Xoka—a sword-master; Jarnulf's former master and teacher

Drukhi—historic figure; son of Queen Utuk'ku and Ekimeniso; killed by mortals

Enkinu—High Anchoress of Nakkiga; mistress of Queen Utuk'ku's body-slaves

Enduya—Viyeki's clan, a middling noble family

Ensume—Sacrifice general of the Northeastern host

Genathi—a blind Celebrant born after the flight from the Garden

Gyrfalcons—a Sacrifice legion

Hamakha—clan of Queen Utuk'ku

Hamakho Wormslayer—historic figure; founder of Queen Utuk'ku's Clan Hamakha; a famous warrior

Hammer-wielders—siege-soldiers who use hammers to knock down walls

Ibi-Khai—member of the Order of Echos and a Sacrifice in Makho's Talon; killed by Diggers

Iyora Clan—Norn clan which included the war hero Suno'ku and Queen Utuk'ku's husband Ekimeniso Blackstaff

Jhindejo—a Sacrifice Scout from Fortress Dark Lantern

Jijibo—a close descendant of Queen Utuk'ku, called "the Dreamer"

Juni'ata, Commander—officer in command of Fortress Dark Lantern

Kemme—a Sacrifice in Makho's Talon

Khimabu, Lady—Lord Viyeki's wife

Kikiti, General—General of the host accompanying Viyeki's builders to Naglimund

Legion Zosho—military legion named after the gyrfalcons of Lake Rumiya

Lord of Dreaming—nickname for Lord Jijibo of Nakkiga

Makho—wounded Hand Chieftain

Nezeru Seyt-Enduya—Daughter of Lord Viyeki and his mistress Tzoja; member of the Queen's Talon led by Makho

Nijin—Hikeda'ya chronicler, source of Tanahaya's parchment

Night Moths—a Sacrifice legion

Nerudade—a Hikeda'ya philosopher credited with the creation or discovery of Unbeing; father of Yedade

Nonao—Lord Viyeki's secretary

Northeastern Host—a little-known Sacrifice army, apparently deployed in mortal lands

Ommu the Whisperer—Singer; member of the Red Hand; resurrected by Queen Utuk'ku

Pratiki—Prince-Templar, member of the Hamakha Clan; relative of Queen Utuk'ku

Queen's Teeth—Queen Utuk'ku's personal guard

Rinde—a scout from the War-Shrikes Legion

Saomeji—member of the Order of Song, Makho's Talon

Sey-Jok'kochi—a Sacrifice legion, part of the Northeastern host, known as "War-Shrikes"

Shun'y'asu of Blue Spirit Peak—a poet

Sogeyu—Host Singer of the Order of Song

Suno'ku—a famous general, killed in the aftermath of the Storm King's War

Utuk'ku Seyt-Hamakha—Norn Queen; Mistress of Nakkiga; oldest being in Osten Ard

Va'ani—Sacrifice Scout from Fortress Dark Lantern

Viyeki seyt-Enduya, Lord—High Magister of the Order of Builders, father of Nezeru

White Foxes—mortal name for Norns

Xaniko sey-Hamakha—writer of the Exile's Letter; member of the Queen's clan

Xohabi—Author of *The Five Fingers Of The Queen's Hand*, a venerated text

Yaarike sey-Kijana, Lord—former High Magister of the Order of Builders, deceased

Ya-Jalamu—a granddaughter of Marshal Muyare

Yansu Clan—noble family; Vordis was born their slave

Yedade—Hikeda'ya philosopher

Yemon—Viyeki's former secretary, executed as a traitor

Zinuzo—a war poet

TINUKEDA'YA

Carry-men—a very tall type of the Tinukeda'ya, used to haul

Chikri—seemingly self-aware dwellers in Aldheorte Forest, somewhat resembling squirrels

Dasa—a member of the Hidden

Delver—a mortal name for the Tinukeda'ya who shape stone

Dwarrows—also called Dvernings, a type of Tinukeda'ya who are skilled at shaping stone

Gan Doha—a Niskie, relative of Gan Itai

Gan Itai—the Niskie who died saving Queen Miriamele many years ago

Gan Lagi—a Niskie; Gan Doha's oldest living relative

Geloë—a wise woman, called "Valada Geloë"; killed at Sesuad'ra during the Storm King's War

Giants—large, shaggy, manlike creatures

Goh Gam Gar—a speaking giant who helped Makho's Talon catch a dragon

Grey—a Chikri

Hidden, the—a faction of Tinukeda'ya, hiding from their masters in Nakkiga

Hunën—Rimmerspakk name for giants

Naya Nos—a member of the Hidden

Niskies—a type of Tinukeda'ya who serve aboard ships
ReeRee—a young Chikri in Aldheorte Forest; Morgan's companion
Ruyan Vé—fabled patriarch of the Tinukeda'ya; called "The Navigator"
Sea Watchers' Guild—another name for the Niskies
Stripe—a Chikri; ReeRee's mother
Tey Seiso—Niskie of Yissola's ship *Li Fosena*
Uvasika—mistress of the Hidden, also known as "the Silent Lady"
Zin-Seyvu—leader of a Tinukeda'ya group traveling through Aldehorte
  Forest

OTHERS

Adversary, the—the Aedonite devil
Creator, the—another name for the Aedonite god
Fortis the Recluse—a 6th-century bishop on Warinsten Island; writer of an
  infamous book
Hyrka—a migrant people from east of Aldheorte Forest
Lightless Ones—dwellers in the depths of Nakkiga; of unknown origin
Madi—a Hyrka guide to Brother Etan
Parlippa—Madi's daughter, also known as Parlip
Plekto—Madi's son, also known as Plek
Sagra—a Kwanitupul neighbor of young Derra and Deornoth
Senigo of Khand—a famous ancient philosopher

CREATURES

Cave-borers—large digging creatures also known as stone-chafers, rock-
  chafers, or earthwicks
Connach—Aelin's horse
Ebur—a large beast of Khand
Falku—Snenneq's ram
Fraxi—a bulldog, full name "Ferax"
Ghants—chitinous Wran-dwelling creatures
Gildreng—Ruzhvang's donkey
Ooki—Sisqi's ram
Orn—Sir Jurgen's horse, a large gray courser
Kilpa—manlike marine creatures
Qallipuk—"River Man"; a water monster
Salt—Jarnulf's horse
Sefstred—a Thrithings horse from Fikolmij's herd
Uro'eni—Sithi name for the ogre of Misty Vale

Vaqana—Binabik's wolf companion
Witiko'ya—a ferocious wolf-like predator of the far north

PLACES

Abaingeat—important trading town in Hernystir, at the coast of the Barraillean River

Abbey of St. Cuthbert—home of Cuff the Scaler in Naglimund

Aelfwent—a great river in Aldheorte Forest; called T'si Suhyasei in Sithi

Aldheorte—also known as Oldheart; a large forest to the north and east of Erkynland

Anitullean Road—major Nabban thoroughfare

Ansis Pellipé—a large city, the capital of Perdruin

Antigine Hill—one of the five hills of Nabban, site of the Domos Benidriyan

Anvijanya—a Sithi settlement

Arbris Sacra—a market town in Nabban

Ardivalis—Benidrivine family lands in northern Nabban

Asu'a—Sithi name of the Hayholt, their most important city before mortals conquered it

Avenue of the Fallen—a street in Nakkiga which runs behind many of the great houses whose estates front on Great Garden Passage

Bellidan—a good-sized town in Nabban

Bishop's Reflection Room—a historic room in the Hayholt

Bitter Moon Castle—Norn fortress on top of Dragon's Reach Pass

Blood Reaches—training grounds for Sacrifices in Nakkiga

Blue Cavern—home of silk-spinning spiders, place of Norn rope production

Blue Knight's Pantry—a corridor in the Hayholt

Blue Mud Lake—a body of water south of the mountains of Yiqanuc

Blue Spirit Peak—mountain near Nakkiga

Breakstaff Square—a place with a gallows in Erchester

Bridvattin—a lake in Rimmersgard

Carn Inbarh—a castle in Hernystir; home of Earl Murdo, Eolair's ally

Chamber of the Well—the heart of Nakkiga; location of The Well and The Breathing Harp

Chaplain's Walking Hall—a room in the Hayholt

Chasu Metessa—a castle in Nabban; Pasevalles' early childhood home

Chasu Orientis—a castle belonging to Earl Drusis at the Nabban-Thrithings border

Chasu Rutilli—a Nabbanai castle-town

Circoille—a huge forest in the northwest of Hernystir

Cloud's Rest—Gardenborn name for Vestivegg Mountains

City of Refuge—another name for Da'ai Chikiza

Cold, Slow Halls—a place of torture in Nakkiga

Commeian Hills—hills in Nabban on the border to the Thrithings

Commeis Valley—a valley in Nabban

Cuihmne Valley—a valley east of Nad Mullach in Hernystir

Da'ai Chikiza—ruined Sithi city in Aldheorte Forest; called "Tree of the Singing Wind", one of the nine Gardenborn cities

Dawnstone Chamber—former home of Da'ai Chikiza's Master Witness

Dellis Latia—a seaport east of the horn of Nabban

Dekusao—a river near Misty Vale, called Narrowdark in Westerling

Dimmerskog—a forest north of Rimmergard

Din's Passage—a corridor in the Hayholt

Domos Bendriyan—the Benidrivine family palace in Nabban; built by the first
Benidrivis some two hundred years ago

Dunath Tower—a guard tower along the Inniscrich near the Hernystir/
Rimmersgard border

Drina—an Earldom in Nabban

Eadne—a large lake as well as an earldom in Nabban

Elvritshalla—the ducal seat in Rimmersgard

Enki e-Shao'saye—one of the nine Gardenborn cities, located at the southern
fringe of Aldheorte Forest

Erchester—capital of Erkynland and seat of the High Throne

Erkynland—kingdom in central Osten Ard

Estrenine Hill—one of Nabban's hills, location of Viscount Matreu's house

Fellmere Castle—an Erkynlandish stronghold west of Laestfinger River

Field of Banners—an open area just outside the gates of Nakkiga

Fields of the Nameless—the graveyard for the disgraced of Nakkiga

Fingerlest—Thrithing name for Laestfinger River

Firannos Bay—a bay south of Nabban; location of many islands

Flowering Hills—a region in Aldheorte Forest; home of Himano

Forbidden Hills—Sithi stronghold, home of Khendraja'aro

Frostmarch, the—a region in northern Hernystir/southern Rimmersgard

Fortress Deeping—a hidden fortress of the Northeastern Host of Nakkiga,
where large Cave-borers are bred

Fortress Dark Lantern—a hidden fortress of the Northeastern Host

Gadrinsett—Erkynlandish city at the border to the High Thrithings

Gate of Cranes—a bridge in Da'ai Chikiza; other bridges there include Tor-
toises, Roosters, Wolves, Ravens, and Stags

Gatherers' Way—the great avenue which leads into Da'ai Chikiza from the north

Garwynswold—a town in eastern Erkynland

Gleniwent—an Erkynlandish river connecting the Kynslagh to the sea

Go-jao'e—Little Boats; name for small Sithi settlements

Grafton—a barony in Erkynland

Granary Tower—a tower in the Hayholt once used to house John Josua's chambers and study

Gratuvask—Rimmersgard river which runs past Elvritshalla

Gray Southwood—a forest southeast of Urmsheim range

Grenefod—a port city in Erkynland

Grianspog—a mountain range in the west of Hernystir

Haestall—barony in Erkynland

Hall of the Dominiate—a building in Nabban erected during the First Imperium

Hall of Memory—a collapsed chamber in Da'ai Chikiza

Harcha—an island in the Bay of Firannos

Harvest District—a section of Nakkiga

Hayholt, the—seat of the High Throne of Osten Ard, located above Erchester

Heartwood—translation of the Norn name for Aldheorte Forest

Hernysadharc—the capital of Hernystir

Hernystir—a kingdom in the west of Osten Ard

Hewenshire—a district in Erkynland, seat of Pasevalles' barony; once home to Josua's friend Deornoth

Hikehikayo—one of the nine Gardenborn cities, located in the far north-west; called Cloud Castle

Himilfells—a mountain range east of Nakkiga

Himnhalla—heavenly home of the Rimmersgarder gods

Hjeldin's Tower—a sealed tower of ominous repute in the Hayholt

H'ran Go-jao—the most easterly of the Go-jao'e (Little Boats)

Hudstad—Rimmersgard market town

Icicle Gallery—a place on Mintahoq

Inniscrich—a valley and river in northern Hernystir, site of the first battle in the Storm King's War

Jao é-Tinukai'i—a hidden Sithi dwelling in Aldheorte, now abandoned

Jhiná-T'seneí—one of the nine Gardenborn cities, lost under the sea

Kementari—one of the nine Gardenborn cities, now lost

Khand—a lost and fabled land; also known as Khandia

Knokkespan, the—mythological bridge over the mythological River Roaring that is to be crossed by the dead

Kwanitupul—the biggest city in the Wran

Kynslagh—a lake in central Erkynland

Kynswood—a small forest adjacent to the Hayholt

Lake Rumiya—a lake on Nakkiga-mountain

Lake Suno'ku—a lake inside Nakkiga discovered after the Storm King's War, which enabled survival when the top of the mountain collapsed

Lakelands, the—an area of Nabban with many lakes and ponds

Laestfinger River—a river on Erkynland's eastern border

Laestmouth—Erkynlandish port city just north of Nabban border

Latria—a town in Nabban

Leaworth—an Erkynlandish barony near the Ymstrecca River

Leymund—"meadow fort"; an Erkynlandish fort

Li Campino—a tavern in Perdruin

Lost Garden—Venyha Do'sae, the fabled place from whose destruction the Keida'ya fled

Mahistrevine Hill—hill on which Sancellan Mahistrevis stands

Mahistrevine Road—road leading to the Sancellan Mahistrevis

Main Row—major thoroughfare in the city of Erchester

Market Square—a marketplace in Erchester

Maze Palace, the—Queen Utuk'ku's labyrinthine home, called Omeiyo Hamakh

Mejuq's Cave—a place on Mintahoq mountain, sacred to the trolls

Meremund—Erkynlandish town on the rivers Greenwade and Gleniwent; birthplace of Queen Miriamele

Mezutu'a—the Silverhome; abandoned Sithi and Dwarrow city beneath the Grianspog Mountains; one of the nine Gardenborn cities

Mintahoq—a mountain of the Trollfells; Binabik's home

Nabban—duchy in the southern part of Osten Ard; former seat of empire

Nad Glehs—home of Countess Rhona in Hernystir

Nad Mullach—Count Eolair's home in eastern Hernystir

Naglimund—a fortress in northern Erkynland; place of battles during the Storm King's War, now a stronghold of the Highward

Nakkiga—Gardenborn city beneath Stormspike Mountain, meaning "Mask of Tears"; home of the Hikeda'ya

Nakkiga-That-Was—city outside Nakkiga mountain; one of the nine Gardenborn cities, now abandoned

Nartha—a river that runs along the base of the Wealdhelm

Nascadu—a desert land in the south

Nearulagh—site of the famous battle where Prester John defeated Benidrivis, the last Imperator of Nabban

Nearulagh Gate—main entrance to the Hayholt

New Gadrinsett—dwelling founded during the Storm King's War by refugees, near Sesu'adra Niskie-town—district of the City of Nabban near the old docks

Nornfells—the northern mountains, home to the Hikeda'ya; also called Nornlands

North Coast Road—Nabbanai road connecting the Commeis Valley to Erkynland

Northithe—county in Erkynland

Onestris—a valley in Nabban

Orangery Garden—a garden that contains an orange orchard, located in the Sancellan Mahistrevis

Osten Ard—mortal kingdom (Rimmerspakk for "Eastern Land")

Perdruin—an island in the Bay of Emettin

Piga Fonto—a mountain village in Perdruin

Place of Sharing Out—a public place in Da'ai Chikiza, beside the river

Place of Silence—the archive chamber of Da'ai Chikiza
Place of Sky-Watching—a ruined domed building in Da'ai Chikiza
Place of Voices—a public chamber in Da'ai Chikiza
Poines—Sir Astrian's birthplace
Porta Antiga—the old harbor of Nabban
Porta Nova—the newer harbor of Nabban
Rasina—a town in Nabban
Redenturine Hill—one of Nabban's hills, with two peaks called Mahistrevine Hill and Sancelline Hill
Red Pig Lagoon—Jesa's home village in the Wran
Refarslod—"The Foxes' Road"; a road in Rimmersgard
Repra Vessina—a Nabbanai town west of Kwanitupul
Rimmersgard—duchy in the north of Osten Ard
Royal Way—ancient road running south from Nakkiga
St. Cusimo's—a church on Almond Tree Hill in Perdruin
St. Cuthbert –a church in Naglimund
St. Granis's—a cathedral in the City of Nabban
St. Sutrin's—the cathedral in Erchester
St. Tankred's—the cathedral in Meremund
St. Tunato's Tower—part of the Sancellan Aedonitis
Sancellan Aedonitis—the palace where the Lector lives, chief seat of the Aedonite Church
Sacelline Hill—the hill on which Sancellan Aedonitis stands
Sancellan Mahistrevis—the ducal palace of Nabban
Shisae'ron—a valley in the southwestern part of Aldheorte Forest; birthplace of Tanahaya
Sea Definite and Internal—a mangled retelling by the Hidden of "the Ocean Indefinite and Eternal", which was crossed by Keida'ya and Tinukeda'ya on their way to Osten Ard
Silent One—a standing stone in the Spirit Hills of the Thrithings
Sina Gavi—a town in the south of Nabban; home of the lector's winter palace
Small Pleasance—a garden in the Hayholt
Spirit Hills—hills surrounding Blood Lake, sacred to the Thrithings clans
Stile, The—ancient abandoned road between Da'ai Chikiza and Naglimund
Sta Mirore—mountain that dominates the island nation of Perdruin
Suthmark—a fortified town near the southern Erkynlandish border
Stormspike—the mountain also known as Nakkiga or Sturmrspeik
Taig, the—a wooden castle; home to Hernystir's ruling family
Tebi Pit—a magical device
Thrithings—plain of grassland in the southeast of Osten Ard, divided into High Thrithings, Meadow Thrithings, and Lake Thrithings
Trevinta—a county in Nabban
T'seya Go-jao—one of the "Little Boats", at the western edge of Aldheorte near the Forbidden Hills

Tumeta'i—northern Sithi city, buried under ice east of Yiqanuc; one of the nine Gardenborn cities
Tzo—the great city in Venyha Do'sae
Urmsheim—a fabled mountain in the far north
Uttersall—barony in northern Erkynland
Varn, the—marshy land north of Kwanitupul
Vea Petranis—an east/west thoroughfare through Nabban
Vea Orentem—an old south/north rode along the edge of the Thrithings
Vellia's Gardens—Gardens in the Sancellan Mahistrevis, built for Vellia Hermis
Venyha Do'sae—original home of Zida'ya, Hikeda'ya, and Tinukeda'ya; called "The Garden"
Vhinansu—a Sithi city, long deserted
Vindirthorp—a town in the east of Rimmersgard
Vissa—a Nabbanai earldom
Warinsten—an island off the coast of Erkynland
Way of the Fountains—a thoroughfare in Nabban
Wealdhelm—a range of hills in Erkynland
Wentmouth—a port town at the mouth of the Gleniwent River
Westworth—an Erkynlandish locale
White Snail Castle—a Hikeda'ya castle on the shoulder of Nakkiga Mountain
Wran, the—marshland in southern Osten Ard
Yasirá—the sacred Sithi meeting place
Yiqanuc—home of the Qanuc people; also known as the Trollfells
Ymstrecca—a river in eastern Erkynland, called Umstreja in Thrithings-tongue; also a battlefield

THINGS

Aedontide—holy time in Decander, celebrating birth of Usires Aedon
Age of Gold—name for Nabbanai era of Anitulles' Second Imperium
Astaline Sisters—members of the Astaline order, a pious lay group who sponsored settlements for women
Book of the Aedon—Aedonite holy book
Book of Prophets—another Aedonite holy book
Cave Icicle—Hikeda'ya name for a white fungus that grows in Nakkiga's depths
Cloudberry Wine—a drink made from fermented berries and a few drops of kei-mi, a rare delicacy in Nakkiga
Cold Root—Makho's witchwood sword, now in Nezeru's possession
Cudomani—an apple brandy made in Nabban
Dance of Sacrifice—Hikeda'ya term for combat
Dawnstone—Master Witness in Da'ai Chikiza, lost during a flood

Day of Weighing Out—Aedonite day of final justice and end of the mortal world

Dead Fingers—a fungus considered a delicacy in Nakkiga

Dika's Jar—a Wranna fable

Dolshire Farmer's Son, The—a war song from the days of the Holly King in Erkynland

Dragonbone Chair—throne of the High King of Osten Ard, unused by King Simon and Queen Miriamele

Drukhi's Day—Hikeda'ya holiday commemorating Queen Utuk'ku's dead son, celebrated during Stone-Listener's Moon

Eadne Cloud—a Nabbanai ship during the Storm King's War

Edict of Gemmia—Imperator Anitulles' proclamation of Nabban as an Aedonite state

Erkynguard—sentries of the Hayholt

Exile's Letter—infamous denunciation written by Xaniko sey-Hamakha

Five Fingers of the Queen's Hand, The—a book of wisdom and instructions, widely read and revered by the Hikeda'ya

Founding Year—year one in the Aedonite calculation of time; the year Nabban was founded.

Gardenborn—all who came from Venyha Do'sae

Garden Endures, The—a greeting that Hikeda'ya give one another

Garden-Root—the witchwood brought from Venyha Do'sae

Genathi's Gift—a fatalistic Hikeda'ya expression, referring to the philosopher Genathi who considered his blindness a gift

Grass Blade—a move in Hikeda'ya combat technique

Great Lodge—Wranna name for the Sancellan Mahistrevis

Great Year—a Gardenborn time span, approximately 60 human years

Hall of Spears—test in Hikeda'ya Sacrifice training

Hermit Ibis cypher—cypher devised by Hikeda'ya philosopher Yedade

High King's Ward—protection of the High Throne over the countries of Osten Ard

Hikeda'yasao—the language of Nakkiga

Hylissa—the ship that brings Queen Miriamele to Nabban, named after her late mother

Hymns of the Precentor—songs of prayer in the Book of Aedon

Hyssop—a plant which is used as an antiseptic and cough reliever

Imperium, the—era of the Nabbanai empire

Keida'ya—the Sithi and Hikeda'ya

Kei-mi—precious powdered witchwood sap

Kei-vishaa—substance used by Gardenborn to make enemies drowsy and weak

Kuriosora blackwood—a tree that grows in forests around Nakkiga, used by the Hikeda'ya for arrows

Landborn—those Sithi and Hikeda'ya born after the arrival in Osten Ard

League of the Scroll—an exclusive and secret society of scholars, seeking and preserving knowledge

Li Fosena—Countess Yissola of Perdruin's flagship

Mamarte and the Deceivers—famous tale from the Book of the Aedon

Meadowsweet—a flowering herb

Mooncloud—a Master Witness

Moonlight—Prince-Templar Prakiti's sword

Moon Trees—part of Himano's lands

Mother Church—the Aedonite church

Motherwort—a healing herb, used for bowel issues and as a sedative

Northern Alliance—a trade organization, in competition with the ancient Sindigato Perdruine

Ocean Indefinite and Eternal—the sea crossed by the Gardenborn to come to Osten Ard

Octander Covenant—pact between the Ingadarine and Benidrivine houses of Nabban

Parting, the—the separation of the Sithi and Norns

Pellarine Table—table of the Small Council of the High Throne; a gift from the Nabbanai Imperator Pellaris to King Tethtain

Pellipan Sisters—an Aedonite religious order

Promissi—"promises", a chapter in the Book of the Aedon

Quarely Maid—a tavern in Erchester, Prince Morgan's favored drinking establishment

Queen's Huntsman—an honorific given by Queen Utuk'ku to a skilled mortal slave-hunter

Quinis-piece—a Nabbanai coin

Red Ruin—a plague

Rhiappa's Bells—an herb used to treat women's pains

Scale—Sithi device for talking over distance, "Witness"

Sacrifice—a Hikeda'ya soldier

Scrollbearers—members of the League of the Scroll, a secret society seeking and preserving knowledge

Shaynat—a Keida'ya strategy game for two players, called Shent by the Sithi

Snakesplitter—Morgan's sword

Spar—a piece of one of the Eight Ships that came from the Garden, sacred to the Niskies

Speakfire—the Master Witness in Hikehikayo

Stag—emblem of Hern's House, the ruling house of Hernystir

Sulian Heresy—King Vargellis Sulis' conjecture, declared heretical, that Usires Aedon was one of the Sithi

Sutrinian Order—Aedonite religious order, whose patron saint is St. Sutrin

Swan of Naglimund—Josua's coat of arms

Talon—a squad of five elite, specially-trained Sacrifices

Thanemoot—a yearly gathering of all Thrithings clans at Blood Lake

Thrithings Wars—a series of wars between the Thrithings and Aedonite kingdoms

Thrones—Erkynlandish gold coins roughly equivalent to Nabbanai gold Imperators

Traveler's Hood—Sithi name of the herb wolfsbane

Treatise on the Aetheric Whispers, A—also called Tractit Eteris Vocinnen; a
banned book

Tree, the—"Holy Tree", or "Execution Tree"; symbol of Usires Aedon's execution and the Aedonite faith

True Faith—the Aedonite religion (as Aedonites see it)

Twin Dragons—House Crest of King Simon and Queen Miriamele

Unbeing—an ancient threat which destroyed Venyha Do'sae

Usirean Brotherhood—a religious order of Aedonite monks

War of Return—Hikeda'ya name for the Storm King's War

Westerling—language originating from Warinsten Island; now the common
tongue of Osten Ard

Windflower—a little white flower, found in woods, flowering in early Spring

Witchwood—rare wood from trees brought from the Garden; as hard as metal

Witchwood Crown, the—Sithi: "kei-jáyha". A circlet for heroes; a group of
witchwood trees; a move in Shaynat/Shent

Witness—a Sithi device to talk over long distances and enter the Road of
Dreams, oftentimes a dragon scale

Wood agrimony—a flowering herb

Word of Resurrection—used to bring life back to a dead body, at least for a
little while

Words of Joining—chanted by Tanahaya to use the Witness

Xari—"scorpions", a kind of Hikeda'ya hand-ax

Yedade's Box—a Hikeda'ya device for testing children

Yerut—fermented mare's milk that the Thrithings-folk have drunk since time
before time

Yrmansol—a festival tree

STARS AND CONSTELLATIONS

Bend of the River—one of the stars of Venyha Do'sae, the Lost Garden

Blade—a star of Venyha Do'sae

Dancer—a star of Venyha Do'sae

Horned Owl—Erkynlandish

Lamp—Erkynlandish

Lantern—Hikeda'ya

Pool—a star of Venyha Do'sae

Staff—Erkylandish

Swallower—a star of Venyha Do'sae

HOLIDAYS

Feyever 2–Candlemansa
Marris 25–Elysiamansa
Marris 31–Fool's Night
Avrel 1–All Fool's Day
Avrel 3–St. Vultinia's Day
Avrel 24–St. Dinan's Day
Avrel 30–Stoning Night
Maia 1–Belthainn Day
Yuven 23–Midsummer's Eve
Tiyagar 15–Saint Sutrin's Day
Anitul 1–Hlafmansa
Septander 29–Saint Granis' Day
Octander 30–Harrows Eve
Novander 1–Soul's Day
Decander 21–Saint Tunath's Day
Decander 24–Aedonmansa

Days of the Week
   Sunday, Moonday, Tiasday, Udunsday, Drorsday, Frayday, Satrinsday

Months of the Year
   Aedonite: Jonever, Feyever, Marris, Avrel, Maia, Yuven, Tiyagar, Anitul, Septander, Octander, Novander, Decander
   Sithi: Raven, Serpent, Hare, Grieving Sister, Nightingale, Lantern, Bearer, Fox, Lynx, Crane, Tortoise, Rooster, Moon-Herald
   Hikeda'ya: Ice-Mother, Serpent, Wind-Child, Dove, Cloud-Song, Otter, Stone-Listener, Lynx, Sky-Singer, Tortoise, Fire-Knight, Wolf
   Thrithing: Second Blue Moon, Third Blue Moon, First Green Moon, Second Green Moon, Third Green Moon, First Yellow Moon, Second Yellow Moon, Third Yellow Moon, First Red Moon, Second Red Moon, Third Red Moon, First Blue Moon

KNUCKLEBONES

Qanuc auguring tools
Patterns include:
   Wingless Bird
   Fish-Spear
   The Shadowed Path
   Torch at the Cave-Mouth
   Balking Ram

Clouds in the Pass
The Black Crevice
Unwrapped Dart
Circle of Stones
Mountains Dancing
Masterless Ram
Slippery Snow
Unexpected Visitor
Unnatural Birth
No Shadow

HIKEDA'YA ORDERS

Order, Ordination, Ordinal
Order House—actual location of Order's school, offices
Orders mentioned: Sacrifices; Whisperers; Echoes; Singers; Builders; Tillers;
    Celebrants; Gatherers
Order hierarchies: Magister or High Magister (Highest official outside Royal
    Household—master of an Order)

THRITHINGS CLANS (AND THEIR THRITHING):

Adder—Lake
Antelope—Meadow
Bison—High
Black Bear—Meadow
Crane or "Kragni"—Lake
Dragonfly—Lake
Fitch—Lake
Fox—High
Grouse—High
Kestrel—Lake
Lynx—Lake
Polecat—Lake
Sparrow—High
Stallion or "Mehrdon"—High
White Spot Deer—Lake
Wood Duck—Lake
Other clans include:
    Badger, Bustard, Otter, Pheasant, Roebuck, Snake, Sparrowhawk, Vulture,
Whipsnake, and Wild Horse

WORDS AND PHRASES

QANUC

Croohok—Rimmersman
Dhoota—an angry, hungry ghost
Kunikuni—name for the creatures Morgan calls "Chikri"
-sa—suffix meaning "dear"

SITHI (KEIDA'YASAO)

A'do-Shao—Unbeing
Hikka Staja—Arrow bearer
Hikeda'ya—Cloud Children
Kayute—word for brush strokes used in Sithi and Hikeda'ya writing
Kei-jáyha—witchwood crown
Seku iye-Sama'an—the Earth-Drake's Back, name for Wealdhelm Mountains
Sudhoda'ya—Sunset Children/mortals
S'huesa—feminine form of S'hue, both terms of respect for a family elder; plural: S'huesae
Tinukeda'ya—Ocean Children
T'si Suhyasei—Her Blood is Cool, name for the river mortals call the Aelfwent
Tzo—star
Zida'ya—Dawn Children

NORN (HIKEDA'YASAO)

Hike—Cloud
Rayu ata na'ara—I hear the Queen in your voice
Ni'iyo—glow-sphere
Ujin é-da Sikhunae—Trap that catches the Hunter, name for the fortress mortals call Naglimund

NABBANAI

Dominiatis Patrisi—"Fathers of the houses"; Nabban's city fathers
Honsa—noble house; plural Honsae

Futústite—fuck yourself
Mansa séa Cuelossan—death mass
Matra sa Duos—Mother of God, a swear word
Patrissi—Fathers, used for the members of the Dominiate (singular Patris)
Podegris—gout
Vindissa—revenge

THRITHINGS SPEECH

Setta—gathering place
Shan—a title meaning "lord of lords"; a leader unifying all Thrithing clans
   under his rule
Skeem—slang for male genitalia
Vilagum. Ves zhu haya.—Welcome. I wish you health.

OTHER

Bunukta—angry winds (Wranna)
Higdaja—giants' name for "Hikeda'ya"
Katulo—spirit knowers (Wranna)
Laup!—jump! (Rimmerspakk)
Settro—neighborhood or district (Perdruinese)
Vao—Tinukeda'ya name for their race
Valada—wise woman (Rimmerspakk)

A GUIDE TO PRONUNCIATION

ERKYNLANDISH

Erkynlandish names are divided into two types, Old Erkynlandish (O.E.) and
Warinstenner. Those names which are based on types from Prester John's native
island of Warinsten (mostly the names of castle servants or John's immediate
family) have been represented as variants on Biblical names (Elias—Elijah,
Ebekah—Rebecca, etc.) Old Erkynlandish names should be pronounced like
modern English, except as follows:

   a—always *ah,* as in "father"
   ae—*ay* of "say"

c—*k* as in "keen"

e—*ai* as in "air," except at the end of names, when it is also sounded, but with an *eh* or *uh* sound, i.e., Hruse—"Rooz-uh"

ea—sounds as *a* in "mark," except at beginning of word or name, where it has the same value as *ae*

g—always hard g, as in "glad"

h—hard *h* of "help"

i—short *i* of "in"

j—hard *j* of "jaw"

o—long but soft *o*, as in "orb"

u—*oo* sound of "wood," never *yoo* as in "music"

HERNYSTIRI

The Hernystiri names and words can be pronounced in largely the same way as the O.E., with a few exceptions:

th—always the *th* in "other," never as in "thing"

ch—a guttural, as in Scottish "loch"

y—pronounce *yr* like "beer," *ye* like "spy"

h—unvoiced except at beginning of word or after *t* or *c*

e—*ay* as in "ray"

ll—same as single *l*: Lluth—Luth

RIMMERSPAKK

Names and words in Rimmerspakk differ from O.E. pronunciation in the following:

j—pronounced *y:* Jarnauga—Yarnauga; Hjeldin—Hyeldin (*H* nearly silent here)

ei—long *i*, as in "crime"

e—*ee*, as in "sweet"

ö—*oo*, as in "coop"

au—*ow*, as in "cow"

NABBANAI

The Nabbanai language holds basically to the rules of a romance language, i.e., the vowels are pronounced "ah-eh-ih-oh-ooh," the consonants are all sounded, etc. There are some exceptions.

i—most names take emphasis on second to last syllable: Ben-i-GAR-is. When this syllable has an *i*, it is sounded long (Ardrivis: Ar-DRY-vis) unless it comes before a double consonant (Antippa: An-TIHP-pa)

    es—at end of name, *es* is sounded long: Gelles—Gel-leez

    y—is pronounced as a long *i*, as in "mild"

QANUC

Troll-language is considerably different than the other human languages. There are three hard "k" sounds, signified by: *c, q,* and *k.* The only difference intelligible to most non-Qanuc is a slight clucking sound on the *q,* but it is not to be encouraged in beginners. For our purposes, all three will sound with the *k* of "keep." Also, the Qanuc *u* is pronounced *uh,* as in "bug." Other interpretations are up to the reader, but he or she will not go far wrong pronouncing phonetically.

SITHI

Even more than the language of Yiqanuc, the language of the Zida'ya is virtually unpronounceable by untrained tongues, and so is easiest rendered phonetically, since the chance of any of us being judged by experts is slight (but not nonexistent, as Binabik learned). These rules may be applied, however.

i—when the first vowel, pronounced *ih,* as in "clip." When later in word, especially at end, pronounced *ee,* as in "fleet": Jiriki—Jih-REE-kee

    ai—pronounced like long *i,* as in "time"

    ' (apostrophe)—represents a clicking sound, and should be not voiced by mortal readers.

EXCEPTIONAL NAMES

Geloë—Her origins are unknown, and so is the source of her name. It is pronounced "Juh-LO-ee" or "Juh-LOY." Both are correct.

Ingen Jegger—He is a Black Rimmersman, and the "J" in Jegger is sounded, just as in "jump."

Miriamele—Although born in the Erkynlandish court, hers is a Nabbanai name that developed a strange pronunciation—perhaps due to some family influence or confusion of her dual heritage—and sounds as "Mih-ree-uh-MEL."

Vorzheva—A Thrithings-woman, her name is pronounced "Vor-SHAY-va," with the *zh* sounding harshly, like the Hungarian *zs*.

C29 0000 0833 840